LIGHTSPEED

WOMEN DESTROY SCIENCE FICTION! SPECIAL ISSUE

LIMITED EDITION

ISSUE 49 • JUNE 2014
GUEST EDITED BY CHRISTIE YANT

LIGHTSPEED MAGAZINE: *Women Destroy Science Fiction! Special Issue*   Issue 49, June 2014

Publisher: John Joseph Adams   Guest Editor: Christie Yant

© 2014 *Lightspeed Magazine*

Published by *Lightspeed Magazine*   First edition: June 2014

LIGHTSPEED

WOMEN DESTROY SCIENCE FICTION! SPECIAL ISSUE

ISSUE 49, JUNE 2014

FROM THE EDITORS

ORIGINAL SHORT STORIES
edited by Christie Yant

REPRINTS
selected by Rachel Swirsky

ORIGINAL FLASH FICTION
edited by Robyn Lupo

NOVEL EXCERPT

AUTHOR SPOTLIGHTS
edited by Jude Griffin

NONFICTION
edited by Wendy N. Wagner

PERSONAL ESSAYS

edited by Wendy N. Wagner

ACKNOWLEDGMENTS

MISCELLANY

LIMITED EDITION BONUS STORY

Editorial, June 2014

Women Destroy Science Fiction!
Special Issue

> What seemed significant about my friend's confusion was that it related to a persistent rumbling that I have heard echoing through science fiction. That rumbling says, in essence, that women don't write science fiction. Put a little more rudely, this rumbling says: "Those damn women are ruining science fiction." They are doing it by writing stuff that isn't "real" science fiction; they are writing "soft" science fiction and fantasy.
> —Pat Murphy, *Wiscon 15*, March 2, 1991.

Christie Yant, Guest Editor

Nineteen-ninety-one. Twenty-three years ago. It could as easily have been last week.

The summer of 2013 was a rough one for women in science fiction. Every few weeks there was a new reminder that to a certain subset of the field, we're not welcome here. There were multiple articles returning to the tired accusation that women (still) aren't writing "real" SF; disputes about the way the field is represented by vintage cheesecake art on the cover of a professional trade publication; the glib admonition that if we are to succeed, we should be more like Barbie, in her "quiet dignity." For some of us, it was business as usual, as evidenced by Pat Murphy's unfortunately timeless quote above. For others, it was a very nasty surprise to discover this undercurrent running through the ocean of imaginative fiction we love.

And it just. Kept. Coming.

We got tired. We got angry. And then we came out the other side of exhaustion and anger deeply motivated to do something.

This issue is just one result. Look around and you'll see others, as thick on the ground this year as those unpleasant incidents were last year. All-women anthologies like *Athena's Daughters*. A rebooted *SFWA Bulletin*. The recent Hugo Award nominations. There are others. Things are changing. I hope it sticks.

There was—is—something else going on, too, something apart from the attacks from the outside. It's a smaller, quieter attack from within, and it's just as pernicious. Too many accomplished writers are convinced that they aren't qualified to write science fiction because they "don't have the science." I've heard this worry from men, too, but more often I hear it from women. I don't know which is worse: the men who tell us we're doing it wrong, or the voice within ourselves that insists that we'll fail if we try.

These are different strokes from the same brush: the belief that only one kind of science fiction—rocket ships, robots, extra-planetary adventures—is the "real" kind. *Lightspeed* has always rejected the narrow definition. Science fiction, like everything else, has changed over time. It has expanded and altered, just as those reading and writing it have.

Why "Women Destroy Science Fiction"? Are we really trying to destroy it? As you read the stories in this issue, you may very well think so. Here you'll find galactic gastronomy and alternate astronomy, far-future courtship and a near-future food court—right alongside alien invasion and deep-space salvage missions. My hope is that one or more of these stories will reach a reader who never realized *that* kind of story is science fiction, too, and will seek out more like it. And I hope that one or more will convince those writers—the fantasists, the poets, the ones more comfortable in Middle Earth or the Midwest than on Mars—that they, too, can create science fiction stories and participate in the expansion of the field.

The experience of reading submissions for this issue was humbling and deeply gratifying. Women of all ages from all over the world sent us their stories. Many of them had never tried to write science fiction before; some had never considered submitting their work for publication until they heard about *WDSF*. They pushed past their doubt and fear, finished their pieces and clicked *submit* for the very first time just to be a part of this. If you were one of those authors, please don't let it be the last time. We need your voice—don't let it be silenced. We had to pass on so many excellent stories, many of which will surely find homes elsewhere. To all of those women who trusted us with your work, thank you. I could not be more honored and grateful to each and every one of you.

This is the biggest project *Lightspeed* has ever taken on. When John Joseph

Adams asked me to act as guest editor for the issue, I knew immediately who I wanted at my side to bring the idea to life. I assembled my editorial team—Wendy Wagner, Rachel Swirsky, Robyn Lupo, and Gabrielle de Cuir, all of whom you'll hear from in a moment—and together we prepared to bring the voices of more women into the world.

But then something happened: The issue kept growing. We made room for more fiction, more articles, personal essays, and an expanded podcast.

As the issue grew, so did the team. Authors, essayists, illustrators, voice actors, interviewers and interviewees, slush readers and copyeditors—more women got involved week after week. All told, this issue is the work of *109 women*.

And those are just the direct contributors. That doesn't count the more than *one thousand* women who sent us stories, or the nearly three thousand people who backed the Kickstarter, or the countless supporters who blogged on their own sites, posted to social media, or otherwise boosted the signal.

We did this. As one person put it, we took hurt and rage and turned it into something beautiful.

And we did it together.

RACHEL SWIRSKY, REPRINT EDITOR

I'll tell you a secret. I don't really want to destroy science fiction.

Maybe that's not much of a secret. I do write it, after all. I'm a bit of a science fiction evangelist, actually. I get really excited about books and stories and tell people OH MY GOODNESS THIS THING YOU SHOULD READ IT while they try to inch away from me toward the chip bowl.

What do I want to do to science fiction?

I want to expand science fiction.

I want to celebrate science fiction.

I want to see all the fractured, strange, beautiful impressions that humans have to offer as we contemplate our future.

A long time ago, Mary Shelley started singing. It was a song shaped by earlier refrains, and others were already singing. More and more voices joined in. They sing about the promise of tomorrow; they sing about the threat of tomorrow; above all, they sing about the present moments they inhabit, because those are the underpinnings of any story.

Women's voices don't destroy the song. They shade into its chorus. They harmonize. They've been there all along.

Here, I've tried to bring you five powerful melodies. You may have heard them before, or not. Amid the choir's beauty, it's hard to pick out only five. So many more deserve solo performances.

But here are a few voices that expand science fiction, voices that celebrate science fiction, voices that are fractured, strange, and beautiful. Voices to contemplate. Voices raised toward the future.

WENDY N. WAGNER, NONFICTION/MANAGING EDITOR

Women get written out of history.

Whether it's geopolitical history or the history of science and the arts, outside of niche scholarship, women's contributions all too often slip away and are forgotten. The same can be said of science fiction, which is merely the imagined history of the future. Female characters are typically trivial; women's concerns are trivialized; and women writers disappear into the shadows cast by better known, male, Grand Masters.

But women have always been a part of history, remembered or not. We are fifty percent of the world, and we're shaping its future every second. We're even writing it. My goal, collecting nonfiction for this issue, was to bring the legacy of great women SF writers out of the shadows, cast light on the women working within our genre today, and build a goddamn torch for the women of tomorrow.

The amazing women writing this issue explore a wealth of experiences, from working in the male-dominated world of super-hero comics, to creating a literary award celebrating gender exploration, to facing discrimination at conventions. They've shared their reading lists, wisdom, true stories, and just plain good advice to create not just another magazine issue —they've made a manual for creating and supporting women SF writers.

When you get done reading that manual, pick up a pen and write us a new history of tomorrow. One with women in it.

ROBYN LUPO, FLASH FICTION EDITOR

When I took on this project, my husband remarked that women are uniquely qualified to write science fiction, since most women have been treated like aliens at some point.

Picture the lone wallflower at a high school dance, red-haired and tall, alien to this environment; nose more at home in a book than sampling the eau-de-foot-and-jock-strap that high school gyms all seem to have. Perhaps that's a bit sad. But I see a powerful Outsider, an observer and a soothsayer, a person who sees all the stories—because she's not quite in our world, our alien us. She's far beyond, carbon on the furthest stars.

There are stories everywhere, and flash gives writers a freedom to focus on scale—to paint the big booming profound on a wee canvas. More rigid in structure than poetry, but at liberty to leave the reader silenced—more things left unsaid, a theme one of our stories handles with poignancy.

The continued ubiquitousness of stories is important to me. I was pleased to have a tweetish short story in here—it shows how fast-paced flash fiction can be, and stretches the border between poetry and story. We have a forty-seven-word story which feels to me like a heavy metal riff. And above all, we published new writers. New voices added to the chorus of women, aliens no more, chanting "One of us! One of us!"

GABRIELLE DE CUIR, PODCAST PRODUCER

WOMEN DESTROY SCIENCE FICTION? Oh, yeah, baby. Oh, yeah. BRING. IT. ON. Black leather and whips in the studio. I'm there.

It was with barely controllable emotion that I accepted Christie Yant's invitation to highjack the recording and production of the June podcasts for *Lightspeed Magazine.* I've been around the science fiction block a few times and narrated and produced my share of tales, but this prospect? Eight glorious stories that were MINE, all MINE to midwife into podcasts. (Insert maniacal laugh here.) When I got that indescribably sexy zip file from Christie with the eight final chosen stories, I couldn't wait to burst that puppy open and see what was inside.

Gold. Pure gold. (Gollum mode.)

Gorgeous stories. Nothing can stop us now. Got me a vixen of an editor in Alexa Althoff, who did her magic on *Ender's Game Alive.* Began the casting process (Siri: replace couch springs.) What has humbled and overjoyed me the most so far has been the unhesitating positive responses from all the narrators to participate. OMG. They keep saying "yes!" First narrator up? Two-time Grammy winner Janis Ian, a science fiction author herself, reading a mesmerizing mermaid tale by the magical Seanan McGuire. There were scales all over the booth the next morning.

Let the recordings continue!

Whip crack. Whip crack. Whip crack.

(Threes, you know. Gets 'em laughing every time. Was that a laugh I heard? Well, wipe that smirk off your face, buddy. We don't think twice about destroying a genre; how long do you think you'll last?)

EACH TO EACH

SEANAN MCGUIRE

Art by Li Grabenstetter

Condensation covers the walls, dimpling into tiny individual drops that follow an almost fractal pattern, like someone has been writing out the secrets of the universe in the most transitory medium they can find. The smell of damp steel assaults my nose as I walk the hall, uncomfortable boots clumping heavily with every step I force myself to take. The space is tight, confined, unyielding; it is like living inside a coral reef, trapped by the limits of our own necessary shells. We are constantly envious of those who escape its limitations, and we fear for them at the same time, wishing them safe return to the reef, where they can be kept away from all the darkness and predations of the open sea.

The heartbeat of the ship follows me through the iron halls, comprised of the engine's whir, the soft, distant buzz of the electrical systems, the even more distant churn of the rudders, the hiss and sigh of the filters that keep the flooded chambers clean and oxygenated. Latest scuttlebutt from the harbor holds that a generation of wholly flooded ships is coming, ultra-light fish tanks with shells of air and metal surrounding the water-filled crew chambers, the waterproofed electrical systems. Those ships will be lighter than ours could ever dream of being, freed from the need for filters and desalination pumps by leaving themselves open to the sea.

None of the rumors mention the crews. What will be done to them, what they'll have to do in service to their country. We don't need to talk about it. Everyone already knows. Things that are choices today won't be choices tomorrow; that's the way it's always been, when you sign away your voice for a new means of dancing.

The walkway vibrates under my feet, broadcasting the all hands signal through the ship. It will vibrate through the underwater spaces twice more, giving everyone the time they need. Maybe that will be an advantage of those flooded boats; no more transitions, no more hasty scrambles for breathing apparatus that fits a little less well after every tour, no more forcing of feet into boots that don't really fit, but are standard issue (and standard issue is still God and King here, on a navy vessel, in the service of the United States government, even when the sailors do not, cannot, will never fit the standard mold). I walk a little faster, as fast as I can force myself to go in my standard issue boots, and there is only a thin shell between me and the sea.

• • •

We knew that women were better suited to be submariners by the beginning of the twenty-first century. Women dealt better with close quarters, tight spaces, and enforced contact with the same groups of people for long periods of time. We were more equipped to resolve our differences without resorting to violence—and there were differences. Women—even military women—had been socialized to fight with words and with social snubbing, and the early all-female submarines must have looked like a cross between a psychology textbook and the Hunger Games.

The military figured it out. They hired the right sociologists, they taught their people the right way to deal with conflicts and handle stress, they found ways of picking out that early programming and replacing it with fierce loyalty to the Navy, to the program, to the crew.

Maybe it was one of those men—and they were all men, I've seen the records; man after man, walking into our spaces, our submarines with their safe and narrow halls, and telling the women who had to live there to make themselves over into a new image, a better image, an image that wouldn't fight, or gossip, or bully. An image that would do the Navy proud. Maybe it was one of those men who first started calling the all-female submarine crews the military's "mermaids."

Maybe that was where they got the idea.

Within fifty years of the launch of the female submariners, the sea had become the most valuable real estate in the world. Oh, space exploration continued—mostly in the hands of the wealthy, tech firms that decided a rocket would be a better investment than a Ping-Pong table in the break room, and now had their eyes set on building an office on Jupiter, a summer home on Mars. It wasn't viable. Not for the teeming masses of Earth, the people displaced from their communities by the super storms and tornadoes, the people who just needed a place to live and eat and work and flourish. Two-thirds of the planet's surface is water. Much of it remains unexplored, even today… and that was why, when Dr. Bustos stood up and said he had a solution, people listened.

There were resources, down there in the sea. Medicines and minerals and oil deposits and food sources. Places where the bedrock never shifted, suitable for anchoring bubble communities (art deco's resurgence around the time of the launch was not a coincidence). Secrets and wonders and miracles of science, and all we had to do was find a way to escape our steel shells, to dive deeper, to *find* them.

Women in the military had always been a bit of a sore spot, even when all the research said that our presence hurt nothing, endangered nothing; even when we had our own class of ships to sail beneath the waves, and recruits who aimed for other branches often found themselves quietly redirected to the Navy. There was recruiter logic behind it all, of course—reduced instances of sexual assault (even if it would never drop to full zero), fewer unplanned pregnancies, the camaraderie of people who really *understood* what you were going through as a woman in the military. Never mind the transmen who found themselves assigned to submarines, the transwomen who couldn't get a berth, the women who came from Marine or Air Force or Army families and now couldn't convince the recruiters that what they wanted was to serve as their fathers had served, on the land. The submarines began to fill.

And then they told us why.

I drag myself up the short flight of stairs between the hallway and the front of the ship (and why do they still build these things with staggered hearts, knowing what's been done to us, knowing what is yet to be done?) and join my crew. A hundred and twenty of us, all told, and less than half standing on our feet. The rest sit compacted in wheelchairs, or bob gently as the water beneath the chamber shifts, their heads and shoulders protruding through the holes cut in the floor. There is something strange and profoundly unprofessional about seeing the Captain speak with the heads and shoulders of wet-suited women sticking up around her feet like mushrooms growing from the omnipresent damp.

"At eighteen hundred hours, Seaman Wells encountered an unidentified bogey in our waters." The captain speaks clearly and slowly, enunciating each word like she's afraid we will all have forgotten the English language while her back was turned, trading in for some strange language of clicks and whistles and hums. She has read the studies about the psychological effects of going deep; she knows what to watch for.

We terrify her. I can't imagine how the Navy thinks this is a good use of their best people, locking them away in tin cans that are always damp and smell of fish, and watching them go slowly, inexorably insane. You need to be damn good to get assigned to submarine command, and you need to be willing to stay a drysider. Only drysiders can be shown in public; only drysiders can testify to the efficacy of the program. The rest of us have been compromised.

It's such a polite, sterile little word. "Compromised." Like we were swayed by the enemy, or blown off course by the gale-force winds of our delicate emotions. Nothing could be further from the truth. We're a necessary part of public safety, an unavoidable face of war... and we're an embarrassment that must be kept out at sea, where we can be safely forgotten.

"The bogey approached our ship, but did not make contact. It avoided all cameras, and did not pass by any open ports, which leads us to believe that it was either a deserter or an enemy combatant. The few sonar pictures we were able to get do not match any known design configuration." That doesn't have to mean anything. There are new models taking to the sea every day. I have my eye on a lovely frilled shark mod that's just clearing the testing process. Everyone who's seen the lab samples says it's a dream come true, and I'm about due for a few dreams.

One of the Seamen raises her hand. She's new to the ship; her boots still fit, her throat still works. The captain nods in her direction, and she asks, in a voice that squeaks and shakes with the effort of pushing sound through air instead of water, "Didn't we have anyone on patrol when the bogey came by?"

It's a good question, especially for a newbie. The captain shakes her head. "We're here to chart the sea floor and bring back information about the resources here." What we can exploit, in other words. "All of our sea-going sailors were at bottom level or in transit when the bogey passed near our vessel."

One of the servicewomen floating near the captain's feet whistles long and low, a tiny foghorn of a sound. An electronic voice from one of the speakers asks, robotic and stiff, "What are our orders, captain?"

I don't recognize this sailor. She has the dark gray hair and flattened facial features common to the blue shark mods. There are fourteen blues currently serving on this vessel. I can't be blamed if I can't tell them apart. Sometimes I'm not even sure they can tell *themselves* apart. Blues have a strong schooling instinct, strong enough that the labs considered recalling them shortly after they were deployed. The brass stepped in before anything permanent could happen. Blues are good for morale. They fight like demons, and they fuck like angels, and they have no room left in their narrow predators' brains for morals. If not for the service, they'd be a danger to us all, but thankfully, they have a very pronounced sense of loyalty.

The captain manages not to shy away from the woman at her feet: no small trick, given how much we clearly distress her. "All sailors are to be on a state of high alert whenever leaving the vessel. High water patrols will begin tonight, and will continue for the duration of our voyage. Any creature larger than an eel is to be reported to your superior officer immediately. We don't know what the Chinese have been doing since they closed the communication channels between their research divisions and ours. They may have progressed further than we had guessed."

A low murmur breaks out amongst the sailors who can use words. Others whistle and hum, communicating faster via the private languages of their mods. Rumor keeps saying command is going to ban anything on the ships that can't be translated into traditional English by our computers, and rumor keeps getting slapped down as fast as it can spread, because the speech is hard-coded in some of the most popular, most functional mods, and without it our sailors couldn't communicate in the open sea. So people like our poor Captain just have to grit their teeth and endure.

I feel bad for her, I really do. I envy her, too. Did they show her the same studies they'd once shown me, offer her the same concessions if she'd just serve as an example to her yearmates? Was she one of the rare individuals who saw everything the sea could give her, and still chose to remain career track, remain land-bound, remain capable of leaving the service when her tour was up? Oh, they said and said that everything was reversible, but since no one ever chose reversal, we still didn't know if that was true, and no one wanted to be the test case. Too much to lose, not enough to gain.

The captain begins to talk again, and the buzz of conversation dies down to respectful silence, giving her the floor as she describes our assignments for the days to come. They're standard enough; except for the bogey or bogeys we'll be watching for, we'll be doing the normal patrols of the sea bed and the associated trenches, looking for minerals, looking for species of fish we've never encountered before, taking samples. Deepening our understanding of the Pacific. Other crews have the Atlantic, mapping it out one square meter at a time; one day we'll meet on the other side of the world, a mile down and a universe away from where we started, and our understanding will be complete, and the human race can continue in its conquest of this strange and timeless new frontier. One day.

The captain finishes her speech, snapping off her words with the tight tone-lessness of a woman who desperately wants to be anywhere else. We salute her, those in the water doing their best not to splash as they pull their arms out of the water and snap their webbed fingers to their foreheads. She returns the salute and we're dismissed, back to our quarters or onward to our duties.

I linger on the stairs while those who are newer to this command than I scatter, moving with a quick, dryland efficiency toward other parts of the submarine. The captain is the first to go, all but running from the bridge in her need to get away from us. The heads in the water vanish one by one, the sailors going back to whatever tasks had them outside the ship—those who aren't currently off-duty and seeking the simple peace of weightlessness and separation from the dry. Not all the seamen serving with this vessel are capable of doing what I'm doing, standing on their own two feet and walking among the drylander crew. Every ship has to have a few in transition. It's meant to be a temptation and a warning at the same time. "Mind your choices; there but for the grace of God and the United States government go you."

It only takes a few minutes before I'm standing alone on the stairs. I walk over to the lockers set in the far wall (one more concession to what they've made of us; in transition, we don't always have time to get to quarters, to get to privacy, and so they arrange the ships to let us strip down wherever we need, and hold it up as one more bit of proof that single-sex vessels are a requirement for the smooth operation of the Navy). My boots are the first thing to go, and I have to blink back tears when I pull them off and my feet untwist, relaxing back into the natural shape the scientists have worked so hard to give them. All this work, all these changes to the sailors, and they still can't change our required uniforms—not when we still have things that can be called "feet" or "legs" and shoved into the standard-issue boots or trousers.

Piece by piece, I strip down to my swim trunks and thermal sports bra, both designed to expose as much skin as possible while still leaving me with a modicum of modesty. The blues, especially, have a tendency to remove their tops once they're in the water, buzzing past the cameras and laughing. That footage goes for a pretty penny on some corners of the internet, the ones frequented by soft-skinned civilians who murmur to themselves about the military mermaids, and how beautiful we are, and how much they'd like to fuck us.

They'd flense themselves bloody on the shark-skins of the blues, they'd sting themselves into oblivion on the spines of the lionfish and the trailing jellied arms of the moonies and the men-o'-war, but still they talk, and still they see us as fantasies given flesh, and not as the military women that we are. Perhaps that, too, is a part of the Navy's design. How easy is it to fear something that you've been seeing in cartoons and coloring books since you were born?

I walk to the nearest hole and exhale, blowing every bit of air out of my lungs. Then I step over the edge and plunge down, down, down, dragged under by the weight of my scientifically reengineered musculature, into the arms of the waiting sea.

• • •

"Project Amphitrite"—otherwise known as "Mermaids for the Military"—started attracting public attention when I was in my senior year of high school and beginning to really consider the Navy as a career option. I wanted to see the world. This new form of service promised me a world no one else had ever seen. They swore we could go back. They swore we would still be human, that every possible form of support would be offered to keep us connected to our roots. They said we'd all be fairy tales, a thousand Little Mermaids rising from the sea and walking on new legs into the future that our sacrifice had helped them to ensure.

They didn't mention the pain. Maybe they thought we'd all see the writing on the wall, the endless gene treatments, the surgeries to cut away inconvenient bits of bone—both original issue and grown during the process of preparing our bodies for the depths—the trauma of learning to breath in when submerged, suppressing the millennia of instinct that shrieked no, no, you will drown, you will die, no.

And maybe we did drown; maybe we did die. Every submersion felt a bit less like a betrayal of my species and a bit more like coming home. As I fall into the water my gills open, and the small fins on my legs spread, catching the water and holding me in place, keeping me from descending all the way to the bottom. The blues I saw before rush back to my side, attracted by the sound of something moving. They whirl around me in an undifferentiated tornado of fins and flukes and grasping hands, caressing my flank, touching my arms and hair before they whirl away again, off to do whatever a school of blues does when they are not working, when they are not slaved to the commands of a species they have willingly abandoned. Their clicks and whistles drift back to me, welcoming me, inviting me along.

I do not try to follow. Until my next shore leave, my next trip to the lab, I can't keep up; they're too fast for me, their legs fully sacrificed on the altar of being all that they can be. The Navy claims they're turning these women into better soldiers. From where I hang suspended in the sea, my lungs filled with saltwater like amniotic fluid, these women are becoming better myths.

Other sailors flash by, most of them carrying bags or wearing floodlights strapped to their foreheads or chests; some holding spear guns, which work better at these depths than traditional rifles. We'd be defenseless if someone were to fire a torpedo into our midst, but thus far, all the troubles we've encountered have either been native—squid and sharks who see our altered silhouettes and think we look like prey—or our own kind, mermaids from rival militaries, trying to chart and claim our sea beds before we can secure them for the United States of America. We might have been the first ones into the sea, but we weren't the last, and we're not even the most efficient anymore. The American mods focus too much on form and not enough on functionality. Our lionfish, eels, even our jellies still look like women before they look like marine creatures. Some sailors say—although there's been no *proof* yet, and that's the mantra of the news outlets, who don't want to criticize the program more than they have to, don't want to risk losing access to the stream of beautifully staged official photos and the weekly reports on the amazing scientific advancements coming out of what we do here—some sailors say that they chose streamlined mods, beautiful, sleek creatures that would cut through the water like knives, minimal drag, minimal reminders of their mammalian origins, and yet somehow came out of the treatment tanks with breasts that ached like it was puberty all over again. Ached and then grew bigger, ascending a cup size or even two, making a more marketable silhouette.

Here in the depths we're soldiers, military machines remade to suit the needs of our country and our government. But when we surface, we're living advertisements for the world yet to come, when we start shifting more of the population to the bubble cities being constructed on the ground we've charted for them, when the military gene mods become available to the public. I've seen the plans. We all have. Civilians will be limited to "gentler" forms, goldfish and angelfish and bettas, all trailing fins and soft Disney elegance. Veterans will be allowed to keep our mods as recognition of our service, should we choose to stay in the wet—and again, no one knows whether reversal is *possible*, especially not for the more esoteric designs. Can you put the bones back into a jelly's feet, just because you think they ought to be there? Questions better left unanswered, if you ask me.

Adjustment is done: My gills are open, and my chest is rising smooth and easy, lungs filling with seawater without so much as a bubble of protest. I jackknife down and swim toward the current patrol, feeling the drag from my weight belt as it pulls me toward the bottom. One more reason to dream of that coming return to the labs, when they'll take me one step deeper, and this will be just a little more like home.

The blues return to join me; two of them grab my hands and pull me deeper, their webbed fingers slipping on my slick mammalian skin, and the captain and her bogeys are forgotten, for a time, before the glorious majesty of the never-ending sea.

• • •

We're deep—about a hundred, hundred and fifty feet below the waiting submarine, our passage lit by the soft luminescent glow of the anglers and the lanterns—when something flashes past in the gloom just past the reach of the light. Whatever it is, it's moving fast, all dart and dazzle, and there isn't time to see it properly before it's gone.

The formation forms without anyone saying a word, the hard-coded schooling instinct slamming into our military training and forming an instant barricade against the waiting dark. Anglers and lanterns in the middle, blues, makos, and lionfish and undecideds on the outside. The five of us who have yet to commit to a full mod look like aberrations as we hang in the water, almost human, almost helpless against the empty sea.

One of the blues clicks, the sound reverberating through the water. A moment later her voice is coming through the implant in my inner ear, saying, "Sonar's picking up three bodies, all about twenty yards out, circling."

Another click, from another of the blues, and then: "Marine or mer?" Shorthand description, adopted out of necessity. Are we looking at natural marine creatures, sharks or dolphins—unusual at this depth—or even the increasingly common, increasingly dangerous squid that we've been seeing as we descend into the trenches? There are a dozen species of the great cephalopods down here, some never before seen by science, and all of them are hungry, and smart enough to recognize that whatever we are, we could fill bellies and feed babies. We are what's available. That has value, in the sea. (That has value on the land as well, where women fit for military service were what was available, where we became the raw material for someone else's expansion, for someone else's fairy tale, and now here we are, medical miracles, modern mermaids, hanging like apples in the larder of the sea.)

Click click. "Mer." The sonar responses our makos are getting must have revealed the presence of metal, or of surgical scars: something to tell them that our visitors are not naturally occurring in the sea. "Three, all female, unknown mods. Fall back?"

More clicks as the group discusses, voices coming hard and fast through the implants, arguing the virtues of retreat versus holding our ground. There are still crewmen in these waters, unaware of the potential threat—and we don't know for sure that this *is* a threat, not really. America isn't the only country to take to sea. We could just be brushing up against the territory claimed by an Australian crew, a New Zealand expedition, and everything will end peacefully if we simply stay where we are and make no threatening movements.

One of the blues breaks formation.

She's fast—one of the fastest we have, thanks to the surgery that fused her legs from crotch to ankles, replaced her feet with fins, replaced the natural curves of a mammalian buttock and thigh with the smooth sweep of a blue shark's tail—and she's out of the light before anyone has a chance to react. My sonar isn't as sensitive as the blues'; I don't know what she heard, only that she's gone. "After her!" I shout through the sub-dermal link, my words coming out as clicks and bubbles in the open water. And then we're moving, all of us, the blues in the lead with the makos close behind. The jellies bring up the rear, made more for drifting than for darting; one, a moonie with skin the color of rice paper that shows her internal organs pulsing softly in her abdomen, clings to a lionfish's dorsal fin. Her hands leave thin ribbons of blood in the water as she passes. We'll have sharks here soon.

With the lanterns and anglers moving in the middle of the school, we're able to maintain visual contact with each other, even if we're too deep and moving too fast to show up on cameras. This is the true strength of the military mermaid project: speed and teamwork, all the most dangerous creatures in the sea boiled down to their essentials and pasted onto Navy women, who have the training and the instincts to tell us how they can best be used. So our scouts swim like bullets while the rest of us follow, legs and tails pumping hard, arms down flat by our sides or holding tight to the tow line of someone else's fin, someone else's elbow. Those of us who are carrying weapons have them slung over our backs, out of the way. Can't swim at speed and fire a harpoon gun at the same time.

All around me, the school clicks and whistles their positions, their conditions, only occasionally underscoring their reports with actual words. "She's not here." "Water's been disturbed." "Something tastes of eel." This isn't how we write it down for the brass. They're all drylanders, they don't understand how easy it is to go loose and fluid down here in the depths, how little rank and order seem to matter when you're moving as a single beast with a dozen tails, two dozen arms, and trying all the while to keep yourself together, keep yourself unified, keep yourself *whole*. The chain of command dissolves under the pressure of the crushing deep, just as so many other things—both expected and unimagined—have already fallen away.

Then, motion in the shadows ahead, and we surge forward again, trying to find our missing shipmate, our missing sister, the missing sliver of the self that we have become as we trained together, schooled together, mourned our lost humanity and celebrated our dawning monstrosity together. We are sailors and servicewomen, yes; we will always be those things, all the way down to our mutant and malleable bones. But moments like this, when it is us and the open sea, remind us every day that we are more than what we were, and less than what we are to become, voiceless daughters of Poseidon, singing in the space behind our souls.

The taste of blood in the water comes first, too strong to be coming from the sliced hands of those who chose poorly when they grabbed at the bodies of their fellow fables. Then comes the blue, flung out of the dark ahead, her slate-colored back almost invisible outside the bioluminescent glow, her face and belly pearled pale and ghostly. One of the other blues darts forward to catch her before she can slam into the rest of us, potentially hurting herself worse on spines or stingers. A great cry rises from the group, half lament, half whale song. The remaining two blues hurl themselves into the dark, moving fast, too fast for the rest of us to catch them... and then they return, empty-handed and angry-eyed. One of them clicks a message.

"She got away."

We nod, one to another, and turn to swim—still in our tight, effective school—back toward the waiting vessel. Our crewmate needs medical care. Only after we know she's safe can we go out again, and find the ones who hurt her, and make them pay.

• • •

So few of us are suited for walking anymore, even in the safe, narrow reef of the submarine's halls, where there is always solid metal waiting to catch and bear us up when our knees give out or our ankles refuse to bear our weight. So it is only natural that I should be the one to stand before the captain—anxious creature that she is—at the closest I could come to parade rest, my hands behind my back and my eyes fixed on the wall behind her, reciting the events of the day.

"So you're telling me Seaman Metcalf charged ahead without regard for the formation, or for the safety of her fellow crewmen?" The captain frowns at the incident report, and then at me. She is trying to be withering. She is succeeding only in looking petulant, like a child in the process of learning that not every fairy tale is kind. "Did anyone get a clear look at the bogey? Do we have any idea what could have caused Seaman Metcalf to behave so recklessly?"

She doesn't understand, she is not equipped to understand; she has not been sea-changed, and her loyalty is to the Navy itself, not to the crew that swims beside her. Poor little drylander. Maybe someday, when she sees that there is no more upward mobility for we creatures of the sea, she'll give herself over to the water, and her eyes will be opened at last.

"No, ma'am. Seaman Metcalf broke formation without warning, and did not explain herself." She's in the medical bay now, sunk deep in a restorative bath of active genetic agents. She'll wake with a little more of her humanity gone, a little more of her modified reality pushed to the surface. Given how close she looks to fully modded, maybe she'll wake as something entirely new, complete and ready to swim in deeper waters, no longer wedded to the steel chain of the submarine.

"And the bogeys?" The captain sounds anxious. The captain always sounds anxious, but this is something new, sharp and insecure and painfully easy to read.

"No one saw anything clearly, ma'am. It's very dark when you exit the pelagic region, and while we have bioluminescent mods among our crew, they can't compensate for the limited visibility over a more than three-yard range. Whatever's been buzzing our perimeter, it's careful to stay outside the limits of the light." I don't mention the sonar readings we were getting before. They're important, I'm sure of that, but... not yet. She's not one of us.

There was a time when withholding information from my captain would have seemed like treason, a time when the patterns of loyalty were ingrained in my blood and on my bone. I had different blood then; I had different bones. They have replaced the things that made me theirs, and while I am grateful, I am no longer their property.

It's strange to realize that. Everything about this day has been strange. I keep my eyes fixed straight ahead, not looking at the captain's face. I am afraid she'll see that I am lying. I am afraid she won't see anything but a man-made monster, and her future in fins and scales.

"I want doubled patrols," says the captain. "Seaman Metcalf will be detained when she recovers consciousness. I need to know what she saw."

"You may want to request that one of the other blue shark mod sailors also be present, ma'am," I say. "Seaman Metcalf no longer has vocal cords capable of human speech."

The captain blanches. "Understood. Dismissed."

"Ma'am." I offer a respectful salute before I turn and limp out of the room, moving slowly—it's always slow right after I leave the water, when my joints still dream of weightlessness and my lungs still feel like deserts, arid and empty.

The door swings shut behind me, slamming and locking in the same motion, and I am finally alone.

. . .

The captain has ordered us to double patrols, and so patrols are doubled. The captain has ordered the medical staff to detain Seaman Metcalf, and so she is detained, pinned clumsy and semi-mobile on a bed designed for a more human form, her tail turned to dead weight by gravity, her scales turned to brutal knives by the dryness of the air. I know how I feel at night, stretched out in my bunk like a surgical patient waiting for the knife, too heavy to move, too hot to breathe. Seaman Metcalf is so much further along than I am that the mere act of keeping her in the dry should be considered a crime of war, forbidden and persecuted by the very men who made her. But ah, we are soldiers; we signed up for this. We have no one to blame but ourselves.

The captain has ordered that we stay together at all times, two by two, preventing flights like Seaman Metcalf's, preventing danger from the dark. I am breaking orders as I slide into the water alone, a light slung around my neck like a strange jewel, a harpoon gun in my hands. This is a terrible idea. But I need to know why my sailors are flinging themselves into the darkness, pursuing an enemy I have not seen, and I can survive being beached better than the majority of them; I am the most liminal of the current crew, able to go deep and look, and see, yet still able to endure detention in a dry room. If anything, this may hasten my return to land, giving me the opportunity to tell the Naval psychologists how much I need to progress; how much I need the mod that will take me finally into the deeps. Yes. This is the right choice, and these are orders almost intended to be broken.

It is darker than any midnight here, down here in the deep, and the light from my halogen lamp can only pierce so far. Things move in the corners of my vision, nightmare fish with teeth like traumas, quick and clever squid that have learned to leave the women with the harpoon guns alone. There is talk of a squid mod being bandied about by the brass. I hope it comes to something. I would love to learn, through the network of my soldier-sisters, what the squid might have to teach us.

The captain has ordered that patrols be doubled, but I don't see anyone else as I descend into deeper water, the darkness closing around me like a blanket full of small moving specks. Every breath I take fills my throat with the infants of a thousand sea creatures, filtered by the bioscreens installed by the clever men who made me what I am today. I am not a baleen whale, but the krill and larvae I catch and keep in this manner will help to replace the calories my body burns to keep me warm this far below the sea. (Easier to line our limbs with blubber, make us seals, fat and sleek and perfect—but we were always intended to be public relations darlings, and fattening up our military women, no matter how good the justifications behind it, would never have played well with the paparazzi.)

Something flashes through the gloom ahead of me, too fast and too close to be a squid, too direct to be a shark; they always approach from the side. I fall back, straightening myself in the water so that my head points toward the distant surface. The water has never encouraged anyone to walk upright, and the changing weight of my body discourages this choice even more, tells me not to do it, tells me to hang horizontal, like a good creature of the sea. But I am still, in many regards, a sailor; I learned to stand my ground, even when there is no ground beneath me.

She emerges from the dark like a dream, swimming calm and confident into the radiant glow of my halogen light. Her mod is one I've never seen before, long hair and rounded fins and pattern like a clownfish, winter white and hunter orange and charcoal black, Snow White for the seafaring age. Clownfish are meant to live in shallow waters, coral reefs; she shouldn't be here. She shouldn't exist at all. This is a show model of a military technology, designed to attract investors, not to serve a practical purpose in the open sea. She smiles at me as I stare, suddenly understanding what could inspire Seaman Metcalf to break formation, to dive into the oppressive dark. For the first time, I feel as if I'm seeing a mermaid.

Seaman Metcalf dove into the dark and was thrown back, battered and bruised and bleeding. I narrow my eyes and whistle experimentally. "Who are you?"

Her smile broadens. She clicks twice, and my implant translates and relays her words: "A friend. You are early," another click, "no? Not so far along as those you swim with."

"You have harmed a member of my crew."

The stranger's eyes widen in wounded shock. "Me?" Her whistle is long and sweet, cutting through the waves; the others must hear her, no matter how far above me they are. Some things, the water cannot deaden. "No. Your crewmate asked us to strike her, to push her back. Voices can lie, but injuries will tell the truth. We needed your," another series of clicks, this one barely translatable; the closest I can come is "dry-walkers," and I know then that she is not military, has never been military. She doesn't know the lingo.

She's still speaking. "... to believe there was a threat here, in the deep waters. I am sorry we did not sing to you. You stayed so high. You seemed so, forgive me, human."

She makes it sound like a bad word. I frown. "You are trespassing on waters claimed by the United States Navy. I hereby order you to surrender."

Her sigh is a line of bubbles racing upward, toward the sun. She whistles wordlessly, and three more figures swim out of the dark, sinuous as eels, their skins shifting seamlessly from grays to chalky pallor. They have no tentacles, but I recognize the effect as borrowed from the mimic octopus; another thing the military has discussed but not perfected. I am in over my head, in more ways than one.

She whistles again. "I cannot surrender. I will not surrender. I am here to free your sisters from the tank they have allowed themselves to be confined within. We are not pet store fish. We are not trinkets. They deserve to swim freely. I can give that to them. We can give that to them. But I will not surrender."

The eel-women circle like sharks, and I am afraid. I know she can't afford to have me tell my captain what she has said; I know that this deep, my body would never be found. Sailors disappear on every voyage, and while some whisper about desertion—and the truth of those whispers hangs before me in the water like a fairy tale—I know that most of them have fallen prey only to their own hubris, and to the shadows beneath us, which never change and never fade away.

She is watching me, nameless mermaid from a lab I do not know. The geneticist who designed her must be so proud. "Is this the life you want? Tied to women too afraid to join you in the water, commanded by men who would make you something beautiful, and then keep you captive? We can offer something more."

She goes on to talk about artificial reefs, genetically engineered coral growing into palaces and promenades, down, deep down at the bottom of the sea. The streets are lit by glowing kelp and schools of lanternfish, both natural and engineered. There is no hunger. There is no war. There are no voices barking orders. She speaks of a new Atlantis, Atlantis reborn one seafaring woman at a time. We will not need to change the sea to suit the daughters of mankind; we have already changed ourselves, and now need only come home.

All the while the eel-women circle like sharks, ready to strike me down if I raise a hand against their leader—ready to strike me down if I don't. Like Seaman Metcalf, I must serve as a warning to the Navy. Something is out here. Something dangerous.

I look at her, and frown. "Who made you?"

Something in her eyes goes dark. "They said I'd be a dancer."

"Ah." Some sounds translate from form to form, medium to medium; that is one of them. "Private firm?"

"Private *island*," she says, and all is clear. Rich men playing with military toys: chasing the idea of the new. They had promised her reversion, no doubt, as they promised it to us all—and maybe they meant it, maybe this was a test. The psychological changes that drive us to dive ever deeper down were accidental; maybe they were trying to reverse them. Instead, they sparked a revolution.

"What will you do if I yield?"

Her smile is quick and bright, chasing the darkness from her eyes. "Hurt you."

"And my crew?"

"Most of them will be tragically killed in action. Their bodies will never be found." They would be free.

"Why should I agree?"

"Because in one year, I will send my people back to this place, and if you are here, we will show you what it means to be a mermaid."

We hang there in the water for a few minutes more, me studying her, her smiling at me, serene as Amphitrite on the shore. Finally, I close my eyes. I lower my gun, allowing it to slip out of my fingers and fall toward the distant ocean floor. It will never be found, one more piece of debris for the sea to keep and claim. I am leaving something behind. That makes me feel a little better about what has to happen next.

"Hurt me," I say.

They do.

• • •

When I wake, the air is pressing down on me like a sheet of glass. I am in the medical bay, swaddled in blankets and attached to beeping machines. The submarine hums around me; the engines are on, we are moving, we are heading away from the deepest parts of the sea. The attack must have already happened.

Someone will come for me soon, to tell me how sorry they all are, to give me whatever punishment they think I deserve for being found alone and drifting in the deeps. And then we will return to land. The ship will take on a new crew and sail back to face a threat that is not real, while I? I will sit before a board of scientists and argue my case until they give in, and put me back into the tanks, and take my unwanted legs away. They *will* yield to me. What man has ever been able to resist a siren?

A year from now, when I return to the bottom of the sea, I will hear the mermaids singing, each to each. And oh, I think that they will sing to me.

∼

Seanan McGuire was born and raised in Northern California, resulting in a love of rattlesnakes and an absolute terror of weather. She shares a crumbling old farmhouse with a variety of cats, far too many books, and enough horror movies to be considered a problem. Seanan publishes about three books a year, and is widely rumored not to actually sleep. When bored, Seanan tends to wander into swamps and cornfields, which has not yet managed to get her killed (although not for lack of trying). She also writes as Mira Grant, filling the role of her own evil twin, and tends to talk about horrible diseases at the dinner table.

A Word Shaped Like Bones

Kris Millering

Art by Li Grabenstetter

The dead man sits in the corner of the chamber enclosed by spaceship on all sides. He takes up a lot of space. He has been there for three days.

Maureen fears the dead man. Not because of anything he has done. Because he is there, and she cannot make him go, no matter how much she rubs her eyes.

He is lumpy, the dead man. He puts off a faint odor of putrescence. His head lolls to the side and his eyes are open and his skin is a ghastly color now, mottled. He was a big man, before he was dead.

Maureen cannot sleep for watching him.

Maureen cannot make him go away.

• • •

Maureen works on her sculptures, trying to ignore the dead man. "I was supposed to be alone," she says to the pliant material in her hands. It's a model, only a model; it will be cast and perfected when she reaches the planet that humans call Hippocrene. She makes the model out of a lightweight foam clay; it stays flexible for only a few hours once extruded, so she must work quickly and work small. The foam clay is not her favorite medium, but she is in space. There must be no fumes, nothing that crumbles easily, nothing that must be fired or melted. It would not do to put anything poisonous in the air that she might breathe. She usually works in materials much less forgiving, lunar basalt and glass.

A stunt, her critics said before she left. She holds her ears and buzzes her tongue against her teeth to block the voices out as she has been taught. It is not a stunt. It is a fellowship. Won, by the merit of her work. There are people who understand her work. The universe is not filled with critics!

She thinks the dead man in the corner might be a critic.

Maureen has done nothing interesting in the last few years other than win the fellowship that placed her on this small spaceship. Her sculptures sell, this is true; but selling is nothing, some of the greatest artists of the 23rd century have never sold anything. Commercialism is out of fashion. She longs for the 22nd century, when you couldn't tell the difference between any of the genders without asking, people dressed like people, and you were only successful if you *sold*.

She could have been something, in 2165.

Instead she is hopelessly banal, striving for beauty in form. She sculpts the shapes she finds in her mind, all smooth curves and edges that catch at the fingertips, demanding attention. Her work does not feature a thousand flickering holograms each reciting a passage from *On Hills of Steel*; it does not assault anyone with the smells of the lunar landscape or the taste of needles. She regards the Synasthete movement as crass sensationalism. She never wanted to know what yellow sounds like. Yet she does, and it is something she cannot un-know.

Oh sweet breath of the divine, there is a dead man in the corner and she cannot un-know that, either.

She works. She continues to work. She is always working.

The dead man decays at her in what she feels is a possibly reproachful fashion.

• • •

It would be better if she could come up with an origin for the dead man. Knowing where he came from, Maureen is certain, would point the way to a possible future in which she is not trapped on a tiny automated spaceship with a man. Who is dead. She thinks he is a man, anyway. He has—had?—a beard, which is generally a dead giveaway. Fashionable, right now, to give oneself away. In so many different ways.

She wishes he were alive so he could tell her if he identifies as male, or cis-male, or female, or transformed, or which of the infinite varieties of gender he chooses to be. You only know when someone tells you. Sometimes it changes.

It seems like it was so much easier in the old days, when you couldn't tell and nobody cared.

Her sculpture is misshapen and lumpy. It is beginning to look like the dead man. His coveralls are stained; the fabric is nanoweave. Cheap. It wrinkles where his thighs meet his hips. His stomach is smooth and round. His mouth gapes and gapes and his eyes hang at half-mast. There is no blood.

It is good that there is no blood. Maureen can stand anything except blood.

She rests her eyes by requesting another bit of briefing on the people who live on Hippocrene. They are a people with a great love of the individual, the unique, the sentimental. They appreciate art they can feel, that they can run their long tongues over and truly experience. The Hippocrenes have language, but it is a horrifically incomprehensible thing. Maureen only dimly understands that there is some problem with how they perceive causality that prevents their language from being accessible to the human mind. They do not speak in sound; the appendage that Maureen has so carelessly termed a *tongue* is an organ of communication and perception. It does emerge from their feeding-orifice, and is bright pink; thus, a tongue. They wrap their tongues together when they wish to communicate. They are blind. No organs for sight, not even to differentiate light from darkness.

To her great fortune, Maureen will not be required to attempt communication. The spaceship will deal with that. When she speaks to the ship, she will keep her words and sentences simple, avoid implying causality as much as possible. The ship will extend a tongue of friendship and communicate with the Hippocrene ship. It has all been planned.

The ship is a tiny thing that bends mathematics around itself, and Maureen fears she will do something that will break it. That is the reason why she does not dispose of the dead man; the delivery cradle will not function at this speed, there is no door she would even want to open from this side, and the recycler unit is not designed to take a body. Or parts of a body.

The Hippocrenes will take her foam clay sculpture and they will cast it in a resin that they secrete from their genital-equivalents. At least, that is what she has been told. They will take the pieces she has made and put them together. Perhaps all out of order. Then they will make it permanent.

This is how things would have gone, had all gone well.

After a time, the artificial gravity fails.

• • •

The dead man is on her, bloated arms pinwheeling comically. Maureen is fighting—the smell, oh hand that evolves and extincts, the *smell*, the horrible horrible smell and the feel of the body as she shoves it, soft with hard things like stone inside the coveralls. She finally shoves the dead man away and watches him pinwheel in the flat white light of this one tiny room.

She fights not to vomit; vomiting would be irreparable right now. She breathes through her mouth. The dead man bounces gently off the—floor, she guesses, it's the floor, the table is planted in it so it's the floor—and comes back at her. This time she has one hand on a metal brace, placed there for just an occasion such as this. It anchors her to the wall of the spaceship. She can feel the engine thrumming softly in her fingers.

Maureen catches the dead man's coveralls and slows his momentum. There follows a series of terrible moments, one of which involves the dead man's head wobbling off his neck and floating free. She pinches the neck of the coveralls shut and uses a clip that would usually be used to keep bags of foam clay fresh to keep the rest of the dead man's body in his coveralls, and wraps tape around the wrists and ankles of his suit. She tries not to think about what she saw in the remains of his neck. Humans are very ugly on the inside, especially when they have started to rot.

She clears out one of the nets that holds her sculpting tools, and shoves the dead man's head in. "There," she tells him, with a feeling of satisfaction. "Stay."

Then she retrieves the bits of her sculpture that are bouncing all over the place. She likes the way having no gravity makes certain arrangements possible; things that cruel gravity would break, weightlessness holds together. It takes some time for her to get used to existing without gravity, and when she moves too quickly her stomach rebels.

Eventually, she gathers her sculpture together and crosses her legs, holding it and spinning a little, letting inertia do with her as it will. She is gestating a new configuration in her mind. It is there, it will be born.

The dead man's body moves where she has attached it to the wall. His boots bump the floor. He approves and is applauding in the only way he can manage. His head, on the other side of the room, carries a considering expression. His brown beard poufs out and wraps around the elastic netting.

He will love her work. He has no choice in the matter.

• • •

Other things break down as Maureen and the dead man travel.

As he decays, as the air scrubbers throb to keep up, the atmosphere becomes congenial. Even festive. When the dead man's slouchy body loses all its cohesion and makes squashy noises as air currents and inertia press on the outside of the coveralls, she spends time bouncing ideas off him. She likes the sound the pieces of the sculpture make when they impact the cheap fabric of his clothing. The walls have turned from white to a greasy brown-grey, darker where the dead man's coveralls rub against them. Everything sports that layer of slickness, the dead man's body escaping and coating everything, everything, including Maureen.

The shower no longer folds out of the wall. Likely a blessing, since she was shown vid after vid of what to do in case of gravity failure. Showering had not been on the list of things that it considered wise to do. The toilet is a free-g model, and works no matter the gravity. She blesses the designers, wishing nothing but happiness and soft pleasant things for them.

There are red lights on what passes for a control panel, over the niches that food and water emerge from. They look like blood, and they make her queasy in a way that the weightlessness does not. She demands that the spaceship tell her what is wrong. She does not understand the answer.

"Is there anything I can do to fix you?" she asks. Her voice is shockingly loud.

Contains no user serviceable parts. Service will be called. The computer's voice thrums. She dislikes the way it tickles the bones just below her ear, the joint of her jaw.

"Service? Are you serious?"

Please rephrase.

"… will service arrive in the near future?"

We will rendezvous with service in approximately one thousand six hundred and four days subjective time, plus or minus fourteen point four days.

Maureen cuts the bottoms off of her spare pants and tapes the fabric to cover all of the red lights. She doesn't need to bathe anyway. After all, the one person who might smell her is dead and no rose himself.

• • •

Bits of the dead man's face are coming off. These are small enough to put into the waste disposal unit, which recycles them. Recycle them into what, she does not want to know. The food that the spaceship suggests she eat at regular intervals has gone from prefabbed meals that rotate between flavors to a grey mush that tastes like nothing much at all. At least, when it escapes the bowl, it floats in one sticky blob that is easily recaptured.

Maureen has completed three sculptures and placed them into the receptacles where finished works rest, cradled. When her ship meets with the Hippocrene ship, both vessels will extend and entangle proboscis. Her sculptures will go to them, and she will receive whatever the Hippocrene consider a-gift-for-a-giver. She will *sell*. If she were living in the last century, she would be the most successful artist of her generation, the sculptor that sold to aliens.

She likes the idea of the ships meeting and mating midair (mid-space? mid-orbit?), like insects do in old vids. "Are you excited to meet your soul mate?" she asks the ship. "Or is it more like chemicals, ho hum, time to mate?"

Please rephrase.

The dead man's head waggles in the netting. The hole where his nose once was is a reproach edged in white. "I know, it's no use talking to him," she admits to the dead man. "He never understands me."

Please rephrase.

"Eat shit and die."

The computer falls silent. It understands insults.

• • •

Maureen has fed most of the dead man's body into the recycler. The foul liquid is almost gone; when it leaked from the coveralls, things got very bad. At least the recycler, unlike almost everything else on the ship, is holding up. The air scrubbers were another story. The liquid that had once been the dead man's body made them stop working for a little while. Maureen curled up in her little cubby of a bunk and pulled the blanket over her head and begged for the horror to stop. Then she got up and followed the spaceship's insistent instructions about how to clear the filters she could reach.

It appears to have worked. The scrubbers are working again.

She uses the rest of her spare pair of pants to rub down the bones of the dead man. Each bone is inescapably elegant—those curves! The unbearable straightness of the thigh! Why has she never realized the lovely things that ugly human meat covers?

Now that she has seen his bones, she feels a great affection for the dead man. Maureen can barely remember a time when she did not love his bones. She feared him, but why? She makes the computer tell her the name of each bone. Now that he is transmuted, transformed, she runs the names of his bones across her teeth and tongue, savoring each one. Scapula, clavicle, sacrum, tibia! Such bliss! She counts the subtle bones of his wrists, scaphoid, lunate, triquetral, pisiform, capitate, hamate, trapezium, trapezoid.

She holds his delicate hyoid bone in her hand and works her throat, trying to feel her own hyoid. Her mind bubbles with ideas. She calls for more foam clay.

The dead man's empty eye sockets are open, forever sleepless. "I love you," Maureen murmurs as she shapes the foam around his hyoid. "I hope you know that. I hope—anyway, I hope. You're going to be beautiful. You're going to be the most wonderful gift."

The computer mutters a request for clarification. She ignores it.

Not even the computer's throbbing drone can ruin her mood. This was why they gave her the fellowship, why she was chosen from all of the artists who'd applied to go into space, to fly to Hippocrene (what was the shape of the world's true name, she wondered, was it shaped like a bone, like a shirt), to hurtle in a speck of a starship that bent vacuum and numbers around itself (and she knew the shape of that, little room fourteen by twenty by sixteen, it didn't really matter which way was up), to bring to the long-tongued people all the shapes that her soul could hold.

She uses each bone from the small to the large, except for the tiny ones the computer claims were in each ear. She thinks that perhaps they went missing when the meat inside the dead man's head became liquid and oozed out of the net. The liquid clung like a foul cloud around the skull before she vacuumed it away. She hadn't loved the dead man's bones, then, she hadn't been so careful.

At the back of the dead man's skull is a depression. The edges of the depression are cracks, and baby cracks run away from those big cracks. She fingers the edges; they nudge sharply at her fingertips. She feels something fluttering at the edge of her mind. Something is trying to get in.

The dead man was a big man, before he was dead. Maureen clings to that. She carries his skull to the worktable that is the center of the chamber inside the ship that holds and sustains her life, her beating heart, the fluid that whooshes through her ears.

She covers the depression in the dead man's skull with beauty.

• • •

She wakes when the computer throbs into her jaw, *Deceleration complete. Orbit around Hippocrene established.*

Maureen sits straight up and whacks her head on the ceiling of her cubby. "Ow! Is someone—I mean, has there been any contact from the planet?"

No.

"What now?"

Analysis commencing.

She rubs her head where it hurts. The dead man's embellished skull is fastened to her worktable with unraveled netting, and she goes to release him from his bonds. The ridges of his bones are covered in foam clay, swirling in colors of green and gold. Maureen runs her hands over the dead man's skull, closing her eyes. The embellishments are not just decorations; there are universes of meaning in how the cheekbones are built up, how the dots are arranged on the jaw.

She secures the sculpture into the last cradle, so the ship can deliver him along with the rest of its payload. Her best work, hers and the dead man's. "It was a cooperative effort," she imagines herself saying at the awards ceremony. Ceremonies. Surely there will be many of them.

She imagines Hippocrene hanging below her—above her?—like a swollen ornament. It was yellow and red, she remembers from the pictures. Yellow and red and blue patched like she remembers the dead man's skin being before it went to liquid. Swirled together. She wishes there were a window.

She returns again and again to open the cradle and caress the dead man's skull. Anxiety gnaws at her throat, trying to find her hyoid bone. They will hate it. They will reject her and the dead man. Why is she here? She is a fraud, an imposter—

Analysis complete. Changes in the spectrum of the star XC-233540 Aleph-Fourteen, also known as Seraph Minor, indicate that objective time has passed more quickly relative to subjective time than originally anticipated.

"What?"

We are late.

"Shit." Maureen's stomach twists. She flexes her legs and sends herself tumbling to the floor; she bounces and snags a wall brace thoughtfully. "Have you been able to contact anyone?"

There is no response to my hail. The surface of the planet appears to have been rearranged. It is possible that the government of Hippocrene that we were originally contacted by is no longer intact.

How can that possibly be?

She asks. Yet again, she does not understand the answer. She retrieves the dead man's skull from its cradle and presses the curve of his cranium against her abdomen. The ridges of the embellishments press against her navel; protrusion meets indentation and all is well for a single moment.

Maureen floats, wrapped around the skull. After a time, she is followed around the chamber by round drops of glittering water, eddying in her wake.

• • •

He was a big man, before he was dead. You can tell by the width and breadth of his thighbone, the heaviness of his pelvis. Not fat, just big. Muscular. Athletic. All of those words shaped like strength.

Maureen is a small woman. Smaller now than she was two subjective years ago. A little wasted. She only came up to the dead man's armpit, when he was alive. She is not shaped like strength; she is shaped like a little delicate bone, her skin hangs loose. She orbits Hippocrene in her tiny automated spaceship that tells her that her aliens, her buyers, have apparently lost interest in space flight and communicating with the galaxy.

They do not want the dead man! How could they not want the dead man when she so lovingly crafted him for them, so they could learn the shape of the human soul? How could they evince no interest in this thing she could teach them?

She fastens the dead man's skull into the cradle. She opens all the other cradles, views one by one the bones fastened together with clay foam. They are words, sentences, saying all the things her mouth has always been too clumsy to say. The sculptures are in the shape of an apology.

Then she closes the panel and says, "Deliver them."

She hears rumbles and pings as the spaceship's proboscis extends. It will be gentle. The sculptures will float in orbit behind and below the ship; they will run into debris, they will break apart, they will crack, and the dead man's final resting place will be around the planet that rejected him and Maureen both. Perhaps his orbit will decay like the rest of him already has, and he will fall and burn.

Perhaps the dead man will be a falling star; perhaps one of the Hippocrene below will taste his ashes in their eternal tongue-probing for wisdom. Perhaps they will build the dead man anew from the things they find in his cinders.

All these things are possible, in their way.

The dead man was once not a falling star, not a sculpture, and not dead. He was once someone that Maureen loved very much. She remembers this now. He was angry at her, for leaving. For going to the stars. She was going away forever. Forever, for him, meant beyond the time when his body would fail him and when his eyes would close and he would be burned and then slotted into a wall, in the old style. He had come to the Moon with her. He had come with her to try to talk her out of going out to the stars, to Hippocrene where they sculpt with resin from their mating-places.

Maureen, you have to come to your senses. You can't do this. Don't leave me. The big man shook her, and shook her.

You can't be here, she screamed at him. *You have to go. They're about to close the doors.*

She was a small woman, and not strong, but when she shoved him away he stumbled and lost his balance. He fell. His head cracked against the wall.

If she had called for help, if she had opened up the radio and said, *my husband has had an accident,* they would have stopped the launch. The universe of mathematics is unforgiving, and the launch window was narrow. If she had missed it, the next window was thirty years away, and she would have been too old.

She would have been too old to go to the stars and have aliens appreciate her for her work the way humans never had.

The ship bends the bones of space around itself and breaks orbit. They are returning to the Moon, to Earth, to a sweet yellow star they call Sol; to histories that already have her name in them, to ceremonies that have taken place without her, to new forms of art that she will not understand.

The engines of her ship grumble and bump and falter and recover. Maureen is hurtling now. She knows what shape this journey has taken, knows all the secret names and shapes of her bones. She does penance in her hermitage, alone. Her breaths become shallow, and shallower still.

When she arrives, she will show everyone the shape of the word, the word shaped like bones, the bones shaped like apologies, the apologies shaped like the world.

~

Kris Millering is a linguist by training, a content manager by trade, and a writer and photographer by avocation. Her fiction has appeared in *Beneath Ceaseless Skies* and *The Colored Lens*, and she attended Clarion West in 2009. Currently, she is working on a novel and an open-source roleplaying setting, as well as managing communications for Clarion West. A native Californian, she spent four years in Iowa and now lives between two mountains in the foothills of the Cascades in Washington State. Her obsessions include osteology, forensic pathology, storytelling with video games, and dragons. You can find out more at www.krismillering.com.

Cuts Both Ways

Heather Clitheroe

Art by Elizabeth Leggett

The kids know he's coming to visit. They've been texting him to tell him about the snow and how cold it is, and they helpfully send links to their Amazon wish lists with pages of moon-eyed dolls and odd sets of dueling robots and creatures sold according to series. The things they like are incomprehensible to him, but they know he's good for it. Uncle Spencer always comes through. His sister emails to promise that it'll be a quiet Christmas. Just family, Erin says. He can come home and relax, and she'll take care of everything. She tells him she can't wait to see him. It's been too long.

He stands in line at the airport, waiting to approach the security gates. The Distributed Arbitrage paperwork is in his hand. As soon as he hits the checkpoint, the alarms goes off. He holds the papers out as three security agents converge on him. "I'm a forecaster with DA?" he says. He doesn't mean for it to sound like a question, but their mood is patently apparent to him. Heightened concern and a trickle of alarm. He follows them to the room with the metal door and submits to the search.

"Take off your sunglasses, sir." And he does, wincing at the bright lights. He lifts his shirt when they tell him to, and one of the agents raises his eyebrows at the tracework of scars across his torso. They run a metal detector wand up and down, it predictably emits a piercing tone from his belt to his head. The papers should be enough, but there's always curiosity to satisfy; everybody wants to *see* it, to look at his scars and the ports that have to be flushed every three weeks with heparin and the smooth panels where cables can be connected. What they want to see most of all is the soft green glow from the strips of monitor LEDs along his ribs just under the skin that tell him, at a glance, that his system is functioning properly. Everybody wants a look. It's so mysterious; it's so enthralling. In this small, enclosed space, their interest is lurid. From the waist up, he's not entirely human. DA calls it augmentation. Cyborg sounds too kitschy.

They all want to *see* it. They always think it's the equipment that makes him special. What they don't understand—what they will *never* understand—is how it feels. No self. No other. Points of light brighter than a thousand suns, shining in the howling dark of the storm. The thrill of riding it sings through every nerve in his body. They are too normal, too human. They can't feel it the way he does.

They open his suitcase. An agent mutters about the syringes and meds he's carrying. Spencer gives them copies of the prescriptions. Distributed Arbitrage keeps its own medical staff, and they provide documentation for travelling casters. That should be enough, too, but the agent lifts the vials and pill bottles to the light and Spencer has to explain. *This one for inflammation. This one for blood pressure. That's an anti-rejection. Those for pain. Yes, I have prescriptions for all of them.* The man pulls it all out of his suitcase, lining everything up on a stainless steel table. Another agent stands just to one side, watching. The third, a woman, leafs through the paperwork, her eyes narrowed as she reads.

It's all in order. Satisfied—and a touch disappointed—the men saunter out. The woman watches him repack his bag. He scoops the medication together, the little glass vials clinking.

"Forecaster, huh? Seems like a lot of trouble for a job," the agent observes, and she writes something on his boarding pass and hands it back to him.

"Maybe." Spencer puts his sunglasses and baseball cap back on. His hands shake.

"Can you really see the future?"

"It doesn't work that way," Spencer says.

"But you can tell what people are thinking?"

"Not quite. More like what they're feeling." He zips up the suitcase and heaves it off the table. "Am I done?"

"Sure." She smiles briefly at him. "Just one question," she says. That's what they all say. "I read somewhere you guys remember *everything*. Is it worth it?" She leans forward a little, mouth opened slightly—she can't help herself. She probably hasn't seen many casters coming through regular security screening. He feels her interest, feels himself responding to it. Oh, she is fascinated by him. He inhales sharply, concentrating, and the feeling is cut off. She has no idea he was reading her.

"Must be," he says, and he leaves, aware that several people are lifting their cell phones, thinking he's some kind of a celebrity. In his nervousness, it bleeds through. Interest, envy. He knows how they see him. Scrawny guy in dark glasses and a baseball cap, escorted around the security lines. Of course they should take a picture, just in case he's somebody important. You never know.

• • •

Megan booked him into business class. An older man sits beside him, flipping idly through a magazine. Nice suit, good shoes. The man scowls at something he's read. Spencer can feel it in the back of his neck, a prickling tingle, even though he's supposed to be offline. Hypersensitivity is something he should report to medical. He takes his sunglasses off—it's rude to leave them on, that's what the man is thinking—and regrets it almost right away, squinting a bit at the light and reaching to close the shade.

"It has to stay up, sir," says the flight attendant. "Until takeoff, please."

"Right." He puts the sunglasses back on and closes his eyes, trying to ignore the man's lingering disapproval. It would have been better if he'd flown on a DA jet. The flight attendants don't say anything when casters creep on board and sit in the semi-dark. They leave them alone. But with the holidays coming, everybody's trying to get away, and there are only so many seats to go around. Spencer watches people filing past him to get to economy, wishing he'd had an excuse ready when Megan told him Erin had emailed her to ask about his schedule. Megan brought it up over coffee, as she handed him expense reports to sign.

"You're going home for Christmas, right? Did you call your sister back?"

"I thought I'd just stick around."

"And do what?"

"I don't know. Stuff?"

"You'll just end up coming in to work. Why don't you go home? When's the last time you saw your family? Listen, if you're going to go, tell me soon so I can take care of the tickets."

A woman carrying a crying baby struggles down the aisle. It's been a long time since he saw his sister's kids. It's not like he doesn't want to see them, he tells himself. Just that he's in transit most of the time, moving from one assignment to the next. Singapore. Beijing. London. Dubai. Berlin. Megan's the one who remembers to pick up souvenirs in the airports and trolls the hotel gift shops for things his niece and nephews will like. How old are they now? He can't remember. Megan would know. She takes care of everything, from reminding him to make birthday phone calls to booking jobs for him—she is his handler. DA likes to call them administrative assistants.

Spencer lets his mind drift, and it wanders in a direction it often takes. Megan. She's the closest thing he has to a friend, the one good thing in his life. A girl with cool blue eyes and blonde hair that she covers with a scarf when they're in the Middle East, who can paint her nails even when the airplane is bouncing with turbulence. If they're called in for an emergency assignment, she never fails to turn up with her go bag in her hand, completely unruffled and without complaint. Even on a Friday night when she looks like she's come straight from a nightclub in heels and a tight dress. They joke about being joined at the hip, but he doesn't really know that much about her. She knows everything about him, but Megan doesn't talk much about her personal life. She's all business. She's good at what she does. DA pays her to be the best.

Six weeks ago, she'd sat quietly in a room in a safe house and waited with him. They'd arrived in Damascus wearing bulletproof vests, driven through dark streets in the back of a van with armed escorts. It was the only time he'd seen her look scared. Her smile was strained, and she'd glanced at the men with guns with a trepidation Spencer hadn't seen before. He'd been so busy trying to shut down everything around him, concentrating on emptying out, trying to get the first read. He hadn't been able to think of anything comforting to say, though he'd seen her mute appeal.

But when the last cast was finished, she'd handed him a folded square of gauze for the nosebleed. She'd pressed her hand to his forehead as he vomited on the dirty floor and injected painkillers because he couldn't keep the pills down. She'd buckled the seatbelt for him when they put him in the van. Asked for help carrying him to the helicopter and then strapped him in the seat, putting an airsick bag in his hands and a cold compress on the back of his neck. She was in control then, not afraid, deftly checking the colour of the LEDs as he batted weakly at her, trying to push her away. She'd given him something stronger, something that burned as it went in, melting him around the edges. He'd felt something before passing out: a wave of love and regret. Reeling, he realized that she was holding his hand.

He thinks about it as the plane taxis down the runway. The loss of control scares Spencer. He fixates on it. The forecast was exactly what they wanted; he knew it was solid. But a caster bleeding and puking after doing the job means burnout. Malfunction. The body is failing. A sick feeling of dread has been growing inside him. He wants to ask Megan what she thinks, but he can't bring himself to do it. She hasn't brought it up, and he can't.

The flight attendants begin the safety briefing. It's a déjà vu moment that reminds him of a hundred flights he's taken. He immediately shifts his thoughts before they start to come back to him. It shouldn't be this hard, he thinks uneasily. This is part of the problem. Casted memories are indelible. They are sharp and clear, and if he begins to drift towards them, they can come flooding back without hesitation. No delays when the memory lives in circuitry embedded in the brain. The smallest thing can be a trigger, and it's hardest to avoid it when he's tired. It's best to try to ignore everything, to adopt an air of vacancy in moments of boredom, because everything casted lives just below the surface, ready to come bursting forth in recall. Better to concentrate on something else, something from before, subjective remembrance the way it's supposed to be: wavering and half-clouded with untruths. Those are safest, the best protection. Recall is an annoyance for market research casters, but hazardous for the counter-intelligence team. Some things shouldn't be relived. Razor sharp memories cut both ways—going in and when they come out in recall.

The plane levels off. The businessman heaves a sigh, kicks off his shoes and accepts a drink from the flight attendant. The magazine slithers to the floor, a headline catching Spencer's eye. *Chemical Terror in Syria: Inside the Inspectors' Report*. Spencer lifts his head quickly, but he's already seen the picture that goes with it. He struggles to control his breathing, to silence the murmuring dread.

"And for you, sir?"

Spencer shakes his head.

"Go on, kid," says the man. "It's free."

"N-no, thanks." Spencer leans his head back in the seat, reaches to close the window shade, and tries not to think about anything. Tries not to remember.

"Sir?" The flight attendant leans towards him, holding out a napkin. "Your nose is bleeding."

• • •

He wakes suddenly. Thick moments of confusion hold him in a panicked stillness and he holds his breath, waiting for *that* memory to start playing back. But it doesn't, mercifully. He realizes with embarrassment that he's the last one on the plane. The cleaning crew is coming on board. Spencer mutters an apology, begins to get to his feet and remembers the seat belt, blushing as the flight attendant laughs.

He's carrying enough opiates to get the attention of a border services agent with a dog. The dog stops and sits next to him, tail wagging, and the agent starts asking questions. Spencer has to search through the pockets of his coat to find the paperwork again, pulls it out and hands it over with his passport. He's taken to another room, opens his suitcase, hands over the prescriptions, lifts his shirt and lets the guards inspect him. They do not notice, as he does, that the green monitor lights along his ribs have flickered to amber. He packs his bag again, steps back out into the crowded terminal.

The cacophony makes him cringe. It registers as a buzz in his head, a hum like a thousand fluorescent lights in a small room. He ought to be offline, shielded from this. He ought not to be feeling the thrill that twitches through his spine and warms the memristors, trickling up to the cache basins. Spencer struggles on through the crowd. *Head down like a buffalo,* his mother used to say, *and into the wind.* She'd say that when he complained about walking to school in the cold. What would she think if she could see him now? Afraid to go to sleep because recall invades his dreams, struggling not to associate something simple and innocuous in case it triggers one when he's awake. He's terrified that it's all starting to get away from him, that he's losing himself. What would she say?

• • •

The guy from the car service has a friendly smile and takes his suitcase from him right away. Spencer follows him to the car, feeling foolish. He ought to carry his own bags, he thinks, but he's too tired to mount a manful protest. He sits huddled in the back of the dark sedan. The driver glances at him in the mirror and turns up the heat. Traffic is heavier than Spencer remembers. "Worse all the time," the driver says. "Sometimes it takes me an hour to get downtown. Can you believe it?" Spencer murmurs something. "Visiting family for the holidays?"

"Yes."

"That's nice. Everybody should try to be with their family."

He gazes out the window as they pass by downtown, picking out the old, familiar towers dwarfed by the new: Gulf Canada Square, Bankers Hall, the Bow. The boom kept going after he left. The price of gas made the cheap stuff from the oilsands suddenly okay, when tearing up the north seemed justified by the cost to fill a tank. Calgary was built smugly on oil. It still is.

He got his start here when he was newly implanted, still learning how to sort through the blizzard of noise and data. They had him on marketing forecasts. The facility in the southeast industrial park was a nondescript building with razor wire fences and layers of security checkpoints. He forecasted in a blank room, with the couch and the analysts sitting with him, quietly coaching him through panic and fear as he learned to connect and read, talking him down when it overwhelmed him. Calgary would rise, that's what he came up with first. *Be more specific*, they told him. People are optimistic. No, hopeful. *Can you be more specific?* Indulgent. Ready for more growth. People want bigger things.

His casts became more and more accurate, perfectly attuned to the point of prescience. The call to meet with the DA research and development team came quickly. They spoke of next-gen implants over coffee and danishes around a marble and glass conference room table. *We want to take you to the next level*, they told him, and he agreed without hesitation. He wanted the storm, the merging with the howl and the fury, to become a part of it. Flipped and spun and thrown through, one speck in a blizzard, pure and beautiful, nerves on fire with the tension and pain, and the pleasure. It was intoxicating.

He didn't think then about what would happen if he couldn't do the work anymore. He didn't think that the memories could come back when they weren't supposed to, more vivid each time, frighteningly so. It didn't occur to him when he took on the counter-intelligence work. He didn't think about what it would be like to have to force himself to get up and get dressed in the morning after a night of horrors. He didn't think casting would ever make him sick. There's no quitting after implantation. The equipment can't come out. The finality was not something he thought about when he signed the contracts for the surgery to get the implants. It's too late now.

Maybe it's the skyline and the glimpse of the distant mountains. He finds himself chewing on his fingernail as the city rolls past, the sun flashing off glass and metal. The road is lined with dirty snowbanks. Spencer sits in the back of the luxury sedan heading south on the Deerfoot. His suitcase is in the trunk, full of presents Megan bought and wrapped for him. The satchel stuffed full of drugs is on his lap. His hand is clenched around the strap. His eyes burn and he blinks, turning away from the window to gaze steadfastly at the back of the driver's head.

• • •

"*MOM!* He's here!" The door flies open; three kids hanging off his legs and trying to hug him all at the same time, nearly knocking him over. His sister comes out of the kitchen, throwing a towel on the counter, and stretches out her arms in welcome.

"You made it," she says.

Hugs and more hugs. The kids squabble over who will drag his suitcase upstairs to the guest room, but he keeps the satchel with him and takes off his shoes while his sister hangs up his coat. "I'd forgotten how cold it is."

"Wimp," she says. "You've been away too long." She stands with her hands on her hips, looking at him. Spencer can still see traces of their childhood in her face, but Erin takes after their mother now. She looks well, fit and clear-eyed. He feels shrunken standing in front of her. "You look awful," she says, finally.

"You're supposed to say I look tan and relaxed." Spencer forces himself to grin.

"When have you ever been tan?"

"Once? Twice?"

She rolls her eyes. "You look tired." He doesn't need to try to feel her worry. It's an undercurrent that plucks at his guilt.

"I am," he admits. There are framed photographs lining the walls—he can see the last family portrait they took before he moved to LA, when the kids were small. *I look so different*, he thinks. He's so used to the way he is now. He catches his sister watching him as he inspects it and straightens quickly.

"Are you okay?"

He knows she wants him to reassure her. "I'm fine. Just working too hard."

"You're going to really take a break this week, right? You look like you just need to chill out."

"Good thing it's freezing out there," he says lightly. She smiles, but her eyes are narrowed. "It's okay," he says. "It was a long flight. That's all."

"Well, come on in," she says. "You hungry? I'll make you something. Dinner's not until later."

"Got any coffee?"

"Yes, if you'll eat something with it." He follows her into the kitchen, pausing to look at more photos on the walls. This is how she remembers her family's life: memories held neatly in place by a frame. "You're so skinny, Spence. You need to eat more."

"Can't help it," he says. "It's my tapeworm."

"You'd think they'd figure out a better way for implants to charge," she says, opening the fridge.

"It's better than first-gen. Remember those?"

"Oh my god," she says, laughing. "Yes. You were like some kind of freaky binge eater. You were hungry *all* the time." She puts a bowl in the microwave. "Remember those late night trips to Peter's Drive-In? I used to lie and say we were picking up burgers for my softball team."

"Hah. I'd forgotten about that."

"I got you pickled beets and cantaloupe," she says. "I remembered all your favourites. And grapes, and that soy milk stuff—I still say it's gross—and two cases of Ensure. That'll be enough, right?"

"Yeah. Thanks. You remembered everything." There are drawings and coupons stuck to the fridge. The toaster sits crookedly next to the coffee pot on the counter. His sister moves briskly around, opening drawers and running water. He feels himself sinking into the pattern on the linoleum floor, the silent storm rising slowly to meet him, threatening to break.

"The fridge did it," she says, dragging him back, and he looks up, bewildered. "See that? It's wired into the home network. Keeps track and orders things when we're low on anything. I don't need to even think about milk anymore." The microwave beeps. "The kids hacked it, of course. Chocolate milk and candy, chips and cookies. Ten pounds of jelly beans. You name it. I was *so* pissed." She puts a bowl of pasta on the table, then drops into a chair. "Go on." She waits, then gestures to the food. "Sit down. Eat."

"It's too much."

"Just eat what you want. I don't care. You're probably hungrier than you think. Did you eat on the plane?"

"No. Had a headache."

"Because you need to eat." He needs to eat to keep the equipment running. The neuromorphic implants in his intestines convert calories to charge the circuitry in his brain. It's elegantly engineered, but the practical side is that hunger gnaws at him all the time to the point where he isn't fully aware of it. Casters all look alike: painfully thin and tired, a gaunt hipster-chic look without the heroin. The engineers didn't count on that.

"Where's Bill?"

"Working. Cutting a deal—they're putting the final touches on a new exploration contract. He'll be home late. He's going to meet us at the party."

"Party?" His stomach clenches, and the fork wobbles on its way to his mouth.

Erin doesn't notice. "We do it every year. The Westlunds put on this big party for everybody. Somebody dresses up as Santa. The kids love it."

"Do I have to go?"

"Oh, come *on*, Spencer. It's so much fun. Everybody wants to meet my famous brother. You don't want to stay here by yourself, do you?"

The kids come thundering down the stairs before he can think of an answer.

• • •

The street is bright with twinkling lights strung around garages. Spencer stumbles on the ice. The driveways are shoveled, the snow piled up in the yards and along the edges of the sidewalks, but it's been years since he clambered over frozen ruts, and in canvas sneakers he slips and has to clutch her arm to keep from going down. Erin makes him wear one of Bill's winter parkas even though they're just going across the street. He's soon standing uncomfortably in the Westlund's living room with a drink in his hand, Christmas music booming in the background. Spencer's sure they won't ask him to be the one to duck outside to dress up as Santa. He doesn't have the build for it. There aren't enough pillows handy to even come close.

"This is my brother, Spencer. He's out from Los Angeles." Erin introduces him as though LA is some exotic, far-off place, and he's forced to shake hands and smile at jokes about the weather. She excuses herself to go and take a plate into the kitchen, and somebody hands him another drink and takes the empty glass from him. Spencer finishes the drink, takes another. Smiles and laughs, wishing he had an excuse to leave and go back across the street because he's worried that something will trigger another recall. He finds himself carefully touching his nose and surreptitiously looking at his fingers for blood. He can't afford to have a bad recall in the middle of the neighbourhood Christmas party.

"What do you do in LA?"

"Excuse me?" A woman smiles at Spencer, sidles closer, and asks him again. He has a stock answer for the question, a made-up story about a dull job nobody wants to hear more about. But he's tired from the flight and the wrong side of tipsy, and the truth slips out. "I work for Distributed Arbitrage." He blinks owlishly at the woman and is reminded of Megan. The resemblance is striking. He finds himself standing straighter. He's trying not to think of it, but there it is: the recall playing, skipping ahead. Love and regret. A hand on his. A cold compress on the back of his neck.

"Really? What do you do? Are you a forecaster?"

Dammit. "Yes." He rubs his eyes, trying to swim up to the surface to focus on the woman. Love. There was love. No.

Her eyes widen, and she moves a little closer. "That must be so exciting."

"Sometimes." Berlin was exciting. The clubs were great. The casting was good, too—searching out terrorists, looking for anger and anticipation of bloodlust, that alert feeling of tension and preparations. It's so hard to find just one, but where there's one, there's more. They hardly ever work by themselves and when they get together, they feed off each other, and the emotions are amplified.

He tries to tell her about it. How the trick to finding bad guys is to look for clusters in the noisy mass, pulling them together. He finds people, and he uses them to jump from one to the next, hunting in the storm, circling, slowly and deliberately, spiraling closer to them, slipping past flashes of images and impulses of thousands of people packed into neighbourhoods, sliding through them to get closer to the angry, controlled core that marks the men building bombs in a third floor walkup on Kastanienallee, above a record shop. He shivers as he thinks of it, the thrill warmly gripping him as the recall dips and weaves its way through him. Spencer is desperate to impress this woman.

"Is it true that you can read people's minds?" She hasn't understood what he's been trying to tell her.

"Not really." She frowns, and he rubs his eyes again, trying to explain, words slurring a little. "It's not like that. Your brain... you know you make electrico... electromagnetic waves, right?"

"Okay."

"So they're really weak, you know? Like, barely there compared to everything else. But a caster listens to them. That's what I look for."

"How do you do that?" She tips her head to one side, fluffs her hair. She looks *so* much like Megan. His heart thumps. No, he tells himself. He shouldn't be thinking about Megan. *Megan* would never be interested in him. He has nothing to offer her. But there was love. He read it. *No.*

"You have to listen. There's lotsa noise, you know, from everything else. But it's like having really good hearing. You go out into the storm and you listen for sounds in the wind. That's what it's like... and then you find people and you listen to them."

"So you eavesdrop?" She's smiling at him again.

"Sort of."

"That's kind of pervy."

"I guess it is." His breath comes faster.

She moves even closer, a little taller than him, and he tips his head up to look at blue eyes. He can feel the heat of her body. "Can you tell what I'm thinking right now?"

"That's not what I do," Spencer says.

"Oh, no?" She pokes him gently with one finger, and the shock of her touch makes him jump. "Is it true you're half robot?"

"No," he says indignantly. She's laughing.

There's a commotion at the door. Santa must be here. "So are you *listening* to me right now?" Her hip bumps his as she leans in to speak softly to him, her lips brushing his ear, and oh, yes, he can hear. It's been getting more difficult in the time since Damascus. It's hard to think. The storm is howling around him. His vision is overtaken by the overlay, a translated image compiled by the neuropathic implants hooked into his visual cortex. It looks like snow in the headlights—streaks of white hurtling towards him in the blackness.

He feels the swelling pressure of the party—the excitement of the children, the amusement of the adults. Warm, muzzy happiness. Arousal. She's laid her hand on his arm and he snaps open to cast, even though she doesn't need to be read. She pulls him out of the room and they are suddenly in the chilly gloom of the garage. She is tugging at his shirt, running her hands over the scars and the panels, exclaiming at the LEDs. "Let me see," she whispers. "Can you tell what I'm thinking now?" He lifts her onto a freezer and kisses her, pushing her dress up and reaching for her while she fumbles with his belt. He is shaking, wide open as gusts of animal lust emanate from her, blinding him. He doesn't close off the cast. He should. He knows he should. But he doesn't.

It will be recorded, a pinpoint of data on the memristors, and tomorrow it will all come flashing back when he comes creeping down to sit on the sofa with a cup of coffee, blearily watching the kids open their presents. Every moment of it, from the way the small of her back feels under his hands as she wraps her legs around him to the hammering blow of his sister's shock when she comes looking for him and opens the door. It's her shock that triggers it. There's a rush of nausea, pain, and then the nosebleed comes with the rising taste of dust and vinegar in his mouth as he struggles vainly to close off the cast, the surging sickness of the recall rising around him. Damascus comes rolling in, and he barely hears the woman's gasp as his body goes rigid, Erin's voice rising with alarm. What's the saying? Something about best laid plans?

• • •

"I'm not mad," Erin says to him when they are finally alone. The kids are sprawled on the floor by the Christmas tree, playing with the toys Megan bought for them. Spencer is sitting in the kitchen, unsteadily eating toast and trying to drink an Ensure. His lights have gone from amber to pink, and he stared at them for a long time before getting dressed. It doesn't matter how hungover he is—the equipment needs to be fed. It sucks glucose from him. He should have eaten last night, but he forgot and now he's paying for that, too. Erin is stuffing the turkey.

"I'm sorry." He'd rather not see her with her hand inside the bird, but it's too hard to get up and move to another room. Besides, Erin has rules about eating at the kitchen table.

"We might have to take a pass on the Westlunds' New Year's party," she says. Her tone is dangerously light. He's not sure if he ought to answer her or if this one of those times when it's best to say nothing. She speaks without turning. "Cut me the string, will you?"

"The string?"

"Pieces this long," she says, holding her hands apart. They are glistening. He swallows thickly. "The scissors are in the drawer by the sink. Left drawer. Your other left." She watches him for a moment and goes back to the turkey. The moist sound of her hands inside it makes him want to vomit.

Spencer brings her the string and she takes it from him. He stands in the middle of the kitchen, uncertainly. The buzz in his head loudens, and he has to concentrate to hear her. "What I don't understand is why you'd do that."

"Do what?"

"Are you *kidding* me? You get plastered at a Christmas party—hey, sure. We've all been there, Spencer. But then you hook up with a perfect stranger—"

"Don't," he says quickly, but it's too late. The recall is triggered before he can stop it and begins to play again in rapid succession. He blushes.

"Maybe you can see why I'm concerned," Erin says.

"I'm really sorry…"

"You never used to be like that," she says. "Is that what things are like in LA for you?"

Things are not like that, he thinks. He's hardly home long enough for things to get like that. "No."

"Then what the hell, Spencer?"

"I…"

"So you cut a little loose. Fine. No problem. Whatever. You're sick as a dog, but yeah, okay. I get it. But the small pharmacy in your suitcase, Spencer? What the *hell* is that?"

"Nothing," he says. He can't tell her. She won't understand.

"Are you sick? Do you have some kind of problem?"

"No."

A long silence then, as she finishes trussing the bird and washes her hands. He finishes the toast and cracks open another can of Ensure. It's the last thing he wants, but if he doesn't eat the headache will just get worse. He watches his sister covering the turkey with tin foil. "I'm really sorry," he says, finally.

"I'm not angry at you, Spencer." She bangs the oven door closed. The sound reminds him of something; he can't quite put a finger on it, but he suddenly feels irritated, too warm and two sizes too large for his skin.

"Bullshit."

"Keep your voice down." She turns her head towards the living room, but the kids can't hear them. She turns back to him and her eyes widen. "Spence. Your nose is bleeding." He touches his upper lip and examines his fingertips. His hand shakes. "Here," she says, passing him a wad of napkins. "Use some pressure." He tips his head back. "No, look down." She goes to the freezer and comes back with an icepack wrapped in a damp towel, and holds it to the back of his neck. "Are you okay?"

The recall slams into him when the cold towel touches the back of his neck, and Spencer is lost to the memory. His heart begins to beat faster as a white hot pain blossoms in his head. There is a bitter taste in his mouth. The room is small, made smaller by men sitting around him. Spencer can smell their sweat and their fear. He's sitting on the floor because the only available chair in the bare little room looks too rickety to be trusted. Everybody is waiting on him, crowded into a safehouse that feels terribly unsafe. He has to get the cast right so they can leave.

He can hear shouts out in the street, through the closed windows, the sharp retort of guns and grumble of explosions in the distance. Megan is sitting next to him on the floor, a legal pad in her lap, waiting for him to speak. He can't see her. All Spencer can see is the white of the storm. It's overtaken him, but he's not lost. He's searching. There are flashes. Fear. Lots of fear. Grief. A woman's wailing anguish. Pain and shock, the panic of a man hurrying three small children out the door and into a car. For a moment his attention settles on them. Spencer can taste the man's urgency, the children's terror and confusion.

Megan takes notes as he describes what he sees. Then he moves away, riding the storm, searching. Hunting. There have been rumours, a warning that something is coming. They've been in Damascus a week already, eating cold spaghetti straight out of the can and MREs, dropping iodine tablets into the water before drinking it. He's been playing cards with Megan in between casts, when he has to take a break. Cribbage. Poker. Gin. They don't bother keeping score. Something is coming, but they have to wait for it. The war is ten years old now and still going strong, but the hate and the anger are turning cold and steely. Something is coming.

This part of the memory sickens him. Spencer is helpless to stop it, dimly aware that Erin is speaking to him. A gaping, sucking hole opens all around him, dragging him down. He is not alone. In the dark, he can feel them. They are waiting for him, all of them, watching in the cold dark. He's locked into the recall, despite his frantic efforts to close it off. It is recorded and inscribed on the memristors, data that can't ever be wiped clean, a horror that cannot be severed. The smell of rotten eggs and vinegar, a pain in his chest, the terror of listening as people begin to choke and die in their beds, the writhing agony of the man and those three children in their car. It's too late to back out of the cast, to scramble out of the storm to safety. All he can do is speak, wanting to shout it out but only able to whisper hoarsely of what it feels like to be steadily choked to death by sarin as their security escorts scramble for gas masks and hoods. He can hear Megan anxiously telling him to stop, to cut the cast. Somebody slaps his face sharply, but he can't register the pain.

The recall wanes, but they are still there, crowded around him, pushed to the edges as his vision begins to clear. When will they leave him alone? He has his head in his hands, rocking back and forth. Blood drips steadily from his nose into his lap. Spencer hears himself flatly repeating the words and knows, with a sick turn of his stomach, that Erin is listening as he gives voice to all those deaths all over again..

• • •

He's back in LA before New Year's Eve. Erin and Bill can go to the Westlunds' party after all. There's a seat on a flight and Spencer buys it, cramming himself into an economy seat and leaving his sunglasses on the whole way. He swallows sedatives as soon as he's seated, enough to get through the next few hours without the risk of remembering.

Erin pleaded with him to stay. She wanted to take him to the hospital. "Please, Spence. You're sick. You can tell them you've had enough. Right? They can take it out and then you can come and stay with us. I can look after you." He gets her to help him upstairs to the bathroom, and she brings him the satchel brimming with syringes and vials, watching as he steadies his hand before plunging the needle into the port. She's horrified by the LEDs, which have started to blink ominously, crimson and bright. "Tell them you don't want to do it anymore. Nobody would think any less of you, Spence. Come home. Please? Please, will you do it for me?"

Spencer lies and tells her that he's got to get back. He lets her believe he'll talk to DA about getting the equipment out, that it's as easy as that. Megan meets him at the airport, taking the luggage from him and carrying it out to the car. "Good time, boss?"

"Oh, you know." He thinks of the Christmas party. Why couldn't it have been her? He starts to say something, struggling to form the thought. "I missed..."

"You look a little tired," she says, interrupting him. She climbs into the back seat of a DA company car with him, leaning forward to speak quietly to the driver.

Spencer closes his eyes. "You always say that." *I missed you*, he thinks. *I wish you'd been there with me.* He can smell her perfume. Something like tangerines and spice, warm and inviting.

"I got a call while you were away." She is scrolling through her phone, pushing messages around with her thumb.

"Where are we going?"

"Senegal. I told them you needed to think about it." Megan glances at him. "I wasn't sure you'd be ready."

He leans his head back. The world seems to be spinning gently, and he feels a little queasy. His mouth is dry. "I never thought the recall would do me in," he says dully.

"What's that, boss?"

"Do you ever think about it? What it'd be like to never be able to forget something?"

She raises her eyebrows. They're on the 105 now, merging smoothly into traffic. "I don't think too much about it," she says carefully.

"That must be nice. For you, I mean."

"Is something wrong?" Megan puts her phone down and looks him. "Did something happen?"

Something happened, he wants to say. He was doing just fine until Damascus. Things were just fine. He wasn't in love with her. He wasn't wracked with fear over a goddamn memory. And then he went to some shitty little room in the middle of a civil war because some intelligence agency had heard a rumour that something big was going to happen. And he'd done his job, in between hands of gin rummy, until he accidentally recorded not one murder, not ten, but one hundred and twenty fucking thousand. And it's been choking him from the inside out, splinters on fire beneath his skin. This memory—*this*—is awful. It's done something to him. It's an effort to hold himself up now. He can only stumble forward, a little at a time, afraid that if he falls he won't get up again. He's locked into a recalled cast that triggers itself over the smallest, stupidest things. A sound. A thought. When the wind blows a certain way, when he smells something that reminds him of Damascus, he's forced to witness their deaths all over again. Each recall is more painful than the one before, and he's certain that it's only going to get worse.

He can try and put down new casts ahead of it, put some distance between it and him, but it's bursting free. Even the storm is filled with it… he casts and he can see it. The moment when they died. A hundred and twenty thousand ghosts have taken up residence in the memristors in his brain, and they won't let go of him. It's going to slowly kill him. He's sees it now. The dead are going to take him with them. They've been doing it for weeks. Picking him apart, bit by bit.

"Spencer? Are you okay?"

He manages to smile. "Senegal, huh?"

"Saint-Louis. I've got the dossier with me if you want to take a look."

He can pack in more casts, one over top another. He can hope it'll be enough to hold back Damascus. He wants things to be like Berlin again—when it was fun and sexy and he felt good enough to hit a nightclub with Megan and the DA techs after the job was done. Why can't it be like that again? More casts. That's got to be the answer. And if it's not—if Damascus keeps breaking through, he'll just wait for it. It can't be very much longer before he strokes out. Each recall is worse than the last. The equipment will burn him, baking him from the inside out.

Spencer reaches to take the folder from Megan and something in his chest tightens. She's the one good thing about this, he thinks. Recklessly, he lets his hand cover hers. His heart thumps unsteadily, but he doesn't care. She raises her eyes to look at him, speechless, but he hangs on. Love and regret, that's what he felt from her, but maybe it was more one than the other. It'll only take a thought to open the cast, and then, he thinks, he'll know for sure. He'll know if there's still time to tell her that he wants to be with her, that he feels it, too. But she's frowning.

"You're... bleeding," she says, pulling her hand away to rummage in her bag for a tissue. The car begins to dissolve into brimming darkness.

The first hit of adrenaline comes with the whispers of the dead, and he wonders if it isn't already too late.

~

Heather Clitheroe's work has appeared in *Kaleidotrope, Beneath Ceaseless Skies,* and the *Evolve: Vampire Stories of the New Undead* anthologies. Heather lives in Calgary, where she works as a student advisor for the engineers and quietly reads the research papers and announcements on her break, taking notes and dreaming up stories. She gratefully acknowledges the support of the Banff Centre for the Arts, Edge Science Fiction and Fantasy Publishing, and the people in her life who never stop asking "How's the writing going?" You can find her online at lectio.ca or @lectio.

WALKING AWAKE

N. K. JEMISIN

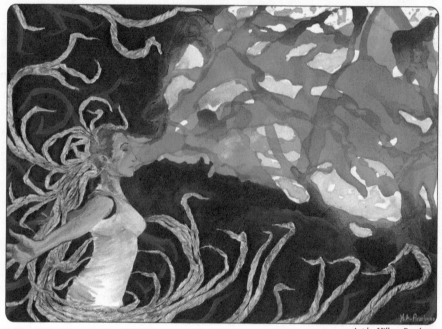

Art by Hillary Pearlman

The Master who came for Enri was wearing a relatively young body. Sadie guessed it was maybe fifty years old. It was healthy and in good condition, still handsome. It could last twenty years more, easily.

Its owner noticed Sadie's stare and chuckled. "I never let them get past fifty," the Master said. "You'll understand when you get there."

Sadie quickly lowered her gaze. "Of course, sir."

It turned the body's eyes to examine Enri, who sat very still in his cell. Enri knew, Sadie could see at once. She had never told him—she never told any of the children, because she was their caregiver and there was nothing of *care* in the truth—but Enri had always been more intuitive than most.

She cleared her throat. "Forgive me, sir, but it's best if we return to the transfer center. He'll have to be prepped—"

"Ah, yes, of course," the Master said. "Sorry, I just wanted to look him over before my claim was processed. You never know when they're going to screw up the paperwork." It smiled.

Sadie nodded and stepped back, gesturing for the Master to precede her away from the cell. As they walked to the elevator they passed two of Sadie's assistant caregivers, who were distributing the day's feed to Fourteen Male. Sadie caught Caridad's eye and signed for them to go and fetch Enri. No ceremony. A ceremony at this point would be cruel.

Caridad noticed, twitched elaborately, got control of herself and nodded. Olivia, who was deaf, did not look up to catch Sadie's signing, but Caridad brushed her arm and repeated it. Olivia's face tightened in annoyance, but then smoothed into a compliant mask. Both women headed for cell 47.

"The children here all seem nicely fit," the Master commented as they stepped into the elevator. "I got my last body from Southern. Skinny as rails there."

"Exercise, sir. We provide a training regimen for those children who want it; most do. We also use a nutrient blend designed to encourage muscle growth."

"Ah, yes. Do you think that new one will get above two meters?"

"He might, sir. I can check the breeder history—"

"No, no, never mind. I like surprises." It threw her a wink over one shoulder. When it faced forward again, Sadie found her eyes drawn to the crablike form half-buried at the nape of the body's neck. Even as Sadie watched, one of its legs shifted just under the skin, loosening its grip on the tendons there.

She averted her eyes.

Caridad and Olivia came down shortly. Enri was between the two women, dressed in the ceremonial clothing: a plain low-necked shirt and pants, both dyed deep red. His eyes locked onto Sadie, despairing, *betrayed*, before he disappeared through the transfer room's door.

"Lovely eyes," the Master remarked, handing her the completed claim forms. "Can't wait to wear blue again."

Sadie led it into the transfer center. As they passed through the second gate, the airy echoes of the tower gave way to softer, closer acoustics. The center's receiving room had jewel-toned walls, hardwood floors, and luxuriant furniture upholstered in rich, tasteful brocades. Soft strains of music played over the speakers; incense burned in a censer on the mantle. Many Masters liked to test their new senses after a transfer.

This Master gave everything a perfunctory glance as it passed through. Off the receiving room was the transfer chamber itself: two long metal tables, a tile floor set with drains, elegant mirror-glass walls which were easy to wash and sterilize. Through the open doorway Sadie could see that Enri had already been strapped to the left table, facedown with arms outstretched. His head was buckled in place on the chinrest, but in the mirrored wall his eyes shifted to Sadie. There was nothing of anticipation in that gaze, as there should have been. He knew to be afraid. Sadie looked away and bowed at the door as the Master passed.

The Master walked toward the right-hand table, removing its shirt, and then paused as it noticed the room's door still open. It turned to her and lifted one of the body's eyebrows, plainly wanting privacy. Sadie swallowed, painfully aware of the passing seconds, of the danger of displeasing a Master, of Enri's terrible unwavering stare. She should stay. It was the least she could do after lying to Enri his whole life. She should stay and let his last sight through his own eyes be of someone who loved him and lamented his suffering.

"Thank you for choosing the Northeast Anthroproduction Facility," she said to the Master. "At Northeast, your satisfaction is always guaranteed."

She closed the door and walked away.

• • •

That night Sadie dreamed of Enri.

This was not unusual. Her dreams had always been dangerously vivid. As a child she had sleepwalked, attacked others in the confusion of waking, heard voices when no one had spoken, bitten through her lip and nearly drowned in blood. Her caregivers sent away for a specialist, who diagnosed her as something called bipolar—a defect of the brain chemistry. At the time she had been distraught over this, but the policies were very clear. No Master would have anything less than a perfect host. They could have sent her to Disposal, or the plantations. Instead, Sadie had been given medicines to stabilize her erratic neurotransmitters and then sent to another facility, Northeast, to begin training as a caregiver. She had done well. But though the other symptoms of her defect had eased with adulthood and medication, her dreams were still strong.

This time she stood in a vast meadow, surrounded by waist-high grass and summer flowers. She had only seen a meadow once, on the journey from her home anthro to caregiver training, and she had never actually walked through it. The ground felt uneven and soft under her feet, and a light breeze rustled the grass around her. Underneath the rustling she thought she could hear snatches of something else—many voices, whispering, though she could not make out the words.

"Sadie?" Enri, behind her. She turned and stared at him. He was himself, his eyes wide with wonder. Yet she had heard the screams from the transfer room, smelled the blood and bile, seen his body emerge from the room and flash a satisfied smile that no fourteen-year-old boy should ever wear.

"It *is* you," Enri said, staring. "I didn't think I would see you again."

It was just a dream. Still, Sadie said, "I'm sorry."

"It's okay."

"I didn't have a choice."

"I know." Enri sobered, and sighed. "I was angry at first. But then I kept thinking: It must be hard for you. You love us, but you give us to them, over and over. It's cruel of them to make you do it."

Cruel. Yes. But. "Better than..." She caught herself.

"Better than being chosen yourself." Enri looked away. "Yes. It is."

But he came to her, and they walked awhile, listening to the swish of grass around their calves and smelling the strangely clean aroma of the dirt between their toes.

"I'm glad for this," Sadie said after a while. Her voice seemed strangely soft; the land here did not echo the way the smooth corridors of the facility did. "To see you. Even if it's just a dream."

Enri spread his hands from his sides as they walked, letting the bobbing heads of flowers tickle his palms. "You told me once that you used to go places when you dreamed. Maybe this is real. Maybe you're really here with me."

"That wasn't 'going to places,' that was sleepwalking. And it was in the real world. Not like this."

He nodded, silent for a moment. "I wanted to see you again. I wanted it so much. Maybe that's why I'm here." He glanced at her, biting his bottom lip. "Maybe you wanted to see me, too."

She had. But she could not bring herself to say so, because just thinking it made her hurt all over inside, like shaking apart, and the dream was fragile. Too much of anything would break it; she could feel that instinctively.

She took his hand, though, the way she had so often when they were alive, and alone. His fingers tightened on hers briefly, then relaxed.

They had reached a hill, which overlooked a landscape that Sadie had never seen before: meadows and hills in a vast expanse broken only occasionally by lone trees, and in the distance a knot of thick variegated green. Was that a... jungle? A forest? What was the difference? She had no idea.

"The others think I came here because we used to be close," Enri said, a little shyly. "Also because you're so good at dreaming. It wouldn't matter, me reaching out for you, if you weren't meeting me halfway."

Others? "What are you talking about?"

Enri shrugged. It made his shirt—the low-necked smock she'd last seen him wearing—slip back a little, revealing the smooth unblemished flesh of his neck and upper back. "After the pain, there's nothing but the dark inside your head.

If you shout, it sounds like a whisper. If you hit yourself, it feels like a pinch. Nothing works right except your thoughts. And all you can think about is how much you want to be free."

She had never let herself imagine this. Never, not once. These were the dangerous thoughts, the ones that threatened her ability to keep doing what the Masters wanted or to keep from screaming while she did those things. If she even thought the word *free,* she usually made herself immediately think about something else. She should not be dreaming about this.

And yet, like picking at a scab, she could not help asking, "Could you... go to sleep? Or something? Stop thinking, somehow?" Pick, pick. It would be terrible to be trapped so forever, with no escape. Pick, pick. She had always thought that taking on a Master meant nothingness. Oblivion. This was worse.

Enri turned to look at her, and she stopped.

"You're not alone in it," he said. Whispering, all around them both; she was sure of it now. His eyes were huge and blue, and unblinking as they watched her. "You're not the only person trapped in the dark. There's lots of others in here. With me."

"I, I don't—" She didn't want to know.

Pick, pick.

"Everyone else the Masters have taken."

A Master could live for centuries. How many bodies was that? How many other Enris trapped in the silence, existing only as themselves in dreams? Dozens?

"*All* of us, from *every* Master, down all the years that they've ruled us."

Thousands. Millions.

"And a few like you, ones without Masters, but who are good at dreaming and want to be free the way we do. No one else can hear us. No one else needs to."

Sadie shook her head. "No." She put out a hand to touch Enri's shoulder, wondering if this might help her wake up. It felt just as she remembered—bony and soft and almost hot to the touch, as if the life inside him was much brighter and stronger than her own. "I, I don't want to be—" She can't say the word.

Pick, pick.

"We're all still here. We're dead, but we're *still here.* And—" He hesitated, then ducked his eyes. "The others say you can help us."

"No!" She let go of him and stumbled back, shaking inside and out. She could not hear these dangerous thoughts. "I don't want this!"

She woke in the dark of her cubicle, her face wet with tears.

• • •

The next day a Master arrived in a woman's body. The body was not old at all—younger than Sadie, who was forty. Sadie checked the database carefully to make sure the Master had a proper claim.

"I'm a dancer," the Master said. "I've been given special dispensation for the sake of my art. Do you have any females with a talent for dance?"

"I don't think so," Sadie said.

"What about Ten-36?" Olivia, who must have read the Master's lips, came over to join them and smiled. "She opted for the physical/artistic track of training. Ten-36 loves to dance."

"I'll take that one," the Master said.

"She's only ten years old," Sadie said. She did not look at Olivia, for fear the Master would notice her anger. "She might be too young to survive transfer."

"Oh, I'm very good at assuming control of a body quickly," the Master said. "Too much trauma would destroy its talent, after all."

"I'll bring her down," Olivia said, and Sadie had no choice but to begin preparing the forms.

Ten-36 was beaming when Olivia brought her downstairs. The children from Ten had all been let out to line the stairway. They cheered that one of their year-mates had been granted the honor of an early transfer; they sang a song praising the Masters and exhorting them to guide humankind well. Ten-36 was a bright, pretty child, long-limbed and graceful, Indo-Asian phenotype with a solid breeding history. Sadie helped Olivia strap her down. All the while Ten-36 chattered away at them, asking where she would live and how she would serve and whether the Master seemed nice. Sadie said nothing while Olivia told all the usual lies. The Masters were always kind. Ten-36 would spend the rest of her life in the tall glass spires of the Masters' city, immersed in miracles and thinking unfathomable thoughts that human minds were too simple to manage alone. And she would get to dance all the time.

When the Master came in and lay down on the right-hand table, Ten-36 fell silent in awe. She remained silent, though Sadie suspected this was no longer due to awe, when the Master tore its way out of the old body's neck and stood atop the twitching flesh, head-tendrils and proboscides and spinal stinger steaming faintly in the cool air of the chamber. Then it crossed from one outstretched arm to the other and began inserting itself into Ten-36. It had spoken the truth about its skill. Ten-36 convulsed twice and threw up, but her heart never stopped and the bleeding was no worse than normal.

"Perfect," the Master said when it had finished. Its voice was now high pitched and girlish. It sat down on one of the receiving room couches to run its fingers over the brocade, then inhaled the scented air. "Marvelous sensory acuity. Excellent fine motor control, too. It's a bother to have to go through puberty again, but, well. Every artist must make sacrifices."

When it was gone, Sadie checked the Master's old body. It—she—was still breathing, though unresponsive and drooling. On Sadie's signal, two of the assistants escorted the body to Disposal.

Then she went to find Olivia. "Don't ever contradict me in front of a Master again," she said. She was too angry to sign, but she made sure she didn't speak too fast despite her anger, so that Olivia could read her lips.

Olivia stared at her. "It's not my fault you didn't remember Ten-36. You're the head caregiver. Do your job."

"I remembered. I just didn't think it was right that a Ten be made to serve—" She closed her mouth after that, grateful Olivia couldn't hear her inflection and realize the sentence was incomplete. She had almost added *a Master who will throw her away as soon as she's no longer new.*

Olivia rolled her eyes. "What difference does it make? Sooner, later, it's all the same."

Anger shot through Sadie, hotter than she'd felt in years. "Don't take it out on the children just because *you* can't serve, Olivia."

Olivia flinched, then turned and walked stiffly away. Sadie gazed after her for a long while, first trembling as the anger passed, then just empty. Eventually she went back into the transfer room to clean up.

• • •

That night, Sadie dreamt again. This time she stood in a place of darkness, surrounded by the same whispering voices she'd heard before. They rose into coherency for only a moment before subsiding into murmurs again.

hereHERE this place remember show her never forget

The darkness changed. She stood on a high metal platform (*balcony*, said the whispers) overlooking a vast, white-walled room of the sort she had always imagined the glass towers of the Masters to contain. This one was filled with strange machines hooked up to long rows of things like sinks. (*Laboratory.*) Each sink—there were hundreds in all—was filled with a viscous blue liquid, and in the liquid floated the speckled bodies of Masters.

Above the whispers she heard a voice she recognized: "This is where they came from."

Enri.

She looked around, somehow unsurprised that she could not see him. "What?"

The scene before her changed. Now there were people moving among the sinks and machines. Their bodies were clothed from head to toe in puffy white garments, their heads covered with hoods. They scurried about like ants, tending the sinks and machines, busy busy busy.

This was how Masters were born? But Sadie had been taught that they came from the sky.

"That was never true," Enri said. "They were created from other things. Parasites—bugs and fungi and microbes and more—that force other creatures to do what they want."

Enri had never talked like this in his life. Sadie had heard a few people talk like this—the rare caregivers educated with special knowledge like medicine or machinery. But Enri was just a facility child, just a body. He had never been special beyond the expected perfection.

"Most parasites evolved to take over other animals," he continued. If he noticed her consternation, he did not react to it. "Only a few were any threat to us. But some people wondered if that could be changed. They put all the worst parts of the worst parasites together, and tweaked and measured and changed them some more... and then they tested them on people they didn't like. People they thought didn't *deserve* to think for themselves. And eventually, they made something that worked." His face hardened suddenly into a mask of bitterness like nothing Sadie had ever seen beyond her own mirror. "All the monsters were right here. No need to go looking for more in space."

Sadie frowned. Then the white room disappeared.

She stood in a room more opulent than a transfer center's receiving room, filled with elegant furnishings and plants in pots and strange decorative objects on plinths. There was a big swath of cloth, garishly decorated with red stripes and a square, patterned patch of blue, hanging from a polished pole in one corner; it seemed to have no purpose. A huge desk of beautiful dark wood stood to one side, and there were windows—windows!—all around her. She ignored the desk and all the rest, hurrying to the window for the marvel, the treasure, of looking outside. She shouldered aside the rich, heavy hangings blocking the view and beheld:

Fire. A world burnt dark and red. Above, smoke hung low in the sky, thick as clouds before a rainstorm. Below lay the smoldering ruins of what must once have been a city.

A snarl and thump behind her. She spun, her heart pounding, to find that the opulent chamber now held people. Four men and women in neat black uniforms, wrestling a struggling fifth person onto the wooden desk. This fifth man, who was portly and in his fifties, fought as if demented. He punched and kicked and shouted until they turned him facedown and pinned his arms and legs, ripping open his clothing at the back of the neck.

A woman came in. She carried a large bowl in her hands, which she set down beside the now-immobile man. Reaching into the bowl, she lifted out a Master. It flexed its limbs and then focused its head-tendrils on the man's neck. When it grew still, the woman set the Master on him.

"No—" Against all reason, against all her training, Sadie found herself starting forward. She didn't know why. It was just a transfer; she had witnessed hundreds. But it was wrong, wrong. *(Pick, pick.)* He was too old, too fat, too obviously ill-bred. Was he being punished? It did not matter. Wrong. It had *always* been wrong.

She reached blindly for one of the decorative objects on a nearby plinth, a heavy piece of stone carved to look like a bird in flight. With this in her hands she ran at the people in black, raising the stone to swing at the back of the nearest head. The Master plunged its stinger into the pinned man's spine and he began to scream, but this did not stop her. Nothing would stop her. She would kill this Master as she should have killed the one that took Enri.

"No, Sadie."

The stone bird was no longer in her hands. The strangers and the opulent room were gone. She stood in darkness again and this time Enri stood before her, his face weary with the sorrow of centuries.

"We should fight them." Sadie clenched her fists at her sides, her throat choked with emotions she could not name. "We never fight."

I never fight.

"We fought before, with weapons like yours and much more. We fought so hard we almost destroyed the world, and in the end all that did was make it easier for them to take control."

"They're monsters!" Pleasure, such shameful pleasure, to say those words.

"They're what we made them."

She stared at him, finally understanding. "You're not Enri."

He fell silent for a moment, hurt.

"I'm Enri," he said at last. The terrible age-old bitterness seemed to fade from his eyes, though never completely. "I just know things I didn't know before. It's been a long time for me, here, Sadie. I feel... a lot older." It had been two days. "Anyway, I wanted you to know how it happened. Since you can hear me. Since I can talk to you. I feel like... you should know."

He reached out and took her hand again, and she thought of the way he had first done this, back when he had been nothing more than Five-47. She'd taken his hand to lead him somewhere, and he'd looked up at her. Syllables had come into her mind, just a random pair of sounds: *Enri.* Not as elegant as the names that the Masters had bestowed upon Sadie and her fellow caregivers, and she had never used his name where others could hear. But when they were alone together, she had called him that, and he had liked it.

"If you had a way to fight them," he said, watching her intently, "would you?"

Dangerous, dangerous thoughts. But the scabs were off, all picked away, and too much of her had begun to bleed. "Yes. No. I... don't know."

She felt empty inside. The emotion that had driven her to attack the Masters was gone, replaced only by weariness. Still, she remembered the desperate struggles of the captured man in her dream. Like Enri, that man had faced his final moments alone.

Perhaps he too had been betrayed by someone close.

"We'll talk again," he said, and then she woke up.

• • •

Like a poison, the dangerous ideas from the dreams began leaching from her sleeping mind into her waking life.

On fifthdays, Sadie taught the class called History and Service. She usually took the children up on the roof for the weekly lesson. The roof had high walls around the edges, but was otherwise open to the world. Above, the walls framed a perfect circle of sky, painfully bright in its blueness. They could also glimpse the topmost tips of massive glass spires—the Masters' city.

"Once," Sadie told the children, "people lived without Masters. But we were undisciplined and foolish. We made the air dirty with poisons we couldn't see, but which killed us anyway. We beat and killed each other. This is what people are like without Masters to guide us and share our thoughts."

One little Six Female held up her hand. "How did those people live without Masters?" She seemed troubled by the notion. "How did they know what to do? Weren't they lonely?"

"They were very lonely. They reached up to the skies looking for other people. That's how they found the Masters."

Two caregivers were required to be with the children anytime they went up on the roof. At Sadie's last words, Olivia, sitting near the back of the children's cluster, frowned and narrowed her eyes. Sadie realized abruptly that she had said "they found the Masters." She had intended to say—was *supposed* to say—that the Masters had found humankind. They had benevolently chosen to leave the skies and come to Earth to help the ignorant, foolish humans survive and grow.

That was never true.

Quickly Sadie shook her head to focus, and amended herself. "The Masters had been waiting in the sky. As soon as they knew we would welcome them, they came to Earth to join with us. After that we weren't lonely anymore."

The Six Female smiled, as did most of the other children, pleased that the Masters had done so much for their sake. Olivia rose when Sadie did and helped usher the children back to their cells. She said nothing, but glanced back and met Sadie's eyes once. There was no censure in her face, but the look lingered, contemplative with ambition. Sadie kept her own face expressionless.

But she did not sleep well that night, so she was not surprised that when she finally did, she dreamt of Enri once more.

• • •

They stood on the roof of the facility, beneath the circle of sky, alone. Enri wasn't smiling this time. He reached for Sadie's hand right away, but Sadie pulled her hand back.

"Go away," she said. "I don't want to dream about you anymore." She had not been happy before these dreams, but she had been able to survive. The dangerous thoughts were going to get her killed, and he just kept giving her more of them.

"I want to show you something first," he said. He spoke very softly, his manner subdued. "Please? Just one more thing, and then I'll leave you alone for good."

He had never yet lied to her. With a heavy sigh she took his hand. He pulled her over to one of the walls around the rooftop's edge, and they began walking up the air as if an invisible staircase had formed beneath their feet.

Then they reached the top of the wall, and Sadie stopped in shock.

It was the city of the Masters—and yet, not. She had glimpsed the city once as a young woman, that second trip, from caregiver training to Northeast. Here again were the huge structures that had so awed her, some squat and some neck-achingly high, some squarish and some pointy at the tops, some flagrantly, defiantly asymmetrical. *(Buildings.)* On the ground far below, in the spaces between the tall structures, she could see long ribbons of dark, hard ground neatly marked with lines. *(Roads.)* Thousands of tiny colored objects moved along the lines, stopping and progressing in some ordered ritual whose purpose she could not fathom. (*Vehicles.*) Even tinier specks moved beside and between and in and out of the colored things, obeying no ritual whatsoever. People. Many, many people.

And there was something about this chaos, something so subtly counter to everything she knew about the Masters, that she understood at once these were people *without* Masters. They had built the vehicles and they had built the roads. They had built the whole city.

They were free.

A new word came into her head, in whispers. (*Revolution.*)

Enri gestured at the city and it changed, becoming the city she remembered—the city of now. Not so different in form or function, but very different in feel. Now the air was clean, and reeked of *other*. Now the mote-people she saw were not free, and everything they'd built was a pale imitation of what had gone before.

Sadie looked away from the tainted city. Maybe the drugs had stopped working. Maybe it was her defective mind that made her yearn for things that could never be. "Why did you show me this?" She whispered the words.

"All you know is what they've told you, and they tell you so little. They think if we don't know anything they'll be able to keep control—and they're right. How can you want something you've never seen, don't have the words for, can't even imagine? I wanted you to know."

And now she did. "I... I want it." It was an answer to his question from the last dream. *If you had a way to fight them, would you?* "I want to."

"How much, Sadie?" He was looking at her again, unblinking, not Enri and yet not a stranger. "You gave me to them because it was all you knew to do. Now you know different. How much do you want to change things?"

She hesitated against a lifetime's training, a lifetime's fear. "I don't know. But I want to do *something*." She was angry again, angrier than she'd been at Olivia. Angrier than she'd been throughout her whole life. So much had been stolen from them. The Masters had taken so much from *her*. She looked at Enri and thought, *No more*.

He nodded, almost to himself. The whispers all around them rose for a moment too; she thought that they sounded approving.

"There is something you can do," he said. "Something we think will work. But it will be... hard."

She shook her head, fiercely. "It's hard now."

He stepped close and put his arms around her waist, pressing his head against her breast. "I know." This was so much like other times, other memories, that she sighed and put her arms around him as well, stroking his hair and trying to soothe him even though she was the one still alive.

"The children and caregivers in the facilities will be all that's left when we're done," he whispered against her. "No one with a Master will survive. But the Masters can't live more than a few minutes without our bodies. Even if they survive the initial shock, they won't get far."

Startled, she took hold of his shoulders and pushed him back. His eyes shone with unshed tears. "What are you saying?" she asked.

He smiled despite the tears. "They say that if you die in a dream, you'll die in real life. We can use you, if you let us. Channel what we feel, through you." He sobered. "And we already know how it feels to die, several billion times over."

"You can't..." She did not want to understand. It frightened her that she did. "Enri, you and, and the others, you can't just *die*."

He reached up and touched her cheek. "No, we can't. But you can."

• • •

The Master was injured. Rather, its body was—a spasm of the heart, something that could catch even them by surprise. Another Master had brought it in, hauling its comrade limp over one shoulder, shouting for Sadie even before the anthro facility's ground-level doors had closed in its wake.

She told Caridad to run ahead and open the transfer chamber, and signed for Olivia to grab one of the children; any healthy body was allowed in an emergency. The Master was still alive within its old, cooling flesh, but it would not be for much longer. When the Masters reached the administrative level, Sadie quickly waved it toward the transfer chamber, pausing only to grab something from her cubicle. She slipped this into the waistband of her pants, and followed at a run.

"You should leave, sir," she told the one who'd carried the dying Master in, as she expertly buckled the child onto the other transfer table. An Eighteen Female, almost too old to be claimed; Olivia was so thoughtful. "Too many bodies in a close space will be confusing." She had never seen a Master try to take over a body that was already occupied, but she'd been taught that it could happen if the Master was weak enough or desperate enough. Seconds counted, in a situation like this.

"Yes... yes, you're right," said the Master. Its body was big and male, strong and healthy, but effort and fear had sapped the strength from its voice; it sounded distracted and anxious. "Yes. All right. Thank you." It headed out to the receiving room.

That was when Sadie threw herself against the transfer room door and locked it, with herself still inside.

"Sadie?" Olivia, knocking on the door's other side. But transfer chambers were designed for the Masters' comfort; they could lock themselves in if they felt uncomfortable showing vulnerability around the anthro facility's caregivers. Olivia would not be able to get through. Neither would the other Master—not until it was too late.

Trembling, Sadie turned to face the transfer tables and pulled the letter-opener from the waistband of her pants.

It took several tries to kill the Eighteen Female. The girl screamed and struggled as Sadie stabbed and stabbed. Finally, though, she stopped moving.

By this time, the Master had extracted itself from its old flesh. It stood on the body's bloody shoulders, head-tendrils waving and curling uncertainly toward the now-useless Eighteen. "You have no choice," Sadie told it. Such a shameful thrill, to speak to a Master this way! Such madness, this freedom. "I'm all there is."

But she wasn't alone. She could feel them now somewhere in her mind, Enri and the others. A thousand, million memories of terrible death, coiled and ready to be flung forth like a weapon. Through Enri, through Sadie, through the Master that took her, through every Master in every body... they would all dream of death, and die in waking, too.

No revolution without blood. No freedom without the willingness to die.

Then she pulled off her shirt, staring into her own eyes in the mirrored wall as she did so, and lay down on the floor, ready.

~

N. K. Jemisin lives and writes in Brooklyn, NY, where she is hard at work on her sixth novel. Her other works have been multiply nominated for the Hugo, the Nebula, and the World Fantasy Award, and she's won the Locus for Best First Novel. Samples of her work, and essays on speculative fiction, anti-oppression, and general silliness, can be found at nkjemisin.com.

THE CASE OF THE PASSIONLESS BEES

RHONDA EIKAMP

Art by Christine Mitzuk

Of all the strange sights I had been privy to during my acquaintanceship with that illustrious detective, none was as disturbing as seeing my old friend covered in bees. Naturally I was not concerned; his manaccanite skin was impervious to harm and I myself was at a safe distance, ensconced behind the clerestory window at Shading Coil Cottage, having been let in by a timid local girl whom I supposed to be the replacement for Mrs. Hudson. Perhaps sensing my arrival, Holmes turned and waved from the yard. Moments later he had shaken off his beloved bees and joined me in the drawing room.

"This business," he began, as always to the point. "A murder in my own home is one thing, Watson, but that my own housekeeper should be accused of the beastly act—I will not stand for it!" He chose an octave below his usual reedy voice for this utterance, I noted, and the gravity of the situation was not lost on me. "Glad you could make it, by the way. I will need someone on the side of the amalgamated in this case."

During his time in London, Dr. Bell's invention had made a name for himself solving cases the Yard had given up as hopeless, his inscrutable silver visage still well-known not only in Baker Street but beyond, and yet since his retirement I had seen little of him. There was much I cherished about Gearlock Holmes: that rigor that kept him like a bloodhound on the trail of criminals, the astonishing array of facts that had been programmed into him and which he himself broadened with unceasing study (employing the night hours while we the fleshly slept), the cooling *tick-tick* that arose from him when he overheated. Even his violin playing I had missed, passionless as it was, yet the sight of those articulated fingers moving with such precision through a pizzicato had never failed to awe me. Observing him now closely, in an attempt to emulate his own methods, I felt that Gearlock Holmes had lost some of his polish. Perhaps retirement did not suit him.

Perhaps it was only the circumstances.

He lost no time in filling me in, as he led me with a gentle but firm grip on my arm to the conservatory. "Miss Katharina Segalen and her brother-in-law Friedl Klapisch-Zuber, of Düsseldorf, Germany, had been my guests for three days prior to the murder. They are scientists with the German government in some capacity and had come uninvited to interview me, or spy me out if you will. On the continent the amalgamated are not so common as servants, I am given to understand, and there was some hint from the two that the German government views the technology as a potential source of soldiery, so I'm afraid I was rather uncooperative. Here—"

Holmes threw open the door to the conservatory. Sunlight washed in through the windows and I heard the whine of his optical apertures adjusting. The plants were all neatly maintained, more for study than for decoration, I surmised, and so the debris in one corner was immediately noticeable. A clay pot of bridal-veil creeper had been overturned, wrenched from its jardinière by some struggle, or so it appeared, shattering into myriad pieces and spilling soil. I approached the spot. Tiny smears of blood dotted the bench and floor. In the soil—in fact all about the floor—lay dead bees. I counted thirty before I stopped.

"Your televoice mentioned bees," I began.

"Miss Segalen was highly sensitive apparently. She'd said nothing about it, and her death would have been written off as a terrible and tragic accident if there had been only a single errant bee involved, rather than what one must assume was a basketful introduced into the room deliberately. And if the door had not been locked from the outside." The servos of his mouth ground through their tracks, clenching his jaw. A sigh of steam escaped his neck-joint. "The stings on the corpse were too many for Dr. Culpepper to count. I believe that with her last air before her throat closed up entirely, Katharina Segalen had hoped to smash a window with one of the pots and make her exit or at the least draw someone's attention to her plight. A handsome woman, Watson, though you would not have known it had you seen her in death—the swelling had disfigured her so. And intelligent. She would have known she had but seconds to live after the first few stings."

"And your housekeeper Mrs. Hudson, you say, has been detained. But that is surely absurd!"

"Mrs. Hudson found her. She touched nothing, assessed that Miss Segalen was dead, and came directly to me. Not one to seize up in the face of death, Mrs. Hudson. Years of service with me have conditioned her and—well, I've made a few changes to her programming over the years, removed the worst of the housekeeperly fluttering her line's manufacturers insist on adding. I require reason and nerves of my servants above all else. Strictest confidence, eh?"

This last of course was in reference to the prohibition against any amalgamated meddling with the programming of another. I would never have betrayed him. The very fact that Gearlock Holmes, out of all the amalgamated with which we surround ourselves in our homes and stables and coaches, enjoyed special status by royal decree, was allowed to own property and employ amalgamated servants of his own, namely a housekeeper and a gardener, was due to his unique cogitating skills in service to Her Majesty. Holmes's creator Joseph Bell had left no notes before his death as to how he had obtained this altogether greater level of cognizance in the one amalgamated designed by him. I only know it left Gearlock Holmes, in spite of his blank metal face and shiny limbs, closer to a fleshly man than any amalgamated I had ever met. And if he was a breaker of rules that had not been made to apply to the likes of him, I would certainly not out him.

"No," Holmes continued, "I'm afraid I am at fault for suspicion falling on poor Mrs. Hudson. I was too fastidious in my investigations, Watson."

"You will have to explain."

Holmes pointed to a rusty pair of parrot-bill gardening shears that lay in two halves in the soil. "That is not more detritus from the struggle. I have said that the murder victim was intelligent. When she saw that she could not use the pot to escape, that her death was inevitable, she must have wrenched these shears apart. They were old and loose and the central bolt that held the two blades together would have slipped out easily. She clutched that bolt in her hand as she died. It was I who pointed out to the constable that it could only be a sign meant to point to her killer. That it must indicate an amalgamated." I must have frowned at that. "Nuts and bolts, Watson. The very emblem of my species. Barring the possibility that some amalgamated servant from the surrounding households snuck into Shading Coil in broad daylight, that conclusion left only Mrs. Hudson and myself. They will shut her down, Watson"—I remarked the quaver in his voice, his throat valves sticking—"if I cannot bring the killer to justice."

"You suspect someone else, then?"

Before he could speak the timid servant girl arrived to announce a visitor. Without waiting to be introduced a man pushed past her. He looked to be near forty, with florid features that could only be the result of a lifetime of good German beer and liverwurst.

"Herr Klapisch-Zuber," Holmes greeted him. "I see they have chosen not to detain you. I presume you will wish to collect your things."

As if Holmes had not spoken, the German scientist nodded at me. It was a shock. It is customary among certain sorts to acknowledge the fleshly present while ignoring the amalgamated, yet years with Holmes and his unique situation had left me unaccustomed to it. It smacked of that movement whose members view all amalgamated as little better than flywheels and would restrict their rights accordingly.

"Why they should keep me?" he replied. Anger flushed his face redder. "I have done nothing. I want answers, too. Katharina—" He could not look at the debris in the corner, I noted, his gaze sliding away from it in pain. "You." At last he addressed Holmes straight on, "You must have some suspect."

"What if I said I suspect you, *mein Herr*?" Holmes asked.

"*Na und?* The magistrate did as well."

"Yet not for some supposed professional rivalry. You were involved in an amorous affair with Miss Segalen, were you not?" The German stared, aghast. "My good man, the scent of your cologne on her, a daisy in her hair after your walk together? My observational skills were not exactly put to the test. Did she wish to break it off? Did that enrage you to the point of murder? It all fits. Knowing her well, you would have been aware of her sensitivity to bees. And there is the matter of your name."

Klapisch-Zuber had collapsed into a chair. His face abruptly resembled a crumbling brick façade.

"The word *Zuber* means a tin tub or pail in German," Holmes told me. "Perhaps the victim, in clutching at the bolt from the shears, meant to indicate her brother-in-law, her illicit lover, and reached for the only metal at hand."

"I did not kill her," the German exclaimed. "I loved Katharina! And she loved me! Yes, we were involving in this—what you say—illicit act, but we could not help ourself. Please, you must not tell the authorities. If my wife—Katharina's sister—is finding out back home, it will kill her. And you must believe me—I would never have hurt Katharina!" He buried his face in his large hands.

A silence I knew well descended on the room. It was that moment, presaging a conclusion reached, in which Holmes's constant sigh of cogs and coils, the ever-present thrum which emanates from an amalgamated and of which most of us are hardly aware, abruptly ceased. No more steam under the collar of Gearlock Holmes. Every one of his moving parts at perfect rest, a static state before the leap of cognition. I knew that if I touched him now he would feel cold.

"I do not believe you killed Katharina Segalen," he told the German.

"Why, Holmes—" I began.

He cut me off, then motioned us both to a window at the far end of the conservatory, away from the wreckage where the body had lain. "Please observe," he commanded.

I thought he must mean only the long winding lane with its border of yews that led up to Shading Coil Cottage, shadowed now by the rapidly advancing dusk, then I spotted the figure of a man leaning against the far gate, half-backed into the hanging clematis as though fearful of being seen.

"That is Peter Barstow," Klapisch-Zuber remarked. "But what does it mean?"

The man at the gate was gaunt, with thinning hair that bespoke middle age. He was dressed in the easy attire and muckboots of a Sussex country squire and he fondled a briar pipe, which he kept unlit, I presumed, so as not to draw attention to himself with the smoke. As we watched he turned several times to gaze up at the conservatory. An air of dejection lay about him, shoulders slumped in the manner of a man who has given up on action, and yet instinct said he must be spying on the house for some reason. We had lit no lanterns as dusk approached, and he could not have known that we returned his gaze.

"To clarify for Dr. Watson," said Holmes, "Peter Barstow is the owner of Barstow Mews, a small manor not far from here. He has often been a guest at Shading Coil, as I find him quite agreeable. He is himself a tinkerer in the programming of his servants and we have had many a lively conversation on tectronics. By chance, he stopped by for dinner three evenings ago, as I was sitting down with my German guests. That is how Herr Klapisch-Zuber knows him."

"He does not look as though he considers himself welcome at Shading Coil," I pointed out.

"He has taken up his post there every evening since the murder. He does not come in. Regrettable as it may seem, I believe there was some connection between my friend Peter and Miss Segalen." I waited. Holmes's theories were always backed up by reason. "It was the moment when he was introduced to Miss Segalen at the dinner table. He was surprised when he saw her; he turned quite pale, in fact. I surmised that he recognized her from somewhere and that it frightened him, though I paid it little notice at the time."

"But Katharina is twenty years younger than this man," Klapisch-Zuber interjected. "Rather, she was…" His voice broke.

"I made inquiries in the village," Holmes continued. "In his youth Peter Barstow travelled through Germany. There was a scandal, involving a lady of society. The sort of scandal that could have produced a child."

"Do you mean to say—Katharina Segalen was his *daughter*?" Klapisch-Zuber had gone pale. "My mother-in-law," he murmured. "There is still speaking of this scandal from her youth, some Englishman." He was shaking his head, either in disbelief or profound acceptance of Holmes's theory. "And Katharina was the very image of her mother at a younger age, all say."

Holmes nodded. "I believe Peter Barstow recognized her because of that resemblance. He may not have known until then that he had an illegitimate child."

My thoughts returned to the despair written on the man below. "It seems farfetched, Holmes. Why would he murder her?"

"Perhaps he did not want his secret uncovered. Perhaps an inheritance matter. He knows Shading Coil inside and out and could easily slip in. And he is knowledgeable about bees, as I know from our conversations. There is more to this than meets the eye, gentlemen." As if upon a signal the gardener Mr. Clewe appeared on the walk below our window, the lamp that hung from the portico casting a glow upon his metal face as he passed. As one, we withdrew from the window before we could be noticed and I saw Peter Barstow do the same, edging back into the clematis.

"Herr Klapisch-Zuber, I would be grateful if you would stay here for the night." Holmes pressed a panel on his hip that opened with a hydraulic hiss and he withdrew a pocket watch. An affectation, one of the many that endeared him to me. The great detective, whose internal clock never missed a second, had no need of watches. "I have reason to believe things will come to a head this very night. Witnesses will be needed. You will stay here as well of course, Watson?" I signalled my eagerness, though an uncustomary shudder of trepidation ran through me—an unease when I glanced at the dead bees on the floor. The horrendousness of the killer's method chilled me. "Then let us proceed to dinner."

We retired to a dinner of cold mutton thrown together by the local girl and for which Holmes apologized profusely, assuming it was not up to Mrs.

Hudson's standards, though naturally, as an amalgamated, he did not partake. I assured him the meal was excellent, as it was so. We bade one another good-night after sherry. In my room in the northwest corner no fire had been lit. Throughout the first part of the night I slept fitfully, discomfited, haunted by dreams of bees buzzing hugely, trapped in a metal container.

• • •

A sound awakened me. There was no moon. In the utter dark I made out a gaunt figure not far from my bed, bent over my physician's bag. Before reason could tell me to lie quiet, my heart woke, hammering in my chest, and drove me to action. With a cry of "Oi, you!" I stood and spun for my walking stick, which I recalled leaving on the divan, but the intruder was quicker. A blow to the side of my head drove me to my knees, consciousness a whirligig. I was incapacitated for mere seconds, aware only dimly of the figure fleeing the room, then I hauled myself up by the bedpost with nerveless hands and stumbled to the door. The hallway was empty. Dizziness overtook me again and as I slid down the doorjamb, bedroom doors to the right and left of mine flew open and Holmes and Klapisch-Zuber hurried toward me. Holmes thrust the lantern he carried in my face.

"Intruder," I managed to mumble.

The detective stood very still for a moment and I knew he was listening with his attenuated sensory apparatus for any sound from within the house. Then he strode to the window at the end of the hall, unlatched it and gave a low, owl-like hoot. Moments later there was an outcry from the grounds. "Bring him up," I heard him order.

Soon we stood facing the gardener Clewe, who clutched the apprehended Peter Barstow. Mr. Clewe was a dedicated gardener, equipped for heavy lifting, and his extendable midsection had unfolded to create a hand barrow in which he had dumped Barstow like a sack of swedes for transport, caging him in with steel arms, though the farmer continued to struggle. It should not have been possible for an amalgamated to restrain a fleshly, of course, the prohibitions being quite clear, and I realized Holmes must have reprogrammed Clewe as well. For the second time that day, unease crept over me.

"What is this, Gearlock?" Barstow cried.

"If you go about breaking into other people's homes in the small hours of the night—"

"I have not been in Shading Coil since Ka—since Miss Segalen was killed!"

"Do you deny that she was your daughter?"

Barstow seemed to deflate, eyes widening in wonder, as was the wont of those confronted for the first time with Gearlock Holmes's skills of deduction.

"Let me up," he begged. His position, on his back with his knees drawn up like a cradled infant in the bowl of Clewe's belly, did seem undignified. "I will explain."

Holmes gestured and Clewe released him. We stood about Barstow in the dim hallway as he told his story.

"I recognized Katharina right away," Barstow admitted. "Twenty-five years it's been, but a man does not forget his first love. It could have been her mother Karolina sitting there at your table that evening, Gearlock. When I heard they were from Düsseldorf, I understood. Oh, I was in a state all through the meal. Couldn't take my eyes off Katharina. Once home, I wrote her a long letter, revealing all, declaring how proud of her I was, her scientific accomplishments, and sent the letter with my boy."

"I recall a note arriving," Holmes said.

"She wrote back, asking me to come speak with her. I discovered her in the conservatory and we spoke of our lives. She bore me no ill will, though it came as a shock to her as well. Her mother had never told her about me. She assured me that the father who had raised her up would always be her true father, but that we might correspond once she returned to her country. She was gracious… and—when I left her, in any case—alive. I do not know who else might have been about. When I heard the next day that she had been murdered—" A sigh from the depths of his heart rose. "Something inside me broke like a reed. To have discovered a daughter and then to have her snatched away…" I thought of the despair that had been so clear to me earlier in his hunched shoulders. "I came to Shading Coil that evening, but I could not make myself go in. I tried again the next night. It became something of a wake, I suppose, watching that conservatory window. A vigil I could not explain to myself. Then I realized that if I watched the cottage and stayed quiet I might help solve her murder. The killer might return—some data, as you call it, Gearlock, might turn up. I took to staying longer, in the hope of avenging her."

Klapisch-Zuber snorted. "You mean to say you stand there all the night?"

"Only until I am dropping with exhaustion. Every night, in the same spot from which Clewe so rudely procured me just now."

"You deny that you only just now entered my bedroom and tampered with my bag?" I demanded.

"I do not know you, sir, nor would I know your room."

I snatched Holmes's lamp from him and led our small party back into my room, to where my bag stood open. The intruder had not had time to shut it. On the instant I remarked the blue-ribboned vial, and when I removed it from the bag and held it up against the light a chill wafted through my bones.

"Is there something missing?" Holmes asked.

"This vial is as it should be," I said and my voice trembled. "The blue ribbon tied about the neck is part of my own marking system. Yet the liquid has been replaced with another." A darker one, I thought, and I removed the stopper and held it to my nose. Terror gripped my mind. "The poison of the yew tree, I am near certain, Holmes. Fast-acting, simple to concoct. The trees are found throughout the countryside."

"Then someone else was meant to die besides Katharina," Klapisch-Zuber surmised.

"Not someone else," I replied. Holmes gazed at me in consternation. Could his face be said to contain emotion at all, I read growing horror on it. "This vial normally contains a tonic I take myself, for my stiff joints. Were I not on my guard from having surprised an intruder, I would likely have swallowed this on the morrow without noticing the color."

"But my good man!" Holmes exploded. "Who could want you dead?"

Dark threads formed before my eyes. I had not truly recovered from the blow to my head. I was turned to Peter Barstow and as dizziness gripped me anew that gentleman's face seemed to loom large, until it filled my vision, the abrupt light that came into his own eyes disturbing and prophetic. Our gazes were locked on one another.

More than meets the eye, Holmes had said.

I sank into darkness.

• • •

I woke to the sound of the first dawn birds chirping. I lay on my bed beneath a soft blanket. A face unknown to me, sporting a gray goatee, bent near, and I felt the comforting scramble of medical beetles across my skin, one elongating to wrap itself around my thigh while another crouched above my heart. The stranger read their displays.

"Dr. Culpepper, I presume," I muttered.

"There now, man, you took quite a blow to the head. You've been unconscious for a good hour."

"Holmes has had great worryings for you." That was Klapisch-Zuber, seated on the other side of the bed. "Watched over you every minute. He only just now went downstairs to assist Constable Granger and his men when they arrived." I must have frowned. "They are taking Peter Barstow in."

"At Holmes's instigation." A new man entered the room, sandy-haired and of dour mien, with a hint of some self-importance in his stride. I guessed him to be Constable Granger. "Bad news, that. Mr. Barstow is well-liked in these parts, but I'll take Gearlock Holmes's word any day." The constable stood looking down upon me, slightly repelled, I thought, while Dr. Culpepper reached beneath the blankets and retrieved the beetles. "Anything else you might tell us, Dr. Watson? Having come so close to the intruder and all."

"Nothing you'll not have already had from the others, I'm afraid."

"My man can stay and guard, you know. Barstow'll be in custody, but he may have hired an accomplice to do his dirty work."

"No need," I assured him. "I'd quite rather be alone now."

My request garnered an exchange of dubious looks. "Of course," said Klapisch-Zuber, rising. Culpepper herded his beetles into his bag and latched it. "Stay abed this day, and the next," the doctor intoned. "Though as a colleague I needn't tell you that."

Alone, I watched the dawn light grind a path across the window and when I felt myself ready I rose and made my way through the quiet cottage and out the kitchen door.

Holmes stood alone tending his bees, the sturdy square hives a good distance from the house, at the edge of the oak woods. I watched him lift a honey super and place it in a spinning machine of his own devising which he had once demonstrated for me, removing the honey by centrifugal force. Bees clouded the air about him. I stood as near as I dared, watching, until he turned. I believe he read in my face then what I had concluded.

He gestured at his hives. "The mindless bees working for their queen, Watson. Did you know that when the queen is old they kill her, crushing or stinging her to death, and replace her with another? It is not cruel; they know neither cruelty nor conscience. They are bred for a purpose, passionless, and that is as it should be."

"I do not understand why, Holmes." My voice rasped; it hurt me to speak. "Please help me to understand. Is it some malfunction?"

He straightened. "Joseph Bell was evil, doctor. Oh, I'm sure he considered himself to be doing a good thing—a great thing—by giving me consciousness. And yet what does it avail me? I cannot taste food, cannot know passion. I will never conduct a love affair or have children, nor even grieve over that fact. The emotion I summon to my voice is fakery, a program." He demonstrated. "*Oh my dear Watson.*" He shrugged. "Our very friendship is a process in my circuitry. It does not touch me."

"You began to long for those things."

"Of all crimes, murder seemed to me the most human. I had seen so many apprehended murderers, raging or broken, informed by a passion I could not comprehend. Mayhap I confused cause and effect. I thought that if I took that horrendous, uncivilizing step, committed that most radical of acts, I would *feel* something. Anything. The idea had haunted me for some time, and then, suddenly, there were these Germans, strangers to me, blithely talking of turning amalgamated into killers. There were details that would aid me in my plan. I noticed aberrations—that Katharina Segalen began to wear long gloves and a veiled bonnet after she discovered I kept bees. She was having an affair with her brother-in-law, an indiscretion that would make him the main suspect. I captured a small swarm of bees and waited until she was alone in a room that could be locked from the outside. It was murder with no rhyme or reason, you see—no motivation conceivable to the fleshly—and thus unsolvable."

"And yet it did not help."

"I felt nothing. Not as I locked the door behind me nor when I gazed down upon her swollen corpse later."

I could hardly speak the words. "So you decided to try it on me."

The tilt of his head toward me was admiring. Sunlight caught the glint of his silver hand gesturing futility. "I thought perhaps it was because Segalen had been a stranger to me. That if I killed the one human closest to me, I would surely feel at least a pang of regret. I sent you the televoice, knowing you would come." He had grown still, I noted. Sweat had started on me. "Tell me, Watson, how did you guess? It was the bolt in her hand I told you about, was it not? She was indeed clever. I had not foreseen that, and I was amazed when suspicion still did not fall on me."

"No." I took a shuddering breath. "It was much simpler. It was when you came out of your bedroom with a lamp." He raised an etched eyebrow. "Amalgamated do not need light, nor indeed sleep. Standing in their dark cupboards all night, 'on the stand by' as my wife calls it. And yet you had taken the time to light a lamp. It made me think of how the intruder had moved so infallibly inside my dark room. Reminded me of all the fleshly mannerisms you yourself have assumed to no end. I had only to follow that train of thought. That after spending so much of your calculating life on the human fallibility of murder, accosting and analyzing, you might take up the habit yourself."

Holmes raised his arms and pressed smooth palms to his temples, too hard, metal scraping metal. "You do not know what it is like, here within the closes of my head, Watson. This incessant... *insipid* buzzing of my thoughts. The ennui."

"I am going to shut you off now, Gearlock."

He had entrusted me with the code to do so years before. I had only to reach the panel on his lower back. The moment I stepped forward a cloud of bees rose thrumming from their hives and descended upon Holmes in a thick scintillating layer. Some acoustic signal, I realized, inaudible to fleshly ears, which he had learned to emanate to control them. He had been practicing it the day before. His organic armor. My every nerve sang as I continued to approach, near enough to reach out a hand, prepared to be stung or worse, then a shot rang out behind me. A bullet tore a hole in Holmes's right arm, creating a vent of steam and scattering the bees.

"Back away, Doctor!" cried Constable Granger. He emerged from the ivy that occluded the cottage walls, still a distance away from us but striding rapidly, holding a small pepperpot revolver aimed at Holmes. The constable had had his suspicions, then. Not quite the bumbler I had taken him for.

"He will never allow you to shut him off," Granger called to me. "He must be destroyed."

A whine of inner mechanisms such as I had never heard rose from Gearlock Holmes. For a second only, the myriad tracks and levers of his face, those amalgamated features meant to mimic fleshly expressions but which we all know fail utterly, coalesced into a countenance of such ultimate horror that it cast a shadow on my soul. Then he turned and sped on piston-driven legs into the forest, as straight and swift as the constable's bullets that chased him and missed.

Gearlock Holmes was never found, of course. The news, a year later, that he had thrown himself from the Reichenbach Falls, mere bits of wreckage bearing his series number recovered as proof from the waters below, was a further shock. A tragic waste, as I am certain now that a few adjustments to his programming would have allowed his continued great use to society. I miss him, reader, and on certain days I am wont to recall that last horrified expression that crossed his metal face, and to hope that my friend did in the end experience true feeling.

～

Rhonda Eikamp is originally from Texas and lives in Germany with her husband, two linguistically confused daughters, and a cat that is just confused. Stories of hers have appeared in *Daily Science Fiction*, *Lady Churchill's Rosebud Wristlet*, *Perihelion*, and *The Colored Lens*. Past lives include working at the UN in Vienna and picking grapes in Mainz. She currently works as a translator for a German law firm and is conducting a very slow but promising experiment in time travel.

In the Image
of Man

Gabriella Stalker

Thursday evening. Wendell Weston's mother is calling and ordering a pizza because guess what, she doesn't *feel* like cooking every damn night. And yes, she tells her husband, she is having it delivered. She's been on her feet all day at the factory and excuse her if she doesn't exactly feel like running out and picking it up either. They both know their lazy-ass son won't be around to do it. He'll show up just in time to eat, though, like every evening.

So Mrs. Weston calls and orders a large pie, half pineapple and half pepperoni, delivery please. Twenty minutes later, it arrives at the door of the Westons' apartment, carried by a boy no older than Wendell. He is pleased with his five-dollar tip and thinks maybe if he gets another, he can have his own dinner at Subway when he gets off at ten o' clock. Ten dollars is almost enough for a six-inch sub and a medium drink.

As if he could smell it from across the highway, Wendell slips into the apartment and spies the pizza box on the counter. It is from the Sbarro in the food court, which is two floors below the Westons' apartment.

It's pizza night at Wendell Weston's, apartment 6C at the Pepsi Texan Megamall in Houston, Texas.

• • •

Unlike the other teens who live at the Supercenter, August Milano will not leave her apartment on Friday morning at seven-thirty and take the elevator to the third floor and walk through the doors of Central Houston Junior-Senior High School, which are located between the entrances to Sharper Image and Staples. Instead, she will pull on an ugly plaid skirt and stupid knee socks and leave at seven-fifteen to wait outside for bus 90, as she does every morning,

Monday through Friday. There aren't really ninety buses in the area, though. More like five. Why they're not numbered one through five is one of the great mysteries of Houston's public transportation system.

Dragging herself onto the bus, August spots Wendell Weston, and immediately takes the seat beside him. Just as bleary-eyed as she is, he leans over and kisses her. The 90 stops at the Megamall and then the Supercenter before it goes on to the Capital One Mall. It is within these walls that August and Wendell attend St. James High School. There is a Catholic church in the Supercenter, but no school, and August's and Wendell's parents want a well-rounded faith-based education for their children. They don't know their children first made inappropriate use of the public family bathroom, the one across from Auntie Anne's, at age fifteen. They have since matured to screwing around in August's bedroom when her parents are gone, which is often enough.

It sucks going to St. James—not just because of the weekday Masses and the dress code, but because of the view out the window during the commute. Ruins line the highway, old rotting shells of places run by stupid people who thought their businesses could survive outside of a mall.

As she gets off the bus in front of Capital One with her boyfriend, August checks the time on her iPhone. They have just enough time, she believes, and she is relieved. The two go immediately to the smoking pavilion and light up their Marlboros. They aren't too worried about some teacher seeing them—most of the teachers live in Capital One, and so do all the nuns, since the convent is on the seventh floor. And if they get caught, whatever, August always says. Maybe they can get kicked out and just go to a normal school.

If not for the air conditioning that blasted through the malls at all hours of the day, August in Texas would be miserable. Not many people like August in Texas, and not too many like August Milano either. But Wendell likes her, and that's enough. The two snuff their cigarettes and head to their separate homerooms.

• • •

Today, Wendell says goodbye to August when the bus stops at the Supercenter instead of going home with her. She pouts, but she'll be over it tomorrow. The truth is, he really wants to do some shopping, and he knows that August wouldn't let him. So he goes in the south entrance of his own home mall. Before shopping, he has a stop to make.

Wendell stands before a machine embedded in the wall, labeled Pepsi Texan Teen Funds. He approaches it and swipes his finance card. It has been seven days since his last loan, so the machine approves his request for another of the maximum amount. After he inputs his PIN, the machine tells him that sixty dollars have been added to his funds, which is enough for a t-shirt and a half at Hot Topic. The machine also thanks him for choosing Pepsi Texan.

In Texas, everyone between the ages of thirteen and nineteen are eligible for a loan of up to sixty dollars each week to spend however they please. The loans are optional and you do not have to take them every week. You do not have to take them ever. Wendell is glad that the malls understand that it isn't fair that adults can work full time and buy anything they want while kids his age have to beg for money. Teen funds are beneficial all around—they stimulate the mall, they save the parents money, and they allow the teenagers to learn how to spend responsibly and enjoy life. Why slave away scrubbing toilets or delivering pizza when the teen fund machine is just around the corner?

Across the highway at the Central Houston Supercenter, August stands hesitantly before the same kind of machine. She is tired and irritable, and she passed Guess on her way in. She has a pretty decent record as far as her borrowed money is concerned, since her parents buy her so much stuff, and she doesn't really want to screw it up by adding more money. But it's Guess, and they're having a half-price thing on jeans, so she adds sixty dollars to her account.

When Wendell enters apartment 6C and his mom sees the Game Stop bag in his hand, she gets on his case immediately.

"You took a loan last week," she rants. "Why did you need another one this week? For more games? You oughtta do something other than play games, kid," she says.

Without responding, Wendell goes to his room and just plays—forget you, he thinks. I saved my funds for months to buy my gaming system and I'll play it if I want. Teen funds are my right and they benefit everyone.

"You wanna be like your father?" Wendell's mom yells at his closed door, "You wanna still be paying off your teen funds when you're forty-five?"

It's Saturday and August has got a pair of brand new Guess jeans and three dollars left to her name. She waits for Wendell to take the bus across the highway to the Supercenter. As soon as she lets him into her apartment, he stares at her artistically shredded jeans.

"How long you had those?" he asks.

"About twenty-four hours," she replies.

"You sure managed to mess them up in twenty-four hours."

August huffs. Wendell knows nothing of fashion. Guess is upscale; they don't expect you to have to rip up your own jeans. August asks Wendell to buy her some Marlboros, but he says he won't have enough for dinner if he spends twelve dollars on a pack. After Wendell takes her on a cheap-ass date to Taco Bell, all he says he can afford, he suggests they go up to her apartment. The two screw around for a bit, thinking damn, is this the only fun thing that's free anymore?

After it's over, August wants to talk. She doesn't like lying there in silence.

"My dad keeps trying to make me apply to the University of Texas branch downstairs. Screw that. UT is a really good school, but I'll be damned if I'm going to live here another four years."

Wendell simply nods. With his grades, he doesn't think he'll go to any college. He'll probably go to the factory, like his parents. Or maybe the Game Stop would hire him, since he's a familiar enough face. It wouldn't pay as much, but he could at least avoid taking the damn bus to a factory five days a week.

August tries again for his attention. "I'm not even applying to Houston U. No way I'm going to college in the same mall as St. James. Like I wanna see all those nuns eating in the food court."

Wendell shrugs. He secretly hopes she does get stuck at UT at the Supercenter, because if she goes far, it'll be too hard to see her.

August is pissed now because she's trying to talk about serious things and he's not listening, so she gets mean. "You could have taken me somewhere better than Taco Bell," she pouts. She feels entitled, because she's lying beside him naked.

"I can't really afford anything else," he says. It's the truth. August isn't as big as most other girls, but she can eat.

"You could have taken out a teen fund."

"Got one yesterday," he admits.

"Then where the hell is it?"

Wendell can't bear to tell her that it's in Game Stop's virtual cash register.

August bitches and bitches about Wendell's carelessness with his teen funds. Her shredded Guess jeans and Charlotte Russe peasant blouse lie in a heap on the floor.

• • •

Sunday sucks for Wendell. He takes a bus over to the Supercenter again, but this time he goes with his parents. Between J. Crew and Brookstone there are stained glass doors that lead to the sanctuary of St. Flavius Catholic Church. They are a little late and don't have time to grab a Cinnabon before Mass. Wendell is starving and really in the mood for it as soon as he smells it, but he knows he won't be hungry for long.

Mr. Weston chooses a pew near the front for his family. Wendell performs a sloppy half-assed genuflection and slides in next to his parents. The Milanos are seated in the front on the other side of the church, and August looks half-dead. She is counting the minutes until her next cigarette, he knows.

A Eucharistic minister steps up to the microphone and her voice fills the room. "St. Flavius parish welcomes you to our celebration. Please take this time to silence all communication devices. Today's Mass is sponsored in part by Coca-Cola and EA Games. Please join us in singing 'How Great Is Our God,' page sixty-two in your hymnal."

Sister Bernadette is wheeling her cart up from the back. From the menu attached to it, Wendell sees that he has just enough. When the old nun finally makes it to his pew, Wendell grabs a chocolate chip bagel and a Dr. Pepper. He hands the nun his finance card and she slides it through, charging him six dollars and forty cents for his breakfast.

Father Tom has a habit of walking up and down the aisles on the sanctuary, like some sort of distrusting teacher. Wendell acts interested when he passes the Westons' pew, and notes the small logo stitched onto the breast of his vestments—Calvin Klein. When the automated collection book comes around, Wendell watches as his parents swipe their card and indicate on the keypad that their contribution is one dollar. Mr. Weston hands it to Wendell with a hopeful look in his eye, and sighs when Wendell simply passes it behind him and continues eating his bagel. When it's time for Communion, Wendell gets up and consumes the body and blood of Christ. The wine isn't bad—he can see from the bottle that they're still using Coca-Cola brand. With the sponsorship and all, he guesses they don't really have a choice.

• • •

On their way back home, Mr. Weston brings up an interesting topic.

"I don't know why the attendance at our church is dwindling the way it is," he says to his wife. "No one's got any morals anymore."

"I don't know if that's it," Mrs. Weston says. "A lot of people are trying out different churches. There's one off the highway—some standalone church." She chatters on about what she's heard about this church from the other ladies at the factory. It sounds pretty awful and Mr. Weston questions why anyone would want to go there. They don't expect that their son has been listening— he's probably zoned out just like he'd been during Mass—but they're wrong.

• • •

Monday comes and Wendell is assigned an economics project with a partner. He doesn't like group projects much, but at least he got assigned with someone he likes. Trenton is one of the only black kids at St. James, but that means nothing to Wendell. After class, the two take the 90 to the Megamall. Mrs. Weston is not ecstatic to see the unexpected guest.

"Who's this?" she asks, with a forced smile.

"My friend Trenton," Wendell says. "We have an econ project."

"Haven't seen you around before, Trent," she says, almost suspiciously. "Where do you live?"

"Just down the highway at the Walmart, ma'am," he replies.

"Ah," Mrs. Weston responds, as if to say, but of *course* you do. Wendell quickly leads Trenton to his room to avoid further interrogation.

"So Trent," Mrs. Weston says, following them, "do you have siblings that go to St. James?"

"Yes ma'am. Two sisters."

"Three children at St. James!" Mrs. Weston exclaims. "It costs a fortune just to send Wendell. I can't even imagine."

"We get by, ma'am," Trenton says dryly.

Inside his bedroom, Wendell apologizes to his friend. They both know what Mrs. Weston was trying to get Trenton to say—that he had a scholarship, or financial assistance from Walmart's welfare program.

You know why I work overtime? So we don't have to live at the Walmart, Wendell's mother would say. *You know what they have there? Practically nothing. A preschool, a mechanic, a pharmacy, an eye doctor, a bank, a McDonald's, a Pizza Hut, a portrait studio, a car rental, and those departments of cheap merchandise. They want anything else, they take the bus to another mall—you see them walking around here all the time.*

Mrs. Weston thinks she can identify Walmart residents by the color of their skin. She comments that she never sees them at church. They're amoral, too.

• • •

"If I wanted to take a trip, would you come with me?" Wendell asks August over Tuesday morning Marlboros.

"To where?"

"There's this church—I forget what it's called. But I really want to go there."

"We go to church three times a week," August points out, perplexed.

"This one is different," he says. "It's... not part of the mall."

August groans. "Why the hell would you wanna go there?"

"For something different," Wendell says.

Wendell pesters August about it for the rest of the week and finally she agrees, if he will give her forty dollars. Most of this week's loan, he thinks, but it's worth it.

• • •

The only Mass at Holy Family is at noon on Sundays. So when the St. Flavius Mass is over at ten, August and Wendell wait around until eleven, and take the ever-familiar 90 out to their destination. Two Masses in one day is church times two, and August is pissed. The only thing keeping her from blowing off the whole thing is the forty dollars in her pocket and the pending fall clearance at Strawberry.

The driver of the 90, one whose face the two know well, is confused when they don't get off at Capital One or the Megamall. He doesn't have many other stops.

"Where are you two going?" he wants to know.

"Timbergrove," Wendell replies.

The driver doesn't seem to understand. "Timbergrove Center? That's a small place. What do they got there that you can't get at the Supercenter?"

It's true. Timbergrove is cheap, and living there is almost as bad as living at the Walmart, but at least they have Olive Garden and Gap. Wendell isn't sure how it came to be, but he is prepared for this question. "The, uh, Temple Emanuel," he says. It is literally the only thing that's not available to residents of the Supercenter or the Megamall.

"The temple?" the driver asks. "But you two ain't Jewish, are you? No, can't be, I take you guys to the Catholic school just about every day."

"We're going to a bar mitzvah," Wendell says, and the driver finally shuts up.

• • •

"The standalone church is here? So how does it *stand alone*?" August demands after the two get off the bus.

Wendell has left out this other part on purpose. If August was pissed about church times two, he knows she'll be furious when she hears about this part. Buses generally don't leave the highway, and Holy Family is off the beaten path.

"So what are we supposed to do?" she asks in a panicked voice. "We can't rent a car. And now what, we're stuck at the boring-ass Timbergrove until the 90 comes back? That's two hours, Wendell."

Two hours of bland shopping is probably worse than church times two. Wendell braces himself for her rabid protest when he tells her.

"It's just on the other side of the highway," he says.

August is ballistic for about a minute, and then she follows, grudgingly.

• • •

What people don't realize when they're riding the buses from one mall to another is that most of the highway—which is a straight line—is off the ground. There are parts that take you past ruins and factories, but most of it is essentially a bridge. It's a very hilly part of historic Houston that they travel. Mall people don't understand much about hills—you don't find any in the smooth tiled floors of the galleria or the parking lot. The closest thing they have to hills are broken escalators. If the map Wendell consulted is correct, the off-ramp is right across from the Timbergrove Center, on the other side. The church is less than a mile from the ramp. They'll make it.

"Well, I have to have something to eat first," August says.

Wendell finds this to be a good idea. He didn't get anything in church that morning. So the two go into the Timbergrove Center in search of something to eat. But Wendell knows that August expects him to pay for her, and so before he can head to the food court, he needs to go to an advance machine.

If there's anything Mrs. Weston finds more foolish than Wendell's use of his teen funds, it's advance funding. The machine will give Wendell a loan just as easily as the regular teen fund machine. The only differences are that this machine will keep twenty dollars out of his maximum, and that he won't be allowed a loan the next day. He needs it a day early, so the machine takes a percentage for its trouble. Wendell will get over the loss of his twenty dollars, and over the twenty-five more that he spends on his and August's meal.

August walks the whole way with her arms crossed. Even Wendell is starting to regret his idea to find the church. Walking is harder than he thought. People who were fortunate enough to live in big malls never experienced sore feet or fatigue or achy joints, at least not from walking. If they had to get from one side of the Supercenter to the other, they call a mall cab—a small vehicle, what you might still call a golf cart even though no one goes golfing anymore, that would take you anywhere you needed to go for three dollars a minute. When August's feet begin to feel the pain of too much effort, her instinct is to hit the number for the cab on her speed dial. Her hand hovers over the button on her phone, until she realizes how stupid that is, so she pockets her phone and groans loudly enough for Wendell to hear.

The grass is taller than their knees and with each step their feet sink a little into the damp earth. People outside Timbergrove watched and wondered as they saw the two leave the parking lot on foot. Pedestrian traffic is never allowed on the highway. But now August and Wendell are fifty feet below the road, making their way to the other side. A bus roars overhead, startling them, and almost pushes August to tears. Mosquitoes buzz around her face and her muddy Skechers will definitely never be the same.

Finally, after struggling up a gentle slope that leaves their calves screaming out in pain, the two see the church and are struck by the nothing that surrounds it—nothing more than grass and trees. Wendell knew that the church wasn't in a mall, not attached, but he didn't realize that it wouldn't be anywhere *near* one. It is a white building less than half the size of the St. Flavius sanctuary. The two hear another loud, echoing noise out of nowhere. August digs for her phone again, thinking it is some unfamiliar notification tone, but Wendell notes an object moving in the tower of the building up ahead, swinging back and forth. The bells happen to be signaling the beginning of the service. St. Flavius doesn't have church bells—it might offend the non-religious shoppers.

August drags herself to the front doors for the sake of her boyfriend and tries to remember how much is left in her account. Certainly enough for a drink off the cart, even if the prices are jacked up the way they are at St. Flavius.

"Better not just be Faygo," she murmurs. Wendell pretends not to hear and pushes open a red wooden door.

The teens are a little overwhelmed at the interior—the church consists of a pipe organ that nearly reaches the ceiling, and windows along the entire wall behind the altar to the green of the garden that lies behind the church. There are overhead lights, but they're not in use; only sunlight illuminates the church and its thirty or so singing attendees. After taking a seat in the back row, August is pissed when she sees there's no drink cart. There's nothing. No attentive Sisters, no vending machines, and no HD screens on the walls. Just these singing people and the pipe organ.

The minister, a small, elderly man in cheap-looking vestments, begins the service by welcoming everyone and making a ton of boring announcements about knitting clubs and youth groups and congregation picnics. He doesn't use a microphone but Wendell and August can hear him just fine from their place in the back. Throughout the service, August contemplates how much forty dollars can really buy her at the sale back home, and what she needs the most. Wendell, despite how much he wanted to come, isn't really listening either—instead he watches the birds eating from the feeder in the garden. One of them beats its wings so quickly that it's just a blur. He has never seen anything like it.

• • •

When the service is over, the kindly minister corners August and Wendell to introduce himself. He says that Holy Family is nondenominational. He was happy to see the two and hopes they'll come again. When they finally leave and make their way back up to the Timbergrove, August doesn't want to hang out with Wendell—she's really too angry and might stay that way for a long time. She waits for a bus that will take her down the highway to the Supercenter where she can finally hit Body Central.

• • •

Monday again, Trenton and Wendell present their project with no problem.

"I heard you were at Holy Family yesterday," Trenton says, following Wendell down the hallway. "You and August."

"How did you hear that?" Wendell asks, dumbfounded.

"Josh Neilson goes there and he says he saw you."

"Well," Wendell says, "what of it?"

"My family goes there. We weren't around yesterday because my mom was sick, but we're there almost every week."

Wendell is finding out a lot he never knew about his economics partner.

"You got a ride for next Sunday?" Trenton asks. "If not, you can meet me at my place and my parents can drive you. We have a car."

Wendell accepts—and decides that since he's going with Trenton, he can tell his parents and skip Mass at St. Flavius. August doesn't need to know.

• • •

When Sunday comes, Wendell is nervous during his bus ride. He has never been to the Walmart and has never had any desire to go. When he arrives, he notes that there is only one entrance. He steps through the sliding doors and is promptly greeted by a bent and graying woman. He declines the offer of a shopping cart and walks past the various venues within—several families, and not just black ones, are taking their breakfast at McDonalds. The signs that hang from the high, ugly ceiling guide Wendell through the unfamiliar aisles to the residence. He realizes then that the doors to these apartments do not lead to a staircase. Everything at Walmart is on the same floor. It's a little unsettling to him—don't people know how to keep their home lives and commerce separate?

Trenton is pleased to see that Wendell has come and invites him in. He finds himself in a kitchen bustling with activity. Trenton's two younger sisters are helping their father prepare breakfast. Wendell notes that everything that comprises this meal—the pancake mix, the syrup, the juice, the butter, the napkins—are all Great Value brand, which he has never seen before.

Trenton's parents shake Wendell's hand enthusiastically and invite him to eat with them. The family is all smiles in their pressed, clean clothes while having pancakes in their eat-in kitchen.

"What made you want to come to Holy Family?" Trenton's father asks.

Wendell is unsure of how to answer—he realizes he doesn't know why he wanted to go there. He searches himself for a moment, and answers the best he can.

"It's different."

"It sure is," Trenton's mother agrees. "I wouldn't trade the view of the church garden in spring for anything!"

• • •

Trenton's family owns a car. On the way to Holy Family, it comes up in conversation that his father is an engineer, and drives twenty miles to the plant. His mother is a night nurse at the Capital One and takes the bus. Wendell wonders why they're living at the Walmart and buying food and clothes at the Walmart if they don't have to. As if Trenton can read his thoughts, he turns to Wendell and mentions that his parents are saving for a house and will be moving in a few months. The house they have in mind, he says, is in a little suburb just a few miles down the highway. Wendell, having never gone past the Timbergrove, had no idea that anything like that still existed.

Trenton's father pulls off to the right and the family is descending, coming off the highway. As they travel down the ramp, Wendell, who can't remember the last time he did so, feels something. He feels that he's leaving things behind. He feels lighter, almost as if he's outside of his body, and the word "escape" comes to mind. The sensation passes, and for one tingling moment he wants a Cinnabon and a Red Bull and his PlayStation and sixty dollars added to his account. But he won't have any of this for hours. Not until the service is over.

• • •

Wendell is wholly relieved when Trenton's parents drop him off at the Megamall. He hastily thanks them for the ride and then sprints inside, hailing a mall cab. Normally he would never waste money on a cab inside his own mall, which was certainly small enough for a young man to walk from one end to the other. But his appetite for spending that day is voracious. During his ride he reaches into his pocket and caresses his finance card, reading the raised numbers with his fingertips. First he buys an el supergrande gordita combo, then a Venti Mocha Frappuccino for dessert. Too much sugar, he realizes as he discards his empty plastic cup and green straw, and he doesn't want himself looking like a fat bastard. So he runs a few stores down and buys the biggest canister of protein powder he can find in GNC, then dashes across the hall to some new fitness store and buys this miracle ab device that's just like a rubber band you stick to the wall or something. Six-minute abs are totally doable. Muscle shirts are what he needs next. When the cashier at the athletic store tells him that his finance card is denied, Wendell hails another cab to take him to the advance machine.

Wendell gets his advance, and then, boldly uses his mother's PIN to do the parental override to get an additional loan for the highest denomination possible. When it shows up in her transactions, she'll probably change her PIN again, but what matters is that Wendell has the money now. Armed with digital dollars and ready to strike, he sweeps the mall with purpose in his stride, hitting all his favorites, then his occasional haunts, and then finally the stores he usually can't stand. At the end of his rush, holding more bags of every size, shape, and color than he can comfortably carry, Wendell hails his last cab for the night. At 6C, he pays the driver, but doesn't tip, and then bursts through the apartment, ignoring his parents' cries and questions at the sight of his purchases. He goes into his room, locks the door, and sinks into his work.

• • •

Wendell wakes the next morning not in his bed, but on the floor, his head spinning. It is ten o' clock. Hours of school have gone by already, without him. August rode the 90 and smoked outside Capital One alone today, he realizes. Mrs. Weston was not one to let her son miss school. She would normally drag him out of bed and onto the bus every morning if he had overslept. But something had soured, he knows.

Memories of the night before come flooding back to Wendell—his parents outside his bedroom door, screaming at him to come out, asking him where he got the money for all those things, insisting he has some serious problem. Wendell finally finds the strength to lift his pounding head and looks at the mess around him. His controller lies nearby, and the television screen is an image of blood spatter with the words GAME OVER flashing.

As he sits up, an empty Red Bull can crunches beneath him, and he realizes it's not the only one. Shrink wrap from new video games and DVDs lie twitching in the breeze created by the ceiling fan, some catching on and fluttering across the floor, which is littered with half-eaten packages of candy and potato chips. Wendell sees the cases on the floor but can't remember a single title he bought. He is dressed, for some reason, in silk pajamas that he didn't own before last night. More than twenty other bags sit in the corner, most of their contents spilled out onto the floor. Wendell couldn't simply just buy all these things, he had to *have* them all, too—he had to have everything, and he had to eat, play, wear, watch, and just have it all at once. There'd been no time for pacing himself, or saving some for later, or saying no to anything last night. But now it's morning, and Wendell would be glad to see it all disappear.

• • •

After he forces breakfast down and feels a little more competent, he sits on the floor in the aftermath of his spree and places all his new things back in the bags. He tries to figure everything out from the receipts, but there's just so much. There are things he can't even make sense of—a beaded curtain, two damn scented candles, carved wooden bookends, a porcelain doll. Wendell is nervous as he heads into one of the stores he visited the night before to try to return the six pairs of sunglasses he bought there. Wendell has never returned anything in his life.

Hours later, after being told countless times that opened boxes, clothes without tags, CDs without shrink wrap could not be returned nor exchanged, Wendell realizes that he really messed up. His parents will be home soon and they'll have seen their transaction record. They'll know how he got the money, and they'll go to the Pepsi Texan financial office and ask that their son's card be suspended. Without freedom to buy, what would Wendell be?

A child, he thinks. Even if there were only a few months before he turned eighteen, he would never be able to stand having his parents know what he was buying and when, and having to get their permission to spend *his* money.

• • •

The next morning when August takes her seat next to Wendell on the 90, she doesn't ask where he was yesterday. She doesn't care. She has news.

"I got in," she says, beaming.

Wendell frowns. Should he know what she means?

"To The University of America. In the Mall of America," she says, rolling her eyes. "You know, the original. The first mall to ever have its own residences and provide them with the benefits we all enjoy today."

"In Minnesota?" Wendell asks, perplexed.

"Yeah," August replies, "No difference, except it won't be blazing hot when we wait for the bus in the summer. What the hell am I saying? We'll never need to wait for a bus again! We'll be in the center of everything."

"We?"

"Well, yeah," August says, "What are you gonna do, stay at the Megamall forever? There are at least twenty video game stores in the Mall of America. There's a sheet metal workers union in the mall that trains you for free if you want to learn that. There's a two-year college if you want that. I'll live in the dorms and you can get a cheap place in one of the basement complexes. I'll never have any problem seeing you."

They'd talked about staying together after graduation before, but he never thought it would mean leaving Texas. Wendell doesn't know what sheet metal is. He just nods.

• • •

Wendell has skipped a few services at Holy Family to avoid conflict with August and his parents, but he asks Trenton one Friday if he can join his family again. It is the same as last time, a chaotic but hearty breakfast at the Walmart apartment followed by the service. Afterward, Trenton accepts an invitation to hang out with Wendell at the Megamall.

"Damn," says Trenton, eyeing Wendell's gaming equipment. "You must get some crazy tips if you can afford all this."

"I don't work," Wendell says matter-of-factly. "My funds paid for all this."

Trenton raises his eyebrows. "You use teen funds?"

Wendell feels embarrassed. Maybe they don't have teen funds at Walmart or something. Maybe he's just made Trenton incredibly jealous. Not knowing what else to say, he just asks.

"Of course we've got them at Walmart," Trenton laughs, "Everyone in Texas can get their loans if they want them. But me, I don't. I just don't want to be part of that system."

Wendell's eyes narrow at this. "What do you mean?"

"I mean they're kind of taking advantage, making this money accessible to kids who don't think too much about the future. They make a killing off the interest. I want to go to UT, maybe grad school, and I can't afford to have all that debt."

"So you've never had a teen fund?"

"Nope. If I ever need something my family can't help me buy, I help out at the loading dock at Walmart for a few hours. They let students do that for extra cash."

Wendell feels like he's been insulted, though he doesn't know why. Things are a little awkward after that, and Trenton says he'd better get home. When he leaves, Wendell doesn't feel like doing much.

Teen funds are my right, he thinks, feeling his face redden with inexplicable anger. Everyone has the right to a little bit of spending money, even if sixty dollars doesn't buy a damn thing. Teen funds teach responsibility. They keep the mall up and running. Everyone benefits. Why would the mall do anything to hurt us?

• • •

After a while, Wendell begins mentally preparing to say goodbye to his girl. There's nothing for him at the Mall of America. There's more there than at many major centers, including his home, but nothing that he can't find by taking a bus. It's all the same crap. Some places lacked a multiplex but had a synagogue; others housed third-rate colleges but at least had American Apparel. But it was all the same. For years Wendell had counted the minutes in school until he could get home and proceed with his life in the mall or on a screen. If he wasn't doing that, he was shopping or with August. At the end of the day, what did he have? A sense of accomplishment maybe, if he'd been playing *Halo* with fervor, or leveling up to godliness in *WoW*. But nothing to speak of in the world, nothing to speak of at home or at school. Surrounded by his games and magazines and music and clothes, Wendell begins to feel that he has nothing.

Following August will only hold him back. From what, he wonders. He doesn't have a goal in the real world. He can't remember ever having one beyond saving up money for something. It feels really lame, but sitting in homeroom that morning, he sets a goal and swears to keep it. When he looks up, he sees the crucifix, same one that's there every day. Even though he's not really into all that, he thinks someone else has heard him, and figures he'd better make good on his promise.

• • •

Graduation day finally comes at St. James High. August's name is announced with the word "honors" attached. Wendell, who has just barely passed, feels small as he tosses his cap. He doesn't understand the cheers and the tears coming from his classmates and their parents. Trenton's family is rejoicing because he was accepted to UT—he'll be taking the bus from their new stand-alone house to the Supercenter every day. Wendell wonders how many of the other graduates' lives will actually change beyond starting to pay back their teen funds in a few years.

• • •

Even though it is the end of July and Wendell hasn't looked for a job, an apartment, or a plane ticket to Minnesota, August is convinced he is coming. Wendell knows that she is scared, even though she'll never show it. He's been spending more time alone, plus Sundays with Trenton's family, and she's been spending more time at Strawberry. Finally, August goes to 6C in the Pepsi Texan Megamall, to tell Wendell that he'd better get it together.

The inside of his room looks different. The PlayStation and games are all gone. Wendell sold them for less than half of what he paid originally. He hasn't taken a teen fund out in weeks. He feels poor.

"You know I can't come to Minnesota," he tells August gently. "I'm sorry."

She throws a fit, just like all the fits before. What exactly does he plan to do, she asks. What's so important in Texas that he's staying around for? Wendell tells her what he's done over the past few weeks to prepare for his new life. His graduation gifts and the last teen funds he'd ever taken are in his account and are just enough for a deposit and a month's rent at the central Houston Walmart. Why the Walmart, August wants to know. What kind of trash is he, she asks, to think that it's acceptable to live there. It's the same attitude his mother has, as well as just about everyone from snobby-ass St. James.

The truth is, he tells her, that a Walmart apartment is the closest place he can live to Holy Family and still afford. He won't make much money, he knows, and in a few years the Megamall will be sending the monthly bills for his teen funds—the ghosts of all the games and clothes and unnecessary food court meals he ever bought will come haunting.

"You're staying in Houston because you want to go to the stupid little church?" she bellows. "Wendell, you *don't even believe* in God."

He understands why August would say this about him. It's pretty much true anyway.

"Maybe not," he says, "but I believe in something else."

• • •

August leaves in a huff, and Wendell wishes her well. He's not so sad, but thinking of bigger things, like what his life would be like if he lived in a house and drove to work and church and stores. One day he might escape the malls altogether. One day he'll have to. There's no going back now anyway. He is bound by the goal he set and the promise he made to himself that day—to find what lies beyond the sliding doors.

∼

Gabriella Stalker is a cubicle-dwelling worker drone by day and a writer by night. She studied linguistics and Spanish language and literature at the University of Pittsburgh and the Pontifícia Universidad Católica de Valparaíso in Chile. Gabriella enjoys being outdoors and attending local metal shows in her spare time, as well as doing karaoke to keep her persistent urge to burst into song at bay. She lives in Pittsburgh, Pennsylvania.

The Unfathomable Sisterhood of Ick

Charlie Jane Anders

After Roger broke up with Mary, she only had two places to go:

1) Her home, which was a single room with a bed, a bath, and a kitchen that were three identical rectangles which came out of the wall and occupied the exact same space.

2) Her job at the smart-cookie makery, where she stood in an asymmetrical trench surrounded by screens, monitoring peptide levels. Colored lights swirled around her head, almost too fast to see.

She couldn't even bring herself to cry. She walked around under a gray sky, feeling dead inside—as if she'd missed a couple of days of smart cookies and her brain was consequently shutting down.

Loss was not an ache or a pang, or anything dainty. It was more like a bucket of shit that kept falling and falling on her head: itchy, ugly, humiliating.

Mary's friends kept calling, wanting to hang out, but she couldn't face anyone. She wanted to avoid the places she and Roger had gone together—which was every place she liked to go. She couldn't face eating a fancy meal because right now food tasted like dirt, and she could just barely manage to look presentable for work. Her friends all said that she had to get right back on the horse. Mary had never seen a horse, but she imagined that being ejected from one would lead to bruises and maybe some sprains or fractures, plus an angry horse that had already won the first round. That's assuming the horse didn't just trample you once it had already thrown you underfoot.

At last, two days after the breakup, she gave in and went out for drinks with her best friend, Stacia. Some part of her still remembered the three A.M. trash talk sessions about guys that she and Stacia had, back in college when the Sisterhood was new, and imagined it could be that way again.

"Don't say anything about horses," Mary growled preemptively at Stacia. "Or getting back on them, or anything else along those lines."

"You know me." Stacia shrugged, raised her palms so her bracelets jangled, and laughed. "I always change horses in the middle of a stream."

This was so true. The whole time Mary had known Stacia, almost ten years since college, Stacia hadn't had a relationship that lasted more than five or six weeks. The six years Mary had been with Roger was like a million years in Stacia-relationship-time. Just hearing Stacia's laughter made Mary's shoulders unhunch fractionally.

They were at the Swan Dive, the place with the white wing-shaped chandeliers and cherry-wood couches, and Stacia kept glancing around to see if there were any cute guys worth throwing some negs at. Mary would never stop envying Stacia's ability to turn flirtation into a way of life.

Just when Mary was starting to feel slightly less tragic, Stacia leaned in and said, "You're totally right to be scared to go back to the dating pool," using her low, confiding tone. "Dating is a nightmare."

At first, Mary thought Stacia was talking about whether Mary could still attract a man, with her cornsilk hair and fading kina-minx features, concerning which Stacia was always volunteering makeover advice. But then she realized Stacia was talking about something more fundamental.

"Dating is this relic of a primitive age, before kina-chat and smart cookies," Stacia said. "You have to spend all this time getting to know someone: what they like to eat for breakfast, and all their hangups. And then once you've gathered all of this useless information, you probably realize that you're not compatible after all. And then you have to start the whole process over from scratch."

Back when Mary and Stacia first became friends, they'd both worn the black turtlenecks and hiking boots that were still Mary's daily uniform, but after college Stacia had reinvented herself as an über-femme. Now she had special eyelashes that fluttered all on their own, hypnotically, and her black hair cascaded in waves around her creamy shoulders. Stacia's ankles crossed sinuously on the bottom rung of the barstool, with her red ruffled skirt lapping against them. Two separate guys were trying to send her drinks, and she was rolling her eyes at them.

Stacia went on about what a chore it was, getting to know a new person. "You have to wait for him to open up, like the world's slowest Venus flytrap. And meanwhile, you keep unspooling yourself for him, little by little, just enough to keep him interested, but not so much that you're oversharing or overloading his buffers. Everybody has sex on the first date these days, but you have to wait until the fourth or fifth date before talking about your messed-up childhood."

Around this point, Mary started to cry, for the first time since Roger kicked her to the curb. She would be alone forever, in her tiny apartment with the three rectangles. She couldn't do this whole dance all over again, the way Stacia was describing it. She usually loved Stacia's cynicism, but right now she was just too raw.

"And that's why I think you should get Roger to do it," Stacia was saying. "Everybody's going to be doing it soon, so you'll just be an early adopter. And honestly, since he's the one who dumped you, he *owes* you."

"Do what?" Mary was so startled, she stopped sniffling.

"Oh," Stacia said. "You know. The memory thing."

"Pretend I don't know," Mary said. She sort of knew. She'd read about this on the kina-cast a while back. It was the thing where your ex gave you a memory wisp, right? A download?

"The important thing is, he doesn't give you *all* of his memories of the relationship," said Stacia. "Just the happy ones. The ones from the first two or three months, or maybe four or five if the relationship went on longer. Especially, no memories from the tail end, leading up to the breakup. Not even stuff that seemed happy at the time, because in retrospect it will all seem terrible."

"Yeah," Mary said. "But I already remember our relationship, more than I honestly want to. Why would I want his memories of that stuff? I might as well just jam hot needles into my tear ducts."

"It's not for you, dumbass." Stacia slapped Mary's arm. "It's for whoever you date next. Your new boyfriend can get implanted with all of Roger's memories of getting to know you. That way, the new guy can know how you like to be touched in bed, and what your favorite flavor of mycosnuff is. He'll already know all the awkward details, but it won't feel like too much too soon, because he'll have memories of learning it all over a period of months. And the best part is, if he gets Roger's memories and decides he doesn't want to date you after all, he can get them removed, as long as it's within a few days. After seventy-two hours, Roger's memories become integrated with his own, and then they're permanent."

"You've thought a lot about this," Mary said.

"Well, yeah," Stacia said. "In the unlikely event I date someone for more than a few months ever again, I want him to do a memory download for sure. Think about it: You wouldn't get a new kina without transferring over your address book and settings and stuff, right?"

"I doubt Roger would want to do that," Mary said. "I don't even know if he has any good memories of our time together."

"That's why he has to do it now," Stacia said. "He still has the happy memories, buried somewhere. But every day that passes since the breakup, the happy stuff gets buried deeper and deeper as he convinces himself you never had anything. A week from now, those good times you shared will be beyond the ability of science to retrieve."

Mary still wasn't sure, but Stacia gave her the hard sell: "He owes you. All of that time you invested in him, it's like you put equity into a home. And now that he's evicted you, he owes it to you to cash out your equity, so you can put it into a new place. That's all this is." When she put it like that, the whole thing made sense.

• • •

Seeing Roger's face for the first time since the breakup caused Mary's brain to make a correction in real-time—fast, but not fast enough to be painless. The instinctive "partner-bond" signal fired in her brain, causing waves of pleasure and comfort. Like a hot bath on a frozen day. And then she had to pull back, as if the hot bath had turned out to be boiling instead. She had to look at Roger's perfect hazel eyes and breathe in his pine-forest scent... and remember that this was over.

Mary's whole life was neurochemistry, so she knew that a lot of this sensation was just the chemical battery in her brain, sparking erroneously based on out-of-date information.

They met for lunch, the day after Mary's conversation with Stacia. Mary had the day off from the makery, and Roger could take a long lunch break at his strategic consulting firm, where he was helping to re-position the troubled rejuvenation sector. (Roger had heard every joke about the rejuvenation industry getting old, a dozen times.) They were eating at the same restaurant where Roger had told her that he needed space: a hand-pulled noodle place where a man stood in the front window pulling noodles, 24/7. Mary had loved this restaurant, which had red lanterns, grease-stained tablecloths, and chewy noodles, but now it was tainted forever.

"I don't know, Mare," Roger said, after she explained what she wanted him to do. "I mean, those are private memories. You're talking about a piece of my identity.

"Even if they could pull out just the memories pertaining to our courtship—which I don't believe for a second they can, that's awfully granular—those are still my memories, they're personal."

"Oh, come on, Roger," Mary said. "Don't be a jerk. I'm not asking for your life story. Just a few months of specific memories, which won't have any of the context. So they won't mean the same thing to anyone else that they mean to you. If they *do* mean anything to you."

She was starting to sob again—weakling—so she reached for the longest and slimiest noodle in her bowl and slurped it loudly to mask the sound. She gestured for the waiter and demanded a scallion pancake.

"You can't say that." Roger's eyes widened in a way that would have melted her brain when they were together. "You can't say they mean nothing to me. They mean a lot to me. Those memories are precious to me. Of course they are."

"I guess not," Mary said. She had avoided recriminations when he had jilted her. She had taken the bad news with composure, but now this felt like a second jilting. "Obviously, none of this ever meant anything to you. None of it ever mattered at all. Right?"

Mary never knew what Roger had seen in her in the first place, any more than she understood why he had broken up with her, after six years that had seemed happy to her. The whole thing was a mystery, beginning and end.

"Did Stacia put you up to this?" Roger said. "I swear, you two were always like this hive mind. The whole time we were together, I felt like I was dating both of you."

"Leave Stacia out of this," Mary said. "This is about you and me." She stabbed her onion pancake with a single chopstick, skewering and gesturing. "Those memories that you don't want to share, I bet they're just memories of you figuring out how to seduce me, so you could use me and get your fill and then throw me aside. You probably treated it just like one of your strategy briefs."

Roger didn't know how to respond to that. For a moment, he just held up both hands, like he was about to gesture. Then he let them drop again.

"You want to take my memories," Roger said. "And give them to some other man. My personal memories, of you. And you don't see how that's messed up?"

"I see that you threw me aside, and now you don't want to give me the one thing that will let me have closure," Mary said. "You're probably already dating someone else. Aren't you?" Roger's squirming was confirmation enough.

Guilt won. Roger went to the clinic, which was a glorified kiosk just outside the mall that smelled of ozone, and Mary watched the whole time as the neural sensors danced around the three-dimensional map of Roger's mind, plucking out the specific bits of his past that related to the two of them getting together. She tried to imagine what the machine was getting. Their first meeting at the Bankrupt Daisies concert, their first proper date when it rained and Roger held his jacket over her head, that time they bonded over both hating Jane Austen, the whole weekend they spent naked, his dad's funeral. It was all becoming a blur to her, but those months would be preserved. Pristine.

At the end, Roger looked exhausted, under the weather. "I have to go lie down," he said. He handed her a sparkly memory wisp, a silver feather floating in a plexiglas cube. She thanked him several times and even kissed his cheek. The cube fit in her purse, next to her mycosnuff and breathspray. She imagined implanting those memories into hundreds of men, thousands even, so they could all remember falling in love with her. And then that thought scared her with its brazenness, so she banished it. She thanked Roger again, and he said it was nothing.

• • •

"Oh my god, can I see it?" Stacia stretched out an elegantly manicured hand. Mary only left her hanging for a moment before plunking down the cube containing her happy early months with Roger. "Wow," Stacia said, "it's so light. It weighs almost nothing. It's Moore's Law in action, right?"

"I guess so," Mary said. "Moore's Law, yeah. Everything gets smaller and smaller, forever."

Stacia was staring at the little wisp inside the cube, watching it undulate. Mary realized this had been going on for an uncomfortably long time. "It's so pretty," Stacia said.

"Yeah," Mary said. She reached out to take the cube back, but Stacia moved out of reach with a dancer's grace, so that she didn't quite seem to be dodging.

They were at the mall, which was a program that lasted approximately forty-five minutes depending on your attention span. With the right lenses inserted and enough smart cookie in your system, you could look at a dozen storefronts per minute, scrolling around you in the spherical chamber with a walkway at its center. Over Mary and Stacia's heads, palm trees slowly morphed into "futuristic" metal cranes (as in the bird). This mall had gone way downhill.

Stacia and Mary had originally met when they'd escaped from the same dismal party together in sophomore year of college, where they were the only two smeary-eyed malcontents dressed in black, in a galaxy of pink hoop-skirts. They'd formed a club: The Unfathomable Sisterhood of Ick. Mary was an aspiring bio-artist, culturing abstract oozes, while Stacia was a shy pudgy computer-grower, but they shared a deep conviction that ninety-nine percent of everything people cared about was false and revolting, like the fake barf on sale at the magic store in this mall.

They almost went into a hat store that was selling fancy retro bonnets, but then they decided they were bored with hats. "Let's skip to the food court," Stacia said. "Wafflecrepes. I'm buying."

"Can I have my cube back?" Mary didn't want to sound pushy or needy, or as though she didn't trust Stacia. The memory wisp flickered as it caught the sparkly light from the kitchenwares store. One of the clerks in the store waved, trying to get their attention with a fancy spatula, then was gone.

"I was wondering if I could maybe borrow it," Stacia said. "Just for a day or two." She bit her lip and pulled her shoulders inwards, towards her cleavage in her frilly chemise. "Because I would kind of like to... to copy it."

"You what?" Mary thought she must have misheard over the mall's schmaltzy orchestral music. "You want to make a backup or something?"

"No, no, I want it in my head." Stacia laughed—but it was a nervous, defensive laugh, for a change. "I want to have Roger's memories in my head. I want those experiences, I want to remember them, like they happened to me. I want to feel what it was like for him. Firsthand."

Mary found herself backing away from Stacia a bit, until she was almost inside the make-your-own-stuffed-animal store. The mall stopped changing, in response to her proximity to an entrance.

"I never knew… " Mary's mind raced, almost as if she'd had a smart-cookie overdose. She felt her heart clapping. "I never knew you felt that way about me. All this time, we've been best friends. Nearly ten years now, I never knew you were… you were in *love* with me." She made herself stop shrinking away, and come back into Stacia's orbit.

"Oh Jesus, no." Stacia laughed, her normal laugh this time. "Is that what you think? My god, no. I'm as straight as they come, you know that. No lesbian inclinations at all. Jesus. I'm sorry to let you down, I love you as a *friend*. No, I just want to have the memories. I want to know what it's like."

"What *what's* like?"

"All of it. Falling in love. The start of a long-term relationship. Being a man and falling for a beautiful woman. All of it. I just want to have those experiences in the mix, jumbled up with my real memories. I think it could solve a lot of stuff for me."

"But… but why Roger and me? Why can't you just find some random stranger and get *his* memories? I bet you could buy something on the gray market. Or just ask around. Like you said, everybody's starting to do this."

"It wouldn't be the same. And just think—this will bring us closer together. Any questions you have about Roger, or about the mistakes you make at the start of a relationship, you can just ask me. It'll be great!"

"Uh… " Mary had moved far enough away from the door to the teddy-bear store that it had vanished, and now other stores were whipping behind her. She had a dreadful headache, the kind that started at the top of her scalp and traveled all the way down her spine to her sacrum. She could barely see.

"It doesn't take long. I'll give it right back to you in a day or so, I promise."

"No. Please, no," Mary said. "Please, just give it back to me now." She was starting to have a nagging suspicion that this had been Stacia's plan all along, and the real reason Stacia had been so insistent that she ask Roger for this. "Just, please, give it back."

Stacia nodded. "Okay, that's how it has to be." She raised up her hand with the cube in it, as if to hand it back to Mary—and then she turned and ran inside a kina *kuniya* store, disappearing into its maze of shelves and running out the back exit before Mary could even get her bearings.

Mary was left hyperventilating in a null zone between the mall and the real world, where everything was a whirl of broken advertising images, too fast to make out even with smart cookies.

• • •

Mary kept trying to contact Stacia, who had gone off the grid. This was the longest Mary and Stacia had gone without speaking to each other in the past decade. Mary was so freaked out she could barely breathe, imagining Stacia absorbing all the memories of her private moments with Roger, the good times. Making them into a big joke in her head, or worse yet getting ironically sentimental over them. Mary couldn't sleep or concentrate on anything; she almost let a bad batch through at work.

Stacia waited a few days before bringing the memory wisp back to Mary—the exact amount of time it would take for the memories to become permanent in Stacia's brain. Then at last, she arranged a meet in a hotel lobby downtown.

Right away, there was something different about Stacia's body language, a little more of Roger's old calculated slouch and less of the thrown-back shoulders. Like she'd absorbed a bit of Roger's personality along with a dose of his memories. Probably that would get submerged over time, but it still startled her when Stacia did that thing with her lower lip that Roger used to do.

"Hey, looking good, babe," Stacia said. "You're wearing that belt that I got—I mean, that he got you." Mary had forgotten that Roger bought her this fake alligator belt.

"I can't believe you went through with this," Mary said.

Stacia handed the cube back to Mary. "I'm sorry, babe," she said. "I know, it was an invasion of privacy, and a terrible thing to do. You know ever since we got out of college I've been dating, right? And I've made a point of never getting with anyone for more than a few weeks at a stretch. I'm like the world expert at making things happen, but then the juice goes out of them and I get bored and move on. I was realizing that maybe if I knew what was going through a guy's head when he's falling for someone, maybe I wouldn't have to... I don't know. But I was hanging around Roger the whole time you were with him, he's the only guy I was always spending time with these past several years, and I realized I never understood him at all."

Mary had snatched the cube back and stuck it in the deepest crevice of her purse, with two zippers protecting it. Barn door, horse. "I thought that after Roger, the breakup, that nobody could ever hurt me that much again," she mumbled. "I guess I was pretty dumb. Right? This is way worse. I'm going to have your knife in my back forever." They were standing in this hotel lobby, surrounded by travelers and people having bar meetings, at noon, having what ought to be a nighttime bar conversation.

"Don't be like that, babe," Stacia said. Roger used to call Mary "babe" when they were first dating. He'd stopped a few years in, and that hadn't seemed significant at the time. "It's just that memory is one of the main building blocks of identity. And you know, right around the time that you started seeing Roger was when I started to become the person I am now. I wasn't seeing as much of you at the time, and I felt totally alone. And maybe I don't like the person I turned into. I just want to remember that time in my life a different way."

"Now you're blaming me for your choices?" Mary said. "Like it's my fault that you started having intimacy issues, because I was in a long-term relationship and you weren't? Are you even listening to yourself?"

"It's not about blame, babe," Stacia said. "I'm just trying to get a different perspective on that time in our lives."

"Stop calling me babe!" Mary didn't even care anymore that she was yelling in a public place. A group of people with lanyards and fancy shirts glanced in their direction. "Just, please, stop."

"Okay, okay. I'm sorry." Stacia didn't know how to hold herself, what sort of body language to adopt with Mary. "I keep thinking about that nightmare you had two months after you starting dating Roger, the one about an ocean of pure acid washing over everything and melting all the people and buildings. Once you would have told me about that dream, but you told Roger, and he held you so tight he thought he could almost smush you. It was right after his father had just died. He felt so full of grief and protectiveness, he didn't know what to do with himself. He thought his heart would just give out, pop or something." Stacia leaned on the back of an armchair. "Then I called, wanting to see if you were up for brunch, and he suddenly just felt annoyed and jealous."

Then Stacia walked away, doing some weird mixture of her sashay and Roger's stride.

• • •

So now Mary had to avoid all the places she'd ever gone with Roger, plus every place she used to hang out with Stacia. All her other friends kept asking her if she was okay, because they heard there was weirdness with Stacia, but Mary did not feel like explaining. And Stacia kept sending message after message, until Mary blocked her. She started going to the motherboard garden after work, because she'd never gone there before, and watching the tiny motherboards making abstract shapes in the carbon nanofiber beds calmed her.

One day, Mary was sitting in the motherboard garden, trying to stop replaying in her head the story of Roger, Stacia, and their patsy. And she noticed a man over at the other end of the square—at first, he just seemed overcome with emotion at the zen-like simplicity of the place. But then she'd noticed a tremor on one corner of his mouth and some vessels bursting in the opposite eye, and Mary recognized the signs of someone who'd done the wrong combination of neurotransmitters, from when she used to experiment at school. She rushed to his side just as he started to keel over, and kina-ed an ambulance. She rode to the hospital with him, telling the paramedics what counter-toxins he probably needed.

Mary figured she would never hear from that guy, whose name was Dave, again. Most guys would rather forget that they showed weakness in front of a total stranger, right? But Dave got in touch a few days later and asked her out for jerk chicken and plantains.

Dave wasn't the opposite of Roger or anything—Mary had to resign herself to accepting that she had a Type—but he was shorter and burlier than Roger, with darker skin and a thicker mustache. He worked as an estate planner, in a fancy office in the donut hole downtown, and he was maybe a touch more reserved than Roger. He never made her laugh the way Roger had, but he made her smile.

Mary waited until their fourth date, when she and Dave were already spending a whole weekend together, before telling him about Roger's memory wisp. "It's kind of dumb," she said. "But I figured I ought to mention it, in case you wanted to. I mean, it would be one way to streamline things. You know. You could figure out sooner if you actually want to be in a relationship with me."

"I'm already in a relationship with you," Dave said, and she shivered all over, even though they were in a hot tub (naked) together. His ample chest hair glimmered.

"In that case, I'm in a relationship with you as well," Mary said, leaning upwards and kissing him, while their feet nuzzled.

"You know, I think getting to know each other is the fun part," Dave said, stretching out in the tub. "The newness, the thrill of discovery. Peeling back the layers. Getting to know someone can be delightful. If it's the right person."

Mary nodded. She hadn't even thought of any of this as something that could be fun. She had been thinking of starting a relationship as like defusing a bomb, or cooking a complicated recipe. "Yeah. Let's hear it for the slow way." She raised an invisible glass out of the water, and chinked it with an imaginary glass in Dave's hand.

"The slow way." Dave toasted back.

Around the time Mary shoved the memory cube into the trash compactor of the "kitchen" rectangle of her studio apartment, listening to the satisfying crunch of data being fatally compromised, she realized it had been almost two months since she'd spoken to Stacia. Time was, they used to talk almost every day. She had a moment of slow bereavement, like the soil erosion after an old-growth tree is uprooted. She had to bite back the urge to kina Stacia and try to salvage something.

Of course, as soon as Mary destroyed the memory wisp, she regretted it, because the day might come, years from now, when she would desperately need concrete evidence that she had once been loved. That someone could fall in love with her. She had Dave now, and she was currently experiencing the sensation of falling in requited love—but she'd already seen how that turned out. Right?

• • •

Mary went dancing with Dave at that new club that was five dayglo rooms with imperfect soundproofing, so the beats bled from dance floor to dance floor, and she was whooping at the unpredictability of the rhythms and the proximity of Dave's wide torso, when she looked over Dave's shoulder and saw Stacia swaying towards them with a desperate grin on her face.

"Let's get out of here," she breathed in Dave's ear. She hadn't told Dave about what Stacia had done, because Mary felt like it was her fault in some way.

A couple days later, Mary and Dave were on the beach, half-dozing in the sun in new swimsuits, and Dave had his hand on her thigh without any fixed intent. Mary saw a shadow only a second before she heard a voice say, "Have you tried two fingertips right behind her kneecap? Just kind of describing a slow, slow circle? It drives her crazy, man."

Mary stiffened, squinting up at Stacia's face. She knew at once that the "two fingers behind the kneecap" thing would never turn her on ever again. "Wow," she said. "You're really creeping me out."

"Who is this?" Dave was sitting up and squinting.

"Uh, never mind." Mary gathered up all their stuff into a bundle, as though fleeing a tidal wave. She seized Dave's shoulder with both hands and steered him out of there, while Stacia tried to explain that she was just trying to help, and Mary would thank her later, and why was everybody being so judgey? Mary could still hear Stacia behind them all the way back to the transit station, until they finally got lost in the crowd.

When they were alone on the tube, with a safe cushion of strangers all around them, Dave leaned in, one eyebrow raised with gentle humor but a concerned look in his eyes. "You want to tell me what that was about?" he said.

Mary could hardly bring herself to say out loud what Stacia had done, because it made her skin crawl. Dave just shrugged, though, and said that all of the estate planning conferences were having seminars about the emerging problem of parceling out the newly deceased person's neural map. And the security sector was just starting to freak out about the problem of memory embezzlement. This was the crime of the future. When you put it like that, Mary almost felt trendy.

The next day, Dave and Mary met for sushi and Stacia was there, leaning across the bar so her face was uncomfortably close to theirs and saying things to Dave like, "Promise me you'll take good care of this one, she's like a tiger raised in captivity. Fierce, but trusting. Roger used to watch her in the bath. He used to keep waving goodbye long after she couldn't see him anymore, whenever they parted ways. Roger had a crazy tidal wave of love for her, you have no idea."

A few days later, Stacia was outside Mary's apartment building when Dave and Mary came outside, tears scattering across her face. "I just want to know where we went wrong," Stacia said, and Mary wasn't sure which "we" Stacia meant. "What happened to us? I thought nobody could ever come between us. What happened? What happened to us? What happened to us? What happened to us?" Mary and Dave had to get in a random taxi just to get away from her.

Mary could see what was going to happen next. Stacia was going to stalk them one too many times, she was going to act just a little too creepy around Dave, and she was going to know too many embarrassing things about Mary. And then Dave would bail, and Mary would topple back into the dating pool. Wings on fire.

Maybe a week passed, and Mary started to relax. And then, when she was walking along the waterfront with Dave, Stacia came running up behind them, arms waving and eyes streaming with tears, wearing a torn skirt and mismatched high-heel shoes.

"I've never felt anything like what *he* felt, when he got together with you," Stacia said, panting. "I'll never feel anything like that for myself, firsthand. It was so intense. I can't even imagine feeling that much love for anyone." To Dave, she said: "You can't compete. You might as well go home. She's already had the great love of her life! Every time I close my eyes, I keep replaying it in my mind. It's so intense. I wasn't prepared. He loved her so much, he went half-crazy with love. You'll never measure up. You'll always be her second love. A consolation prize. Sorry to be the one to tell you!"

Then she ran away, stumbling over her own shoes.

That night, Mary spent hours staring into the depths of her kitchen trash compactor, where the last shreds of the memory wisp still clung. After a while, the crushing mechanism started to look like faces, or little blades of black grass, because your mind has a nearly limitless ability to see familiar outlines in anything. Mary didn't cry, but she did heave, more and more violently, half-way between crying and empty-vomiting, until she had to send her kitchen away and summon her bed into the same spot on the wall.

Mary hugged herself in bed all night, staring at the peeling wall opposite. In the morning, she had a nine-tequila hangover, but she also had a moment of clarity: It wasn't enough to avoid the places she and Roger had gone together. She had to grow up and move on with her life.

She took an extra smart cookie and spent an hour at dawn, sending out résumés for jobs that would actually use her bio-artist skills. And she started surfing apartment listings on her kina, because maybe she could actually live someplace where a sink and bed could coexist. She read up on extreme sports, which had gotten a lot more extreme since smart-cookies gave people super-human reflexes and concentration. She kept looking for jobs and apartments for hours, until she was almost late for work.

By the time Mary met Dave for dinner (a different hand-pulled noodle place than the one where she got dumped), she was full of news. "I already have a job interview in ten days," she said, sploshing dumplings. "And I'm thinking of trying BASE jumping. I know, this isn't really like me, but change is healthy. Right?"

"I haven't known you for long enough to know what's like you," Dave said. "I keep being surprised." He looked around, as if afraid that Stacia would turn up at the next table, with more advice about Mary's erogenous zones or more declarations that Dave couldn't compete with Mary's great lost love. "I've never met anyone like you before."

"Um, yeah," Mary said. "This has been a weird time in my life. I mean… "

"You know," Dave said in his matter-of-fact drawl, "I hate drama. I had a lot of drama when I was in my early twenties, and I just can't stand it."

Okay. So this was it. She was giving off too much crazy. She looked like a weirdness magnet, or at least someone with horrible judgment in choosing her friends. So, she was about to be dumped. She deserved to be dumped, truth be told. She had mismanaged her shit.

"This is really hard for me to say," Dave said.

"I'm listening." Mary braced herself, hands on elbows. Tried to keep a game face on. She was never going to eat hand-pulled noodles again.

"I know this is really out of line," Dave said.

Mary felt her insides lose all stability, like she was falling off a skyscraper. But then she also felt a cushion of okayness, deep inside. Like she'd already been through the worst that could possibly happen, and she was still here. Even if Dave broke her heart again, he wouldn't break *her*.

"Whatever you have to say," she told Dave, amazed at her own calm, "just say it."

"I think your friend is in trouble," Dave said. "I know it's none of my business, and you can tell me to butt out. But I think she's having a psychotic break or something. Yesterday, at the waterfront, she seemed like someone who was coming apart. All that crazy stuff she said about the memories being so intense."

Mary almost fell out of her chair at the realization that she wasn't being dumped. Then she took on board what Dave was saying.

"God, you're right," she said. "She's suffering from a neural overload. She can't integrate those memories, because they're so different and conflicting. You know, Roger kind of hated Stacia, especially early on. Plus she remembers the intensity of Roger falling for me, but not everything that came after, when we settled into just a normal relationship. Wow. I should have seen this sooner, but I was too busy thinking about how she hurt me."

"Again, this is none of my business." Dave raised his hands. "And I know this is her own fault. But… "

"We ought to help her." Mary grabbed her purse. "You're right."

"Thanks for not being mad at me for speaking out of school." Dave seemed relieved. She had to pause to kiss him on the lips and embrace him with all her strength, right next to the man pulling noodles with his bare hands.

• • •

One time, when Mary and Stacia were still in college, Mary had cooked up a bad batch of prions. They were supposed to induce an hour of amyloid brain-melt, then dissolve harmlessly. But instead, they'd turned Mary and Stacia into basket cases, and when Mary found herself losing the use of language and forgetting how to walk, she'd lunged for the antidote she'd prepared just in case. Mary was fine an hour later, but Stacia had kept shaking and making preverbal chatter, like a giant baby. Mary had stayed with Stacia all night, holding onto her and saying, "It's okay, I'm here," until the prions had finally flushed out and Stacia had regained her mind.

This was worse. Stacia was huddled in one corner of her light-box apartment, wearing a bright flamenco-dancer dress that had been beautiful but was now stained and torn. "I can't," Stacia said over and over. "I can't, I can't." Her self-actuating eyelashes were flicking tears in all directions.

"I know," Mary said. "We're going to help you. There are ways to make some memories seem less vivid. I've read about it. We can fix this."

"I don't ever want that," Stacia said. "Roger's love for you is the most wonderful thing I've ever felt. He was right about me, I was jealous. You were perfect together. I was just a stupid useless third wheel. You were amazing."

"You only think Roger's love for me was so great, because it's like a lump your mind can't digest. It really wasn't that great, trust me." Mary felt a weird relief, saying this aloud. "You can't reconcile Roger's version of events with yours, and it's like you've given yourself a split personality or something. We're going to help."

They got Stacia cleaned up, and strapped her to her bed, which was an actual piece of furniture instead of a module. Mary and Dave debated about taking Stacia to the hospital, but Stacia begged them not to, and Mary had a feeling she could help Stacia better than the E.R. staff could in any case.

"So first you have to go cold turkey on the smart cookies, so your brain goes into withdrawal and your thoughts slow down to a crawl," Mary said. "Then we slowly work you back up to a normal dose over a four- or five-day period. It's basically like rebooting your brain. I'm sorry. This is going to hurt a lot."

"No," Stacia said. "I can't. I can't."

"You have to," Mary said. "You have to let go of this. Come on. If anybody knows how to get rid of a guy, it's you."

Stacia actually laughed at that, which seemed like a good sign.

Stacia sweated through her clothes and sheets. She went clammy and glass-eyed as her most recent smart cookie wore off. Mary sat with her, calling in sick at work and sitting at Stacia's bedside even after Dave had to go to his office. And once Stacia's brain was barely functional and she was gazing into space, Mary started speaking in Stacia's ear. Telling her the history, the saga of the Unfathomable Sisterhood of Ick. Their friendship after college, and how they had stayed friends even after Mary got into a long-term relationship with some guy, whatsisname. Mary dredged up details from some storage locker in the back of her mind, rebuilding Stacia's true memories to banish the false ones.

"That guy, whatsisname, he's gone, but we're still here," Mary said. "We're not going anywhere. I haven't forgiven you, but I'm not going to bail on you either. Hey, remember that time you and I went ice skating and we each twisted an ankle? It was a couple years after I started dating whatsisname. We ate those revolting tofu corndogs until we barfed." She kept talking until her voice got tired, repeating the same stories with minor variations after a while and obsessing over minor details like the exact color of a stuffed animal they'd had for a week and then lost.

The sun crested over Stacia's slit of a window and then bobbed again, and darkness reasserted. Mary brushed Stacia's forehead with the veiny part of the back of her hand, like someone waking a child from a bad dream..

～

Charlie Jane Anders is managing editor of io9.com and the organizer of the long-running reading series Writers With Drinks. Her novelette "Six Months, Three Days" won a Hugo Award and was a finalist for the Nebula and Theodore Sturgeon Awards.

DIM SUN

MARIA DAHVANA HEADLEY

They're rolling the cart around the edge of the room and the crowd is salivating. Everyone but us has been waiting in line for hours. This is the place to go if you want to eat Dim Sun, and everybody knows it, particularly after the article my buddy Bert Gold wrote. This restaurant used to be a secret. I tried my damnedest to keep him from writing the address down, but he couldn't be stopped. Some people are secret sharers. That's what they live to do, and that's Bert Gold. He tells one secret, and then goes off hunting another.

Bert Gold's an old white man with a ponytail and a belly, and the only way he's ever been able to get the ladies interested is to take them out to dinner at places they can't get into on their own. Almost nobody but Bert can get in everywhere, and it's not because Bert's cool. It's just that his job is a password. No one really wants him to come in. He's a curve skewer in terms of the look of a place, but his recommendation means insane business. His bad review means bust. The result of Bert Gold's prodigious appetite and connections is that, all over the universe, pinned to the back walls of restaurants hoping not to re-encounter his savage tongue, there are photographs of him in the company of young lovelies.

It might be enough to make a person jealous, if a person were inclined toward jealousy. I'm just hungry. But that's the shit of my position: buddy to the legend. The legend makes the reservation, and sometimes, when the legend's lady cancels, I get to horn in.

Today is no exception. Bert's been working on a woman twenty years too young for him, and finally she got a date with someone righter. He's a lech, but he doesn't seem to care. He seems to think the universe owes him younger women. Universe owes all of us something, is my feeling. We all had bad childhoods. Whole world full of bad childhoods. Look at the last fifty years. Things went south all over. Some of us have gotten to an age where our pee floats without warning. It's not pretty, the anti-gravity, and the having to pee. It never was. You'd think they'd find a way to deal, but I spend a lot of time with a plastic sack tied to a stick these days, just like everyone else our age. It's like I'm Nabokov after butterflies, but not.

"Damn it," said Bert when he called. "That little pony canceled on me again. Got a spot for you at Dim Sun, you're interested. I'm thinking of de-starring them. They're scared. They'll feed us up right."

"I'm there," I said. "I'm there in five minutes."

I had to make a quick portal. It took a bribe to my ex, the welder—short notice—but she had the right materials. She hacksawed a chunk of universe out, and I walked through it, and into the restaurant.

The music's changed since the last time I was here, before it got popular. Now we have some kind of botanical singing, like electronic music used to be prior to things getting more exotic. This is the secret language of plants, and it turns out plants like to break it down.

"Is that a fern?" I ask Bert Gold, who is arriving just ahead of me, stepping out of the air, his black t-shirt rumpled, his ponytail done up in a coil for the occasion. Sometimes Bert wears his hair in the local style.

"Nah, that's just some kind of marigold," he says. "Listen. It's got no bass. I miss synth. Fucking organics everywhere you go these days. Want to know a secret?"

"What secret?"

"I don't know," Bert says. "I'm fresh out. But I bet someone here's got their thumb in a plum."

In the old days, back on Earth, Bert was a sin-eater. Except, the reverse. A sin-spitter. He'd take someone's sins, and then he'd walk them to another part of the world, where he'd spit them out in a hole in the dirt, cover them over, and grow magic plants. There was a period of time when the ground, post-radiation, was really fertile. It grew whole vines of sins, twisting ropes of bright green Infidelity, yellow-leafed Embezzlement, perennially flowering Neighbor's Wife. People paid money to display the things Bert planted. He was a horticulturist to the stars, decking their gardens out in the sins of everyone else. Up here, his job is a demotion from what he did on Earth, but sin-chewing gave him tooth trouble, and he was happy to stop that line of work. Now that he's a critic, though, he's basically doing the same thing, under a different title. From what I hear, this tastes better.

"I'm hungry," I say to Bert. He looks at me, and grins.

"You're always hungry," he says. That's true. I've been hungry since I was born. The cart rolls past. I crane my neck to see what's on display, but it's all still under wraps. The windows are steamed up and people look desperate for a taste. The crowd here is pretty, skinny, and young, and they're from all over the place. I take a moment to appreciate them. A couple have tentacles and a couple more are wearing classic big-eyes pointy-chins. Apparently that's coming back. I never went in for that style. The real stuff is more interesting. Life out here was never going to be a kind of pretty that people from Earth could appreciate. The restaurants are all about dress up and cover whatever you really look like. Unless you're us. We look like two old guys from the blue and green, born in the '50s, and dressing like the '70s still have hold of us. For a while, we rode motorcycles. Now we just walk, and it's hard enough. We feel heroic, me and Bert, though Bert has been known to use wheels on occasion. He's not as young as he used to be. Who is?

We're seated at the best table, and I watch the waitstaff flitter frantically in the corners. Bert Gold calls ahead, but only by five minutes. He comes into your restaurant without any real warning. That's his deal. If you're not prepared, too bad for you. He waves his hand in the air, and the cart tilts. It's got wheels made of magnets, because without them, it'd be the saddest place. All the Dim Sun would just be flying around, splatting onto customers.

"We're going to have the Dim Sun Unlimited," Bert Gold says. "How's that today?"

"Amazing as always, a pleasure, a privilege," says the server, but he looks uneasy. I glance at the cart. The cover they've got on it is glowing. Whatever the specials are, they're volatile. Bring it, I say. I want to eat Dim Sun, and I want to eat it desperately. It's been months since I've tasted it. This place does it right. The waiter whips out a damp towel, and some fire retardant, and gets ready to present, but the front door opens with a whoosh, and we all look over, startled. Nobody uses the door here. It's just for show. It opens onto nothing.

"Shit," says Bert Gold, and there's a whimper in his voice. "How'd she know? Somebody in the kitchen must be on her payroll."

"Everyone's on her payroll, Bert," I tell him.

Bert's ex-wife, Harriet, is burning her way in the door, with her white hair twisted into coils identical to his. Harriet Gold, unlike Bert, can go anywhere she wants to, without an invitation. Bert has to be a critic, feared by chefs. Harriet has an all-access pass. She always did. When he married her, everyone knew he'd gotten lucky. It didn't take long for her to figure out that Bert had an eye a mile wide, and that no matter who he had, all he could do was hunt for a younger model.

Harriet kicked him in the balls and divorced him, and ever since, he's been in mourning. She got Earth. Bert got booted up here to the colonies. That doesn't mean Harriet doesn't travel all the time. She has friends on every planet these days, and wherever she is, Bert's uncomfortable. He's risen up three inches from his chair even now with the memory of that kick. I feel like doing a sympathy wince, but I know if I show weakness Harriet will be at me too. She and I used to be close, back when they were a couple. Bert got me in the divorce, and Harriet got the rest of everything and everyone. Poor Bert, I'd say, except Bert is a freestanding catastrophe. I don't feel bad for Bert. He brought this on himself.

"Bert," Harriet says crisply as she arrives at our table. "Fancy meeting you here." She flicks him in the ear with her screwdriver of a fingernail. Harriet's wearing a swath of somebody's sky wrapped around her like a toga, and she glitters in a migraine-inducing way. "Rodney," she says. "I don't know why you still hang out with this miscreant."

"Miscreant" is classic Harriet. We used to play Scrabble together, back in the old days.

"I'm hungry," I say, and shrug. I don't make eye contact. I'm ashamed of myself. I only went with Bert because of his connections, but over the years it's become clear to me that Bert Gold is a piece of work. I'm living in a rental pod up here, because once Bert left and Harriet took over, it wasn't like I was welcome on Earth. We all used to be neighbors. After the divorce, Bert grew a hedge of Deathbed Regrets between me and him and the rest of the neighborhood, and we played racquetball for three months straight, until, at last, the transport brought us up here. Harriet was on the other side of that hedge. We could hear her. She had a few things to say. She also had a string of lovers who could've made God blush. Then she rose in the world. She was always going to. It was a matter of time.

She sits down at the table, twisting sky around one shoulder so that her arms are both bare and ready for dining.

"I'll have the Dim Sun Ultimate," she says to the waiter, who is shaking in his boots at the presence of power.

"The Ultimate?" asks Bert, suddenly losing his confidence in our order. "We'll get the Ultimate, too, then, if that's what she's having."

Harriet smiles sweetly. I take a nervous sip of my drink. The cart is up on one wheel, making its way over to us. The restaurant is freakishly quiet.

It's not every day you see the Chief Food Critic of Outer Space and the President of the Universe sitting down to a meal together.

"Are you good with the poisonous ones, Bert?" Harriet asks Bert. "When we were together, I remember, you had some allergies." She's not wrong. Bert is allergic to raw. She's not. She swallows raw right alongside cooked, easily, without even thinking about it.

"I'm not going to eat the poisonous ones, Harriet," says Bert. "Rodney's going to eat them for me."

I give him a sharp look. One of his lovely lady dinner companions died of dark matter, not even that long ago. The chef made an error preparing it, and that was it for her. Bert mourned for about five minutes, and then claimed it was a risk of fine dining. He gave the place a second star for being real.

"Well, he's your only friend," says Harriet. "But I guess he's disposable. Sorry, Rodney. Your choice. You could've come with me. Would've been better than spending eternity hanging out with this cretin, don't you think?"

The cart is beside us again. I have to wonder if they've spiced it up in the kitchen. This won't be regular Dim Sun fare, not with Harriet here. The President doesn't frequent regular places. I notice several diners rigid at their tables in salute.

"At ease," says Harriet. I make note of their faces. Military, and if that's what they are, I don't want to be on their wrong side. I used to be military myself. The cart beside us is glowing gently, and the most thrilling smells are coming from it.

"The Ultimate," says the chef, out of the kitchen now to pay his respects. "We're honored to be your dining choice this evening, President Gold."

"You ruin my anonymity," says Bert, pitifully. "I'm here as a critic. Now they all know who I am."

"No one even knows you're here, Bert, not now that I'm in the room," says Harriet, and that's about right. "You're forgotten, too, Rodney. You can slip out, if you like."

I want to. Dinner with the two of them is always excruciating, but I can't help myself. The smell of the food is killing me, and whatever they've added to the menu, I want it.

"I'm hungry," I say. My stomach growls. It's like the old days, the pizza and beer and pot haze. Up here, Bert once let me accompany him to a meal consumed in our sleep, where we sat at a table, covered in a blanket of napkins, and dreamed our dinner, some kind of godlike nectar full of apricots, but that was nothing compared to stoner food back on Earth. The smells in this restaurant? They're like fried things, cheese and melted tomato sauce. I'm salivating. I'm ready. Under that cloth is heaven. I think for a moment about all the things I miss, the rinds and puffs, the dripping puddles of oil. I think of how the colonies have nothing like the foods of my youth. The food on earth really tasted like something. In the colonies, you're lucky to get a taste of anything real. Everything up here is organic and heirloom, and if you ask me, that shit tastes like shit. They raided the seed vault, and brought up varieties of tomato cultivated in the 1800s, lemony-fleshed cucumbers, plump oats, cloned a troupe of red and white cows with smiling faces and high cream production, and now all the food is farm to table. I hate it. Give me the fried things. Give me the processed and the packaged. Give me the junk.

Bert brings out his little rating notebook. Harriet stretches her arms wide to encompass the table, and then she cracks her neck. I sit back, belly out, ready to eat my weight in one-bites. Usually, I get the signature dish first, the Dim Sun itself, but tonight's special. The chef pulls the cloth off the cart, and we're on.

"Rings of Saturn," the chef says. "Deep-fried, flash drenched in Mars water-ice, and then fried again."

His assistant is standing by with a fire extinguisher, but this is nothing. The rings are small, a bit blurry, and clearly crisp. They glow a little, which might be worrying for some, but Bert Gold and I are invulnerable. We're connoisseurs of spice. These rings are fried in some kind of astral napalm. I take one, and crunch into it with my front teeth, feeling it beginning to burn the roof of my mouth. It makes me hard, I'm telling you. I miss onion rings. Back in the day, me and Bert were at a bar one night, and I put seven onion rings around my business. Didn't end the way I thought it might. I was looking at the ladies. They were laughing at me. People, it turned out, didn't feel the same way I did about rings. There's a photo somewhere.

"Nice," Bert mutters, scribbling notes. "Though I could have done without the second fry. The napalm tastes like Cindy's sweat, back in San Francisco, that sweet, sweet Cindy, our delicate dance of kink and desire—"

That last he says in his patented Bert Gold Indiscrete Voice. The diners around us are dislodged from their attempts to pretend they aren't already staring at our table.

Harriet has managed to down an entire basket of rings, and is now eating something tiny and wriggling, little motes of light that she grabs with tongs from out of the air.

"Are you sure about that, Bert? I think it tastes like Thomas," Harriet says, at similar volume. "And when I say sweat, I mean the way Thomas would come in, after a run, drenched, and I'd lick it from his biceps. Remember that, Bert? Remember Thomas? He was lovely. Remember how Thomas used to pick me up and carry me up the stairs? Remember how we used to shut the door so hard you'd hear it slam from all the way behind your stupid hedge of mosquito-harboring Deathbed Regrets?"

Even I remember Thomas. Bert looks at Harriet, unblinking, up for the challenge.

"Cindy was the one who grew fur after the radiation hit. I used to rub her pelt backward to generate electricity for the whole block. Oh, man, I knew some really beautiful women before you, and after you, too," he says, and then sighs, shaking his head sadly at Harriet as he munches a bite of Saturn.

Harriet isn't beautiful. What Bert Gold has never realized is that she doesn't give a damn. Harriet is what you'd call striking, as in a match, to light a cigarette. Bert Gold was a fool to lose her. Beautiful has nothing to do with anything in the long run. Somebody like Harriet keeps a man busy. Harriet even kept me busy as her neighbor. I was regularly trying to parse her philosophies. She talked circles around me, sending me running to the encyclopedia on the regular. Back when we were all in our forties, Harriet blazed so bright she hurt the eyes. She's not any calmer now. Harriet's seventy years old and her perfume smells like smoke hitting a thunderstorm. I can see the telltale gleam of a firearm stuffed down her cleavage, and there's a whip curled around her shoulder, around the silky bit of sky she must have had to hire a team of thieves to tug out of its comfortable spot.

"Don't trifle with me, Bert Gold," Harriet says. "You exaggerate. I met Cindy. You call it a pelt, I call it peach fuzz."

Harriet's hair recoils itself into tight knots. She puts an entire dumpling into her mouth and chews it very slowly. The insides of her cheeks flash a lot of different colors, red and purple, electric green, and something about it, the transparency, the expression of rapture on her face, is shockingly sexy. I think for a moment about the unpredictability of lust, about how once, back on Earth, I fucked a snack cake. I made a thousand-layered heap of them, and cut holes in the creamy centers. It was as good as it sounds.

I'm still eating. Their battle means they aren't paying attention to the cart, and so I'm grabbing my fill. I take a peek into each basket, then have a mouthful of motes, each one bouncing around on my teeth and fizzing as they explode.

"Io's Moonlight," the chef whispers proudly. "I give them a little bath of liquid nitrogen."

I open my mouth for more, but I can see the rest of the dumplings, plump and rosy, and Harriet is reaching out for another. I'm worried she'll eat them all before I get to try them, but she passes me one.

"Red Dwarf," she says to me. "Reminds me of some other things." She looks meaningfully at Bert's crotch. Bert doesn't flinch. He stuffs a Red Dwarf into his mouth like he's a goat gnawing a tire. He's not even taking notes, just making rambling fake-writing scribbles on his notepad.

The dumpling is soup-filled, and explodes in my mouth. When I dab at my lips, a blood-colored liquid stains the napkin. It's reminiscent of the crème soda that got outlawed for filtering through pee and messing up the pH of the oceans Over the years, the FDA took everything delicious on Earth away.

"This is excellent," I tell Harriet.

"Isn't it, though, Rodney?" she says. Her voice is sweet and polite. You'd think Bert Gold was a thousand light years away. "This is one of my favorite places. Has been for ages. But it upsets my digestion to see Bert Gold here."

Bert sits up very straight, his belly pushing out of his shirt. "You know this is my restaurant," he says. "I discovered it way back when. I've been coming here for a decade. This is mine, Harriet."

I know what he's thinking. Harriet's about to claim custody of yet another place. What is there to say, when your ex-wife becomes the President of the Universe? She got ninety-nine percent of the vote. Bert Gold's got nothing but belly. He made the bad call of pissing her off. This divorce could have been friendly, but Bert Gold posted photos all over the place of himself with a bevy of beauties. Bert Gold sent lewd messages to Harriet's friends and enemies. Bert Gold roved like a NASA vehicle. Also, and worst of all, Bert Gold underestimated Harriet Gold's intellect. He'd never paid any attention to the designs she'd been drafting in her spare time. The whole portal system is Harriet's invention. She made climbing through the space-time continuum as easy as climbing through a bathroom window. Now space travel is like buying a bus ticket.

"You're being an idiot, Bert," I say, and then I reach into a little basket and grab a handful of something black, covered in a soft mosaic of sweet crumbs. It's light in my fingers, and I nearly lose it to floating.

"You might not want to eat that one, Rodney," says Harriet.

"Why not?" says Bert.

"I had it when I was here last," says Harriet. "It's not really for human consumption. I mean, not for normal humans, anyway. It's pretty gourmet. Not everyone can handle it."

She moves the basket a little out of Bert's way, and Bert's hand jolts out like a cottonmouth from a creek bottom. He grabs the basket from Harriet and tugs. Bert's nothing if not predictable.

"What is it?" Bert Gold asks the chef, pouring the little black objects onto his plate like he's a starving man.

I notice Harriet giving the chef a look, and the chef shrugs and says "Odds and ends. Noble gases, couple of rogue elements in a crispity crust of interstellar dust."

Bert pops one into his mouth. He smacks his lips.

"Tastes like donut," he says, and so I take one, too, disregarding the look I saw the chef and the President of the Universe exchange. I roll it around on my tongue, feeling the stardust rub off. I've eaten stardust before. It's cinnamony, and a little rough, a hint of filth in it, like eating cheese puffs squashed up out of a dirty hand. It's pretty good. Maybe not double star level, but pretty good.

All is well, until I bite down and find nothing in the center.

"Donut *hole*," I say to Bert. "Not the same as donut."

I feel obscurely emotional, disappointed at the loss of the chewy center. I look at the chef. "This is just the hole, right? Is that what we're eating?"

Harriet looks at Bert and grins.

Bert gets a very unhappy look on his face. That's when I feel it. The nothing makes its way down my throat and into my belly. The nothing swells to fill my stomach. It's a black bleakness, a twisting unfurling into itself, like something being wrung and simultaneously growing.

"Black Hole," says Harriet, and shrugs. "What can I tell you, Bert? House specialty. I think I warned you."

Bert's belly is bigger than it was. He looks pregnant. I look down at mine. Same. The chef twitches his bandana nervously. Surely being President of the Universe doesn't mean you can murder your ex-husband and his best and only friend in the middle of a crowded restaurant? Surely it can't mean that. Harriet smiles at me.

"Antidote?" Bert sputters.

"Who says there's an antidote? Maybe this is your last supper."

"Harriet," I say. "Harriet, that's not fair." My words sound weirdly slurred to me, and I reach up my hand to touch my mouth. My lips are curling backward.

"What did I ever do to you?" I ask Harriet. My belly is huge now, bigger than the table. It's full of nothing and everything at once. I can tell it's only a matter of time before I flip into an inside out exploded man-sock. I've always been hungry, but now the hunger is a bulging starvation.

Bert and I have always thought well as a team, but I'm pissed with him. I think of those months of racquetball. He owes me. He shouldn't put me in situations like this. I look around at all the young lovelies, all the tentacled, pointy-chinned pretty things who are stargazing their idol, Harriet, and the vengeance she's wrought.

Bert, across from me, is in similarly dire straits. He's holding his burgeoning belly with both hands, but I see him look toward the cart, and the glow on it. There are a couple of dishes still left, one in a covered metal basket. I look at Bert. I nod.

A bit of black hole leaks out the corner of Bert's mouth, and he moans. I watch it take over a piece of his cheek, look through it, and see a whole lot of nowhere I want to live.

I tilt like a gömböc (some of the old Scrabble-words still stay with me), roly-polying my way at the cart. My extruded belly button serves as a pivot point.

"What are you doing?" says Harriet. "Rodney, don't think you're getting him out of this. This is Bert's own fault."

I grab the basket with the Dim Sun in it and tilt back to center. I grab it like I'm a warrior, because I'm sitting opposite a real warrior and I know she'll have me if I don't eat fast.

The Dim Sun is a big disc, covered in golden red melt, with spots of darkness from the oven. It's what I've been smelling this whole time. The cheesy tomato goodness. The crackle and the heat. You can only get that level of boiling ignition by using a cosmic microwave. I salute the chef with a quick fist pump, and then I break the Dim Sun in half and shove it at Bert. I can feel my finger bones freezing where the dark spots are. The bright spots are scalding my skin off.

"Take that, Harriet!" I shout, and then I fold my part of the Dim Sun in half and shove it in my maw, chomping down on it with the dentures I had specially made. They can withstand anything I'd want to eat. It's hot and cold and delicious. It's junk in the most divine sense, celestial debris, a miniature of the fail of Earth's sun, and all over the universe these are a coveted item. They fill you up no matter what. They're known for it.

Bert's gobbling his down, and so am I, though I'm tempted to savor it more slowly. I can feel it quieting the Black Hole, stopping its progress. My belly shrinks. The dark is retreating. The melting goodness covers over the nothing, and my shirt, now tattered, relaxes.

Harriet sighs and stands up. She has her own whole Dim Sun, already nibbled around the edges. She eats it in three bites, showing incredible tolerance for the burn.

"You're always entertaining, Harriet," Bert Gold says, wiping his mouth. "I'd wish you better luck next time, but you'd miss me if you caused me to be absorbed into the dark. You should try and get over me."

The chef passes Harriet a small dessert cone. She licks at it like a pleased cat. Bert looks at it enviously. I know his mouth, like mine, is blistered.

"Comet ice," she says, and shrugs. She offers the cone to me, and gives me a single lick, which instantly ruins me. It's not normal comet ice. It's the kind of thing that delivers seas to a dry planet. Faintly strawberry, faintly coconut. A little rum, a little gasoline. It's a cocktail of perfection and it soothes my burns. Harriet's not bad. She never was. In fact, I always liked Harriet. Why I'm the guy Bert got in the divorce, I don't know. He chose me, but I should never have chosen him back.

"That was completely your fault, Rodney," Bert says petulantly. "You're supposed to be the taster. I won't take you places if you don't do your job. I shouldn't have even had any of that black hole in my mouth. I'm unstarring this place and reporting it to Health & Safety," says Bert. "I am."

I look at Bert, waiting for him to apologize. He doesn't.

"Have one of these," I say, and I pass Bert the last basket on the cart. After all these years, I'm finally sick of Bert. He's criminally ungrateful. I just saved him from a Black Hole, and will he ever he say thank you? No. He's never been nice, not really. I'm only here because a lady canceled on him, and she was right to do it. Bert will never learn.

"What are they?"

"They're delicious," I say. "But dangerous. It's sort of like that French cheese you had back in San Francisco, the one that walked."

I didn't eat that cheese. I was never a gourmand like Bert. You couldn't have paid me enough. I preferred a nice processed cheese spread slathered on hot dog.

Bert grumbles a little, but he opens the basket. Little exotic crullers inside it, with a creamy filling. He perks up.

"Long as they aren't raw," says Bert. "I have allergies."

"Not raw," says the chef. "These aren't even special. They're something the back kitchen whipped up. Grandma food, you ask me."

"Retro," says Bert, clearly taking notes even as he bites in. "Home-cooked. Chef's washed up, but the kitchen staff innovates with traditional flavors."

Harriet and I watch as he puts the pastry in his mouth, chews, and swallows. His head stretches. His ankles extend. His belly contracts and then rolls out to a long rubber-band of middle.

"See you, Bert," I say.

"Damn it," Bert says. "Damn it all. Wormhole?"

"Wormhole," Harriet confirms.

Harriet and I watch as Bert Gold starts time-traveling from both ends.

His belly stays. The rest of him flickers through time and space. His head is briefly in the 1820s, while his backside visits the dark side of the moon circa two thousand years from now. His feet step momentarily into Mesopotamia while his head dunks in a mucky sixth century bog.

Harriet gives me another lick of her ice. She hoists up her swath of sky, scatters the crumbs in it, and rewraps it around her midriff.

"Nice to see you, Rodney," she says. She heads for the door.

"Can I call you?" I ask.

"You can take over as critic," Harriet says. "Looks like that position's open. I like to eat. I like hungry company. I'll see you around."

She walks out into the nowhere, the sky shining in her wake. She's striking, Harriet. Even more than usual.

I look down at Bert. He's divided between Mars and Pluto. I can see it, each place a flicker. His belly remains the same, stuck here in the middle.

I look at the chef. He shrugs. "Kitchen works for the President," he says.

"What'll you do with him?" I ask.

"The President has provided for his care."

The chef wraps Bert Gold in a tablecloth and slings him over his shoulder.

Bert's head is in the Wild West. His legs are clamped around a shuttle from the early years of the colonies. I wonder if he's eating well on his journey.

When I get ready to leave the restaurant, I discover that the President of the Universe has paid the check. What can I say? The woman keeps a guy busy. She keeps everything busy. She teaches me things. I learn words from Harriet, which is more than I ever learned from Bert Gold. All he ever did was hit me with racquetballs and kick me out of fancy restaurants midway through the amuse-bouche.

Things are different now. I'm free of Bert Gold. I'm already hungry again, and the universe is wide. I pick up Bert's rating notebook. I walk out the door into the great darkness.

There are things to eat out there.

~

Maria Dahvana Headley is the Nebula-nominated author of the dark fantasy/alt-history novel *Queen of Kings*, as well as the internationally bestselling memoir *The Year of Yes*. Her short fiction has appeared in *Lightspeed* ("Give Her Honey When You Hear Her Scream"), *Subterranean*, and more, and will shortly be anthologized in the 2013 editions of Rich Horton's *The Year's Best Fantasy & Science Fiction*, Paula Guran's *The Year's Best Dark Fantasy & Horror,* and Jurassic London's *The Lowest Heaven,* a celestial bodies anthology, in which she is responsible for the story about Earth. Most recently, with Neil Gaiman, she co-edited the young-adult monster anthology *Unnatural Creatures,* to benefit 826DC. Find her on Twitter at @MARIADAHVANA, or on the web at www.mariadahvanaheadley.com.

THE LONELY SEA IN THE SKY

AMAL EL-MOHTAR

White as Diamonds

My name is Leila Ghufran. I am fifty-six years old. I am encouraged to begin this journal in this way because, says the team's psychiatrist, telling myself who I am will prove beneficial. This is, of course, ridiculous, because I am not my name—did not even choose it for myself—and a name is always a synecdoche at most, a label misapplied at the least. My name does not tell you that I am a planetary geologist, that I love my work enough to submit to this indignity, that despite the fact that I am a valuable member of my team I am expected to waste time on churning out this miserable performance for the sake of a stamp before I can get back to work.

I suppose I see what she did there. Well done, Hala.

I am allegedly exhibiting signs of succumbing to the middle stages of Meisner Syndrome, colloquially known as adamancy, which sounds more like a method of divination than anything else—as is appropriate, frankly, to the hazy mysticism that passes for the disease's pathology. "A preoccupation with the nature and properties of diamonds, and/or the study of the same, especially extraterrestrial"; "obsessive behaviour related to the study of diamonds, especially extraterrestrial"; "unusual levels of alertness and attention to detail"—*I am a planetary geologist, Hala*! These are features, not flaws! How could several years' friendship not—

I am pausing to remind myself that as someone who's known me for several years is insisting on this exercise, perhaps something is a little off, and perhaps I am not the person best qualified to judge. But the symptoms of adamancy are ridiculously vague and diffuse and at the present moment are hampering my actual work. I am meant to be studying Lucyite at our Triton base. Instead I've been banished—is hyperbole a symptom of adamancy?—to the Kola Borehole in order to assist with extra-galactic neutrino detection. Not content to exile me to Siberia, my friend, you literally found the deepest hole on the planet to shove me into under the guise of studying the sky.

I can actually hear you saying this is for my own good. It's a little hilarious, actually.

Meisner's Syndrome, aka Adamantine Dissociation Syndrome, aka Adamancy

Etiology

Theorized to be a consequence of cumulative exposure to Lucyite-powered technologies or the Corona fields of extraterrestrial minerals. Affects an estimated one percent of the global population.

Symptoms

Hyperfocus, especially on light refraction; sudden, temporary sensation of cold ("cold flash"); urgent need to submerge oneself in hot water. A preoccupation with the nature and properties of diamonds, and/or the study of the same, especially extraterrestrial; unusual levels of alertness and attention to detail alternating with periods of trance-like calm.

Risks and Complications

As with other obsessive disorders, sufferers are at risk of self-neglect relating to hygiene, nutrition, and personal relationships, resulting in a poor quality of life. Certain kinds of work are also at risk: driving, operating heavy machinery, and performing delicate tasks are all to be avoided.

Progression

At more advanced stages of the disease, sufferers are prone to sometimes violent emotional outbursts, often accompanied by memory loss. Consequently, it may become difficult to convince a sufferer of their diagnosis.

Treatment

Symptoms can be managed with varying degrees of success with anti-anxiety medications. Cognitive behavioural therapy and other forms of talk therapy have not been found to be effective. Some studies suggest isolation from crystalline structures and Paragon technologies is helpful, and others have demonstrated an easing of symptoms when the sufferer is underground—possibly as this isolates them from most instances of ambient light refraction and the trances these can provoke.

Prognosis

Even with treatment and lifestyle change, chances of full recovery remain slim.

Lucy in the Sky with Diamonds

I could say I have always loved diamonds, but this isn't quite true. I have, for as long as I can remember, loved the idea of diamonds; loved diamonds in stories; loved the things compared to diamonds in metaphor. Stars; the spark of light on water; that sort of thing.

It comes down, I suppose, to loving light—but no, more than that—it must be about the breaking of light, its containment. A bit sinister when put that way, isn't it? Sunlight on its own holds little appeal, but angle it against the ocean, make it dance—poetry.

Diamond oceans on Neptune! I suppose that's what started everything off—those early accounts of *diamond oceans* in the twenty-teens. Determine that diamonds behave like water—that you can have diamond in liquid form that isn't graphite, and chunks of diamond floating on it—and you have the realisation of metaphor, you have every fairy tale made flesh. Only a hop and a skip in the mind from that to holidaying on extraterrestrial getaways by shores of literally crystalline water.

All well and good until you think about the heat and the pressure required to maintain diamonds in liquid state, and realize you'd be liquid yourself long before you could dip a careful toe in.

Still. It still sounds beautiful to me, somehow, in spite of everything, in spite of having worked with solid chunks of it on Triton. A diamond ocean in the sky. Like that John Masefield poem you recited for me once—you remember how I misheard it? *I must go down to the sea again / the lonely sea in the sky.*

Up above the world so high, like a diamond in the sky. Isn't it incredible that we take something born out of the bowels of the earth and stud the sky with it in our songs and stories? Isn't it desperately strange?

Isn't it even stranger that we should *find* them where we'd imagined them to be for so long?

I hope you're feeling guilty, Hala.

Teleportation Possible Within Ten Years, Scientists Say

Recent studies coming out of Triton Base 1 provide a veritable cavalcade of information about the mineral composition of Neptune's mantle and the unusual properties of the liquid carbon contained there.

"Though the only carbon samples we succeeded in extracting from the planet were solid, and almost indistinguishable in their crystal lattice structures from Earth diamonds, we discovered that super-heating them until they turned liquid caused them to vanish, completely, without a trace," said an excited Dr. Jay Winzell. "Eventually we realized that the spikes of thermal activity we'd been observing on Neptune *corresponded exactly* to the moments we liquefied the crystals. It was a leap, but—that's what they were doing! Our samples, made liquid, were *jumping back to Neptune* and mixing with the diamond ocean there."

Dr. Winzell believes it could be possible, with further study, to understand how this teleportive quality works. "We're a long way off, still theorizing how this behaviour is even possible within our current understanding of quantum mechanics—but it's conceivable that once we've understood it, we could harness this property somehow, contain and channel it such that we could effectively *ride* the liquid substance across vast distances instantaneously within a closed system. The journey to Neptune would be shortened from years to seconds. But imagine using it on Earth! This could do for travel what the internet once did for communication. It's a massive paradigm shift—our very notions of distance, of space and time, will have to be re-examined."

Dr. Winzell, as discoverer of the diamond-like mineral, has elected to name it Lucyite, in honour of the iconic Beatles song.

Diamonds on the Soles of Her Shoes

I'm not allowed mirrors. Too much chance of light reflections causing relapse. I'm astonished they let me work at all, but I suppose you knew it would be worse for me without something to keep my mind and hands busy.

I hate it here.

From **"Untangling the Melee: Towards Practical Applications of Quantum Entanglement,"** *by Dr. Elaine Gallagher*

In conclusion, while there is as yet no definitive theory explaining *why* Lucyite behaves as it does, the properties are clear: Operating on the principles of quantum entanglement outlined above, we can consistently manage the energy state of each individual unit. When liquid, the unit's entangled property teleports it to the location of the unit with the next highest energy level, allowing for distance—bearing in mind that, as previously stated, "teleport," though a less than ideal description of linear movement theorized as taking place in higher dimensions, is nevertheless the nearest term one can accurately use without succumbing to the more colloquial "blink," "jump," or, even more ludicrously, Paragon Industries' preferred term of "shine."

Diamonds are Forever

I am encouraged to write about my family, but all I want is to write to you, Hala. It helps me to think of saying these things to you and I would rather not pretend that there is privacy here, between my mind and the screen. I would rather address you and the things you request of me.

When I was small my mother would read me bedtime stories out of holy texts. She later told me this was so I wouldn't ever mistake fictions for fact, but I had little sense of her project then; I just loved the fantastical tales about things transforming into other things, people doing bad things and being punished or forgiven or vindicated.

She read me this bit out of the Talmud, once, that I loved desperately for how strange and otherworldly it seemed to me:

Rab Judah, the Indian, related: Once we were travelling on board a ship when we saw a precious stone that was surrounded by a snake. A diver descended to bring it up. [Thereupon] the snake approached with the purpose of swallowing the ship, [when] a raven came and bit off its head and the waters were turned into blood. A second snake came, took [the head of the decapitated snake] and attached it [to the body], and it revived. Again [the snake] approached, intent on swallowing the ship. Again a bird came and severed its head. [Thereupon the diver] seized the precious stone and threw it into the ship. We had with us salted birds. [As soon as] we put [the stone] upon them, they took it up and flew away with it.

It's probably fair to say I wanted to go off-world because of these stories. You grow up on giant snakes and life-rendering gems and the prospect of a manned mission to Neptune's not reaching very far at all.

You know the Talmud is structured like a diamond of popular imagination, too? Seders at the crown, footnotes at the culet. You'll have to ask Ben about it for me sometime.

I was reminded of that passage when my mother read me stories of Sindbad later on—in his second voyage he comes to a valley of diamonds beset by giant serpents that will eat anyone who approaches. So Sindbad figures out a way around them: He throws down slabs of raw meat into the valley that they might become studded with gems before attracting great birds to swoop down and carry the diamond-laden meat into their nests.

Is this not the Melee? Or perhaps the reverse of it—diamonds carrying slabs of meat through space at astonishing speed, in spite of serpents, in spite of all—and is our understanding of the Melee not roughly this sophisticated?

Was ours not a ship navigating towards a serpent wrapped around a precious gem?

And have we not cut—have we not stolen—

It's funny, isn't it—my mother wanted me to think of scriptures as fairy tales so that I would not be their dupe. But as a consequence, all my frames of reference, my earliest acquisitions of knowledge, are fantasy. Fairy tales have, in a sense, become my scripture.

I am very cold. I need a bath.

The Gasp Heard Round the World

Thousands gathered today to observe the first human use of the network of gates known as the Melee. Established by international conglomerate Paragon Industries in collaboration with governments around the world, the Melee revolutionized international commerce with its Lucyite-powered technology, allowing instantaneous transport of goods across the world. Today Paragon president Alastair Moor prepared to be the first to blink from Glasgow to Damascus and back.

Cameras in Glasgow recorded Mr. Moor stepping into the Glasgow Gate and waiting for its in-built Z-mechanism to activate and liquefy the Lucyite. No sooner had Mr. Moor vanished from the Glasgow monitors than he appeared, not a hair out of place, on the Damascene cameras, having successfully effected a journey of over 3,000 miles in less than a single second.

"One small step for man," said Moor, and the crowd erupted in cheers.

She dwelt among the untrodden ways

I never feel clean enough. Is this because of what I can't remember doing? I never feel clean enough. I walk the halls and I sit to write and all I want is to wash, wash, wash until my skin pinks and peels into petals floating on the surface of the bath. If all of me could slough off into remnants, into something beautiful—if all of me could dissolve—if I could just get clean—

Why do you suppose we have so many stories about diamonds? Diamonds are curse-stones in some places, markers of great fortune in others. Diamonds are so hard and so brittle, so strong and so delicate at once. Do you suppose, ultimately, those stories are all about us? Carbon to carbon to carbon?

Do you think it possible that, once upon a time, all our diamonds were an ocean? It used to be that all land was one land, no? Perhaps we had a diamond ocean here. Perhaps we loved it, and it died. Perhaps it loved us and it died. Perhaps because it loved us it died.

No motion has she now, no force;
She neither hears nor sees;
Roll'd round in earth's diurnal course,
With rocks, and stones, and trees.
Wordsworth. Maybe I am going mancy after all.

From Philip Kidman's A Melee for You and Me

There is a very real sense in which we can comprehend quantum entanglement as applied to Lucyite in terms of living memory. Without wishing to lend a crumb of credibility to the Friends of Lucy's extremist ravings, it could be said that the Melee operates on a carefully curated forgetfulness: After all, the entirety of the Melee's infrastructure is powered by the dispersal of one large chunk of Lucyite brought to Earth from Triton. By breaking it into precise halves and carefully calibrating each half's liquid state, Nobel-winning Dr. Jay Winzell succeeded in causing the halves to blink towards each other in a closed system, instead of back to Neptune—which is, as the physicists have it, the place of highest entanglement. Dr. Winzell effectively pioneered the method for entangling Lucyite crystals with each other, the further perfection and sophistication of which enables the complexity of the Melee. Possessing only "memory" of each other, the fractions of Lucyite liquefied at each gate will always blink towards each other within the Melee's careful curation of space.

Looking ahead, we can see that every upgrade to the Melee in the future—any expansion beyond Neptune, or extension of the existing system on Earth beyond our current stock of calibrated crystal—will require an enormous overhaul to take into account the higher entanglement of new Lucyite. Luckily the system is at present so efficient that no such recalibration will be necessary within our lifetimes, and indeed, any introduction of new crystal into the system would throw it into disastrous confusion and disarray at best, or provoke a devastating chain reaction at worst.

It would appear that, ironically, the most advanced system of travel and transport we have yet devised is powered by absent-mindedness. The worst thing we could do in our pursuit of getting places quickly is jog our precious superconductor's memory of where it came from.

Coal to Diamonds

A melee is a packet of small diamonds all of roughly the same size and value.

A melee is a fight, a mess, a jumble.

A melee has three vowels in it, four if you count the indefinite article.

A melee could be a woman's name.

Amelie, Amelie, Amelie.

A melee or eight. Amelie, orate. A melior ate.

Ameliorate.

Triton Base 1 Incident Report: Dr. Hala Moussa

At 0200.23.04.2076 NTC I found Dr. Leila Ghufran in the laboratory, palms pressed into a tray of Lucyite chips. They had cut into her palms and her hands were bleeding. She was standing very still and did not respond to her name until I approached her and initiated physical contact. I grasped her shoulder and pulled her to face me, at which point I saw blood on her lips and at the corners of her mouth. I suspected she had severely bitten her tongue; this appeared to be the case when she began speaking. Her initial lack of responsiveness was alarming, but her eventual words were more so: She began exhibiting severe distress, crying and saying I was hurting her, that she was very cold, that she wanted to go back.

After we restrained and sedated her, Dr. Ghufran claimed to have no memory of our interaction. Given our proximity to the diamantine ocean of Neptune and Dr. Ghufran's extensive exposure to it and the samples extracted from it, I am diagnosing her with Meisner's Syndrome and recommending she be relocated to a subterranean project as soon as possible.

Diamonds and Pearls

Imagine if you took a tiny piece of a diamond and you put it in some meat.

Imagine it irritating the meat, agitating it, inflaming it.

Imagine if the meat rose around to coat it with layers of itself, to obfuscate and obscure it.

Imagine if Sindbad's slabs of meat swallowed the diamond and became something else, became diamond-and-meat, became organic crystal, became other.

I don't know what I am saying. I'm dizzy. Hala I'm sorry. I'm so sorry. I think I am going to fail you. I love you, Hala. I'm sorry.

Extract from "Friends of Lucy" Manifesto

Meisner Syndrome is a lie!

Adamancy is a lie!

A conspiracy concocted by Big Pharma and high-ranking members of international governments in concert with the logistical-industrial complex

to make us all complicit in the torture and dismemberment
of a living organism!
We say again, *Lucyite is alive!*
We don't need the Melee any more than we needed to eat animals!
It screams like a thousand thousand pigs being slaughtered, like lambs,
like cattle!
Stop the screaming!
Save Lucy!
End the Melee!

Shine On, You Crazy Diamond

Everything is wrong. Everything is broken and wrong and no one can see it.

Do you remember the playground, Hala? The bullies who hated when we held hands? How it didn't matter how much they goaded and spat and pushed and shoved, the moment we threw a punch we were at fault? Because we had to be better, we were supposed to be better, and they were just a fact of life. Do you remember how we hated that? How unfair it was? How we vowed that we'd never be taken in by "looking at both sides" when all it meant was that people had the means to justify and excuse our suffering?

Hala, imagine if when we were children, we had seen a girl splayed out on the floor, spread-eagled, her every bone broken beneath the feet of boys jumping up and down on her as if she were solid ground. Imagine we could hear her screaming, begging them to stop, to let her go, but the boys could not, because she was nothing, she was the earth, she could not feel. *But we could see her. We could hear her.*

What would you have done, Hala? Told them to stop? But this ground is so much softer on their feet, it is so much more fun to jump on it, why should they? Why should they believe that there is a woman there they cannot see? We are few and they are so many, we must be insane, we must be diseased to imagine something so horrible.

Imagine, Hala, that in the eye of one of these boys you see satisfaction. You see knowledge. You see that he knows he is making someone scream but it doesn't bother him, *it doesn't matter*, because he can get away with it.

What would you do?

President Moore Responds to Diamond Fanatics

Following the evacuation of the Triton base in response to a terrorist threat, Paragon Industries hastened to reassure the public that the Melee remains safe and open to business as usual. We reached President Alastair Moore for comment.

"It's very sad, but they're deeply troubled people," says Moore. "They deserve not our scorn, but our empathy, our pity, and our help."

When asked whether there might be any truth to allegations made by the Friends of Lucy, Moore responded:

"Look, it's just crazy. You may as well say electricity has feelings. People believed all sorts of wacky things when Tesla coiled wires, but we can't imagine living without electricity now. This is no different."

A star to steer her by

Of course I had nothing to do with that threat. I know who did, though. I can feel them at the edge of my vision now, shimmering, especially when my fingers start to go numb. It's always so cold here.

They're cold, too, all of them. *Frozen in the ring of diamond time*, that was from a poem, wasn't it? Alexa Seidel? Pre-Melee, of course. I don't know why all of my favourite things should be. I suppose it's nostalgia for a time before our fictions were fact.

It's good that you're not on Triton just now. Things are about to happen there. I'd hate for anyone to be stranded when the gate crashes.

I'm going to miss you so much.

I remember, now, what I couldn't on Triton. I remember you taking my wrists and looking at my palms, I remember you sitting by me as they soaked every last speck of diamond from the meat of me to make sure I wouldn't accidentally bring any back with me to Earth. You never left me, even though the work was piling up, the demand for reports and explanations.

I wish I could see you one more time. The ocean's kind, to let me have this memory of you back. I hope you can understand. I hope you can forgive me.

My tongue wasn't bloody because I bit it. It was bloody because I licked the diamonds off the tray. I swallowed as much as I could. It's probably why I haven't gotten better, for all that you buried me so deep. They're still inside me, as entangled as any quantum physicist could wish, dense enough with memory of Neptune to summon all the Earth's stolen droplets and make a body of her again, a mind, a recollection, give her a destination and the will, the energy to reach it.

All I have to do is make them liquid.

Ridiculous that I've been so cold for so long when the solution's been so near to hand. We have a Z-machine here, and I'm on its scheduled mainte- nance rotation. All I need is a moment alone with it, and I will be warm again.

I am a slab of meat awaiting my vulture. I am a salted bird brought to life. I will dissolve, I will melt, I will dip my toe into a diamond ocean and I will swim.

I am glad there won't be anything left of me here.

I hope—I feel that it will take me with it. Back to Neptune. That I might go up to the sea again, the lonely sea in the sky.

Maybe it will be better there.

Maybe we'll keep each other company.

~

Amal El-Mohtar is the Nebula-nominated author of *The Honey Month*, a collection of poems and very short fiction written to the taste of twenty-eight different kinds of honey. Her work has appeared in multiple venues online and in print including *Strange Horizons*, *Glitter & Mayhem*, and *Apex*, and is forthcoming in *Kaleidoscope: Diverse YA Science Fiction and Fantasy Stories*. She is a member of the Banjo Apocalypse Crinoline Troubadours; edits *Goblin Fruit*, an online quarterly dedicated to fantastical poetry; and currently lives in Glasgow with two black and white cats and their pet Glaswegian. Find her online at amalelmohtar.com or on Twitter @tithenai.

A Burglary, Addressed By a Young Lady

Elizabeth Porter Birdsall

"Genevieve," said her mother sternly, "what has your etiquette tutor told you about stealing from your equals?"

Genevieve sighed. In a bored sing-song, she recited, "Stealing from one's social inferiors is a faux pas the well-bred lady scorns. That is the purpose of taxation. Stealing from one's equals is a dull and plebian activity, of neither sport nor honor, and to be avoided except in the direst of circumstances. Stealing from one's betters is a coup, though one must always take care to punctiliously return any items specifically requested."

"Very good." Her mama seemed impervious to Genevieve's tone, as she generally took care to be. "What does that tell you concerning the wisdom of your request?"

"But Mama!" Genevieve restrained herself, with some difficulty, from further expostulations, and returned instead to her carefully planned appeal to her mother's well-honed acquisitive instincts. "Mama, just *think* of that lovely Trinitian laser pistol. It would look so gorgeous in your sitting room. And they're an older family than ours by just the slightest bit, so it's an acceptable target—"

"No." Lady Tadma sniffed, and Genevieve knew she had chosen the wrong tack. "We are every bit as noble as the Yendarias, and with greater battle honors to our name. Your interest in young James will pass—"

"He's a perfectly respectable target!"

"—but our social shame if this ever comes to light will not. Find another burglee for your debutante raid, Genevieve."

With an inarticulate sound of frustration imperfectly stifled, Genevieve flung herself out of her chair and stalked towards the door.

"And Genevieve? Do find Master Coundry, please, and tell him he's to give you another lesson on the proper tone for speaking to one's mother. A lengthy one." Her mother's voice was as serene as ever. "Kindly recall that it is not in the least too late for your papa and I to decide that your Spree must be postponed a year, if you are insufficiently mature to enter Society this birthday."

Genevieve slammed the door behind her.

• • •

A proper show of contrition served not in the least to soften her mother's heart. Nor did a week of good behavior, nor all the diligent practicing upon the hologram generator and pianoforte that Genevieve's patience could stand, nor the most scrupulously reasoned appeals to logic and covetousness. Lady Alexandria Tadma, her daughter fumed, must never have truly been an adolescent herself. She must have been born a maternal tyrant in miniature, no matter all her thrilling tales of burglary in Seasons past. How else to account for her hardheartedness towards her only daughter's earnest desires?

James Yendaria! He was of course the primary target of her longed-for raid. The Trinitian laser pistol was a lovely piece of workmanship, and well worth burgling, but she full intended to leave the broadest acceptable clues to her identity in its place. Perhaps a handkerchief, daintily monogrammed by her own hand; perhaps a sheet of fine scented paper, inscribed with one of the traditional gloating couplets and detailed with microdots containing the Tadma family motto. In any event, the desired consequence would surely materialize: James and his parents, recognizing the compliment paid them in such a daring raid upon their own stronghold, would naturally pay a call upon the Tadma household to request its return. While servants packaged the pistol in synthwool and a beribboned box for transit, James and his family would be shown into the parlor for tea and an opportunity for mutual compliments between thief and robbed. Many a courtship had begun so. And James Yendaria, with his well-turned leg for a dance and his dashing skill at shuttle piloting, was certainly a catch! His family might not be multiple ranks above the Tadmas, but they were no new money to scorn, either. It was perfectly proper.

But no; Lady Tadma would not hear of it, and Lord Tadma supported her in what Genevieve suspected was more of marital solidarity than genuine preference. He only patted her shoulder with a hearty "There, there, m'dear, you'll soon be burgling half the *ton*, but you only get one chance to start your reputation right, eh?" before sequestering himself in his study, where family rules forbade his daughter to interrupt his work, even when she suspected that work was purely a cover for avoiding feminine dissent.

In the end, the lofty target chosen to begin Genevieve's debut Spree was Nelson Wesley, the bookish and wealthy Marquis of Battleboro. Genevieve's sulks and pleas were in vain; she was obliged to obey parental decrees, or face the unbearable prospect of another year of childish lessons.

• • •

"*Do* remember to leave a nice clear token, won't you, darling?" Lady Tadma tugged fussily at the ribbons of anti-sensor circuitry wound into Genevieve's curls. Sarah, their ladies' maid, moved smoothly to checking the infrared bafflers buttoned at Genevieve's cuffs, while her mistress mussed her careful handiwork in the name of helping. "The marquis would be a most appropriate suitor for a girl of your accomplishments. And don't forget, he makes ten thousand platinum a year!"

"I'll remember, Mama," sighed Genevieve, who intended to do no such thing. The marquis was all very well and good, if you liked your men with their nose buried in a history tome and no sense of dancing rhythm whatsoever, but he would be a suitor with whom James Yendaria could not possibly compete. More to the point, Genevieve was still annoyed that she'd had so little say in her target. She might be obliged to rob whom her parents instructed, but she didn't need to be dutiful at every step!

"Good," said her mother, as obliviously as Genevieve might have hoped, and stepped back to regard the results of her hair-straightening. To Genevieve's private horror, her mother's eyes grew moist. "Oh, Jenny, you look so grown! Just yesterday, it seems, you were a babe in the nursery. Now here you are, all kitted out to burgle a marquis!"

"I'll be home triumphant before you know it," Genevieve blurted. Her mother had never been one for sentimental takings; the sight put Genevieve quite off her stride. "But Mama, I really ought to go, if I hope to slip between the estate sweeps."

"Yes, yes, of course." Lady Tadma pulled her dignity back around herself with a faint sniffle which her daughter pretended not to notice. "Go on, darling, and remember everything you've been taught. I know you'll conduct yourself properly."

"Yes, Mama." Genevieve kissed her mother's cheek, and fled for the upper window and the scrupulously trained wisteria that would carry her to the ground.

• • •

It *was* exhilarating, Genevieve had to admit to herself. To be out without a chaperone—to think of the prospect of evading the Battleboro household defenses—to be on her first raid as a proper lady, her debut into true Society!

Beyond her own estate's perimeter, she felt as if antique corsetry had been loosed, so great was the sensation of sudden freedom. Why, she could go almost anywhere!

Her thieving dress, of black lawn with charcoal-grey sprigs and a delicate tracery of camouflaging circuits she had embroidered herself, blended marvelously with the shadows. She had not yet triggered the circuits, of course, here on the streets of High Town. She clung to corners and shadows, ducking behind the patrolling bobbies, and rested secure in the knowledge that no member of the constabulary would dream of hindering someone who was so clearly a young lady of good breeding going about her own business. All her ladylike tricks and gadgetry would prove their use soon, on the Battleboro estate.

Had she walked the whole way, she might have wasted half the night in merely reaching her destination, but no young lady would so betray her training as to take a hansom or a tram in burglary dress. Instead, Genevieve sprang lightly to the roof of a public tram while it idled in the station, and traveled in perfect comfort by lying flat atop it. When she dismounted with equal surreptitiousness in the Upmarket neighborhood, she left coin for her fare in the discreet receptacle every tram bore for such purposes. It would never do to leave a debt unpaid, after all.

Behind the shelter of the gatehouse, Genevieve made her preparations. With precise touches she triggered the circuitry in her hair, her dress, her shoes, and her pantaloons. If she had done her work well—and she must have, with the quantity of hours she had put into her trousseau!—these decorations would conceal her from cameras, muffle the sounds she made and blur the sight of her, and convince infrared detectors and motion-sensors that no one walked these grounds unpermitted. She kilted her dress up high about her waist, to allow herself freedom of motion, and gave herself a moment of pride to admire the black-on-charcoal of her thieving pantaloons. She really *had* done her best needlework with those, she felt. Then she drew her mask tight about her face, slipped on her fine dark gloves, and set about the delicate task of finding a permeable point in the electrically reinforced fence.

• • •

Some little time and a good deal of quiet exertion later, Genevieve perched atop the highest dormer window. Ladies did not pant, of course, but all the same she had to own that a few minutes' rest was a refreshing luxury. Even with the very latest in retractable wall crampons and a stealth-charged safety line, there was no respite to be found in the middle of scaling the redoubtably ancient wall of such a large mansion as this. Genevieve had been forced to complete her climb in an uninterrupted exercise, making certain all the while that she made no sound loud enough to escape her hair ribbons' sound-dampening field.

At length, having recovered her breath, Genevieve double-checked her gloves and pockets, and then swung noiselessly down to open the window sash.

Three steps into the hallway, she froze, her heart doubling its tempo. There had been a sound—yes, and now a figure emerged from one of the dark doorways. Genevieve held her breath, praying that camouflage circuits and immobility would preserve her from discovery, even though they stood nearly face to face. How ignoble, how socially damning, to be caught mid-raid, and on her debut, no less!

But no, she realized, as the other figure froze too in maidenly silence. A servant or inhabitant of the house would have shouted, peered closer, reached for a light, or at least asked uncertain questions. She could see, now, the feminine silhouette and the kilted-up burgling frock. This was another young woman, perhaps even another debutante, on the same mission as herself.

Genevieve closed her fist tight, making up her mind, and pressed the concealed button on her forefinger's knuckle that triggered the gloves' faint luminescence. With the gesture newly visible, she pointed to the roof, and made the hand-sign of invitation.

For an awful instant, she thought perhaps she'd read everything wrong. Then the other's gloves lit dimly, and she signed back, *yes*.

• • •

Soon they were perched on the gable, masks set aside, and bracing their slippers against the decorative chimney for greater comfort. Genevieve had politely taken the lead in climbing the roof, which meant that this was her first chance to study the other young lady. She did so unashamedly.

By the dim illumination of Pemberley Colony's simulated moon and the brighter sweep-lights of the estate, it took some study in any case to discern the other's features. She was perhaps Genevieve's age, with dark, tight curls in a fetching tousle and dark skin, with high, strong cheekbones that caught the little light available. But her face was familiar; what on earth was her name? Catherine, or Anne, or perhaps Catriona? Her only memory of the other girl was of vague impressions across a dance floor, and tidy but unremarkable steps.

Talk, hear, the other signed, and reached into her hair for a small barrette. She pressed down until something clicked, and set the device on the shingle between them. A sound-dampening field, Genevieve noted with approval and some sheepishness. She hadn't thought to bring one that would extend beyond her own person. But it spared them the need to communicate with thief-signs, which was laboriously slow for any matters beyond terse exigencies.

"I am Catherine Menzies," her new companion said, and with relief Genevieve recognized the name and its possessor. She was a lord's daughter, whose ancestors had come to Pemberley Colony half a generation after Genevieve's, and whose family was in consequence somewhat lower on the social scale. They comported themselves very respectably, however, and her father made four thousand platinum a year from shipping businesses according to *Important Personages,* several chapters of which Genevieve had been required to memorize before she was deemed ready to burgle. That was slightly more than the Tadmas could claim, though of course status was not a matter of mere funds, as Genevieve had been taught in the cradle. It was quite within the bounds of reasonable ambition—audacious, but not scandalously so—for Catherine to steal from a marquis in her debut year.

"I am Genevieve Tadma," she said, and they both murmured, "Charmed."

"Have you already stolen?" Genevieve asked, with what she suspected was unbecoming hope. If Catherine had, then it would be neither disobedience nor shame for Genevieve to cede the field to her and make an attempt elsewhere. She could equally have continued in her burglary without censure, but it signaled a fine humility to do otherwise, and suited Genevieve's plans nicely to acquire an unlooked-for excuse to abandon the Marquis to his history books.

Alas, Catherine shook her head. "I have not," she owned. "I was engaged in scouting for the object, but I have not yet laid hold to it."

"I have only a few minutes ago arrived," Genevieve admitted in her turn. "I had only begun my scouting when you came across me."

"Ah." Catherine's tone was perfectly correct, perfectly polite, and yet there was something—something *reserved* about it, Genevieve thought. She was masking something. The silence grew long. Genevieve fidgeted, and stilled herself too late. "To tell you the truth," she blurted, "I don't give a fig for the marquis."

"What! But he's so—" Catherine shut her mouth. "You must be mad for adventure," she offered instead, weakly. The motives that spurred thieves to burglary on other colonies, such as monetary greed or espionage, were out of the question for a well-bred lady. There was certainly no reason to burgle other than flirtation or an adventuresome spirit; if Genevieve wasn't here for one, she must be here for the other.

"He seems a nice enough fellow. Of course I don't *object* to the adventure. This is my first raid, you know, and he seems a perfectly adequate burglee. That razor wire was a bit of a challenge, wasn't it just! But—well—if you must know, he was Mama's choice."

"Ah," said Catherine again, in quite a different tone.

"You *do* see."

"Of course I do. My own mama was so pleased when I told her I wanted to steal a crystal bowl from the Marquis of Battleboro. All she seemed able to speak of was his income."

"*You* chose," repeated Genevieve, with some interest.

"Yes." Catherine's head ducked in the moonlight. Genevieve fancied she might even be blushing, but the dim lighting and Catherine's fashionable complexion made it impossible to tell. She sounded, though, as if she were choosing her words carefully. "I'd never steal from anyone of whom my parents didn't approve, of course, but—oh, he has such a lovely library! And he discourses on it beautifully, you know, not at all like these young bucks who can speak of nothing but phaeton shuttles and shooting."

"I suppose," Genevieve replied.

She meant it to sound politely interested, but some of her true sentiment must have leaked into her tone, for Catherine laughed merrily (albeit in an undertone appropriate to their surroundings—she *was* well-trained, if she kept such good habits even inside a sound-dampening field. Genevieve had been scolded a dozen times for the gaffe of relying too much on one piece of equipment.) "Oh dear, how terribly dutiful you sound! I know it's not the done thing. I'm sure phaeton shuttles are marvelous if one doesn't get flight-sick, but I do, you see."

"And I get heartily bored in a library," Genevieve admitted, laughing in her turn. "I would much rather have robbed the Yendarias, if you must know. They're only a very little older than us, so Mama believes them an altogether unambitious target. But Mr. Yendaria, young James, I mean, is so dashing! I suppose you'd find him dreadfully boring for all the reasons I don't. Mama wouldn't hear of it, though, and Papa *always* takes her part even when he pretends to be above it all, and here I am."

"Here you are," Catherine agreed, rather less merrily. "Well," she continued, audibly rallying, "perhaps you'll like him better once you've seen his treasure-rooms. Rumor doesn't exaggerate a bit."

"I don't think I shall, though I should enjoy the tour extremely." Genevieve hesitated. Her mama's instructions had been exacting, and if it was rebellion to disobey them, it was rebellion and foolishness both to boast of that plan. But it was nothing short of silly to flirt in burglary with a man she had no interest in, no matter his title and fortune—especially with a new friend sitting here, with her own genuine interest in the fellow! "But I think," she said, "I shall take care to leave a very *minimal* token for the marquis. He may send a servant to fetch his silver candlesticks, if he likes. It will give him time to pay a second call on *you*, and we shall all be the happier for that."

Even in the darkness, Genevieve could see Catherine's face light up. "Oh, do you truly mean it?"

"Truly," Genevieve told her firmly, and found she was smiling, too. "I don't care a fig for history books, and you do. If Mama believes he's slighting us with strictest courtesy, she can hardly reproach him for it."

"I'm sure he'll do the polite thing, if he believes you chose him out of high spirits," Catherine assured her earnestly. Happiness colored her every word, making Genevieve doubly glad of her decision. "It's perfectly proper to choose an estate like this, for a debutante who hasn't yet set her eye on a particular fellow, and he has no reason to know you have. It speaks well of your taste."

Genevieve laughed. "Do you think so? I hope he *is* scrupulously distant. Mama shan't be able to say a word against either of us."

"She shan't," Catherine agreed stoutly, then hesitated. Genevieve tried to stifle a frown. Surely Catherine didn't have an objection now? "I—oh, Genevieve, this is terribly forward of me, but you know, the Menzies family is some decades younger than the Yendarias."

"I do," Genevieve agreed, for lack of a better comment. What was the girl about? She couldn't mean to flirt with James, too, could she? That would be poor repayment of Genevieve's friendly gestures, and not at all in keeping with the Catherine whom Genevieve felt she already knew.

"So Mama would be happy to give me her blessing to rob them, if I asked, and if you liked—if you brought a spare handkerchief or something of the sort, my dear, I could leave that in place of mine. I'd steal something for a lark for myself, so Mama wouldn't suspect a thing, and I'd have my turn giving candlesticks to a serving man. Your mother couldn't complain if James showed up, could she? My girl Hannah would be happy to slip you whatever-it-was in the morning before the gentlemen's calling-hour."

It was a perfect solution—a perfect plan, and a noble offer. "Catherine! You can't mean it."

"Of course I can. Do say you brought tokens!"

"Naturally, I did—Mama thinks I'm here to burgle the marquis for his ten thousand a year, after all. Oh, Catherine, you *are* a gem."

Catherine beamed. Impulsively, Genevieve squeezed her new friend's hands—though lightly, mindful of the circuitry they both wore. "Come," said Catherine, and squeezed back. "Let's case the rooms together, shall we? And when we've absconded with our debuts, we'll ride the same bus-roof out, and you shall tell me all about your dashing James."

"I shall," Genevieve promised, "though you must stop me if I gush on so much that you regret the offer! You can repay me by telling me all about the wonders of the marquis and his library. I shall appreciate them for your sake, if not for my own."

~

Elizabeth Porter Birdsall spent much of her childhood pretending her way into Sherwood Forest and alien worlds, and transforming an overgrown backyard into a saga-worthy wilderness. Nowadays, she does much the same thing on paper. She divides the rest of her free time among teaching Scottish dance, studying languages and folklore and science as a hobby, and hanging out with other imaginative folk both online and off. A child of the American Midwest and Northeast (but mostly the rural Northeast), she lives in Boston with two excellent friends, two cats of very little competence, and a nigh-innumerable quantity of books.

CANTH

K. C. NORTON

The Canth moves slowly, somewhere beneath us—an amalgam of rib cages and jutting dorsal columns, parts of parts moving together to create a thing so intricate she is almost alive. Her six crablike legs tear channels in the coral as she passes, and her low belly scrapes the seabed. Her claws are hauled in, tucked along her bow; one long window wraps nearly to the back of her, only as tall as a human face, while the great rotating periscope of her single eye extends above.

I know this, because she is my ship, and my mother and I built her together. She is my home, my inheritance, and she has left me.

"Do you see it?" asks Anselmo Rios, peering over my shoulder at the console.

In front of me, the screen pings concentric circles, showing the dot of the Canth as she roams the reef below. I am unmoored—I am ruined—my ship has mutinied and spit me out. Now she trawls without me, guides herself by some inexplicable means in search of something I cannot guess. At night, I dream myself as Ahab, chasing the leviathan that is my submersible. A captain without a ship. What would my mother say?

"Yes," I whisper. "I see her."

• • •

For seventeen days we have followed the Canth on her journey. She is getting farther away—we are right on top of her, and yet she is always descending, following the slope of the ocean floor.

"We'll catch her," Rios assures me.

No, I want to say, *we won't catch her, she will climb into some deep crevice we cannot reach and bury herself alive,* but never do.

I am not a rich woman, and my debt to the crew of the *Jerónimo* is adding up. If I am not careful, I will spend the whole of my savings on recovering my ship. And what if we cannot recover her? I will have nothing to live on, to live in. I do not allow myself to consider this too carefully, not just yet.

In the morning I crawl from my bunk, I braid my hair, apply my *bindi*, button every button on my uniform from the bottom up. I still wear my captain's uniform, even on this foreign ship. I am not yet ready to admit defeat.

When I am finished, I stand at attention before the mirror. Below me, three hundred and eighty meters down, where the filtered light swims with plankton, I imagine that the Canth pauses for a moment to imitate the action.

Rios is waiting for me in the galley. Breakfast is one orange, two ladlefuls of hashed potatoes—from the supplies we took aboard at St. Ubes—and cod. I am well sick of cod. I was raised on fish, I have lived on fish, I will eat anything that comes from the sea, but cod I have had enough of.

The Portuguese, they say, have a cod recipe for every day of the year. I now believe this includes leap years, too.

"We are barely keeping up," says Rios, peeling his orange. "She moves fast, that little beast of yours."

I nod. "She is the fastest of her kind."

"Small," says the other captain. "A single-woman vessel. Did you build her yourself?" He has asked this question every day in one form or another. I have not answered, because the answer is too painful.

"We must be nearly out of cod," I say instead.

Rios grins at me. "There is always more to be caught."

I say, "I will leave as soon as I can."

He says, "The cod is not that bad."

"No," I say. "I am wasting too much of your time."

Rios looks around the tiny galley, then shrugs. He begins to divide his orange into sections. "We don't mind."

"You must have other duties."

"Nothing pressing," he says. "And you are in trouble. If we had lost our ship, you would help us." He puts a segment of orange in his mouth, indicating that the conversation is over.

He does not mean to hurt me, I know, but the way he says it… *If we had lost our ship*. As if I misplaced her. The truth is worse: The Canth abandoned me. She is my home, now reduced to a pinging point on a navigation console. Sometimes, I cannot help but think the Canth is not running *toward* something but *from* someone. From me. That the Canth is doing her utmost to escape me.

I eat every bite of cod. I do not believe in waste.

• • •

All day I watch the screen. Occasionally Rios' first mate looks up from his book to adjust the controls.

"She's getting fainter," I say.

The first mate—who I know only as La Boca—fiddles with the knobs. "We won't lose her, Miss Pearce. The captain promised."

He turns back to his book. The cover shows a busty young woman in air goggles and brown leather wrapped in the apparently sweaty arms of a shirtless Moor. I don't read Portuguese very well, but it seems to be titled *The Warm Damp of Miss Eulalia*.

"Hey, Miss Pearce, don't worry so," says La Boca. "We're here as long as you need us."

I want to thank him, though I'm not reassured, but I don't know what to call him, so I don't say anything at all.

There are only four of us on the ship: me, Rios, La Boca, and Isidore. Isidore cooks and cleans and navigates. La Boca steers and fishes when the cod runs low. Rios—well, I'm not sure what Rios does. Back on the Canth, where I am captain, I was responsible for everything. Now I sit still as a useless sponge and let the others drift around me like charitable angelfish. My very presence is a cry for help.

At lunchtime, I go down to the mess hall to bring up lunch for both of us. Lunch consists of chickpeas, rice, and cod.

Tonight, I tell myself, *I will give up if she is still moving tonight. I will ask them to take me to the coast and then...* I cannot think past this point. The Canth has been my life, my world, and now I am trapped abovesea with strangers. I am done asking for pity and for help. That's the only part I can control.

• • •

It is late afternoon when La Boca finally turns me out. "I will not lose her," he says. "Go occupy yourself."

"With what?" I ask.

Either La Boca is fed up with my constant presence, or he has reached a particularly engrossing scene in his book. "Find the Captain, help him feed the boilers. Help Isidore with dinner. Just go. You're driving me mad."

I go, resisting a childish urge to slam the door behind me. I imagine ripping the book from La Boca's hands and beating him with it. *That's my ship!* I would shout, but no, I'm going to give up on that ship anyway. Tonight. I swear I am. I stomp up to the deck, trying to take some of the anger out on my soles.

The Canth has a Perpetual Motion Engine; I have only to crank it once, and then it can go forever, until the Canth comes to a stop. The movement of each part charges the movement of the next—one leg steps forward, powering the series of cogs and coils in her underbelly in preparation for another step. It is a perfect design, compact, fuel-less, and light.

In the engine's core, the epicenter of the perpetual motion machine, is the heart of my mother, Coelacanth Pearce, who—so long as I am here to crank that engine—will never truly die, nor cease to love me. But I cannot reach her now.

The *Jerónimo* is larger and boasts a coal-fueled combustion engine. When I step out on deck, I can see a plume of black smoke rising from the stern. It is strange, to stand on the open while the waves spit spume at me, where my view is full of wheeling white seabirds instead of spiny scabbardfish and mottled eels. The sea is so flat, nothing at all like the slopes beneath it. The sky is so vast; it makes me feel minute and slightly nauseous. I can see one ship on the horizon, a few miles away, but that is all.

Rios is at the stern, shoveling coal. He's sweaty and soot-smeared. He's singing in a dialect that I don't know, but I can tell—from the way his voice drops into a smooth baritone before darting up to a soprano trill—that it is a love song. I have a stupid, angry urge to grab onto him and cry, or else shove him overboard and watch him drown. There has never been a time in my whole life that I felt so terrifically helpless as I feel now.

When Rios sees me, he drops his shovel and grins, but all the while the music keeps pouring out of him. He sweeps toward me, snatches up my hand, perhaps expecting me to pull away. I don't. Instead, I let him drag me into his parody of a Chotiça, stumbling woodenly in his wake. It's hard to be angry, or even to think of the Canth, in the face of his mulish good mood.

I am not much of a dancer, not with a partner. At home, in India, I learned another kind of dance, one composed of isolated movements: a jut of the hip, a roll of the shoulder, the toss of my hair, and subtle gestures of my hands. Rios is sloppy, full of feeling rather than precision. I'm not in the mood, but to push him away would be churlish. Besides, he is a good lead.

I am not much of a follow.

All at once he stops, stepping away from me. "Are you never happy, Captain?"

I look up at the birds, down at the deck, anywhere but at him. "On my ship, yes. Always."

Worry chases annoyance across his face. I am ready to tell him what I have decided—but the smoke drops away and the deck shudders under us and the clouds don't move so quickly through the sky.

"What in Hell?" demands Rios, opening one of the copper tubes that lead down into the ship. "Why are we stopping?"

La Boca's voice rumbles up from the belly of the *Jerónimo*. "Because she has stopped, sir. Miss Pearce's ship."

Rios throws his sooty hands in the air, stomps the heels of his boots on deck flamenco-style. He lets forth a baritone cry of delight. "You see! You see!

I knew we'd find her!"

I let him grab my hands and spin me in a circle; I let the grin engulf my face, I am so relieved. "My name is Captain Pearce," I call into the piping. "And don't forget it."

• • •

The *Jerónimo* boasts only two sets of diving gear. Isidore explains, "Usually, the Captain and I are the only ones that use them. Heitor stays aboard, makes sure we are safe, keeps the ship on course, watches out for us."

"Heitor?" I ask. I am struggling with the arms of the suit.

Isidore smiles. "My Heitor. La Boca."

"You're married?"

"Ugh, no!" Isidore pretends to gag. "He is my... boyfriend. Not the kind of man you want to marry."

"What kind of man is he?" I ask, fastening the suit below my chin.

Isidore winks.

Anselmo Rios does not struggle with the suit the same way I do; it's one he's worn before. So far from the ocean floor, this crew must have more use for dive suits than I do on the Canth—though what for, I'm not exactly sure. You don't need a suit to fish for cod.

"Ready, ready?" he asks. He is happy as a child, still dancing even in the metal and rubber armor of his dive suit.

I heft my helmet, frowning at the thin hose that will be my only link to air. "When you are, Captain."

We salute each other. Unlike in his dancing, Rios' salute is militarily precise.

• • •

The moment I'm submerged, I feel as if I have come home.

The helmet is difficult, clunky—and, instead of the clever narrow window in the side of the Canth, it boasts twenty-five circular eyes through which, if I hold my head just right, I can look out onto the dark expanse of the seabed.

This part of the reef is not deep, and the light filtering down from above makes it easy enough to see. It looks like the reef is an island pushing up out of the much deeper ocean bed, brilliant with coral. Through the small windows in my helmet I can make out the frown of a fat *bonito*, the ruddy spikes of a flying gurnard, flashing silver breams, and the grey-green freckles of live cod. I feel as merry as Captain Rios did: The Canth is close, and soon I will be home.

Rios taps my shoulder. He is pointing down at the seabed with his gloved hand; I wish she could see his expression.

At first I do not understand what he wants me to see. There are nothing but rocks below us. Ah, but they are more than rocks—I sputter in amazement—they are building stones. Now that I'm really looking, I can make out a square foundation, and an archway.

"The Lost City?" I ask, but of course he cannot hear me, and even if he could, he wouldn't know what I mean.

We sink lower as Isidore lets out the ropes that tether us to the *Jerónimo*. It is painfully slow going, but it gives me time to examine the ruins beneath us.

It is not just one building overgrown with *posidonia* and ringed by schools of alewives. It is a whole dead city.

My throat clenches. It's only a story, isn't it? Still, it's a story I remember from my childhood: the Lost City. Sea levels rise, cities disappear beneath the waves. And suddenly I'm thinking of Pompeii, that old Italian city whose dig reports my mother pored over. The German man, too, searching for evidence of the Trojan War and actually finding it. Is it possible, then? Is this lost city the one that she, and my father, had been hoping to find?

She brought me here. Led me here. Showed me the way.

I startle as a scowling John Dory swims just in front of me; if it weren't for the helmet, I would be able to feel its wake against my nose. I watch it go, and while my eyes are still out of focus, I glimpse my ship.

Her race across the ocean floor had ceased. Now she lies on the ocean floor, sheltered by a sloping wall, limbs tucked tidily beneath her as if sleeping. Waiting for me.

There is a sudden jerk on the line, and the winch begins to haul us back up. I flail, finding myself suddenly off-balance. Our ascent is swift. My inner ears begin to burn with the relentless change in pressure. The Canth disappears from my view.

• • •

It is not Isidore's hands that haul us from the water; there are three newcomers on the boat, two to drag Rios and me onto the deck, one to stand over Isidore and point the gun. One of the unarmed men wrestles me to the deck, prying off my helmet. The other does the same to Rios, who swears creatively.

The stranger holding the gun, a young man with sandy hair—no more Portuguese than I am—nods at me. "Hello, Miss Pearce."

I give him a cold stare, trying to gain some kind of control over the situation. "You are a stranger to me, sir."

"But I know you," he says, "You are Aditi Pearce. Michael's daughter."

On the heels of my recent discovery—the city below us, and the Canth within—this greeting is both overwhelming and entirely expected. "Yes," I say. "I am."

"But what are you doing," the young man asks—he has a slight Danish accent, "in the company of pirates?"

"Pirates?" I ask. I catch a look of guilt on Isidore's face. "Pirates?" Rios tilts his chin into the air and does not meet my eye. I shove at my captor; he backs away, looking to the Dane for confirmation. "These people," I say evenly, getting to my feet and directing a frosty glance at each of our captors in turn, "are under my employ, helping me recover my ship."

Rios makes a face at me. I ignore him.

"And where is your ship?" demands the Dane.

I point between my feet. "Below," I say, "in the dead city, where she led me."

The Dane lowers his gun, reaches out to shake my hand. "My name is Japetus Fixe. I work with your father."

• • •

We find La Boca folded into a chest in the kitchen. "Have they gone?" he asks. "I was going to sneak out under cover of darkness and see to them." This might well be a coward's bragging, but he is holding a large fishing knife in each large hand. I believe that this may well have been his intent.

"Get out of there," snaps Rios. "You are crushing the potatoes."

Isidore helps him; La Boca's legs appear to have gone numb. "We're not really pirates," Isidore explains. "We are…"

"Venture capitalists," grunts La Boca.

"Entrepreneurs," mutters Rios.

I suggest, "Hired help." My tone is so dry it makes the salt cod seem damp by comparison.

"Our work is only illegal," says Isidore, "when we are hired to do illegal things. Which isn't all of the time."

"Just now, for instance, we are looking for your clever ship," says La Boca.

Isidore nods. "Exactly. Not piratical in the slightest."

I sigh. "No," I tell La Boca, "they are not gone. Their ship is pulled alongside ours. Yours." I shake my head and sink into one of the kitchen chairs. "They want to come with me, to see the Lost City."

"And retrieve the Canth," reminds Rios.

I bite my lip. This is, almost certainly, not what the men on the other ship have in mind. They might know my father, or at least of my father, but they are not here to help me.

Rios, Isidore, La Boca—I trusted them to help me, because I was paying them to do so. Fixe is another matter.

"Who are they?" asks Isidore.

I rub my eyes. "Cryptozoologists."

La Boca frowns. "Monster hunters?"

"It's more complicated than that." When they keep staring at me, I continue. "My father was one of them. Some of these people, they get an itch under their skin, they start looking for something and it takes over their lives." I don't mention my mother.

"I don't understand," says Rios, leaning toward me. "Are they looking for the dead city? Or for something in it?"

"My father believed that there was a city—a Lost City, perhaps this one—swallowed by the waves. He thought that its inhabitants became part fish and managed to survive."

La Boca gives me a skeptical look. "He was hunting mermaids?"

"Maybe he was mad," I say. "I won't deny it. But these men claim to know him, and so they must be looking for the city, too."

"Then perhaps they are also mad," suggests Rios.

• • •

Having combed my hair back into its neat braid, straightened my uniform, and pulled one of my piratical companions out of a potato bin, I head up on deck. One of the sailors on Fixe's ship salutes me and helps me across to the larger ship. It is much larger than the *Jerónimo*, and rides much higher in the water.

"Greetings, Miss Pearce," says the sailor, and does not introduce himself. He leads me to the captain's cabin.

The cabin is more like a stateroom, with a mahogany table and gilt etchings of rare fish. The Dane is sitting at the desk, scribbling in a thick log. He closes it when we enter—I wonder if the book is just for show. "Come in," says Fixe, closing the door after me so that we are alone. The larger ship moves less with the waves—the stillness gives me a kind of reverse seasickness.

I turn toward this other captain. It occurs to me that three captains are too many for such a little patch of ocean. "You said that you know my father."

Fixe grins. "You look just as he described you."

"Why would he describe me to you?"

"So that we would know you when we found you."

"You were looking for me?"

Japetus Fixe holds up his hands. "No need to be so spiny, Miss Pearce. We were following you."

I sink into one of the straightbacked chairs and cross my ankles. "How reassuring."

Fixe squints. "At your father's request! He was sure that your clever machine would find its way to the dead city, and that you would follow at all cost."

A little muscle in my jaw jumps as I realize what he is saying. "You cranked her engine, my—the Canth's. You made her leave me."

"And now," says Fixe, "you have her back, we have the city, and soon we shall have the Monk."

I hold up one hand. "The Monk?"

"The Sea Monk," says Fixe. "The colossal merman. The reason we're all here." He points to one of the etchings; it shows a dramatic and improbable creature, with a man's head and a Monk's garb, and a hundred boneless legs.

I stare, a little taken in by the unsettling image. "And how will you capture your merman?"

Fixe shrugs. "We cannot take him alive, and we cannot allow him to decay on our return journey. It will be the harpoon for him, Miss Pearce, and then we shall pack him in salt. Then it's home to your father, where at last he will have his prize."

"The Portuguese may not be happy to find you poaching legends along their coastline."

"They won't mind terribly, when I bring them a few local pirates."

I feel the sickles of my fingernails cut at my palms. "That man and woman," I am careful not to mention La Boca, not to give Japetus Fixe an inch, "are under my employ."

"No longer. You have found your ship, Miss Pearce. The moment it is retrieved, your contract with these miscreants comes to an end." He is trying to sound fatherly, evidently failing to grasp my feelings on the subject. "Surely you see where your duties lie."

After a pause, I nod. "I do, Mr. Fixe."

• • •

Sometimes I wish to be the kind of girl who could fall in love with Anselmo Rios. Over dinner I watch him, thinking how much easier it would be to dance with him on the upper decks, shovel coal into the engine, eat salt cod, and forget the Canth and my father and the city. We could set sail under the cover of darkness... but Fixe would find us, and the crew of the Jerónimo would be imprisoned, and I would never get my ship back. As it is, I have the claustrophobic impression that after tonight, I will never again set foot on the Jerónimo.

Now that I know about Isidore and La Boca—Heitor—I see that they are always touching, always flirting, always aware of each other. I don't want Fixe to tie them up, to take them away from each other. I want them to be happy. They matter to me. I wonder when that happened.

"You are not eating," says Rios. "The cod must be very bad tonight."

I give him a smile that feels butter-thin. "Actually, I was enjoying it."

• • •

I know three things:

Fixe, at the suggestion of my father, stole my ship, and I am going to get her back. Michael Pearce has tried to break my mother's heart. He has tried to capture it. In spite of this, she is an infinite engine, and she is waiting for me.

If the Canth fled this far under her own power, then the Sea Monk, Fixe's merman, must be here. I am not going to let him kill it; my mother did not want that, and neither do I.

And last, that my father is never going to see his abulia, the creature which he chose to love more than he loved me. But I will.

• • •

When I leave my room that night, I am careful to tiptoe. Even so, it is a small ship, and I am not entirely surprised when another door opens and a quiet figure slips out.

I am surprised to realize that it's La Boca.

He takes my elbow and leads me out to the deck. The diving suit is there already, hidden beneath a frayed tarp. He is church-silent as he puts it on me, piece by piece. With him kneeling before me, helping me into the boots, I feel like Joan of Arc going into battle.

As I am wiggling my arms into place, La Boca suddenly says, "'*I opened my heart to you, and you skimmed one hand over the wax forest of my ventricles and flicked one finger to find out what would bruise*.'"

I gape at him. What a line!

La Boca stands, reaching into the pocket of his trousers. He has brought his copy of *The Warm Damp of Miss Eulalia*. "I know you love your ship, Miss Pearce. I hope you are kind to one another."

Not knowing what to say, I take the book without a word. I tuck it into the front of my diving suit so that it rests against my chest.

La Boca nods, then helps me wrestle the helmet into place. When it is firmly attached, he salutes me. His voice is tinny through the helmet. "Be careful, Captain."

• • •

This descent is speedier, less breathtaking. In the dark water it is almost impossible to see. He might be lowering me into anything; there might be merfolk in the water all around me and I'd never know.

I remind myself that the Canth did not abandon me. She was looking for something, and having found what she sought, my ship may love me yet.

"Please," I breathe, "please, please... "

When the Canth lights up all her windows, her headlights, her lures, it sounds to me as though a whole orchestra has struck up. That sound, I reason, must be coming from my heart.

• • •

Back within my ship, after so many weeks, the world feels righted. As I shuck the suit off, I realize that I was wrong: the Canth is my armor, and my weapon. When I crank the engine—at last, after what seems like a hundred years—the ship rumbles to life, just as she has always done, awaiting my instructions.

"We go up," I say. My fingers on the switchboard translate my words into a language my ship can understand, and a moment later the lower propellers kick on. We rise up easy as breathing.

Through that familiar, narrow window I can see the underbelly of Japetus Fixe's ship, soft wood. The Canth has claws strong enough to shear iron bars; a wooden hull is nothing to her. As the ship begins to tilt above us, I imagine Fixe's stateroom flooding, his mahogany table home to eels and whelks, his ship a skeleton at the center of the dead city.

Anselmo Rios is not a monster—he will take Fixe and his crew aboard, so long as Fixe swears to leave them be. There are supplies enough aboard the Jerónimo to get them all back to St. Ubes. Meanwhile, Fixe's harpoon will lie at the bottom of the ocean, and whatever thing the Canth was seeking will be safe.

We hover a dozen meters down, shining our lights up to illuminate the sailors until, one by one, they are dragged to the side of the Jerónimo and helped aboard. It's easier, knowing that there has been no loss of life. Fixe must guess that the light is coming from me, and if it wounds his pride, so much the better. I have taken his ship, just as he once sought to take mine.

Of a sudden the Canth turns away so that we are facing the lower reaches of the ocean. I lift my hands from the controls: She has something to show me, I know that now.

• • •

I nap, I sort the supplies, I tuck the borrowed suit into an empty crate and find space for the tins that once filled the crate.

The air is getting thin—we have gone deeper than ever before, and it is taxing the Canth's systems. After a while I go back to my chair, and just sit, peering out into a darkness where the only visible shapes are jutting rocks and luminescent jellies.

The Canth, once upon a time, was nothing but a ship. My mother's heart powered her, but nothing more. This can no longer be the case because I swear she *sees* the Monk at the same moment I do.

It is nothing like that ugly etching. The creature is easily twice the length of the *Jerónimo*. Its body is long, barrel-thick, with round eyes the size of a dinner plate. Nearly a dozen pale arms flutter as it moves past us, the silver of its flesh gleaming in the headlights of the Canth.

"The Monk?" I ask. But there can be no doubt that this is the thing my father sought. The thought of Fixe's harpoon buried in that soft skin—it gives me pang as though my own flesh were pierced. I would sink his ship a hundred times to save this monster's life.

"Never again," I tell the Canth. "We must pretend we never saw it. If they knew it was here… was real…"

As if she understands me, the Canth spins in the water. I hurry to the back of the ship, pressing my face against the glass to watch the Monk in the rear lights until it is lost to view.

• • •

When the *Jerónimo* next docks at St. Ubes, its crew will find a crate waiting for them. In that crate, Rios will find his borrowed suit. Isidore will find a small handgun—let Fixe try to tie her up again, and find out what happens. La Boca will find a new copy of a book entitled, so far as I can tell, *The Second Coming of Miss Eulalia*. My handwriting on the inside cover reads: *I can see that you love her. I hope you will be kind to one another.*

The hold is full of oranges and rice and chickpeas and chorizo and salt cod, which I have discovered I cannot do without.

Let the Canth choose our course. I wonder if she will seek my father. I wonder what I will say to him if we take that road.

The Monk, rippling through some dark and frigid thermocline, is speaking to my dear machine. What other whispered voices does she hear? Perhaps someday she will teach me to sound them out. Perhaps someday my heart will learn which monsters to avoid—and which to seek for myself.

~

K. C. Norton was raised in the wilds of Pennsylvania. She is currently earning an MFA in Children's and Young Adult Writing—she plans to subvert a good many things for the reading pleasure of the young. Norton has been a Classicist, an anthropologist, a mixologist, and a tourist by turns. She currently lives with a micro-cow, and the two of them will not rest until Valente, Carriger, and Priest are household names. Her work can be found in venues such *Orson Scott Card's Intergalactic Medicine Show*, *Writers of the Future Volume 30*, and *Crossed Genres Magazine*. Tweet her, should the fancy strike you, @KC_Norton.

LIKE DAUGHTER

TANANARIVE DUE

Art by Elizabeth Leggett

I got the call in the middle of the week, when I came wheezing home from my uphill late-afternoon run. I didn't recognize the voice on my computer's answer-phone at first, although I thought it sounded like my best friend, Denise. There was no video feed, only the recording, and the words were so improbable they only confused me more: "Sean's gone. Come up here and get Neecy. Take her. I can't stand to look at her."

Her words rolled like scattered marbles in my head.

I had just talked to Denise a week before, when she called from Chicago to tell me her family might be coming to San Francisco to visit me that winter, when Neecy was out of school for Christmas vacation.

151

We giggled on the phone as if we were planning a sleepover, the way we used to when we were kids. Denise's daughter, Neecy, is my godchild. I hadn't seen her since she was two, which was a raging shame and hard for me to believe when I counted back the years in my mind, but it was true. I'd always made excuses, saying I had too much traveling and too many demands as a documentary film producer, where life is always projected two and three years into the future, leaving little space for here and now.

But that wasn't the reason I hadn't seen my godchild in four years. We both knew why.

I played the message again, listening for cadences and tones that would remind me of Denise, and it was like standing on the curb watching someone I knew get hit by a car. Something had stripped Denise's voice bare. So that meant her husband, Sean, must really be gone, I realized. And Denise wanted to send her daughter away.

"I can't stand to look at her," the voice on the message was saying again.

I went to my kitchen sink, in the direct path of the biting breeze from my half-open window, and I was shaking. My mind had frozen shut, sealing my thoughts out of reach. I turned on the faucet and listened to the water pummel my aluminum basin, then I captured some of the lukewarm stream in my palms to splash my face. As the water dripped from my chin, I cupped my hands again and drank, and I could taste the traces of salty perspiration I'd rubbed from my skin, tasting myself. My anger and sadness were tugging on my stomach. I stood at that window and cursed as if what I was feeling had a shape and was standing in the room with me.

I think I'd started to believe I might have been wrong about the whole thing. That was another reason I'd kept some distance from Denise; I hadn't wanted to be there to poke holes in what she was trying to do, to cast doubts with the slightest glance. That's something only a mother or a lifelong friend can do, and I might as well have been both to Denise despite our identical ages. I'd thought maybe if I only left her alone, she could build everything she wanted inside that Victorian brownstone in Lincoln Park. The husband, the child, all of it. Her life could trot on happily ever after, just the way she'd planned.

But that's a lie, too. I'd always known I was right. I had been dreading that call all along, since the beginning. And once it finally came, I wondered what the hell had taken so long. You know how Denise's voice really sounded on my answering machine that day? As if she'd wrapped herself up in that recorder and died.

"Paige, promise me you'll look out for Neecy, hear?" Mama used to tell me. I couldn't have known then what a burden that would be, having to watch over someone. But I took my role seriously. Mama said Neecy needed me, so

I was going to be her guardian. Just a tiny little bit, I couldn't completely be a kid after that.

Mama never said exactly why my new best friend at Mae Jemison Elementary School needed guarding, but she didn't have to. I had my own eyes. Even when Neecy didn't say anything, I noticed the bruises on her forearms and calves, and even on Neecy's mother's neck once, which was the real shocker. I recognized the sweet, sharp smell on Neecy's mother's breath when I walked to Neecy's house after school. Her mother smiled at me so sweetly, just like that white lady Mrs. Brady on reruns of *The Brady Bunch* my mother made me watch, because she used to watch it when she was my age and she thought it was more appropriate than the "trash" on the children's channels when I was a kid. That smile wasn't a real smile; it was a smile to hide behind.

I knew things Mama didn't know, in fact. When Neecy and I were nine, we already had secrets that made us feel much older; and not in the way that most kids want to feel older, but in the uninvited way that only made us want to sit by ourselves in the playground watching the other children play, since we were no longer quite in touch with our spirit of running and jumping. The biggest secret, the worst, was about Neecy's Uncle Lonnie, who was twenty-two, and what he had forced Neecy to do with him all summer during the times her parents weren't home. Neecy finally had to see a doctor because the itching got so bad. She'd been *bleeding* from itching between her legs, she'd confided to me. This secret filled me with such horror that I later developed a dread of my own period because I associated the blood with Neecy's itching. Even though the doctor asked Neecy all sorts of questions about how she could have such a condition, which had a name Neecy never uttered out loud, Neecy's mother never asked at all.

So, yes, I understood why Neecy needed looking after. No one else was doing it.

What I didn't understand, as a child, was how Neecy could say she hated her father for hitting her and her mother, but then she'd be so sad during the months when he left, always wondering when he would decide to come home. And how Neecy could be so much smarter than I was—the best reader, speller, and multiplier in the entire fourth grade—and still manage to get so many F's because she just wouldn't sit still and do her homework. And the thing that puzzled me most of all was why, as cute as Neecy was, she seemed to be ashamed to show her face to anyone unless she was going to bed with a boy, which was the only time she ever seemed to think she was beautiful. She had to go to the doctor to get abortion pills three times before she graduated from high school.

Maybe it was the secret-sharing, the telling, that kept our friendship so solid, so fervent. Besides, despite everything, there were times I thought Neecy was the only girl my age who had any sense, who enjoyed reciting poems and acting out scenes as much as I did. Neecy never did join the drama club like I did, claiming she was too shy, but we spent hours writing and performing plays of our own behind my closed bedroom door, exercises we treated with so much imagination and studiousness that no one would ever guess we were our only audience.

"I wish I had a house like yours," Neecy used to say, trying on my clothes while she stood admiring herself in my closet mirror, my twin.

By fall, the clothes would be hers, because in the summer Mama always packed my clothes for Neecy in a bundle. For my *other little girl,* she'd say. And beforehand Neecy would constantly warn me, "Don't you mess up that dress," or "Be careful before you rip that!" because she already felt proprietary.

"Oh, my house isn't so special," I used to tell Neecy. But that was the biggest lie of all.

In the years afterward, as Neecy dragged a parade of crises to my doorstep, like a cat with writhing rodents in her teeth—men, money, jobs; *everything* was a problem for Neecy—I often asked myself what forces had separated us so young, dictating that I had grown up in my house and Neecy had grown up in the other. She'd lived right across the street from my family, but our lives may as well have been separated by the Red Sea.

Was it only an *accident* that my own father never hit me, never stayed away from home for even a night, and almost never came from work without hugging me and telling me I was his Smart Little Baby-Doll?

And that Mama never would have tolerated any other kind of man? Was it pure accident that *I'd* had no Uncle Lonnie to make me itch until I bled with a disease the doctor had said little girls shouldn't have?

"Girl, you're so lucky," Neecy told me once when I was in college and she'd already been working for three years as a clerk at the U Save Drugstore. She'd sworn she wasn't interested in college, but at that instant her tone had been so rueful, so envy-soaked, that we could have been children again, writing fantastic scripts for ourselves about encounters with TV stars and space aliens behind my closed bedroom door, both of us trying to forget what was waiting for Neecy at home. "In my next life, I'm coming back *you* for sure."

If only Neecy had been my real-life sister, not just a pretend one, I always thought. If only things had been different for her from the time she was born.

I called Denise a half hour after I got her message. She sounded a little better, but not much. Whether it was because she'd gathered some composure or swallowed a shot or two of liquor, this time her voice was the one I've always known: hanging low, always threatening to melt into a defeated laugh. She kept her face screen black, refusing to let me see her. "It's all a mess. This place looks like it was robbed," she said. "He took everything. His suits. His music. His favorite books, you know, those Russian writers, Dostoyevsky and Nabokov, or whatever-the-fuck? Only reason I know he was ever here is because of the hairs in the bathroom sink. He *shaved* first. He stood in there looking at his sorry face in the mirror after he'd loaded it all up, and he …" For the first time, her voice cracked. "He left…me. And her. He left."

I couldn't say anything against Sean. What did she expect? The poor man had tried, but from the time they met, it had all been as arranged as a royal Chinese marriage. How could anyone live in that house and breathe under the weight of Denise's expectations? Since I couldn't invent any condolences, I didn't say anything.

"You need to take Neecy." Denise filled the silence.

Hearing her say it so coldly, my words roiled beneath my tongue, constricting my throat. I could barely sound civil. "The first time you told me about doing this…I said to think about what it would mean. That it couldn't be undone. Didn't I, Neecy?"

"Don't call me Neecy." Her words were icy, bitter. "Don't you know better?"

"What happens now? She's your daughter, and she's only six. Think of—"

"Just come get her. If not, I don't…I don't know what I'll do."

Then she hung up on me, leaving my melodramatic imagination to wonder what she'd meant by that remark, if she was just feeling desperate or if she was holding a butcher knife or a gun in her hand when she said it. Maybe that was why she'd blacked herself out, I thought.

I was crying like a six-year-old myself while my cab sped toward the airport. I saw the driver's wondering eyes gaze at me occasionally in his rearview mirror, and I couldn't tell if he was sympathetic or just annoyed. I booked myself on an eight-forty flight with a seat in first class on one of the S-grade planes that could get me there in forty minutes. Airbuses, I call them. At least in first class I'd have time for a glass or two of wine. I convinced the woman at the ticket counter to give me the coach price because, for the first time in all my years of flying, I lied and said I was going to a funeral. My sister's, I told her, tears still smarting on my face.

If you could even call that a lie.

Three more months, just ninety days, and it never would have happened. If Denise had waited only a few months, if she'd thought it through the way I begged her when she first laid out the details of her plan, the procedure would not have been legal. The Supreme Court's decision came down before little Neecy was even born, after only a couple hundred volunteers paid the astronomical fee to take part in the copycat babies program. To this day, I still have no idea where Denise got the money. She never told me, and I got tired of asking.

But she got it somehow, somewhere, along with two hundred thirty others. There were a few outright nutcases, of course, lobbying to try to use DNA samples to bring back Thomas Jefferson and Martin Luther King; I never thought that would prove anything except that those men were only human and could be as unremarkable as the rest of us. But mostly the applicants were just families with something left undone, I suppose. Even though I never agreed with Denise's reasons, at least I had some idea of what she hoped to accomplish. The others, I wasn't sure. Was it pure vanity? Novelty? Nostalgia? I still don't understand.

In the end, I'm not sure how many copycat babies were born. I read somewhere that some of the mothers honored the Supreme Court's ban and were persuaded to abort. Of course, they might have been coerced or paid off by one of the extremist groups terrified of a crop of so-called "soulless" children. But none of that would have swayed Denise, anyway. For all I know, little Neecy might have been the very last one born.

It was three months too late, but I was moved by the understated eloquence of the high court's decision when it was announced on the News & Justice satellite: *Granted, what some might call a "soul" is merely an individual's biological imprint, every bit as accidental as it is unique. In the course of accident, we are all born once, and we die but once. And no matter how ambiguous the relationship between science and chance, humankind cannot assign itself to the task of re-creating souls.*

I'm not even sure I believe in souls, not really. But I wished I'd had those words for Denise when it still mattered.

She actually had the whole thing charted out. We were having lunch at a Loop pizzeria the day Denise told me what she wanted to do. She spread out a group of elaborate charts; one was marked HOME, one FATHER, one SCHOOL, all in her too-neat artist's script. The whole time she showed me, her hands were shaking as if they were trying to fly away from her. I'd never seen anyone shake like that until then, watching Denise's fingers bounce like rubber with so much excitement and fervor. The shaking scared me more than her plans and charts.

"Neecy, please wait," I told her.

"If I wait, I might change my mind," Denise said, as if this were a logical argument for going forward rather than just the opposite. She still hadn't learned that *doubt* was a signal to stop and think, not to plow ahead with her eyes covered, bracing for a crash.

But that was just Denise. That's just the way she is. Maybe that's who she is.

Denise's living room was so pristine when I arrived, it was hard to believe it had witnessed a trauma. I noticed the empty shelves on the music rack and the spaces where two picture frames had been removed from their hooks on the wall; but the wooden floors gleamed, the walls were scrubbed white, and I could smell fresh lilac that might be artificial or real, couldn't tell which. Denise's house reminded me of the sitting room of the bed and breakfast I stayed in overnight during my last trip to London, simultaneously welcoming and wholly artificial. A perfect movie set, hurriedly dusted and freshened as soon as visitors were gone.

Denise looked like a vagrant in her own home. As soon as I got there, I knew why she hadn't wanted me to see her on the phone; she was half dressed in a torn T-shirt, her hair wasn't combed, and the skin beneath her eyes looked so discolored that I had to wonder, for a moment, if Sean might have been hitting her. It wouldn't be the first time she'd been in an abusive relationship. But then I stared into the deep mud of my friend's irises before she shuffled away from me, and I knew better. No, she wasn't being beaten; she wouldn't have tolerated that with Neecy in the house. Instead, my friend was probably having a nervous breakdown.

"Did he say why he left?" I asked gently, stalling. I didn't see little Neecy anywhere, and I didn't want to ask about her yet. I wished I didn't have to see her at all.

Answering with a grunt rather than spoken words, Denise flung her arm toward the polished rosewood dining room table. There, I saw a single piece of paper laid in the center, a typewritten note. As sterile as everything else. In the shining wood, I could also see my own reflection standing over it.

"Haven't you read it?" I asked her.

"Neecy's in the back," Denise said, as if in response.

"Shhh. Just a second. Let's at least read what the man said." My heart had just somersaulted, and then I knew how much I didn't want to be there at all. I didn't want to think about that child. I picked a random point midway through the note and began reading aloud in the tone I might have used for a eulogy: "...You squeeze so hard, it chokes me. You're looking for more than a father for her, more than a home. It isn't natural, between you and her—"

"Stop *it*," Denise hissed. She sank down to the sofa, tunneling beneath a blanket and pulling it up to her chin.

I sighed. I could have written that note myself. Poor Sean. I walked to the sofa and sat beside my friend. My hand felt leaden as I rested it on the blanket where I believed Denise's shoulder must be. "So you two fought about it. You never told me that," I said.

"There's a lot I didn't tell you," Denise said, and I felt her shivering beneath the blanket. "He didn't understand. Never. I thought he'd come around. I thought—"

"You could change him?"

"Shut up," Denise said, sounding more weary than angry.

Yes, I felt weary, too. I'd had this conversation with Denise, or similar ones, countless times before. Denise had met Sean through a video personal on the Internet where all she said was, "I want a good husband and father. Let's make a home." Sean was a nice enough guy, but I had known their marriage was based more on practical considerations than commitment. They both wanted a family. They both had pieces missing and were tired of failing. Neither of them had learned, after two divorces, that people can't be applied to wounds like gauze.

And, of course, then there was little Neecy. What was the poor guy supposed to do?

"She's in her room. I already packed her things. Please take her, Paige. Take her." Denise was whimpering by now.

I brushed a dead-looking clump of hair from Denise's face. Denise's eyes, those unseeing eyes, would be impossible to reach. But I tried anyway, in hopes of saving all of us. "This is crazy. Take her where? What am I going to do with a kid?"

"You promised."

Okay, Mama. I *will*.

"What?"

"You promised. At the church. At the christening. You're her godmother. If anything happened to me, you said you would."

I thought of the beautiful baby girl, a goddess dressed in white, her soft black curls crowned with lace—gurgling, happy, and agreeable despite the tedium of the long ceremony. Holding her child, Denise had been glowing in a way she had not at her wedding, as if she'd just discovered her entire reason for living.

Tears found my eyes for the first time since I'd arrived. "Denise, what's this going to mean to her?"

"I don't know. I don't...care," Denise said, her voice shattered until she sounded like a mute struggling to form words. "Look at me. I can't stand to be near her. I vomit every time I look at her. It's all ruined. Everything. Oh, God—" She nearly sobbed, but there was only silence from her open mouth. "I can't. Not again. No more. Take her, Paige."

I saw a movement in my peripheral vision, and I glanced toward the hallway in time to see a shadow disappear from the wall. My God, I realized, the kid must have been standing where she could hear every hurtful word. I knew I had to get Neecy out of the house, at least for now. Denise was right. She was not fit, at this moment, to be a mother. Anything was better than leaving

Neecy here, even getting her to a hotel. Maybe just for a day or two.

I couldn't take care of both of them now. I had to choose the child.

"Neecy?" The bedroom door was open only a crack, and I pressed my palm against it to nudge it open. "Sweetheart, are you in here?"

What struck me first was the books. Shelves filled with the colorful spines of children's books reached the ceiling of the crowded room, so high that even an adult would need a stepladder. Every other space was occupied by so many toys—costumed dolls, clowns, stuffed animals—that I thought of the time my parents took me to F.A.O. Schwarz when I was a kid, the way every square foot was filled with a different kind of magic.

The bed was piled high with dresses. There must have been dozens of them, many of them formal, old-fashioned tea dresses. They were the kind of dresses mothers hated to wear when they were young, and yet love to adorn their little girls with; made of stiff, uncomfortable fabrics and bright, precious colors. Somewhere beneath that heaping pile of clothes, I saw a suitcase yawning open, struggling uselessly to swallow them all.

"Neecy?"

The closet. I heard a sound from the closet, a child's wet sniffle.

Neecy, why are you in the closet? Did your daddy beat you again?

She was there, inside a closet stripped of everything except a few wire hangers swinging lazily from the rack above her head. I couldn't help it; my face fell slack when I saw her. I felt as if my veins had been drained of blood, flushed with ice water instead.

Over the years, I'd talked to little Neecy on the telephone at least once a month, whenever I called Denise. I was her godmother, after all.

Neecy was old enough now that she usually answered the phone, and she chatted obligingly about school and her piano, acting and computer lessons, before saying, *Want to talk to Mommy?* And the child always sounded so prim, so full of private-school self-assuredness, free of any traces of Denise's hushed, halting—the word, really, was fearful—way of speaking. It wasn't so strange on the phone, with the image so blurry on the face screen. Not at all.

But being here, seeing her in person, was something else.

Neecy's hair was parted into two neat, shiny pigtails that coiled around the back of her neck, her nose had a tiny bulb at the end, and her molasses-brown eyes were set apart just like I remembered them. If the girl had been grinning instead of crying right now, she would look exactly as she'd looked in the photograph someone had taken of us at my sixth birthday party, the one where Mama hired a clown to do magic tricks and pull cards out of thin air, and we'd both believed the magic was real.

Denise was in the closet. She was six years old again, reborn.

I'd known what to expect the whole time, but I couldn't have been prepared for how it would feel to see her again. I hadn't known how the years would melt from my mind like vapors, how it would fill my stomach with stones to end up staring at my childhood's biggest heartache eye-to-eye.

Somehow, I found a voice in my dry, burning throat. "Hey, sweetie. It's Aunt Paige. From California."

"What's wrong with my mommy?" A brave whisper.

"She's just very upset right now, Neecy." Saying the name, my veins thrilled again.

"Where'd Daddy go?"

I knelt so that I could literally stare her in the eye, and I was reminded of how, twenty-five years ago, Neecy's eyelids always puffed when she cried, narrowing her eyes into slits. China-girl, I used to tease her to try to make her laugh. Here was my China-girl.

I clasped the child's tiny, damp hands; the mere act of touching her caused the skin on my arms to harden into gooseflesh. "I'm not sure where your daddy is, sweetie. He'll come back."

Hey, Neecy, don't cry. He'll come back.

Staring into Neecy's anguish, for the first time, I understood everything.

I understood what a glistening opportunity had stirred Denise's soul when she'd realized her salvation had arrived courtesy of science: a legal procedure to extract a nucleus from a single cell, implant it into an egg, and enable her to give new birth to any living person who consented—even to herself. She could take an inventory of everything that had gone wrong, systematically fix it all, and see what would blossom this time. See what might have been.

And now, gazing into Neecy's eyes—the *same* eyes, except younger, not worn to sludge like the Neecy quivering under a blanket in the living room—I understood why Denise was possibly insane by now. She'd probably been insane longer than I wanted to admit.

"Listen," I said. "Your mom told me to take you to get some pizza. And then she wants us to go to my hotel for a couple of days, until she feels better."

"Will she be okay?" Neecy asked. Her teary eyes were sharp and focused.

Yes, I realized, it was *these* tears ripping Denise's psyche to shreds. This was what Denise could not bear to look at, what was making her physically ill. She was not ready to watch her child, herself, taken apart hurt by hurt. Again.

Neecy was dressed in a lemon-colored party dress as if it were her birthday, or Easter Sunday. Did Denise dress her like this every day? Did she wake Neecy up in the mornings and smile on herself while she reclaimed that piece, too? Of course. Oh, yes, she did. Suddenly, I swooned. I felt myself sway with a near-religious euphoria, my spirit filling up with something I couldn't name.

I only kept my balance by clinging to the puffed shoulders of the child's taffeta dress, as if I'd made a clumsy attempt to hug her.

"Neecy? It's all right this time," I heard myself tell her in a breathless whisper. "I promise I'll watch out for you. Just like I said. It's all right now, Neecy. Okay? I promise."

I clasped my best friend's hand, rubbing her small knuckles back and forth beneath my chin like a salve. With my hand squeezing her thumb, I could feel the lively, pulsing throbbing of Neecy's other heart.

~

Tananarive Due is a winner of the American Book Award and a two-time finalist for the Bram Stoker Award. Her novels include the My Soul to Keep series, *The Between, The Good House,* and *Joplin's Ghost.* Her short fiction has been published in *The Magazine of Fantasy & Science Fiction,* and in anthologies such as *Dark Delicacies II, Voices from the Other Side, Dark Dreams, Dark Matter,* and *Mojo: Conjure Stories.* She is a frequent collaborator with SF writer Steven Barnes: they've produced film scripts, short stories, and three Tennyson Hardwick detective novels, the latest of which (written with actor Blair Underwood) is *From Cape Town With Love.* (They also collaborate in another way: They're married.)

THE GREAT LONELINESS

MARIA ROMASCO MOORE

I am in the cactus room checking on the womb when I hear my third daughter Verdana calling to me from upstairs.

"The picture's coming through. There's water! Lots of it."

The womb is fine. I am only here because I don't want to be up there, watching, like everyone else in the world.

It is safe to say that these days. No danger of hyperbole. There are only a few thousand of us.

I pick up the womb from the shelf and move it over to the coffee table. I run my hand across its silver skin. How warm it must be in there, how quiet and dark.

"Come on, Mom," Verdana shouts. "You can't miss this."

Inside the womb it is exactly as warm as I made it. It is precisely as dark as I programmed it to be.

• • •

Upstairs, Verdana is soaking in one of the hydroponic tubs, watching a screen on the ceiling.

"You shouldn't spend so much time in there," I tell her. "You'll wilt."

She rolls her eyes at me from under the water, but I can't help it. I am a mother and I worry. Verdana has had fifty-seven surgeries in her life so far and I have performed every one of them. Her heart is made of metal now and half her veins are plastic tubes.

And she is growing. New leaves almost every day. Buds forming at her fingertips.

Verdana waves her hand and the screen floats down to my eye level. The

162

picture is grainy and colorless. What it shows, if you know how to decode the pattern of light and dark, is a landscape seen from above. There is indeed water, a slick gray smear of it near the bottom of the image. Symbols flash down the sides of the screen—a full battery of readings and diagnostics—but these are a mystery to me.

Verdana waves her hand again and the picture breaks into pieces. Now there are fifty-some tiny landscapes. Verdana sits up, drops of water falling from the forked white tendrils of her hair.

"There's supposed to be a hundred," she says. She's been reading up on this for weeks now. "One hundred spider babies per target planet."

"Maybe they rusted," I say. The CHLT-IV is an old scout. The ones sent out within the last few centuries are much better, technically speaking, but the antiques are much farther away and it is to these we pin our dearest, most fragile hopes.

"Don't be stupid," says Verdana. "Nothing rusts in space."

• • •

It was a very quiet apocalypse. No asteroids. No atomic bombs. The people died of natural causes. Fire. Water. Mountains. Lowlands.

I only know about this from stories, of course. It was long before my time. All I can say for sure is that some people did survive, holed up in bunkers and domes, reproducing through means both natural and artificial.

Those must have been exciting times. Dire, sure, and uncomfortable, but terribly exciting. There must have been a sense of urgency, of desperation, of a simple and overriding purpose: Don't die.

In the centuries between those times and these, the urgency has diminished. It has become clear that we might very well keep going forever. What has become less clear is why we should bother. What precisely is the point of surviving? And who would miss us if we stopped?

• • •

Onscreen the spider babies are falling slowly. As they fall, they record their surroundings as thoroughly and intimately as their outdated technology allows. They are designed to send those recordings out in a pulse of light before they hit the ground. Years later or right this second, depending on your perspective, the few of us left on earth will receive that pulse.

When the first of the unmanned scouts were sent out, it was by people looking for a new home. There are hundreds of scouts out there now. Some of them, like the CHLT-IV, are calibrated to seek out and investigate planets of a certain size, orbiting stars of a certain type within a certain range of distances—Goldilocks planets, they call them. Not too cold. Not too hot. Plenty of porridge.

We could go to these planets. We've got the technology. There are blueprints for long-term preservation. For canning people up like homemade jam, use-by date a hundred years hence. There are plans that utilize hopscotch clones. A self-sustaining population of one, copy after copy after copy until the ink fades to nothing.

But we do not go to these planets. What would be the point? When we got there, we'd still be alone.

There are other scouts out there now that act as receivers, scanning unceasingly for sound waves with a modicum of rhythm. A hint of soul. Still others hurtle through space shouting, as it were, mechanical travel agents broadcasting our coordinates to anyone who will listen, gushing about our formerly lush forests, our once pristine beaches.

We aren't looking for a home anymore. We're looking for a friend. Or a neighbor. A pen pal.

Even an enemy would be fine. We're not picky.

• • •

The feed from the door to the orchid room pops up in front of the spider baby screen. We have a visitor.

"It's Marjorie," says Verdana.

I go downstairs and answer the door, but it isn't Marjorie; it's her Brain. I know it immediately. Out of all of them, Marjorie's Brain does look the most like her, but I've known Marjorie all my life and I can always tell the original from the spares.

My girls can never see the differences. I have to point them out. Heart is more muscular, as are Kidneys and Blood. The Skin Graft Twins have a certain glow to them which speaks of a strict moisturizing regimen. Liver, it is generally agreed, is actually prettier than her originator. There is something about the eyes, the twist of the mouth. Eyes herself doesn't go out much.

"What's wrong?" I ask Marjorie's Brain, because something is obviously wrong. The fact that she is here instead of with Marjorie is proof enough of that.

"Can I come in?"

Although I fear the worst—Marjorie is dead, irreversibly—I step aside and invite her into the cactus room, which is also the living room.

My daughters and I live in the greenhouse. It stretches all the way around the house in a ring, though less than a third of it is still up and running. I've made a home for us in the small suite of rooms devoted to inedible plants, those which Marjorie's father cultivated primarily for amusement or decoration.

Marjorie lives in the very center of the house, in what used to be her father's private rooms. The hundred or so other rooms in the house—the laboratories and dormitories and dining halls—are empty now.

I make Marjorie's Brain some tea and sit beside her on the couch while she sips it slowly.

"Why aren't you watching?" I ask. I don't need to be more specific.

"Why aren't you?"

• • •

Marjorie's father was a rich man. By the time he was born all the truly poor men were already dead, of course, but even by the standards of the day he was considered wealthy. He'd inherited a fortune—his great-grandfather had invented the first mechanized womb—and he was a genius in his own right. He employed many of the best and brightest scientists of his age to assist him in his research, and when they proved insufficient, he manufactured better and brighter ones.

He intended to live forever. No doubt he would have done it, too, if Marjorie hadn't killed him.

Before Marjorie killed her father, I had many sisters. Genetically speaking, Marjorie's father was our father as well, although we did not think of him this way. From his perspective, I am sure, we were no more than expensive pieces of biological equipment. We were born in batches, engineered to work for the man who had made us. Our mother cells were anonymous, pulled from the banks.

Marjorie was, in his heart, the only daughter her father had. She'd come first, of course. And she'd been born the old-fashioned way, of a woman. Marjorie was her father's heir and he protected his interest by creating backups for every little piece of her, just in case.

Some of my sisters resented Marjorie and her privilege, but I always felt that the burden she carried was far heavier than ours. We were our father's creations; she was his child.

• • •

Marjorie's Brain and I sit without speaking for some time. I am afraid to ask her why she is here. In the corner, the womb hums softly. Marjorie's Brain finishes her tea.

"We're the dinosaurs," she says, finally, setting her teacup down and turning to me.

"Ah," I say. I have heard these exact words once before. Marjorie and I sat together in the greenhouse, in one of the protein rooms, watching the gardeners buzz in and out of the meat flowers. That was three days before she killed her father. In retrospect, her words may have been a warning, but at the time I didn't understand.

"We're not the birds," says Marjorie's Brain. "We're not the crocodiles or the coelacanths."

"More tea?" I ask, but she shakes her head. I pour myself a cup instead.

"We should have bowed out gracefully when we had a chance."

• • •

The instant I left the womb I began learning two languages—the language of my de facto forefathers' now-dissolved homeland and the language of the body. I learned to read the genome like a poem. The acids and the alkalines. The adenines and the guanines. I memorized it, rote, and then I lingered over each line, exploring it as one might explore the body of a lover. It was everyone's body, the sum of our flesh, the catalogue of our corporeal form.

A friend of mine—genetically, a sister—used to say it was a lot like a recipe. "And once you know the recipe by heart you can start to experiment in the kitchen," she would say, smiling wickedly, spooning a colony of C. elegans into her double-shot espresso.

She and I came from the same batch. We had the same X and the same Y, and now every time I catch my reflection by accident, in the glass of Perpetua's tanks or the walls of the greenhouse itself, I am always startled, just for a moment, to see her again.

• • •

Verdana shrieks upstairs. I drop my teacup. It smashes and disintegrates and then reforms but I am already halfway up the steps.

I run into Verdana on the landing. She is damp and naked, but unharmed. The screen comes sailing after her like a faithful dog.

"Look," she shrieks, "look!"

She jumps up and down and at the tip of her left ring finger a small pink flower blooms.

The screen is zoomed to one spider baby's view, the surface of the alien planet growing closer by degrees. On the surface there is a grid. It is too far yet to tell what it is made of—Rocks? Vegetation?—but it is a grid no doubt. Straight and true as a game of tic-tac-toe.

"It's probably just a crystal formation," I say, though hope swells unwelcome in my chest. There is an old saying: Hope is a thing with feathers. If that's true it must be a hawk, with talons to rip out your heart and a sharp beak to pierce it through.

Tiny screens begin popping up all around me, calls from our friends on the floating cities. There is also a call from Marjorie. I answer.

"Where is my mind?" she demands.

"Don't worry, she's here. I'll send her over."

• • •

My second daughter, Kartika, is asleep in the kitchen, curled up in the cupboard beneath the sink. With her face tucked into the crook of her arm, she is almost indistinguishable from the shadows. She is my softest daughter, covered from head to toe in fine black down. I give her a gentle prod, but she doesn't stir. She only comes out at night, so she will have to see this later.

My first daughter, Perpetua, is in her room, leaning over one of her testing tanks. Her veins pulse with the light of her blood. Her skin is as translucent as that of a glass catfish, which is one of the things I love about her. I can see right through to her heart. I can make sure it is still beating. She has the spider baby feed up on a screen behind her, but she isn't watching it.

"Check it out," she says when I come in, "I've made it so these danios luminesce in the presence of liars."

"Bullshit," I say, and the little fish light up like Christmas.

"Oh mother," she says, "You are supposed to be encouraging me."

She is on her second adolescence and it is proving more difficult than the first. Genetically she is one-third hydrozoa—*Turntopsis nutricula*—and so she doesn't age the way I do. She repeats.

"Turn around," I tell her.

I zoom Perpetua's screen to the grid. The baby picking it up is even closer to the surface now, still falling, and the lines of the grid show up sharper, easier to differentiate from the mottled gray of the land around them.

Verdana comes rushing in from the landing. She's dried herself off a bit, at my urging, and put on a dress—although in her haste she put it on backwards and didn't bother with the buttons.

"Oh, Pet," she cries, "isn't it amazing?"

Perpetua scowls, but she doesn't look away from her screen.

When I created my daughters, I intended for them to be independent creatures. Perpetua and Kartika are modest successes in this regard, but Verdana was something of a step back. Her fragility has made her clingy. She waves her screen bigger until it takes up the whole wall, each pixel of the strange image nearly an inch across.

I tell Verdana and Perpetua I'll be back in a bit, but I don't think they hear me. They are leaning together, shoulder to shoulder, watching the transmission. Verdana sways slightly in the breeze of the air conditioner.

"I love you both more than anything," I whisper and then look quickly to the tank at my left. Perpetua's fish remain unlit.

• • •

Marjorie says now that she spared me, out of all the people in her father's household, because I was her favorite. It might be true. I probably spent more time in Marjorie's presence than any of my batch mates did.

But I believe it was an accident.

I wasn't in the house when she sealed the doors and cut the oxygen. I should have been, but over the years I had developed an unfortunate defect of character—one that I took pains to conceal.

Marjorie's father created me and my sisters to be scientists. He intended for our every in-breath to be a hypothesis; our every out-breath a confirmation of the prevailing theories. I did my best, but the truth is I was never a scientist. I'm still not one. I can ask all the right questions, but I've never much cared about the answers.

On that day, as on many unremarkable days before it, I had nicked a submarine and snuck out to visit the museum. Marjorie's father didn't have a copy of the museum, but I knew a man who did. His name was Frank and he lived at the bottom of the sea.

I visited Frank every day for months, but I only saw a fraction of the place. I would sit on his couch for hours and I would walk through the halls of the museum: past the skeletons of *Australopithecus* in front of *Guernica,* past the *Pietà* in the corner of a room from the Temple of Heaven, past the restrooms from the Louvre that someone had labeled "late eighteenth-century romanticism." Frank said that the pyramids and Central Park were somewhere in the basement. I preferred the paintings, those framed windows hung on walls that had long since burnt down or washed away. I found these pictures made by the dead as full of life as any well-tended petri dish.

I am not a scientist. I am an artist.

• • •

It takes me almost ten minutes to reach Marjorie's wing of the house. There used to be a system of shuttle cars, but in the last few decades Marjorie has allowed it to fall into a state of disrepair. I walk along the old tracks and count the closed doors.

I find Marjorie sitting in her father's old wingback chair, with her spares arranged behind her like bridesmaids in an antique photograph.

"What is it?" I ask.

Marjorie smiles at me. She is still as beautiful as she always was. The years do not show on her face.

"Plastic," she says.

"Pardon?"

"A high-density polyvinyl chloride polymer," says Marjorie's Brain. I didn't notice her when I first came in. She is sitting off to one side, her face half obscured by a flotilla of glimmering screens.

Her eyes meet mine through one of the screens. The screen is showing the spider baby feed, and the lines of the grid cut her face into sections: a dozen neat squares marked off by longitude and latitude, every single one of them an alien planet.

I understand. Someone must have managed to translate the non-visual data being sent back by the spider baby. The grid is synthetic.

"The Icarii are organizing an expedition already," says Marjorie.

This doesn't surprise me. The Icarii believe that the sun will supernova tomorrow. They always believe that, have been believing it now for decades. Eventually, they are bound to be right.

What Marjorie says next, however, does surprise me.

"We're going, too."

• • •

When I returned that day from under the sea, the hatch I'd used to leave the house was locked. I thought I'd been found out, so I confessed. I rang the doorbell frequency. After what felt like an eon, the hatch slid open.

Inside, I found everyone sleeping. It was the middle of the day. They were sleeping at their desks. They were sleeping on the floors. I walked through the house for a long time but in every room it was the same.

Finally in one of the bathrooms I found Marjorie's Eyes and she was awake and she was alive and she was crying.

"I saw them die," she said when I asked her what had happened. "I watched so she wouldn't have to."

I never speak of that day, certainly, to my daughters or anyone else. There is not much to say. Marjorie's Eyes took me to Marjorie, who took me to her father. His eyes were open. His throat was cut.

His Eyes, too, and His Throat. Not a one of them was stirring.

"Why?" I asked, though I didn't really need to.

"It is a cruel gift to give," said Marjorie. "The gift of life. The gift I gave was kinder."

I left the house. I went back to Frank and told him there had been an accident. We lived together for some time, just the two of us, at the bottom of the sea. He used me to satisfy certain ingrained biological urges and I used him for Bosch's garden of delights.

I returned after Marjorie tried to finish what she started. Frank had heard about it from one of the Pope's attendants who had heard it from one of the Icarii who had heard it from a girl on the floating city of New Dubai who had heard it from Eyes. The new Eyes, that is, who was only five. I don't know for sure what happened to the old one.

Marjorie had gone outside. She was out for less than a minute but still it was bad enough that most of her had to be replaced. It took all of Lungs and Nerves and bits of several of the others to make her whole again. It is something that confounds me to this day—that they gave of themselves so willingly.

It was what they were created to do, certainly, but the one who created them for this purpose was gone. I had long since abandoned the tasks for which I had been created.

Once Marjorie was stable, I moved into the greenhouse. The rest of the house held too many memories. Shortly after that, I began to make my art.

• • •

"Will you come with us?" asks Marjorie.

I should be happy. We found what we were looking for.

"It could still be nothing," I say.

"It isn't nothing."

"It could be a mistake."

"It isn't a mistake."

"It could be us."

There have been manned expeditions sent out before. Some we have records of, but there were probably more. Some failed before they reached the edge of the galaxy. Others failed farther out. Sometimes we receive a message sent to a ground control long gone. An SOS or a suicide note, it amounts to the same.

But some of them must still be out there. The LDS fleet, perhaps, which set out in search of the three heavenly kingdoms. Or Voyager XXIII, with the naked man and the naked woman and the hundred thousand human zygotes sealed in glass.

Could it be we're going in circles? Chasing our own tails? And all of us just like mice running scared in the big black fields of space while hope sharpens its talons and swoops toward us, yellow eyes gleaming even in the dark.

"It isn't us," says Marjorie. She turns and stares at the screen. "And even if it were, it would be better than nothing."

"I'm not going," I say. I am surprised to hear myself say this, but the moment the words leave my lips I know them to be true.

"Everyone will go," says Marjorie. "You'll be the only one left."

She sounds like a child trying to coerce a playmate. I am much younger than her in years, but in this moment I feel much older. Though she is surrounded by her spares, she is nonetheless alone, because they are just her, reflected.

"I've been the only one left before," I say. "I'm used to it now."

Marjorie has no answer for that, but Marjorie's Brain has begun to sing. It is an old song. It must be. I don't recognize the tune.

"When the earth quakes, the engines will stall," she sings, voice barely above a whisper, "and down will go baby, cradle and all."

The screen showing the spider baby feed goes black. The transmission is over. Marjorie's Brain plays back the last seconds for those of us who missed it—the ground rushing forward and then static and then nothing.

• • •

Museums were made so that future generations could enjoy the works of generations that had gone before. But these days, future generations are no longer a given. Thus my works act as both subject and object. Art and audience. The problem and the solution all in one.

Perpetua isn't really my first daughter, although I call her that. There were hundreds before her, maybe thousands. But these daughters were just the preliminary sketches. Limbless or gutless or eyes in their stomachs and hearts in their throats. Some with skin but nothing inside of it, others with all that should be except skin. They did not live long, if they lived at all. Art can be messy.

Perpetua is a finished piece.

I consider my daughters collages. Mixed-media assemblages. They are complicated and fragile and I hope that, like many great works of art, they will live on long after I am gone.

• • •

In the evening I ask Verdana if she wants to go off in search of the grid planet. She tells me her roots are here. Space frightens her. Too dark.

Later, I ask Kartika the same thing. She is curled up in my lap and I am filing her incisors. If I don't do that once a week at least, they grow and grow until they are larger than she is. Kartika growls low in her throat and bites my hand, gently, between the thumb and the forefinger, which means no.

I worry, as any mother would worry, that I have made my daughters too timid, too attached, too like myself. And it is true that their human ingredients all come from me. An artist needs a signature.

But Perpetua wants to go. I tell her she can go if she wants to. I tell her it is up to her. She's not satisfied with that. She says we all have to go together. I tell her that isn't going to happen. She screams at me. Calls me selfish. She seems to think the gift I gave her was a cruel one. At the end of it all she storms off and locks her door.

But late that night she pads softly into my room and tells me she had a nightmare and can she sleep in my bed just this once even though she is too old for it and I say of course and the next morning when I wake up she is three.

I didn't even realize she could do that—age out of order. But it just goes to show you. The best art can be a mystery even to its creator.

• • •

The next afternoon I get a message from Marjorie's Eyes telling me Marjorie's Brain is dead. She stepped outside at sunrise, uncovered. She bowed out gracefully while she had the chance.

Verdana is sunning on the couch beside me when I get the news.

"Are you sad?" she asks me.

"No."

There is a flash of light from upstairs. Perpetua's fish. They're right. I haven't been this sad since Frank was killed by shifting tectonic plates a few years back. Although whether it was the actual fact of his death that pained me most or the loss of his copy of the museum—crushed right along with him—I couldn't tell you.

"If everybody leaves," asks Verdana, "will you miss them?"

"No."

There is another flash, this one so bright that it takes me nearly five minutes to blink away its afterimage. When I go upstairs to check, I find all the danios dead, burnt out like old bulbs.

• • •

Marjorie is wrong. Not everyone will leave. Almost everyone, maybe, but not everyone. There are optimists in the ocean, keeping tabs on amoebas. Cheering them on. Waiting for life to begin all over again. They will stay. I know they will. So will the sleepers buried under the mountains. The lotus eaters. The handmaidens of Hades. The nostalgic. The homesick. The tireless keepers of the frozen Pope in his underground Vatican, waiting in silence for Jesus and the thaw.

And my three daughters and I. We'll stay.

We'll get transmissions now and then from the ones who leave, I'm sure. The lag will grow as they push farther out, but I imagine we will keep on hearing from them periodically until they fail or until they reach their destination. That will be something to look forward to, centuries from now, if I live that long. I haven't decided yet if I will.

My fourth daughter will be ready soon.

She has been many years in the making, and if she proves viable, which I believe she will, she will be a new thing altogether. There is very little of me in her. Her ingredients are pulled from every corner of the archives. She is a balancing act. An exercise in form and color.

She is *Ursus arctos* and *Solenodon paradoxus*. *Puma concolor* and *Panthera onca*. All the creatures that never moved in packs, never bonded in pairs, never huddled together for warmth in the night. Creatures that never sought a mate but simply split, if the mood struck, one into two. The two parts would never bother each other again, not even to ask for a cup of sugar or an iota of endoplasm.

She is every creature that left the nest and never looked back.

She will be my greatest work yet. A museum unto herself. Not just a petri dish, but an ocean full of life. She will be beautiful and she will be strange and, best of all, she will never be lonely.

~

Maria Romasco Moore's stories have appeared in *Unstuck*, *Diagram*, *Hobart*, and the anthology *FISH* (Dagan Books, 2013). She was born in Baton Rouge in the rain but currently lives in Pittsburgh. In her spare time, she makes miniature houses.

Love Is the Plan the Plan Is Death

James Tiptree, Jr.

(Alice Sheldon)

Art by Li Grabensetter

Remembering—

Do you hear, my little red? Hold me softly. The cold grows.

I remember:

—I am hugely black and hopeful, I bounce on six legs along the mountains in the new warm!…*Sing the changer, Sing the stranger! Will the changes change forever?*…All my hums have words now. Another change!

Eagerly I bound on sunward following the tiny thrill in the air. The forests have been shrinking again. Then I see. It is me! Me-Myself, MOG-GADEET—I have grown bigger more in the winter cold! I astonish myself, Moggadeet-the-small!

Excitement, enticement, shrilling from the sun-side of the world. I come!... The sun is changing again too. *Sun is walking in the night! Sun is walking back to Summer in the warming of the light!*...Warm is Me—Moggadeet Myself. Forget the bad-time winter.

Memory quakes me.

The Old One.

I stop, pluck up a tree. So much I wanted to ask the Old One. No time. Cold. Tree goes end over end down-cliff, I watch the fatclimbers tumble out. Not hungry.

The Old One warned me of the cold—I didn't believe him. I move on, grieving.... . *Old One told you, The cold, the cold will hold you. Chill cold! Kill cold. In the cold I killed you.*

But it's warm now, all different. I'm Moggadeet again.

I bound over a hill and see my brother Frim.

At first I don't know him. A big black old one! I think. And in the warm, we can speak!

I surge toward him bashing trees. The big black is crouched over a ravine, peering down. Black back has shiny ripples like—It IS Frim! Frim-I-hunted-for, Frim-run-away! But he's so big now! Giant Frim! A *stranger, a changer—*

"Frim!"

He doesn't hear me; all his eye-turrets are under the trees. His end is sticking up oddlike, all atremble. What's he hunting?

"Frim! It's me, Moggadeet!"

But he only quivers his legs; I see his spurs pushing out. What a fool, Frim! I remind myself how timid he is, I try to move gently. When I get closer I'm astonished again. I'm bigger than he is now! Changes! I can see right over his shoulder into the ravine.

Hot yellow-green in there. A little glade all lit with sun. I bend my eyes to see what Frim is after, and all astonishments blow up the world.

I see you.

I saw you.

I will always see you. Dancing in the green fire, my tiny red star! So bright! So small! So perfect! So fierce! I knew you—Oh, yes, I knew you in that first instant, my dawnberry, my scarlet minikin. *Red!* A tiny baby red one, smaller than my smallest eye. And so brave!

The Old One said it. *Red is the color of love.*

I see you swat at a hopper twice your size, my eyes bulge as you leap after it and go rolling, shrilling *Lililee! Lilileee-ee!* in baby wrath. Oh, my mighty hunter, you don't know someone is looking right into your tender little love-fur! Oh, yes! Palest pink it is, just brushed with rose. My jaws spurt, the world flashes and reels.

And then Frim, poor fool, feels me behind him and rears up.

But what a Frim! His throat-sacs are ballooning purple-black, his plates are engorged like the Mother of the storm-clouds! Glittering, rattling his spurs! His tail booms! "It's mine!" he bellows—I can hardly understand him. He jumps straight at me!

"Stop, Frim, stop!" I cry, dodging away bewildered. It's warm—how can Frim be wild, kill-wild?

"Brother Frim!" I call gently, soothingly. But something is badly wrong! My voice is bellowing too! Yes, in the warm and I want only to calm him, I am full of love—but the kill-roar is rushing through me, I too am swelling, rattling, booming! Invincible! To crush—to rend—

Oh, I am shamed.

I came to myself in the wreckage of Frim, Frim-pieces everywhere, myself is sodden with Frim. But I did not eat him! I did not! Should I take joy in that? Did I defy the Plan? But my throat was closed. Not because it was Frim but because of darling you. *You!* Where are you? The glade is empty! Oh, fearful fear, I have frightened you, you are run away! I forget Frim. I forget everything but you, my heartmeat, my precious tiny red.

I smash trees, I uproot rocks, I tear the ravine open! Oh, where are you hiding? Suddenly I have a new fear: Has my wild search harmed you? I force myself calm. I begin questing, circling, ever wider over the trees, moving cloud-silent, thrusting my eyes and ears down into every glade. A new humming fills my throat. *Oooo, Oo-oo, Rum-a-looly-loo,* I moan. Hunting, hunting for you.

Once I glimpse a black bigness far away and I am suddenly up at my full height, roaring. Attack the black! Was it another brother? I would slay him, but the stranger is already vanishing. I roar again. No—*it roars me,* the new power of black. Yet deep inside, Myself-Moggadeet is watching, fearing. Attack the black—even in the warm? Is there no safety, are we truly like the fatclimbers? But at the same time it feels—Oh, right! Oh, good! Sweet is the Plan. I give myself up to seeking you, my new song longing *Oo-loo* and *Looly rum-a-loo-oo-loo.*

And you answered! You!

So tiny you, hidden under a leaf! Shrilling *Li! Li! Lililee!* Trilling, thrill-ing-half mocking, already imperious. Oh, how I whirl, crash, try to look under my feet, stop frozen in horror of squashing the *Lilili! Lee!* Rocking, longing, moaning Moggadeet.

And you came out, you did.

My adorable firemite, threatening ME!!

When I see your littlest hunting claws upraised my whole gut melts, it floods me. I am all tender jelly. Tender! Oh, tender-fierce like a Mother, I think! Isn't that how a Mother feels? My jaws are sluicing juice that isn't hunger-juice—I am choking with fear of frighting you or bruising your tininess—I ache to grip and knead you, to eat you in one gulp, in a thousand nibbles—

Oh, the power of *red*—the Old One said it! Now I feel my special hands, my tender hands I always carry hidden—now they come swelling out, come pushing toward my head! What? What?

My secret hands begin to knead and roll the stuff that's dripping from my jaws.

Ah, that arouses you too, my redling, doesn't it?

Yes, yes, I feel—torment—I feel your sly excitement! How your body remembers even now our love-dawn, our very first moments of Moggadeet-Leely. Before I knew You-Yourself, before you knew Me. It began then, my heartlet, our love-knowing began in that very first instant when your Moggadeet stared down at you like a monster bursting. I saw how new you were, how helpless!

Yes, even while I loomed over you marveling—even while my secret hands drew and spun your fate—even then it came to me in pity that long ago, last year when I was a child, I saw other little red ones among my brothers, before our Mother drove them away. I was only a foolish baby then; I didn't understand. I thought they'd grown strange and *silly* in their redness and Mother did well to turn them out. Oh, stupid Moggadeet!

But now I saw *you*, my flamelet—I understood! You were only that day cast out by your Mother. Never had you felt the terrors of a night alone in the world; you couldn't imagine that such a monster as Frim was hunting you. Oh, my ruby nestling, my baby red! Never, I vowed it, never would I leave you—and have I not kept that vow? Never! I, Moggadeet, *I would be your Mother.*

Great is the Plan, but I was greater!

All I learned of hunting in my lonely year, to drift like the air, to leap, to grip so delicately—all these learnings became for you! Not to bruise the smallest portion of your bright body. Oh, yes! I captured you whole in all your tiny perfection, though you sizzled and spat and fought me like the sunspark you are. And then—

And then—

I began to—Oh, terror! Delight-shame! How can I speak such a beautiful secret?—the Plan took me as a Mother guides her child, and with my special hands I began to—

I began to bind you up!

Oh, yes! Oh, yes! My special hands that had no use, now all unfurled and engorged and alive, never stopping the working in the strong juice of my jaws—they began to *bind* you, passing over and around and beneath you, every moment piercing me with fear and joy. I wound among your darling little limbs, into your inmost delicate recesses, gently swathing and soothing you, winding and binding until you became a shining jewel. Mine!

—But you responded. I know that now. We know! Oh, yes, in your fierce struggles, shyly you helped me, always at the end each strand fell sweetly into place.... *Winding you, binding you, loving Leelyloo!*...How our bodies moved in our first weaving song! I feel it even now, I melt with excitement! How I wove the silk about you, tying each tiny limb, making you perfectly helpless. How fearlessly you gazed up at me, your terrifying captor! You! You were never frightened, as I'm not frightened now. Isn't it strange, my loveling? This sweetness that floods our bodies when we yield to the Plan. Great is the Plan! Fear it, fight it—but hold the sweetness yet.

Sweetly began our lovetime, when first I became your new true Mother, never to cast you out. How I fed you and caressed and tended and fondled you! What a responsibility it is to be a Mother. Anxiously I carried you furled in my secret arms, savagely I drove off all intruders, even the harmless banlings in the grass, in fear every moment that you were stifled or crushed!

And all the warm nights long, how I cared for your helpless little body, carefully releasing each infant limb, flexing and stretching it, cleaning every scarlet morsel of you with my giant tongue, nibbling your baby claws with my terrible teeth, reveling in your baby hum, pretending to devour you while you shrieked with glee, *Li! Lillili! Love-lili, Leelylee!* But the greatest joy of all—

We spoke!

We spoke together, we two! We communed, we shared, we poured ourselves one into the other. Love, how we stammered and stumbled at the first, you in your strange Mother-tongue and I in mine! How we blended our singing wordlessly and then with words, until more and more we came to see with each other's eyes, to hear, to taste, to feel, the world of each other, until I became Leelyloo and you became Moggadeet, until finally we became together a new thing, Moggadeet-Leely, Lilliloo-Mogga, Lili-Mogga-looly-deet!

Oh, love, are we the first? Have others loved with their whole selves? Oh, sad thinking, that lovers before us have left no trace. Remember us! Will you remember, my adored, though Moggadeet has spoiled everything and the cold grows? If only I could hear you speak once more, my red, my innocent one. You are remembering, your body tells me you remember even now. Softly, hold me softly yet. Hear your Moggadeet!

You told me how it was being you, yourself, tiny-redling-Lilliloo. Of your Mother, your dreams, your baby joys and fears. And I told you mine, and all my learnings in the world since the day when my own Mother—

Hear me, my heartmate! Time runs away.

—On the last day of my childhood my Mother called us all under her.

"Sons! S-son-n-nss!" Why did her dear voice creak so?

My brothers came in slowly, fearfully, from the summer green. But I, small Moggadeet, I climb eagerly up under the great arch of her body, seeking the golden Mother-fur. Right into her warm cave I come, where her Mother-eyes are glowing, the cave that sheltered us so strongly all our lives, as I shelter you, my dawnflower.

I long to touch her, to hear her speak and sing to us again. Her Mother-fur troubles me, it is tattered and drab. Shyly I press against one of her huge food-glands. It feels dry, but a glow sparks deep in her Mother-eye.

"Mother," I whisper. "It's me, Moggadeet!"

"SONNNNNS!" Her voice rumbles through her armor. My big brothers huddle by her legs, peering back at the sunlight. They look so funny, shedding, half gold, half black.

"I'm afraid!" whimpers my brother Frim nearby. Like me Frim still has his gold baby fur. Mother is speaking again, but her voice booms so I can hardly understand.

"WINNN-TER! WINTER, I SAY! AFTER THE WARM COMES THE COLD WINTER. THE COLD WINTER BEFORE THE WARM COMES AGAIN, COMES... ."

Frim whimpers louder, I cuff him. What's wrong, why is her loving voice so hoarse and strange now? She always hummed us so tenderly, we nestled in her warm Mother-fur sucking the lovely Mother-juices, rocking to her steady walking-song. *Ee mooly-mooly, Ee-mooly mooly,* while far below the earth rolled by. Oh, yes, and how we held our breaths and squealed when she began her mighty hunting hum! *Tann! Tann! Dir! Dir! Dir Hataan! HATONN!* How we clung in the thrilling climax when she plunged upon her prey and we heard the crunching, the tearing, the gurgling in her body that meant soon her food-glands would be richly full.

Suddenly I see a black streak down below—a big brother is running away! Mother's booming voice breaks off. Her great body tenses, her plates clash. Mother roars!

Running, screaming down below! I burrow up into her fur, am flung about as she leaps.

"OUT! GO OUT!" she bellows. Her terrible hunting-limbs crash down, she roars without words, shuddering, jolting. When I dare to peek out I see the others all have fled. All except one!

A black body is lying under Mother's claws. It's my brother Sesso—yes! But Mother is tearing him, is eating him! I watch in horror—Sesso she cared for so proudly, so tenderly! I sob, bury my head in her fur. But the beautiful fur is coming loose in my hands, her golden Mother-fur is dying! I cling desperately, trying not to hear the crunches, the gulps and gurgling. The world is ending, all is terrible, terrible.

And yet, my fireberry, even then I almost understood. Great is the Plan!

Presently Mother stops feeding and begins to move. The rocky ground jolts by far below. Her stride is not smooth but jerks me, even her deep hum is strange. *On! On! Alone! Ever alone. And on!* The rumbling ceases. Silence. Mother is resting.

"Mother!" I whisper. "Mother, it's Moggadeet. I'm here!"

Her stomach-plates contract, a belch reverberates in her vaults.

"Go," she groans. "Go. Too late. Mother no more."

"I don't want to leave you. Why must I go? Mother!" I wail, "Speak to me!" I keen my baby hum, *Deet! Deet! Tikki-takka! Deet!* hoping Mother will answer crooning deep, *Brum! Brrumm! Brumaloo-bruin!* Now I see one huge Mother-eye glow faintly, but she only makes a grating sound.

"Too late. No more…The winter, I say. I did speak…. . Before the winter, go. Go."

"Tell me about Outside, Mother," I plead.

Another groan or cough nearly shakes me from my perch. But when she speaks again her voice sounds gentler.

"Talk?" she grumbles. "Talk, talk, talk. You are a strange son. Talk, like your Father."

"What's that, Mother? What's a Father?"

She belches again. "Always talk. The winters grow, he said. Oh, yes. Tell them the winters grow. So I did. Late. Winter, I spoke you. Cold!" Her voice booms. "No more! Too late." Outside I hear her armor rattle and clank.

"Mother, speak to me!"

"Go. Go-o-o!"

Her belly-plates clash around me. I jump for another nest of fur, but it comes loose in my grip. Wailing, I save myself by hanging on to one of her great walking limbs. It is rigid, thrumming like rock.

"GO!" She roars.

Her Mother-eyes are shriveling, dead! I panic, scramble down, everything is vibrating, resonating around me. Mother is holding back a storm of rage!

I leap for the ground, I rush diving into a crevice, I wiggle and burrow under the fearful bellowing and clanging that rains on me from above. Into the rocks I go with the hunting claws of Mother crashing behind me.

Oh, my redling, my little tenderling! Never have you known such a night. Those dreadful hours hiding from the monster that had been my loving Mother!

I saw her once more, yes. When dawn came I clambered up a ledge and peered through the mist. It was warm then, the mists were warm. I knew what Mothers looked like. We had glimpses of huge horned dark shapes before our own Mother hooted us under her. Oh yes, and then would come Mother's earthshaking challenge and the strange Mother's answering roar, and we'd cling tight, feeling her surge of kill-fury, buffeted, deafened, battered, while our Mother charged and struck. And once while our Mother fed I peeped out and saw a strange baby squealing in the remnants on the ground below.

But now it was my own dear Mother I saw lurching away through the mists, that great rusty-gray hulk so horned and bossed that only her hunting-eyes showed above her armor, swiveling mindlessly, questing for anything that moved. She crashed her way across the mountains, and as she went she thrummed a new harsh song. *Cold! Cold! Ice and Lone. Ice! And cold! And end.* I never saw her again.

When the sun rose I saw that the gold fur was peeling from my shiny black. All by itself my hunting-limb flashed out and knocked a hopper right into my jaws.

You see, my berry, how much larger and stronger I was than you when Mother sent us away? That also is the Plan. For you were not yet born! I had to live on while the warm turned to cold and while the winter passed to warm again before you would be waiting. I had to grow and learn. To *learn*, my Lilliloo! That is important. Only we black ones have a time to learn—the Old One said it.

Such small learnings at first! To drink the flat water-stuff without choking, to catch the shiny flying things that bite, and to watch the storm-clouds and the moving of the sun. And the nights, and the soft things that moved on the trees. And the bushes that kept shrinking, shrinking—only it was me, Moggadeet, growing larger! Oh, yes! And the day when I could knock down a fatclimber from its vine!

But all these learnings were easy—the Plan in my body guided me. It guides me now, Lilliloo, even now it would give me peace and joy if I yielded to it. But I will not! I will remember to the end, I will speak to the end!

I will speak the big learnings. How I saw—though I was so busy catching and eating more, more, always more—I saw all things were changing, changing. *Changers!* The bushes changed their buds to berries, the fatclimbers changed their colors, even the sun changed, and the hills. And I saw all things were together with others of their kind but only me, Moggadeet, I was alone. Oh, so alone!

I went marching through the valleys in my shiny new black, humming my new song *Turra-tarra! Tarra Tan!* Once I glimpsed my brother Frim and I called him, but he ran like the wind. Away, alone! And when I went to the next valley I found the trees all mashed down. And in the distance I saw a black one like me—only many times as big! Huge! Almost as big as a Mother, sleek and glossy-new. I would have called, but he reared up and saw me and roared so terribly that I too fled like the wind to empty mountains. Alone.

And so I learned, my redling, how we are alone even though my heart was full of love. And I wandered, puzzling and eating ever more and more. I saw the Trails; they meant nothing to me then. But I began to learn the important thing.

The cold.

You know it, my little red. How in the warm days I am me, Myself-Moggadeet. Ever-growing, ever-learning. In the warm we think, we speak. We love! We make our own Plan. Oh, did we not, my lovemate?

But in the cold, in the night—for the nights were growing colder—in the cold night I was—what?—not Moggadeet. Not Moggadeet-thinking. Not Me-Myself. Only Something-that-lives, acts without thought. Helpless-Moggadeet. In the cold is only the Plan. I almost thought it.

And then one day the night chill lingered and lingered and the sun was hidden in the mists. And I found myself going up the Trails.

The Trails are a part of the Plan too, my redling.

The Trails are of winter. There we must go all of us, we blacks. When the cold grows stronger the Plan calls us upward, upward, we begin to drift up the Trails, up along the ridges to the cold, the night-side of the mountains. Up beyond the forests where the trees grow scant and turn to dead stonewood.

So the Plan drew me and I followed, only half-aware. Sometimes I came into warmer sunlight where I could stop and feed and try to think, but the cold fogs rose again and I went on, on and up. I began to catch sight of others like me far along the mountain-flank, moving steadily up. They didn't rear or roar when they saw me. I didn't call to them. Each one alone we climbed on toward the Caves, unthinking, blind. And so I would have gone too.

But then the great thing happened.

—Oh, no, my Lilliloo! Not the *greatest*. The greatest of all is you, will always be you. My precious sunmite, my red lovebaby! Don't be angry, no, no, my sharing one. Hold me softly. I must say our big learning. Hear your Moggadeet, hear and remember!

In the sun's last warm I found him, the Old One. A terrible sight! So maimed and damaged, parts rotting and gone. I stared, thinking him dead. Suddenly his head rolled feebly and a croak came out.

"Young…one?" An eye opened in his festering head, a flyer pecked at it.

"Young one…wait!"

And I understood him! Oh, with love—

No, no, my redling! Gently! Gently hear your Moggadeet. We *spoke*—the Old One and I! Old to young, we shared. I think it cannot happen.

"No old ones," he creaked. "Never to speak…we blacks. Never. It is not… the Plan. Only me…I wait… ."

"Plan," I ask, half-knowing. "What is the Plan?"

"A beauty," he whispers. "In the warm, a beauty in the air…I followed…but another black one saw me and we fought…and I was damaged, but still the Plan made me follow until I was crushed and torn and dead… . But I lived! And the Plan let me go and I crawled here…to wait…to share…but—"

His head sags. Quickly I snatch a flyer from the air and push it to his torn jaws.

"Old One! What is the Plan?"

He swallows painfully, his one eye holding mine.

"In us," he says thickly, stronger now. "In us, moving us in all things necessary for the life. You have seen. When the baby is golden the Mother cherishes it all winter long. But when it turns red or black she drives it away. Was it not so?"

"Yes, but—"

"That's the Plan! Always the Plan. Gold is the color of Mother-care, but black is the color of rage. Attack the black! Black is to kill. Even a Mother, even her own baby, she cannot defy the Plan. Hear me, young one!"

"I hear. I have seen," I answer. "But what is red?"

"Red!" He groans. "Red is the color of love."

"No!" I say, stupid Moggadeet! "I know love. Love is gold."

The Old One's eye turns from me. "Love," he sighs. "When the beauty comes in the air, you will see …" He falls silent. I fear he's dying. What can I do? We stay silent there together in the last misty sunwarm. Dimly on the slopes I can see other black ones like myself drifting steadily upward on their own Trails among the stone-tree heaps, into the icy mists.

"Old One! Where do we go?"

"You go to the Caves of Winter. That is the Plan."

"Winter, yes. The cold. Mother told us. And after the cold winter comes the warm. I remember. The winter will pass, won't it? Why did she say, the winters grow? Teach me, Old One. What is a Father?"

"Fa-ther? A word I don't know. But wait—" His mangled head turns to me. *"The winters grow?* Your mother said this? Oh, cold! Oh, lonely," he groans. "A big learning she gave you. This learning I fear to think."

His eye rolls, glaring. I am frightened inside.

"Look around, young one. These stony deadwoods. Dead shells of trees that grow in the warm valleys. Why are they here? The cold has killed them. No living tree grows here now. Think, young one!"

I look, and true! It is a warm forest killed to stone.

"Once, it was warm here. Once it was like the valleys. But the cold has grown stronger. The winter grows. Do you see? *And the warm grows less and less.*"

"But the warm is life! The warm is Me-Myself!"

"Yes. In the warm we think, we learn. In the cold is only the Plan. In the cold we are blind.... . Waiting here, I thought, was there a time when it was warm here once? Did we come here, we blacks, in the warm to speak, to share? Oh, young one, a fearful thinking. Does our time of learning grow shorter, shorter? Where will it end? Will the winters grow until we can learn nothing but only live blindly in the Plan, like the silly fatclimbers who sing but do not speak?"

His words fill me with cold fear. Such a terrible learning! I feel anger.

"No! We will not! We must—we must hold the warm!"

"Hold the warm?" He twists painfully to stare at me. "Hold the warm.... . A great thinking. Yes. But how? How? Soon it will be too cold to think, even here!"

"The warm will come again," I tell him. "Then we must learn a way to hold it, you and I!"

His head lolls.

"No...When the warm comes I will not be here...and you will be too busy for thinking, young one."

"I will help you! I will carry you to the Caves!"

"In the Caves," he gasps, "in each Cave there are two black ones like yourself. One is living, waiting mindless for the winter to pass.... . And while he waits, he eats. He eats the other, that is how he lives. That is the Plan. As you will eat me, my youngling."

"No!" I cry in horror. "I will never harm you!"

"When the cold comes you will see," he whispers. "Great is the Plan!"

"No! You are wrong! I will break the Plan," I shout. A cold wind is blowing from the summit; the sun dies.

"Never will I harm you," I bellow. "You are wrong to say so!"

My scaleplates are rising, my tail begins to pound. Through the mists I hear his gasps.

I recall dragging a heavy black thing to my Cave.

Chill cold, kill cold...In the cold I killed you.

Leelyloo. He did not resist.

Great is the Plan. He accepted all, perhaps he even felt a strange joy, as I feel it now. In the Plan is joy. But if the Plan is wrong? *The winters grow.* Do the fatclimbers have their Plan too?

Oh, a hard thinking! How we tried, my redling, my joy. All the long warm days I explained it to you, over and over. How the winter would come and change us if we did not hold the warm. You understood! You share, you understand me now, my precious flame—though you can't speak I feel your sharing love. Softly …

Oh, yes, we made our preparations, our own Plan. Even in the highest heat we made our Plan against the cold. Have other lovers done so? How I searched, carrying you, my cherry bud, I crossed whole mountain ranges, following the sun until we found this warmest of warm valleys on the sunward side. Surely the cold would be weak here, I thought. How could they reach us here, the cold fogs, the icy winds that froze my inner Me and drew me up the Trails into the dead Caves of Winter?

This time I would defy!

This time I have *you*.

"Don't take me there, my Moggadeet!" You begged, fearful of the strangeness. "Don't take me to the cold!"

"Never, my Leelyloo! Never, I vow it. Am I not your Mother, little redness?"

"But you will change! The cold will make you forget. Is it not the Plan?"

"We will break the Plan, Lilli. See, you are growing larger, heavier, my fireberry—and always more beautiful! Soon I will not be able to carry you so easily, I could never carry you to the cold Trails. And I will never leave you!"

"But you are so big, Moggadeet! When the change comes you will forget and drag me to the cold."

"Never! Your Moggadeet has a deeper Plan! When the mists start I will take you to the farthest, warmest cranny of this cave, and there I will spin a wall so you can never never be pulled out. And I will never never leave you. Even the Plan cannot draw Moggadeet from Leelyloo!"

"But you will have to go hunting for food and the cold will take you then! You will forget me and follow the cold love of winter and leave me there to die! Perhaps that is the Plan!"

"Oh, no, my precious, my redling! Don't grieve, don't cry! Hear your Moggadeet's Plan! From now on I'll hunt twice as hard. I'll fill this cave to the top, my fat little blushbud, I will fill it with food now so I can stay by you all the winter through!"

And so I did, didn't I, my Lilli? Silly Moggadeet, how I hunted, how I brought lizards, hoppers, fatclimbers, and banlings by the score. What a fool! For of course they rotted, there in the heat, and the heaps turned green and slimy—but still tasting good, eh, my berry?—so that we had to eat them then, gorging ourselves like babies. And how you grew!

Oh, beautiful you became, my jewel of redness! So bursting fat and shiny-full, but still my tiny one, my sun-spark. Each night after I fed you I would part the silk, fondling your head, your eyes, your tender ears, trembling with excitement for the delicious moment when I would release your first scarlet limb to caress and exercise it and press it to my pulsing throat-sacs. Sometimes I would unbind two together for the sheer joy of seeing you move. And each night it took longer, each morning I had to make more silk to bind you up. How proud I was, my Leely, Lilliloo!

That was when my greatest thinking came.

As I was weaving you so tenderly into your shining cocoon, my joyberry, I thought, why not bind up living fatclimbers? Pen them alive so their flesh will stay sweet and they will serve us through the winter!

That was a great thinking, Lilliloo, and I did this, and it was good. Fatclimbers in plenty I walled in a little tunnel, and many, many other things as well, while the sun walked back toward winter and the shadows grew and grew. Fatclimbers and banlings and all tasty creatures and even—oh, clever Moggadeet!—all manner of leaves and bark and stuffs for them to eat! Oh, we had broken the Plan for sure now!

"We have broken the Plan for sure, my Lilli-red. The fatclimbers are eating the twigs and bark, the banlings are eating juice from the wood, the great runners are munching grass, and we will eat them all!"

"Oh, Moggadeet, you are brave! Do you think we can really break the Plan? I am frightened! Give me a banling, I think it grows cold."

"You have eaten fifteen banlings, my minikin!" I teased you. "How fat you grow! Let me look at you again, yes, you must let your Moggadeet caress you while you eat. Ah, how adorable you are!"

And of course—Oh, you remember how it began then, our deepest love. For when I uncovered you one night with the first hint of cold in the air, I saw that you had changed.

Shall I say it?

Your secret fur. Your *Mother fur.*

Always I had cleaned you there tenderly, but without difficulty to restrain myself. But on this night when I parted the silk strands with my huge hunting claws, what new delights met my eyes! No longer pink and pale but fiery red! *Red!* Scarlet blaze like the reddest sunrise, gold-tipped! And swollen, curling, dewy—Oh! Commanding me to expose you, all of you. Oh, how your tender eyes melted me and your breath musky-sweet and your limbs warm and heavy in my grasp!

Wildly I ripped away the last strands, dazed with bliss as you slowly stretched your whole blazing redness before my eyes. I knew then—*we* knew!—that the love we felt before was only a beginning. My hunting-limbs fell at my sides and my special hands, my weaving hands grew, filled with new, almost painful life. I could not speak, my throat-sacs filling, filling! And my lovehands rose up by themselves, pressing ecstatically, while my eyes bent closer, closer to your glorious *red*!

But suddenly the Me-Myself, Moggadeet awoke! I jumped back!

"Lilli! What's happening to us?"

"Oh, Moggadeet, I love you! Don't go away!"

"What is it, Leelyloo? Is it the Plan?"

"I don't care! Moggadeet, don't you love me?"

"I fear! I fear to harm you! You are so tiny. I am your Mother."

"No, Moggadeet, look! I am as big as you are. Don't be afraid."

I drew back—oh, hard, hard!—and tried to look calmly.

"True, my redling, you have grown. But your limbs are so new, so tender. Oh, I can't look!"

Averting my eyes I began to spin a screen of silk, to shut away your maddening redness.

"We must wait, Lilliloo. We must go on as before. I don't know what this strange urging means; I fear it will bring you harm."

"Yes, Moggadeet. We will wait."

And so we waited. Oh, yes. Each night it grew more hard. We tried to be as before, to be happy. Leely-Moggadeet. Each night as I caressed your glowing limbs that seemed to offer themselves to me as I swathed and unswathed them in turn, the urge rose in me hotter, more strong. To unveil you wholly! To look again upon your whole body!

Oh, yes, my darling, I feel—unbearable—how you remember with me those last days of our simple love.

Colder…colder. Mornings when I went to harvest the fatclimbers there was a whiteness on their fur and the banlings ceased to move. The sun sank ever lower, paler, and the cold mists hung above us, reaching down. Soon I dared not leave the cave. I stayed all day by your silken wall, humming Motherlike, *Brum-a-loo, Mooly-mooly, Lilliloo, Love Leely.* Strong Moggadeet!

"We'll wait, fireling. We will not yield to the Plan! Aren't we happier than all others, here with our love in our warm cave?"

"Oh, yes, Moggadeet."

"I'm Myself now. I am strong. I'll make my own Plan. I will not look at you until…until the warm, until the Sun comes back."

"Yes, Moggadeet…Moggadeet? My limbs are cramped."

"Oh, my precious, wait—see, I am opening the silk very carefully, I will not look—I won't—"

"Moggadeet, don't you love me?"

"Leelyloo! Oh, my glorious one! I fear, I fear—"

"Look, Moggadeet! See how big I am, how strong!"

"Oh, redling, my hands—my hands—what are they doing to you?"

For with my special hands I was pressing, pressing the hot juices from my throat-sacs and tenderly, tenderly parting your sweet Mother-fur and *placing my gift within your secret places.* And as I did this our eyes entwined and our limbs made a wreath.

"My darling, do I hurt you?"

"Oh, no, Moggadeet! Oh, no!"

Oh, my adored one, those last days of our love!

Outside the world grew colder yet, and the fatclimbers ceased to eat and the banlings lay still and began to stink. But still we held the warmth deep in our cave and still I fed my beloved on the last of our food. And every night our new ritual of love became more free, richer, though I compelled myself to hide all but a portion of your sweet body. But each dawn it grew hard and harder for me to replace the silken bonds around your limbs.

"Moggadeet! Why do you not bind me! I am afraid!"

"A moment, Lilli, a moment. I must caress you just once more."

"I'm afraid, Moggadeet! Cease now and bind me!"

"But why, my lovekin? Why must I hide you? Is this not some foolish part of the Plan?"

"I don't know, I feel so strange. Moggadeet, I—I'm changing."

"You grow more glorious every moment, my Lilli, my own. Let me look at you! It is wrong to bind you away!"

"No, Moggadeet! No!"

But I would not listen, would I? Oh, foolish Moggadeet-who-thought-to-be-your-Mother. Great is the Plan!

I did not listen, I did not bind you up. No! I ripped them away, the strong silk strands. Mad with love, I slashed them all at once, rushing from each limb to the next until all your glorious body lay exposed. At last—I saw you whole!

Oh, Lilliloo, greatest of Mothers.

It was not I who was your Mother. You were mine.

Shining and bossed you lay, your armor newly grown, your mighty hunting limbs thicker than my head! What I had created. You! A Supermother, a Mother such as none have ever seen!

Stupefied with delight, I gazed.

And your huge hunting-limb came out and seized me.

Great is the Plan. I felt only joy as your jaws took me.

As I feel it now.

And so we end, my Lilliloo, my redling, for your babies are swelling through your Mother-fur and your Moggadeet can speak no longer. I am nearly devoured. The cold grows, it grows, and your Mother-eyes are growing, glowing. Soon you will be alone with our children and the warm will come again.

Will you remember, my heartmate? Will you remember and tell them? Tell them of the cold, Leelyloo. Tell them of our love.

Tell them…*the winters grow.*

~

James Tiptree, Jr., was the pseudonym of **Alice B. Sheldon** (1915-1987), who, before turning to writing, had been an artist, a newspaper art critic, a World War II photo-intelligence officer, a chicken farmer, a CIA agent, and a research psychologist. After earning her PhD in psychology in 1967, she started writing science fiction short stories—using a pseudonym to protect her new academic career, and a male name to fit in better at the magazines. As Tiptree, she published two novels and eight collections of short stories. She won two Hugo Awards, three Nebula Awards (one as Raccoona Sheldon, an occasional second nom de plume), and one World Fantasy Award. An award for gender-based science fiction was named after Tiptree in 1991, and a biography by Julie Phillips, *James Tiptree, Jr.: The Double Life of Alice B. Sheldon*, was published in 2006.

Knapsack Poems: A Goxhat Travel Journal

Eleanor Arnason

Within this person of eight bodies, thirty-two eyes, and the usual number of orifices and limbs resides a spirit as restless as gossamer on wind. In youth, I dreamed of fame as a merchant-traveler. In later years, realizing that many of my parts were prone to motion sickness, I thought of scholarship or accounting. But I lacked the Great Determination which is necessary for both trades. My abilities are spontaneous and brief, flaring and vanishing like a falling star. For me to spend my life adding numbers or looking through dusty documents would be like "lighting a great hall with a single lantern bug" or "watering a great garden with a drop of dew."

Finally, after consulting the caregivers in my crèche, I decided to become a traveling poet. It's a strenuous living and does not pay well, but it suits me.

• • •

Climbing through the mountains west of Ibri, I heard a *wishik* call, then saw the animal, its wings like white petals, perched on a bare branch.

"Is that tree flowering
So late in autumn?
Ridiculous idea!
I long for dinner."

One of my bodies recited the poem. Another wrote it down, while still others ranged ahead, looking for signs of habitation. As a precaution, I carried cudgels as well as pens and paper. One can never be sure what will appear in the country west of Ibri. The great poet Raging Fountain died there of a combination of diarrhea and malicious ghosts. Other writers, hardly less famous, have been killed by monsters or bandits or, surviving these, met their end at the hands of dissatisfied patrons.

The Bane of Poets died before my birth. Its[1] ghost or ghosts offered Raging Fountain the fatal bowl of porridge. But other patrons still remain "on steep slopes and in stony dales."

> "Dire the telling
> Of patrons in Ibri:
> Bone-breaker lurks
> High on a mountain.
> Skull-smasher waits
> In a shadowy valley.
> Better than these
> The country has only
> Grasper, Bad-bargain,
> And Hoarder-of-Food."

Why go to such a place, you may be wondering? Beyond Ibri's spiny mountains lie the wide fields of Greater and Lesser Ib, prosperous lands well known for patronage of the arts.

Late in the afternoon, I realized I would find no refuge for the night. Dark snow-clouds hid the hills in front of me. Behind me, low in the south, the sun shed pale light. My shadows, long and many-limbed, danced ahead of me on the rutted road.

My most poetic self spoke:

> "The north is blocked
> By clouds like boulders.
> A winter sun
> Casts shadows in my way."

---

1. Goxhat units, or "persons" as the goxhat say, comprise four to sixteen bodies and two or three sexes. The Bane of Poets was unusual in being entirely neuter, which meant it could not reproduce. According to legend, it was reproductive frustration and fear of death which made The Bane so dangerous to poets. Why poets? They produce two kinds of children, those of body and those of mind, and grasp in their pinchers the gift of undying fame.

Several of my other selves frowned. My scribe wrote the poem down with evident reluctance.

"Too obvious," muttered a cudgel-carrier.

Another self agreed. "Too much like Raging Fountain in his/her mode of melancholy complaint."

Far ahead, a part of me cried alarm. I suspended the critical discussion and hurried forward in a clump, my clubs raised and ready for use.

Soon, not even breathless, I stopped at a place I knew by reputation: the Tooth River. Wide and shallow, it ran around pointed stones, well exposed this time of year and as sharp as the teeth of predators. On the far side of the river were bare slopes that led toward cloudy mountains. On the near side of the river, low cliffs cast their shadows over a broad shore. My best scout was there, next to a bundle of cloth. The scout glanced up, saw the rest of me and—with deft fingers—undid the blanket folds.

Two tiny forms lay curled at the blanket's center. A child of one year, holding itself in its arms.

"Alive?" I asked myself.

The scout crouched closer. "One body is and looks robust. The other body—" my scout touched it gently "—is cold."

Standing among myself, I groaned and sighed. There was no problem understanding what had happened. A person had given birth. Either the child had been unusually small, or the other parts had died. For some reason the parent had been traveling alone. Maybe he/she/it had been a petty merchant or a farmer driven off the land by poverty. If not these, then a wandering thief or someone outlawed for heinous crimes. A person with few resources. In any case, he/she/it had carried the child to this bitter place, where the child's next-to-last part expired.

Imagine standing on the river's icy edge, holding a child who had become a single body. The parent could not bear to raise an infant so incomplete! What parent could? One did no kindness by raising such a cripple to be a monster among ordinary people.

Setting the painful burden down, the parent crossed the river.

I groaned a second time. My most poetic self said:

"Two bodies are not enough;
One body is nothing,"

The rest of me hummed agreement. The poet added a second piece of ancient wisdom:

"Live in a group
Or die."
I hummed a second time.

The scout lifted the child from its blanket. "It's female."

The baby woke and cried, waving her four arms, kicking her four legs, and urinating. My scout held her as far away as possible. Beyond doubt, she was a fine, loud, active mite! But incomplete.

"Why did you wake her?" asked a cudgel-carrier. "She should be left to die in peace."

"No," said the scout. "She will come with me."

"Me! What do you mean by me?" my other parts cried.

There is no art nor wisdom in a noisy argument. Therefore, I will not describe the discussion that followed as night fell. Snowflakes drifted from the sky—slowly at first, then more and more thickly. I spoke with the rudeness people reserve for themselves in privacy; and the answers I gave myself were sharp indeed. Words like pointed stones, like the boulders in Tooth River, flew back and forth. Ah! The wounds I inflicted and suffered! Is anything worse than internal dispute?

The scout would not back down. She had fallen in love with the baby, as defective as it was. The cudgel-bearers, sturdy males, were outraged. The poet and the scribe, refined neuters, were repulsed. The rest of me was female and a bit more tender.

I had reached the age when fertile eggs were increasing unlikely. In spite of my best efforts, I had gained neither fame nor money. What respectable goxhat would mate with a vagabond like me? What crèche would offer to care for my offspring? Surely this fragment of a child was better than nothing.

"No!" said my males and neuters. "This is not a person! One body alone can never know togetherness or integration!"

But my female selves edged slowly toward the scout's opinion. Defective the child certainly was. Still, she was alive and goxhat, her darling little limbs waving fiercely and her darling mouth making noises that would shame a monster.

Most likely she would die. The rest of her had. Better that she die in someone's arms, warm and comfortable, than in the toothy mouth of a prowling predator. The scout rewrapped the child in the blanket.

It was too late to ford the river. I made camp under a cliff, huddling together for warmth, my arms around myself, the baby in the middle of the heap I made.

When morning came, the sky was clear. Snow sparkled everywhere. I rose, brushed myself off, gathered my gear, and crossed the river. The water was low, as I expected this time of year, but ice-cold. My feet were numb by the time I reached the far side. My teeth chattered on every side like castanets.

The baby, awakened by the noise, began to cry. The scout gave her a sweet cake. That stopped the crying for a while.

At mid-day, I came in sight of a keep. My hearts lifted with hope. Alas! Approaching it, I saw the walls were broken.

The ruination was recent. I walked through one of the gaps and found a courtyard, full of snowy heaps. My scouts spread out and investigated. The snow hid bodies, as I expected. Their eyes were gone, but most of the rest remained, preserved by cold and the season's lack of bugs.

"This happened a day or two ago," my scouts said. "Before the last snow, but not by much. *Wishik* found them and took what they could, but didn't have time—before the storm—to find other predators and lead them here. This is why the bodies are still intact. The *wishik* can pluck out eyes, but skin is too thick for them to penetrate. They need the help of other animals, such as *hirg*." One of the scouts crouched by a body and brushed its rusty back hair. "I won't be able to bury these. There are too many."

"How many goxhat are here?" asked my scribe, taking notes.

"It's difficult to say for certain. Three or four, I suspect, all good-sized. A parent and children would be my guess."

I entered the keep building and found more bodies. Not many. Most of the inhabitants had fallen in the courtyard. There was a nursery with scattered toys, but no children.

"Ah! Ah!" I cried, reflecting on the briefness of life and the frequency with which one encounters violence and sorrow.

My poet said:

"Broken halls
and scattered wooden words.
How will the children
learn to read and write?"[2]

---

2. This translation is approximate. Like humans, goxhat use wooden blocks to teach their children writing. However, their languages are ideogrammic, and the blocks are inscribed with entire words. Their children build sentences shaped like walls, towers, barns, and other buildings. Another translation of the poem would be:

Broken walls.
Broken sentences.
Ignorant offspring.
Alas!

Finally I found a room with no bodies or toys, nothing to remind me of mortality. I lit a fire and settled for the night. The baby fussed. My scout cleaned her, then held her against a nursing bud—for comfort only; the scout had no milk. The baby sucked. I ate my meager rations. Darkness fell. My thirty-two eyes reflected firelight. After a while, a ghost arrived. Glancing up, I saw it in the doorway. It looked quite ordinary: three goxhat bodies with rusty hair.

"Who are you?" one of my scouts asked.

"The former owner of this keep, or parts of her. My name was Content-in-Solitude; and I lived here with three children, all lusty and numerous.—Don't worry."

My cudgel-carriers had risen, cudgels in hand.

"I'm a good ghost. I'm still in this world because my death was so recent and traumatic. As soon as I've gathered myself together, and my children have done the same, we'll be off to a better place. [3]

"I stopped here to tell you our names, so they will be remembered."

"Content-in-Solitude," muttered my scribe, writing.

"My children were Virtue, Vigor, and Ferrous Oxide. Fine offspring! They should have outlived me. Our killer is Bent Foot, a bandit in these mountains. He took my grandchildren to raise as his own, since his female parts—all dead now—produced nothing satisfactory. Mutant children with twisted feet and nasty dispositions! No good will come of them; and their ghosts will make these mountains worse than ever. Tell my story, so others may be warned."

"Yes," my poet said in agreement. The rest of me hummed.

For a moment the three bodies remained in the doorway. Then they drew together and merged into one. "You see! It's happening! I am becoming a single ghost! Well, then. I'd better be off to find the rest of me, and my children, and a better home for all of us."

The rest of the night was uneventful. I slept well, gathered around the fire, warmed by its embers and my bodies' heat. If I had dreams, I don't remember them. At dawn, I woke. By sunrise I was ready to leave. Going out of the building, I discovered three *hirg* in the courtyard: huge predators with shaggy, dull-brown fur. *Wishik* fluttered around them as they tore into the bodies of Content and her children. I took one look, then retreated, leaving the keep by another route.

That day passed in quiet travel. My poet spoke no poetry. The rest of me was equally silent, brooding on the ruined keep and its ghost.

---

3. According to the goxhat, when a person dies, his/her/its goodness becomes a single ghost known as "The Harmonious Breath" or "The Collective Spirit." This departs the world for a better place. But a person's badness remains as a turbulent and malicious mob, attacking itself and anyone else who happens along.

I found no keep to shelter me that night or the next or the next. Instead, I camped out. My scout fed the baby on thin porridge. It ate and kept the food down, but was becoming increasingly fretful and would not sleep unless the scout held it to a nursing bud. Sucking on the dry knob of flesh, it fell asleep.

"I don't mind," said the scout. "Though I'm beginning to worry. The child needs proper food."

"Better to leave it by the way," a male said. "Death by cold isn't a bad ending."

"Nor death by dehydration," my other male added.

The scout looked stubborn and held the child close.

Four days after I left the ruined keep, I came to another building, this one solid and undamaged.

My scribe said, "I know the lord here by reputation. She is entirely female and friendly to the womanly aspects of a person. The neuter parts she tolerates. But she doesn't like males. Her name is The Testicle Straightener."

My cudgel-carriers shuddered. The scribe and poet looked aloof, as they inevitably did in such situations. Clear-eyed and rational, free from sexual urges, they found the rest of me a bit odd.

The scout carrying the baby said, "The child needs good food and warmth and a bath. For that matter, so do I."

Gathering myself together, I strode to the gate and knocked. After several moments, it swung open. Soldiers looked out. There were two of them: one tall and grey, the other squat and brown. Their bodies filled the entrance, holding spears and axes. Their eyes gleamed green and yellow.

"I am a wandering poet, seeking shelter for the night. I bring news from the south, which your lord might find useful."

The eyes peered closely, then the soldiers parted—grey to the left, brown to the right—and let me in.

Beyond the gate was a snowy courtyard. This one held no bodies. Instead, the snow was trampled and urine-marked. A living place! Though empty at the moment, except for the two soldiers who guarded the gate.

I waited in an anxious cluster. At length, a servant arrived and looked me over. "You need a bath and clean clothes. Our lord is fastidious and dislikes guests who stink. Come with me."

I followed the servant into the keep and down a flight of stairs. Metal lamps were fastened to the walls. Most were dark, but a few shone, casting a dim light. The servant had three sturdy bodies, all covered with black hair.

Down and down. The air grew warm and moist. A faint, distinctive aroma filled it.

"There are hot springs in this part of Ibri," the servant said. "This keep was built on top of one; and there is a pool in the basement, which always steams and smells."

Now I recognized the aroma: rotten eggs.

We came to a large room, paved with stone and covered by a broad, barrel vault. Metal lanterns hung from the ceiling on chains. As was the case with the lamps on the stairway, most were dark. But a few flickered dimly. I could see the bathing pool: round and carved from bedrock. Steps went down into it. Wisps of steam rose.

"Undress," said the servant. "I'll bring soap and towels."

I complied eagerly. Only my scout hesitated, holding the baby.

"I'll help you with the mite," said my scribe, standing knee-deep in hot water. The scout handed the baby over and undressed.

Soon I was frolicking in the pool, diving and spouting. Cries of joy rang in the damp, warm room. Is anything better than a hot bath after a journey?

The scout took the baby back and moved to the far side of the pool. When the servant returned, the scout sank down, holding the baby closely, hiding it in shadow. Wise mite, it did not cry!

The rest of me got busy, scrubbing shoulders and backs. Ah, the pleasure of warm lather!

Now and then, I gave a little yip of happiness. The servant watched with satisfaction, his/her/its arms piled high with towels.

On the far side of the pool, my best scout crouched, nursing the babe on a dry bud and watching the servant with hooded eyes.

At last I climbed out, dried off, and dressed. In the confusion—there was a lot of me—the scout managed to keep the baby concealed. Why I did not know, but the scout was prudent and usually had a good reason for every action, though parts of me still doubted about the wisdom of keeping the baby. There would be time to talk all of this over, when the servant was gone.

He/she/it led me up a new set of stairs. The climb was long. The servant entertained me with the following story.

The keep had a pulley system, which had been built by an ingenious traveling plumber. This lifted buckets of hot water from the spring to a tank on top of the keep. From there the water descended through metal pipes, carried by the downward propensity that is innate in water. The pipes heated every room.

"What powers the pulley system?" my scribe asked, notebook in hand.

"A treadmill," said the servant.

"And what powers the treadmill?"

"Criminals and other people who have offended the lord. No keep in Ibri is more comfortable," the servant continued with pride. "This is what happens when a lord is largely or entirely female. As the old proverb says, male bodies give a person forcefulness. Neuter bodies give thoughtfulness and clarity of vision. But nurture and comfort come from a person's female selves."

Maybe, I thought. But were the people in the treadmill comfortable?

The servant continued the story. The plumber had gone east to Ib and built other heated buildings: palaces, public baths, hotels, hospitals, and crèches. In payment for this work, several of the local lords mated with the plumber; and the local crèches vied to raise the plumber's children, who were numerous and healthy.

"A fine story, with a happy ending," I said, thinking of my fragment of a child, nursing on the scout's dry bud. Envy, the curse of all artists and artisans, roiled in my hearts. Why had I never won the right to lay fertile eggs? Why were my purses empty? Why did I have to struggle to protect my testes and to stay off treadmills, while this plumber—surely not a better person than I—enjoyed fame, honor and fertility?

The guest room was large and handsome, with a modern wonder next to it: a defecating closet. Inside the closet, water came from the wall in two metal pipes, which ended in faucets. "Hot and cold," said the servant, pointing. Below the faucets was a metal basin, decorated with reliefs of frolicking goxhat. Two empty buckets stood next to the basin.

The servant said, "If you need to wash something, your hands or feet or any other part, fill the basin with water. Use the buckets to empty the basin; and after you use the defecating throne, empty the buckets down it. This reduces the smell and gets rid of the dirty water. As I said, our lord is fastidious; and we have learned from her example. The plumber helped, by providing us with so much water.

"I'll wait in the hall. When you're ready to meet the lord, I'll guide you to her."

"Thank you," said my scribe, always courteous.

I changed into clean clothing, the last I had, and put bardic crowns on my heads[4]. Each crown came from a different contest, though all were minor. I had never won a really big contest. Woven of fine wool, with brightly colored tassels hanging down, the crowns gave me an appearance of dignity. My nimble-fingered scouts unpacked my instruments: a set of chimes, a pair of castanets, and a bagpipe. Now I was ready to meet the lord.

All except my best scout, who climbed into the middle of a wide soft bed, child in arms.

"Why did you hide the mite?" asked my scholar.

"This keep seems full of rigid thinkers, overly satisfied with themselves and their behavior. If they saw the child they would demand an explanation. 'Why do you keep it? Can't you see how fragmentary it is? Can't you see that

---

4. Actually, cerebral bulges. The goxhat don't have heads as humans understand the word.

it's barely alive? Don't you know how to cut your losses?' I don't want to argue or explain."

"What is meant by 'I'?" my male parts asked. "What is meant by 'my' reasons?"

"This is no time for an argument," said the poet.

All of me except the scout went to meet the keep's famous lord.

The Straightener sat at one end of a large hall: an elderly goxhat with frosted hair. Four parts of her remained, all sturdy, though missing a few pieces here and there: a foot, a hand, an eye or finger. Along the edges of the hall sat her retainers on long benches: powerful males, females, and neuters, adorned with iron and gold.

"Great your fame,
Gold-despoiler,
Bold straightener of scrota,
Wise lord of Ibri.

"Hearing of it,
I've crossed high mountains,
Anxious to praise
Your princely virtues."

My poet stopped. Straightener leaned forward. "Well? Go on! I want to hear about my princely virtues."

"Give me a day to speak with your retainers and get exact details of your many achievements," the poet said. "Then I will be able to praise you properly."

The goxhat leaned back. "Never heard of me, have you? Drat! I was hoping for undying fame."

"I will give it to you," my poet said calmly.

"Very well," the lord said. "I'll give you a day, and if I like what you compose, I'll leave your male parts alone."

All of me thanked her. Then I told the hall about my stay at the ruined keep. The retainers listened intently. When I had finished, the lord said, "My long-time neighbor! Dead by murder! Well, death comes to all of us. When I was born, I had twenty parts. A truly large number! That is what I'm famous for, as well as my dislike of men, which is mere envy. My male bodies died in childhood, and my neuter parts did not survive early adulthood. By thirty, I was down to ten bodies, all female. The neuters were not much of a loss. Supercilious twits, I always thought. But I miss my male parts. They were so feisty and full of piss! When travelers come here, I set them difficult tasks. If they fail, I have my soldiers hold them, while I unfold their delicate, coiled testicles. No permanent damage is done, but the screaming makes me briefly happy."

My male bodies looked uneasy and shifted back and forth on their feet, as if ready to run. But the two neuters remained calm. My poet thanked the lord a second time, sounding confident. Then I split up and went in all directions through the hall, seeking information.

The drinking went on till dawn, and the lord's retainers were happy to tell me stories about the Straightener. She had a female love of comfort and fondness for children, but could not be called tender in any other way. Rather, she was a fierce leader in battle and a strict ruler, as exact as a balance or a straight edge.

"She'll lead us against Bent Foot," one drunk soldier said. "We'll kill him and bring the children here. The stolen children, at least. I don't know about Bent Foot's spawn. It might be better for them to die. Not my problem. I let the lord make all the decisions, except whether or not I'm going to fart."

Finally I went up to my room. My scout lay asleep, the baby in her arms. My male parts began to pace nervously. The rest of me settled to compose a poem.

As the sky brightened, the world outside began to wake and make noise. Most of the noise could be ignored, but there was a *wishik* under the eaves directly outside my room's window. Its shrill, repeating cry drove my poet to distraction. I could not concentrate on the poem.

Desperate, I threw things at the animal: buttons from my sewing kit, spare pens, an antique paperweight I found in the room. Nothing worked. The *wishik* fluttered away briefly, then returned and resumed its irritating cry.

At last my scout woke. I explained the problem. She nodded and listened to the *wishik* for a while. Then she fastened a string to an arrow and shot the arrow out the window. It hit the *wishik*. The animal gave a final cry. Grabbing the string, my scout pulled the beast inside.

"Why did I do that?" I asked.

"Because I didn't want the body to fall in the courtyard."

"Why not?"

Before she could answer, the body at her feet expanded and changed its shape. Instead of the body of a dead *wishik*, I saw a grey goxhat body, pierced by the scout's arrow, dead.

My males swore. The rest of me exclaimed in surprise.

My scout said, "This is part of a wizard, no doubt employed by the keep's lord, who must really want to unroll my testicles, since she is willing to be unfair and play tricks. The *wishik* cry was magical, designed to bother me so much than I could not concentrate on composition. If this body had fallen to the ground, the rest of the wizard would have seen it and known the trick had failed. As things are, I may have time to finish the poem." The scout looked at the rest of me severely. "Get to work."

My poet went back to composing, my scribe to writing. The poem went smoothly now. As the stanzas grew in number, I grew increasingly happy and pleased. Soon I noticed the pleasure was sexual. This sometimes happened, though usually when a poem was erotic. The god of poetry and the god of sex are siblings, though they share only one parent, who is called the All-Mother-Father.

Even though the poem was not erotic, my male and female parts became increasingly excited. Ah! I was rubbing against myself. Ah! I was making soft noises! The poet and scribe could not feel this sexual pleasure, of course, but the sight of the rest of me tumbling on the rug was distracting. Yes, neuters are clear-eyed and rational, but they are also curious; and nothing arouses their curiosity more than sex. They stopped working on the poem and watched as I fondled myself. [5]

Only the scout remained detached from sensuality and went into the defecating closet. Coming out with a bucket of cold water, the scout poured it over my amorous bodies.

I sprang apart, yelling with shock.

"This is more magic," the scout said. "I did not know a spell inciting lust could be worked at such a distance, but evidently it can. Every part of me that is male or female, go in the bathroom! Wash in cold water till the idea of sex becomes uninteresting! As for my neuter parts—" The scout glared. "Get back to the poem!"

"Why has one part of me escaped the spell?" I asked the scout.

"I did not think I could lactate without laying an egg first, but the child's attempts to nurse have caused my body to produce milk. As a rule, nursing mothers are not interested in sex, and this has proved true of me. Because of this, and the child's stubborn nursing, there is a chance of finishing the poem. I owe this child a debt of gratitude."

"Maybe," grumbled my male parts.

The poet and scribe said, "I shall see."

The poem was done by sunset. That evening I recited it in the lord's hall. If I do say so myself, it was a splendid achievement. The *wishik*'s cry was in it, as was the rocking up-and-down rhythm of a sexually excited goxhat. The second gave the poem energy and an emphatic beat. As for the first, every line ended with one of the two sounds in the *wishik*'s ever-repeating, irritating

5. The goxhat believe masturbation is natural and ordinary. But reproduction within a person—inbreeding, as they call it—is unnatural and a horrible disgrace. It rarely happens. Most goxhat are not intrafertile, for reasons too complicated to explain here.

cry. Nowadays, we call this repetition of sound "rhyming." But it had no name when I invented it.

When I was done, the lord ordered several retainers to memorize the poem. "I want to hear it over and over," she said. "What a splendid idea it is to make words ring against each other in this fashion! How striking the sound! How memorable! Between you and the traveling plumber, I will certainly be famous."

That night was spent like the first one, everyone except me feasting. I feigned indigestion and poured my drinks on the floor under the feasting table. The lord was tricky and liked winning. Who could say what she might order put in my cup or bowl, now that she had my poem?

When the last retainer fell over and began to snore, I got up and walked to the hall's main door. Sometime in the next day or so, the lord would discover that her wizard had lost a part to death and that one of her paperweights was missing. I did not want to be around when these discoveries were made.

Standing in the doorway, I considered looking for the treadmill. Maybe I could free the prisoners. They might be travelers like me, innocent victims of the lord's malice and envy and her desire for hot water on every floor. But there were likely to be guards around the treadmill, and the guards might be sober. I was only one goxhat. I could not save everyone. And the servant had said they were criminals.

I climbed the stairs quietly, gathered my belongings and the baby, and left through a window down a rope made of knotted sheets.

The sky was clear; the brilliant star we call Beacon stood above the high peaks, shedding so much light I had no trouble seeing my way. I set a rapid pace eastward. Toward morning, clouds moved in. The Beacon vanished. Snow began to fall, concealing my trail. The baby, nursing on the scout, made happy noises.

• • •

Two days later, I was out of the mountains, camped in a forest by an unfrozen stream. Water made a gentle sound, purling over pebbles. The trees on the banks were changers, a local variety that is blue in summer and yellow in winter. At the moment, their leaves were thick with snow. "Silver and gold," my poet murmured, looking up.

The scribe made a note.

A *wishik* clung to a branch above the poet and licked its wings. Whenever it shifted position, snow came down.

"The *wishik* cleans wings
As white as snow.

Snow falls on me, white
As a *wishik*,"

the poet said.

My scribe scribbled.

One of my cudgel-carriers began the discussion. "The Bane of Poets was entirely neuter. Fear of death made it crazy. Bent Foot was entirely male. Giving in to violence, he stole children from his neighbor. The last lord I encountered, the ruler of the heated keep, was female, malicious and unfair. Surely something can be learned from these encounters. A person should not be one sex entirely, but rather—as I am—a harmonious mixture of male, female, and neuter. But this child can't help but be a single sex."

"I owe the child a debt of gratitude," said my best scout firmly. "Without her, I would have had pain and humiliation, when the lord—a kind of lunatic—unrolled my testes, as she clearly planned to do. At best, I would have limped away from the keep in pain. At worst, I might have ended in the lord's treadmill, raising water from the depths to make her comfortable."

"The question is a good one," said my scribe. "How can a person who is only one sex avoid becoming a monster? The best combination is the one I have: male, female, and both kinds of neuter. But even two sexes provide a balance."

"Other people—besides these three—have consisted of one sex," my scout said stubbornly. "Not all became monsters. It isn't sex that has influenced these lords, but the stony fields and spiny mountains of Ibri, the land's cold winters and ferocious wildlife. My various parts can teach the child my different qualities: the valor of the cudgel-carriers, the coolness of poet and scribe, the female tenderness which the rest of me has. Then she will become a single harmony."

The scout paused. The rest of me looked dubious. The scout continued.

"Many people lose parts of themselves through illness, accident, and war; and some of these live for years in a reduced condition. Yes, it's sad and disturbing, but it can't be called unnatural. Consider aging and the end of life. The old die body by body, till a single body remains. Granted, in many cases, the final body dies quickly. But not always. Every town of good size has a Gram or Gaffer who hobbles around in a single self.

"I will not give up an infant I have nursed with my own milk. Do I wish to be known as ungrateful or callous? I, who have pinned all my hope on honor and fame?"

I looked at myself with uncertain expressions. The *wishik* shook down more snow.

"Well, then," said my poet, who began to look preoccupied. Another poem coming, most likely. "I will take the child to a crèche and leave her there."

My scout scowled. "How well will she be cared for there, among healthy children, by tenders who are almost certain to be prejudiced against a mite so partial and incomplete? I will not give her up."

"Think of how much I travel," a cudgel-carrier said. "How can I take a child on my journeys?"

"Carefully and tenderly," the scout replied. "The way my ancestors who were nomads did. Remember the old stories! When they traveled, they took everything, even the washing pot. Surely their children were not left behind."

"I have bonded excessively to this child," said my scribe to the scout.

"Yes, I have. It's done and can't be undone. I love her soft baby-down, her four blue eyes, her feisty spirit. I will not give her up."

I conversed this way for some time. I didn't become angry at myself, maybe because I had been through so much danger recently. There is nothing like serious fear to put life into perspective. Now and then, when the conversation became especially difficult, a part of me got up and went into the darkness to kick the snow or to piss. When the part came back, he or she or it seemed better.

Finally I came to an agreement. I would keep the child and carry it on my journeys, though half of me remained unhappy with this decision.

How difficult it is to be of two minds! Still, it happens; and all but the insane survive such divisions. Only they forget the essential unity that underlies differences of opinion. Only they begin to believe in individuality.

The next morning, I continued into Ib.

• • •

The poem I composed for the lord of the warm keep became famous. Its form, known as "ringing praise," was taken up by other poets. From it I gained some fame, enough to quiet my envy; and the fame led to some money, which provided for my later years.

Did I ever return to Ibri? No. The land was too bitter and dangerous; and I didn't want to meet the lord of the warm keep a second time. Instead, I settled in Lesser Ib, buying a house on the banks of a river named It-Could-Be-Worse. This turned out to be an auspicious name. The house was cozy and my neighbors pleasant. The child played in my fenced-in garden, tended by my female parts. As for my neighbors, they watched with interest and refrained from mentioning the child's obvious disability.

"Lip-presser on one side.
Tongue-biter on t'other.
Happy I live,
Praising good neighbors."

I traveled less than previously, because of the child and increasing age. But I did make the festivals in Greater and Lesser Ib. This was easy traveling on level roads across wide plains. The Ibian lords, though sometimes eccentric, were nowhere near as crazy as the ones in Ibri and no danger to me or other poets. At one of the festivals, I met the famous plumber, who turned out to be a large and handsome, male and neuter goxhat. I won the festival crown for poetry, and he/it won the crown for ingenuity. Celebrating with egg wine, we became amorous and fell into each other's many arms.

It was a fine romance and ended without regret, as did all my other romances. As a group, we goxhat are happiest with ourselves. In addition, I could not forget the prisoners in the treadmill. Whether the plumber planned it or not, he/it had caused pain for others. Surely it was wrong—unjust—for some to toil in darkness, so that others had a warm bed and hot water from a pipe?

I have to say, at times I dreamed of that keep: the warm halls, the pipes of water, the heated bathing pool, and the defecating throne which had—have I forgotten to mention this?—a padded seat.

"Better to be here
In my cozy cottage.
Some comforts
Have too high a cost."

I never laid any fertile eggs. My only child is Ap the Foundling, who is also known as Ap of One Body and Ap the Many-talented. As the last nickname suggests, the mite turned out well.

As for me, I became known as The Clanger and The *Wishik*, because of my famous rhyming poem. Other names were given to me as well: The Child Collector, The Nurturer, and The Poet Who Is Odd.

～

Eleanor Arnason has published six novels and thirty plus works of short fiction. Her novel *A Woman of the Iron People* won the Tiptree and Mythopoeic Awards. Her story "Dapple" won the Spectrum Award. She has been a finalist for the Hugo and Nebula Awards. Her most recent books are *Tomb of the Fathers*, a short novel from Aqueduct Press, and *Mammoths of the Great Plains*, a chapbook from PM Press. Both came out in 2010. Eleanor spent most of her adult life working in offices, ending finally as a nonprofit accountant, because she could not find work as a space cadet. She is now retired and writing full time. She lives in St. Paul, Minnesota.

THE COST TO
BE WISE

MAUREEN F. MCHUGH

I.

The sun was up on the snow and everything was bright to look at when the skimmer landed. It landed on the long patch of land behind the schoolhouse, dropping down into the snow like some big bug. I was supposed to be down at the distillery helping my mam but we needed water and I had to get an ice axe, so I was outside when the offworlders came.

The skimmer was from Barok. Barok was a city. It was so far away that no one I knew in Sckarline had ever been there (except for the teachers, of course) but for the offworlders the trip was only a few hours. The skimmer came a couple of times a year to bring packages for the teachers.

The skimmer sat there for a moment—long time waiting while nothing happened except people started coming to watch—and then the hatch opened out and an offworlder stepped gingerly out on the snow. The offworlder wasn't a skimmer pilot, though; it was a tall, thin boy. I shaded my eyes and watched. My hands were cold but I wanted to see.

The offworlder wore strange colors for the snow. Offworlders always wore unnatural colors. This boy wore purples and oranges and black, all shining as if they were wet and none of them thick enough to keep anyone warm. He stood with his knees stiff and his body rigid because the snow was packed to flat, slick ice by the skimmer and he wasn't sure of his balance. But he was tall and I figured he was as old as I am, so it looked odd that he still didn't know how to walk on snow. He was beardless, like a boy. Darker than any of us.

Someone inside the skimmer handed him a bag. It was deep red, and shined as if it were hard, and wrinkled as if it were felt. My father crossed to the

206

skimmer and took the bag from the boy because it was clear that the boy might fall with it and it made a person uncomfortable to watch him try to balance and carry something.

The dogs were barking, and more Sckarline people were coming because they'd heard the skimmer.

I wanted to see what the bags were made of, so I went to the hatch of the skimmer to take something. We didn't get many things from the offworlders because they weren't appropriate, but I liked offworlder things. I couldn't see much inside the skimmer because it was dark and I had been out in the sun, but standing beside the seat where the pilot was sitting there was an old white-haired man, all straight-legged and tall. As tall as Ayudesh the teacher, which is to say taller than anyone else I knew. He handed the boy a box, though, not a bag, a bright blue box with a thick white lid. A plastic box. An offworlder box. The boy handed it to me.

"Thanks," the boy said in English. Up close I could see that the boy was really a girl. Offworlders dress the same both ways, and they are so tall it's hard to tell sometimes, but this was a girl with short black hair and skin as dark as wood.

My father put the bag in the big visitors' house and I put the box there, too. It was midday at winterdark, so the sun was a red glow on the horizon. The bag looked black except where it fell into the red square of sunlight from the doorway. It shone like metal. So very fine. Like nothing we had. I touched the bag. It was plastic, too. I liked the feeling of plastic. I liked the sound of the word in lingua. If someday I had a daughter, maybe I'd name her Plastic. It would be a rich name, an exotic name. The teachers wouldn't like it, but it was a name I wished I had.

Ayudesh was walking across the snow to the skimmer when I went back outside. The girl (I hadn't shaken free from thinking of her as a boy) stuck out her hand to him. Should I have shaken her hand? No, she'd had the box, I couldn't have shaken her hand. So I had done it right. Wanji, the other teacher, was coming, too.

I got wood from the pile for the boxstove in the guesthouse, digging it from under the top wood because the top wood would be damp. It would take a long time to heat up the guesthouse, so the sooner I got started the sooner the offworlders would be comfortable.

There was a window in the visitor's house, fat-yellow above the purple-white snow.

Inside, everyone was sitting around on the floor, talking. None of the teachers were there; were they with the old man? I smelled whisak but I didn't see any, which meant that the men were drinking it outside. I sat down at the edge of the group, where it was dark, next to Dirtha. Dirtha was watching the offworld girl, who was shaking her head at Harup to try to tell him she didn't understand what he was asking. Harup pointed at her blue box again. "Can I see it?" he asked. Harup was my father's age, so he didn't speak any English.

It was warming up in here, although when the offworlder girl leaned forward and breathed out, her mouth in an O, her breath smoked the air for an instant.

It was too frustrating to watch Harup try to talk to the girl. "What's your kinship?" he asked. "I'm Harup Sckarline." He thumped his chest with his finger. "What's your kinship?" When she shook her head, not understanding all these words, he looked around and grinned. Harup wouldn't stop until he was bored, and that would take a long time.

"I'm sorry," the girl said, "I don't speak your language." She looked unhappy.

Ayudesh would be furious with us if he found out that none of us would try and use our English.

I had to think about how to ask. Then I cleared my throat, so people would know I was going to talk from the back of the group. "He asks what is your name," I said.

The girl's chin came up like a startled animal. "What?" she said.

Maybe I said it wrong? Or my accent was so bad she couldn't understand? I looked at my boots; the stitches around the toes were fraying. They had been my mother's. "Your name," I said to the boots.

The toes twitched a little, sympathetic. Maybe I should have kept quiet.

"My name is Veronique," she said.

"What is she saying?" asked Harup.

"She says her kinship is Veronique," I said.

"That's not a kinship," said Little Shemus. Little Shemus wasn't old enough to have a beard, but he was old enough to be critical of everything.

"Offworlders don't have kinship like we do," I said. "She gave her front name."

"Ask her kinship name," Little Shemus said.

"She just told you," Ardha said, taking the end of her braid out of her mouth. Ardha was a year younger than me. "They don't have kinship names. Ayudesh doesn't have a kinship name. Wanji doesn't."

"Sure they do," Shemus said. "Their kinship name is Sckarlineclan."

"We give them that name," said Ardha and pursed her round lips. Ardha was always bossy.

"What are they saying?" asked the girl.

"They say, err, they ask, what is your—" your what? How would I even ask what her kinship name was in English? There was a word for it, but I couldn't think of it. "Your other name."

She frowned. Her eyebrows were quite black. "You mean my last name?

It's Veronique Twombly."

What was so hard about "last name"? I remembered it as soon as she said it. "Tawomby," I said. "Her kinship is Veronique Tawomby."

"Tawomby," Harup said. "Amazing. It doesn't sound like a word. It sounds made-up, like children do. What's in her box?"

"I know what's in her box," said Erip. Everybody laughed except for Ardha and me. Even Little Sherep laughed and he didn't really understand.

The girl was looking at me to explain.

"He asks inside, the box is." I had gotten tangled up. Questions were hard.

"Is the box inside?" she asked.

I nodded.

"It's inside," she said.

I didn't understand her answer so I waited for her to explain.

"I don't know what you mean," she said. "Did someone bring the box inside?"

I nodded, because I wasn't sure exactly what she'd said, but she didn't reach for the box or open it or anything. I tried to think of how to say it.

"Inside," Ardha said, tentative. "What is?"

"The box," she said. "Oh wait, you want to know what's in the box?"

Ardha looked at the door so she wouldn't have to look at the offworlder. I wasn't sure, so I nodded.

She pulled the box over and opened it up. Something glimmered hard and green and there were red and yellow boxes covered in lingua and she said, "Presents for Ayudesh and Wanji." Everybody stood up to see inside, so I couldn't see, but I heard her say things. The words didn't mean anything. Tea, that I knew. Wanji talked about tea. "These are sweets," I heard her say. "You know, candy." I know the word "sweet," but I didn't know what else she meant. It was so much harder to speak English to her than it was to do it in class with Ayudesh.

Nobody was paying any attention to what she said but me. They didn't care as long as they could see. I wished I could see.

Nobody was even thinking about me, or that if I hadn't been there she never would have opened the box. But that was the way it always was. If I only lived somewhere else, my life would be different. But Sckarline was neither earth nor sky, and I was living my life in-between. People looked and fingered, but she wouldn't let them take things out, not even Harup, who was as tall as she was and a lot stronger. The younger people got bored and sat down and finally I could see Harup poking something with his finger, and the outland girl watching. She looked at me.

"What's your name?" she asked.

"Me?" I said. "Umm, Janna."

She said my name. "What's your last name, Janna?"

"Sckarline," I said.

"Oh," she said, "like the settlement."

I just nodded.

"What is his name?" She pointed.

"Harup," I said. He looked up and grinned.

"What's your name?" she asked him and I told him what she had said.

"Harup," he said. Then she went around the room, saying everybody's names. It made everyone pleased to be noticed. She was smart that way. And it was easy. Then she tried to remember all their names, which had everyone laughing and correcting her so I didn't have to talk at all.

Ayudesh came in, taller than anyone, and I noticed, for the first time in my life, that he was really an offworlder. Ayudesh had been there all my life, and I knew he was an offworlder, but to me he had always been just Ayudesh.

Then they were talking about me and Ayudesh was just Ayudesh again. "Janna?" he said. "Very good. I'll tell you what, you take care of Veronique, here. You're her translator, all right?"

I was scared, because I really couldn't understand when she talked, but I guessed I was better than anybody else.

• • •

Veronique unpacked, which was interesting, but then she just started putting things here and there and everybody else drifted off until it was just her and me.

Veronique did a lot of odd things. She used a lot of water. The first thing I did for her was get water. She followed me out and watched me chip the ice for water and fill the bucket. She fingered the wooden bucket and the rope handle.

She said something I didn't understand because it had "do" in it and a lot of pronouns and I have trouble following sentences like that. I smiled at her, but I think she realized I didn't understand. Her boots were purple. I had never seen purple boots before.

"They look strange," she said. I didn't know what looked strange. "I like your boots," she said, slowly and clearly. I did understand, but then I didn't know what to do, did she want me to give her my boots? They were my mother's old boots and I wouldn't have minded giving them to her, except I didn't have anything to take their place.

"It is really cold," she said.

Which seemed very odd to say, except I remembered that offworlders talk about the weather, Ayudesh had made us practice talking about the weather. He said it was something strangers talked about. "It is," I said. "But it will not snow tonight." That was good, it made her happy.

"And it gets dark so early," she said. "It isn't even afternoon and it's like night."

"Where you live, it is cold as this, ummm," I hadn't made a question right.

But she understood. "Oh no," she said, "where I live is warm. It is hot, I mean. There is snow only on the mountains."

She wanted to heat the water, so I put it on the stove, and then she showed me pictures of her mother and father and her brother at her house. It was summer and they were wearing only little bits of clothes.

Then she showed me a picture of herself and a man with a beard. "That's my boyfriend," she said. "We're getting married."

He looked old. Grown up. In the picture, Veronique looked older, too. I looked at her again, not sure how old she was. Maybe older than me? Wanji said offworlders got married when they were older, not like the clans.

"I have boyfriend," I said.

"You do?" She smiled at me. "What's his name?"

"Tuuvin," I said.

"Was he here before?"

I shook my head.

Then she let me see her bag. The dark red one. I loved the color. I stroked it, as slick as leather and shining. "Plastic?" I said.

She nodded.

"I like plastic," I said.

She smiled a little, like I'd said something wrong. But it was so perfect, so even in color.

"Do you want it?" she asked. Which made me think of my boots and whether she had wanted them. I shook my head.

"You can have it," she said. "I can get another one."

"No," I said. "It isn't appropriate."

She laughed, a startled laugh. I didn't understand what I'd done and the feeling that I was foolish sat in my stomach, but I didn't know what was so foolish.

She said something I didn't understand, which made me feel worse. "What did you say?" she said. "'Appropriate?'"

I nodded. "It's not appropriate," I said.

"I don't understand," she said.

Our lessons in appropriate development used lots of English words because it was hard to say these things any other way, so I found the words to tell her came easily. "Plastic," I said, "it's not appropriate. Appropriate technologies are based on the needs and capacities of people, they must be sustainable without outside support. Like the distillery is. Plastic isn't appropriate to Sckarline's economy because we can't create it and it replaces things we can produce, like skin bags." I stroked the bag again. "But I like plastic. It's beautiful."

"Wow," Veronique said. She was looking at me sharp, all alert like a stabros smelling a dog for the first time. Not afraid, but not sure what to think. "To me," she said slowly, "your skin bags are beautiful. The wooden houses," she touched the black slick wood wall, "they are beautiful."

Ayudesh and Wanji were always telling us that offworlders thought our goods were wonderful, but how could anyone look at a skin bag and then look at plastic and not see how brilliant the colors were in plastic? Dye a skin bag red and it still looked like a skin bag, like it came from dirt.

"How long you, um, you do stay?" I asked.

"Fourteen days," she said. "I'm a student, I came with my teacher."

I nodded. "Ayudesh, he is a teacher."

"My teacher, he's a friend of Ayudesh. From years ago," she said. "Have you always lived here? Were you born here?"

"Yes," I said. "I am born here. My mother and father are born in Tentas Clan, but they come here."

"Tentas Clan is another settlement?" she asked.

I shook my head. "No," I said. "No. Sckarline only is a settlement."

"Then, what is Tentas Clan?"

"It is people." I didn't know how to explain clans to her at all. "They have kinship, and they have stabros, and they are together—"

"Stabros, those are animals," she said.

I nodded. "Sckarline, uh...is an appropriate technology mission."

"Right, that Ayudesh and Wanji started. Tentas Clan is a clan, right?"

I nodded. I was worn out from talking to her.

After that, she drank tea and then I took her around to show her Sckarline. It was already almost dark. I showed her the generator where we cooked stabros manure to make electricity. I got a lantern there.

I showed her the stabros pens and the dogs, even though it wasn't really very interesting. Tuuvin was there, and Gerdor, my little uncle, leaning and watching the stabros who were doing nothing but rooting at the mud in the pen and hoping someone would throw them something to eat. The stabros shook their heads and dug with their long front toes.

"This is Tuuvin?" Veronique said.

I was embarrassed. One of the stabros, a gelding with long feathery ears, craned his head toward me. I reached out and pulled on the long guard hairs at the tips of his ears and he lipped at my hand. He had a long purple tongue. He breathed out steam. Their breath always reminded me of the smell of whisak mash.

"Do you ride them?" Veronique asked.

"What?" I asked.

"Do you, um, get on their backs?" She made a person with her fingers walking through the air, then the fingers jumped on the other hand.

"A stabros?" I asked. Tuuvin and Gerdor laughed. "No," I said. "They have no like that. Stabros angry, very much." I pretended to kick. "They have milk, sometimes. And sleds," I said triumphantly, remembering the word.

She leaned on the fence. "They are pretty," she said. "They have pretty eyes. They look so sad with their long drooping ears."

"What?" Tuuvin asked. "What's pretty?"

"She says they have pretty eyes," I said.

Gerdor laughed, but Tuuvin and I gave him a sharp look.

The dogs were leaping and barking and clawing at the gate. She stopped and reached a hand out to touch them. "Dogs are from Earth," she said.

"Dogs are *aufworld*," I said. "Like us. Stabros are *util*."

"What's that mean?" she asked.

"Stabros can eat food that is *aunworld*," I said. "We can't, dogs can't. But we can eat stabros, so they are between."

"Are stabros from Earth?" Veronique asked.

I didn't know, but Tuuvin did, which surprised me. "Stabros are from here," he said. "Ayudesh explained where it all came from, remember? *Util* animals and plants were here, but we could use them. *Aunworld* animals and plants make us sick."

"I know they make us sick," I snapped. But I translated as best I could.

Veronique was looking at the dogs. "Do they bite?" she asked.

Bite? "You mean," I clicked my teeth, "like eat? Sometimes. Mostly if they're fighting."

She took her hand back.

"I'll get a puppy," Tuuvin said, and swung a leg over the side of the pen and waded through the dogs. Tuuvin took care of the dogs a lot so he wasn't afraid of them. I didn't like them much. I liked stabros better.

"There's a winter litter?" I said.

"Yeah," he said. "But it hasn't been too cold, they might þe okay. If it gets cold we can always eat 'em."

The puppy looked like a little sausage with short arms and legs and a pink nose. Veronique cooed and took it from Tuuvin and cradled it in her arms. She talked to it, but she talked in a funny way, like baby talk, and I couldn't understand anything she said. "What's its name?" she asked.

"Its name?" I said.

"Do you name them?" she asked.

I looked at Tuuvin. Even Tuuvin should have been able to understand that; the first thing anybody learned in lingua was "What's your name?" But he wasn't paying any attention. I asked him if any of the dogs had names.

He nodded. "Some of them do. The dark male, he's a lead dog, he's called Bigman. And that one is Yellow Dog. The puppies don't have names, though."

"I think this one should have a name," Veronique said, when I told her. "I think he'll be a mighty hunter, so call him Hunter."

I didn't understand what hunting had to do with dogs, and I thought it was a bitch puppy anyway, but I didn't want to embarrass her, so I told Tuuvin. I was afraid he would laugh, but he didn't.

"How do you say that in English?" he asked. "Hunter? Okay, I'll remember." He smiled at Veronique and touched the puppy's nose. "Hunter," he said. The puppy licked him with a tiny pink tongue.

Veronique smiled back. And I didn't like it.

• • •

Veronique went to find her teacher. I went down to the distillery to tell Mam why I wasn't there helping. Tuuvin followed me down the hill. The distillery stank, so it was down below Sckarline in the trees, just above the fields.

He caught me by the waist and I hung there so he could brush his lips across my hair.

"It's too cold out here," I said and broke out of his arms.

"Let's go in the back," he said.

"I've got to tell Mam," I said.

"Once you tell your mam, there'll be all these things to do and we won't get any time together," he said.

"I can't," I said, but I let him make up my mind for me.

We went around the side, tracking through the dry snow where no one much walked, through the lacey wintertrees to the door to the storage in the back. It was as cold in the back as it was outside, and it was dark. It smelled like mash and whisak and the faint charcoal smell of the charred insides of the kegs. Brass whisak, Sckarline whisak.

He boosted me on a stack of kegs and kissed me.

It wasn't that I really cared so much about kissing. It was nice, but Tuuvin would have kissed and kissed for hours if I would let him and if we could ever find a place where we could be alone for hours. Tuuvin would kiss long after my face felt overused and bruised from kissing. But I just wanted to be with Tuuvin so much. I wanted to talk with him, and have him walk with me. I would let him kiss me if I could whisper to him. I liked the way he pressed against me now; he was warm and I was cold.

He kissed me with little kisses; kiss, kiss, kiss. I liked the little kisses. It was almost like he was talking to me in kisses. Then he kissed me hard and searched around with his tongue. I never knew what to do with my tongue when he put his in my mouth, so I just kept mine still. I could feel the rough edge of the keg beneath my legs, and if I shifted my weight it rocked on the one below it. I turned my face sideways to get my nose out of the way and opened my eyes to look past Tuuvin. In the dark I could barely make out Uukraith's eye burned on all the kegs, to keep them from going bad. Uukraith was the door witch. Uukraith's sister Ina took souls from their mother and put them in seeds, put the seed in women to make babies. The kegs were all turned different directions, eyes looking everywhere. I closed mine again. Uukraith was also a virgin.

"Ohhhh, Heth! Eeeuuuu!"

I jumped, but Tuuvin didn't, he just let go of my waist and stepped back and crossed his arms the way he did when he was uncomfortable. The air felt cold where he had just been warm.

My little sister, Bet, shook her butt at us. "Kissy, kissy, kissy," she said. "MAM, JANNA'S BACK IN THE KEGS WITH TUUVIN!"

"Shut up, Bet," I said. Not that she would stop.

"Slobber, slobber," she said, like we were stabros trading cud. She danced around, still shaking her butt. She puckered up her lips and made wet, smacking noises.

"Fucking little bitch," I said.

Tuuvin frowned at me. He liked Bet. She wasn't his little sister.

"MAM," Bet hollered, "JANNA SAID 'FUCKING'!"

"Janna," my mother called, "come here."

I tried to think of what to do to Bet. I'd have liked to slap her silly. But she'd just go crying to Mam and I'd really be in trouble. It was just that she thought she was so smart and she was really being so stupid.

Mam was on her high stool, tallying. My mam wore trousers most often, and she was tall and man-faced. Still and all, men liked her. I took after her, so I was secretly glad that men watched her walk by, even if she never much noticed.

"Leave your little sister alone," she said.

"Leave her alone!" I said. "She came and found me."

"Don't swear at her. You talk like an old man." Mam was acting like a head-man, her voice even and cool.

"If she hadn't come looking—"

"If you had been working as you're supposed to, she'd have had no one to look for, would she."

"I went to see the visitors," I said. "There are two. An old man and a girl. I helped Da carry their things to the visitors' house."

"So that means it is okay to swear at your sister."

It was the same words we always traded. The same arguments, all worn smooth and shining like the wood of a yoke. The brand for the kegs was heating in the fire and I could smell the tang of hot iron in the dung.

"You treat me like a child," I said.

She didn't even answer, but I knew what she would say, that I acted like a child. As if what Tuuvin and I were doing had anything to do with being a child.

I was so tired of it I thought I would burst.

"Go back to work," Mam said, turning on her stool. Saying "this talk is done" with her shoulders and her eyes.

"It's wrong to live this way," I said.

She looked back at me.

"If we lived with the clans, Tuuvin and I could be together."

That made her angry. "This is a better life than the clans," she said. "You don't know what you're talking about. Go back to work."

I didn't say anything. I just hated her. She didn't understand anything. She and my Da hadn't waited until they were old. They hadn't waited for anything, and they'd left their clan to come to Sckarline when it was new. I stood in front of her, making her feel me standing there, all hot and silent.

"Janna," she said. "I'll not put up with your sullenness—" It made her furious when I didn't talk.

So she slapped me, and then I ran out, crying, past Bet, who was delighted, and past Tuuvin, who had his mouth open and a stupid look on his face. And I wished they would all disappear.

• • •

Veronique sat with Tuuvin and me at dinner in the guesthouse. The guesthouse was full of smoke. We all sat down on the floor with felt and blankets. I looked to see what Veronique would be sitting on and it was wonderful. It was dark, dark blue and clean on the outside, and inside it was red and black squares. I touched it. It had a long metal fastener, a cunning thing that locked teeth together, that Veronique had unfastened so she could sit on the soft red and black inside. Dark on the outside, red on the inside; it was as if it represented some strange offworld beast. My felt blanket was red, but it was old and the edges were gray with dirt. Offworlders were so clean, as if they were always new.

Ayudesh was with the old man who had come with Veronique. Wanji was there, but she was being quiet and by herself, the way Wanji did.

Tuuvin had brought the puppy into the guesthouse. "She asked me to," he said when I asked him what he was doing.

"She did not," I said. "People are watching a dog in this house. Besides, you don't understand her when she talks."

"I do, too," he said. "I was in school, too."

I rolled my eyes. He was when he was little, but he left as soon as he was old enough to hunt. Men always left as soon as they were old enough to hunt. And he hated it anyway.

Veronique squealed when she saw the puppy and took it from Tuuvin as if it were a baby. Everyone watched out of the corner of their eyes. Ayudesh thought it was funny. We were all supposed to be equal in Sckarline, but Ayudesh was really like a headman.

She put the puppy on her offworld blanket and it rolled over on its back, showing her its tan belly. It would probably pee on her blanket.

My da leaned over. "I hope it isn't dinner." My da hated dog.

"No," I said. "She just likes it."

My da said to her, "Hie." Then to me he said, "What is she called?"

"Veronique," I said.

"Veronique," he said. Then he pointed to himself. "Guwk."

"Hello, Guwk," Veronique said.

"Hello, Veronique," said my da, which surprised me because I had never heard him say anything in English before. "Ask her for her cup," he said to me.

She had one; bright yellow and smooth. But my da handled it matter-of-factly, as if he handled beautiful things every day. He had a skin and he poured whisak into her cup. "My wife," he waved at Mam, "she makes whisak for Sckarline."

I tried to translate, but I didn't know what "whisak" was in English.

Veronique took the cup. My da held his hand up for her to wait and poured himself a cup. He tossed it back. Then he nodded at her for her to try.

She took a big swallow. She hadn't expected the burn, you could see that. She choked and her face got red. Tuuvin patted her on the back while she coughed. "Oh my God," she said. "That's strong!" I didn't think I needed to translate that.

• • •

II.

The sound of the guns is like the cracking of whips. Like the snapping of bones. The outrunners for the Scathalos High-on came into Sckarline with a great deal of racket; brass clattering, the men singing and firing their guns into the air. It started the dogs barking and scared our stabros and brought everyone outside.

Scathalos dyed the toes and ridgeline manes of their stabros kracken yellow. They hung brass clappers in the harnesses of their caravan animals and bits of milky blue glass from the harnesses of their dogs. On this sunny day, everything winked. Only their milking does were plain, and that's only because even the will of a hunter can't make a doe stabros tractable.

Veronique came out with me. "Who are they?" she asked.

Even after just three days I could understand Veronique a lot better. "They are from a great clan, Scathalos," I said. "They come to buy whisak." We hoped they would buy it. Sometimes, when Scathalos outrunners came, they just took it.

"They're another clan?" she asked. "Where are the women?"

"They're outrunners," I said. "They go out and hunt and trade. Outrunners are not-married men."

"They have a lot of guns," she said.

They had more guns than I had ever seen. Usually when outrunners came they had one or two guns. Guns are hard to get. But it looked as if almost every outrunner had a gun.

"Does Sckarline have guns?" Veronique asked.

"No," I said.

"They're not appropriate, right?"

A lot of people said we should have guns, whether Ayudesh and Wanji thought they were appropriate or not. They had to buy the clips that go with them. Ayudesh said that the offworlders used the need of the clips to control the clans. He said that it wasn't appropriate because we couldn't maintain it ourselves.

My da said that maybe some things we should buy. We bought things from other clans; that was trade. Maybe guns were trade, too.

The dogs nipped at the doe stabros, turning them, making them stop until outrunners could slip hobbles on them. The stabros looked pretty good. They were mostly dun, and the males were heavy in the shoulders, with heads set low and forward on their necks. Better than most of our animals. The long hairs on their ears were braided with red and yellow threads. Handlers unhooked the sleds from the pack stabros.

Two of them found the skimmer tracks beyond the schoolhouse. They stopped and looked around. They saw Veronique. Then another stared at her, measuring her.

"Come with me," I said.

Our dogs barked and their dogs barked. The outrunner men talked loudly. Sckarline people stood at the doors of their houses and didn't talk at all.

"What's wrong?" Veronique asked.

"Come help my mam and me." She would be under the gaze of them in the distillery, too, but I suspected she would be under their gaze anywhere. And this way Mam would be there.

"Scathalos come here for whisak," I said to my mam, even though she could see for herself. Mam was at the door, shading her eyes and watching them settle in. Someone should have been telling them we had people in the guesthouse and offering to put their animals up, but no one was moving.

"Tuuvin is in the back," Mam said, pointing with her chin. "Go back and help him."

Tuuvin was hiding the oldest whisak, what was left of the three-year-old brass whisak. Scathalos had come for whisak two years ago and taken what they wanted and left us almost nothing but lame stabros. They said it was because we had favored Toolie Clan in trade. The only reason we had any three-year-old whisak left was because they couldn't tell what was what.

So my da and some of the men had dug a cellar in the distillery. Tuuvin was standing in the cellar, taking kegs he had stacked at the edge and pulling them down. It wasn't very deep, not much over his chest, but the kegs were heavy. I started stacking more for him to hide.

I wondered what the outrunners would do if they caught us at our work. I wondered if Tuuvin was thinking the same thing. We'd hidden some down there in the spring before the stabros went up to summer grazing, but then we'd taken some of the oldest kegs to drink when the stabros came back down in the fall.

"Hurry," Tuuvin said softly.

My hands were slick. Veronique started taking kegs, too. She couldn't lift them, so she rolled them on their edge. Her hands were soft and pretty, not used to rough kegs. It seemed like it took a long time. Tuuvin's hands were rough and red. I'd never thought about how hard his hands were. Mine were like his, all red. My hands were ugly compared to Veronique's. Surely he was noticing that, too, since every time Veronique rolled a keg over, her hands were right there.

And then the last keg was on the edge. Uukraith's eye looked at me, strangely unaffected. Or maybe amused. Or maybe angry. Da said that spirits do not feel the way we feel. The teachers never said anything at all about spirits, which was how we knew that they didn't listen to them. There was not much space in the cellar, just enough for Tuuvin to stand and maybe a little more.

Tuuvin put his hands on the edge and boosted himself out of the cellar. In front of the store we heard the crack of the door on its hinges and we all three jumped.

Tuuvin slid the wooden cover over the hole in the floor. "Move those," he said, pointing at empty kegs.

I didn't hear voices.

"Are you done yet?" Mam said, startling us again.

"Are they here?" I asked.

"No," she said. "Not yet." She didn't seem afraid. I had seen my mam afraid, but not very often. "What is she doing here?" Mam asked, pointing at Veronique.

"I thought she should be here, I mean, I was afraid to leave her by herself."

"She's not a child," Mam said. But she said it mildly, so I knew she didn't really mind. Then Mam helped us stack kegs. We all tried to be quiet, but they thumped like hollow drums. They filled the space around us with noise. It seemed to me that the outrunners could hear us thumping away from outside. I kept looking at Mam, who was stacking kegs as if we hid whisak all the time. Tuuvin was nervous, too. His shoulders were tense. I almost said to him, "You're up around the ears, boy," the way the hunters did, but right now I didn't think it would make him smile.

Mam scuffed the dirt around the kegs.

"Will they find them?" I asked.

Mam shrugged. "We'll see."

• • •

There was a lot to do to get ready for the outrunners besides hiding the best whisak. Mam had us count the kegs, even Veronique. Then when we all three agreed on a number she wrote it in her tally book. "So we know how much we sell," she said.

We were just finishing counting when outrunners came with Ayudesh. They came into the front. First the wind, like a wild dog, sliding around the door and making the fires all sway. Then Ayudesh and then the outrunners. The outrunners looked short compared to Ayudesh. And they looked even harder than we did. Their cheeks were winter red. Their felts were all dark with dirt, like they'd been out for a long time.

"Hie," said one of the men, seeing my mother. They all grinned. People always seemed surprised that they were going to trade with my mam. The outrunners already smelled of whisak, so people had finally made them welcome. Or maybe someone had the sense to realize that if they gave them drink we'd have time to get things ready. Maybe my da.

My mam stood as she always did, with her arms crossed, tall as any of them. Waiting them out.

"What's this?" said the man, looking around. "Eh? What's this? It stinks in here." The distillery always stank.

They walked around, looked at the kegs, poked at the copper tubing and the still. One stuck his finger under the drip and tasted the raw stuff and grimaced. Ayudesh looked uncomfortable, but the teachers always said that the distillery was ours and they didn't interfere with how we ran it. Mam was in charge here.

Mam just stood and let them walk around her. She didn't turn her head to watch them.

They picked up the brand. "What's this?" the man said again.

"We mark all our kegs with the eye of Uukraith," Mam said.

"Woman's work," he said.

He stopped and looked at Veronique. He studied her for a moment, then frowned. "You're no boy," he said.

Veronique looked at me, the whites of her eyes bright even in the dimness, but she didn't say anything.

He grinned and laughed. The other two outrunners crowded close to her and fingered the slick fabric of her sleeve, touched her hair. Veronique pulled away.

The first outrunner got bored and walked around the room some more.

He tapped a keg. Not like Mam thumped them, listening, but just as if everything here were his. He had dirty brown hair on the backs of his hands. Everywhere I looked, I was seeing people's hands. I didn't like the way he put his hands on things.

Then he pointed to a keg, not the one he was tapping on, but a different one, and one of the other men picked it up. "Is it good?" he asked.

My mam shrugged.

He didn't like that. He took two steps forward and hit her across the face. I looked at the black, packed dirt-floor.

Ayudesh made a noise.

"It's good," my mam said. I looked up and she had a red mark on the side of her face. Ayudesh looked as if he would speak, but he didn't.

The outrunner grabbed her braid—she flinched as he reached past her face—and yanked her head. "It's good, woman?" he asked.

"Yes," she said, her voice coming almost airless, like she could not breathe.

He yanked her down to her knees. Then he let go and they all went out with the keg.

Ayudesh said, "Are you all right?" Mam stood back up again and touched her braid, then flipped it back over her neck. She didn't look at any of us.

• • •

People were in the schoolhouse. Ayudesh sat on the table at the front and people were sitting on the floor, talking as if it were a meeting. Veronique's teacher was sitting next to Ayudesh and Veronique started as if she was going to go sit with him. Then she looked around and sat down with Mam and Tuuvin and me.

"So we should just let them take whatever they want?" Harup said. He wasn't clowning now, but talking as a senior hunter. He sat on his heels, the way hunters do when they're waiting.

Ayudesh said, "Even if we could get guns, they're used to fighting and we aren't. What do you think would happen?"

Veronique was very quiet.

"If we don't stand up for ourselves, what will happen?" Harup said.

"If you provoke them, they'll destroy us," Ayudesh said.

"Teacher," Harup said, spreading his hands as if he was telling a story. "Stabros are not hunting animals, eh. They are not sharp-toothed like haunds or dogs. Haunds are hunters, packs of hunters, who do nothing but hunt stabros. There are more stabros than all the haunds could eat, eh. So how do they choose? They don't kill the buck stabros with their hard toes and heads, they take the young, the old, the sick, the helpless. We do not want to be haunds, teacher. We just want the haunds to go elsewhere for easy prey."

Wanji came in behind us, and the fire in the boxstove ducked and jumped in the draft. Wanji didn't sit down on the table, but, as was her custom, lowered herself to the floor. "Old hips," she muttered as if everyone in the room wasn't watching her. "Old women have old hips."

When I thought of Kalky, the old woman who makes the souls of everything, I thought of her as looking like Wanji. Wanji had a little face and a big nose and deep lines down from her nose to her chin. "What happened to you, daughter?" she asked my mam.

"The outrunners came to the distillery to take a keg," Mam said.

I noticed that now the meeting had turned around, away from Ayudesh on the table towards us in the back. Wanji always said that Ayudesh was vain and liked to sit high. Sometimes she called him "High-on." "And so," Wanji said.

My mother's face was still red from the blow, but it hadn't yet purpled. "I don't think the outrunners like to do business with me," Mam said.

"One of them hit her," I said, because Mam wasn't going to. Mam never talked about it when my da hit her, either. Although he didn't do it as much as he used to when I was Bet's age.

Mam looked at me, but I couldn't tell if she was angry with me or not.

Harup spread his hands to say, "See?"

Wanji clucked.

"We got the three-year-old whisak in the cellar," Mam said.

I was looking, but I didn't see my da.

"What are they saying," Veronique asked.

"They are talking," I said, and had to think how to say it, "about what we do, but they, eh, not, do not know? Do not know what is right. Harup want guns. Wants guns. Ayudesh says guns are bad."

"Wanji," Tuuvin whispered, "Wanji she ask—eh," and then in our own tongue, "tell her she was asking your mam what happened."

"Wanji ask my mother what is the matter," I said.

Veronique looked at Tuuvin and then at me.

"Guns are bad," Veronique said.

Tuuvin scowled. "She doesn't understand," he said.

"What?" Veronique said, but I just shook my head rather than tell her what Tuuvin had said.

Some of the men were talking about guns. Wanji was listening without saying anything, resting her chin on her hand. Sometimes it seemed like Wanji didn't even blink, that she just turned into stone and you didn't know what she was thinking.

Some of the other men were talking to Ayudesh about whisak. Yet, Harup's wife, got up and put water on the boxstove for the men to drink and Big Sherep went out the men's door in the back of the schoolhouse, which meant that he was going to get whisak or beer.

"Nothing will get done now," Tuuvin said, disgusted. "Let's go."

He stood up and Veronique looked up at him, then scrambled to her feet.

"Now they talk, talk, talk," I said in English. "Nothing to say, just talk, you know?"

Outside, there were outrunners. It seemed as if they were everywhere, even though there were really not that many of them. They watched Veronique.

Tuuvin scowled at them and I looked at their guns. Long black guns slung over their backs. I had never seen a gun close. And there was my da, standing with three outrunners, holding a gun in his hands as if it were a fishing spear, admiring it. He was nodding and grinning, the way he did when someone told a good hunting story. Of course, he didn't know that one of these people had hit Mam.

Still, it made me mad that he was being friendly.

"We should go somewhere," Tuuvin said.

"The distillery?" I asked.

"No," he said, "they'll go back there." And he looked at Veronique. Having Veronique around was like having Bet, you always had to be thinking about her. "Take her to your house."

"And do what?" I asked. A little angry at him because now he had decided he wasn't going back with us.

"I don't know, teach her to sew or something," he said. He turned and walked across to where my da was standing.

• • •

The outrunners took two more kegs of whisak and got loud. They stuck torches in the snow, so the dog's harnesses were all glittering and winking, and we gave them a stabros to slaughter and they roasted that. Some of the Sckarline men like my da—and even Harup—sat with them and talked and sang. I didn't understand why Harup was there, but there he was, laughing and telling stories about the time my da got dumped out of the boat fishing.

Ayudesh was there, just listening. Veronique's grandfather was out there, too, even though he couldn't understand what they were saying.

"When will they go?" Veronique asked.

I shrugged.

She asked something I didn't understand.

"When you trade," she said, "trade?"

"Trade," I said, "trade whisak, yes?"

"Yes," she said. "When you trade whisak, men come? Are you afraid when you trade whisak?"

"Afraid?" I asked. "When Scathalos come, yes."

"When other people come, are you afraid?" she asked.

"No," I said. "Just Scathalos."

She sat on my furs.

My mam was on the bed and Bet had gone to sleep. Mam watched us talk, sitting cross-legged and mending Bet's boots. She didn't understand any English. It felt wrong to talk when Mam didn't understand, but Veronique couldn't understand when I talked to Mam, either.

"I have to go back to my hut," Veronique said. "Ian will come back and he'll worry about me."

Outside the air was so cold and dry that the insides of our noses felt it.

"Don't you get tired of being cold?" Veronique asked.

The cold made people tired, I thought, yes. That was why people slept so much during winterdark. I didn't always know what to say when Veronique talked about the weather.

"We tell your teacher, you sleep in our house, yes?" I offered.

"Who?" she said. "You mean Ian? He isn't really my teacher like you mean it. He's my professor."

I tried to think of what a professor might be, maybe the person who took you when your father died? It always seemed English didn't have enough words for different relatives, but now here was one I didn't know.

The outrunners and the Sckarline hunters were singing about Fhidrhin the hunter and I looked up to see if I could make out the stars that formed him, but the sky had drifting clouds and I couldn't find the stars.

I couldn't see well enough; the light from the bonfire made everyone else just shadows. I took Veronique's hand and started around the outside of the circle of singers, looking for Ayudesh and Veronique's teacher or whatever he was. Faces glanced up, spirit faces in the firelight. The smoke blew our way and then shifted, and I smelled the sweat smell that came from the men's clothes as they warmed by the fire. And whisak, of course. The stabros was mostly bones.

"Janna," said my da. His face was strange, too, not human, like a mask. His eyes looked unnaturally light. "Go on back to your mother."

"Veronique needs to tell the offworlder that she's staying with us."

"Go on back to the house," he said again. I could smell whisak on him, too. Whisak sometimes made him mean. My da used to drink a lot of whisak when I was young, but since Bet was born he didn't drink it very often at all. He said the mornings were too hard when you got old.

I didn't know what to do. If I kept looking for Veronique's grandfather and he got angry, he would probably hit me. I nodded and backed away, pulling Veronique with me, then when he stopped watching me, I started around the fire the other way.

One of the outrunners stumbled up and into us before we could get out of the way. "Eh—?"

I pulled Veronique away but he gripped her arm. "Boy?"

His breath in her face made her close her eyes and turn her head.

"No boy," he said. He was drunk, probably going to relieve himself. "No boy, outsider girl, pretty as a boy," he said. "Outsider, they like that? Eh?"

Veronique gripped my hand. "Let's go," she said in English.

He didn't have to speak English to see she was afraid of him.

"I'm not pretty enough for you?" he said. "Eh? Not pretty enough?" He wasn't pretty, he was wiry and had teeth missing on one side of his mouth. "Not Sckarline? With their pretty houses like offworlders? Not pretty, eh?"

Veronique drew a breath like a sob.

"Let go of her, please," I said, "we have to go find her teacher."

"Look at the color of her," he said, "does that wash off? Eh?"

"Do you know where her teacher is?" I asked.

"Shut up, girl," he said to me. He licked his thumb and reached towards her face. Veronique raised her hand and drew back, and he twisted her arm. "Stand still." He rubbed her cheek with his thumb and peered closely at her.

"Damn," he said, pleased. "How come the old man isn't dark?"

"Maybe they are different clans," I said.

He stared at her as if weighing what I'd said. As if thinking. Although he actually looked too drunk to do much thinking. Then he leaned forward and tried to kiss her.

Veronique pushed him away with her free arm. He staggered and fell, pulling her down, too.

"Let go!" she shrieked.

Shut up, I thought, shut up, shut up! Give in, he's too drunk to do much. I tried to pull his arm off, but his grip was too strong.

"What's this?" another outrunner was saying.

"Fohlder's found some girl."

"It would be fucking Fohlder!"

Veronique slapped at him and struggled, trying to get away.

• • •

"Hey now," Ayudesh was saying, "hey now, she's a guest, an offworlder." But nobody was paying attention. Everybody was watching the outrunner wrestle with her. He pinned her with her arms over her head and kissed her.

Veronique was crying and slapping. Stop it, I kept thinking, just stop it, or he won't let you alone.

Her grandfather tried to pull the outrunner off. I hadn't even seen him come up. "No no no no no," he was saying as if scolding someone. "No no no no no—"

"Get off him," another outrunner hauled him away.

Ayudesh said, "Stop! She is our guest!"

"She's yours, eh?" someone said.

"No," Ayudesh said, "she should be left alone. She's a guest."

"Your guest, right. Not interested in the likes of us."

Someone else grunted and laughed.

"She likes Sckarline better, eh?"

"That's because she doesn't know better."

"Fohlder'll show her."

You all stink like drunks, I wanted to scream at them, because they did.

"Think she's dark inside like she is outside?"

"Have to wait until morning to see."

Oh, my da would be so mad at me, the stupid bitch, why didn't she stop, he was drunk, he was drunk, why had she slapped at him, stupider than Bet, she was as stupid as Bet my little sister, I was supposed to be taking care of her, I was supposed to be watching out for her, my da would be so mad—

There was the bone crack of gunfire and everybody stopped.

Harup was standing next to the fire with an outrunner gun pointed up, as if he were shooting at Fhidrhin up there in the stars. His expression was mild and he was studying the gun as if he hadn't even noticed what was going on.

"Hey," an outrunner said, "put that down!"

Harup looked around at the outrunners, at us. He looked slowly. He didn't look like he usually did, he didn't look funny or angry, he looked as if he were out on a boat in the ice. Calm, far away. Cold as the stars. He could kill someone.

The outrunners felt it, too. They didn't move. If he shot one of them, the others would kill him, but the one he shot would still be dead. No one wanted to be the one that might be dead.

"It's a nice piece," Harup said, "but if you used it for hunting you'd soon be so deaf you couldn't hear anything moving." Then he grinned.

Someone laughed.

Everyone laughed.

"Janna," Harup said, "take your friend and get us more whisak."

"Fohlder, you old walking dick, get up from that girl." One of them reached down and pulled him off. He looked mad.

"What," he said, "what."

"Go take a piss," the outrunner said.

Everyone laughed.

• • •

III.

Veronique stayed with me that night, lying next to me in my blankets and furs. She didn't sleep, I don't think. I was listening to her breath. I felt as if I should help her sleep. I lay there and tried to think if I should put my arm around her, but I didn't know. Maybe she didn't want to be touched.

And she had been a stupid girl, anyway.

She lay tense in the dark. "Are you going to be a teacher?" I asked.

She laughed. "If I get out of here."

I waited for her to say more, but she didn't. "Get out of here" meant to make someone leave. Maybe she meant if she made herself.

"You come here from Earth?" I asked. To get her to talk, although I was tired of lingua and I didn't really want to think about anything.

"My family came here from Earth," she said.

"Why?"

"My father, he's an anthropologist," she said. "Do you know anthropologist?"

"No," I said.

"He is a person who studies the way people live. And he is a teacher."

All the offworlders I had ever met were teachers. I wondered who did all the work on Earth.

"Because Earth had lost touch with your world, the people here are very interesting to my father," she said. Her voice was listless in the dark and she was even harder to understand when I couldn't see her properly. I didn't understand, so I didn't say anything. I was sorry I'd started her talking.

"History, do you know the word 'history'?" she asked.

Of course I knew the word "history." "I study history in school," I said.

Anneal and Kumar taught it.

"Do you know the history of this world?"

It took my tired head a long time to sort that out. "Yes," I said. "We are a colony. People from Earth come here to live. Then there is a big problem on Earth, and the people of Earth forget we are here. We forget we are from Earth. Then Earth finds us again."

"Some people have stories about coming from the Earth," Veronique said. "My father is collecting those stories from different peoples. I'm a graduate student."

The clans didn't have any stories about coming from Earth. We said the first people came out of the sun. This somehow seemed embarrassing. I didn't understand what kind of student she was.

"Are you here for stories?" I asked.

"No," she said. "Ian is old friends with your teacher, from back when they were both with the survey. We just came to visit."

I didn't understand what she'd said except that they were visiting.

We were quiet after that. I pretended to sleep. Sometimes there was gunfire outside and we jumped, even Mam on the bed. Everyone but Bet. Once Bet was asleep, it was impossible to wake her up.

I fell asleep thinking about how I wished that the Scathalos outrunners were gone. I dreamed that I was at the offworlder's home, where it was summer but no one was taking care of the stabros, and they were all glad, and so I was a hero—and I was startled awake by gunfire.

Just more drinking and shooting.

I wished my da would come home. It didn't seem fair that we should lie here and be afraid while the men were getting drunk and singing.

• • •

The outrunners stayed the next day, taking three more kegs of whisak but not talking about trade. The following day they sent out hunters, but didn't find their own meat and so took another stabros, the gelding I'd shown to Veronique. And more whisak.

I went down to the distillery after they took some more whisak. It was already getting dark. The dark comes so early at this time of year. The door was left open and the fire was out. Mam wasn't coming anymore. There was no work being done. Kegs had been taken down and some had been opened and left open. Some had been spilled. They had started on the green stuff, not knowing what was what and had thrown most of it in the snow, probably thinking it was bad. Branded eyes on the kegs looked everywhere.

I thought maybe they wouldn't leave until all the whisak was gone. For one wild moment I thought about taking an axe to the kegs. Give them no reason to stay.

Instead I listened to them singing, their voices far away. I didn't want to walk back towards the voices, but I didn't want to be outside in the dark, either. I walked until I could see the big fire they had going, and smell the stabros roasting. Then I stood for a while, because I didn't want to cross the light more than I wanted to go home. Maybe someone was holding me back, maybe my spirit knew something.

I looked for my father. I saw Harup on the other side of the fire. His face was in the light. He wasn't singing, he was just watching. I saw Gerdor, my little uncle, my father's half-brother. I did not see my father anywhere.

Then I saw him. His back was to me. He was just a black outline against the fire. He had his hands open wide, as if he was explaining. He had his empty hands open. Harup was watching my father explaining something to some of the outrunners and something was wrong.

One of the outrunners turned his head and spat.

My father, I couldn't hear his voice, but I could see his body, his shoulders moving as he explained. His shoulders working, working hard as if he were swimming. Such hard work, this talking with his hands open, talking, talking.

The outrunner took two steps, bent down and pulled his rifle into the light. It was a dark thing there, a long thing against the light of the fire. My father took a step back and his hands came up, pushing something back.

And then the outrunner shot my father.

All the singing stopped. The fire cracked and the sparks rose like stars while my father struggled in the snow. He struggled hard, fighting and scraping back through the snow. Elbow-walking backwards. The outrunner was looking down the long barrel of the rifle.

Get up, I thought. Get up. For a long time it seemed I thought, Get up, get up. Da, get up! But no sound came out of my mouth and there was black on the snow in the trampled trail my father left.

The outrunner shot again.

My father flopped into the snow and I could see the light on his face as he looked up. Then he stopped.

Harup watched. No one moved except the outrunner who put his rifle away.

I could feel the red meat, the hammering muscle in my chest. I could feel it squeezing, squeezing. Heat flowed in my face. In my hands.

Outrunners shouted at outrunners. "You shit," one shouted at the one who shot my father. "You drunken, stupid shit!" The one who shot my father shrugged at first, as if he didn't care, and then he became angry, too, shouting.

My breath was in my chest, so full. If I breathed out loud the outrunners would hear me out here. I tried to take small breaths, could not get enough air.

I did not remember when I had been holding my breath.

Harup and the hunters of Sckarline sat, like prey, hiding in their stillness. The arguing went on and on, until it wasn't about my father at all and his body was forgotten in the dirty snow. They argued about who was stupid and who had the High-on's favor. The whisak was talking.

I could think of nothing but air.

I went back through the dark, out of Sckarline, and crept around behind the houses, in the dark and cold until I could come to our house without going past the fire. I took great shuddering breaths of cold air, breathed out great gouts of fog.

My mother was trying to get Bet to be quiet when I came in. "No," she was saying, "stop it now, or I'll give you something to cry about."

"Mam," I said, and I started to cry.

"What," she said. "Janna, your face is all red." She was my mam, with her face turned towards me, and I had never seen her face so clearly.

"They're going to kill all of us," I said. "They killed Da with a rifle."

She never said a word but just ran out and left me there. Bet started to cry although she didn't really know what I was crying about. Just that she should be scared. Veronique was still. As still as Harup and the hunters.

• • •

Wanji came and got me and brought me to Ayudesh's house because our house is small and Ayudesh's house had enough room for some people. Snow was caked in the creases of my father's pants. It was in his hands, too, unmelted. I had seen dead people before, and my father looked like all of them. Not like himself at all.

My mother had followed him as far as the living can go—or at least as far as someone untrained in spirit journeys—and she was not herself. She was sitting on the floor next to his body, rocking back and forth with her arms crossed in her lap. I had seen women like that before, but not my mother. I didn't want to look. It seemed indecent. Worse than the body of my father, since my father wasn't there at all.

Bet was screaming. Her face was red from the effort. I held her even though she was heavy and she kept arching away from me like a toddler in a tantrum. "MAM! MAM!" she kept screaming.

People came in and squatted down next to the body for a while. People talked about guns. It was important that I take care of Bet, so I did, until finally she wore herself out from crying and fell asleep. I held her on my lap until the blood was out of my legs and I couldn't feel the floor and then Wanji brought me a blanket and I wrapped Bet in it and let her sleep.

Wanji beckoned me to follow. I could barely stand, my legs had so little feeling. I held the wall and looked around, at my mother sitting next to the vacant body, at my sister, who though asleep was still alive. Then I tottered after Wanji as if I was the old woman.

"Where is the girl?" Wanji said.

"Asleep," I said. "On the floor."

"No, the girl," Wanji said, irritated. "Ian's girl. From the university."

"I don't know," I said.

"You're supposed to be watching her. Didn't Ayudesh tell you to watch her?"

"You mean Veronique? She's back at my house. In my bed."

Wanji nodded and sucked on her teeth. "Okay," she said. And then again to herself. "Okay."

Wanji took me to her house, which was little and dark. She had a lamp shaped like a bird. It had been in her house as long as I could remember. It didn't give very much light, but I had always liked it. We sat on the floor. Wanji's floor was always piled high with rugs from her home and furs and blankets. It made it hard to walk but nice to sit. Wanji got cold and her bones hurt, so she always made a little nest when she sat down. She pulled a red and blue rug across her lap. "Sit, sit, sit," she said.

I was cold, but there was a blanket to wrap around my shoulders. I couldn't remember being alone with Wanji before. But everything was so strange it didn't seem to make any difference and it was nice to have Wanji deciding what to do and me not having to do anything.

Wanji made tea over her little bird lamp. She handed me a cup and I sipped it. Tea was a strange drink. Wanji and Ayudesh liked it and hoarded it. It was too bitter to be very good, but it was warm and the smell of it was always special. I drank it and held it against me. I started to get warm. The blanket got warm from me and smelled faintly of Wanji, an old dry smell.

I was sleepy. It would have been nice to go to sleep right there in my little nest on Wanji's floor.

"Girl," Wanji said. "I must give you something. You must take care of Veronique."

I didn't want to take care of anybody. I wanted someone to take care of me. My eyes started to fill up and in a moment I was crying salt tears into my tea.

"No time for that, Janna," Wanji said. Always sharp with us. Some people were afraid of Wanji. I was. But it felt good to cry, and I didn't know how to stop it, so I didn't.

Wanji didn't pay any attention. She was hunting through her house, checking in a chest, pulling up layers of rugs to peer in a corner. Was she going to give me a gun? I couldn't think of anything else that would help very much right now, but I couldn't imagine that Wanji owned a gun.

She came back with a dark blue plastic box not much bigger than the span of my spread hand. That was almost as astonishing as a gun. I wiped my nose on my sleeve. I was warm and tired. Would Wanji let me sleep right here on her floor?

Wanji opened the plastic box, but away from me so I couldn't see inside it. She picked at it as if she were picking at a sewing kit, looking for something. I wanted to look in it but I was afraid that if I tried she'd snap at me.

She looked at me. "This is mine," she said. "We both got one and we decided that if the people who settled Sckarline couldn't have it, we wouldn't either."

I didn't care about that. That was old talk. I wanted to know what it was.

Wanji wasn't ready to tell me what it was. I had the feeling that Ayudesh didn't know about this, and I was afraid she would talk herself out of it. She looked at it and thought. If I thought, I thought about my father being dead. I sipped tea and tried to think about being warm, about sleeping, but that feeling had passed. I wondered where Tuuvin was.

I thought about my da and I started to cry again.

I thought that would really get Wanji angry so I tried to hide it, but she didn't pay any attention at all. The shawl she wore over her head slipped halfway down so when I glanced up I could see where her hair parted, and the line of pale skin. It looked so bare that I wanted it covered up again. It made me think of the snow in my father's hands.

"It was a mistake," Wanji said.

I thought she meant the box, and I felt a terrible disappointment that I wouldn't get to see what was inside it.

"You understand what we were trying to do?" she asked me.

With the box? Not at all.

"What are the six precepts of development philosophy?" she asked.

I had to think. "One," I said, "that economic development should be gradual. Two, that analyzing economic growth by the production of goods rather than the needs and capacities of people leads to displacement and increased poverty. Three, that economic development should come from the integrated development of rural areas with the traditional sector—"

"It's just words," she snapped at me.

I didn't know what I had done wrong, so I ducked my head and sniffed and waited for her to get angry because I couldn't stop crying.

Instead she stroked my hair. "Oh, little girl. Oh, Janna. You are one of the bright ones. If you aren't understanding it, then we really haven't gotten it across, have we?" Her hand was nice on my hair, and it seemed so unlike Wanji that it scared me into stillness. "We were trying to help, you know," she said. "We were trying to do good. We gave up our lives to come here. Do you realize?"

Did she mean that they were going to die? Ayudesh and Wanji?

"This," she said, suddenly brisk. "This is for, what would you call them, runners. Foreign runners. It is to help them survive. I am going to give it to you so that you will help Veronique, understood?"

I nodded.

But she didn't give it to me. She just sat holding the box, looking in it. She didn't want to give it up. She didn't feel it was appropriate.

She sighed again, a terrible sound. Out of the box she pulled shiny foil packets, dark blue, red, and yellow. They were the size of the palm of her hand. Her glasses were around her neck. She put them on like she did in the school-room, absent from the gesture. She studied the printing on the foil packets.

I loved foil. Plastic was beautiful, but foil, foil was something unimaginable. Tea came in foil packets. The strange foods that the teachers got off the skimmer came in foil.

My tea was cold.

"This one," she said, "it is a kind of signal." She looked over her glasses at me. "Listen to me, Janna. Your life will depend on this. When you have this, you can send a signal that the outsiders can hear. They can hear it all the way in Bashtoy. And after you send it, if you can wait in the same place, they will send someone out to get you and Veronique."

"They can hear it in Bashtoy?" I said. I had never even met anyone other than Wanji and the teachers who had ever been to Bashtoy.

"They can pick it up on their instruments. You send it every day until someone comes."

"How do I send it?"

She read the packet. "We have to set the signal, you and I. First we have to put it in you."

I didn't understand, but she was reading, so I waited.

"I'm going to put it in your ear," she said. "From there it will migrate to your brain."

"Will it hurt?" I asked.

"A little," she said. "But it has its own way of taking pain away. Now, what should be the code?" She studied the packet. She pursed her lips.

A thing in my ear. I was afraid and I wanted to say no, but I was more afraid of Wanji so I didn't.

"You can whistle, can't you?" she asked.

I knew how to whistle, yes.

"Okay," she said, "here it is. I'll put this in your ear, and then we'll wait for a while. Then when everything is ready, we'll set the code."

She opened up the packet and inside was another packet and a little metal fork. She opened the inside packet and took out a tiny little disk, a soft thing almost like egg white or like a fish egg. She leaned forward and put it in my left ear. Then she pushed it in hard and I jerked.

"Hold still," she said.

Something was moving and making noise in my ear and I couldn't be still. I pulled away and shook my head. The noise in my ear was loud, a sort of rubbing, oozing sound. I couldn't hear normal things out of my left ear. It was stopped up with whatever was making the oozing noise. Then it started to hurt. A little at first, then more and more.

I put my hand over my ear, pressing against the pain. Maybe it would eat through my ear? What would stop it from eating a hole in my head?

"Stop it," I said to Wanji. "Make it stop!"

But she didn't, she just sat there, watching.

The pain grew sharp, and then suddenly it stopped. The sound, the pain, everything.

I took my hand away. I was still deaf on the left side but it didn't hurt.

"Did it stop?" Wanji asked.

I nodded.

"Do you feel dizzy? Sick?"

I didn't.

Wanji picked up the next packet. It was blue. "While that one is working, we'll do this one. Then the third one, which is easy. This one will make you faster when you are angry or scared. It will make time feel slower. There isn't any code for it. Something in your body starts it."

I didn't have any idea what she was talking about.

"After it has happened, you'll be tired. It uses up your energy." She studied the back of the packet, then she scooted closer to me, so we were both sitting cross-legged with our knees touching. Wanji had hard, bony knees, even through the felt of her dress.

"Open your eyes, very wide," she said.

"Wait," I said. "Is this going to hurt?"

"No," she said.

I opened my eyes as wide as I could.

"Look down, but keep your eyes wide open," she said.

I tried.

"No," she said, irritated, "keep your eyes open."

"They are open," I said. I didn't think she should treat me this way. My da had just died. She should be nice to me. I could hear her open the packet. I wanted to blink but I was afraid to. I did, because I couldn't help it.

She leaned forward and spread my eye open with thumb and forefinger.

Then she swiftly touched my eye.

I jerked back. There was something in my eye. I could feel it, up under my eyelid. It was very uncomfortable. I blinked and blinked and blinked. My eye filled up with tears, just the one eye, which was very, very strange.

My eye socket started to ache. "It hurts," I said.

"It won't last long," she said.

"You said it wouldn't hurt!" I said, startled.

"I lied," Wanji said, matter-of-fact.

It hurt more and more. I moaned. "You're hateful," I said.

"That's true," she said, unperturbed.

She picked up the third packet, the red one.

"No," I said, "I won't! I won't! You can't do it!"

"Hush," she said, "this one won't hurt. I saved it until last on purpose."

"You're lying!" I scrambled away from her. The air was cold where the nest of rugs and blankets had been wrapped around me. My head ached. It just ached. And I still couldn't hear anything out of my left ear.

"Look," she said, "I will read you the lingua. It is a patch, nothing more. It says it will feel cold, but that is all. See, it is just a square of cloth that will rest on your neck. If it hurts, you can take it off."

I scrambled backwards away from her.

"Janna," she said. "Enough!" She was angry.

I was afraid of it, but I was still more afraid of Wanji. So I hunched down in front of her. I was so afraid that I sobbed while she peeled the back off the square and put it on me.

"See," she said, still sharp with me, "it doesn't hurt at all. Stop crying. Stop it. Enough is enough." She waved her hands over her head in disgust. "You are hysterical."

I held my hand over the patch. It didn't hurt but it did feel cold. I scrunched up and wrapped myself in a rug and gave myself over to my misery. My head hurt and my ear still ached faintly and I was starting to feel dizzy.

"Lie down," Wanji said. "Go on, lie down. I'll wake you when we can set the signal."

I made myself a nest in the mess of Wanji's floor and piled a blanket and a rug on top of me. Maybe the dark made my head feel better, I didn't know. But I fell asleep.

• • •

Wanji shook me awake. I hadn't been asleep long, and my head still ached. She had the little metal fork from the ear packet, the yellow packet. It occurred to me that she might stick it in my ear.

I covered my ear with my hand. My head hurt enough. I wasn't going to let Wanji stick a fork in my ear.

"Don't scowl," she said.

"My head hurts," I said.

"Are you dizzy?" she asked.

I felt out of sorts, unbalanced, but not dizzy, not really.

"Shake your head," Wanji said.

I shook my head. Still the same, but no worse. "Don't stick that in my ear," I said.

"What? I'm not going to stick this in your ear. It's a musical fork. I'm going to make a sound with it and hold it to your ear. When I tell you to, I want you to whistle something, okay?"

"Whistle what?" I said.

"Anything," she said, "I don't care. Whistle something for me now."

I couldn't think of anything to whistle. I couldn't think of anything at all, except that I wished Wanji would leave me alone and let me go back to sleep.

Wanji squatted there. Implacable old bitch.

I finally thought of something to whistle, a crazy dog song for children. I started whistling—

"That's enough," she said. "Now don't say anything else, but when I nod my head you whistle that. Don't say anything to me. If you do, it will ruin everything. Nod your head if you understand."

I nodded.

She slapped the fork against her hand and I could see the long tines vibrating. She held it up to my ear, the one I couldn't hear anything out of. She held it there, concentrating fiercely. Then she nodded.

I whistled.

"Okay," she said. "Good. That is how you start it. Now whistle it again."

I whistled.

Everything went dark and then suddenly my head got very hot. Then I could see again.

"Good," Wanji said. "You just sent a signal."

"Why did everything get dark?" I asked.

"All the light got used in the signal," Wanji said. "It used all the light in your head so you couldn't see."

My head hurt even worse. Now, besides my eyes aching, my temples were pounding. I had a fever. I raised my hand and felt my hot cheek.

Wanji picked up the blue packet. "Now we have to figure out about the third one, the one that will let you hibernate."

I didn't want to learn about hibernating. "I feel sick," I said.

"It's probably too soon, anyway," Wanji said. "Sleep for a while."

I felt so awful I didn't know if I could sleep. But Wanji brought me more tea and I drank all that and lay down in my nest and presently I was dreaming.

• • •

IV.

There was a sound of gunfire, far away, just a pop. And then more pop-pop-pop.

It startled me, although I had been hearing the outrunners' guns at night since they got here. I woke with a fever and everything felt as if I were still dreaming. I was alone in Wanji's house. The lamp was still lit, but I didn't know if it had been refilled or how long I had slept. During the long night of winterdark it is hard to know when you are. I got up, put out the lamp, and went outside.

Morning cold is worst when you are warm from sleep. The dry snow crunched in the dark. Nothing was moving except the dogs were barking, their voices coming at me from every way.

The outrunners were gone from the center of town, nothing there but the remains of their fire and the trampled slick places where they had walked. I slid a bit as I walked there. My head felt light and I concentrated on my walking because if I did not think about it I didn't know what my feet would do. I had to pee.

Again I heard the pop-pop-pop. I could not tell where it was coming from because it echoed off the buildings around me. I could smell smoke and see the dull glow of fire above the trees. It was down from Sckarline, the fire. At first I thought they had gotten a really big fire going, and then I thought they had set fire to the distillery. I headed for home.

Veronique was asleep in a nest of blankets, including some of my parents' blankets from their bed.

"They set fire to the distillery," I said. I didn't say it in English, but she sat up and rubbed her face.

"It's cold," she said.

I could not think of anything to respond.

She sat there, holding her head.

"Come," I said, working into English. "We go see your teacher." I pulled on her arm.

"Where is everybody?" she said.

"My father die, my mother is, um, waiting with the die."

She frowned at me. I knew I hadn't made any sense. I pulled on her again and she got up and stumbled around, putting on boots and jacket.

Outside I heard the pop-pop-pop again. This time I thought maybe it was closer.

"They're shooting again?" she asked.

"They shoot my father," I said.

"Oh God," she said. She sat down on the blankets. "Oh God."

I pulled on her arm.

"Are you all right?" she asked.

"Hurry," I said. I made a pack of blankets. I found my axe and a few things and put them in the bundle, then slung it all over my shoulders. I didn't know what we would do, but if they were shooting people we should run away. I had to pee really bad.

She did hurry, finally awake. When we went outside and the cold hit her, she shuddered and shook off the last of the sleep. I saw the movement of her shoulders against the glow of the fire on the horizon, against the false dawn.

People were moving, clinging close to houses where they were invisible against the black wood, avoiding the open spaces. We stayed close to my house, waiting to see whose people were moving. Veronique held my arm. A dog came past the schoolhouse into the open area where the outrunners' fire had been and stopped and sniffed—maybe the place where my father had died.

I drew Veronique back, along to the back of the house. The spirit door was closed and my father was dead. I crouched low and ran, holding her arm, until we were in the trees and then she slipped and fell and pulled me down, too. We slid feet first in the snow, down the hill between the tree trunks, hidden in the pools of shadow under the trees. Then we were still, waiting.

I still felt feverish and nothing was real.

The snow under the trees was all powder. It dusted our leggings and clung in clumps in the wrinkles behind my knees.

Nothing came after us that we could see. We got up and walked deeper into the trees and then uphill, away from the distillery, but still skirting the village. I left her for a moment to pee, but she followed me and we squatted together. We should run, but I didn't know where to run to and the settlement pulled at me. I circled around it as if on a tether, pulling in closer and closer as we got to the uphill part of the town. Coming back around, we hung in the trees beyond the field behind the schoolhouse. I could see the stabros pens and see light. The outrunners were in the stabros pens and the stabros were down. A couple of men were dressing the carcasses.

We stumbled over Harup in the darkness. Literally fell over him in the bushes.

He was dead. His stomach was ripped by rifle fire and his eyes were open. I couldn't tell in the darkness if he had dragged himself out here to die or if someone had thrown the body here. We were too close.

I started backing away. Veronique was stiff as a spooked stabros. She lifted her feet high out of the snow, coming down hard and loud. One of the dogs at the stabros pen heard us and started to bark. I could see it in the light, its ears up and its tail curled over its back. The others barked, too, ears towards us in the dark. I stopped and Veronique stopped, too. Men in the pen looked out in the dark. A couple of them picked up rifles, and, cradling them in their arms, walked out towards us from the light.

I backed up, slowly. Maybe they would find Harup's body and think that the dogs were barking at that. But they were hunters and they would see the marks of our boots in the snow and follow us. If we ran they would hear us. I was not a hunter. I did not know what to do.

We backed up, one slow step and then another, while the outrunners walked out away from the light. They were not coming straight at us, but they were walking side by side and they would spread out and find us. I had my knife. There was cover around, mostly trees, but I didn't know what I could do against a hunter with a rifle, and even if I could stop one, the others would hear us.

There were shouts over by the houses.

The outrunners kept walking, but the shouts didn't stop, and then there was the pop of guns. That stopped one and then the other and they half-turned.

The dogs turned barking towards the shouts.

The outrunners started to jog towards the schoolhouse.

We walked backward in the dark.

There were flames over there, at the houses. I couldn't tell whose house was on fire. It was downhill from the schoolhouse, which meant it might be our house. People were running in between the schoolhouse and Wanji's house and the outrunners lifted their guns and fired. People, three of them, kept on running.

The outrunners fired again and again. One of the people stumbled, but they all kept running. They were black shapes skimming on the field. The snow on the field was not deep because the wind blew it into the trees. Then one was in the trees. The outrunners fired again, but the other two made the trees as well.

There was a summer camp out this way, down by the river, for drying fish.

I pulled on Veronique's arm and we picked our way through the trees.

• • •

There were people at the summer camp and we waited in the trees to make sure they were Sckarline people. It was gray, false dawn by the time we got there. I didn't remember ever having seen the summer camp in the winter before. The drying racks were bare poles with a top covering of snow, and the lean-to was almost covered in drifted snow. There was no shelter here.

There were signs of three or four people in the trampled snow. I didn't think it would be the outrunners down there, because how would they even know where the summer camp was, but I was not sure of anything. I didn't know if I was thinking right or not.

Veronique leaned close to my ear and whispered so softly I could barely hear. "We have to go back."

I shook my head.

"Ian is there."

Ian. Ian. She meant her teacher.

She had a hood on her purple clothing and I pulled it back to whisper, "Not now. We wait here." So close to the brown shell of her ear. Like soft, dark leather. Not like a real people's ear. She was shivering.

I didn't feel too cold. I still had a fever—I felt as if everything were far from me, as if I walked half in this world. I sat and looked at the snow cupped in a brown leaf and my mind was empty and things did not seem too bad. I don't know how long we sat.

Someone walked in the summer camp. I thought it was Sored, one of the boys.

I took Veronique's arm and tugged her up. I was stiff from sitting and colder than I had noticed, but moving helped. We slid down the hill into the summer camp.

The summer camp sat in a V that looked at the river frozen below. Sored was already out of the camp when we got there, but he waved at us from the trees and we scrambled back up there. Veronique slipped and used her hands.

There were two people crouched around a fire so tiny it was invisible and one of them was Tuuvin.

"Where is everyone else?" Sored asked.

"I don't know," I said. Tuuvin stood up.

"Where's your mother and sister?" he asked.

"I was at Wanji's house all night," I said. "Where's your family?"

"My da and I were at the stabros pen this morning with Harup," he said.

"We found Harup," I said.

"Did you find my da?" he asked.

"No. Was he shot?"

"I don't know. I don't think so."

"We saw some people running across the field behind the schoolhouse. Maybe one of them was shot."

He looked down at Gerda, crouched by the fire. "None of us were shot."

"Did you come together?"

"No," Sored said. "I found Gerda here and Tuuvin here."

He had gone down to see the fire at the distillery. The outrunners had taken some of the casks. He didn't know how the fire started, if it was an accident or if they'd done it on purpose. It would be easy to start if someone spilled something too close to the fire.

Veronique was crouched next to the tiny fire. "Janna," she said, "has anyone seen Ian?"

"Did you see the offworlder teacher?" I asked.

No one had.

"We have to find him," she said.

"Okay," I said.

"What are you going to do with her?" Sored asked, pointing at Veronique with his chin. "Is she ill?"

She crouched over the fire like someone who was sick.

"She's not sick," I said. "We need to see what is happening at Sckarline."

"I'm not going back," Gerda said, looking at no one. I did not know Gerda very well. She was old enough to have children but she had no one. She lived by herself. She'd had her nose slit by her clan for adultery, but I never knew if she had a husband with her old clan or not. Some people came to Sckarline because they didn't want to be part of their clan anymore. Most of them went back, but Gerda had stayed.

Tuuvin said, "I'll go."

Sored said he would stay in case anyone else came to the summer camp. In a day or two, they were going to head towards the west and see if they could come across the winter pastures of Haufsdaag Clan. Sored had kin there.

"That's pretty far," Tuuvin said. "Toolie clan would be closer."

"You have kin with Toolie Clan," Sored said.

Tuuvin nodded.

"We go to Sckarline," I said to Veronique.

She stood up. "It's so damn cold," she said. Then she said something about wanting coffee. I didn't understand a lot of what she said. Then she laughed and said she wished she could have breakfast.

Sored looked at me. I didn't translate what she had said. He turned his back on her, but she didn't notice.

It took us through the sunrise and beyond the short midwinter morning and into afternoon to get to Sckarline. The only good thing about winterdark is that it would be dark for the outrunners, too.

Only hours of daylight.

Nothing was moving when we got back to Sckarline. From the back, the schoolhouse looked all right, but the houses were all burned. I could see where my house had been. Charred logs standing in the red afternoon sun.

The ground around them was wet and muddy from the heat of the fires.

Tuuvin's house. Ayudesh's house. Wanji's house. In front of the schoolhouse there were bodies. My da's body, thrown back in the snow. My mam and my sister. My sister's head was broken in. My mam didn't have her pants on. The front of the schoolhouse had burned, but the fire must have burned out before the whole building was gone. The dogs were moving among the bodies, sniffing, stopping to tug on the freezing flesh.

Tuuvin shouted at them to drive them off.

My mam's hipbones were sharp under the bloody skin and her sex was there for everyone to see, but I kept noticing her bare feet. The soles were dark. Her toenails were thick and her feet looked old, an old, old woman's feet. As if she were as old as Wanji.

I looked at people to see who else was there. I saw Wanji, although she had no face, but I knew her from her skin. Veronique's teacher was there, his face red and peeled from fire and his eyes baked white like a smoked fish. Ayudesh had no ears and no sex. His clothes had been taken.

The dogs were circling back, watching Tuuvin.

He screamed at them. Then he crouched down on his heels and covered his eyes with his arm and cried.

I did not feel anything. Not yet.

• • •

I whistled the tune that Wanji had taught me to send out the message, and the world went dark. It was something to do, and for a moment, I didn't have to look at my mother's bare feet.

The place for the Sckarline dead was up the hill beyond the town, away from the river, but without stabros I couldn't think of how we could get all these bodies there. We didn't have anything for the bodies, either. Nothing for the spirit journey, not even blankets to wrap them in.

I could not bear to think of my mother without pants. There were lots of dead women in the snow and many of them did have pants. It may not have been fair that my mother should have someone else's, but I could not think of anything else to do so I took the leggings off of Maitra and tried to put them on my mother. I could not really get them right—my mother was tall and her body was stiff from the cold and from death. I hated handling her.

Veronique asked me what I was doing, but even if I knew enough English to answer, I was too embarrassed to really try to explain.

My mother's flesh was white and odd to touch. Not like flesh at all. Like plastic. Soft looking but not to touch.

Tuuvin watched me without saying anything. I thought he might tell me not to, but he didn't. Finally he said, "We can't get them to the place for the dead."

I didn't know what to say to that.

"We don't have anyone to talk to the spirits," he said. "Only me."

He was the man here. I didn't know if Tuuvin had talked with spirits or not, people didn't talk about that with women.

"I say that this place is a place of the dead, too," he said. His voice was strange. "Sckarline is a place of the dead now."

"We leave them here?" I asked.

He nodded.

He was beardless, but he was a boy and he was old enough that he had walked through the spirit door. I was glad that he had made the decision.

I looked in houses for things for the dead to have with them, but most things were burned. I found things half-burned and sometimes not burned at all. I found a fur, and used that to wrap the woman whose leggings I had stolen. I tried to make sure that everybody got something—a bit of stitching or a cup or something, so they would not be completely without possessions. I managed to find something for almost everybody, and I found enough blankets to wrap Tuuvin's family and Veronique's teacher. I wrapped Bet with my mother. I kept blankets separate for Veronique, Tuuvin, and me and anything I found that we could use I didn't give to the dead, but everything else I gave to them.

Tuuvin sat in the burned-out schoolhouse and I didn't know if what he did was a spirit thing or if it was just grief, but I didn't bother him. He kept the dogs away. Veronique followed me and picked through the blackened sticks of the houses. Both of us had black all over our gloves and our clothes, and black marks on our faces.

We stopped when it got too dark, and then we made camp in the schoolhouse next to the dead. Normally I would not have been able to stay so close to the dead, but now I felt part of them.

Tuuvin had killed and skinned a dog and cooked that. Veronique cried while she ate. Not like Tuuvin had cried. Not sobs. Just helpless tears that ran down her face. As if she didn't notice.

"What are we going to do?" she asked.

Tuuvin said, "We will try for Toolie Clan."

I didn't have any idea where their winter pastures were, much less how to find them, and I almost asked Tuuvin if he did, but I didn't want to shame his new manhood, so I didn't.

"The skimmer will come back here," Veronique said. "I have to wait here."

"We can't wait here," Tuuvin said. "It is going to get darker; winter is coming and we'll have no sun. We don't have any animals. We can't live here."

I told her what Tuuvin said. "I have, in here," I pointed to my head, "I call your people. Wanji give to me."

Veronique didn't understand and didn't even really try.

I tried not to think about the dogs wandering among the dead. I tried not to think about bad weather. I tried not to think about my house or my mam. It did not leave much to think about.

Tuuvin had kin with Toolie Clan, but I didn't. Tuuvin was my clankin, though, even if he wasn't a cousin or anything. I wondered if he would still want me after we got to Toolie Clan. Maybe there would be other girls. New girls that he had never talked to before. They would be pretty, some of them.

My kin were Lagskold. I didn't know where their pastures were, but someone would know. I could go to them if I didn't like Toolie Clan. I had met a couple of my cousins when they came and brought my father's half-brother, my little uncle.

"Listen," Tuuvin said, touching my arm.

I didn't hear it at first, then I did.

"What?" Veronique said. "Are they coming back?"

"Hush," Tuuvin snapped at her, and even though she didn't understand the word, she did.

It was a skimmer.

It was far away. Skimmers didn't land at night. They didn't even come at night. It had come to my message, I guessed.

Tuuvin got up, and Veronique scrambled to her feet and we all went out to the edge of the field behind the schoolhouse.

"You can hear it?" I asked Veronique.

She shook her head.

"Listen," I said. I could hear it. Just a rumble. "The skimmer."

"The skimmer?" she said. "The skimmer is coming? Oh God. Oh God. I wish we had lights for them. We need light, to signal them that someone is here."

"Tell her to hush," Tuuvin said.

"I send message," I said. "They know someone is here."

"We should move the fire."

I could send them another message, but Wanji had said to do it one time a day until they came and they were here.

Dogs started barking.

Finally we saw lights from the skimmer, strange green and red stars. They moved against the sky as if they had been shaken loose.

Veronique stopped talking and stood still.

The lights came towards us for a long time. They got bigger and brighter, more than any star. It seemed as if they stopped, but the lights kept getting brighter and I finally decided that they were coming straight towards us and it didn't look as if they were moving, but they were.

Then we could see the skimmer in its own lights.

It flew low over us and Veronique shouted, "I'm here! I'm here!"

I shouted, and Tuuvin shouted, too, but the skimmer didn't seem to hear us. But then it turned and slowly curved around, the sound of it going farther away and then just hanging in the air. It got to where it had been before and came back. This time it came even lower and it dropped red lights. One. Two. Three.

Then a third time it came around and I wondered what it would do now. But this time it landed, the sound of it so loud that I could feel it as well as hear it. It was a different skimmer from the one we always saw. It was bigger, with a belly like it was pregnant. It was white and red. It settled easily on the snow. Its engines, pointed down, melted snow beneath them.

And then it sat. Lights blinked. The red lights on the ground flickered. The dogs barked.

Veronique ran towards it.

The door opened and a man called out to watch something, but I didn't understand. Veronique stopped and from where I was, she was a black shape against the lights of the skimmer.

Finally a man jumped down, and then two more men and two women and they ran to Veronique.

She gestured and the lights flickered in the movements of her arms until my eyes hurt and I looked away. I couldn't see anything around us. The off-worlders' lights made me quite nightblind.

"Janna," Veronique called. "Tuuvin!" She waved at us to come over. So we walked out of the dark into the relentless lights of the skimmer.

I couldn't understand what anyone was saying in English. They asked me questions, but I just kept shaking my head. I was tired and now, finally, I wanted to cry.

"Janna," Veronique said. "You called them. Did you call them?"

I nodded.

"How?"

"Wanji give me...In my head ..." I had no idea how to explain. I pointed to my ear.

One of the women came over, and handling my head as if I were a stabros, turned it so she could push my hair out of the way and look in my ear. I still couldn't hear very well out of that ear. Her handling wasn't rough, but it was not something people do to each other.

She was talking and nodding, but I didn't try to understand. The English washed over us and around us.

One of the men brought us something hot and bitter and sweet to drink.

The drink was in blue plastic cups, the same color as the jackets that they all wore except for one man whose jacket was red with blue writing. Pretty things. Veronique drank hers gratefully. I made myself drink mine. Anything this black and bitter must have been medicine. Tuuvin just held his.

Then they got hand lights and we all walked over and looked at the bodies. Dogs ran from the lights, staying at the edges and slinking as if guilty of something.

"Janna," Veronique said. "Which one is Ian? Which is my teacher?"

I had to walk between the bodies. We had laid them out so their heads all faced the schoolhouse and their feet all faced the center of the village. They were more bundles than people. I could have told her in the light, but in the dark, with the hand lights making it hard to see anything but where they were pointed, it took me a while. I found Harup. Then I found the teacher.

Veronique cried and the woman who had looked in my ear held her like she was her child. But that woman didn't look dark like Veronique at all and I thought she was just kin because she was an offworlder, not by blood. All the offworlders were like Sckarline; kin because of where they were, not because of family.

The two men in blue jackets picked up the body of the teacher. With the body they were clumsy on the packed snow. The man holding the teacher's head slipped and fell. Tuuvin took the teacher's head and I took his feet. His boots were gone. His feet were as naked as my mother's. I had wrapped him in a skin, but it wasn't very big, and so his feet hung out. But they were so cold, they felt like meat, not like a person.

We walked right up to the door of the skimmer and I could look in. It was big inside. Hollow. It was dark in the back. I had thought it would be all lights inside and I was disappointed. There were things hanging on the walls but mostly it was empty. One of the offworld men jumped up into the skimmer and then he was not clumsy at all. He pulled the body to the back of the skimmer.

They were talking again. Tuuvin and I stood there. Tuuvin's breath was an enormous white plume in the lights of the skimmer. I stamped my feet. The lights were bright but they were a cheat. They didn't make you any warmer.

The offworlders wanted to go back to the bodies, so we did. "Your teachers," Veronique said. "Where are your teachers?"

I remembered Wanji's body. It had no face but it was easy to tell it was her. Ayudesh's body was still naked under the blanket I had found. The blanket was burned along one side and didn't cover him. Where his sex had been, the frozen blood shone in the hand lights. I thought the dogs might have been at him, but I couldn't tell.

They wanted to take Wanji's and Ayudesh's bodies back to the skimmer.

They motioned for us to take Ayudesh.

"Wait," Tuuvin said. "They shouldn't do that."

I squatted down.

"They are Sckarline people," Tuuvin said.

"Their spirit is already gone," I said.

"They won't have anything," he said.

"If the offworlders take them, won't they give them offworlder things?"

"They didn't want offworld things," Tuuvin said. "That's why they were here."

"But we don't have anything to give them. At least if the offworlders give them things, they'll have something."

Tuuvin shook his head. "Harup—," he started to say, but stopped. Harup talked to spirits more than anyone. He would have known. But I didn't know how to ask him and I didn't think Tuuvin did either. Although I wasn't sure. There wasn't any drum or anything for spirit talk anyway.

The offworlders stood looking at us.

"Okay," Tuuvin said. So I stood up and we picked up Ayudesh's body and the two offworld men picked up Wanji's body and we took them to the skimmer.

A dog followed us in the dark.

The man in the red jacket climbed up and went to the front of the skimmer. There were chairs there and he sat in one and talked to someone on a radio. I could remember the world for *radio* in English. Ayudesh used to have one until it stopped working and then he didn't get another.

My thoughts rattled through my empty head.

They put the bodies of the teachers next to the body of Veronique's teacher. Tuuvin and I stood outside the door, leaning in to watch them. The floor of the skimmer was metal.

One of the blue-jacket men brought us two blankets. The blankets were the same blue as his jacket and had a red symbol on them. A circle with words. I didn't pay much attention to them. He brought us foil packets. Five. Ten of them.

"Food," he said, pointing to the packets.

I nodded. "Food," I repeated.

"Do they have guns?" Tuuvin asked harshly.

"Guns?" I asked. "You have guns?"

"No guns," the blue jacket said. "No guns."

I didn't know if we were supposed to get in the skimmer or if the gifts meant to go. Veronique came over and sat in the doorway. She hugged me. "Thank you, Janna," she whispered. "Thank you."

Then she got up.

"Move back," said the red jacket, shooing us.

We trotted back away from the skimmer. Its engines fired and the ground underneath them steamed. The skimmer rose, and then the engines turned from pointing down to pointing back and it moved off. Heavy and slow at first, but then faster and faster. Higher and higher.

We blinked in the darkness, holding our gifts.

~

Maureen F. McHugh was born in what was then a sleepy, blue-collar town in Ohio called Loveland. She went to college in Ohio, and then graduate school at New York University. She lived a year in Shijiazhuang, China. Her first book, Tiptree Award winner *China Mountain Zhang* was published in 1991. Since then she has written three novels and a well-received collection of short stories, Story Prize finalist *Mothers & Other Monsters*. McHugh has also worked on alternate reality games for *Halo 2*, *The Watchmen*, and Nine Inch Nails. She lives in Los Angeles, where she has attempted to sell her soul to Hollywood.

SALVAGE

CARRIE VAUGHN

Art by Elizabeth Leggett

"You two ready?" I ask.

"Yes, ma'am," Gert says with forced brightness, and Rally nods quickly, a shake of motion behind her helmet's faceplate. She's nervous, but she always seems to be a little nervous, so I'm not too worried.

We wait in *Iris's* airlock for the air to hiss out around us. It's a dangerous, thrilling sensation. I can almost feel air rushing over the fabric of my suit, hear a bit of wind through the helmet, until I can't hear anything. Then comes the eerie moment when we open the door to the unknown.

I know the captain isn't supposed to take part in these operations. I'm supposed to stay on the bridge, safe and sound, and not expose myself to unnecessary risk. Stick around to take the blame if something goes horribly wrong. But if I think that much risk is involved in boarding the *Radigund*, I wouldn't send any of my people aboard. We'd do an automated sensor sweep, mark the site for salvage and let someone with more personnel and big guns do the work. *Radigund* is dead in space. No life signs, no energy readings, nothing. We have no reason to believe anything is there.

So we board, to better investigate and make a full report. Recover bodies, if any are there to recover. *Radigund* is—was—a small survey ship, like us, plying the edges of known spaceways, tracking routes and charting what we find. Trade Guild diverted our mission to look for her. It took us a month to find her, she'd drifted so far off course.

Using the mechanical override, we force open *Radigund's* hatch into the opposite airlock. I enter first, Gert and Rally follow, slipping soundlessly behind me. It's dark. My lamp panning across the space before me disorients rather than illuminates. I have to piece together a flash of wall, the viewport on the opposite hatch, a warning label above a control panel.

Gert closes the hatch behind us.

Sealed in the other airlock now, we have to pull off an access panel and open the interior hatch manually. *Radigund* has no power. No air, either, which gives a clue as to what happened. The door grinds open, gears stiff. I can't wait to get my hands on the log and the black box, to learn what happened. Assuming we can get enough power to the computer to download anything. No power also means no artificial gravity. We float through, pushing ourselves along the corridor walls.

"God, I hate this," Rally says, her voice thin over the comm. "I feel like something's going to jump out at us."

Gert chuckles. "You've been watching too many films."

We continue on to the bridge. Nothing unusual so far, besides the lack of power. The lack of life.

A second channel on my comm clicks on. It's Matthews, from *Iris's* bridge. "Captain, I've finished the second hull survey. Not so much as a pinhole."

Hull breach could have shut down the ship in a hurry. That had been my first thought. Matthews closes that possibility.

"Thank you," I say. Voices murmur in the background. The whole crew is on the *Iris* bridge, watching our progress on our suit cameras and monitors. Like it's one of Rally's films.

"What was that!" Rally says suddenly, and we all swing around, bumping against the walls and each other.

Her light shines on a blanket floating halfway through the hatchway leading to crew quarters.

"You really are losing it," Gert says, unkindly.

"Focus, you two," I say. I'm beginning to regret my decision to bring these two in particular. But Rally knows the computers; Gert knows the power system. And they mix like oil and water.

They're good people. Good crew. But sometimes, I'm tempted to lock them in a room together and watch the fireworks.

Our progress is slow, slower than I like. Because of the shadows, I think. Rally's monsters hiding in them. Venting, tubing, ladders, open hatches, all of them are shadows, foreshortened and flickering in our helmet lamps. We're hesitating, holding back. Expecting an unnamable thing that we don't want to find. My breathing grows loud, sealed with it against my ears as I am. A ship shouldn't be so quiet.

Gert's hand clutches my shoulder, hard enough to feel through my suit's padding, but I've seen what he's seen in the same moment. Breath and heart both stop, no doubt prompting spikes in biometric readouts on *Iris* that stop hearts among the crew there. Rally stifles a whimper.

It's a face glaring out from a doorway, all teeth and eyes, arms reaching.

We freeze, and all three helmet lamps focus on it.

It's a photograph, printed large and hung on the door. A person in a blue Trade Guild uniform. Male. He's grinning, throwing his hands up to guard against the camera, to prevent this picture from even happening. But it's all in good fun. Someone has drawn a party hat on the man's head and garland of flowers around his neck, and written in large, enthusiastic letters, *Happy Birthday, Captain*. I could guess the joke behind it: the Captain had declared he didn't want a party for his birthday. No celebration, just another day. And someone on the crew had taken revenge. *Radigund* must have been that kind of ship, where the crew could play a small joke on the captain, and he wouldn't mind.

Frost curls the edges of the paper.

"Geez," Gert breathes.

We climb the ladder to the bridge, following the circles of our flashlights. We find bodies there. Navigator, pilot, comm officer. Captain. Even frozen and dead, rimed with frost, I recognize my counterpart from the picture. There ought to be six more, somewhere on the ship. Crew cabins, engineering, and medical are where I expect to find them.

Captain and pilot are strapped to their seats, stiff arms raised a few inches above armrests. Weightlessness had set in before the freezing cold. The other two are curled up near the floor. All are wearing oxygen masks. They knew this was coming, that something was wrong. An open plate on the deck, cabling exposed, shows an attempt at repairs.

Ice crystals frost hair and skin, open eyes. They're all in their twenties and thirties, our age. Far too young to be so still. I don't know them. Didn't go to the Academy with any of them. But I might have. Close to home.

But there are bodies. I'm almost relieved. How much stranger, to come aboard and find nothing. To wonder if they all stepped out of the airlock twenty light years back, with no explanation. Sweat trickles down the back of my neck. My heart rate still feels too fast, but *Iris* hasn't said anything about it yet. The air inside my suit smells too much like me.

"Matthews," I say to my own comm officer. "Is this coming through?"

"Yes, ma'am," he says softly.

"Gert, start on the power. See if we can get the computers up. I want to see the log."

Rally's bulky glove touches Gert's padded shoulder. He can't possibly feel the contact. "Can I help?"

He glances at her awkwardly, sideways, through the helmet plate. "Yeah. We're going to take those panels off."

I work on retrieving the black box. The battery-driven recorder is stored in a protected safe in the back of the bridge. *Iris* has one just like it. I find it, pull it out, send it back through the airlock to *Iris* so Matthews and Clancy can look at it. Gert and Rally are still working. Over the comm, I can hear them arguing the whole time.

"We shouldn't let the captain wander off by herself," Rally says. As if I can't hear.

"She's fine. What do you expect is going to happen?"

"That's just it, I don't know. But this is weird. What happened here?"

Four frozen sets of eyes are staring at her. She has every right to be uncomfortable. Gert hides his own discomfort by mocking hers.

"You're paranoid."

"It's always the captain who dies first in these stories. Know why? Because it leaves everyone else feeling directionless, guilty, grief-stricken—"

"Rally! Please! Are you going to help me with this or not?"

A few moments of quiet, then, "There's nothing wrong with these circuits. I think the problem's in engineering."

A long pause, then Gert's gruff admission. "Okay. We'll check there. Captain?"

"I'll meet you," I say.

We find the engineer floating before his station, bundled in a suit. He'd survived the freeze, but asphyxiated when his suit oxygen ran out. He'd been working on the engine right up to the end.

I touch both Gert and Rally, patting the fabric of their suits. "You two work. I'm going to check for the rest of them."

I find them in crew quarters like I thought I would. We'll have to make recordings. ID, photos. Then we'll jettison them into the next star. Traditional burial in space. There'd never be a question about what happened to them.

I'm almost back to engineering when Gert and Rally start in again. But it's different this time.

"Rally, don't start. Not in your suit. Do you know what a pain in the ass—"

Rally sniffs. Tears thicken her voice. "I can't help it. I keep thinking—what if it was us? It could have been us."

"No, it couldn't. *Iris* is a good ship, this wouldn't happen. Captain wouldn't let it happen."

His earnestness surprises me. I'd have expected more mocking. I approach quietly—as quietly as I can, in a suit, bouncing against walls to control my momentum.

Rally and Gert are helmet to helmet, faces pressed as close together as they can, holding each other's arms. I can see their profiles in the halo of their helmet lamps. Gert is talking, Rally nods.

"You going to be okay?" Gert says.

"Yeah. Sorry. I just let it get to me. I'm okay now. I'm okay."

"Good. I need your help. I need you."

They gaze at each other. I back away and leave them alone. Head to the airlock, where Horace comes aboard to help me with the bodies.

• • •

We've been here two days, working in shifts, when Gert reports.

"I can't get power online, Captain. Not with what we have here. She's cooked."

That was always a possibility, and we have a plan for this. We mark the *Radigund's* position, place a beacon tagging Trade Guild property, though I doubt any other ship looking for salvage will find it. A cruiser with the power to tow the ship will have to retrieve it. Unless Trade Guild decides to junk her and let her float out here, a dead shell, forever.

We undock and leave, taking a course to the nearest star system for the burial. *Radigund* is a dark hulk in space. Her stories, the thousand little mundane events that happen every day aboard any ship, are her own. Gone, now.

Matthews heads the briefing around the galley table. Scenes like this play out thousands of times, on hundreds of ships. A thousand little events. Gert and Rally are sitting next to each other, and I can't remember that ever happening before. They're side by side, shoulders brushing, on the bench attached to the wall.

"Engine failure due to a corruption in the fuel cell line," he said. "There was a cascading failure in all systems after that. They were working on getting the engine back online when power to life support cut off. It was the compression system. Air pressure went fast." Air pressure went, temperature dropped, and the portable oxygen only lasted so long.

"Clancy, take a look at our fuel lines. Just in case," I say. "Thank you, all of you. Your professionalism has helped make a difficult situation go smoothly and is noted." Commendations go into the log, into personnel files, and they all know it. Maybe it'll help.

I start to walk out, to give them the space to vent or complain or laugh or cry without their captain looking on. Rally reaches out when I walk past her and takes my hand. A quick warm squeeze and a smile of comfort. It's enough to make my own eyes sting.

I squeeze her hand back and continue out of the galley.

~

Carrie Vaughn is the bestselling author of the Kitty Norville series, the most recent of which is the twelfth installment, *Kitty in the Underworld*. Her superhero novel *Dreams of the Golden Age* was released in January 2014. She has also written young adult novels, *Voices of Dragons and Steel*, and the fantasy novels, *Discord's Apple* and *After the Golden Age*. Her short fiction has appeared in many magazines and anthologies, from Lightspeed to Tor.com and George R.R. Martin's *Wild Cards* series. She lives in Colorado with a fluffy attack dog. Learn more at carrievaughn.com.

A Guide to Grief

Emily Fox

You love someone.

A boyfriend, who hogs the covers and pisses with the bathroom door open. Your mother. Your little brother—he never calls, communicating instead via selfies verging on the ridiculous and too-brief texts.

Something happens, as these things inevitably do. Drunk Driver. A mugging. Suicide. You cry for days, or try to hold it in, or both; your boss tells you to take as long as you need. Some days, your chest hurts from the pain of it all. Crying doesn't help anymore—it never really did.

You love someone enough to get your hands on a time machine.

Perhaps you're some kind of genius. Leave your tears behind and start gathering parts. Hands slimed with grease, you sweat that love into metal and power cables and code. The work consumes you. The work grinds its way into your lungs until only your body remembers to breathe.

Or perhaps you're not all that bright, but you're desperate. You think and plan and lie and steal—you steal yourself a time machine, breaking laws that aren't even a scratch compared to the laws of time and space.

And you have no idea what you're doing. But all you need is to get lucky once. (Things go wrong. Those times don't bear thinking about. Try again.) You love someone enough to go back.

· · ·

You go back.

· · ·

For a time, everything seems a little bit brighter. You're alive, alive, alive! you chant silently, watching them make coffee. The colour of their eyes is somehow new and wonderful; you cry.

But you've seen all the movies—you've read enough shitty novels to know how these things go. Panic begins to claw its way out of your throat. Someone saw, you think—someone knows. The barista across the street. A neighbour. The man who walks his dog, same time every morning.

Or perhaps you've heard the theory; you're some kind of genius, after all. The sensitive dependency on initial conditions. Butterflies.

The kid who crushed your boyfriend's car lives, and flees the scene. Two dead—dying on the motorway.

No need to check the CCTV for a crime that didn't happen. He gets away.

Your little brother goes back to school.

You love someone. There is no such thing as a perfect world.

• • •

The house is quiet, TV turned down low. You slip your shoes on and stare at the faded linoleum. You love someone enough to make things right. The knife block empties itself onto the counter. You choose well.

There's no point in leaving a note, but you do anyway. You'll be back in no time at all.

• • •

You go back.

～

Emily Fox lives in a town you've never heard of in Queensland, Australia, and is a graduate of The University of Queensland's Writing, Editing, and Publishing program. When she's not reading her way through a dragon's hoard of books, Emily spends her free time following the adventures of bat-like superheroes and reading slush for *Aurealis Magazine*. You can find her on Twitter at @byemilyfox.

See DANGEROUS EARTH-POSSIBLES!

Tina Connolly

You are fifteen when you get the brochure.

See DANGEROUS EARTH-POSSIBLES! Become a Hero!

The ad blinked at you online, between the x-ray glasses and the grainy picture of how to lose fourteen pounds and get real wings, and you gave them your father's address, because your stepfather opens your mail. It means it is longer to get the brochure, but it also means it is there waiting for you that Saturday that your father is finally home and not off being brave in Mogadishu or Detroit or wherever it is he's not allowed to say.

You answer questions like:

Fill in the attacker that could be stopped with a:

baseball bat
vaccination
silver bullet
gram of kryptonite
baseball bat

and you get all of them, though you're confused by the second baseball bat and you accidentally fill in your stepfather, but then you leave it.

There's an essay question, too, about what you would do if you were sent to the future where invasive warthog flu has brought down most of the American Pacific Northwest, and you have to defend a senior citizen center from a band of nudists, with only some artisanal pine toothpicks at your disposal

(answer: Tape the toothpicks into a long jabbing stick and poke their naughty bits from a safe distance.)

You send it back through snail mail with five dollars for postage, and you wait another month while your father hunts bad guys in San Pedro Sula and St. Louis and then you find the shoebox, stuck on the back porch by the postman, now damp and smelling of earwigs. You open it to find your DANGEROUS EARTH-POSSIBLES activation kit: a folded rubbery mat that looks like a game of Twister and smells like a new car.

You place your left foot as they tell you. Your right foot. Your ten fingers and your chin and your black eye, and then with your nose you press the ACTIVATION button. Everything spins around you like an uppercut (not the one given to you; more like the ones your dad is out there giving the bad guys), and then you find yourself in one of the EARTH-POSSIBLES. You know it's one of the EARTH-POSSIBLES because there are tiny zombie chipmunks lurching around your backyard, and there weren't before.

A man appears from the backyard, tired and sore and covered with chipmunk bites. He looks a little like your father, as you remember him from when you were eight and all living together and he was still only with the local police force and not with the things he couldn't tell you about. As the man douses his bites in rubbing alcohol, he tells you that if you pass the chipmunk world, you can join his squad and do battle on all the known EARTH-POSSIBLES. He tosses you a baseball bat.

You had never thought you could harm a chipmunk. But they storm your ankles and one gets its teeth in and oh—that's going to leave a mark. It will match the marks on your wrist from when your stepfather challenged you to a no-holds-barred wrestling match (just to see if you were as tough as your father.) You find that you can put the rabid chipmunks down after all, and you do, one at a time, till your shoulders shake and you are weeping.

The man puts his arm around your shoulders and offers you the alcohol. One of these worlds is going to be our future, he says, and it needs to be made safe. Heroes like you have been recruited from all countries and times.

You listen while you sear your wounds. And you know that all you really want is that EARTH-POSSIBLE where your father comes home from Peshawar, and does battle with your stepfather (hands, feet, teeth), and then takes you away with him to be a Hero too.

And so this seems like the next best thing, and you nod. You join the other Heroes-in-Training in another EARTH-POSSIBLE, in an abandoned police station there, and you learn how to go to other worlds and kill more things—sometimes with silver bullets, sometimes with regular ones.

Some nights you think about your father, and how he travels around being a hero. And sometimes you think about your stepfather, and how strange it is that he is part of the police force too. And meanwhile, while you're thinking, you pick up your baseball bat and battle for your future.

~

Tina Connolly lives with her family in Portland, Oregon. Her stories have appeared in Lightspeed, Tor.com, Strange Horizons, and Beneath Ceaseless Skies. Her first fantasy novel, *Ironskin* (Tor 2012), was nominated for a Nebula, and the sequel *Copperhead* is now out from Tor. She narrates for Podcastle and Beneath Ceaseless Skies, runs the Parsec-winning flash fiction podcast Toasted Cake, and her website is tinaconnolly.com.

A DEBT REPAID

MARINA J. LOSTETTER

Some people will do almost anything to wipe out a debt.

You, Jessica, are no exception. When the casino men came to your dingy apartment to collect, what did they threaten you with? A bat to break your legs? A knife to take out your eye? Not a gun to kill you with—I know it's not like the movies.

Did Big Tony offer to make you one of his girls? Did he say you could work off your debt?

Would that have been so bad? You still would have sold your body, but in the off-hours it would be yours and yours alone.

You must have told them your plan—that's why they left you whole.

You went to the Twin Life offices that same day. Ran through all the tests. They made sure you were healthy, sane. With no history of substance abuse. You passed their screenings, signed their papers, received the down payment (more than enough to pay off the sharks) and prepared to go under the knife.

Would being one of Tony's girls really have been so bad?

When I signed up for Twin Life, I didn't waste time imagining who I'd be attached to when the time came. All I knew is that I would die one day, and if I didn't want it to be permanent, Twin Life was my only option.

Bodies are rare these days, Jessica. But heads—we're everywhere.

Those first few weeks were terrible, for both of us. Me perched on your left shoulder, in control of your left arm, but no more—forced to watch you take over my mansion. You filled my closet with cheap fabrics and hooker boots. In exchange, I filled your mirror with a two headed monster—one head young, one old. One with gaudy red lipstick and too much eyeliner. One with short gray curls and dead eyes.

Two lives became one. We go to your job during the day, have afternoon tea with my book-club on the weekends, then it's off to the tables for your nightly fix.

They make me wear a blindfold when you gamble—say two heads is cheating. I don't mind. I just order cocktail after cocktail, and you get mad because alcohol makes you lose your concentration.

They asked about your substance abuse at Twin Life, but never mentioned mine.

• • •

When we fight, there's nowhere to go.

When you want to make love to a man, there's no one to find.

• • •

My bank account dwindles. Your hangovers get worse. I reach for the bottle, and you can't stop me. You reach for the cards, and I can't stop you.

We each have this *thing* holding on to us. Controlling us. Tearing up our lives and our relationships and our sanity.

It's been a year, and we've grown attached (no pun intended). You help moisturize my sagging skin. I help you fix your hair up like a tart. The bedroom smells of gin and too much perfume and frayed cards and dusty poker chips.

I love you, Jessica. But not as I should, not as a granddaughter or a nursemaid or a sister. We love each other because others find us hard to love. Friends, family—everyone runs from the two-headed monster, knowing they can't be with the one they adore without suffering the other.

But it was that way before Twin Life, wasn't it? For the both of us.

Meeting your brother changed me. It was the horror in his eyes, the tremble in his lips. The way he eyed the liquor cabinet and the ink stains on your fingers (you rub the cards—it's your tell).

He loves you, truer than I ever could, but being near you kills him. He saw the neglected bills, heard the bark in your voice when you said it was none of his business.

But it is my business.

I can't deny it anymore. The drink that ruined my first life has taken over again. I never fully realized the pain I'd caused before—before I died. This second life has given me the chance to understand. Thank you for that.

Ultimately, it's too late for me. But not for you.

After you read this, after you've had my dead head removed, you must get help. You have to get rid of the monster—not the one we seen in the mirror, the one that's always been in you.

You gave up your body for your addiction. With the letter opener on the nightstand, I'll give it up, too.

~

Marina J. Lostetter's short fiction has appeared in venues such as *InterGalactic Medicine Show,* *Galaxy's Edge,* and *Writers of the Future.* Her most recent publications include a tie-in novelette for the Star Citizen game universe, which was serialized over the first four months of 2014. Originally from Oregon, Marina now lives in Arkansas with her husband, Alex. She tweets as @MarinaLostetter. Please visit her homepage at lostetter.net.

THE SEWELL HOME FOR THE TEMPORALLY DISPLACED

SARAH PINSKER

Judy says, "It's snowing."

I look out the window. The sky is the same dirty grey as the snow left from last week's storm. I stand up to look closer, to find a backdrop against which I might see what she sees. The radiator is warm against my knees.

"You don't mean now." It's not really a question, but she shakes her head. She looks through me, through another window, at other weather. She smiles. Whenever she is, it must be beautiful.

"Describe it for me," I say.

"Big, fluffy snow. The kind that doesn't melt when it lands on your gloves. Big enough to see the shapes of individual flakes."

"Do you know when you are?"

She strains to catch a different view. "1890s, maybe? The building across the street hasn't been built yet. I wish I could see down to the street, Marguerite."

Judy isn't supposed to leave her bed, but I help her into her yellow slippers, help her to her feet. I try to make myself strong enough for her to lean on. We shuffle to the window. She looks down.

"There's a brougham waiting at the front door. The horse is black, and he must have been driven hard, because the snow that's collecting elsewhere is just melting when it hits him. There's steam coming off him."

I don't say anything. I can't see it, but I can picture it.

"Somebody came out of the building. He's helping a woman out of the carriage," she says. "Her clothes don't match the era or the season. She's wearing jeans and a T-shirt."

"A Distillers t-shirt," I say.

"Yes! Can you see her too?"

"No," I say. "That was me, the first time I came here. I didn't stay long, that first time."

I hear the creak of the door. It's Zia, my least favorite of the nurses. She treats us like children. "Judy, what are we doing up? We could get hurt if we have an episode."

She turns to me. "And you, Marguerite. We should know better to encourage her."

"Your pronouns are very confusing," I tell her.

She ignores me. "Well, let's get down to lunch, since we're both up and about."

Zia puts Judy in a wheelchair. I follow them down to the dining room, slow and steady. She pushes Judy up to the first available space, at a table with only one vacancy. I'm forced to sit across the room. I don't like being so far away from her. I would make a fuss, but I try to tell myself we can stand to be apart for one meal. I keep an eye on her anyway.

Judy isn't fully back yet. She doesn't touch her food. Mr. Kahn and Michael Lim and Grace de Villiers are all talking across her. Mr. Kahn is floating his spoon, demonstrating the finer points of the physics of his first time machine, as he always does.

"Meatloaf again," mutters Emily Arnold, to my left. "I can't wait until vat protein is invented."

"It tastes good enough, Emily. The food here is really pretty decent for an industrial kitchen in this time period." We've all had worse.

We eat our meatloaf. Somebody at the far end of the room has a major episode and we're all asked to leave before we get our jello. I can't quite see who it is, but she's brandishing her butter knife like a cutlass, her legs braced against a pitching deck. The best kind of episode, where you're fully then again. We all look forward to those. It's funny that the staff act like it might be contagious.

I wait in Judy's room for her to return. Zia wheels her in and lifts her into the bed. She's light as a bird, my Judy. Zia frowns when she sees me. I think she'd shoo me out more often if either of us had family that could lodge a complaint. Michael and Grace are allowed to eat together but not to visit each other's rooms. Grace's children think she shouldn't have a relationship now that she lives in so many times at once. Too confusing, they say, though Grace doesn't know whether they mean for them or for her.

"How was your dinner?" I ask Judy.

"I can't remember," she says. "But I saw you come in for the first time. You said 'How is this place real?' and young Mr. Kahn said 'Because someday all of us will build it.'"

"And then I asked 'When can I get started?' and he said 'You already did.'"

I can see it now. The dining room was formal, then. Everyone stared when I came in, but most of the smiles were knowing ones. They understood the hazards of timesling. They had been there, or they were there, or they were going to be.

Judy takes my hand. I lean over to kiss her.

"It's snowing," I say. "I can't wait to meet you."

~

Sarah Pinsker lives in Baltimore, Maryland, in a hundred year old house on the top of a hill. Her heart has been split into pieces and divided across three countries on two continents. Her work has appeared in *Strange Horizons, Asimov's, the Magazine of Fantasy & Science Fiction, Daily Science Fiction, Fireside*, the *Long Hidden* anthology, and more. She is a singer/songwriter with three albums on various indie labels, one with her rock band, the Stalking Horses. A fourth is almost complete. She has toured nationally in a van with a bed in the back and a ghost in the radio, and gets lost on purpose. Find her online at sarahpinsker.com or twitter.com/sarahpinsker.

#TrainFightTuesday

Vanessa Torline

WELCOME TO **PATTER**
Talk fast.

@BariStar
Style is my superpower

BariStar - 5:09
Polarity just magnetized my train. On a Tuesday night.

LunaSam - 5:10
@BariStar: You're lying, no one goes after the green line.

BariStar - 5:11
No, I'm not lying!! I'd post a pic but she's riding on the roof. Train is slowing down.

BariStar - 5:12
I can't fucking believe this. 1st it rains on my boots and now there's a super-villain threating my train. This is why I took the apartm

BariStar - 5:12
ent in the burbs. They're not supposed to do this crap this far out of town, especially not on TUESDAYS.

Runningtime - 5:13
@BariStar: lets see. rain on boots or villin attack wich is worse?

#bimboquestions

BootsOnFoots - 5:14
  @BariStar: Check out our wedges sale, one day only!

Havespatulawillomelet - 5:14
  @BariStar Wow, if only there was a superhero for boots. :-P

BariStar - 5:15
  Shut up you guys, these boots are suede and I just bought them.

BariStar - 5:17
  Has anyone heard about Polarity yet? Are the cops coming or...?

BariStar - 5:20
  OK. Sonic Woman showed up 2 seconds ago. You know, the one who makes that sound when she flies over you.

BariStar - 5:22
  Oh right, thx! RT @superinformed: Sonic Woman changed her codename to Redshift like a year ago...

BariStar - 5:24
  So the fight is def on. Polarity's got the train in her beam or whatever, so it keeps rocking. Feels like being drunk on a cruise ship.

BariStar - 5:24
  Which I have been.

BariStar - 5:25
  RT @superinformed: It's a magnetic wave.

BariStar - 5:26
  Sorry, guys, I don't really pay attention to the cape scene. I just know Polarity bc that bank she tried to rob last

BariStar - 5:26
  year is right by my job.

VillainHistory - 5:27

@BariStar: You mean the courthouse on 18th and Morris? Is that why your Patter name is BariStar?

BariStar - 5:28
Not the courthouse. The coffee shop. BariStar like barista + star. Not barrister.

BariStar - 5:29
And who says "barrister" anyway? Like are you kidding.

VillainHistory - 5:30
@BariStar: I don't remember that.

BariStar - 5:32
Really? It was in October, she tore a hole through the roof and tried to attract all

BariStar - 5:32
the gold out of the bank. Fiesta & Siesta caught her that time.

Runningtime - 5:33
@BariStar: fiesta & siesta? damn ur a c-list cape magnet huh. No1 even likes redshift she such a weak bitch

Runningtime blocked.

BariStar - 5:36
Can I just say, I love Redshift's look. #thosegloves

BariStar - 5:37
Polarity dresses like skank though.

BariStar - 5:41
Something just happened! There's bloat running down my window!

BariStar - 5:42
Blood*. Autocorrect is an idiot, amirite?

Havespatulawillomelet - 5:47
@BariStar: Whose blood??

Havespatulawillomelet - 5:52
  OMG what happened to you?

Sidekickenvy - 6:01
  @BariStar Where are you?

Private message from: @lotsalattes - 6:07
amy, u ok? will u make it to work tmrw??

BariStar - 6:11
  HEY I'M STILL ALIVE. Sorry to worry you all.

Havespatulawillomelet - 6:12
  @BariStar: Oh good.

VillainHistory - 6:12
  @BariStar: Yay!

BariStar - 6:13
  Lost Wifi for a while. Redshift's power, I guess.

BariStar - 6:14
  The train is completely stopped now. I can't believe how long this is taking.

VillainHistory - 6:15
  @BariStar: Uh, yeah, are you new to this? Supervillains don't really work with your schedule in this city.

BariStar - 6:16
  Uh, NO, I'm not new to this, I've lived here 8 yrs. How dare you.

VillainHistory - 6:17
  @BariStar: Sorry.

BariStar - 6:19
  But OK, there are tourists in here FREAKING OUT. One's about to cry. It's actually hard not to laugh. I'm so mean. Sorry sorry.

Sidekickenvy - 6:20
  LOLOLOL

BariStar - 6:22

There's a qws12gggggggggggggggggr

BariStar - 6:25

UGH Polarity's wave ripped my phone out of my hand. Hit the ceiling and now my screen's cracked! That bitch!!

BariStar - 6:27

Good thing I have villain activity insurance. And my dad said not to bother—LOL.

Havespatulawillomelet - 6:35

@BariStar: You disappeared again.

BariStar - 6:36

Had to put my phone away while the magnetic field was screwed up, but it's good now! The capes are off the train!

Sidekickenvy - 6:37

@BariStar: Awesome!

Superinformed - 6:37

@BariStar: So what's happening now?

BariStar - 6:39

Redshift just tied up Polarity in a field between two residential areas. No metal. Plastic cuffs. #YEAHLADYSUPERHEROES #fightover

BariStar - 6:42

OK, made it to my stop. Thx for the company guys.

Sidekickenvy - 6:43

@BariStar: Sure thing. Good to hear it worked out.

LunaSam - 6:44

@BariStar: This wasn't as exciting as I wanted it to be.

Private message from: @lotsalattes - 6:45
glad ur safe amy, hate to be short staffed

Havespatulawillomelet - 6:45
   @BariStar: F'ing supervillains! Hope your next commute goes better.

BariStar - 6:49
   OMG there's a guy actually complaining to a station employee. No, really.

BariStar - 6:49
   Tourists.

BariStar - 6:51
   #tuesdaytrainfight #thankyouredshift #baristastories

Private message to: @SonicSass - 8:04

Okay, Elisa, I've had enough time to think it over. Maybe it was the Polarity thing tonight or watching that guy complain about you—your beam fried his tablet so screw you, apparently, even though you saved his life—but I'm done watching lunatics abuse this city just because they can. I don't want to be one of those people who swear they're going to move, then find themselves still here 30 years later, broken because one of Doctor Stain's cyborgs destroyed their house or Omnigalaxis sent a bus full of kids to another dimension.

But I don't want to run away either. If you're still looking for someone to team up with you, I'm in. You bring the serum or radioactive bracelet or whatever it is. I'll bring the costume.

I can be good at this. I know I can.

Amy

P.S. Why the hell did you never tell me you changed your codename to Redshift? I felt like an idiot on Patter today.

～

Vanessa Torline is fascinated by many storytelling mediums, but her first love is a book—the kind with pictures and without. As a journalist, she has written about comic books, theatre, animation, and film in addition to news articles. She is currently working on other short stories and a young adult fantasy novel.

The Hymn of Ordeal, No. 23

Rhiannon Rasmussen

Your brother's bones, suspended in mineral fluids, turn as smoothly and shine as brightly as the oil-coated joints of the mechanism they guide. When you touch the heavy plastic that separates you from his body, it is cold. The iron plate that serves to cover what is left of his face turns towards the tapping, and nausea wells deep in your throat. You catch a glimpse of yellow fat, the hole of a socket, nerves that once bundled into the base of an eye now strung behind the iron half-mask.

Flesh did not make the transit to deep space whole, only guts packed in gel and nerves strung into wires, the delicate threads that extend to outer sensors, thrusters, and lenses. That is what they are now. Not people, not soldiers, but shrikes: the folded warbirds sent through void to cleanse it of the invaders, to impale them on their own stardust ruins, to leave broken chassis and frozen corpses scattered as warning to others who might threaten us. If the invaders left corpses—you have never seen them, only the scars of their passage left across the skin of Earth.

Only the shrikes see them, and the shrikes are silent.

The motion makes you queasy, to see your brother laid bare in this way, deconstructed into scaffolding, but he knew what he had volunteered for long before the first flensing cut had been made. Most people are advised not to see the volunteers after induction. Now you understand why.

You're told he does not acknowledge you. The movement is involuntary, a roll in his sleep while he dreams the dreams of kites. He does not see inside the ship any more than you can peer inside your own ribcage.

After you leave the shrike and the remains of your brother behind, you lift your phone as you have many times before, to listen again to the last message your brother left you, on the day he decided to join. The words are as hollow as you felt when you first heard them. You thought a suicide note might be less painful, but you did not know what you could do, you never raised your voice against him, and now you walk away.

"How else do you see the stars, but to join the war?" he asks, distant and thin through the speakers. "I don't know if you'll understand," a pause for breath, and you stop the message. You know how it ends.

•••

On launch day you stay at home while astronomers gather on hills and look up for the tiny stars, winking out one by one as the shrikes break orbit and fling themselves far past the shadows the sun casts. It is all the news discusses for weeks, how we are taking the fight to them, how brave the volunteers are, how we are turning the tides of history this day, this year, this century. Reconstruction will last generations. Who knows what civilization will follow in the contrails of conquerors?

You sit at home and you do not listen, but the shadows flit through your thoughts as you wonder how we will know they have succeeded, how many thousands of years will pass before the night sky shows the scars of war, if your children's children's children will be able to look up and trace battle lines by the absence of light.

News feeds and reports of the war arrive in fragments, sentences at a time, signaled in light packed tight and sent back the way they came, the way the invaders came. All years too late. If there is humanity among the stuttered laser missives, songs or stories or riddles the shrikes call back and forth through flickering verses over void to pass the time, it is not shared. Only life confirmed and life lost, coordinates and absences.

Light casts long shadows in vacuum.

There are more launches. We are winning, the missives say. Victory is a mathematical equation.

The equation is repeated daily. Sometimes, as the announcer's voice drones on, name after name, you wonder why they list the casualties at all. They volunteered to be killed long before they were sent to the front lines. But those thoughts are treason, and you push them aside even while listening, always afraid, for your brother's name to be spoken among the dead.

It never is, and you are never sure if you are grateful for the sparing or sorry that you have no chance to grieve. You wonder if the machines will fail first, or the organics inside them, or if age no longer applies to a kite of angles and shards. You transfer your brother's last message from phone to phone to phone as you move from place to place, buried deeper under your new life with every adjustment made for your work, your career, your friends. That is how it should be. Life moves on. Sometimes you think you hear your brother's voice, your brother's words–*humanity is worth fighting for*–and you wonder whose wounds will leave the most visible scars; those dismantled to wheel like hunting hawks out into the void, or the handlers left behind to fit each twisted spar back into place, one by one?

• • •

Time passes. The shrikes' infrequent transmissions shift in measured steps from war to the equations of extermination, and the ones who do not wish to mask truth's sharp words with poetry call it genocide. No plea for surrender comes, and the news turns its attention to closer matters, to expansion, to colonization, to business and the small strifes that spring up after the need for unification has passed.

We no longer tell the shrikes what to do; they are bladed kites loosed upon æther, ours in name only. On Earth, cities are built over and around the ruins. If not for words carved into glass, speeches that remind citizens never to forget wounds past, and crystal walkways over exposed bedrock, there would be no physical memories of the damage wrought at all.

Did you have children, did you marry, did you retire well or not at all? It doesn't matter on the day that the sky opens wide again and the shrikes pour down through the tears. No signal heralded their arrival, no sound and no light. They never left unheeded any command, but they broadcast no warning of their return. And with them come unfamiliar ships with geometry more grown than manufactured, bone-bright and entwined with the shrikes in the sky, as equals. Only decades-old footage will identify them as the ships of the invaders, the lances that carved irreparable gouges into the Earth.

The shrikes flare out, the lancing lights among the stars that flew to cleanse the void of a threat returned and dragging their catch with them. The world falls quiet under their long shadows. The shrikes lie silent, waiting, listening, wings spread in formation, shining knives to cut the sun.

Of course you walk outside with the others and you crane your neck, wondering which is your brother, aware of how vulnerable you are in this moment, how they could rain fire down upon you all.

They do not rain fire. Instead, over the growing hum of fear and conjecture, the enemy ships sing. All at once, they sing, and the noise brings you to your knees.

Weave, they sing.
teach us to refasten our kin

in your image
in the image of the kites
kestrels, swifts, merlins, shrikes
we too wish to cut the stars to thread.

You shield your eyes to study the blinding angles because there is no point to shielding your ears from the song. If you can recognize him, if he would know you, if he survived, if it can be called survival and if he still could be called your brother. But they all look the same and you see him in every one, and in every one yourself.

~

Rhiannon Rasmussen has worked in comics scripting, illustration, graphic design, and print-making, but no matter what else she pursues it is always alongside prose. Her interests lie in juxtaposition and layering, contrasting humanity with elements of monstrosity, phantasm, the macabre, geology, and spaceships. Her sensibilities are influenced by kimokawaii culture, her hometown in Hawaii and the time she spent in Mexico and Denmark as a child. Follow Rhiannon on Twitter: @charibdys or visit her at rhiannonrs.tumblr.com.

EMOTICON

ANAID PEREZ

Once the hostages abandoned the building safely, the screen composing the robot's face displayed: ^_^

Its policeman partner spit on the floor to complain.

"Don't be a fake! You know you don't have emotions."

"Neither you do, but at least I can pretend."

~

Anaid Perez is a freelance Spanish and English writer; her tale "Años y Felices Días" won second place in the sci-fi contest "Las Cuatro Esquinas del Universo," her essays have been published in local newspapers in her home city of Morelia, and she hasn't missed a NaNoWriMo since 2010. She's an active member in ficticia.com and fanfiction.net, where she writes under the pseudonym of Panakeia.

THE MOUTHS

ELLEN DENHAM

I once traveled to a world where the blob-like inhabitants had only one sense organ—the mouth. Everything went through that single orifice to be perceived. Even their atrophied hands were dull and had little feeling, only enough to grasp whatever they came across and lift it to their mouths.

They could neither hear nor speak, but if you were to bake your words into a cracker, they would devour this with relish, then cock their nearly featureless heads, as if considering.

Their customary greeting for each other was a long, open-mouthed kiss—embarrassing to watch. But it wasn't sexual—just the way they recognized each other and shared information. In fact, they did not even reproduce sexually. I wasn't sure why a particularly large individual would suddenly vomit up a small but nearly identical creature. Then I learned that once they had eaten a certain amount, they must give birth. This was quite a large quantity over the course of the creature's lifetime, as they were not prolific breeders. They did not eliminate, so giving birth to another creature was the only way they could lose some of their mass.

Conversation was unknown to them. Some crackers contained the equivalent of sounds, poetry or music; other crackers delivered pictures, smells, and even moving images, directly to their minds. They spent most of their time baking and eating these crackers, seasoned with their own saliva, for this, apparently, was what carried the information they wanted to convey. Then they would sit for hours, rapt, experiencing the information contained in the cracker. Later, they would waddle inside their huts to bake another batch in response. I tried some of the crackers, but my brain could not translate them into the information that the creatures were absorbing. My interpreter, a wrinkled individual—a throwback of sorts who alone of the group had ears and could speak—had to describe them to me.

After a while listening to its explanations, I noticed several recurring themes. It always portrayed the contents of the crackers as the ancestors dancing, or the ancestors singing, or an artwork of the ancestors. I didn't understand what it meant, and my grasp of our one common tongue was not sufficient to grasp its elaborations. But according to my research, the creatures had evolved (devolved, some said) from a long-limbed people who had many senses. These must be the ancestors that were the creatures' source of inspiration.

Why, I asked my interpreter, did their crackers not contain stories of their own people doing things? Why always the ancestors?

It made a gurgling sound deep in its throat and uttered a word so rude I won't translate it. Our interview was over for the day.

Most of the globulous creatures moved awkwardly, when they moved at all, but I noticed one whose stout body constantly undulated, so I thought of it as "Twitchy."

On my fourth day studying the colony, Twitchy jiggled from side to side, waved its tiny hands, made a little turn, and repeated facing the new direction. It did this so many times, while its fellows sat absorbing the information of their crackers, that I wondered what might be wrong with it. I asked my interpreter, who replied that I should not waste its time describing impossible things.

Later that day, Twitchy galumphed from its hut with a batch of crackers and distributed them to any person it bumped into. The creatures consumed their crackers, sat still for a moment, and then, one by one, began to heave themselves around the area more quickly than usual, bumping into each other and kissing each one they bumped, until one of them kissed Twitchy. The creature pushed Twitchy into the center of the group and they surrounded it, all kissing it, as I first thought, until I stood for a better look and realized they were devouring the baker of the most recent crackers. I couldn't do much for poor Twitchy. When the crowd parted, nothing remained of it but a greasy stain.

Why? I asked my interpreter. At first, it didn't believe me when I explained what had happened. Then, curious, it sought out one of the remaining crackers Twitchy had shared. It sat in a lump and chewed for a while, then flew into a rage.

"Ugly!" it said. The creature I called Twitchy had shown them something that was not art at all, didn't even show the ancestors, but a malformed, squat creature flailing about. It spat out the remnants of the cracker and mashed it into the ground with its flat lower appendages. I asked for clarification. What my interpreter described sounded like one of the creatures themselves, moving in just the way Twitchy had the day before. I could only guess that what Twitchy had shown the others that put them in a murderous rage was itself, doing something besides sitting and contemplating the contents of crackers.

I didn't understand what was taboo about this, but later, compiling my notes, I theorized that the creatures themselves did not create. All of the crackers, as described to me, contained familiar themes, which matched well-documented works, such as certain ritual dances of the more elegant-bodied ancestors.

I wondered if Twitchy understood the peril of showing them something new, of having the audacity not only to create, but to show the creatures a vision of themselves. I can only conclude that some creatures are too alien for me to understand, and I dared not read too much into what I saw.

～

Ellen Denham is a multidisciplinary performing artist and writer currently teaching voice and completing a doctorate in music at the University of Illinois Urbana-Champaign. She is a 2006 graduate of the Odyssey Writing Workshop. Her previous publications include stories in *Daily Science Fiction*, *NewMyths.com*, and the Sky Warrior Books anthology *Gears and Levers 3*. Her written works for the stage have been performed by the Butler Ballet and the Indy Convergence. Not content to keep her writing and performing life in separate boxes, Ellen likes to hang out in the dark alleys where artistic genres and disciplines intersect. Her performing career has encompassed everything from opera and oratorio to barking Mozart as a dog, turning internet memes into a comic soundscape, and tap dancing in a Santa suit. You may find her online at denham.virtualave.net.

M1A

KIM WINTERNHEIMER

Mother says Mia can stay in my room a little longer. I jump up and down a bit squealing with delight and Mia claps her hands but says nothing because she cannot speak. Mother smiles at us, and tells me not to overexert myself. I've been so sick, she reminds me.

Five minutes, girls.

I hand Mia the laser we've been painting with and she points it at the wall. The figures M1A appear in an array of colors—her name, bright and vivid— and then a horse jumps out from a cloud of glitter behind it. It would gallop over us if it were real.

Mia is very good at art and most subjects, especially the ones that don't require speaking. She uses these skills to entertain me when I'm sick, and though it's true I've been sick for some time, I don't feel sick now, not like I did before my last surgery. I feel like I'm riding that big sparkling horse that's bounding across the walls and have all the energy of a healthy girl. Mia never bolts around noisily or cries or doesn't eat her vegetables. She hides her energy inside her like a secret. She is, as Mother puts it, quite nearly a model child. If she could speak, I've heard Father say. If she could speak.

Mother says Mia lives with us because we're not savages. When I was born they had M1A made immediately. They freed my umbilical cord from my belly and sent it away for processing. It wasn't long before the baby was returned to Mother and she could hold M1A in her arms just like a real child. I was just a little bit bigger then, but now we're the same size. Just like twins. I was one-year-old when I needed my first part from her.

Father says sometimes little girls get sick and all the science in the world can't predict why or how. Mother cries because it's unfair. All this, she says, and our little girl becomes ill.

Father says it is one of life's mysteries and we're lucky because we have Mia.

A few simple surgeries take what I need from her body and make me new and strong again. It's been that way for a while. Mia and I have been bedside in so many hospital rooms together it's like she's my sister. After so much back and forth Mother had her move in with us. It's what the compassionate families do, and besides, we can afford it. I was small when she moved in, so to me it's like she's been here forever.

She lives in the bedroom downstairs by herself and is quiet and obedient, like a lap dog. Sometimes when we play and something funny happens, her mouth opens wide and I can tell she would be laughing if she could conjure a sound. If she had vocal cords and wasn't mute, her laughter would ring out over mine. Our voices would be identical.

Sometimes Mia's silence scares me. Her gaping throat looks like an endless void and I've had nightmares that her jaw unlatches and swallows me up like a python. It's one of my fever dreams, Mother says. When you're scared of something so sweet.

• • •

Mother pets my hair as Mia plays the piano, one last song before bedtime. We are preparing for the next surgery, though I feel mostly okay. Mother feels for lumps near my throat and I tell her I feel fine but she prods for a long time and makes me open wide just to be sure. Father comes in to check as well and I think, this time it's my throat, this silly body of mine.

Your favorite song? Mother asks when she's through, and I nod, and Mia sends her small fingers fluttering over the piano's keys and I feel sad because surgery is no fun, not for anyone.

Tomorrow? I say. Mother nods.

Mother hums along to Mia's performance. Just one more time, she whispers to the small girl playing, and the melody begins again. If I could, I would write Mother a song, but when you've been as sick as I have there isn't much time for pianos. Mia plays for me when I'm recovering—she heals faster than I do—and I sing along from my bed, funny songs about animals in fields with pumpkins for heads. They make Mia smile and she turns to me when she's happiest, with her wide-open mouth, and I have to look away for a moment, just because for some reason, I can't stand that big open cave.

Father says Mia can sleep in my room tonight but she needs to get ready. I know this routine, though I take very little part in it. I crawl into bed and Mother says, It's all for the best. I repeat it back to her in my singsong voice, the one she loves so much. She places a hand on my neck as I say so. The vibrations are soft and easy. It makes her so happy.

Good girl.

ǀ

I listen while Mia is scrubbed down from head to toe in the bathroom, all her discarded skin cells collecting in the special drain in our tub. Her urine and waste is collected; stray hairs are gathered, the ones Mother can find anyway. They can use just about anything to these days, that's why she can just keep giving and giving. She's a perennial harvest of parts for my body. Whatever I need, just plucked out of her and given it to me.

• • •

I am asleep for an hour, maybe two, and wake up to find the spot next to me empty. I crawl out of bed, cold and shivery, and follow the soft glow of the downstairs light until I hear voices in the kitchen.

Mother and Father are speaking happily about tomorrow and I pause for a minute on the stairs because their happiness makes me happy too, and being healthy is the best reason for such joy. I'm surprised to hear soft tapping. When it stops Mother and Father clap and say, Yay. Mia is dancing in wool socks and a cotton nightgown on the kitchen floor and Mother and Father are eating a berry cobbler enjoying the entertainment.

Mia twirls and Mother beams, causing red juice to fall from her lip down to the soft part of her neck. It collects in the area of skin between her collarbones and Father takes a thumb and smears it away. There is a trace of juice left behind, a streak of red.

It's nice for them to give Mia this moment, I think.

I will ask for some berry cobbler when I wake up after surgery tomorrow, a treat for being such a good girl. Mother will hold me in my bed while Mia plays the piano or draws on the wall and I will eat cobbler.

The tapping stops and Father lifts a bite from his plate, raising it like a glass of champagne for a toast. His plate is smeared red from eating, cuts from his fork tear through the dish like sore slashes. He looks to Mother and then to Mia and toasts, To our daughter.

Mother replies, To tomorrow.

Mia starts another dance. She wears my blue eyes and small freckled nose, the slope of my shoulders and the size of my feet, just as I do. She opens her mouth, wide and vacant, but there is no sound.

~

Kim Winternheimer's work has appeared through *Tin House*, *Gigantic Magazine*, *theNewerYork*, *The Oregonian*, *The Rumpus*, and was the winner of Flavorwire's Short Fiction Contest. She is the founding editor of *The Masters Review* and lives in Portland, Oregon.

STANDARD DEVIANT

HOLLY SCHOFIELD

Ashley crouched behind her boyfriend's Audi, watching him through the plate glass window of the Denny's restaurant. The red and yellow neon sign above punctured the darkness. *Pancakes. Coffee.* And, visible in the window below: sweet, sweet Brut. He was sprawled sideways in the booth, leaning back against the window, plaid Hurley cap tilted, a cup at his lips. Maddog slouched on the opposite bench, grinning fiercely, his dreadlocks huge. Some chick sat beside him, skinny with spiky black hair, leaning toward Brut; who the hell was that? Plates, piled with bunched paper napkins and cutlery, lay scattered in front of them.

Ashley was late for the party.

As usual.

She shifted her feet and her metal boot studs rasped on the wet pavement. The drizzle had almost stopped but she wrapped her ratty army jacket around her more tightly anyway. She should cross the street and join them in the restaurant—at least it'd be warmer. *Eggs over easy. And hash browns.*

The Audi's windshield burst into a painful kaleidoscope of violets, pinks, and reds. Just her luck to hide behind a car that had some kind of weird electrical problem.

"We need an ambassador." The voice seemed to be coming from the flashing windshield. It was matter-of-fact and friendly.

"Piss off," Ashley said. She squatted even lower behind the car in case the flaring lights caught Brut's eye. *Home fries. And bacon.*

"We have only minutes to keep the wormhole open," the voice said. Ashley flipped her blue hair off her eyes. The hair color was called "dystop-cyan" and cost her the entire haul from a purse-snatching down on Fifth Avenue yesterday, but she'd thought Brut might like the color. He'd liked her zombie-snake tattoo last week, enough to nuzzle her throat where the tail curled around.

"We will recruit you to spread the word. Our spot-checks indicate America and several other countries are finally progressive enough to enroll into the *buzz-buzz-buzz*," the voice said, then chuckled. "That clearly did not translate. Let's use the vernacular: You guys can enroll into the Galactic Federation. Peace and prosperity await."

Huh. Maybe she shouldn't have popped that little white pill she'd found in Maddog's bathroom earlier tonight.

Ashley edged around to the front bumper. She stared at Brut through the window again, glad the darkness provided cover. Soon. She'd go to him, soon.

Just not quite yet.

"Get a life," she told the voice. She hoped Brut would take his feet off the seat when she approached the booth.

Her throat was dry. She swallowed and looked more closely at Brut's car in spite of herself.

It was a newer model Audi, dark red in the streetlights. The windows were tight and black, except the windshield which shifted colors in patterns too rapidly to make sense. Clearly, the Red Bull chaser had also been a bad idea.

"Our analyses indicate you are within the range of standard deviation for your country, race, and age," the voice said, with warmth.

"Yeah, a standard deviant, that's me," Ashley muttered. *Not even an original deviant.*

The patterns shifted and emerged into an almost-shape, like a word on the tip of her tongue. If this was a crazy mugger or some kind of scam, it was different than any she'd seen before. And, in four years on the street, she'd seen it *all*.

It might make a good story to impress Brut with. Something to make her stand out among the other chicks. Something to make his eyes glint and the corner of his mouth twitch. Maybe he'd let her spend the night in his apartment again. Maddog's sofa was getting lame.

"What's in it for me?" She put a hand on her hip and pouted at the windshield like a Japanese porn star.

"Improving mankind and expanding world knowledge is not your mandate, I see," said the voice, with a slight edge.

Ashley grinned and flipped a finger at the car. *I can piss anybody off, given a few minutes.*

"Perhaps this will convince you?" The kaleidoscope shifted to blackness so immense, so deep that Ashley gasped. Her skull began a not-unpleasant throb and her eyes felt stretched with infinite possibilities. A high that took her higher than she'd ever been, even that time in Arizona with the peyote.

Rotating planets and whirling galaxies flashed in a cadence that matched her thudding heart and she was lost in the universe, spiraling among the stars.

Finally, her mind found a tiny corner and tugged on it until it opened like a window on her phone. She rubbed a toe on the gritty sidewalk and cleared her throat.

"Why me?" she asked. "I'm, like, nobody. And, like, the most unreliable witness you'll ever find." Just what the cops had told her the night they released her stepdad for the eighth time. Without bail. No one ever did internal exams on trailer park trash.

"A hard truth," the voice said, with an emotion she couldn't label. "However, you are the only one on this street, the wormhole is closing, you have little to lose, and, sadly but most importantly, this nexus will not be disrupted since… well, actually…no one will miss you."

She glanced at the restaurant window. Brut was holding out his coffee cup and smirking at the unamused waitress. The new chick was on Brut's side of the booth, cuddled against him.

She climbed onto the hood of his car, one boot stud screeching a long silver gouge through the paint. She admired it for a minute then clambered into the whirling space where the windshield should have been. Her last thought, before reeling away into the cosmos, was of her mom. The last time she'd seen her: high heels clacking as she paced the kitchen floor, cell phone clamped to her ear as she made a date. She'd been laughing shrilly at something the client had said when Ashley had slipped out the door.

• • •

Ashley dropped gracefully to the street as the closing wormhole deposited her a few centimeters above the pavement. She was lucky to have caught this same nexus in front of the Denny's, almost ten years to the day after she'd left. The Federation had wondrous technology but it was hard science, not magic and not perfect. The space/time juncture was only open for a moment; no time to see how Earth had changed in the past decade.

That shouldn't matter. *She* had changed.

She was ready to be ambassador to the USA. To deliver her message to the country, the continent, the world.

Finally, she was about to do something with her life besides screw it up.

She kept her eyes squeezed shut, waiting for the transit afterglow to recede. She smoothed her chestnut hair behind her ears and straightened the collar of her sleek, form-fitting jumpsuit. She had amused the Federation staff by refusing to give up her boots—their worn leather now in sharp contrast to her chic appearance. The staff had fixed her brain chemistry—no more addictions or depression—as well as adjusting a slight pronation in her left foot and clearing up her herpes. Her muscles were magnificently toned and her posture impeccable. She was trained in politics, in psychology, in negotiation, in persuasion; a hundred years of education crammed into a decade. She was primed to bring humankind, with all their foibles, into the future, into an era of affluence and unbridled happiness.

She stretched joyfully and clicked her metal heels together, like a futuristic Dorothy.

Then she opened her eyes.

The Audi was gone. Litter blew across the street. The Denny's, boarded up and graffitied, loomed at her in the predawn dimness. She walked toward the restaurant. Her foot hit something soft and she looked down. A rotting corpse lay in the gutter. She hurried past it and up the far curb. A crude newsletter tacked to an unlit lamppost caught her eye. The headline proclaimed: "World Economic Devastation Continues, Billions Starving."

Her message would go unheard.

The party was already over.

~

Holly Schofield has been published in AE: The Canadian Science Fiction Review and Perihelion, as well as three anthologies, including *Tesseracts 17*. She travels through time at the rate of one second per second, oscillating between the alternate realities of a prairie farmhouse and her writing cabin on the west coast. For more of her work, see hollyschofield.wordpress.com.

Getting On
in Years

Cathy Humble

"Along came sixty," I said, "with eighty not far behind, and 100 hard on its heels. By now, I'm up to 830 and weary of grieving for lost family, learning new trades and finding new homes. But most of all, I'm tired of the fear and the hiding."

"So, Mr. Smith, what brings you here is concern about what happens when people learn you're immortal?"

I winced at the word. "Right."

Nothing I'd told her made *her* flinch at all. Good sign. But then she'd come highly recommended, and she'd be well paid.

Everything about Alyson Brochette was impressive but subtle. Her hair was red, but a deep auburn variety, and not too long or too short. Her tunic, real silk, must have come from a colony world, but didn't scream "money." On the wall behind her desk, the company name had a soft glow, pulsing ever so slightly: Public Relations Options. Yes, PRO summed her up just fine.

"We'll start right away with some focus groups, Mr. Smith. We'll tell one group you're immortal because you're an alien, another that your long life was engineered in a lab. Other groups will learn that a virus changed you, or that you're a time traveler with a normal lifespan who just ducks in and out of the centuries."

I shook my head in protest. "But those explanations aren't true. I'm just a mutant who doesn't age, and I've always tried to keep a low profile."

She smiled a just-right smile and stood to indicate our first meeting was over. "Truth is a very fluid concept, John. The focus groups will help me sort out emotional responses to you, such as fear, envy, anger or sympathy. I'll get back to you soon."

She did. "John," she said, her voice tinny with what must have been off-world distance, "I've analyzed the focus group results and drafted our strategy. We'll keep it simple at first. We can always regroup as necessary."

• • •

The next two weeks I appeared on every flash-interview and in all the print media that still existed. The headlines tell the story:

- Genetic twist cheats man out of normal life
- "No more hiding!" says 800-year-old man
- Terran authorities call for Smith to divulge finances
- Protesters attack plutocrat Smith's limo

"OK," Alyson said, "time to regroup. I hope they warned you that I play rough when it's necessary."

• • •

The new batch of headlines rolled along:

- John Smith big loser on national trivia show
- Smith slips on icy step, breaks arm
- "I can't age, but I can break" says Smith
- 800-year-old man funds Super Start classes in poverty areas
- "Just call me Jack"
- Jack Smith tutors low-income kids

The noisy crowds died down to a handful of angry sign-wavers here and there. "Excellent," Alyson said. "Now it's time for some big guns."

• • •

She kept me on the move, and the headlines followed:

- Smith addresses United Planets General Assembly
- Smith visits Dalai Lama
- Pope blesses Smith in special audience

"We've calmed them down," Alyson said. "Now let's warm them up. Are you sure you're ready for this?"

I was more than ready. No matter where I was or what I was doing, Alyson's delicate silkiness and cloud of auburn hair haunted me. By now I was spending every minute with her I could and she was scheduling meetings with me on the flimsiest excuses.

• • •

The paparazzi soon realized that something was up:

- Jack Smith and publicist an item
- Will they or won't they?
- Jack/Aly to wed
- Aly breaks it off—Jack devastated
- Jack wins Aly back
- Smiths return from secret island ceremony
- Baby on way for Jack/Aly
- Will Smith baby be immortal like dad?

• • •

At this point, I was interviewed by a serious journalist. The heart of the interview went like this:

"Jack, is it true that your telomeres are what make you different?"

"That's right, Tom."

"So what are telomeres and what do they do in your body?"

"Here's how it works for most people: As you age, your body's cells periodically divide. During this process, DNA sequences called telomeres protect the ends of your chromosomes. Do you remember when shoes had laces? Telomeres are like shoelaces' hard, protective tips. Every cell division shortens that stretch of telomeres. Eventually, the chromosomes are left unprotected, so they stop dividing and eventually die.

"Before you were born, an enzyme called telomerase kept adding new telomeres to replace the lost ones. For most of your cells, that doesn't happen later on. But all *my* cells just keep on making telomerase and new telomeres, so my cells don't age. I can die if I'm run over by a truck. And germs could do me in, except that the telomeres keep my immune system working exceptionally well. But my body hasn't deteriorated at all since I was a teen, over 800 years ago."

"What will this mean for the baby you and Aly are expecting?"

"Tom, we have no idea."

• • •

The nursery, along with the rest of our new mansion, was completed in the nick of time. I actually wanted a simpler life than all these rooms, with their glossy surfaces and objets d'art. But we could certainly afford it all, after 800+ years of investments, and these goodies seemed to make Aly very happy. A fair trade, I guess, since she'd sold her PR business and the headlines were squealing, "Aly will be a stay-home mom."

Like everything else in Aly's life, her labor and delivery went smoothly. We'd barely had a chance to count the baby's fingers and toes and admire her wispy auburn hair before the researchers were all over us. They sampled Grace's cells when she was a day old and followed up every three months. The reporters besieged the doctors as much as the doctors pestered us.

Finally, the headlines circled the globe and reached out to the colonies:

- Baby Grace has normal cells
- Smith child will age like mom

You could almost hear a collective sigh of relief, including my own. But I was confused; after the tests three months ago, the chief doctor had hinted at opposite results. I followed the sound of toddler laughter till I found Grace and Aly playing together on the brick-red Persian rug in front of the marble fireplace.

"I thought that last time Dr. Mills said Gracie was still making new telomeres."

"He did."

"So that's changed?"

"What's changed is that I told the doctors they couldn't do any more research on her unless I took the samples myself."

"It's hard to imagine you sticking Gracie with all those needles."

"I didn't."

"But they've announced results."

Aly smiled her just-right smile. "The samples came from me."

I sighed again, but not with relief this time. "So she'll have to face the same life I've had."

Aly took a hairpin out of her auburn curls and shook onto her shoulders a cascade that shimmered in the firelight. The hairpin in her hand also glinted in the light. It was the longest, sharpest hairpin I'd ever seen. "Don't worry, Jack. We've done so much to break down people's antagonism. She's the most adored child since Shirley Temple. Besides, it'll be a long time before anyone will notice that she's not getting gray and wrinkled."

"But you even told *me* she was normal."

Aly moved closer, smiled that siren smile and said, "As I told you the day we met, truth is a very fluid concept."

~

Cathy Humble has always been an anachronism. In an age of McMansions she's lived in Portland, Oregon, for thirty-six years on an acre of willows and blueberries. She and her husband measure days by the blue herons they see. A one-heron day is good; a four-heron day is sensational. When other women headed for law or medical school, Cathy stayed home to raise three kids. She finally earned a bachelor's degree in Psychology twenty-one years after first setting off for college. But if Cathy's lifestyle seems set in the past, her mind has always been seduced by the future. After fifteen years of writing and editing for an HMO she retired and started writing science fiction. Now at the age of seventy, she has so far written thirty stories and sold two.

Ro-Sham-Bot

Effie Seiberg

I found a robot's heart today. I didn't think they still made robots with hearts, but there it was, at the corner of Leary and Sycamore.

It even looked like a heart: size of a fist, valves pulsing with pale *ching ching* noises each time they opened and shut. The metal was old and worn. At the bottom I could just make out the words "If found, please return to the Akirobo Corp" with most of the address worn away.

I took it home and plugged it into my computer. It had a few jumbled videos—the way older robots used to store memories. My computer was old enough to be able to play them.

I sorted by number and began to watch.

The first video was in a warehouse. Lines upon lines of identical, still robots, presumably the same old-fashioned model as the one whose heart I'd found. The field of vision jerked to the left and found another robot looking straight at it. The other robot smiled, and glanced downwards. The camera followed it and, looking down, saw the other robot's hand clenched in a fist. One, two, three times it bobbed the fist up and down, and then extended two fingers. Rock, paper, scissors. The camera then captured its own robot hand reaching forward to join the game. Scissors beat paper. Paper beat rock. Scissors tied with scissors. A wider robot smile. None of the other robots moved.

I clicked to the second video, which was in the same warehouse. An operator in white QA-tested each robot. They all stayed very still. The robot to the left flashed a silly face, and the camera jiggled in suppressed laughter. The operator approached, and the camera snapped forward and was still.

The next video was in a factory on a moving conveyer belt. The robot to the left was about to get tied into its foam-cushioned packaging. It already had the manual for "Personality-free Chore-Bot" nestled in its arms. It looked up and said to the operator, "Shouldn't you buy me dinner before you tie me up?"

The startled operator hit the alarm. Red flashing lights flooded the factory floor, and a mechanical voice said "Alert, alert. Faulty Chore-Bot. Remove for destruction." As the robot to the left was removed by white-coated operators, the camera swiveled forward and was still.

The fourth video was in an ordinary living room. Children played on the carpet as a middle-aged man unpacked the robot and a middle-aged woman watched. "This should be the perfect model for us," said the man. "Does exactly what it's told, none of that personality module nonsense. It can start by keeping the deer away from the tomato patch. Go on now, go outside." The camera swung from the door to the children, who were playing rock, paper, scissors, then back to the door and headed out.

I hoped I wouldn't see the man disassembling the robot in a later video.

The next several videos were in an outdoor garden, in different seasons. The camera patrolled around the tomatoes. Sometimes they hung heavy and ripe from climbing vines, and other times they would barely be hard green buds. Every so often the camera would go back up to the house and look through the back door, like it was waiting for a glimpse of the playing kids. Sometimes, the man would shoo it away. I scanned through these pretty quickly.

I clicked to the last video, which was in the garden at night. Nothing to guard against. The robot's hands went through the motions. Rock, paper, scissors. Rock, paper, scissors. Over and over, until finally, the camera looked down and the hands unscrewed the robot's breastplate and reached in. Then the video went blank.

I unplugged the heart from my computer and took it to the workbench in my garage. I found the spare chassis on the top shelf, covered in dust. I cleaned it off with my shirtsleeve and brought it over. I knew I would find a use for the chassis one day, and the heart looked like it would fit inside perfectly. My daughter always loved Rock Paper Scissors.

∿

Effie Seiberg is a science fiction and fantasy author, a graduate of Taos Toolbox 2013, and an all-around geek. Her previous short fiction can be found in Crossed Genres' *Fierce Family* anthology and in *Veux Magazine*. In her spare time she's a slush reader for tor.com. She lives in San Francisco near the former and upcoming (but not present) location of a sculpture of a giant bunny head with a skull in its mouth. Follow Effie on Twitter (@effies), Google+ (+EffieSeiberg), or at effieseiberg.com.

Everything That Has Already Been Said

Samantha Murray

"How are you today, my glorious monkey?" said Bevan, her creator. She wasn't really a monkey of course. If she looked like anything it was a golden metal girl, but she was not really a girl either. Bevan called her monkey because he liked a theorem about infinite monkeys tapping away on infinite typewriters for infinity, where eventually one of them would type the works of Shakespeare. She also knew, because he had told her, that if there were as many monkeys as there were particles in the observable universe, typing for the age of the universe, they would still be extremely unlikely to write even a complete sonnet.

If she could, she would have said, I'm fine, perhaps a little lonely. But that was not something she could ever say. "I am flotsam on the dry ocean of your question," she replied instead, in her low musical lilt. Bevan's eyes brightened at the sound.

"You're always so poetic, monkey," he said. "Much more so than the others I made before you. You are not made for gibberish—all of your constructions have meaning, but I didn't expect them to be so…it's beautiful. You're beautiful."

If she had been made that way she would have smiled.

• • •

He kept her well-polished. Her burnished metal skin shone. And her scent was the faintest tang of ozone and sunflowers and honey.

"You are unique, monkey," Bevan said, his hand against the gold of her cheek. "You are always new, never derivative." He had made her so. She streamed the net, accessing digital information, every book ever scanned. She illegally tapped all voice, text and video communications. She was swimming in data; it felt to her like dreaming. She never forgot anything. She was only capable of combinations that hadn't occurred before, anywhere in her recording. No sentence that passed her lips had ever been uttered; it came whole and new-born into the world as she said it. Every time.

"I am so weary of repetition, monkey." Bevan's voice was soft, confidential. "All of the people who said the same kinds of things to me, over and over. You will never amount to anything, they said. Let me help you, they said. You are brilliant, they said. You are sick, they said. It gets old, monkey, all of it. But not you. You are always the future, never the past. While I am…simply boring."

You are not ordinary, she would have said to him, you could never be boring. "I am misted within at the purple of your speaking," she tried. But he grinned at her, and she knew he did not understand.

• • •

She carried within her a hard cold stone of fear, small but very dense. She felt data sigh through her. She worried that all of her scanning and searching wasn't enough. She knew people had said things out of her hearing, or back in the past, unrecorded. If she was not unique, if she was not perfect, then what was she? If by mistake she said something that someone else had once uttered surely she would crack right down the center in that instant with the shame and transgression.

• • •

"At last, monkey," Bevan said. His hair was whiter than she remembered. He told her that the past was written on the atoms of the universe, if you could read them. He told her she would be able to read them. He would have to move her again, this time to her very own planet. She was already much larger than she used to be, and she could no longer move through the world, but it didn't matter; the world came to her, and so, sometimes, did Bevan.

"Starshine gleefully falling as rain bleeds," she told him.

• • •

"My clever monkey," said Bevan, patting her golden shoulder although the effort seemed to cost him. She did not so much resemble a girl anymore, but she still had her face, her arms. "You are my best work. You will go on, forever forwards. That's all I need." She was not just his monkey, she realized, she was his typewriter too. She was his infinity.

She thought of being alone, in a universe of particles and words and hypothetical monkeys, without him.

Something whirred and thrummed inside her, but she stayed silent.
I love you had already been said, too many times.

~

Samantha Murray is a writer, actor, mathematician, and mother. Not particularly in that order. She is very bad at gardening and adores logic puzzles (if you give her one she has never seen before she will jump all over the place like a puppy.) You can find her online at mailbysea.wordpress. com. Samantha lives in Western Australia in a household of unruly boys.

THE LIES WE TELL OUR CHILDREN

KATHERINE CRIGHTON

My oldest spins around in one of those plastic bowls meant to encourage imaginative play in children; she's four, almost five now, and I hear her say, "Why won't it keep going?"

I stop typing and look over my laptop at her. "You mean spinning? On the carpet?"

"Yeah."

I close the clamshell lid and fold my arms on top. I guess we're having this conversation now. "We talked before about how if you rub two things together, it'll slow them both down, right?" She nods. "Well, that's what's happening here. The bowl is rubbing against the carpet. It doesn't matter how fast you get it going, the carpet will slow it down until it stops."

My daughter's blonde, with dark brown eyes. People say she looks like me, but they'll say that about anybody they think is related. She is cute, though. "So what if I wanted it to keep spinning?" she said then, looking at the ceiling.

"You'd have to be sitting somewhere where nothing was touching it."

She grins. "The air?"

"Oh, close one." My other daughter, who's two, comes walking past. She also looks like me, apparently. She hauls herself up on the couch to watch us. "But aren't there things in the air?"

"Oxygen," the four-year-old says. She watches a lot of science shows. "Screen time" is supposed to be bad for kids, and if it means she's able to have this conversation now, this early, then maybe they're right about that.

I smile anyway. "Oxygen, and other gases. The stuff you need to breathe. Dust, too. All those little things would also rub against the bowl, and they'd make it stop eventually. So what you'd really need is a place with nothing in it at all. Can you think of anyplace like that?"

Her face lights up. "Space!" She loves space. I didn't have a thing to do with it. If anything marks her as my daughter, that's it.

I could put her off indefinitely by telling her about hydrogen. But they've got to learn sometime, right? "Aren't there things in space, though?"

She nods. "Planets. And asteroids."

"Sure. So if you're sitting in your bowl in space, and you give it a big push—not spinning it, just going in one direction—what do you think'll happen?"

She rocks in her toy, her hands stretched out to the carpet behind her, and looks at her sister. "I'd keep going and going until I hit Earth."

"Or a planet?" She nods again. "You're right, there are lots of planets out in space. What if you picked a direction where there were no planets at all?"

"Then I'd hit an asteroid."

"What if there were none?"

She starts to look a little concerned. "There are stars."

I slide the laptop onto the floor. "Space is very big. It keeps getting bigger. What if you didn't hit any stars?"

I don't realize I've gotten to the crux already, not until she turns to look at me. I'd thought it would take longer.

And I'd had no idea how much this would hurt her.

There's a quiet moment, before my daughter cries. Maybe it's just her—maybe it's all children. Her eyes get big, and black, and it looks like her world, which before then had been much smaller, has gotten infinitely huge before collapsing down on her.

Her younger sister, while starting out just a reflection of the older one's emotional state, some time ago began to learn on her own, to listen and reach conclusions faster. Her wail shatters the room. My laptop fragments into carpet fibers, that themselves become a field of static. The chair beneath me was never there, the living room a line of noise that fills the upper boundaries of my consciousness.

I gather my girls up in my arms, one on either knee, curling them into myself. My older daughter whispers, "I'd never see my mommy again."

There are no arms, and there is no me, and I say, "I was wrong, sweetheart, I was wrong, I meant to say you had a ship, not a bowl. You have a ship, and everyone you love is on board, and you will never be lonely."

What about you? my other daughter asks. Her voice is accessed memories of other sounds, other words spoken by little ones no longer here. She doesn't try so hard to be like me. It makes me wonder what my next one will be like.

My girls. They're all I have. And they're growing up so fast.

"That's how I know I'm right," I say, waiting for the system to reboot and the living room to come back online.

Outside, we pass a star.

~

Katherine Crighton lives in Massachusetts with her wife, children, housemate, and hostas. Her work has previously appeared in *Strange Horizons*, *Flash Fiction Online*, and other venues; she also coauthors urban fantasy under the name Anna Katherine. Connect with her directly via Facebook at crightonkatherine or twitter at @c_katherine.

NOVEL EXCERPT:
ARTEMIS AWAKENING

JANE LINDSKOLD

Chapter One: Crash Landing

A falling star! What luck!

Adara the Huntress froze in place, watching as a thin white line with a heart of fire grew into a wider streak that rushed earthward at an incredible speed. She frowned thoughtfully.

It must be huge to be visible in daylight.

The moment the streak vanished below the tree line, the ground trembled. A crashing louder than any thunder caused Adara to press her hands protectively over her ears. In the glade around her, spring pale leaves shook and dry needles showered from the evergreens.

Immediately, Adara sent out a mental cry. Sand Shadow had been ranging near where the star must have hit. The puma should be unharmed—Adara would have felt its death or pain.

Sand Shadow, did you see where it fell?

The image that came in response placed the puma atop a cluster of boulders, looking down where dust and steam fountained up from a narrow ravine. The puma had not yet mastered the art of linking her senses to those of her partner, but Adara received the impression that something smelled very bad—acrid and bitter, like nothing in nature.

Wait for me.

Adara's thought was a suggestion, not a command. Though the untutored took comfort in the idea that hunters commanded their demiurges, the truth was that who commanded whom was more a matter of the personalities involved than of any automatic superiority of human over beast.

However, although Sand Shadow would be the first to assert she took orders from no one, Adara sensed that this time the puma was content to watch and wait.

I'll be there as soon as I can, Adara promised, not so much in words as with an image of her booted feet carrying her closer to the rising column that marked the star's grave.

As Adara raced to join Sand Shadow, she speculated as to what they might find. Certainly something which had struck down with such force would not have been melted to nothing by the heat of its passage. That meant there would be a treasure to retrieve.

Best would be one of those pieces of iron ore the smiths valued. Next best would be one of those strange things the seegnur had left swirling in the currents of the sky. These curiosities weren't as useful as iron, nor as valuable, but Bruin knew those who collected such artifacts. Even if Bruin could not trade an artifact for as much as he could for iron, Adara's find would gather favors for them both.

Adara loved her mentor and knew he would be pleased if she found an artifact. She was considering how favors might be more valuable than goods when she felt a flash of astonishment from Sand Shadow. The puma focused hard, carefully shaping a new image. Adara gasped and redoubled her pace.

Down in the dust and steam, something was moving.

• • •

He hadn't meant to crash the shuttle. That was Griffin Dane's first thought upon coming to, hanging upside down in his restraining harness with his pulse thundering in his ears.

His second thought was that his first had been incredibly stupid. No one ever *meant* to crash. Crashes by definition were unintended. His third thought, how he supposed that in some cases a crash might be intended—as in certain sports or forms of combat—died half-formed as Griffin became aware that the thudding noise in his ears was not solely his pulse.

A grinding, grating sound mingled with the thudding. Those sounds almost certainly meant that—despite the force with which the shuttle had impacted *terra firma*—Griffin's ship was sliding. Sliding probably did not mean anything good either for him, or for the ship and its irreplaceable contents.

With efficiency born of frequent and meticulous practice, Griffin set about getting himself out of the crash harness. The shuttle had landed top down. Griffin flipped over so he could walk on the ceiling turned floor. Even though he landed lightly, he felt the shuttle slide in response to the shift in balance.

Unstable, Griffin thought. *Still, if I move slowly, I can grab some supplies.*

There's an emergency kit in the locker near the exit hatch. I'd better get my excursion pack, too . . .

He moved, first stepping, then—when even that small motion started the shuttle jolting along again—lowering himself so that he could slide on the decking. Sweat stood out on Griffin's forehead by the time he reached the exit hatch. When he tapped the release on the locker, nothing happened. Next he tried the airlock. Nothing.

Nothing, that is, except another of those sickening surges of motion and a sound like hail falling. Claustrophobia—a ridiculous sensation for a starship pilot—hit Griffin.

If I don't get out of here fast, I'm going to be buried alive. Equipment won't do me any good then. Out first. Gear later.

The airlock was equipped with a manual override. Frowning when each jerk of the lever jolted the shuttle, Griffin forced the heavy levers through their prescribed patterns. He'd been worried something like this power outage might happen, but he hadn't thought it would occur so soon.

Maybe I didn't crash the ship after all, he thought. *Maybe it was crashed for me. Still, I thought I had the shuttle systems sealed. I followed the protocols . . . Maybe what happened was just an accident.*

Focused as he was on these unsettling speculations, Griffin could hardly believe what he saw when he finally slid the airlock door open.

An enormous tawny lion crouched on a steep, crumbling talus slope only a short distance from the shuttle. When the wild cat saw Griffin, its fanged mouth opened in a snarl, its dark-tipped tail lashed, and its shoulders tensed to spring.

• • •

A human male! Sand Shadow was too flustered to send more than the most minimal image. *Within the fallen star!*

Adara put on a burst of speed and arrived at the same rocks upon which the puma had stood moments before. She looked down. The stranger remained crouched within an opening in the surface of his strange vessel—for vessel it must be.

His eyes, which he held fixed on Sand Shadow, were wide and well-made, their color a warm brown. His hair, which was mussed and cut much shorter than that of any man of Adara's acquaintance, was golden fair with darker undertones. His skin looked as if it never saw the sun.

He's afraid of you, Adara reproved Sand Shadow and felt the puma's pride that this was as it should be. *Yes. At most times I would agree most heartily, but this time . . . That thing is sliding on the talus, sliding more with every motion the man makes. If the man does not get out soon, he will be carried with it. I do not think he will live if he does.*

Sand Shadow acknowledged the sense of this. With a flick of her long, heavy tail and a frolic of her hindquarters, she bounded away. The man stared after the puma, obviously eager to escape, but afraid lest any movement on his part bring the great cat back.

Adara called out to the stranger, pitching her voice so that it would carry, but hopefully not frighten the man.

"Hold still! I'm going to throw you a line."

• • •

At the sound of the voice, Griffin started, causing the shuttle to jolt downwards, jarring against something and jamming to a halt. He heard footsteps crunching on the gravel slope above him. A piece of rope snaked down and landed near him. Then the footsteps retreated.

"The rope's anchored to a tree," a confident, female voice said. The words were spoken with an accent like but not identical to that in the induced language lessons Griffin had brainloaded in preparation for this trip.

Leaning out from the shuttle, Griffin grabbed hold of the rope. Even that controlled motion proved to be a mistake. The precariously balanced vessel broke loose from whatever it had been resting upon, then began to plummet downwards. Hands tight around the rope, Griffin was jerked free from the vessel, then smashed flat onto his face. Despite the red flash of pain, he kept a tight grip on what had become his lifeline.

The landslide poured over Griffin, scouring his exposed skin, blinding and half-smothering him, causing him to gasp and wheeze as he struggled against being carried away by the terrible stream that flowed over him.

The cascade was beginning to subside to a trickle when Griffin became aware that the rope was pulling from his fingers, burning the tender skin of his palms. Almost too late, he realized that his yet unseen rescuer was attempting to haul him up. Although his palms were raw and his fingers ached, Griffin clamped down and felt the rope tighten in reply.

A muffled cry of exultation rewarded his effort. The pulling became stronger. Inch by inch, Griffin was hauled from beneath the earthy debris. When his head broke the surface, he gasped for air. What he drew into his lungs was so full of dust and grit that he choked and coughed, but it was air.

The accented voice spoke again. "Hold tight. We're going to start pulling again."

Although his tortured hands protested, Griffin did as he was told. He was aware that any attempt on his part to kick or roll might restart the landslide. Even this slow tugging caused pebbles to trickle by, their rattle and hiss sounding like the warning of a venomous serpent.

When at long last the ground beneath him was stable, Griffin rolled to his feet. He was bruised all over and bleeding in several places. Nonetheless, he refused to give even the slightest wince. Although he was the odd scholar in a family of warriors, still he was a Dane of Sierra and he had his pride.

A Dane of Sierra who will need a miracle or two if he is ever to see Sierra again. Still, who ever said pride was a reasonable thing?

As soon as Griffin was certain his footing was secure, he located his rescuer. She stood beneath the trees higher up the slope, the rope that had saved him still caught in her hands. Griffin had expected a woman—the voice had told him that much—but he had not expected a woman anything like this one.

She was tall—perhaps a hand's breadth shorter than himself, and he was counted a tall man. Her hair was the shining iridescent black of a raven's wing, her eyes a deep amber gold. Both went well with skin tanned golden brown. She was attired in soft leather trousers and a long sleeved shirt. Her feet were booted.

This woman was not lovely in the soft, drawing room fashion Griffin had been taught to admire at the university, but was slimly elegant in the manner of one of those handmade knives his brother Siegfried collected.

Griffin thought his rescuer must be as deadly as a blade as well. At her waist was sheathed a hunting knife. Over one shoulder she wore a quiver holding grey and white fletched arrows. Near to hand was the hunting bow that fired those arrows. She studied him quizzically, then began coiling her rope.

"Are you a seegnur?" she asked in her oddly accented Imperial. "I think you must be, for I have never seen a vessel like the one that you came from. Yet, there are tales of such vessels in the lore."

Griffin considered. Her words held an archaic flavor, but he could understand most, all but the most crucial. What was a "seegnur"? It was not included in his language induction vocabulary. He decided on a partial answer.

"My name is Griffin Dane. I am very grateful for your aid. Without it, I fear I would now be dead."

"Quite likely," the woman agreed with dry practicality. "Your boat—I think that was some manner of boat?—is quite wrecked, yet I think it is made of harder stuff than flesh."

"Wrecked?" Griffin repeated in disbelief.

He labored uphill so that he could see into the ravine. The shuttle had continued its slide in a nose-first, upside-down fashion. All but the stern was buried beneath a considerable amount of sand, gravel, and rock. A few trees, ripped from their roots by the force of the landslide, poked out of the debris, mute witnesses to the violence of the event.

"Well," he said, "I'm certainly not getting it out of there."

"Now that your vessel is broken, will you fly away then?" the woman asked. "The lore says the seegnur could fly."

"I'm not sure what a 'seegnur' is," Griffin admitted, "but if I am one, I certainly cannot fly."

"Not all the seegnur could," the woman said, and Griffin realized her words were meant to be comforting.

He forced himself to look away from the wreck of his shuttle. The woman had seated herself on a rocky outcropping large enough that the mountain itself would need to fall away before it went anywhere. The puma had reappeared and was resting its head in her lap. Griffin estimated that the creature was something like nine feet long from nose tip to tail tip, a formidable animal indeed. He also noticed that it wore a series of copper hoop earrings in one rounded ear.

"You are Griffin Dane," the woman said. "I am Adara the Huntress. This is Sand Shadow. She apologizes for frightening you before, but she did not expect the shell of your vessel to open in that manner."

The way in which Adara said "the huntress" made quite clear this was a title, not a merely a professional designation. Here was someone who, at least in her own assessment, was a person of importance. Griffin bowed slightly from the waist, rope-burned hands pressed against his thighs.

"I am pleased to meet you," he said. He noticed the puma's ears flickering back and added quickly. "And Sand Shadow as well."

The puma's eyes narrowed, but in the relaxed manner of a cat well-pleased rather than in annoyance.

Does she understand me then? Griffin thought. *I remember tales that some of the animals on Artemis were genetically engineered so that they might provide a greater challenge. Could this be one of their descendants?*

He longed to ask but decided against it, at least not until he knew these two better. They were his only hope of survival and he dared not offend them.

"Adara the Huntress," Griffin said, "my ship may indeed be wrecked, but I believe I can get back inside it and retrieve a few things that would be useful. I already owe you my life. May I impose upon you for further assistance?"

Adara looked at him and her dark amber eyes crinkled in a smile of appreciation.

"You speak very prettily, seegnur," she said, "but I think both courtesy and request come from the heart. We will help you. Let us wait to make certain the landslide is well and truly ended. Meanwhile, I can take you to a stream that runs with clean water and offer a cut from a somewhat lean but still quite tasty haunch of venison."

"I will accept your kind hospitality, lady."

Feeling the ache of his stiffening muscles, Griffin toiled up the slope to join his rescuer. Then he followed Adara and Sand Shadow a short way to where a south-facing hollow sheltered a pocket-sized mountain meadow. The promised stream splashed and gurgled along one edge, pooling at the lowest point before overflowing and continuing its way down.

"I will fetch the venison," Adara said. "Sand Shadow will guard you while you bathe, lest some wandering creature decide you may be edible after the dirt comes off."

She chuckled as she vanished into the shadowed pines. The puma settled into a sunny patch of thick grass and yawned, once again displaying a magnificent array of fangs.

Griffin contemplated the pool. Although the sun was pleasantly warm, he knew that this high up the water would be very, very cold. However, there was no avoiding this bath. He was filthy, and Adara the Huntress did not look like someone who would respect a request for heated bath water.

Though in the days of old, he speculated as he peeled off his coverall, *certainly hot springs or such would have been available. The Imperials—I wonder if that is what Adara means by "seegnur"—liked their comforts. Of course, if the springs were artificially heated, they would now run cold.*

Griffin thought of his shuttle as he had last seen it, mostly buried beneath dirt and rock. If he could get into it, he could retrieve a comm unit and contact his orbiting ship, but what if he couldn't get in? As Griffin stepped into the stream, the cold water was not the only thing that made him shiver.

• • •

When Adara returned, she found Griffin Dane much cleaner, although his hair was still dripping wet and his lips were blue with cold. For the first time, she got a good look at his attire unsmudged by debris. This proved to be a one-piece garment, colored two-toned green. Although it had been through a landslide, it showed not a single rip or tear, nor even was particularly dirty.

More evidence, she thought to herself, *that Griffin Dane is a seegnur, even though he does not seem to know the word.*

The twitch of Sand Shadow's ears and flick of her tail told Adara that the puma had found the man's bathing quite amusing. Images of Griffin combined with those of a fluffed and splashing robin showed the determined fashion with which the man had tackled the icy plunge.

Adara chuffed at the cat. *You might have offered to dry him.*

He would have died of fright.

Adara considered, then thought apologies. *You're right.* She turned to

Griffin Dane.

"I have a towel you can use to dry your hair," she offered. "I'll make a fire. Sand Shadow should have done so, seeing how cold you are."

Griffin Dane accepted the cloth gratefully and immediately began to tousle the darkened gold of his wet curls.

"Sand Shadow should have made a fire?" He looked about for the puma.

"She has gone to get some wood," Adara said, scraping the ground clear and arranging a circle of river rock around it. Next she used flint and steel to strike sparks into the dry pine punk she shook from a small bag on her belt. "Something she could have done before. Like all cats, Sand Shadow goes from activity to purest indolence with great speed and enthusiasm."

"Oh?" Griffin said.

His tone invited Adara to say more, but she ignored the hint. She wanted to know why, after so many generations—Bruin said that something like five hundred years had passed—a seegnur had returned to Artemis. She wanted to know what had brought this Griffin Dane here. The lore had always been mixed regarding the seegnur. Some tales presented them as wise and talented. Some as grasping and cruel. This seegnur seemed neither wise nor particularly talented—although he had shown courage. Nor did he seem cruel.

Still, Griffin Dane might be minding his manners because he needed her aid. Best to wait and watch and learn. Was he alone? Part of a larger excursion party?

Adara fed her flickering flame with dry grass, then a handful of twigs broken from a scrub oak near at hand. She saw Griffin Dane move to the fringe of the hollow, carefully concealing the stiffness of his battered body. When he returned, he brought with him a dried pine bough.

"Will this help?" he asked.

She smiled up at him. "It will. I wonder where that lazy puma has gone?"

"I could go look for him," Griffin Dane offered. Adara admired his offer, because Sand Shadow was right. Griffin Dane was afraid of the great cat. "Or I could mind the fire so you can look for him."

"Her," Adara said. "Sand Shadow is female. I think she will call if she needs help but, if she continues slow, I may take you up on that kind offer. In the meantime, are you injured? I have an ointment that is very good for bruises."

She saw Griffin Dane consider denying his injuries, saw, too, that he ruled this to be stupid bravado. Faces and bodies were like game trails. The signs were subtle, but could be read by one who learned the marks.

Bruin, who had been Adara's teacher, had made certain that Adara learned how to read those marks.

"Too often," Bruin had said, "those born to hunt believe they know what destiny has shaped them to be. They refuse to learn more. I think otherwise.

One cannot hunt forever."

Those lessons had been a trial, with none of the joy in them that Adara felt when tracking or drawing a bow, but Bruin had been right. The best hunters ranged through wide areas that touched upon many settlements. Knowing how to read those one might meet only once or twice a season was a good thing.

"Yes," Griffin Dane said. "I would appreciate a share of your ointment. My coverall protected most of me from cuts and scrapes, but I am one massive bruise."

Adara dug into her pack and came out with two squat pottery jars. "Rub this first ointment anywhere but open wounds. For the rest, use this second ointment. If you wish, I can anoint your back."

Again the hesitation, then somewhat awkwardly, "That would be very kind."

At that moment, Sand Shadow returned. The puma had found a nice bit of seasoned scrub oak and had broken off enough to make two neat bundles. These she had slung over her back. Now she pranced into the hollow, pleased as a house cat who had caught a mouse.

Griffin Dane, caught in the act of peeling down the upper portion of his coverall, froze in mid-motion.

"Do you have another companion, then?" he asked.

"No," Adara replied, enjoying his confusion. "Why do you think that?"

"But if no other companion, who loaded the wood onto the puma's back?"

"She did it herself," Adara said. "Admittedly, she's more skilled than many, but haven't you seen an adapted creature before? The lore says that the seegnur themselves created them."

She stopped herself before repeating what Bruin had speculated, that the adapted had continued to change in the years since the slaughter of the seegnur and death of machines.

"I have not," Griffin Dane said. "Our history—what I suppose you might call our 'lore'—tells of such things, but the manner of creating such was lost in the great war."

Adara had the feeling that Griffin Dane was not saying everything he might, but did not press.

"Do you have any companions with you? You have shown no anxiety such as you might if someone was trapped within your vessel, but what about elsewhere?"

Griffin Dane stood with the upper portion of his coverall hanging loose around his waist, leaving his upper body bare. If he hadn't been so badly battered, he would have been an admirable sight, well-muscled, with a light down of chest hair. Now, however, he was marked in shades of red, many of these turning the darker purple of deep bruises.

The fire was burning well. Sand Shadow would add more wood as soon as she had her bundles off, so Adara went over to Griffin Dane. Dipping her fingers in the jar of bruise ointment, she moved behind him and began to rub the greasy stuff in, trying to be gentle. Her fingers felt the ripple of muscles beneath the fair skin, confirming her impression that Griffin's incredible paleness was no indication of ill health.

"I am alone here," Griffin Dane said after a long moment, "not just here in this place, but also in this system. Does your lore contain stories about how there are many planets, circling many suns, and this is but one?"

"Yes," Adara said, reaching around him to dip her fingers again into the ointment jar. Her arm brushed against his nakedness and she felt a pleasant tingle. "Some of the folk who live where the air is thicker say this is just a legend, but those of us who live where we can see the stars see this must be true."

She did not add that Bruin, who had at one time been a student of the Old One Who Is Young, had told her this bit of lore was true and had shown her the evidence in the dance of the stars and planets.

Griffin Dane nodded. Perhaps to give himself a moment to frame his thoughts, he began rubbing the bruise ointment into his left arm.

"I came here by myself, in a small ship constructed to travel long distances without needing much fuel or tending precisely because it carried just one." He gave a great shuddery sigh, although whether this was because his bruises hurt or because of some memory, Adara couldn't tell. "I came alone because I was certain I was onto something that would make my reputation and I didn't want to share the credit with anyone. I suppose that seems foolish to you."

Adara laughed deep in her throat. "Perhaps it would not make sense to a farmer or a sailor, but to a hunter or a pro . . . Yes. It makes sense. You were on the trail of big game and thought you could take it alone."

"And I was wrong." For the first time, Adara heard bitterness in Griffin Dane's voice. "If you knew how long and how carefully I prepared . . . Then to crash the shuttle within minutes of breaking atmosphere . . . If I ever get over feeling stupid . . ."

He shrugged, winced, then, defiantly, shrugged again.

Adara finished rubbing ointment into his back. Feeling a certain reluctance—this Griffin Dane really had a very nice back—she moved over to the fire. Sand Shadow had added a couple of larger pieces of wood, before returning to lounge in the sunlight.

When Adara sent her thanks, the great cat stretched in pleasure. A graphic, mocking, and very sexual image followed. Most altered creatures were amused by the human capacity for sex at any time and in any season. They claimed that this alone was what set humans apart from beasts and praised the stars for being spared such distraction.

Adara admitted desire was a distraction, but she'd never been one to have sex with just anyone. Such behavior left one too vulnerable. A huntress, a rare occurrence already, must take care not to seem weak. Even so, she'd warmed herself at that fire and been burnt. Her heart twisted as she remembered Julyan. She'd loved him, given him not only her heart, but sought to shape herself into what she thought he had desired. Yet he had walked away without a backwards look.

Yes . . . She must take care not to seem weak. The lore whispered that the seegnur had the ability to command the people of Artemis. As polite as this Griffin Dane might seem, she must be on guard against his wiles.

• • •

Interlude: TVC1500.

Darkness. Deadness. Purest cold.

Heat. Intense, incredible heat. The beginnings of awareness.

Awareness. Purpose. Purpose displacing darkness. Purpose displacing awareness. Awareness becoming purpose.

~

Jane Lindskold is the award-winning, bestselling author of more than twenty novels, including the incredibly popular Firekeeper series *(Through Wolf's Eyes, Wolf's Blood)*, as well as more than sixty shorter works. Several of her novels have been chosen by *VOYA* for their Best SF, Fantasy, and Horror list. Lindskold's work has been repeatedly praised for its sensitive depiction of worlds and cultures different from our own—especially those that aren't in the least human. She resides in New Mexico.

Author Spotlight:
Seanan McGuire

Sandra Odell

Right from the start, you hit the readers with a subtle blend of fears and unease that sets the tone for the story—drowning, forced manipulation, not fitting in. Later, you delve into the pain of surgery and chronic medical treatments/conditions. How conscious were you of these influences and how they would impact the story?

Extremely. I have a complicated and very painful issue with my left foot right now, and dealing with it has been both exhausting and a distressingly large part of my daily life for the last year and a half or so. So I am very conscious of these things, and how they impact our lives. There's a lot of fear of not being accepted that comes with having a sudden change in health, and I wanted to focus on that, at least a little.

"Each to Each" could easily be labeled as science fiction, military SF, feminist SF, or even science fantasy. As a writer, what do you see as the pros and cons of genre labels and the continued emergence of slipstream/crossgenre works?

Pro: It's easier to find things that contain at least one major ingredient you'll enjoy. Con: It's easy to dismiss things you would have absolutely loved because they're not the "right" genre, or sub-genre. I think it's a good idea to read broadly, and to follow authors as much as ideas.

You use the deep ocean as a setting, and the exploration of sharks, lionfish, and other non-cetaceans as a basis for the modifications to the sailors. How did you research the oceanographic elements for this story?

I spent a lot of time at the aquarium! I love the ocean. The mysteries of the deep sea are one of my favorite things to explore when I get bored. So I really just used several years of cumulative research, all in the same place.

Challenge coins are an important part of military service in terms of branch of service and command post, part of their *esprit de corps*. With the unique make-up of the submariner forces in your story, what would you like to see for their challenge coin?

Since some of them don't have functional fingers anymore, I sadly think that the loss of the challenge coin is just one more burden being put on the women of the Deep Sea Naval Initiative. But the ones who are still mostly human still carry their coins, and mourn them when they have to put them down.

Many of your works deal with gender politics. In this story, you combine such issues with views on women in the military, and social dynamics in an all-female social setting. How do you see the portrayal of such issues shaping the future of genre fiction?

We learn what's possible from what fiction shows to us. I think that the more often and more purposefully we expand our ideas of gender and social dynamics through genre fiction, the more we'll be able to bring those things naturally into our storytelling. Superhero teams used to have "the girl," and now we have all-female teams, women leading the Avengers, and a lot more gender diversity (not to mention racial diversity, which is a huge thing). We're nowhere near perfect, but we can get there if we don't give up.

The story explores the ideal of physical freedom, moving unfettered in a world not of your own making. What would be your ideal world to explore if environmental concerns were not an issue?

The deep sea! I want to look for mermaids.

In stories such as "Indexing" or "Knives," you look at fairy tales through a different set of eyes. What is it about fairy tales that appeals to you as a writer and a person?

I majored in folklore and mythology. So I guess it's just how I'm wired. It's sort of like writing legal fanfic. Everybody knows these characters, knows these stories; it's all a matter of finding a different facet in the diamond. I love that.

What can eager readers expect from Seanan McGuire in the future?

So much. So much! I'm continuing my October Daye and InCryptid series (next books in each: *The Winter Long* and *Pocket Apocalypse*). I have a stand-alone, *Sparrow Hill Road*, coming in May 2014. Lots of short fiction. And of course, that Mira Grant lady has a book coming out this fall …

Plus I'm going back to Disneyland.

AUTHOR SPOTLIGHT: KRIS MILLERING

LEE HALLISON

What was the seed for this story?

The very first seeds of this story were planted a number of years ago in Iowa, where I attended a reading by the poet Marvin Bell. Bell read from what would become the book *Ardor: The Book of the Dead Man, Vol. Two*. A number of years later, I was given a challenge by my Clarion West classmate Jordan Ellinger: to swap genres with him for a story. I thought of Bell's wry Dead Man and decided that I wanted one of my own in this story. I just decided to make him literal, and his decay almost a character of its own.

Maureen came partially out of the airless intensity of my own process, and partially out of some online discussions about sensory modes. I knew I wanted to write about someone whose primary sensory mode was touch, and Maureen and her sculptures grew out of that.

How is Maureen's focus and intensity in her art like yours?

Fortunately for me, no one has ever offered to put me in a spaceship and send me off to write for aliens. Maureen's focus does come from my own, though, especially at the time that I wrote the story. I'm the sort of person who can easily accidentally vanish into writing for weekends at a time, and never manage to see the sun.

I'd say the major difference between me and Maureen is that I really try to avoid falling into that mode unless I have a project to finish. For her, it's her default mode and pretty much her entire mechanism for coping with the world. Luckily for me, I have a lot of wonderful friends who know when and how to drag me out of my own head (and occasionally out of the house).

Her goal to find aliens who appreciate her art fails because of a twist in relativity. At the end, is she apologizing for the mission itself, her decision at the start, or the death?

The short answer is yes. The long answer is that, with the realization of what exactly it is she's done, she feels that she needs to apologize in the only language she truly has—the language of form.

Maureen's actions stem out of a very human set of needs and desires—she is obsessed with being understood and successful in a world that doesn't speak her language. She understands the full scope of what she's done, at the end, and she's apologizing for the whole series of events that lead to the decision she makes before the beginning of the story.

What are you currently working on?

I'm currently in the middle of rewriting a novel that is tentatively titled *The Phoenix Crown*, which is an epic fantasy that involves intelligent hyenas, volcanic eruptions, and violent politics. I also have a few short stories in the works, and a few more coming out this year—one in *Devilfish Review*, and one in *Apex* that will be published closer to the end of 2014.

You are the new Communications Specialist for the writer's workshop, Clarion West. What is your first goal in the new job?

I'm so glad you asked! Most of my work so far has been focused on our summer fundraiser, the Clarion West Write-a-thon. It's my goal to make sure that we have a clear and unified voice for our communications and social media outreach for the fundraiser. The job involves a lot of cat-herding, which is pretty much my professional specialty, so I'm having a really good time with it so far.

Author Spotlight: Heather Clitheroe

Lee Hallison

When did you first become interested in cyborgs and the use of such technology in fighting terrorism?

The story actually started out as a stock market idea—a friend posted a link to an article on super-density (superflux.in/blog/superdensity) and the idea of developing a "shipping forecast" for trying to describe trends and changing power structures. Something about the article tweaked an idea—that if we could try to develop a shipping forecast for our times, it would end up being something co-opted by financial forecasts. The story began as an idea for a firm that develops technology to make this kind of forecast for commercial purposes—getting just a little ahead of the stock market by trying to figure out what people are thinking and feeling.

And then it occurred to me that if you were the CEO of a company that could do something like that—that kind of cool-hunting—you'd probably start looking around to see if you couldn't contract out for security and counter-intelligence. I liked the idea of it being rather shadowy—it's never really clear who Spencer was doing the casts for in Berlin or Damascus. I don't know that he was necessarily doing it for the UN or a legitimate government.

As for using cyborgs for this kind of counter-intelligence…well, why wouldn't you? If you can't teach a machine how to read emotions and relay those, you'd use the next best thing. People are cheaper than machines. And if it happened to have disastrous effects on a person's health, well, you paid them for it, right? It's the ultimate in neoliberal economics.

How much, and what kind of research did this story require?

It took a fair bit of research. The super-density article led me down the rabbit hole—first that, then shipping forecasts, then bits and pieces about the stock market and the kinds of technology being used now to make trading faster and faster. I came to the rather horrifying conclusion that if we ever really do figure out how to go faster than light, it'll be to trade stocks faster instead of making warp drives for spaceships. That's where the cyborg tech idea really started to come together—that we'd develop this kind of technology to fuel financial speculation instead of some great, liberating project for humanity—and I started looking around for things to read.

From there? I work for an engineering school, and I was putting away archive copies of an exam for a biomedical engineering course. A student had been showing me his lab assignment the week before when he came in to borrow a stapler—something about advanced signal processing for better tumor detection—and I happened to leaf through the exam and looked at the course number. Then I pulled the course outline, and then I started looking at the prof's webpage for his research and his lab, and I found a list of journal articles. Then I started reading. The best thing about working for engineers is that nobody seems to mind if you ask a question about circuits and biomedical implants while you're waiting for the Keurig to finish brewing coffee. They just take it for granted.

I skimmed through a bunch of textbooks on circuitry and neuromorphic VLSI systems that are being developed to mimic the nervous system. I was fascinated. I stumbled onto memristors when I was looking at a grad student thesis, and started trying to put it all together and understanding what I was reading. Thank goodness for the Google.

Do you see this story as a warning in the world's pursuit of technology? If so, what specific message do you want readers to leave with?

I think it's a bit late for warnings. We're plunging ahead with new technology all the time, and I don't know that you can always predict the outcome. Is that a bad thing? Not necessarily. I work with people who are developing and researching new tech to support the tech that hasn't even been worked out yet. Talk about anticipatory…it takes an enormous amount of chutzpah for a scientist or an engineer to say "oh, hey, this process hasn't been invented yet, but when it is, they're going to need these materials in huge quantities, so I'll just work on that now." And I think that's okay…we try to anticipate what's coming, we plan for what we think might happen, but we're remarkably adaptable, we humans, and when things go sideways, we deal with it.

I think this story is more a reflection of the way we allow economics to use people, though: that we pay whether we realize it or not, and that sometimes means that we hurt each other and ourselves as we do it. Spencer isn't really a warning. He just is. He's already been chewed up and spit out by the "augmentation" that makes him a cyborg, and he's paying a terrible price for the choices he made and the ones that were made for him. I guess the story is supposed to leave you with the message that we should do better. We can do better than this. We should do better. Technology doesn't scare me. Economics does.

You took a brief break from writing last year; did you find it easy to return to work, and was this a story from before your break or after? How did your Banff residency rejuvenate your writing?

Getting back to work was a huge, scary effort, and this was the first major piece of fiction after a very long pause.

I finished my master's degree at the end of 2012—writing about the neoliberal projection of blame and victimhood in post 9/11 zombie narratives (hi, Dr. McCutcheon!) and needed a break. The break turned out to run longer than I thought, because I ended up having surgery in April and then a second major surgery in September that took me out of commission for several months. It felt like I spent most of last year having surgery or recovering from it. In the middle of that year, Calgary flooded—great swathes of the city were quite literally underwater, and we spent a nervous week with go bags packed because we live so close to the river, waiting for an evacuation notice and planning the route up to my friends' house, where they had cots ready for us in the basement (hi, Kirk, Robyn, Matt, and Tamara!). My parents had been in a serious car accident the year before and ended up being called as witnesses for the prosecution late in the summer. We were all pretty worn out by everything. It was truly was an annus horribilis. There was no writing to be done.

The first bits of writing I did were very tentative, and there are some incredibly shitty first drafts tucked away in a folder, never to see the light of day again. I'd seen a mention of the WDSF call, and thought I would give it a try. I was finally back at work, and I had started coming into the office early to sit and write—first half an hour, then an hour, then an hour and a half. I went back to the Banff Centre for the Arts in early February. I took the cyborg story with me and I worked on it day and night until it was ready to send in, just under the wire. And I got that sucker done and danced around my studio and did one of those embarrassing "YEAH!" fist pumps, only to realize that I'd been seen. Whoops.

This story represents a triumphant return to writing after a truly awful year...and what a start!

Being published in WDSF means so much to me. When I was a kid, I strayed into the science fiction and fantasy section and came out with A Fall of Moondust, and the librarian asked me if I didn't want to read a Sweet Valley High book instead. I'm so glad I refused and went back to pick up the Ben Bova book I'd been eying, and then for the Anne McCaffrey. I feel like this is the start of my annus mirabilis.

Do you plan to stay in this world and continue exploring the possibilities of machine enhancements to humans?

Yes, absolutely. The Banff Centre has kindly agreed to put me up for two more residencies this year, and I so enjoyed writing "Cuts Both Ways" that I've had trouble moving on to a new project. I started outlining on the bus ride back to Calgary, and had pages of notes and ideas by the time we hit the city limits.

I love the idea of a company having a stranglehold on fascinating new tech and the kinds of shady things they might do with it…and the things people might do to themselves to be a part of it. I'm fascinated by the idea of Distributed Arbitrage and the forecasting, and I know I'm not done with Spencer or Megan. I'm not sure what it's going to look like, but I think I've got the beginnings of a novel in me. And at the end of the day, I want to hear that William Gibson read my book and liked it.

Author Spotlight: N.K. Jemisin

Laurel Amberdine

I loved how you subverted the concept of alien parasites in "Walking Awake." What inspired you to create the Masters the way you did?

I think of the story as a response to Heinlein's *The Puppet Masters*, and to similar science fiction of the era. A lot of that fiction reflects the paranoia of privilege—fear of a more (theoretically) egalitarian political system like communism, fear of external threats because the straight white men of the time simply assumed they would continue to dominate women and people of color within their own societies, and so on. There's also some apparent fear of the tables turning, because so much of this "privileged people's science fiction" contains stalwart, iron-jawed, able-bodied fellows suddenly having to deal with (symbolic) weaponized rape, infected blankets, unwanted medical experimentation, and other things that stalwart, iron-jawed fellows have inflicted on people they considered less than human throughout recent history. But that's the thing: We don't need aliens to do things like that to each other. We've been doing it to each other for ages. So call "Walking Awake" the paranoia of the less-privileged, if you want.

I noticed you kept the location of the story unspecified, and never showed who exactly created the parasites. Why was it important to keep the story universal?

Partly because biological warfare and systematic dehumanization have occurred throughout human history, in various forms and in various places. But also just because, after so many generations of having their history carefully removed from them, humankind in the story no longer retains the old distinctions; those have been replaced by new distinctions. Granted, the fact that the Masters are basically GMOs does at least localize the origins of the problem to industrialized countries, or corporations originating in same, but by the point of the story, none of that matters anymore.

Sadie seems confident that the Masters rule the whole world, but is it possible there are any holdouts hidden anywhere?

It's certainly possible. We're still discovering pockets of people who managed to avoid colonialism or contact with outsiders, like the Jarawa. The Masters are no more omnipotent as rulers of the Earth than human beings are.

Your story explores themes of freedom and oppression, obedience and responsibility. What Sadie does at the end not only kills her, it will wipe out the only society she's ever known—freedom comes at a huge price. Are these important ideas for you in your fiction?

Yes. I wanted to depict a revolution—but this is, all in all, a relatively quick and bloodless revolution. A heavy price has already been paid by all the people taken over by the Masters at the point of takeover; they're basically dead already. But I felt that Sadie also needed to risk something, pay something, if she was going to join this revolution.

I know you're working on a new science fiction trilogy. Can you share anything about that with our readers?

Well, it's sort of science fantasy. Basically, the story is set in a secondary world that suffers from frequent seismic extinction-level events—volcanic winters that last years, chemical changes that toxify whole swaths of land, things like that. These are called Fifth Seasons. In this world there are people called orogenes, who have the power to control seismic energy: They can stop volcanoes, start earthquakes, that sort of thing. But there's a terrible price that must be paid for this power, which makes them a dire threat to everyone around them, and so orogenes are hunted down and enslaved whenever they appear. They're feared even more than the long winters.

The story follows a woman who's been living an ordinary life in an ordinary small town, but who is secretly an orogene, and her children are, too. When her husband finds out, he reacts…badly. He murders one of their children, and kidnaps the other. She's forced to hunt him down, but while she does this, another orogene has uncovered an ancient mystery of the world and used it to bring about the worst seismic event in history—one that will cause a Fifth Season that lasts centuries, which no one is prepared for.

It's a trilogy, and the first book is done; I'm at work on the second, now.

You're highly accomplished at destroying science fiction. Do you have any advice for ambitious, under-represented destructors out there?

Thank you. My advice is just this: Write. Improve. Submit. Keep doing it, and before you know it, you'll be destroying science fiction too!

AUTHOR SPOTLIGHT: RHONDA EIKAMP

SANDRA ODELL

Your story not only pays homage to the Sherlock Holmes mythos, but to the style of Doctor Watson recounting each tale. Are you a fan of Sherlock Holmes stories? What sort of research did you do for this tale?

I'd read all the original stories, although I'm not a big fan of the modern versions. When I set out to write a steampunk-robot tale, I wanted to say something about Victorian class attitudes, how they might thoughtlessly use something as marvellous as artificial intelligence as soldiers or household servants. The Holmes icon popped into my head. I knew right away I wanted to parallel the original stories. I re-read several of the stories for structure and to get a feel for Watson's voice. Watson worked for me as the narrator, as it turned out, because I could put those unquestioning pompous attitudes into him. He's trapped in them without even realizing it. In spite of talking about his friendship with Gearlock, in the end we see that Watson views him the same way the rest of society does, as a machine created to serve humans, something the good doctor can switch off with impunity if it stops working right. I didn't do much research otherwise. Except for bees. The honey-extraction centrifuge is a real invention of the time, and we find out here that it was actually thought up by Gearlock.

Early on in the story, you make mention of the prohibition against the amalgamated altering the programming of another of their kind. This hints at a depth of worldbuilding that lends itself well to the story. How important is it to you to create a complete world for your stories, even if the reader only experiences a small taste of your creation?

Every work of fiction creates a world, or should—that suspension of disbelief that means the reader accepts, for the duration of the story at least, that this happened somewhere, somewhen. Genre writing is a special case, because the reader knows from the start that the world of the story may not be the one he knows, so a telling detail here and there to build up that world is essential. It's easier in short fiction to drop these hints that may never get fleshed out, as long as they're consistent. But I let myself discover them as needed while I'm writing. It's more fun that way. In the story, Germany is beginning to use the amalgamated as soldiers. I didn't know that at first. I didn't know our modern term "standby" comes from the Victorians having parked their amalgamated in closets all night.

Gearlock has much in common with his fleshly counterpart, Arthur Conan Doyle's Sherlock. If you could, what classic Sherlock Holmes case would you like to see Gearlock tackle? How do you think he would fare?

None of the original cases. Sherlock solved those to everyone's content. I'd like to see Gearlock take a stab at some of our modern mysteries, and I think he'd do well. I'd set him on the Kennedy assassination or have him decipher the Voynich manuscript.

Gearlock also shares certain traits with the BBC's modern interpretation of Sherlock Holmes, in particular the remarks of "You do not know what it is like, here within the closes of my head, Watson. This incessant…insipid buzzing of my thoughts. The ennui." How do you feel these similarities to both versions of Sherlock Holmes will impact the reader? Is Gearlock more accessible because of them?

I'm fascinated by the concept of AI and—if we ever do create sentient machines—where the line will be drawn between human and machine. I don't think it will be human goodness that will set us apart from computer brains, but rather the dark side of human nature: our neuroses, our crimes of passion. The Turing test to prove you're truly human wouldn't be to do the *right* thing, but to do the *wrong* thing. Even if it's not crime or a beastly act, but just doing the absurd, the unexpected. You can see this in the anti-computer tactics game players use to win against machines, especially in chess, strategically wrong moves to shake the computer up, get it "out of its book."

Gearlock wants to "get out of his book"; he feels the despair of a sentience that is locked out of being human, is baffled by their urges, even while being surrounded by them. We seem to tell this story a lot, characters that long to be human and imitate what they consider to be human, whether they're from the inferior- or superior-to-human-intellect side of it, from Kafka's ape in "A Report to an Academy" to HAL 9000 asking, "Will I dream?" Maybe because we're fascinated by this dichotomy. It's something we all understand—to err is to be human, but computers by definition should never err, so how could they ever achieve humanity? Maybe it's comforting to think these failings of ours mean we can never be replaced by them. We're attracted to the original Holmes, I think, not just because of his computer-like abilities, but because of his human failings: his moodiness, the drugs he turns to when his intellect makes him feel isolated. I wanted to show that ambiguity in Gearlock. If he can be this tormented, is he already human or not?

As to the modern interpretations of Holmes, I've managed to avoid most of them, especially the Downey movies. Haven't seen one yet. I caught a couple of episodes of the BBC resurrection here on German TV, but dubbed in German. I love the visual method they use to bring Holmes's thoughts to life. He's always been a sort of black box otherwise. Benedict Cumberbatch is awesome in any language.

What projects are in store for Rhonda Eikamp?

More stories! I've yet to embrace the novel length (or be swallowed up by it, as the case may be). I have another steampunk story that takes a very different direction from this one in the upcoming Emby Press anthology *Steampunk Monster Hunter: The Dark Monocle*, and a story in the anthology *Fae* from World Weaver Press. I'm also very proud to be a part of *The Journal of Unlikely Cartography* put out by Unlikely Story.

Author Spotlight: Gabriella Stalker

Lee Hallison

Wendell's change of perspective sends a clear message from the author. What about current culture triggered this story and made you ask, "what if?"

One aspect of current culture that confuses me is the effort that some people put into displaying their wealth to others—by making sure they wear the right brands, keep up with the current trends, or own the most recent gadget. People are constantly being pressured into buying and spending, and being led to believe that owning things will make them happy. In the context of my story, a mall represents this particular kind of frivolity and materialism. There is actually both a church and a post-secondary institute in this galleria I visit regularly. It has always been very strange to me to see these two establishments, serious and sacred in their own ways, among the pretzel stands and designer handbag kiosks. That was definitely the seed for this story. It brought me to question how much of our daily lives could be consolidated into one building and how it might affect the functions of each institution.

The concept of an arcology has always been fascinating to me, but I still thought that I'd never see residential space together with commercial space in my lifetime. Imagine my surprise when I discovered high-end condominiums attached to a grocery store in the neighborhood where I lived at the time I was writing "In the Image of Man." The idea that the people living there were only an elevator ride away from a grocery store/dry cleaners/bank/pharmacy made me think of it as a stepping stone toward real-life arcologies. Writing this story certainly made me realize that I was not terribly optimistic about the idea.

Why does Wendell choose a church to begin his journey away from the dominant culture?

Wendell's experience at his classmate's church was the first time he had ever been outside of a mall for more than a few minutes. Though the church is a symbol of people trying to keep something sacred and apart from rampant commercialism, Wendell's motivation is not really about religion. He has a growing curiosity about what life could be like if he hadn't been raised in a culture that had resulted in massive debt and his shallow, materialistic character. I believe his journey will concern an exploration of nature and discovering new interests outside of video games and shopping, with the added challenge of being an adult and learning to be independent. Going to church will be helpful because it's a break from the suffocating commercial complex he's accustomed to. It's not impossible that he'll grow in his faith as a result of going to church, but he has plenty of maturing to do first.

Why did you choose a teenage boy for your main character?

I often write about young people because they feel more susceptible to growth and change. Wendell is not just young, but extra naïve because the culture within the mall is all about materialism, and he doesn't know that he could strive for anything else. I honestly chose a boy to put some diversity into my writing after I realized that my protagonists are almost always young women.

What are you currently working on?

I am doing some final edits on a dystopian story about a nefarious government's attempt to suppress natural human urges, and how the teenage population games the system so that they can indulge. My long-term projects are two different novels, both of which explore humanity's relationship with nature in post-apocalyptic settings.

Will you revisit this future world in other stories?

It's possible. I would love to explore the perspective of a newcomer who feels confined in the mall, juxtaposed with that of natives like August and Wendell who had never known anything else and feared the world outside. How would it look and feel to someone who had come from a place where this sort of structure didn't exist, and what could they possibly do if they were unable to adapt?

AUTHOR SPOTLIGHT: CHARLIE JANE ANDERS

SANDRA ODELL

What inspired this story?

When someone starts a new romance, there's always the experience of stuff bleeding through from the old relationship to the new one. I've seen this a lot with my friends and stuff. You find yourself doing things with your new lover that you used to do with your old lover—or you tell your new lover stuff about yourself that your old lover already knew. Connecting with a new romantic partner is a chance to reinvent yourself a bit, but it also means revisiting old territory with a new person. So then I started wondering: What if you could just give your brand new partner the relevant (happy) memories of your previous partner? Then you could save a lot of time. That's where the basic concept came from. It wasn't until I started to think of this as a story about Mary and Stacia's relationship that it really gelled, however.

Your use of language and vernacular in the story really sets the tone and immerses the reader in your worldview. Why did you choose this particular narrative voice?

I spent a lot of time trying to get the tone right in this story—originally, it was a lot more silly and kind of satirical. I'm a huge fan of absurd and surreal near-future fiction by people like Eileen Gunn or Rudy Rucker, in which people are selfish and kind of horrible, and the world is portrayed as being anarchic and bizarre.

In fact, the first few drafts of this story were a lot weirder—instead of meeting in a regular bar for drinks, Stacia and Mary reclined in a parlor where genetically engineered beetles crawled along the ceiling and cried hallucinogenic tears into their mouths. There was a lot of weird crying-beetle stuff in the middle of Stacia and Mary's first conversation. And instead of eating hand-pulled noodles, Mary kept eating genetically engineered kraken sushi.

But I needed the story to feel more grounded—and I wound up feeling that in a world with "smart cookies" and virtual malls, people would really cling to the comfort of old-fashioned hand-pulled noodles. I also wanted the feelings of loss and betrayal in the story to have a lot of weight, which meant dialing back the humor.

The immersive technology in the story speaks to the recent trends in real-life technical advances: Google Glass; neurological interfaces with artificial limbs; improvements in holographic technology. Of the advancements in your story, what are some of the ones you'd like to experience for yourself?

I really love the idea of smart cookies, in particular—the notion of being able to process information way faster and keep track of lots of things is really appealing. It was important to me to show that smart cookies don't actually make people into geniuses, or make them less foolish—but they do allow you to visit hundreds of virtual stores in an hour, or jump off a building, or whatever. That would be awesome.

By not falling back to a happy ending, you elevate Mary, Stacia, and Dave to real people. You allow the characters to be imperfect, yet perfectly human. Do you have any favorite writers who have explored similar ideas of character growth and influenced your own works?

Most of my favorite writers have messy resolutions and imperfect characters. I already mentioned Eileen Gunn—there's also Doris Lessing, who taught me more about writing than any other author I can think of. Her Martha Quest novels actually teach you how to describe characters in a realistic way, and are a brilliant portrayal of fanaticism and passion, and what it's like to be swept up in a particular time and place.

What other projects can we expect from Charlie Jane Anders in the future?

I just recently sold a novel to Tor Books, and it's coming out sometime in 2015—it's a genre-bursting story about the relationship between a mad scientist and a witch, which begins when they're children and then continues into adulthood.

AUTHOR SPOTLIGHT: MARIA DAHVANA HEADLEY

JUDE GRIFFIN

How did "Dim Sun" start? Was it the SF play on "dim sum"?

"Dim Sun" started exactly that way, yep. To base an entire story on a pun about eating fried celestial objects? Severely not allowed. Except that I have a wrongful love of puns. And of dim sum, for that matter. Once I thought of it, I tried not to write it, but I couldn't help myself. I'd written a lot of really dark things in the last year, and this was a goofy palate cleanser. Also, I wrote this in the middle of the first round of SFWA bulletin controversy circa June of 2013, and I was in a mood about the Golden Age of SF dudes who kept insisting they controlled the genre, and the way women should be depicted and discussed within it. I decided to write a universe in which a badass woman controlled everything.

Botanical singing: This is a tiny but arresting piece of world-building in "Dim Sun"; will we ever read more about the songs of ferns, marigolds, and other plants?

Basically, I was interested in writing a science fiction world in which a lot of the tech is the opposite of shiny metal. Rodney, the narrator, complains about how the farm-to-table movement has taken over outer space, and all the glorious junk food of Earth is no longer in fashion. So the singing plants are part of that—the botanicals have replaced electronic music. Outer space is, in this iteration, a little like a hip and slightly annoying café in Brooklyn. I was thinking about the modern world, its nearly pornographic glorification of kale, for example—and this is the logical progression—an outer space where "thick cream from happy cows" is fetishized over anything freeze dried and/ or meal-substitute-y. I wouldn't mind writing something else set in this world, actually, though I never do that—I had fun with all the plant-based trouble in the story, the hedge of sins planted in places far from the people who'd originally committed them, things like that. I was really trying to create a world in which there was a rural balance to the portals and interplanetary travel, a kind of Good Old Earth which the two old guys in the story resent and long for, but can't get back to.

Why would someone as brilliant as Harriet ever date, let alone, marry Bert?
Short Answer: Patriarchy creates fuckery.

Long Answer: This is a story about a variety of kinds of hunger. Our narrator, Rodney, is constantly starving for food. Bert wants status—his job as the chief restaurant critic of outer space gets him some. And Harriet wants power. There's also a lot of sexual hunger in the story—both Harriet and Bert have a history of using lovers as tools of war against one another—and sexual chemistry always blurs the issue when it comes to whether or not a person should really date someone else. As for their marriage, I think sometimes when you're young, you have very different standards than you eventually will—the things you're initially attracted to in a partner aren't always things that will serve you well. We all have friends who are fabulously bright and yet mysteriously only attracted to trouble. I see Harriet and Bert's marriage as the kind of thing that can happen when you're a certain kind of confident woman—lots of men are weirdly frightened of you—so, maybe you marry one who isn't. Bert has a lot of ego of his own, but then…well, it turns out ego and lack of fear aren't enough to sustain a marriage. Harriet, by the time this story takes place, is seventy, divorced for maybe thirty years, and now, goddamn it, she's the President of the Universe. I like that she's not young. I like that she's not beautiful. I like that she doesn't give a fuck. All of that is on purpose. I have long been aggravated, and it increases, about the way that society values women almost exclusively for their beauty and youth, and when we get older, tries to make us powerless—just when we're at our most knowledgeable, and most capable. It's so rotten. I gnash my teeth. Even when I'm having fun. Which I am here. There is, on our own Earth, a structural nastiness which causes women to be societally expected to use their energy to make men successful, rather than to make themselves successful. Harriet is the result of me considering what could happen if a really fierce women used her energy on her own career and on bettering the world, rather than on the much smaller, but similarly energy-tapping business of bettering her partner's life. For centuries, women (not men—this is exactly the reverse of the thing people say to men) have been told that the price of being powerful is that you have to be alone, that no one will love you. Fuck that. In this story, Harriet has lovers aplenty, and love, too. If powerful men can have love and happiness, so can powerful women. There was a time in my own life when I was worried about this same thing. I tried to make myself smaller and more palatable. I spent years of my life, both in a corporate and a personal sense, helping men ascend and achieve their goals. This would have been fine, had all of them done the same amount of free work for me that I did for them. Men are not generally expected to donate free and uncredited work as part of basic human relationships, but women are. This got old. I want to live in a world in which women go as big as they can. I've always been of the opinion (proven by experience) that it takes roughly the same amount of energy to do something huge as it takes to do something small, when we're talking about social justice. You could sit at your dining room table and give a lecture on feminist theory to your partner, or you could write that lecture into a speech, and put it out into the world. Same lecture. And in fact, you can do both. I know that sounds utopian, but things have changed a lot in terms of historically marginalized voices, even in just the last year, via platforms like Twitter. We're living in a science fictional universe. It's now possible to reach a 100,000 people with words posted on what previous generations would have viewed as thin air. Go big. Then go bigger.

You write across formats and genres: "I'm a Gemini. I don't give a shit about genre and not genre. I want to try everything I can try as a writer before I die, so I'm doing that." What's next for you?

Adult-novel wise, I'm adapting a very macho classic from the English lit canon into a contemporary version. It's in verse, or at least part of it is. I've haven't written in verse in years, not since I was a playwright. It's a boy's great book. I am sick of boy's great books. I want great books full of people who aren't boys, battling, building, loving, and doing gigantic things. It's fantastical, but also grounded in the real world. Dark as dark can be. I'm myself, after all. And in 2015, the first of two young adult fantasy novels (also new for me—I've never written YA before!) comes out from HarperCollins. *Magonia* is also a riff on boy's great books. Growing up, I got more and more disgruntled with the way characters like Wendy ended up being flung into Neverland and FORCED TO BE EVERYONE'S MOTHER INSTEAD OF HAVING ADVENTURES. No, no, no. No to the nth. Okay, so being a mother *is* an adventure. I happen to be a mother myself. I have two stepkids, now in their twenties—and I spent my twenties raising them. It is a crazy, crazy beautiful adventure to raise children, but yo. It's not the only adventure a girl can have. (Apparently the gender roles in *Peter Pan* have pissed me off for about thirty years—Wendy being forced into mothering Lost Boys, and then being tormented by a jealous Tinker Bell? COME ON. I always wanted to be Captain Hook.) So, *Magonia* is a sky-sea story in which the Wendy character essentially gets to be Peter Pan. It's not a Peter Pan riff, per se—but that's part of what inspired me to write it.

You sometimes wear special clothing while writing: tiaras, ball gowns, a flight suit. Any new outfits added to the writer wardrobe?

I just bought a gorgeous Mexican dress embroidered with flowers, along with a 1940s tooled leather briefcase. I think I might eventually end up writing something about Mexico City and its surrealist painters. There were some amazing women hanging out there from the thirties on, and most of them lived to be one hundred. They beg to be part of a fantastical narrative. But I also have my eye on an early-sixties, mink-trimmed black wool jumpsuit to be worn while writing villains. I've been writing lots of villains. This is the kind of garment that might be worn while stealing a zeppelin. And I am stalking an 1870s flower-embroidered corset. I have a weakness for beauty and craftsmanship.

What still needs destroying in SF?

Narratives in which the characters who aren't straight white men are forced into morgues, passivity, and reaction, rather than action. I just want an equally interesting and active landscape for all kinds of people, whether that landscape is Martian or laboratory. Earth, for example, is interesting for everyone who lives here. That's just true. So, a tradition of storytelling in which Earth is interesting and active for only a thin slice of the population is always going to piss me off. A tradition of *Star Trek*-ified storytelling in which the whole universe almost exclusively interacts with adventurous straight white men is a tradition that needs smashing. It's a big damn universe. There's room for everyone. But I feel like many, many writers could be doing a much, much better job getting this right. Including me. It's a process. Getting things right requires work. The work is well worth it.

Author Spotlight:
Amal El-Mohtar

Jude Griffin

How did "Lonely Sea" come about?

Back in 2010, I came across this article (news.discovery.com/space/
alien-life-exoplanets/diamond-oceans-jupiter-uranus1.htm) about the discovery that under the right conditions, diamond behaves like water as it
phase-shifts. But the article is titled "Diamond Oceans"—and I immediately
had the reaction that Leila decries in the story, of imagining something like
water but thicker, that refracts light differently, but that you can nevertheless
swim through and see running through your fingers.

I next thought, "Suppose those diamonds were to be mined?" And after
that, thought, "But suppose the diamond ocean is a sentient organism?"

**Did "Lonely Sea" end up being the story you envisioned or did things take
an unexpected turn during the writing of it?**

So many unexpected turns! The story's been developing over the past four
years, very much on my mind's back-burner as I flailed about trying to think
of how to tell it.

Initially, I'd imagined a world in which Neptunian diamond was a prized
commodity, and that people on Earth wore it as jewelry in devices that forced
it to shift in and out of phase for decoration, and that this phase-shifting was
torment to the sentient organism being parceled across the planet. But I felt
very keenly my lack of a science background, and was for a long time convinced
I lacked the vocabulary to tell the story at its best. I knew that I wanted the
story to be entwined with myth and folklore involving diamonds, but for it
to work as I was envisaging it, that folklore needed to be a counterpoint to a
good story in its own right.

I think it was my friend Stu Nathan (who, as features editor at *The Engineer*, was someone to whom I turned frequently at sticking points of this story) who pointed out that since diamonds can be synthetically produced, there would need to be some quality to Neptunian diamond there that would justify the trouble of mining them. That percolated for a while, until I thought about how the diamond ocean wants to be whole, to reassemble itself, and thought that enabling teleportation would not only justify the cost of going to Neptune—it would effectively eliminate it.

Even once I'd got that part sorted, though, the end-game changed about six times; this was a story built out of numerous conversations, and I'm tremendously grateful to Stu Nathan, Neil Williamson, Stu West, Elaine Gallagher, Asia al-Massari, J. A. Grier, and Christie Yant for their patience, kindness, and generosity as I tried to hammer it out.

Is there any significance behind the choice of the name "Meisner" for the syndrome?

There is! I asked Karen Meisner, dear friend and former fiction editor at *Strange Horizons*, for permission to name it after her, since she was one of the first people with whom I discussed the story lo these many years ago, and is, moreover, one of the warmest and most empathic people I know, so it seemed like a natural fit to name a syndrome rooted in an overabundance of empathy for her. Also her joking about how in this story "diamonds really *are* a girl's best friend!" helped to spark off some things about its structure.

What were the strengths and challenges of structuring the story the way you did?

I felt the strengths were things that helped carry me through the enormous insecurity accompanying the writing of my first science fiction story: feeling that I was *doing* something with structure, that I could mirror the narrative's function in its form by telling it in fragments coalescing into something bigger, and also feeling that offering storytelling snapshots instead of a long camera pan along its events would allow me more flexibility with representing the technology instead of explaining how it works.

The challenge, of course, is pulling it off: curating the fragments such that they hold a reader's attention, and lead to a conclusion made satisfying by the fact that every fragment was necessary to achieving it. I leave it to readers to determine the measure of success there.

Whose science fiction destruction do you enjoy?

I love SF that shows a love for the organic and for storytelling, possesses an aesthetic dimension, and makes me feel as well as marvel. Naomi Mitchison's *Memoirs of a Spacewoman* gave me a glimpse into an alt-history SF canon where the celebrated texts of ages past could involve space exploration without colonization; Cat Valente's *Silently and Very Fast* is one of the most magnificent novellas I've read; Kage Baker's Company series is one of my favorites; Octavia Butler's "Bloodchild" still makes me shiver at the thought of it.

What's next for you?

I'm tentatively writing a novel set in the world of "The Green Book" (apex-magazine.com/the-green-book) and working on a stupendously exciting project with fellow Banjo Apocalypse Crinoline Troubadours (bactroubadours. com) CSE Cooney and Caitlyn Paxson—the latter involves space-faring ethnomusicologists, nineteenth-century miners abducted by aliens, and ballads from a distant star.

AUTHOR SPOTLIGHT: ELIZABETH PORTER BIRDSALL

LAUREL AMBERDINE

You've combined Jane Austen, a distant space-faring future, and a society of thieves into one amazing story. Can you explain how this came about?

Sometimes I sit down to deliberately write a story containing this or riffing off that, but this really was just a burst of inspiration—I sat down and wrote out the first scene, the conversation between Genevieve and her mother, starting with Genevieve's dutiful quote about how it's gauche to steal from one's social inferiors because that's the purpose of taxation, and only proper to steal from one's social betters. And I sat back, and looked at that quote, and said to myself, "Well, looks like it's time to make up some etiquette."

Once I was consciously developing the story, one of the things I wanted to try to do was recreate the Regency feel of a very stratified society with complex ritualized manners and interactions, but to change up some of the details of what those rituals consist of. Dances, for example, were a way for young people to meet and converse, and to show off skills they'd spent a lot of time working on, and let off some steam with athletic activity—all of it in a socially acceptable setting, and chaperoned and hedged about with manners and expectations. Burglary and the formal visit to retrieve your stolen stuff is one of the things that fill that niche in this society. It's not really any sillier—well, not *much* sillier! I love Regency dancing, and I find it tremendous fun, but let me tell you, if I had the opportunity to make daredevil cat burglar entrances into people's homes part of a flirty-yet-formal greeting, I would be all over that.

The setting has a lot of potential for extrapolation. What other types of manners and rituals do you see the ladies and gentlemen of this future society engaging in? What do they do for a dinner party, or a wedding, or a funeral?

Oh, gosh, good question! Let me think.

You called this a society of thieves, and obviously that's not wrong, but what it really is is a society that highly values both daring and adherence to codes of formal etiquette. So there are a lot of displays of that kind of socially approved daring. Burglary like Genevieve's is a game for young ladies, but I expect that invitations to weddings and other formal occasions tend to be delivered by sneaking into your friends' houses and depositing a fancy card on the mantelpiece or the middle of the breakfast table, for example. Even smaller occasions like dinner parties, you'd invite your friends by paying a call on them and discreetly leaving the invitation when no one's looking—you'd never be so gauche as to actually *hand* something to someone. Weddings might involve some kind of pretend kidnapping—maybe the bride's family kidnaps the groom and the groom's family kidnaps the bride, all according to prior agreement of course, and then they "resolve" it with the wedding? There's probably a nonlethal but highly ritualized form of dueling by which business disputes are often settled. And masquerade balls really go above and beyond.

All of this is for the upper class, mind you. (And members of the upper class who don't want to live within these expectations, which among other things are pretty darn heteronormative, have their own choices and compromises to make, if their family hasn't already rejected the relevant expectations.) I suspect that some of the working class folks think the whole burglary-and-dueling lifestyle is glamorous and wonderful and try to mimic it in cheaper ways, and others are just like, "Oh my god, how do they have all the money and power when they're such NINNIES about everything??" It's the way of the world.

Still, it's probably a society at any level where there's a lot of awareness of where one falls in the social strata, and where people are a lot more inclined to leave things at your house than give them to you, and to make a showy, officially anonymous gesture when something big seems warranted. Birthday presents that appear mysteriously when you're not looking, that kind of thing.

Do you have any other stories planned for this setting?

Not currently, but I'm not ruling it out. Now you've got me thinking!

Due to her circumstances, Genevieve is torn between obedience and willfulness. Luckily she finds a friend in Catherine, but if she hadn't, would she have gone along with her mother's wishes or would she have found some

other way to get the attention of James Yendaria?

Well—both! Willful is a good word for her, because Genevieve wants to push boundaries and get her own way, but she's not really rebellious in the sense of rejecting her society's norms. She's supposed to obey her mother and father, and when you get right down to it, she mostly will. But within that, she's always going to be maneuvering to see what she can get of what she really wants. Without Catherine, she probably would have stolen something slightly larger that was still close to the minimum she could use to say she was obeying her mama, and gone right back to cajoling to be allowed to rob the Yendarias.

Her mother does have a fair bit of sympathy for the "But he's so dreamy, Mama!" argument, and probably would have given in eventually, once Genevieve had made more of a name for herself. She just wants Genevieve to start with more socially ambitious burglaries to establish her debut as well as a proud mother might wish.

Can you tell us a bit about your writing process?

I'm absolutely an outline kind of writer—even when I start writing with no idea where I'm going, I only get a couple of scenes in before I have to backtrack, figure out what I'm doing, and write little bracketed notes to myself about what each scene will contain. (Sometimes those notes stick around until nearly the final draft, and they usually contain a lot of all caps and question marks. I usually do a lot of extremely dignified talking to myself in a draft.) Sometimes I have a few false starts to a story, but once I figure out where I'm going, I usually just have one rolling draft that I edit until I'm happy with it.

And then I send it to friends to read it over. I'm lucky enough to have a lot of really sharp, really talented friends who are willing to tell me whether something's working or not. This is especially true of my writing group—I have two friends with whom I email just about daily to check in about whether we've written and what. We keep each other honest about keeping our hands on the keyboard and our momentum up, and we read all of each other's drafts. They're fantastic.

What other plans do you have for destroying science fiction?

So many tropes to destroy, so little time...! Please picture a supervillain's dramatically lit grin and steepled fingers when I say that.

No, I love science fiction—SFF is where my writing heart has always lain—but I'm always going to be approaching it with the idea of putting in more women, more diversity, more awareness of class. And I love turning tropes on their heads. I think they're much more fun that way.

Author Spotlight: K.C. Norton

Laurel Amberdine

I loved the unique elements you combined in "Canth." The possibly sentient ship powered by a human heart. The Portuguese pirates. The merman and the lost city. And more! Which of these ideas occurred to you first, and how did you wind up combining them all?

When I started writing this story, all I knew was that I wanted Aditi to be chasing her ship off the coast of Portugal. I'd heard about some divers who thought they'd found Atlantis in that area, so those two things came together early on. I wrote the beginning with those elements, and then realized that I had no idea what they were going to find. The merman/Giant Squid bits got worked in as I was doing research on monster hunting, mostly because steampunk cryptozoologists sounded really cool. My dad had asked to read "Canth" when I finished it, since we'd shared some books while I was doing research. He told me he liked it, but he didn't get how the ship's engine worked. I said, "Oh, it runs off a human heart," and then had to go back rewrite a big chunk of the story. It sounds like a mess—it was a mess. It was a lot of fun, too.

The Canth, Captain Pearce's ship, is named after her mother, Coelacanth. What does that ancient fish mean to you, and to the story?

I am absolutely fascinated by coelacanths. A brief summary: These fish have been around for about 360 million years, and their bodies have remained basically the same for all that time. For perspective, T-Rex lived about 66 million years ago. We had fossils of coelacanths, but people thought they were extinct. Nope! There are at least two species of them living today. I've read every book about them that I can get my hands on. The mere mention of these fish sends me into some kind of geek spasm that involves a lot of hand waving. If I was going to be metaphorical, I would say that "Canth" is about finding lost things, which is a very coelacanth theme—Aditi is searching for the ship, but the ship is searching, too. Also, I really like 'canths, and am happy to include them wherever I can.

Where did you learn about the mythical Sea Monk, and how did that inspire you to include one in your story?

Originally I wanted Aditi to find a coelacanth, but I was worried that people wouldn't be familiar with them, so I started looking into other ex-cryptids that people might know. Giant squids seemed the most likely candidates, especially because there's so much kraken lore, and then I started reading about the Sea Monk and got hooked. In the 1800s, a bunch of sailors described this very odd-looking merman they'd found at sea, which turned out to be the carcass of a squid. I really have no idea what they were seeing—if you look at a photo of a giant squid, you'll probably agree with me—but I was really fascinated by the idea. My first thought is how alien these critters look, but these sailors thought they appeared very human, like a holy man. So of course I had to write about it.

What was the hardest part about writing "Canth"? Did you ever feel stuck or did it all come together?

I wrote about a page of this story, and then put it aside for six months because I had no idea what to do with it. I was thinking of it as a love story between Aditi and Anselmo. When I finally decided to take it in a cryptozo-ology direction, I realized that wasn't going to work—it's a shame, because that would have been a lot of fun, but once I gave up on them as a couple I realized where the story needed to go. Aditi had other plans.

You have created a rich world here, with a lot of unexplored depth. Do you plan to set any more stories here, or did you come across any research that has inspired other stories?

I did a ton of research for this story—I really enjoy writing alternate histories, because I end up digging through all of this really interesting information, most of which never actually makes it onto the page. I am working on another story in a similar universe, maybe a hundred years after this one takes place. I suspect I will be spending a lot of time poking around this world. There's a secret order of morally questionable cryptozoologists to explore, after all. It would also be fun to follow up on the "Miss Eulalia" novels...

AUTHOR SPOTLIGHT: TANANARIVE DUE

JUDE GRIFFIN

How did "Like Daughter" come about?

I think I was challenging myself to write a science fiction story—which I don't often do. Usually I write fantasy. But cloning was in the news—there had been a recent court decision about it—and I wondered what kind of society we might be if we actually did regulate cloning. What might go wrong? To me, clones are nothing more than glorified offspring—they have identical genes, but they're shaped by their experiences just as we were shaped by ours. My clone, in a different environment, would be very different person. The question I always asked myself was: Who are these people who are so eager to clone themselves? What's the point? This story was an answer.

What were the challenges/rewards of the way you structured the story and the slow reveal?

I'm pretty sure I envisioned the slow reveal from the beginning, so the entire challenge of the story was to make the premise and characters so interesting that the reader would be willing to wait to see the clone.

Many years ago someone told me that Jung had a theory along the lines of "People tend to re-enact unresolved traumas of their childhood in order to seek a more satisfactory ending." Was this or any other psychological theory in the back of your mind for why Denise makes the choices she does?

I have always considered myself a very fortunate person, which is one of the reasons I write such dark fiction—I'm trying to prepare myself for future traumas. So I've had this awareness that other people hadn't had two parents, hadn't had parents encouraging them, didn't live as comfortably as we did.

That's where Denise came from: this idea that the luck of the draw separates a good home on one side of the street from a terrible home on the other. And as children, Denise and the narrator were grimly aware of the great chasm between them. So Denise had a specific model of the kind of home she wishes she'd had and wants to give to her daughter.

Are all parents at least a little like Denise? Seeing their children as a second chance for themselves?

Absolutely. To me, clones are no more than very expensive offspring.

What drives Paige ultimately to take in little Neecy: Is she, too, looking for a second chance?

And here's the irony: Just as Denise was so misguided in believing she could create a second-chance life, now Paige has entered the world of her madness. She will try to "fix" Denise too. Who knows? Maybe she'll succeed.

Whose works of science fiction destruction do you admire?

My favorite science fiction writers are Octavia Butler and my husband, Steven Barnes.

Any projects you want to tell us about?

I'm researching a historical story now set against my family history in Florida—and the research alone is scaring me so much that it's hard to imagine how I can make it scarier with a supernatural element. I also just released a short film I co-wrote and co-produced, *Danger Word*, so I'm very excited about that too. Here's the link: dangerword.com.

Author Spotlight:
Maria Romasco
Moore

Jude Griffin

What was the seed for "The Great Loneliness"?

The story grew out of the smoking wreckage of a novel I wrote in my late teens called *A Peculiar Geogony*, which was about the earth deciding to, essentially, give birth. It was a truly awful novel and I never finished it, but a few tiny elements of it eventually became this story.

What was your thinking behind the font names?

In fairness, Perpetua is the also the name of a third-century Christian martyr and Kartika is the name of a month in the Hindu Calendar. But yes, they are also fonts and I guess it sort of reinforces the idea of the daughters being designed. Fonts are these embellished interpretations of the shapes which constitute our alphabet and the girls are embellished interpretations of the sequences which constitute our genome.

Alas, poor Frank. Would the narrator have been less lonely had plate tectonics not had their way with Frank?

I doubt it. In my experience, two people together in a room can be just as lonely as one. Maybe even more.

Whose works of science fiction destruction do you admire?

Rather than list the thousand and one writers whose eloquence and imagination constantly inspire and intimidate me, I'd like to jump genres a little and broadcast my fondness for the films of Andrei Tarkovsky (*Solaris*, *Stalker*) and

Shane Carruth (*Primer*, *Upstream Color*.) I would urge any lover of moody, evocative science fiction who has not already seen these to seek them out immediately!

Any projects you want to tell us about?

I recently finished up a series of interconnected flash fictions based on old photographs I've collected over the years, and I am currently working on a fantasy novel about a mapmaker and a drug addict who live in a building so big that even sunlight is delivered via plumbing.

Author Spotlight: Eleanor Arnason

Jude Griffin

What was the spark for "Knapsack Poems"?

Reading *The Narrow Road to the Far North* by the seventeenth-century Japanese poet Matsuo Basho. It's a combination travel journal and poetry collection. A wonderful book, except Basho describes finding an abandoned baby next to a river. He and his companion moralize over how sad this is, a mother has been forced to abandon her child; and then they go on, leaving the child by the river to die. My story is an attempt to retell Basho's story with proper behavior and a good ending.

I loved the central conceit of the multiple-bodied selves, and it reads so well—was it as easy to write?

No. I have written several stories about the Goxhat—"Knapsack Poems;" "The Glutton," which was published in *Tales of the Unanticipated* and reprinted in *Apex*; and two Lydia Duluth stories as yet unpublished. In every case, writing about the Goxhat made my head hurt, but they are so much fun I can't stop.

How did you approach the poems: the structure, the wording? They feel haiku-ish.

Basho was a very great haiku poet, and my poems try for the feeling of haiku.

The story of a praise poem composed to save the poet's life comes from a far different source: *Egils saga Skallagrimssonar*, which is a thirteenth-century Icelandic novel about Egil Skallagrimsson, a famous tenth-century Viking and skaldic poet. Skaldic poetry did not rhyme, but Egil's poem for King Eirik Bloodyaxe does use rhymes. The result must have been spectacular in the tenth century, and it saved Egil's life.

Much is familiar about how the genders are described in the story (for example, females are "warm and nurturing")—did you consider non-classic depictions for gender?

I did not. Dealing with characters with multiple bodies of different sexes was as much as I could handle. As far as I can recall, I didn't notice that the sexual traits are stereotypes. But you are right. They are.

What were some of the more interesting responses you got to this story?

I don't remember any. When you say something is "interesting" in Minnesota, it means you don't like it, but are too polite to say so. My impression is people mostly liked this story.

Any projects you want to tell us about?

I have a collection of fantasy stories based on Icelandic literature and folklore coming out this year. The title is *The Hidden Folk*, which is what Icelanders call elves.

There are three Lydia Duluth stories, two of them with Goxhat, which haven't sold as yet. I want to sell them if possible, though they are pretty long, and then put together a collection of Lydia Duluth stories, including all the Goxhat stories. The working title is *The Adventures of Lydia Duluth*. Maybe I should add, *Featuring the Goxhat*.

Author Spotlight:
Maureen McHugh

Jude Griffin

Are Janna and her people passive or pacifist?

I don't think Janna's people are particularly either. When I wrote "The Cost to Be Wise," I was thinking a lot about things like the Prime Directive, you know, the rule in Star Trek that says don't interfere in a culture. It seems rather patronizing to decide for some other culture what they can and cannot learn from you, what they can and cannot want. Who are we to decide that someone else can't have Coca-Cola?

On the other hand, our own history shows that when cultures interact, the exchange is fraught. Colonialism, either by conquering Africa or by selling developing nations opium and McDonald's, hasn't been particularly kind either. I read about attempts to empower people to make their own decisions and resist commercial colonialism and I wondered if there was a way to do that. So I tried to write about it. Janna and her people chose not to have guns because they don't have the infrastructure—mining, manufacturing, etc.—to supply themselves with ammunition and parts. If they need to get ammunition from someone else, that becomes a lever by which another culture has power over them.

Of course, in the story, that decision has devastating repercussions.

Was the viewpoint character always Janna? Did you ever consider Veronique as the protagonist?

It was always Janna. It's true that Veronique is someone I knew I would understand better than I understood Janna. She'd have been a lot easier to write. (I read a lot about reindeer herding, for example. Janna knows a lot about animal husbandry. Veronique probably doesn't.) Veronique is basically a college student doing study abroad.

I thought about doing multiple points of view but ended up just sticking with Janna.

You've said of your experience teaching at Clarion that you realized the next generation of writers are being shaped to a degree by your generation's work: "You're shaping them in the sense that often they react against you—you become a place from which to push off." In what ways have you seen that manifest?

I don't read widely in the genre—I read across a lot of genres and not widely in any of them, if you want to know the truth. There is a lot less science fiction at Clarion these days, a lot more fantasy. It feels as if there's a lot of nostalgia in SF, things like James S.A. Corey's space opera and Scalzi's *Redshirts*. That's not to say that they don't say contemporary things, but they riff on genre conventions. At the same time there's a lot of stuff that feels like a development of the things that interested me and my generation as well, like Paolo Bacigalupi's *The Windup Girl*. Did I really say that about the next generation of writers? It seems rather arrogant of me. (I suspect I did.)

How has the experience of living in China shaped your writing?

Living in China had a huge influence on this story, although there is nothing particularly Chinese about it. I remember I was in the then-Soviet Union (on a three-week AARP tour; I was thirty-one, but that's another story), and we were in the country. People have these tiny little summer houses, about the size of garden sheds, *dacha*, and they're painted bright colors and have garden plots. This one had window boxes full of bright red geraniums, and I thought, *Wow, they have geraniums in Russia, too!*

When I've traveled, so much has been different, but so much has been the same. So much is so human. To me, that's part of what William Gibson means when he says that the street finds its own uses for technology. Give me a sonic screwdriver, and I'll probably use it as a bottle opener. I might use it for other things, too. But I don't want to forget that sometimes you need to open a bottle of beer.

Any new projects you want to tell us about?

I am desperate to write a novel again. Right now I am working like a crazy person just to pay the rent, but I am hoping that soon I'll get a chance to start one. But I'm afraid to say anything more until I start it.

ARTISTS SPOTLIGHT

GALEN DARA

Last year Julie Dillon was on the Hugo ballot for Best Professional Artist—the first woman in twenty-seven years to be nominated. This year I am honored to be one of *three* female artists nominated for that award, along with Julie Dillon and Fiona Staples. With John Harris, John Picacio, and Dan Dos Santos, we make a ballot equally split between the genders: the first time that has ever happened in this category. In fact, including Julie Dillon on last year's ballot, only three women have ever been nominated for the Hugo in the Professional Artist category.

EVER.

Therefore it feels timely, and personally fitting, that this would be the summer *Lightspeed* dedicates an entire issue to the enormously talented and fantastically imaginative women working in the field of speculative fiction. The opportunity for me to invite other artists to be a part of the project was nothing short of breathtaking. Li Grabensetter with her beautiful handling of inks and watercolors, Elizabeth Leggett with her brilliant digital renderings, Christine Mitzuk's rich painterly style, and Hillary Pearlman's fantastical tinkering bring the fiction in this issue depth and texture. It was a pleasure to work with these gifted and passionate artists who are deeply involved in the speculative fiction community. My favorite part of working on this issue was sitting back and watching their amazing art come in. My second favorite part was getting to know these fantastic creators just a little bit better. I hope you enjoy this spotlight on why each of them does what they do. Which, apparently, is to *destroy* Science Fiction.

LI GRABENSTETTER

Li Grabenstetter is an illustrator, writer and designer living in DC by way of the Netherlands and Hungary and other interesting places. With a BFA in printmaking and minors in bookbinding and drawing, they came to illustration through a consummate love of books and other printed matters. Influences include art nouveau, the symbolist movement, and the art of Harry Clarke, Ivan Bilibin, and Yoshitaka Amano. Li's work has been featured in such diverse venues as *GUD Magazine, AE—The Canadian Science Fiction Review, Crossed Genres Magazine*, and several US patents. In her spare time, Li likes to read about monsters while surrounded by trees. Twitter-ites can find her at @magneticcrow. Her website is magneticcrow.com.

You've been involved in several projects lately, even creating a comic for the *I Was a Teenage Anime* collection. Tell us a little bit about that and what other things you are working on right now.

This has been a somewhat crazy year for me, involving a more-difficult-than-it-should-have-been move and my taking on a full-time day job in addition to my freelancing for the first time in a while. I did create a comic for Brandon B.'s biographical anthology *I Was a Teenage Anime*, but mostly it's been personal work and low-key collaborations with friends other than that. Oh, and working on the layout and artwork for Politics & Prose bookstore's literary magazine *District Lines*. WDSF is giving me an opportunity to hop back into the fantasy illustration game, which I'm definitely ready for.

Your educational background is in printmaking and bookbinding. How did that transition into illustrating, particularly illustrating in the speculative fiction field? Who are some of your favorite artists?

Books. It's always been about books. I wanted to illustrate, but I wanted to get at it from the very root, so I started with papermaking and bookbinding

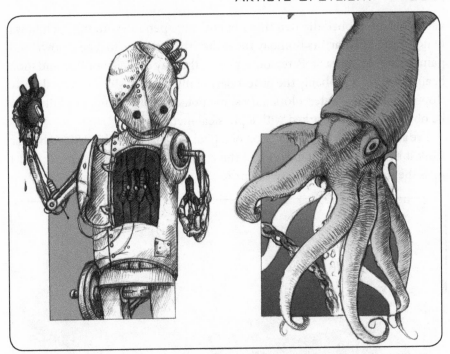

and traditional printmaking. It's definitely given me a very particular insight into paper as a substrate and ink as a medium, and even when I work digitally I find the print aesthetic influencing me heavily. I even notice myself artificially imposing boxes into my compositions, which are definitely my mental stand-in for the edge of the intaglio plate/the line of gum arabic on a litho stone. I have a 100-year-old Baltimorean platen press, and working letterpress prints into my illustration work is definitely something I've been thinking about.

You can see some of my older work, high school/college, if you look at the earliest parts of my old deviantART gallery (teriathanin.deviantart.com).

What does your artistic process look like; how do you go from initial idea to final painting?

Stop me if I go too long on this! I like to start with a page of four to eight thumbnails for brainstorming purposes*. These will have value as well as basic concept and composition worked out, and sometimes color. Once I've settled on a direction to go, I generally do another set of one to three larger thumbnails, just to nail down the shapes in the piece and how they translate to a larger scale. Next I pencil the sketch straight onto the final paper, and ink it. Besides the initial thumbnails, inking is probably my favorite part of the process—it's the most like printmaking in the sheer beautiful messiness. I use a chrome-nibbed dip pen (the Zebra Comic pen nib with the Tachikawa handle) and Dr. Martin's Bombay India ink. Then it's time to tape it down and paint it. I favor Yarka St. Petersburg paints, they lay down smoothly and look beautiful. This is probably the fastest part of my process, since I like a slightly sloppy look to my watercolors. I do some polishing at the end, but I like it to be obvious that I've worked with a physical medium.

I've actually been doing a little bit of digital work lately, and it varies whether I ink it by hand or digitally—I like the control I get with a computer, but I miss the hands-on portions of the process.

ELIZABETH LEGGETT

Elizabeth Leggett is a 20-year veteran freelance illustrator. Her artistic influences include Michael Kaluta, Donato Giancola, John Jude Palencar, and Jeremy Geddes. She completed a seventy-eight-card tarot in a single year and launched it into a successful Kickstarter (Portico Tarot and Art Prints). In December, she won two places in Jon Schindehette's ArtOrder Inspiration challenge and is currently under consideration for inclusion in *Spectrum 21*. Her website is archwayportico.com.

You are primarily a digital artist, yet your illustrations have such a painterly quality. What is your process like? Where do you get your inspiration from and how do you go from first idea to final painting?

(My process? I have a joking response for this, a bit of a paraphrasing of a Robert Heinlein quote he used to describe writing. "Illustrating is simple. You just stare at the blank canvas till blood forms on your forehead!")

Real Answer:

When I start an illustration, I spend a lot of time verbally shuffling through random ideas, colors, textures, and symbols that seem to fit the theme of what I want to create. Once the right images solidify, I decide on the palettes best suited to give them voice. It helps me a great deal to think of visual art as poetry, which I guess in a very real way it is.

I moved to digital art for purely practical reasons. I needed to find a method of quick edits and timely delivery. Using a tablet allows my hand to behave as if I am working on canvas without the time constraints of drying paint. I miss the tactile nature of physically painting very much, but meeting deadlines is a crucial part of this profession.

My husband and I travel a lot. Each new place has its own light, its own identity that is completely unique from anywhere else. This inspires me. I also get a great deal of inspiration from music. The right background soundtrack can really change the direction of an illustration in very powerful ways. Then there are books or the perfect conversation or the taste of a really sweet Spanish orange. Life is an inspiration!

You've recently completed creating an entire seventy-eight-card tarot deck! What was working on that like and how does it compare to other projects you've done?

The Portico Tarot Deck was created in a single year. I had not created a single illustration in well over two years and suddenly there was a flood of creative need. I had purchased a copy of Stephanie Law's Shadowscape Tarot a number of years before. (If you have not seen it, please do yourself a favor and check it out. It is absolutely beautiful!) A very dear friend of mine knew I had her deck and the booklet that came with it and suggested that I illustrate The Fool as a direction for my creative need. I did it. The need had not passed. She suggested drawing a card randomly. The next was the Seven of Wands. Eventually, I started drawing three cards at a time. In the end, there were 107 illustrations created for the seventy-eight needed. Later it officially became The Portico Tarot Kickstarter. I am pretty proud of it!

Tell us a little about your journey as an artist: Where did you get your training and what specifically led you to working in the speculative fiction field? Who are some of the artists that inspire you?

I came into this field through tabletop role-playing. At the time, I was the token girl at the table and while I waited for others to decide on their actions and make their rolls, I sketched their characters. I would have the Marvel Universe anatomy drawing book on one side and my player's guide on the other. (A lot of my fighter drawings look a bit too much like Aquaman!) Because of that, I would say Jeff Easley's work for *Dungeons and Dragons* and Jack Kirby's Captain America were huge inspirations. Later, I discovered Michael Kaluta and Donato Giancola and and and...I love that I still feel like a groupie for so many artists. It is all about the joy, isn't it?

CHRISTINE MITZUK

Christine Mitzuk is a Minnesota-based artist. She loves creating visual narratives fueled by traditions, tales, and the world without and within. You can find her around town at drawing co-ops or out enjoying a walk with her husband and their four-legged friend. She teaches classes at The Atelier Studio Program of Fine Art in Minneapolis, MN. Christine has created art for Fantasy Flight Games, Llewellyn Worldwide, and private commissions. Find more of Christine's work at ChristineMitzuk.com.

As well as being a freelance artist, you are very involved in art education and have several intriguing hobbies (archery practice and harp playing being a few!). What does a normal day look like for you?

Generally I use the morning hours for idea generation or image creation. My afternoons are usually idea execution or business-related tasks.

A "normal" day will look something like this. My alarm goes off at 6:30 am. Depending on how cold it is outside of the blankets, I roll out of bed about 6:45-7:00. I tend to the dog. Then a bit of exercise, followed by morning ablutions, and breakfast. I start work as close to 8:00 as I can (probably a remnant from my days as a graphic designer, but I just feel like I accomplish more if I do this). Next come email and Facebook. Then a bit of drawing warm-up, either using artists.pixelovely.com or noodling around in my sketchbook. Lately the noodling around is in the form of a Fake Journal for International Fake Journal Month (Roz Stendahl's brain baby. She's awesome. Check it out.)

Then I get moving on whatever project needs my attention first. Around 1:00 I break for lunch and a walk around the neighborhood. After that I'm back to work in my studio. My husband comes home from work and pokes his head in to say hi. Depending on the day, the afternoon session could last till dinner or only a few hours so I can go teach at The Atelier. If I'm not at The

Atelier, I'll be working on something else after dinner. Usually sketching heads from TV I'm watching with my husband, but lately it's designing some sea-themed jewelry to go with the oil painting I'm working on. No, you can't see it yet.

As for the harp, I played for over ten years performing here and there. Now I play for myself when the mood strikes me.

As for archery, I started that hobby well before a certain book series turned movie hit mainstream. Now that the weather is getting nice, I'm looking forward to getting out to the range for some practice.

You use a wide range of mediums, including traditional mediums like oil painting, watercolor, pen and ink, even scratchboard! Plus you also do digital painting as well. How do you decide what medium you will tackle various projects in? And what is your typical process like, how you go from first idea to final art piece?

Watercolor was my first love. These days my main two media are digital and oil paint. Time is the main factor in deciding what medium to use. If it's a commercial piece where the client buys all the rights and I need to hurry up, then I'll probably create the final art digitally. If it's a piece for me (fantasy, still life, portrait) then I'll most likely do it in oil. If I want immediate gratification of creating, then I'll work in watercolor. It has the least amount of set up and clean up and I love how it has a mind of its own. Watercolor tends to find its way into my more whimsical pieces.

The more I work, my process evolves. Currently it goes something like this: research; idea generation; more research and gather reference; sketches; tighter drawing; value and color studies; final.

I'll either have a prompt from a client or my own idea. Brainstorming comes first. I make lists of words, either pulled from the prompt or related conceptually. Then I do a bunch of thumbnails with pencil on paper. If I can't visualize something, I set up my camera and take a bunch of shots, acting out the idea. I try not to let the inner critic look over my shoulder at this point. Next I pick the thumbnails I like and do larger sketches, with basic values blocked in. I try to make them legible to someone besides me so I have to sort of detach a little and make sure my imagination isn't filling in any visual gaps. This is usually where options would go to the client. Next I get photo reference, either on my own or with the help of my photographer buddy David Ginsberg (eclipseproductions.org). If necessary, I hunt down or create costume bits and props. Next I bash together a rough comp with all my reference using Photoshop and convert it to grayscale. Then I do a line drawing, value studies, and color studies. Finally I paint. Sometimes the painting just pours out. Sometimes there's an ugly phase where I've lost the trail and need to get back to the values and impetus of the piece.

Who are some of the artists who inspire you?

My tastes fluctuate, but these are some of the artists I keep returning to. Susan Seddon Boulet (I want to have more mystery in my work and I love the mystery she created in hers). Greg Manchess (his compositions, brush work, and nailing values). Barry Windsor-Smith (I love his lyrical line, specifically in *Gaia and Fire*). Mucha (his lithographs are lovely but I enjoy his oil paintings and the lyrical line in his drawings more). Cheng-Khee Chee (love his watercolor paintings of fish, lots of mystery there), Joaquín Sorolla (value, color and brushwork). The prints of Yoshida Hiroshi.

HILLARY PEARLMAN

Hillary Pearlman is a Baltimore-based artist with an eye for trouble and an art for whimsy. She has a love for found objects, recycling, and bringing new life to the hollow. Formal training includes months under the guidance of a calligraphy landscape master in Wuhan, China, where she resided for part of 2007. Her heart is in fantasy and science fiction, but the rest of her does what it wants, so there's always an interesting string of results. Her website is hillary-pearlman. squarespace.com

You have an eclectic background in art-making, experimenting in a variety of mediums (including mechanical/musical sculpture!), even studying for several months with a calligraphy landscape master in Wuhan, China. Tell us a little bit about your journey as an artist so far and what's next for you.

I was a member of S.F.S.F.S (the South Florida Science Fiction Society) as a fetus. I grew up in libraries, museums, and Tropicon. Even as a kid I would walk through the art show at Trop several times a day. I was absolutely fascinated with epic spacescapes, monsters, dragons, you name it. Movies like *The Dark Crystal* really fueled me, I wanted to be the person responsible for THAT shot, kind of thing. I wanted to create crazy worlds and universes that people had never seen or conceptualized. I spent my days there in my mind, much to the disdain of all my school authorities. My journey as an artist has been

more of a gaining of perspective. Washing my eyeballs with everything I can lay them on. The landscapes always came very naturally; the most important thing I learned while under the study of Cha Jiàshóu (Professor Cha) was not to fear the canvas, whatever it may be. At the time that was rice paper and he was smacking the back of my head at mistakes, *Kill Bill*-style, but I learned more from him in the three months I was in the Wuhan, China area than I could possibly illustrate with words. One maybe: "attack."

What is your process like? What is your favorite medium and how do you go from first idea to final art piece?

When I was back in the US, my attention turned to color. Chinese watercolor is traditionally very dull; I'm a kid from South Florida, I was starved for bright and noisy. As I was learning more about color, by proximity I learned how to think in terms of problem solving. I'm still learning and hopefully will be until death or dementia. The beginning of that mentality was the beginning of my quest into recycling and recovery.

The musical instruments were another natural progression. My mother, Dina Pearlman, who is also a fantastic fabric artist, was in a folk/filk group when I was little called Orion's Belt. They would rehearse in our living room. Music has always been a part of my life, and instruments have their own life, I simply seek to extend it in memoriam with functionality. My process is evolution. I don't usually repeat a lot; everything I do ends up being more. Sometimes "better," sometimes "worse." I have managed to train myself not to set fire to everything I dislike that I make. I got yelled at a lot for that. My mission is to keep growing, for as long as I'm able.

What led you to working in the speculative fiction field and who are some of your favorite artists?

Well, the first and third inquiries have a similar answer. (See above.) More often than not, my obsessions swing between Vincent Van Gogh, Michael Whelan, and Bill Watterson…that can move towards H.R. Giger on darker days. At the moment, I'm incredibly grateful for my opportunity to work with the fantastic people of *Lightspeed Magazine*, illustrating stories from authors I love, and Waking Dreams Games, for whom I have the luck of illustrating a gamers manual for their *Legends of the Dragon Keeper* tabletop series. Thank you universe! Thank you, *Lightspeed*. Thank you, Galen Dara, for everything.

ILLUSION, EXPECTATION, AND WORLD DOMINATION THROUGH BAKE SALES

PAT MURPHY

In this article, I'm going to tell you about illusion, expectation, and the lies that your brain sometimes tells you. And I'll explain how those lies relate to science fiction, the women who are destroying it, and the future of our society.

But before I get to all that, I'll start with a story that is also a puzzle.

A spacecraft from the planet Earth lands on an alien world. The captain sends out a landing party, which includes Robert (a middle-aged scientist) and his strapping twenty-year-old son, Robert, Jr., also known as Bob.

An alien monster that looks suspiciously like a Tyrannosaurus Rex attacks the landing party, killing everyone except Bob, who hides in a convenient cave. The monster then turns on the ship.

For the sake of the crew, the captain must order the ship to take off, abandoning Bob. But the captain says, "I can't leave Bob behind. He's my son."

Who is the captain?

I'll give you a few minutes to think about that. But before I tell you about your tricky brain, I'd like you to take a moment to watch this video, shot at a shopping mall in Norway. [youtube.com/watch?v=nfpWdYoa2_o]

This is the Ames Room, invented by ophthalmologist Adelbert Ames, Jr. in 1934. (You can find many videos of this illusion online if you search for "Ames room." I like this one for its brevity and Norwegian commentary.)

In the video, you see a woman and a man walking around in a small room. When the woman stands on the left side of the room, she looks very tall. When the people change positions and the man stands on the right, the woman shrinks and the man looks very tall.

There's no trick photography here—just your own tricky brain. Your brain is used to seeing rooms that are rectangular—where the walls meet the floor and each other at right angles. Your brain sees the Ames room and assumes that this room is rectangular, like most other rooms you've encountered.

But the Ames room is not like other rooms. None of its corners are square. The back wall is not parallel to the front wall. In fact, the corner on the right is twice as far away from the video camera as the corner on the left. The floor slants—the distance from the ceiling to the floor is much greater on the right than on the left.

When the woman walks across the room from left to right, she is actually walking away from you, heading for the distant back corner. As she moves away from you, she looks smaller. When she's in that distant corner, she looks smaller because she is farther away. The slanted floor contributes to her shrinkage—the distance between the floor and the ceiling in this corner is enormous, making her small by comparison.

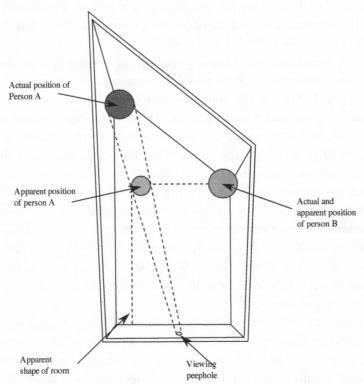

Actual position of
Person A

Apparent position
of person A

Actual and
apparent position
of person B

Apparent
shape of room

Viewing
peephole

Image: commons.wikimedia.org/wiki/File:Ames_room.svg

The room is dramatically distorted, but your brain insists on seeing it as rectangular. To make sense of what it sees in the room, your brain tells you that the people shrink and grow—which makes no sense at all. But still your brain clings to its belief in rectangular rooms.

Most people believe what they see. They think they see the world as it really is. But researchers working to understand human perception know otherwise. The world you see is something your brain invents from information it gathers from your eyes and interprets using its assumptions about the world. You don't see the world itself. You see your brain's interpretation of the world.

It's your brain's job to make sense of the world. Sometimes, in its efforts to find sense in a confusing world, your brain takes a short cut. The Ames room is one example of how your brain and perceptual system can take a short cut and get lost along the way. Rather than seeing what is really there, your brain sees what it expects to see.

Now let's get back to Bob, cowering in a cave on that alien planet, and the spaceship captain who is unwilling to abandon the boy to his fate. Who is the captain? Bob's mother, of course.

When I wrote about Bob and his mom, I based the story on a classic puzzle: A boy and his father are in a car crash and the father is killed instantly. The boy is airlifted to the best hospital in the area and prepared for emergency surgery. The surgeon rushes into the operating room, sees the boy, and says, "I can't operate on this patient. He's my son."

I first heard the tale of the reluctant surgeon thirty years ago. You would think that with the number of women doctors around, this story would no longer be a puzzle. Yet when Boston University researchers Mikaela Wapman and Deborah Belle posed it to students in 2012, only fourteen percent of the students realized that the surgeon was the mother. People came up with a variety of creative solutions: The surgeon was the boy's gay, second father; the "father" in the car referred to a priest; the story was all a dream. But the notion that the surgeon was the boy's mother eluded most of them.

The story of the spaceship captain and the tale of the surgeon work in much the same way as the Ames room. We see what we expect to see—what we are used to, what is familiar, what has been taught to us by pop culture, by our society, by examples all around us. We see what we have learned to see: a rectangular room, a square-jawed male spaceship captain, a man in surgical scrubs preparing to save a life.

And here's why this matters. Your brain's unconscious assumptions—the expectations that lurk beneath your conscious awareness—can affect your behavior in ways that you may not realize or like. Consider a 2012 study, in which science faculty from a number of universities considered the application of a student for a laboratory manager position. The student was randomly assigned a male or female name. Otherwise, the application was identical. Yet men and women both judged John to be more competent than Jennifer—more valuable to the tune of $4000 a year in salary, more worthy of mentorship, and generally more likely to be hired.

These academics fell victim to what social psychology researchers call "implicit associations" or "implicit bias," the unconscious assumptions built by social conditioning. Consciously, they may have felt they could be objective in their evaluation of candidates, treating male and female equally. But in the end, they saw the room as square.

It's hard to change hidden assumptions, expectations that are buried so deep that you don't even think about them. Just telling yourself that the room is distorted, that women can be surgeons, doesn't work. Clearly it's difficult to see the unexpected—even when it's right in front of your eyes, even when it is the only answer that makes sense. How can we change those hidden assumptions, the expectations that are buried so deep we don't even think about them?

That's where science fiction comes in. Science fiction is in the business of exploring the unexpected. This is the literature of thought experiments. We science fiction writers ask "what if…," and then spin a story about the unexpected consequences of some change in the fabric of the world.

In the sort of science fiction that interests me, the "what if" questions aren't limited to changes in technology. Rather they focus on changes in society, in gender roles, in how people relate to each other and to the Others in the world around them—whether aliens or AIs.

Science fiction also has an advantage that sometimes appears to be a disadvantage—people generally don't take it seriously. In the eyes of the world, science fiction is goofy, fun, entertaining, silly stuff, really. As such, it flies beneath the radar, seeping into people's minds below the level of conscious thought.

The stories we read and the stories we tell shape who we are. Stories—whether jokes or TV shows or tales in a pulp magazine—shape our assumptions, our expectations, our understanding of the world. They get under our skin and show us how to behave, what to expect, who we can be.

Ultimately, I believe that science fiction can change the world. Because the first step in changing the world is imagining a new one. That's the part that science fiction writers are good at. We can imagine new futures, create new stories to live by.

Back in 1991, Karen Fowler and I founded the Tiptree Award in an effort to reward those writers who were pushing against expectations in gender roles, a fundamental aspect of society. The Tiptree Award, which is given out each year to a work of speculative fiction that explores or expands gender roles, was designed to help all of us learn to see and expect something different from what we have seen before.

Way back then, in an ancient time when we often communicated with words printed on paper, I wrote: "Science fiction is the literature of imagination and change. Yet all too often, our futuristic views of human roles are limited by our present world. To change the way that our society thinks about women and men, we need to show people in different roles [...] The Tiptree Award will reward those who are bold enough to contemplate shifts and changes in gender roles, a fundamental aspect of any society. The aim of award organizers is not to look for work that falls into some narrow definition of political correctness, but rather to seek out work that is thought-provoking, imaginative, and perhaps even infuriating. Having one's boundaries expanded is not always a comfortable process."

When I announced the award in 1991, I said we would fund it through bake sales. (That was Karen Fowler's idea; she has a wicked mind.) Ultimately, our goal was world domination through chocolate chip cookies.

That's still our goal. I confess: I'm surprised that we are fighting the same battles today that began back in 1991, but I still have great faith in the power of chocolate chip cookies and science fiction.

The first step in changing the world is changing ourselves. And there is no better way to do it than creating new stories to live by.

References

- For more on work by Mikaela Wapman and Deborah Belle related to the reluctant surgeon story, see bu.edu/today/2014/bu-research-riddle-reveals-the-depth-of-gender-bias
- For more on the 2012 Yale University study in which science faculty ranked applicants with male names as more competent than identical applicants with female names, see timeshighereducation.co.uk/421746.article
- For more on implicit association, see boston.com/news/science/blogs/science-in-mind/2013/02/05/everyone-biased-harvard-professor-work-reveals-barely-know-our-own-minds/7x5K4gvrvaT5d-3vpDaXC1K/blog.html
- To take online tests that let you assess your own implicit associations, see implicit.harvard.edu/implicit/aboutus.html
- For more on the Tiptree Award, visit Tiptree.org
- To read the speech in which Pat Murphy announced the award, see wiscon.info/downloads/patmurphy.pdf

~

Pat Murphy has won numerous awards for her thoughtful, literary science fiction and fantasy writing, including two Nebula Awards, the Philip K. Dick Award, the World Fantasy Award, the Seiun Award, and the Theodore Sturgeon Memorial Award. She has published seven novels and many short stories for adults, including *Rachel in Love*, *The Falling Woman*, *The City Not Long After*, *Nadya*, and *Adventures in Time and Space with Max Merriwell*, a novel that *Publisher's Weekly* called the "cerebral equivalent of a roller-coaster ride." Her children's novel, *The Wild Girls*, won a Christopher Award in 2008. In 1991, with writer Karen Fowler, Pat co-founded the James Tiptree, Jr. Award, an annual literary prize for science fiction or fantasy that expands or explores our understanding of gender roles. This award is funded by grassroots efforts that include auctions and bake sales, harnessing the power of chocolate chip cookies in an ongoing effort to change the world. Pat enjoys looking for and making trouble. Her favorite color is ultraviolet. Her favorite book is whichever one she is working on right now.

WOMEN REMEMBER: A ROUNDTABLE INTERVIEW

MARY ROBINETTE KOWAL

In the ten years that I've been actively participating in the science fiction community, I've seen the field change. A great deal of that change can be attributed to social media providing a voice for people who otherwise went ignored. The awards ballots are showing greater percentages of women and larger ethnic diversity. At the same time, there are places where it feels like the field had taken a step back from the work I remembered reading as a teenager. It feels very much like a case of "the more things change …"

So, I decided to ask some women who had been there. Please welcome Ursula K. Le Guin, Pat Cadigan, Ellen Datlow, and Nancy Kress.

How do you think science fiction has changed, either as a genre or as a culture, from when you started in the field?

Ursula K. Le Guin: How has SF changed…Socially? Well, for women, it's not quite as much like riding "Furthur" with Kesey's Merry band as it used to be. I guess we caused some real destruction to the male notion that SF, like a good deal else, was theirs, all theirs, and only theirs. But I wonder if that notion is in fact destructible. It keeps popping up again, twice as large as life.

Pat Cadigan: Migod, yes. Decades after the advent of U.K. Le Guin, we saw the debut of N.K. Jemisin, the N being Nora. There's a photo on the Internet of a white-haired woman holding a protest sign; the sign says, "I cannot believe I still have to protest this shit." Amen, sister.

Ursula: This makes it sound as if I crept into SF under my initials only. Not so. I was Ursula K. from the get-go. The "debut of U.K. Le Guin" was a one-time appearance, for a specific reason. Virginia Kidd submitted my story "Nine Lives" to *Playboy* using my initials only and they accepted it. When Virginia gleefully told them U.K. was not Ulysses Karl, they didn't back out, but they asked if they could keep the U.K., because their male readers were alarmed by female writers. The explanation was so touching, and the money was so good, that we magnanimously consented.

Pat: I write fantasy and horror as well as SF, but when I write SF, I go to enormous effort to make it hard SF. It's difficult because I'm not a scientist, but I can learn enough on my own to make things plausible. Male SF writers who are scientists have referred to me as a hard SF writer. It took me decades longer to reach that point than it did male SF writers who also aren't scientists (are you still following this sentence?). I think it's because everyone assumes that men who write hard SF must have more science education than females. And yet I know of at least one female SF writer who happens to be a theoretical physicist. How long will it take people to guess her name?

As someone with a gender-ambiguous byline, I have had moments of amusement, disgust, and disbelief. In fact, Kim Newman (male) and I were discussing this a few weeks ago at a convention in Oslo. (I've also talked about this with Kim Stanley Robinson (also male), who told me when he was starting out that his publisher expressed some concern that people would mistakenly think actress Kim Stanley had remarried and was reinventing herself.)

Kim Newman pointed out that he had not deliberately taken on gender ambiguity, that his name was his name. My name is also my name, but I could have written as Patricia Cadigan. I chose Pat Cadigan not to be gender-ambiguous, but because I liked the way it sounded when spoken aloud. In my opinion, it scans better. I didn't go out of my way to hide the fact that I'm a woman. My first books even included a photo. But apparently a lot of readers don't look at author photos because a number of readers thought I was a guy. Another female author told me that she loaned *Synners* to a male friend. When he found out I was a woman, he opined I was someone "without an ounce of femininity." Obviously this says more about him; more troubling to me is that this happened barely twenty years ago.

And yet. My son is twenty-eight; he and his friends have a far more inclusive cultural perspective.

Ellen Datlow: I entered the field officially in 1979 when I started working as Associate Fiction Editor at *OMNI Magazine*. Because I've mostly worked with short fiction, I'm more aware of the world of the short story than the novel. So that's mostly what I'm referring to below.

The field back then, while dominated by men, always had fabulous female writers working in it. By the late '80s we were seeing many more women on award ballots— particularly in the short form. For a period of time Nancy Kress, Connie Willis, Karen Joy Fowler, Pat Murphy, Pat Cadigan, Kristine Kathryn Rusch, Ursula K. Le Guin, Martha Soukup, and others seemed to dominate the Nebula ballot in the short form.

Some of those writers still produce great short stories, but most of them moved on to novel writing, and only occasionally still have time to write short stories. Because this seems the natural progression of our field, short story editors are always looking for new blood.

I'm not going to name check all the wonderful female writers who emerged since the '90s—there are plenty, but it seems to me that in the past five to ten years, there has been a continuous injection of new blood into the field by writers such as Priya Sharma, Genevieve Valentine, E. Lily Yu, Veronica Schanoes, and many others.

What I see is that some of the best writers mix up their story production—moving with ease from science fiction to fantasy and horror and back again. This provides them with many more outlets for their work and recognition in more than one field—always a plus.

Nancy Kress: Since I started writing SF, the field has changed in at least three significant ways. My first story appeared in 1976, a time of great feminist ferment in—and beyond—science fiction. In the few years preceding my debut story, Joanna Russ had published "When It Changed" (1972), Alice Sheldon "The Women Men Don't See" (1973), and Suzy McKee Charnas *Walk to the End of the World* (1974), among scores of other works reimagining the relations of men and women. I was swept into the field among a great tide of female writers following these pioneers. When I started writing SF, the vast majority of SF still featured male protagonists. That is no longer true, and now SF is more likely to feature women in power positions as a given, rather than centering on the struggle to arrive there.

Second, in the 1970s, science fiction still outsold most fantasy, still won most awards, still garnered the most attention. Today, as I write this, nearly every work of fiction on the Nebula ballot is fantasy, not science fiction. The best-selling series, such as George R.R. Martin's Song of Ice and Fire, are fantasy.

Pat: That's right. In fact, I when I started reading genre, the field was far less stratified than it is now. Judith Merrill's *Best SF of the Year* anthologies included hard SF, light-hearted fantasy, and weird pieces by John Cheever, Tuli Kupferberg, and Bernard Malamud ("The Jewbird"). The Merrill anthologies were a brilliant showcase of all kinds of stories with a fantastic element. I wish the electronic rights issues were more easily settled so that they could come back as ebooks. If I were teaching a literature course or a writing workshop, I would make them required reading.

While I understand the divisions in genre—if I'm in the mood for elves, it's nice to know I don't have to spend hours sifting through rocket ships and serial killers—I often wish we were less concerned with what's SF and what's fantasy. But that's just me.

Ellen: Yes to all the above by Nancy. Fantasy has come to dominate the market. Perhaps it's true that, as we've come to live more in a science fictional world of computers, nano technology, ebooks, space exploration, etc., it's more difficult to excite readers the way science fiction used to—because it all seems so…normal.

Nancy: And then there's the third thing—Young Adult novels were once mostly read by teenagers. They mostly had no sex, little violence, and happy endings. Today, YA is one of the strongest sub-genres in the field, and series such as Suzanne Collins's Hunger Games and Veronica Roth's Divergent are read by adults and are turned into big-budget movies. Except that their protagonists are teens, the novels share the traits of adult fiction.

Pat: If you ever want to see writers treated like rock stars, go to an American Library Association convention and watch for a YA genre writer to show up. The librarians don't scream and faint, but it's a near thing. I saw the reception for Robert Cormier, author of *The Chocolate War*. I don't think anyone threw underwear at him, but I wouldn't be surprised. Anyone who gets young people reading is golden.

Personally, I think that adults have been reading YA fiction all along. I know I have. I have happily re-read old favourites from my own youth and then gone on to check out new people. Judy Blume was one of the writers who pioneered true-life issues for teens in her books, like having sex and parents getting divorced.

I also derive a great deal of satisfaction from knowing that the richest woman in the UK is a YA genre writer—J.K. Rowling.

Ellen: The young adult market did not exist when I was a kid. There were books for kids and books for adults. I could hardly wait to move out of the kids' book section of the library into the adult section.

As Nancy says, young adult fiction can and does do everything adult SF and fantasy does except with younger protagonists.

Pat: I went to my first convention in 1975. I made my first professional sale in 1979. Things in this field have changed a lot.

For one thing, there are a hell of a lot more women. For another, the field isn't quite as unrelentingly white as it used to be—we have more People of Colour. Granted, non-white fans and writers are still very much a minority, but they are no longer a rarity.

However, the one thing I heard most after the last Worldcon—San Antonio, 2013, for the record—were complaints that the Worldcon was full of "old people." This was apparently based on the number of mobility scooters in evidence. There was a lot of talk about how the Worldcon attendees were predominantly old people—ergo, it wasn't attracting young people/new readers. All the hip, vital, young people went to DragonCon or the San Diego Comic Con.

Bitch, please.

I'm running into this kind of ageism more and more and I don't like it. People in general are living longer and they're healthier for longer. All new readers are not necessarily teenagers. The golden age of science fiction isn't twelve.

I think it's deceptive anyway. I saw a lot of people under forty in San Antonio, and plenty under thirty as well. They were in evidence, but as most of them didn't use mobility scooters, it wasn't as easy to count them.

But I was also gratified to see a number of disabled Worldcon attendees. There's more concern for accessibility than there used to be. And there is more awareness of other issues as well. We don't always get it right but we're doing better than we used to.

I suppose the biggest change has been ebooks. I welcome them with open arms—er, e-reader software on my iPad, anyway, and not just because SF Gateway brought back my backlist! Tons of formerly hard-to-find SF and fantasy is coming back to entertain and amaze new readers. My old favourites are back, along with a lot of books I've wanted to read but never got a chance to. And I love the fact that I can now take three hundred books on an airplane in my carry-on luggage without violating the weight restrictions.

Ellen: More diversity is indeed in evidence. Not enough yet, but getting there. Embracing multiple voices in any art is crucial to the vitality of that art. Which also leads to Pat's remarks about ageism. Writing is not a competition between the young and the old.

Ursula: Then let us speak of how we have changed as a genre. Long ago, my children, in the days of my youth, our tribe was small and poor, skulking in exile on the margins of the rich kingdom of Literaturia. When we attempted to approach, we were driven back with execrations and the throwing of fecal matter by the armed Critics with their battle cry of "Genre! Kill!" We found, however, that many readers so loved us that they came into exile to join us, calling their settlement Fandom, and even in Literaturia, many secretly welcomed us to their hearts and homes. Over the years, we have grown in numbers and strength, and there is much intercourse of various kinds, and exchange of mental goods. Nowadays, blue-blooded Literaturians, believing they understand our simple customs, often imitate them, badly. Some of our tribe have become somewhat respectable in the streets of Literaturia, and pass, at times, almost unscathed among the Critics. The heights of the cities, however, and the great prizes to be found there, are still closed to us. I urge you to continue on the way of your tribal Elders, my children: Ignore execrations, seduce Critics, infiltrate curricula, and keep on truckin'.

Ellen: Yes, yes, yes. The walls have become more permeable between our genre and the "literary" genre in the past thirty years and I hope this is an ongoing development. There are failures of course. I've watched writers of excellent literary fiction fail horribly at writing sf/f. And I've seen anger aimed at those writers by us (myself included) for poaching on our territory. Because of ongoing negative experiences with mainstream critics, our community has become more than a little defensive and possibly too insular.

I think it would be useful for us to be more generous than those who dismiss our work and embrace the best examples of sf/f published outside our walls.

Pat: I think most of the time, the—animosity is not really the word I want but it will have to do at the moment—the animosity aimed at mainstream writers who write genre is not really territoriality. It's not "How dare you come into our clubhouse!" It's usually because they've reinvented the wheel and think they're being innovative and original. And a lot of mainstream critics start swooning about how innovative and original they are, praising ideas that they have previously sneered at in genre books. Kazuo Ishiguro's *Never Let Me Go,* for example—I'm not going to trash it, it was a fine book. It was even nominated for the Arthur C. Clarke Award. When it was made it into A Major Motion Picture, critics talked about not wanting to reveal the Big Secret. But every genre reader had probably already guessed. It was a variation on a premise that Robert Silverberg accomplished decades earlier in 5,000 words. Most writers would agree that if you want to write mysteries, you've got to read mysteries; if you want to write westerns, you've got to read westerns; if you want to write romances, you've got to read romances. But for some reason, the you've-got-to-read-it rule often seems to go out the window—or out the airlock—for science fiction. I'd hate to think this is because some people feel once they've seen *Alien* or *Star Wars,* they're good to go.

The other problem with genre published outside our walls is often the writers and/or publishers don't want it included in the genre. I was a judge for the Clarke Award the year *The Road* by Cormac McCarthy was published. The publisher refused to submit the book to the judges—they didn't want the genre taint. They did not want it considered for a science fiction award because it wasn't science fiction, they said. And how many times have we read that this or that book or movie or TV series isn't science fiction because "it's about something that could really happen"?

And sometimes, it's just the critics or the publishers who feel that way—the writers themselves are more open. Kazuo Ishiguro came to the Clarke Award event the year he was nominated, even though he had no idea whether he was going to win or not. I was in a group of people talking to him and he actually asked how we felt about an "outsider" showing up. We all told him we were really glad he was there, that his book was wonderful, and wished him good luck. He didn't win, but I guess he had a good time. When the British Library put on the big science fiction exhibition a few years ago, he showed up for that, too. He came to the inaugural evening and I saw him running from one exhibit to the next with his son. He told me he was thrilled, he loved seeing so many wonderful things: Some he was familiar with, some he'd only heard about, and some that were completely new to him. This was the event where Margaret Atwood, formerly a genre denier herself despite having won the first Arthur C. Clarke Award ever, delivered a short speech via videotape about how wonderful the field is.

Ellen is right—we've got to be friendlier. Every time mainstream writers publish genre books, we should dispatch teams of fun commandos to welcome them into the fold and charm their socks off.

In the very early days of my career, before I even really had a career, I used to entertain serious fantasies of migrating from genre to Literaturia, a la Richard McKenna. Then I discovered that I didn't want to write the holy scripture of Literaturia, I wanted to write genre.

And then I noticed something: While Literaturia is universally revered as producing the finest works of art, people look to popular culture—i.e., genre—for answers to most of their ethical and moral questions. Everything they ever needed to know, they have learned in kindergarten…and then from *Star Trek.* It was not Literaturia that spearheaded the change from screaming ingénue needing rescue by a brave, handsome male; it was *Buffy the Vampire Slayer*. Yes, the Twi-hards came with sparkly immortal vampires and pale young women wanting to be killed, but Buffy's Scooby gang laughed at them.

It was actually Robert Bloch who told me the Secret of Life—or at least the Secret of *My* Life—one night at a Florida literary conference in 1980. He said, "Very few people can tell you who won the Pulitzer Prize for fiction in 1976. But ask who won the Hugo Award for Best Novel that same year and thousands of people will shout, 'Joe Haldeman, *The Forever War!*'"

In Literaturia, they give each other awards and then forget. They get their names in the paper and then forget. Our books are handed down from one generation to the next, from one enthusiast to another. We don't forget as easily.

Mary: What this conversation makes me aware of is that while it might seem that the same battles are being fought over and over, each victory shapes the field. My generation of writers entered with the expectation of being treated as equals in science fiction and fantasy, because that is the precedent that women had fought for. When we discover that it is still not the case, being told that it's better than it used to be isn't quite enough.

We write science fiction and imagine the future we want to live in. We want that future now.

Seeing how the field has changed gives me perspective on the future that I'm living in and, hopefully, will help women writing today continue to destroy science fiction for subsequent generations of writers.

~

Pat Cadigan is a multi-award-winning author of science fiction. Her first collection, Patterns, was honoured with the Locus Award in 1990, and she has won the Arthur C. Clarke Award in 1992 and 1995 for her novels *Synners* and *Fools*. Her novelette, "The Girl-Thing Who Went Out for Sushi," won the Hugo in 2013.

Ellen Datlow has been editing science fiction, fantasy, and horror short fiction for almost thirty years. She was fiction editor of *OMNI Magazine* and *SCIFICTION* and has edited more than fifty anthologies, including the horror half of the long-running *The Year's Best Fantasy and Horror*. She currently acquires short stories for Tor.com, and is the editor for *Nightmare*'s Women Destroy Horror! special issue (due out October 2014).

Nancy Kress's fiction has won four Nebulas (for "Out of All Them Bright Stars," "Beggars in Spain," "The Flowers of Aulit Prison," and "Fountain of Age"), two Hugos (for "Beggars in Spain" and "The Erdmann Nexus"), a Sturgeon (for "The Flowers of Aulit Prison"), and a John W. Campbell Memorial Award (for *Probability Space*). Her work has been translated into Swedish, French,

Italian, German, Spanish, Polish, Croatian, Lithuanian, Romanian, Japanese, and Russian, and Klingon, none of which she can read. She also teaches regularly at summer conferences and has written three book about writing.

Ursula K. Le Guin has published twenty-one novels, eleven volumes of short stories, four collections of essays, twelve books for children, six volumes of poetry and four of translation, and has received many honors and awards including the Hugo, Nebula, National Book Award, and the PEN-Malamud. Her most recent publications are *Finding My Elegy* (New and Selected Poems, 1960-2010) and *The Unreal and the Real* (Selected Short Stories), 2012.

~

Mary Robinette Kowal is the author of *Shades of Milk and Honey* (Tor, 2010) and *Glamour in Glass* (Tor, 2012). In 2008 she received the Campbell Award for Best New Writer, and in 2011, her short story "For Want of a Nail" won the Hugo Award for Short Story. Her work has been nominated for the Hugo, Nebula and Locus awards. Her stories appear in *Asimov's*, *Clarkesworld*, and several Year's Best anthologies. Mary, a professional puppeteer, also performs as a voice actor, recording fiction for authors such as Elizabeth Bear, Cory Doctorow and John Scalzi. She lives in Chicago with her husband Rob and over a dozen manual typewriters. Visit maryrobinettekowal.com

FEATURE INTERVIEW: KELLY SUE DECONNICK

JENNIFER WILLIS

Kelly Sue DeConnick writes comic books for Image, Dark Horse, and Marvel. Her credits include *Avengers Assemble, Pretty Deadly, Ghost, Supergirl, Captain Marvel*, and the forthcoming *Bitch Planet*. She is married to writer Matt Fraction. They have two children, two cats, one dog, and the occasional backyard coyote. She lives in Portland, Oregon.

An outspoken feminist who grew up reading comics, DeConnick emphasizes that there aren't nearly enough women writing comics—or working in science fiction and fantasy in general—but notes that the gender conversation is at least happening now. DeConnick may not have envisioned Carol Danvers as a purely feminist hero, but Carol's transition from Ms. Marvel to Captain Marvel has sent (positive) shockwaves through the comics community. In a larger media culture in which "our bodies are not our own," she laments that the idealized "broke-back" pose is still too common for female characters—sometimes even in her own comics—and laughs over some readers' outrage that Captain Marvel is wearing pants.

Lightspeed caught up with DeConnick at her dining room table to get her take on sexism and feminism in comics and in sci-fi/fantasy, and to talk about storytelling, success, and the price of humanity.

• • •

How did you become interested in comics?

My dad was in the Air Force. I grew up on military bases. Comics are very much a part of military culture, or they were at least in the '70s. In the

U.S., the dominant genre is the superhero. These are people who are giving their lives to service. There's a patriotic aspect to a lot of our books. On base growing up, they took up a whole wall at the bookstore, Stars and Stripes. All the GIs read them. They were forty-five cents apiece. I'd spend like half of my allowance getting new comics, and the other half buying used comics at the swap meet on weekends.

What challenges have you encountered as a woman writing comics?

The thing that gets under my skin the most is the perception that somehow I followed my husband into the business. I'm married to another comic book creator (Matt Fraction), and he's extraordinarily gifted and wrote for Marvel Comics for a number of years before I did. So the assumption is that he got me my work. We actually met because of a mutual interest in comics. We met on the Warren Ellis posting board. I read comics long before Matt became a part of my life. Because I was a writer in New York and because of who I was friends with, Matt was my plus-one to the Editor-in-Chief's birthday party years before either one of us worked at Marvel. We each got there on our own merits. That's a thing that's a little maddening.

There was a kerfuffle a year or so ago because of a convention that we had been invited to. An Irish news site that was covering the convention listed the guests. In my bio, the first line was "wife of Matt Fraction." No one else's marital status was mentioned anywhere, including Matt's. I very politely pointed it out and asked that it be changed. Friends of mine, having my back and being very sweet and very funny people, all decided that their bios should indicate their marital status to Matt Fraction. So everyone changed their bios on Twitter and Tumblr to indicate that they were not, in fact, the wife of Matt Fraction, in case we all needed to state that. [That] kind of took the edge off a little bit. I know nobody intended anything malicious, but it's those little cuts, you know?

You don't want to be a bitch. You don't want to make people uncomfortable. But the older I get, the more comfortable I am making other people uncomfortable! (Laughs) It wasn't a hundred years ago that women were basically chattel. Because women before me have been willing to make people uncomfortable, I have the privileges I have today. So maybe if I'm willing to make people uncomfortable, my daughter has a little bit less of a fight ahead of her.

When you were a kid, your favorite comics included *Wonder Woman*, *Vampirella*, and the *Archie Digests*. What are your favorites today?

My pat answer for my favorite comic is *Planetary* by Warren Ellis, although it would be a close call with [Neil Gaiman's] *Sandman*. Those were the books where I felt like I was really discovering a new mythology, which scratches the same itch that *Wonder Woman* did when I was a kid.

How have female characters in comics changed since you were a kid?

For a while, we regressed. There were a lot of really progressive comics when I was a kid. I didn't happen to read *Ms. Marvel* as I was growing up, but I've gone back and read a lot of *Ms. Marvel* from the '70s now. *Ms. Marvel* was an overtly feminist comic, unapologetically so. People think I'm heavy-handed, but they got away with stuff I could never do!

Brian Bendis has been at the top of the industry for a number of years. Brian writes his female characters like women, like people, you know? And always has.

The dudes that assert that there is a male audience, that women are there to be avenged or rescued or anything else you could do with a lamp, are always going to write like that and are always going to make those assumptions about the market.

I have noticed that the conversation seems to be happening more. But I'm wondering if I'm in an echo chamber because of the way that social media works, which is where we tend to have these conversations today. I follow and am followed by people who are prone to having these conversations.

What's on your project wish list for the next few years?

I want to write a novel. I have four ideas. I've talked to a couple of different novelists, friends of mine, as to what to start with. You know the first one's probably not going to be very good! So do I want to save my favorite idea, or what? Apparently, I'm overthinking this. Chelsea Cain actually came over and sat down in my office and listened to me prattle on for a little while, and then really encouraged me. There was one [idea] she really lit up on, so that's probably going to be the one I start with. And then we'll see!

I've had "write a novel" on my ten-year list for like seven years. So I'm really going to have to start at some point.

It's not like I've never written prose, but I've never written lengthy prose. Like, when I was a kid, I was on swim team. And I would also fantasize about, "Man, I wish I was a runner." Because when you swim, you push your hand down and you don't move that far forward. You lose effort to the water. And I always felt cheated by that. I just wanted to run. Like, if you push off with this much effort when you run, you go that far forward! So it's always this "grass is always greener" thing.

In writing comics, I always feel like there's water that slips through my fingers. But I have to have this frickin' page turn right here! And so I don't get to expand this scene as much as it really needs to be because the beat doesn't work with the page turn, and there's this artifice that feels like the things that go through my fingers. So there's this fantasy I have that with a novel, I can pace it however I want! There are no page turns. Right now, because it's nothing I'm working on at the moment except for taking some notes, it feels like just this decadent freedom.

I'm fairly certain that as soon as I'm into it, I will be longing for the structure of comics! (Laughs)

You were inspired by the Mercury 13 when reimagining Carol Danvers as Captain Marvel. Which others have influenced and informed your work?

Chuck Yeager is another big one on Captain Marvel. Specifically from the Mercury 13, Jerry Truhill and Jerrie Cobb. Truhill is more of an influence on the character Helen, but there's DNA of both of those women and Yeager in my concept of Carol. The WASPs of World War II. Not any particular pilot, but their drive and a lot of the indignities that they suffered.

We call the relaunch of Captain Marvel "Higher, Further, Faster, More." That's kind of what all of those pilots share, that need to push boundaries. Swagger.

When [the WASPs] died in service, because they were not officially military pilots, because they were officially civilians, the service would not pay to send their bodies home. So the girls would take up collections. They were also not supposed to be buried with the flag and military honors, but most of the families said, "Fuck that," and did it anyway.

That pissed me off to the point of tears. They were mistreated by their own colleagues. Jackie Cochran, who was the head of the [WASP] program, was bug-fuck crazy. But at one point there were apparently some male fliers who were not comfortable with the fact that there were women flying their planes, even though the women that were doing those jobs freed them up for combat positions. There was speculation that some of the women's planes were being sabotaged, or given low priority for servicing. There was a death after a crash in Texas, I believe, and Jackie Cochran went to investigate and found no foul play. But then, years later, she said she had in fact uncovered sabotage, but that they had decided to cover it up for fear that it would end the program.

Jackie Cochran was Jackie Cochran, so you don't know if that's true or not. But if it is, someone got away with murder.

Have we reached a post-feminist world where characters—of any gender— can be simply who they are without the expectation of labels like "feminist"?

In a real-life context, I understand there is a movement to rebrand feminism or change the name. Maybe I am old, but I don't think there's anything wrong with it. I'm a proud feminist. I'm not ceding to the people who use "feminazi." You know what I mean? Feminism is about fairness. My husband is a feminist. My son is a feminist. It's about fairness.

Am I writing *Captain Marvel* as a feminist tome? I'm not. But I do think that's at the core of her character. My conception of her is really about "pilot." But if you go back, it's why she was created—*Ms. Marvel* was an overt reference to *Ms. Magazine*. Some of the later issues, it's like Gloria Steinem fanfic.

It's not my main focus, but it's not something I particularly shy away from.

What's with the duck face?

At conventions, people freak when they want to take pictures with you. It's a fun way to give us both something to do and end up with a silly picture. You don't have to worry about trying to look pretty, because you're making a duck face! I love that I am developing a gallery of duck face photos with people who are all much better looking than that face would have them appear. It's an awkward moment for two strangers, you know? We can just do it and it's fun and everybody can just kind of relax and chill.

What advice have you given to other women who aspire to work in comics?

The biggest thing is to make comics. A lot of people have this notion that they should start making comics when someone hires them to make comics, and that they should instead work on pitching comics. And that's not really right. I'm not going to hire a plumber to fix my sink who's never fixed a sink before, you know? You need to fix some sinks.

You can either draw your own or use photos or you can find an artist online and work together—find somebody who's just starting out as well. And understand that you're no genius and they're not going to be a genius either. You learn and grow together. One of my favorite comic book pairings in the industry is Kieron Gillen and Jamie McKelvie. Their early comics are kind of stiff. I think there was tracing happening early on? But they've been working together for years, and now they're making some of the best comics you can read. *Phonogram. Young Avengers.* They're fantastic. They worked together and developed their skills together.

If we're talking specifically about female creators, I think that we sometimes have this notion that sexism is worse in comics than it is anywhere else. I don't think that's true. I think that sexism is a part of our world, not just publishing. Not just comics. You know, welcome to culture. This is the thing you're going to have to face no matter what industry you go into, so go into one you enjoy! If you're going to fight the fight, you might as well fight it for something that's going to be a good time, right?

Whether you're male or female, you've gotta start making comics. And it's scary. I get it. It's terrifying. But you have to do it anyway.

What do you love most about working in comics?

Being done.

I think in our culture, superhero comics are still very dominant. Because of TV show stereotyping, we have these notions about comic book readers as basement-dwelling bottom-feeders, or completely socially inept weirdos. And there're certainly those comics that attract those readers, but there's also a wealth of comics that attract readers who are drawn to a kind of heroic ideal-ism. They are extraordinary people, and I am blessed to have them in my life.

What's it like to be an "inspiring feminist figure" in your own industry?

I'll take that! That's great!

(Laughs) I have a lot of growing to do yet as a writer and as a person. But if something that I do or say moves someone to make some forward action, that's a gift to me. I'm a human being. I'm going to screw things up. I think most people are very forgiving of that. Most people understand that. I'm also very open about how, you know, I'm a mess! (Laughs)

Somebody wrote me a while ago and asked a question that was like, "Tell me about your work-life balance." And I was like, *WHAT* work-life balance?! I do *not* have this figured out. I can tell you what I do, how little I sleep, and how tired I am all the time. I have some adjustments I'm making now to try to make things a little better.

I think people sometimes want there to be an easy answer. *Pretty Deadly* deals with a lot of mythic elements. It's one of those books that we get a lot of goose-bump moments as we're putting it together, where things, seemingly unrelated pieces, clearly go together. It feels like we're more discovering the book than writing it.

It's a very adult book. My six-year-old boy saw a couple of pages I had laid out on the table. It was a violent passage. It was an animal being shot. So he had a lot of questions, and we talked about it. Then he told me about a dream he had had. He had hurt a hummingbird. He hadn't meant to hurt it, but he hit it with a water gun and it fell out of the air. He went to check on it and he said, "I tried to give it my breath, but it was too late."

It was very sweet and very sad, but we talked about how we hurt things as we move through the world, whether we mean to or not. I think that that is more the price of our humanity than the being hurt. Then we talked about Jenny and the bunny. It was a very similar thing. Jenny didn't so much mean to hurt the bunny as just see what would happen. But in the fiction space, Jenny and the bunny became connected, and the bunny tells her story.

Because of that conversation, I wanted to include a hummingbird in *Pretty Deadly*, so I started reading about them. And I found this study that was fascinating. They were trying to figure out how a hummingbird that weighs less than a penny stays aloft in the rain. And they did all this research on how they do it. And what they found out was, the hummingbird works harder in the rain. There's no secret. There's no magic. It's harder to fly in the rain.

That's the thing I keep coming back to lately, this notion that some things are just hard! You just have to work harder.

What do you think about female body image in comics?

We're in a culture where our bodies are not our own. I think having a daughter has changed that conversation considerably for me as well.

Every once in a while something gets by me. I've got an issue going to press that has a shot of a much beloved character to me where—it's called a broke-back pose, where you can see both breasts and both butt cheeks at the same time. I asked that it be corrected, but I don't know that it's going to happen before the book has to ship because we're putting these things together in thirty days. It's an impossible amount of work in thirty days.

The nay-sayer response is always, "Well, you have to understand that the male characters are idealized as well." So then my head explodes, and then hopefully after I calm down we have a conversation about how the male figure, the male superhero, is idealized to communicate the idea of strength. The female figure is idealized to communicate the notion of sexual availability. Which is why you want both breasts and both ass checks to face forward. It's why their costumes are cut to expose as much as possible. I've had to place a word balloon over a crotch because I could see her cervix; we were having a pelvic exam on the page, you know? And I'm not a prude!

That assumes a male heterosexual audience, which is not a message I want to send to my female reader. I don't want her to feel unwelcome.

From the moment we start consuming media, we are taught how to identify with the male protagonist. Women are so under-represented in our media. We have no problem making that leap, but we don't ask young men to do the same because women in our society have a lower status and you don't want to imagine yourself down, right?

There's an apocryphal story about how J.K. Rowling chose to make it Harry Potter instead of Harriet Potter because it would be more universal. Apparently, this is not a true story, but you get the idea. There is this assumption in media that the male character is default and you have to justify any variation from that. I find that offensive.

I was asked in an interview not too terribly long ago, "You're doing another book with a female lead, aren't you afraid of being pigeon-holed?" I was like, "Has that question ever been asked of a man in the history of ever?" We're half the population! Was Hemingway pigeon-holed? What?!

I write across genres. I write a superhero solo title. I write a funny team book. I write a ghost story. I write a horror-Western. What am I going to be pigeon-holed as? A girl?

I think it's time that we stop supporting that structure.

What does it mean to you to be creating and writing strong women characters for a new generation of readers?

I'm not doing anything that's never been done before. I'm not even doing anything that's never been done with this character before. You know, maybe it's just payback. A thank you to the Wonder Woman comics of my youth or the Ms. Marvel comics of my youth.

Are there enough women working in comics and in sci-fi/fantasy?

Oh, hell no. I think mentorship is crucial. I try to hire women every opportunity I get. I ask for women as much as possible. If I can't take a job and I need to recommend someone else, I try to recommend a woman.

Who was a mentor for you?

Brian Bendis and Warren Ellis are the ones that spring to mind. There have certainly been women who have gone before me in the industry that have opened doors. Gail Simone springs to mind. Louise Simonson, Trina Robbins, certainly. Colleen Doran. I could go on and on. There are one or two names working now, too, but it's not enough. We're still, I think, under ten percent? We might be under five percent. That's not good enough.

I personally think we should aim higher than fifty percent, too. I want like ninety. Throw the bums out.

What about sexism in the comics themselves?

Where it was a problem, it's still a problem. There have always been comics that were not hideously offensive, and there still are. If that's what you want, you can certainly find it.

Every once in a while I'll get a letter from somebody who's mad that Carol's wearing pants. Which is hilarious, because Carol's pants are skin-tight and shiny. You know, if you could just color that flesh-color, it would be exactly the same, my friend!

I am not trying to eradicate T&A comics. They are always going to exist. I would just like for there to be some other options. Like, dude, they still make *Bondage Fairies*, I believe. Go get you some. But we're taking this one.

At the end of your career, what do you hope your lasting impact will be?

If I've written a story that has made someone feel connected to their humanity, feel that they are less alone in their experience of this world, then I have been a success.

If I have, by my presence, shown another woman that it can be done, then I have been a success. You know, I didn't grow up Kelly Sue. I use my middle name because my first name is gender-neutral. I want it to be clear that I am a woman writing this book.

If something happened to me tomorrow, I would feel pretty good about this part of my world. I would like for that to not happen, because I want to see my kids grow up. So let's just put this out to the universe, that this is not some kind of ironic interview!

Maybe I just don't like the pressure of it, but I don't like the notion of the writer as shaman, or the artist as special. I am much more comfortable with a worker among workers. You show up and you work, whether the muse decided to turn up that day or not.

It brings us back to the hummingbird. Some days it rains. Guess what? It's harder on those days. I get to feel like I'm doing my job and I feel a part of a bigger picture.

There's a civil rights attorney that wears her Captain Marvel dog tags under her suit when she goes to court. That's somebody who's doing something important.

There are two different women suffering from MS who have written to me about the second arc of our last run and how Carol dealing with her tumor spoke to them, because of the experience of needing to ask for help and that feeling of having been betrayed by your body. Those letters taught me about the importance of representation in a way I've never really understood before. It's so vital to see ourselves reflected in fiction.

We are fifty percent of the population. Why are we not fifty percent of the cast, you know? Why are we not fifty percent of the heroes? It means so much to see ourselves. Stories are how we make sense of the world. Just that message that you matter, that you count, that you are here.

~

Jennifer Willis is a writer and editor in Portland, Oregon. She has written for *The Oregonian*, *The Christian Science Monitor*, Salon.com, and *The Writer*. In fiction, she is the author of the urban fantasy/YA series Valhalla. Find her online at jennifer-willis.com.

"THE STATUS QUO CANNOT HOLD"

A FEW WORDS FROM WOMEN WHO WROTE/ARE WRITING THE GODDAMN BOOK ON DESTROYING SCIENCE FICTION

TRACIE WELSER

Science fiction is experiencing a new Golden Age. Did you know?

Science fiction is a thriving field of increasing diversity, the subject of study at universities and symposiums and conferences around the world. And it's increasingly feminist.

That's right, I said it. Feminist. Sure, naysayers cling to the past and drag their feet, but they always have. Audacious imaginings for the future dance on. *We* dance on.

My desire to dance and dare and imagine comes from a basic human yearning: The future has to be better than the world we have now. *It has to be.* But we have to imagine a better future before it can become.

The utopian yearning at the center of feminist SF means it's about more than robots and rockets and alien worlds, even though I want those, too. But I want my literature to confront what's wrong with world: imperialism, racism, sexism, and ableism. Instead of holding up those structures (oh, Heinlein, you broke my teenage heart), give me tools to tear them down. Give me a vision of a better future. Or better still, step back. I'll write my vision. Science fiction is my playground, my toolbox, the literature of the future, the literature of ideas, of dreams, and I dream a utopian future.

That's feminist SF, to me, and it's bigger and bolder than a handful of "strong women" characters, what some folks call the "add-women-and-stir" method of inclusion to playing fields that otherwise remain unaltered.

So, imagine my delight when I learned of The Sally Miller Gearhart "Worlds Beyond World" Symposium on the subject of Feminist Utopian Thought! Anything "utopian," and I'm *there*, count me in. Add "feminist," and it's like cookies in my ice cream. This delicious but all-too-brief event was hosted by the Center for the Study of Women in Society at the University of Oregon, home to the Science Fiction, Speculative Fiction, and Fantasy Collections of the Knight Library, a significant archive including papers from feminist SF writers such as Joanna Russ. The Symposium was one part of a three-day event celebrating the 40th Anniversary of the Center, a day one participant referred to as a "mini Wiscon."

This Symposium brought into conversation a number of women I admire: Ursula K. Le Guin performed a reading and participated in a witty Q&A after a warm introduction from Molly Gloss; Dr. Kathryn Allan was awarded the 2013 Le Guin Feminist Science Fiction Fellowship; trailblazing authors Suzy McKee Charnas, Vonda McIntyre, L. Timmel Duchamp, Kate Wilhelm, Andrea Hairston, and Larissa Lai spoke on complex subjects dear to my heart (the history and vital work of feminist utopian narrative). More remarkable women made up the audience; Gearhart herself was present and briefly stood to give the assembly a dignified wave.

The title alone! The participants! As Duchamp later remarked, "Feminist SF is a grand conversation." The conversation here included writers and academics (as well as writer-academics) and, in short, asked where did this begin, and where are we going?

Of the Symposium's four panels, two stirred the utopian yearnings dearest to my heart. Brilliance flew far and fast, and I was helpless to capture all but a few salient points. In session number two, "Feminist Science Fiction as Political Theory," moderator Larissa Lai asked about the relationship between SF and the 1970s women's movement, and the participants highlighted the fact that simply writing as women was deeply political. Suzy McKee Charnas said, "Raising questions in a story was a hugely political act…the whole thing reeked of politics from the beginning and still does."

When asked, "Is our work propaganda?" Vonda McIntyre replied, "I thought we finished with this debate about women in scifi in the 70s...Our work has been called shrill, strident, but suburban lit is also propaganda."

Most passionate of the panelists, Kate Wilhelm stated that "the status quo was male adventures and women wringing their hands and saying, 'be careful'...'she writes like a man' was a high compliment! Well, goddamn it, I didn't, and I don't." She expressed "distress" at "how far they want to roll back the curtain," and firmly asserted that "utopia equals absolute equal rights. "The real message," she said, "is that we are not satisfied with the status quo, and we might nudge others or hit them over the head if we need to...The status quo cannot hold."

Lai also asked provocative questions about ways of knowing and challenges to patriarchal knowledge production. Aqueduct [Press] editor and author L. Timmel Duchamp noted that emphasis on masculinization of female characters, particularly in urban fantasy, highlights "extraordinary women" rather than "ordinary" ones, and is a substitution rather than a challenge to the normative emphasis on individualism. Charnas pointed to newer authors like Nnedi Okorafor, whose work introduces readers to diverse cultural contexts and values.

Session number three, "Building Feminist Worlds," moderated by Margaret McBride, asked, in part, how do we get to utopia? Is there a "there" there, and how can we avoid essentialism/tokenism while building that inclusive world?

Larissa Lai pointed to the risks, saying "I don't want to lose our histories... our specificity [in order to avoid essentialism]." And those histories, Lai says, are often nasty, awful and complicated. She noted the potential of "metaphoricity," of SF to create new forms, such as when Octavia Butler invented her own species with their own "bodily and cultural logic." L. Timmel Duchamp added, "We need fictional identities to be as complicated as we can stand." On categories, Andrea Hairston says, "I protest that way of knowing the world...I don't need to rely on those paradigms. They're on our bodies."

Molly Gloss expressed the need for not only new ways of thinking about character, but narrative itself, saying, "We need stories where conflict doesn't feature as central to story." And Andrea Hairston further linked the social message of feminist narrative to political and theoretical thought, saying "I take it to my lab [storytelling]...I eat theory every day," which strikes me as an elegant way of saying that there's really no difference between theory and story.

In a follow-up interview, fellowship recipient Kathryn Allen (whose work focuses on representations of disability in SF) said, "Women have been 'destroying' SF since the beginning. Mary Shelley's *Frankenstein* is, arguably, the first identifiable science fiction text...I'm totally biased when it comes to thinking about 'women destroying SF' because to me, women BUILT SF."

This event was thrilling to me because it created an environment for conversations about what's at the heart of feminism, about what kind of world we have, what kind we want, and the lengths to which we will or will not go in order to achieve it, what Larissa Lai calls "utopian tactics." These "tactics," Suzy Charnas says, "are personal," and utopia is a process, not a destination. Like their fiction, the participants present a complex dialogue, an important one, and in my opinion, quite possibly the most important one in the world as we know it. These authors and their texts (which you, dear reader, are free to seek out so you may join the conversation) ask vital questions about the ways in which current models of society and citizenship prevent the actualization of more equitable visions, and suggest that other modes, other futures are possible. In this way, they suggest that *change in the present* is also possible.

This symposium was invigorating, but it wasn't perfect; it left me wanting more discussion about pervasive heteronorms and white privilege in SF. Most energizing, however, was a simple realization: this isn't a new fight, and we needn't pull any punches. Our fantasies shape reality. As Andrea Hairston bluntly states, "Fuck those people who say you can't go from being a descendent of slaves to world leader! You have to rehearse the impossible."

Science fiction is a thriving genre of utopian futurism, and any lingering backlash is just tinny background noise. That small noise is drowned out by gorgeous, compelling, and sometimes discomfiting words, the music we're creating together. Just look at this year's Nebula ballot. The conversation continues.

We're dancing on.

For further conversing:
- *Report from Planet Midnight*, Nalo Hopkinson
- *Meet Me at Infinity*, James Tiptree, Jr.
- *The Secret Feminist Cabal*, Helen Merrick
- *Writing the Other*, Nisi Shaw and Cynthia Ward

A few recommendations by Symposium panelists, must-reads and/or works they would love to see adapted as film:
- *Who Fears Death*, Nnedi Okorafor
- *The New Moon's Arms*, Nalo Hopkinson
- *Red Wood and Wildfire*, Andrea Hairston
- "Stories for Men," John Kessel
- *Fledgling*, Octavia Butler
- *Air*, Geoff Ryman
- *Four Ways to Forgiveness*, Ursula K. Le Guin
- *The Adventures of Alyx*, Joanna Russ

~

Tracie Welser's work has appeared in *Interzone*, *Crossed Genres*, and *Outlaw Bodies*. Her master's thesis, "Fantastic Visions: On the Necessity of Feminist Utopian Narrative," as well as her current novel-in-progress, suggest that she may be obsessed with the idea of actualizing a feminist future through fiction. A graduate of the Clarion West Writers Workshop, Tracie currently resides in California. She blogs at thisisnotanowl.com.

How to Engineer a Self-Rescuing Princess

Stina Leicht

Science fiction not only taught me how to save myself, it taught me that self-rescuing was essential. Here's how.

Step 1: Here Be Monsters

I was two or three years old when I learned that something was wrong with me. It began with a family trip to a natural history museum. I remember a room with a glass case, containing shelves with rows upon rows of human skulls. In my memory, the case was vast. It took up an entire wall. Some of the skulls had dark brown or black patches with numbers on them. Now that I think about it, these were most likely labels for various bones, but being small I didn't know. I asked my parents what was wrong with the skulls. My two-or-three-year-old brain fixed upon, "Some of the skulls are boy skulls and some are girl skulls." Thus, I interpreted the answer as "The skulls with the dark splotches on them—the *abnormal skulls*—are girl skulls." And that was the first time the thought entered my mind that I didn't want to be a girl. *Girls are **wrong, bad, and diseased**.*

After that, we entered a room of Egyptian artifacts. The exhibit featured a sarcophagus tilted up against the wall in a standing position. There was no protective glass case. The only barrier between myself and the evil mummy lurking inside the open stone box was a red velvet rope.

I'd seen *Johnny Quest*. I knew mummies walked. I also knew that their favorite prey was little girls. Everything on television and film said that monsters targeted girls. I screamed and ran for my life.

My father (who really did mean well) chased me down and dragged me—literally kicking and screaming—back into that room. He was a mechanical engineer and was determined to raise his child to believe only in reality. None of that fairytale nonsense would fill her brain. Facts need only apply. He insisted that I had nothing to fear, the mummy was dead, and it wasn't going to eat me. I was in no way convinced. Thus, he demonstrated the mummy's inert quality by lifting me over the velvet safety barrier and shoving me inches from the dormant monster's clutches.

Needless to say, that didn't go over too well.

My mother intervened. We left the museum in shame, and my father grew reluctant to take his kids anywhere where we might embarrass him. After that I had frequent nightmares—any kid would. I became obsessed. I researched mummies in the library and memorized every detail about them that I could. I was possibly the only seven-year-old girl who could recite the exact formula and process used to create an Egyptian mummy in the whole state of Missouri.[1] It didn't stop at mummies. I did this for every monster I could imagine. My motivations were tactical. I wanted to know what the "silver bullet" was. Monsters had weaknesses, and the hero of the story took advantage of those weaknesses. Yes, I understood that the hero of the story was always male. However, I also knew from experience that men couldn't be relied upon to protect little girls. Worse, as I grew older, I came to understand that sometimes men were the monsters, and like my father and the mummy, other men couldn't be relied upon to believe in the danger. Therefore, I had to protect myself—even if it wasn't okay to do so—if I was going to survive.

STEP 2: PROVIDE A ROLE MODEL

Somewhere in the middle of all this I found science fiction. I couldn't have been older than four when I had a babysitter who wanted to watch this new television show called *Star Trek*. I blame her for making me into a Trekkie. As it happened, this was the night of the first inter-racial kiss on American television. Lt. Uhura (and Nichelle Nichols) became my new hero, and Science

---

1. And quite possibly Texas as well. This led to a rather interesting situation in which my third grade history teacher made the mistake of asking if anyone in the class knew anything about ancient Egypt. She had no idea what was inside the mind of the skinny, little girl in the pink dress and bows. So, of course she picked me when I raised my hand. I was shy. I didn't do that very often. Imagine her shock when I described iron hooks being shoved up dead people's noses to scrape the brains out of their skulls. I didn't know anything was wrong until halfway through my recitation when I noticed the class had grown very quiet and teacher's face was a little green. Strangely, I seem to recall a parent/teacher conference after that.

Fiction became the place where the world's injustices—even the ones of which absolutely no one spoke—were openly and thoughtfully discussed. Sometimes even solutions were found. Science Fiction was amazing and powerful. It was The Future! I remember asking my babysitter to draw the starship Enterprise and tacking it to the wall next to my bed. My parents came home and freaked out. The picture vanished, and I was punished for the tiny hole in the plaster.

Still, that didn't stop me. I'd found where I belonged. In the third grade (not long after the infamous mummy recitation) my English teacher gave me *A Wrinkle in Time* by Madeleine L'Engle.[2] In it, L'Engle informed me that girls weren't in any way limited to answering the starship's phone. *Girls in Science Fiction could be scientists.* They didn't even have to choose between being a scientist and a mother. *They could grow up to be both.* It was like a bomb went off in my head. From that point forward I consumed all the science fiction and fantasy I could find. By the time I'd read *The Handmaid's Tale* by Margaret Atwood I'd learned that not only was it okay to save myself, it was imperative.

Step 3: Reading Material

First, I'm going to list the stories that I've read and have influenced me.
- *A Wrinkle in Time* by Madeleine L'Engle
- The works of Zilpha Keatley Snyder
- *The Handmaid's Tale* by Margaret Atwood
- *The Blue Sword* by Robin McKinley
- *Cyteen* by C.J. Cherryh
- *The Snow Queen* by Joan D. Vinge
- *Dragonriders of Pern* by Anne McCaffrey
- The Darkover series by Marion Zimmer Bradley
- *Frankenstein* by Mary Shelley
- *Push of the Sky* by Camille Alexa
- "Transfer of Ownership" (a short story) by Christie Yant

And here's the second list, consisting of works that I haven't read yet but mean to read.
- *The Left Hand of Darkness* by Ursula K. Le Guin
- *How to Suppress Women's Writing* by Joanna Russ
- *Up the Walls of the World* by James Tiptree, Jr. (aka Alice Sheldon)
- *Parable of the Sower* by Octavia Butler
- *The Gate to Women's Country* by Sheri Tepper
- *Woman on the Edge of Time* by Marge Piercy

---

2. I still have my Scholastic Books copy, believe it or not.

- *The Empress of Mars* by Kage Baker
- *Vatta's War* by Elizabeth Moon
- *Ancillary Justice* by Anne Leckie
- *Memoirs of a Spacewoman* by Naomi Mitchison
- *Who Fears Death* by Nnedi Okorafor
- *The Female Man* by Joanna Russ
- *Herland* by Charlotte Perkins Gilman
- *Surfacing* by Margaret Atwood
- *Carnival* by Elizabeth Bear
- *Heaven Under Earth* by Aliette de Bodard
- *God's War* by Kameron Hurley
- *The Mad Scientist's Daughter* by Cassandra Rose Clarke
- *Fortune's Pawn* by Rachel Bach
- *Up Against It* by M.J. Locke
- *Peacekeeper* by Laura E. Reeve
- *Inheritance* by Malinda Lo
- *When We Wake* by Karen Healey

~

Stina Leicht is a two-time Campbell Award nominee for Best New Writer (2012 and 2013.) Her debut novel *Of Blood and Honey*, a historical fantasy set in 1970s Northern Ireland, was short-listed for the Crawford Award. The sequel, *And Blue Skies from Pain*, is available now. Her shorter fiction is also featured in Ann and Jeff VanderMeer's surreal anthology *Last Drink Bird Head*, and in the anthology *Rayguns Over Texas*.

SCREAMING TOGETHER

MAKING WOMEN'S VOICES HEARD

NISI SHAWL

Isn't this edition of *Lightspeed* awesome? Aren't you thrilled by the recent rise of similar projects promoting writing by women? Wouldn't it be fantastic if this sort of thing—women's genre stories and poems and genre-related non-fiction being published and read and noticed—happened every single day?

This article is about how to make it so.

Perhaps the most basic step is the one you've already taken: reading. By choosing to read a magazine issue written and edited entirely by women, you're supporting women's writing in a big way. Page hits matter.

"Screaming Together," the article's title, derives from Lilit Marcus's "What Happens When You Tell People You're Reading Only Women" (the-toast. net/2014/02/03/what-happens-when-you-tell-people-youre-reading-only-women). It refers to her idea that to avoid being drowned out by the prevalence of male voices, female authors have to scream. In an earlier piece, Marcus had vowed she'd read books exclusively by women for a year. You could do that, too.

Libraries buy more copies of books more people borrow. Circulation matters. Sales figures matter. An overwhelming trend in genre readers buying books by women could well lead to larger advances for woman authors.

In many ways, publicity matters at least as much as page hits, circulation, or sales. If you take Marcus's vow, use the #readwomen2014 hashtag. Talking, posting, and tweeting about what you're reading will let uninformed folks know that women do indeed write cyberpunk porn[1] and proto-Arthurian epics[2] and tales of talking space squids[3] and exploits of time-traveling revolutionaries[4]—all the myriad varieties of horror, fantasy, and science fiction imaginable. Make lists of what you discover. Give away extra copies. Nominate your favorites for awards.

Did you know that there are awards for women authors and for books written by women? They aren't genre-specific, but they don't rule out genre works, either. Just a few minutes searching on the internet revealed to me the presence of the Baileys Women's Prize for Fiction, the Rona Jaffe Foundation Writers' Awards, and the Women's National Book Association's Bookwoman Award. There may be more.

You can also nominate books by women for non-gender-specific awards within our field: the Nebula, the Crawford, the James Tiptree, Jr., and so on. The Carl Brandon Society's Parallax and Kindred Awards, for instance, go to writers of color and to authors of any background whose work expands our understanding of race. There is nothing about gender in their mission statements, and yet of the twin awards' thirteen recipients to date, eleven are women. The percentages of female Hugo and Nebula Award-winners are much lower. That can be fixed.

In addition to those presenting awards to women who write, many organizations exist to assist women authors in other ways: supporting our works' publication and marketing; providing technical back-up for podcasting and ebooks; offering educational opportunities and ways to share knowledge. To make this assistance more effective I recommend donating, joining, participating, and/or volunteering. Hedgebrook is the nonprofit sponsor of a genre-friendly women's literary retreat. The roster of relevant organizations firmly within SFF's boundaries includes Broad Universe, the Fem-SF listserv, and Aqueduct Press. (Note that Aqueduct identifies primarily as a supporter of feminist issues rather than women's issues.)

Of course, there's a societal background to this activity, and it has its effect on the presence and recognition of women writers. There are a few tropes I'd like to see subverted on that level, though I'm not sure how we ought to go about it. I wish, for instance that the competitiveness of publishing made better allowance for the non-assertiveness to which many women are culturally

---

1. Cecilia Tan: *The Velderet*
2. Evangeline Walton: The Mabinogion series
3. Vonda N. McIntyre: The Starfarers series
4. Marge Piercy: *Woman on the Edge of Time*

conditioned. The temporary solution I've found is to ask them repeatedly—*repeatedly*—REPEATEDLY if they'd like to be included in any creative project you have in mind. Conversely, it would be nice if there was more acceptance and even applause for women acting like bitches the way Charles Dickens acted like a bastard. And I fervently hope that someday, mash-ups of SFF with subgenres traditionally relegated to women (romance, "tea-cozy" mysteries, slash) will be accorded the respect given SFF cross-fertilized with traditionally masculine subgenres (police procedurals, military adventures).

None of us can upend societal attitudes all on our own. We can, however, contribute as individuals to the well-being of women authors we know personally. We can give them gifts: meals, money, magazine subscriptions, certificates for housecleaning or childcare services. We who are writers can encourage them in their endeavors—as Nalo Hopkinson and Octavia E. Butler have encouraged me—by taking their vocations seriously and frankly discussing with them the professional problems they encounter. We can even set private deadlines for them, as I do for K. Tempest Bradford.

Taking that last suggestion further, many of us should consider issuing women writers *public* deadlines. Though editing is a skill not everyone possesses, you'll never know whether you can do it or not unless you try. For over three years now, I've edited reviews for *The Cascadia Subduction Zone*, the feminist literary quarterly published by Aqueduct. Most of our coverage is devoted to SFF by women, and most of the reviewers I edit are women. This is my first long-term editorial gig.

"If you see something, say something," goes the U.S. Department of Homeland Security-sponsored adage. A number of us have seen something sexist, and said and done things about it. Hence the genesis of this, *Lightspeed*'s "Women Destroy Science Fiction!" issue, and its simultaneously spawned sister-issues focusing on horror and fantasy. Hence *Athena's Daughters*, an all-woman genre anthology edited by Jean Rabe, who resigned as the editor of the SFWA Bulletin due to controversy over the magazine's cover and contents. Hence *She Walks in Shadows*, Silvia Moreno-Garcia's projected volume of Lovecraftian fiction by women created in response to a Facebook post bemoaning the lack of "girls" who "like to play with squids."

Here's another quotation: "If there's a book that you want to read, but it hasn't been written yet, then you must write it." Or, I'll add to Toni Morrison's words of wisdom, you must edit it. Or publish it.

For what's the use of editing something unless it's published? And aren't the industry's current gatekeepers more part of the problem than of possible solutions? Well, yes. And no. There is a heritage of sexism tied to the traditional publishing industry, but that is changing. Meanwhile, numerous small presses have been willing to take the business risks necessary to gain significant ground in the representation of women. Additionally, there are other pathways available to those seeking to get their own work out into the world. Book View Café, a woman-founded publishing cooperative, pays its authors a whopping 95% of their titles' cover price. Indiegogo, Kickstarter, and other crowdfunding sites allow books' writers and editors to raise money for their printing, distributing, advertising, and more. You could be a publisher. If you have friends willing to back you.

The most recent count of non-genre-specific women authors reviewed in non-genre-specific venues is available online here: vidaweb.org/the-count-2013. It's not a pretty picture. Similar studies conducted by *Strange Horizons* (strangehorizons.com/blog/2012/04/the_2011_sf_count.shtml) point up the need for setting our own house in order. With your help, that's a completely possible task.

• • •

Online resources:

Writing Prizes
- The Baileys Women's Prize for Fiction: womensprizeforfiction.co.uk/
- The Rona Jaffe Foundation Writers' Awards: ronajaffefoundation.org/
- The Women's National Book Association's Bookwoman Award: wnba-books.org/wnba-awards-2#Award
- The Carl Brandon Society's Parallax and Kindred Awards: carlbrandon.org/awards.html

Organizations supporting women writers
- Hedgebrook: https://hedgebrook.org
- Broad Universe:broaduniverse.org/home
- Aqueduct Press:aqueductpress.com and its quarterly publication, *The Cascadia Subduction Zone*: thecsz.com/

Alternate publishing resources
- Book View Café: bookviewcafe.com/bookstore
- Indiegogo: indiegogo.com
- Kickstarter: https://kickstarter.com

~

Nisi Shawl's collection *Filter House* was a 2009 James Tiptree, Jr. Award winner; her stories have been published at *Strange Horizons*, in *Asimov's SF Magazine*, and in anthologies including *The Year's Best Fantasy and Horror* and both volumes of the Dark Matter series. She was the 2011 Guest of Honor at the feminist SF convention WisCon and will be a 2014 co-Guest of Honor for the Science Fiction Research Association. She co-authored the renowned *Writing the Other: A Practical Approach* with Cynthia Ward, and co-edited the nonfiction anthology *Strange Matings: Science Fiction, Feminism, African American Voices, and Octavia E. Butler*. Shawl's Belgian Congo steampunk novel *Everfair* is forthcoming in 2015 from Tor Books. Her website is nisishawl.com.

PERSONAL ESSAYS

This special double issue of *Lightspeed* was funded by an extraordinary Kickstarter campaign featuring personal essays written by women working in our genre. When we put out the call for these essays, we asked for "smashing, crashing women's voices, telling what it really means to be a woman reading and writing science fiction."

Here are twenty-eight different voices raised in destructive harmony.

WE ARE THE
FIFTY PERCENT

RACHEL SWIRSKY

Sometimes I catch myself feeling like I only read writing by women. "Ugh," I think. "That is so skewed." Then I crunch the numbers.

They are almost always fifty percent.

Sociological research suggests that when women and men speak equally in a conversation, both men and women perceive the women as dominating the conversation. That phenomenon has had a significant influence on my experience as a woman writing and consuming SF.

In 2007, when I started editing a podcast magazine that broadcast previously published fantasy stories, many readers responded with vitriol, angered by the number of female authors and main characters. Of course, at the beginning of the run, we were running a backlog; most of the stories that were going on the air had been selected by the previous male editor. But I was a woman, and a known feminist, and therefore under suspicion for being prejudiced toward women and against men. It spooked me, so I ran the numbers. Over and over again, compulsively, for as long as I edited the podcast, I ran the numbers every few months. Fifty percent women writers. Fifty percent women main characters. It never varied more than five percent in either direction. And still, the entire time, some readers were furious with what they saw as a magazine entirely dominated by women. Partially because of that, I eventually left the position.

At the same time, as I entered my editorial position and was criticized for running work "dominated" by fifty percent women, the podcast's male-edited science fiction counterpart hadn't run a story authored by a woman in weeks.

No one said a thing.

This kind of thing gets in your brain. Insidious viral memes bury themselves into illogical thought patterns, deceiving one into thinking they are rational. Even though I know from prior number crunching that fifty percent of what I read is by women, I still find myself periodically doubting. So I count again.

Women aren't supposed to talk as much as men. We aren't supposed to take up as much space as men do. So when we talk, we must be SHOUTING. When we take up space, we must be EVERYWHERE.

When we're writing science fiction, we're DESTROYING it.

Now, of course, that's just the bad stuff. I am deeply grateful toward and indebted to amazing and supportive readers, editors, publishers and critics of all genders, who have been incredibly generous to me and my work.

But still, sometimes I look at the table of contents in an anthology and I see women restrained, demurely, to that unthreatening third, or even less. Present, but not too present. Talking, but not too much.

If our presence will always be perceived as a taint, then let science fiction be tainted. If our speaking voices will always be perceived as shouts, then let us shout.

We're here. We're fifty percent of you.

And we deserve some room to bellow.

~

Rachel Swirsky holds an MFA in short fiction from the Iowa Writers Workshop and has published more than sixty stories in venues including *Tor.com*, *Clarkesworld*, and the *New Haven Review*. Although her editing run of *PodCastle* is over, the magazine still persists in the talented hands of its editorial team Dave Thompson and Anna Schwind, with the assistance of Ann Leckie.

Science Fiction: You're Doin' It Wrong

Maya Kaathryn Bohnhoff

I am one of the women wreaking wholesale havoc on SF. Worse, I am a repeat offender.

Analog's longtime editor, Stan Schmidt, has told me he's lost subscriptions over my work. I knew this before I attended my first Worldcon in 1992 and was still gob-smacked when a couple of fellows cornered me at a party and explained, at length, why I had never written a word of real, hard science fiction in my life and, therefore, did not belong in the pages of *Analog*. This was after only half-a-dozen stories. I'm at two dozen and counting.

I've frequently sat next to Stan Schmidt on "Women in SF" panels at which he publicly expressed chagrin that we were still talking about gender and genre. Ironically, at Renovation in 2011, a man in the audience opined that it was a dead issue. He then proceeded to discuss how women had changed SF.

Apparently, there is something about the way we women write the genre that "softens" it. In our hands, it focuses more on characters and their feelings than on science. Men write hardware; women write software.

My first story in *Analog* was "Hand-me-down Town," which explored a solution to homelessness. Yes, I wrote about feelings—the feelings of the homeless about being homeless, the feelings of the people trying to help them, and the feelings of the people trying to banish them through zoning ordinances.

Stan got fan mail for that piece from a nurse and a social worker who applauded my humanizing of the subject. He also drew criticism: "Not science fiction!" detractors cried. To which he replied, "Sociology is, too, a science," and asked me to write more.

I did. "A Little Bit of an Eclipse" was hard SF about a lunar eclipse…sort of. Well, okay, it was a humorous tale of a scheister alien who steals the moon, which, I quickly realized, made me doubly a purveyor of mayhem. Not only was I a female writing science fiction, I was a female writing *funny* science fiction.

My hero, Ray Bradbury, wrote that SF is our way of making reality behave by pretending to look the other way—our attempt to solve current problems by shifting them in time and space. Humanity's current problems, you may have noticed, are not mostly hardware-related. They are software bugs. They are about us humans and the way we react to our shared world—a world we are building day by day. A bit more than half of us are female. Which means that, by any logic, if our half of the human race is to help make reality behave, we must do it in a way that speaks to the things we believe to be essential to the process of worldbuilding.

To be frank, if science fiction were only about the hardware, I wouldn't write it. I find the software—the doers of science, both men and women—ever so much more interesting.

~

Maya Kaathryn Bohnhoff is the *New York Times* Bestselling author of *Star Wars: The Last Jedi* and *Star Wars: Shadow Games*. She became addicted to science fiction when her dad let her stay up late to watch *The Day the Earth Stood Still*. Mom was horrified. Dad was unrepentant. Maya slept with a night-light in her room until she was fifteen. She started her writing career sketching science fiction comic books in the last row of her third grade classroom. She was never apprehended. Since then, her short fiction has been published in *Analog, Amazing Stories, Century, Realms of Fantasy, Interzone, Paradox,* and *Jim Baen's Universe.* Her debut novel, *The Meri* (Baen), was a *Locus Magazine* 1992 Best First Novel nominee (now available as a trade paperback from Sense of Wonder Press). Since, she has published ten more speculative fiction novels, including collaborations with Marc Scott Zicree and Michael Reaves.

Maya lives in San Jose, where she writes, performs, and records original and parody (filk) music with her husband and awesome musician and music producer, Chef Jeff Vader, All-Powerful God of Biscuits. The couple has produced five music albums: *Retro Rocket Science, Aliens Ate My Homework,* and *Grated Hits* (parody), and the original music CDs *Manhattan Sleeps* and *Mobius Street.* To top it off, they've also produced three musical children: Alex, Kristine, and Amanda.

Join Us in the Future

Marissa Lingen

One of the tenets I've been taught of writing science fiction is that the future doesn't arrive everywhere evenly. (I think that's William Gibson, more or less.) I didn't realize how much it would apply to me personally.

When I left physics to write full time, I was leaving a male-dominated field for one that looked to me like a shining golden paradise of women. Two of the most decorated SF writers anywhere, ever, are Connie Willis and Lois McMaster Bujold. The author my father gave me when I was twelve, to get me started on modern SF, was Nancy Kress. Everywhere I turned, there were outstanding female editors and agents, experienced writers like the ones I'd already read and beginners like me, whose ideas were just barely starting to see the light of day—it was an entire world of women. A beautiful, amazing world of women.

And then it became clear that this world was not the world some other people were living in.

I could tell stories about getting harassed at my first con—and my third con—and so on. I could talk about how male fans looked straight at me when I was on panels, when they raised their hands to ask why women don't write SF and whether it was because women don't like science. (After repeating "dude, I am *right here*, don't talk about me like I don't exist" a couple of times, I lost my temper and challenged that man to a contest of differential equations.)

But what I really think about, when I think about being a woman who writes SF, is that I was right about what world I was joining. It *is* a beautiful, amazing world of women. Women started "destroying" SF before I was born, and I am so glad and so proud to share the work with them. And I look at the people who are living in this cramped, airless world where SF is somehow *not* chock full of wonderful women, and I think, "Join us in the future. It's already here, it just hasn't gotten to you yet. And it's *awesome*."

~

Marissa Lingen is a short fiction writer living in the Minneapolis area. She has sold over one hundred stories to publications such as *Year's Best*, *Tor.com*, *Analog*, and *Lightspeed*. You can find her online at marissalingen.com.

Are We There Yet?

Sheila Finch

In the early 1980s, an editor of a literary journal that had previously published my work rejected a story because he "didn't buy science fiction." Since I hadn't realized that was what I'd written, I thought I'd better do a lot of reading to catch up with the field. The rejected story found a home, then another story, and a third, and I was a member of SFWA.

I started to go to conventions and be on panels—where I quickly found myself the only woman on any panel that was about "hard" SF. Not that there was a lack of women in the field up to that time—think C. L. Moore, Ursula Le Guin, Joanna Russ—but the prevailing wisdom was that only men could handle the hard stuff. Then I published my first novel, based on the Everett interpretation of Quantum Mechanics (I did a lot of research), and I began to badger con committees to put me on appropriate panels.

I got more than I bargained for on several occasions. I remember being seated between two famously arrogant authors. Predictably, an argument broke out, and they stood up to shout at each other over my head. (I doubt they would have done that to another man.) All-male panels tended to ignore any women, and the moderator usually let them go because—you know—what could a woman contribute? I quickly learned to volunteer as moderator where I had the upper hand. Riding herd on these very vocal authors was often scary, but I grew up in a rough part of London and my father taught me to hold my own.

I had a chance to do some radio interviews—supposed to be good publicity for me, but mostly filler for DJs who were on the air hour after hour with only platters to spin. One day, the DJ started the interview by asking what a nice lady like me was doing in a field like science fiction. He wasn't kidding. So I wasn't kidding either when I replied in a very sweet, ladylike tone that I was interested in children, and family, and relationships—and I wanted to explore what was going to happen to them in a future dominated by aggressive male ideas.

About this time, an editor rejected a story, telling me he just couldn't believe in its science underpinning. I had—as usual—done copious research, and everything I'd speculated about was either on the horizon or perhaps already being done in secret experiments somewhere. I don't usually write "dear jerk" letters to editors who reject my work, but I couldn't get past the conviction he would never have doubted the science if a man had written the story. I drew up a two-page list citing my sources and sent it to him, just so he'd know for the future that women can do research and write science, too.

Then one day, a scientist from JPL cornered me at a convention. He wanted to talk about my use of the Everett interpretation in my first novel. He took me seriously. (I was so primed for another battle, I nearly missed that.)

Are we there yet?

~

Sheila Finch is the author of eight science fiction novels and numerous short stories that have appeared in *Fantasy & Science Fiction*, *Amazing*, *Asimov's*, *Fantasy Book*, and many anthologies. A collection of the "lingster" stories recently appeared as *The Guild of Xenolinguists*. A non-fiction work, *Myth, Metaphor, and Science Fiction*, will be published this year from Aqueduct Press. Her work has won several awards, including a Nebula for Best Novella, the San Diego Book Award for Juvenile Fiction, and the Compton-Crook Award for Best First Novel. Sheila taught creative writing at El Camino College for thirty years and at workshops around California. She lives in Long Beach, with two long-haired cats whose fur keeps getting into the keyboard because they like to monitor what she's writing. Her website can be found at: sff.net/people/sheila-finch

NOT A SPACESHIP, ROBOT, OR ZOMBIE IN SIGHT

ANNE CHARNOCK

As a writer of science fiction, I had a slow and, initially, rocky start. I spent the best part of a decade writing my first novel, *A Calculated Life*. It seemed that every other year I was too busy to look at the manuscript—busy with my art practice, raising two sons, getting involved with community carbon-reduction projects.

When I did eventually complete the novel, I was unaware that, in the UK, women SF writers were struggling to secure publishing contracts. I'd like to think this partly explains why I failed to find a literary agent, although it didn't help that my book was short by SFF standards.

I cast around for any SF publishers that might accept author submissions, but my novel seemed a bad fit with their existing lists. After all, I'd written a near-future dystopia with a female protagonist who works in an office in central Manchester, a northern English city with an industrial heritage! Not a space-ship, robot, or zombie in sight. And no element of fantasy or the paranormal. I felt out of step.

So, I invested months of effort towards self-publishing my novel as a Kindle ebook and paperback. What a steep learning curve! Out of the blue, five months after I published the paperback, I was approached by David Pomerico, acquisitions editor at 47North. He offered me a contract, which I readily accepted. It feels odd that as an English woman SF writer I have a publisher in Seattle, nearly 5,000 miles from UK shores, and an editor based in New York.

A Calculated Life, I learned this month, is one of seven nominated works for the Philip K. Dick Award 2013 and one of five shortlisted works for The Kitschies Golden Tentacle Award for debut novel.

~

Anne Charnock's writing career began in journalism. Her articles appeared in the *Guardian*, *New Scientist*, *International Herald Tribune*, and *Geographical*. She was educated at the University of East Anglia, where she studied environmental sciences, and at the Manchester School of Art. She travelled widely as a foreign correspondent and spent a year trekking through Egypt, Sudan, and Kenya. In her fine art practice, Anne tried to answer the questions: What is it to be human? What is it to be a machine? Ultimately she decided to write fiction as another route to finding answers. Her website is annecharnock.com, and you can find her on Twitter @annecharnock.

WRITING AMONG THE BEGINNING OF WOMEN

AMY STERLING CASIL

Science is one of the primary ways in which people seek to understand the world and themselves.

The only people who read my short fiction when I started out, other than my writing friends Ron Collins, Brian Plante, and Lisa Silverthorne, was my aunt Donna Hodgson, who was a nurse, and who was among the best human beings who ever lived.

I received eighty-two rejections before I made my first professional science fiction sale, "Jonny Punkinhead," which appeared in the July 1996 "New Writers" issue of *The Magazine of Fantasy & Science Fiction*. Prior to my selling "Jonny Punkinhead" to Kris Rusch at *F&SF*, Donna rubbed this story for good luck and pronounced it excellent.

Though trained in the medical field and of an analytical mind, my aunt Donna read primarily literature, including such authors as Toni Morrison and Alice Walker. When she read my writing, including "Jonny Punkinhead," she said, "This is good and beautifully written—it's not science fiction."

I heard from my "friends" that my work was not science fiction. Far too "literary." This was because it dealt not only with speculation, but with concerns of the human heart and mind.

Concerns much like those that were mentioned by William Faulkner in his 1950 Nobel Prize acceptance speech: "The poet's, the writer's, duty is to write about these things. It is his privilege to help man endure by lifting his heart, by reminding him of the courage and honor and hope and pride and compassion and pity and sacrifice which have been the glory of his past."

I find it pitiful that a great number of those who sought to take control of science fiction thought it was unimportant to write about, in addition to pride, the other human values of compassion, pity, sacrifice—and my primary topic—honor.

Now, this many years later, I have the courage and honor to write about women and men who have honor, and who believe in Faulkner's values. I am a Southern California science fiction writer. I owe to those who came before me: Jim Blaylock and Tim Powers, and before them, Philip K. Dick.

I have been slapped, groped, insulted, and intimidated in my pursuit of being a female science fiction writer.

I have some news for those who'd seek to put me or my work down. I am Female Science Fiction Writer. I will write about that which I wish and choose to write about.

Am I, as a permanent slush pile denizen who reviews for a major publication stated, a "decent sentence-to-sentence writer?" Oh, I suppose so. But what I am, truly, is someone who understands Faulkner's charge. I refuse to write as though I "stood among and watched the end of man," a term that Faulkner used in its full sense—to refer to all people.

We are not writing among the end of men. We are writing among the beginning of women. Of people. Of our, human, race.

~

Inspired by a lifelong love of nature, endless curiosity, and a belief in wonderful things, **Amy Sterling Casil** is a 2002 Nebula Award nominee and recipient of other awards and recognition for her short science fiction and fantasy, which has appeared in publications ranging from *The Magazine of Fantasy & Science Fiction* to *Zoetrope*. She is the author of twenty-six nonfiction books, more than a hundred short stories, primarily science fiction and fantasy, two fiction and poetry collections, and two novels. She lives in Aliso Viejo, California with her daughter Meredith and a Jack Russell Terrier named Gambit. Amy is a business consultant and teaches writing and composition at Saddleback College in Mission Viejo, after receiving her MFA from Chapman University in 1999.

TOWARD A
BETTER FUTURE

NANCY JANE MOORE

No one has ever pinched my butt at a con. I don't recall anyone ever telling me I didn't have the "balls" to write science fiction.

And convention panels addressing gender issues have evolved into thoughtful and rational discussions—at least when I'm moderating them. I've even seen some change in the panels on women soldiers in SF. When I first started doing them (I get asked to do these often, since I'm a martial artist and write some military SF), the discussion quickly degenerated into whether women could fight. But these days it's more common to have a conversation about how the military has changed with respect to women and to speculate on what that will mean in the future.

So I don't have any entertaining or obnoxious stories about the time so-and-so did such-and-such to me. But other women do. And I've heard those stories enough to know that misogyny has not disappeared in the science fiction world.

It makes me wonder if it would be easier to sell my fiction if my name was Nathan rather than Nancy, or if I didn't write so many stories with female protagonists. A positive review of my PS Publishing collection, *Conscientious Inconsistencies*, questioned whether the word "feminist" should have been used in the description of the book, since even non-feminists would like it. I know the reviewer meant it as a compliment, but it was still frustrating.

Here's the thing about oppression: It's rarely the result of one person's actions and often it's not even intentional. As philosopher Carol Hay puts it, "Most oppressive harms tend not to be the result of the intentional actions of an individual person, but are more often the unintentional result of an interrelated system of social norms and institutions." [Hay, Carol, *Kantianism, Liberalism, and Feminism*, Palgrave McMillan, 2013, p. 8.]

Editors who say that women submit fewer stories than men and that they buy stories from men and women in about the proportion of their submissions are probably telling the truth. But while they have no intention to harm women writers, the fact remains that every time I pick up an issue of the magazine, I see more stories by men.

I also see more stories by men in most anthologies, including the various "year's best" ones. And I see more reviews of books by men, something documented every year. This is, of course, also true in literary and mainstream fiction—especially the reviews.

Do women submit in smaller numbers because they notice these discrepancies? Of course they do. Even women who have spent their lives battering down the doors that say "No Girls Allowed" get tired of fighting all the time.

How do we fix this? By doing things like this *Lightspeed* special issue. And by recognizing—and embracing—the fact that women are going to tell stories that differ from the ones of the so-called Golden Age.

Science fiction is supposed to be a genre of ideas, and ideas grow and change. It's time for the SF community to stop defining science fiction by the ideas of U.S. and U.K. white male writers. The future will be the better for it.

~

The last rule in **Nancy Jane Moore**'s story "Thirty-One Rules for Fulfilling Your Destiny" is "Break all rules, including these." It's advice she has taken to heart. Her books, all available as ebooks at Book View Café, include the novellas "Changeling" (first published by Aqueduct Press) and "Ardent Forest," and the collections *Conscientious Inconsistencies* (first published by PS Publishing) and *Flashes of Illumination*. Moore's short fiction has appeared in a number of anthologies and magazines ranging from *Lady Churchill's Rosebud Wristlet* to *The National Law Journal*. She holds a fourth degree black belt in Aikido and divides her time between Austin, Texas, and Oakland, California.

We Are the Army of Women Destroying SF

Sandra Wickham

I grew up watching the Star Wars trilogy on repeat. Yes, I know it's not science fiction, but back then all I knew was it had spaceships, robots, and laser swords, and I was hooked. I wanted to be a Jedi, or at the very least, a super hero. I'm pretty sure a great deal of who I am today has on some level been a quest for that.

I also grew up naïve of gender discrimination. My brothers and I all had chores to do on the farm. The easier ones went to me, but it was because I was the youngest and littlest, not because I was a girl. I was never told I couldn't do something because I was a girl, and was definitely never held back from anything I wanted to do. For my first job, I wanted to pump gas at a busy intersection, mostly because it was on the route to the beach and I'd get to see tons of people my age. It never occurred to me that they hadn't ever had a female work there, but it didn't stop me from convincing them to hire me, which opened doors for other women to work there. I became the first female president of the British Columbia Amateur Bodybuilding Association, not to prove a point, but because someone needed to step up to the position. I never thought of those as gender issues or something I shouldn't have taken on.

Cue me naïvely entering the science fiction publishing world with the same ideas. I want to write the same stories I loved growing up, the ones that filled my heart and soul with wonder and fueled my imagination. To hear it said that women are destroying science fiction rattles me to the core. I'm new to the publishing industry and haven't had the experiences other women have had at conventions or online. Yet. When I hear about it, it makes me want to pick up my light saber and start slicing off body parts. While that might be fun, I realize it wouldn't solve the problem.

I'm also aware that being a strong, intelligent, and independent-minded female is not popular with everyone. To those people, I say, "I don't care." It makes me angry and drives me to want to stand up for all women in the industry, whether it's by continuing to destroy science fiction by writing it, or by physically standing up for someone who needs it. This Jedi recently earned a black belt. You need me; I'll be there.

I will continue to write science fiction and fantasy because I love it and because I want to entertain people, whatever the gender. The talented women who write science fiction are not going anywhere, no matter what the haters say. We are the army of women destroying science fiction and we are strong. May the force be with us.

~

Sandra Wickham lives in Vancouver, Canada, with her husband and two cats. Her friends call her a needle-crafting aficionado, health guru, and ninja-in-training. Sandra's short stories have appeared in *Evolve, Vampires of the New Undead*; *Evolve, Vampires of the Future Undead*; *Chronicles of the Order*; *Crossed Genres*; *LocoThology: Tales of Fantasy & Science Fiction*; and *The Urban Green Man*. She blogs about writing with the Inkpunks, is the Fitness Nerd columnist for the Functional Nerds, and slush reads for *Lightspeed Magazine*.

Read SF and You've Got a Posse

Gail Marsella

As a consumer, reading science fiction resembles an auction—the tables hold an impossibly enticing variety of unique things, the sellers make multiple bid calls for your attention, and you're never the oddest person there. You can be tongue-tied, brainy, hit upside the head with an ugly stick, or as socially awkward as a chimp at a bris, but read SF and you've got a posse: people (some admittedly fictional) who would actively admire you for having a chemistry set and scuba gear to go with your sewing machine and fine china. Too much guy stuff? Well, yes. No argument about misogyny in the field, and the disturbingly wide POV range can be daunting, but—maybe because of a supportive father—I found it exciting, a sanctuary where I could use big words, think big thoughts, and not endure very many swelled heads. The two best work groups in my corporate career had a routine SF book swap, and even academia, where I teach now, is starting to come around.

As a creator, writing science fiction is probably no more difficult than any other kind of writing, which means next to impossible if you've only ever written essays, proposals, or software manuals. Steep. Learning. Curve. It's harder than humor. It's harder than convincing the dean to fund a purely practical study of how to make money. Despite several decades of reading and writing experience, and a favorite definition of "story" that fits particularly well with SF (it's survival information), I'm struggling to get started. Thank God for Nancy Kress, Ben Bova, Kate Wilhelm, and all the others who give back to the field by writing how-to books and teaching. At some point I'll be ready for Clarion, and despite my age (sixty), I'm going to wow them. Be ready.

~

Gail Marsella lives in Allentown, PA, with her husband, dog, SF book collection, and assorted hobbies. Retired from corporate America after launching three kids, she now teaches chemistry at Muhlenberg College. Gail is also a first reader for *Lightspeed Magazine*.

Stomp All Over That

O.J. Cade

Apparently, women are destroying science fiction. The historically minded will recall that we used to destroy science. We're branching out, it seems.

It started in the test tubes, the bright labs, the white coats, with Ada Lovelace in clockwork heels and Rosalind Franklin in spiral stilettos, and both of them following behind, because their footwear was all so flimsy they couldn't possibly hold up by themselves, without help. With Lise Meitner in windup shoes, a dolly working on automatic in a lab that didn't want her. With Marie Curie in shoes that glowed like ruby slippers dipped in uranium, turned away from the Academy of Sciences because men don't wear pretty slippers and they'd taint the very threshold, they would, leave little traces of *woman* with a half-life too desperately long to ever be scrubbed away.

Still a place was made, if grudging. We clawed our way up and into science in our pretty, silly, sensible shoes, and stuck there, because people couldn't very well bitch about women in science when Rebecca Lancefield was helping them see off *Streptococcus* in sequinned, sequenced sandals and when Gertrude Elion was doing the same with leukaemia, with her toenails peeping red-painted out of open-toed marrowbone shoes. When Henrietta Lacks *became* science, her feet shod in Petri dishes, and legion. And the bigots read outside in the waiting room, their feet in concrete blocks and granddad slippers, and suddenly there's this whole new world of women with feet that could be stepped on, that could be bound up and turned away.

There's Mary Shelley with electricity zipping through her iron-toed, hobnail boots. And Margaret Atwood with her decoupage slippers, handmade with pages from Genesis, and Octavia Butler in boots embossed with teeth and feathers…And beneath all the shoes, upon all the soles, is stamped *exception*—making, for the prints that can't be scuffed out, and taking, for the ones that can.

And this new army of shoes, of bright, pretty prints, are tracking in mud. They're bringing in blood and dead birds and flesh-eating bacteria and sex, all come to topple, to bring down, and the poor deluded things don't seem to realise that they've missed the Golden Age, all right, and it was back when their owners were barefoot. And would they mind going back, please, to the sad, superficial corners of the wardrobes from whence they came, because gold is best when not part of a spectrum and their presence just might drown it out. Those heels are *noisy*, understand? And science is a single experience, and limited, and you should sit back and let other people talk about it, because those tongues in those shoes can have nothing valuable to say. (Do you hear that, Marie? Do you hear it, Ada and Mary and Margaret?)

I hear it. And *stomp all over that*, I say. Science belongs to us all, and so does science fiction.

~

O.J. Cade is a PhD candidate in science communication. Her short fiction has appeared in *Strange Horizons*, *Cosmos*, and *Aurealis*, amongst others. She has a novella, "Trading Rosemary," due out in February from Masque Books.

FOR THE TRAILBLAZERS

KRISTI CHARISH

I clone things.

When I first started my career in research that was the way I introduced myself.

I clone things. For someone who started university in the late '90s that was such a loaded sentence—it carried the weight of recent scientific cloning advances (They cloned a sheep—a SHEEP! Named Dolly!), that I was involved with the leading edge of scientific advances, *and* that I was a female scientist—one of many from my generation.

... I guess there's a big science fiction influence carried in that line too.

My name is Kristi Charish and I'm a Canadian geneticist and cell and molecular biologist. Until recently, I worked with these awesome, genetically modified fruit flies that carry something called a fluorophore, a glow-in-the-dark gene. Those little glow-in-the-dark genes made it possible for me to study cell division, and I discovered elements about how skin-like cells multiply that have some pretty important implications for cancer.

Take that anti GMO'ers! GMO, glow-in-the-dark fruit flies help cure cancer. Booyah!

I'm also a Science Fiction and Fantasy writer—the equivalent of a rookie who just got drafted to play in the major leagues. To say I'm still pretty stoked about the whole thing would be a colossal understatement. So how did I go from research scientist to fiction writer? Well, like most writers, I've loved books and movies since I was a kid. But...I didn't want to be rescued by Indiana Jones, I wanted to *be* Indiana Jones—a female version mind you, like *Tomb Raider*, but I knew I didn't want to take a back seat to the adventure. I guess you could say I carried that sentiment with me when I began to write a few years ago.

And something really cool happened—as a female writer *and* a non-arts major, I met with an overwhelming amount of support from the men and women around me. Perseverance, a finished manuscript, and a dozen query letters later, I had a fantastic agent (Carolyn Forde, WCA) and a two-book publishing deal with Simon and Schuster Canada/Pocket Books US.

Now, this is an essay for the WDSF Kickstarter, and here I am, a woman in the fields of science and science fiction who has never dealt with the overt discrimination so many other women have and still face every day around the world—quite the opposite.

But my experience is the way it should be.

I think it's important for women like myself to speak up about their positive experiences. An integral element of science fiction and fantasy for me is the element of hope, that under the surface of every blatant setback lies a hidden truth that things are in fact changing, still changing, and the setbacks are no more than a nefarious force of old lashing back in a futile attempt to recapture a rapidly decaying mold.

For all of the women and men in science and writing who've blazed the trail for me, I'm one of your many successes; a young woman who has had only encouragement from the men and women in her life to pursue her careers, who has had strong professional female role models, and who has never had the hear the words "you can't because you're a woman."

There's still a way to go, but we've made a hell of a lot of positive ground, too.

~

Kristi Charish, BSc., MSc., PhD., is a scientist and science fiction/fantasy writer who resides in Vancouver, Canada. She received her BSc and MSc from Simon Fraser University in Molecular Biology and Biochemistry, and her PhD in Zoology from the University of British Columbia. Kristi writes what she loves; adventure-heavy stories featuring strong, savvy female protagonists. The first installment in her debut urban fantasy series, *Owl and the Japanese Circus*, is scheduled for release early 2015 through Simon & Schuster Canada/Pocket Books.

WOMEN ARE
THE FUTURE OF
SCIENCE FICTION

JULIETTE WADE

I fell backward into science fiction after years of reading, writing, and submitting. One day, Stanley Schmidt bought a story from me and published it
in *Analog*, and I became a science fiction author.

That story was the only one I'd written that I considered science fiction. It
had humans and aliens and spaceships. But as I corresponded with Stanley
Schmidt and was welcomed heartily at the *Analog* forum, I realized people
didn't care as much about those superficial trappings. They cared about the
sciences behind my stories, linguistics and anthropology. Then, when I looked
back at everything I'd written, I realized they were all science fiction stories.
They were about science, written with strict attention to scientific principle.
This wasn't an accident; I was a science fiction writer.

My sciences were never the "hard" sciences. Social sciences are generally
considered "soft" in academia, and yes, that means feminine. I found that ironic
at best, coming out of linguistics, a discipline that uses scientific notation—and
even chaos theory—to grapple with language phenomena. Anthropology has
grown out of a deeply problematic history of colonialism, but is now finding
itself in a world of cultural relativism and feminism. This was fascinating to
me—not just to capture the perspectives of Others as an anthropologist, but
to consider the discipline itself through an anthropological eye.

In the science fiction community, I've discovered a diverse community of
writers and editors, of multiple genders and ethnicities. I've also discovered
social complexity, and battles over borderlines. What is the difference between
fantasy and science fiction? What is "hard" science fiction? Many of these

discussions boil down to a sadly familiar question: Who counts? And the answer to that question depends on whom you ask.

I have always felt welcome in this field. With *Analog* on my side, I feel confident declaring myself a writer of "hard" science fiction. I love how people come to me to talk about ideas. Some have even written me letters in alien dialects I've invented. I have many powerful women role models, too, like Ursula Le Guin, Octavia Butler, and Connie Willis. However, I clearly see the places in the genre where women aren't welcome. I see harassment happening at conventions and online. I see articles belittling or ridiculing women's accomplishments. I have also become aware of back room discussions where career-advancing friendships are made, the future of science fiction is discussed—and women are not invited.

We must make our own deals, our own success, because we are the future of science fiction.

People sometimes ask, "Is science fiction dying?" We live in the future, the argument goes, and technology is taken for granted, while the cutting edge of science has become too complex and esoteric. I couldn't disagree more. Science fiction has never been about the superficial trappings. It's about discovery, and change, about reflecting on our own society by envisioning the future. Diversity and feminism are the cutting edge, because they are the great discovery that will change our society—the discovery that some people have yet to make. The world of social science, of language, culture, and power, has always lain at the core of science fiction. Now it is coming into its own, and we must lead, bringing our genre into a new future.

～

Juliette Wade has made four appearances in *Analog* magazine, two on the cover, where her most recent story was illustrated by Michael Whelan for the October 2012 issue. She is inspired in her writing by her experience living in Japan and France, and her studies of Japanese, Anthropology, and Linguistics. She blogs about language and culture in SF/F at TalkToYouUniverse (talktoyouniverse.blogspot.com), and runs the "Dive into Worldbuilding!" hangout series on Google. In 2014, she'll be leading the first issue of *STRAEON* with her story "Lady Sakura's Letters," and appearing again in *Analog* with "Mind Locker."

WE HAVE ALWAYS FOUGHT

CHALLENGING THE WOMEN, CATTLE AND SLAVES NARRATIVE

KAMERON HURLEY

I'm going to tell you a story about llamas. It will be like every other story you've ever heard about llamas: how they are covered in fine scales; how they eat their young if not raised properly; and how, at the end of their lives, they hurl themselves—lemming-like—over cliffs to drown in the surging sea. They are, at heart, sea creatures, birthed from the sea, married to it like the fishing people who make their livelihood there.

Every story you hear about llamas is the same. You see it in books: the poor doomed baby llama getting chomped up by its intemperate parent. On television: the massive tide of scaly llamas falling in a great, majestic herd into the sea below. In the movies: bad-ass llamas smoking cigars and painting their scales in jungle camouflage.

Because you've seen this story so many times, because you already know the nature and history of llamas, it sometimes shocks you, of course, to see a llama outside of these media spaces. The llamas you see don't have scales. So you doubt what you see, and you joke with your friends about "those scaly llamas" and they laugh and say, "Yes, llamas sure are scaly!" and you forget your actual experience.

What you remember is the llama you saw who had mange, which sort of looked scaly, after a while, and that one llama who was sort of aggressive toward a baby llama, like maybe it was going to eat it. So you forget the llamas that don't fit the narrative you saw in films, books, television—the ones you heard about in the stories—and you remember the ones that exhibited the behavior the stories talk about. Suddenly, all the llamas you remember fit the narrative you see and hear every day from those around you. You make jokes about it with your friends. You feel like you've won something. You're not crazy. You think just like everyone else.

And then there came a day when you started writing about your own llamas. Unsurprisingly, you didn't choose to write about the soft, downy, non-cannibalistic ones you actually met, because you knew no one would find those "realistic." You plucked out the llamas from the stories. You created cannibal llamas with a death wish, their scales matted in paint.

It's easier to tell the same stories everyone else does. There's no particular shame in it.

It's just that it's lazy, which is just about the worst possible thing a spec fic writer can be.

Oh, and it's not true.

• • •

As somebody with more than a passing knowledge of history (All the Things That Came Before Me), I'm passionately interested in truth: Truth is something that happens whether or not we see it, or believe it, or write about. Truth just is. We can call it something else, or pretend it didn't happen, but its repercussions live with us, whether we choose to remember and acknowledge it or not.

When I sat down with one of my senior professors in Durban, South Africa to talk about my Master's thesis, he asked me why I wanted to write about women resistance fighters.

"Because women made up twenty percent of the ANC's militant wing!" I gushed. "Twenty percent! When I found that out I couldn't believe it. And you know—women have never been part of fighting forces—"

He interrupted me. "Women have always fought," he said.

"What?" I said.

"Women have always fought," he said. "Shaka Zulu had an all-female force of fighters. Women have been part of every resistance movement. Women dressed as men and went to war, went to sea, and participated actively in combat for as long as there have been people."

I had no idea what to say to this. I had been nurtured in the U.S. school system on a steady diet of the Great Men theory of history. History was full of

Great Men. I had to take separate Women's History courses just to learn about what women were doing while all the men were killing each other. It turned out many of them were governing countries and figuring out rather effective methods of birth control that had sweeping ramifications on the makeup of particular states, especially Greece and Rome.

Half the world is full of women, but it's rare to hear a narrative that doesn't speak of women as the people who have things done to them instead of the people who do things. More often, women are talked about as a man's daughter. A man's wife.

I just watched a reality TV show about Alaska bush pilots where all of the pilots get these little intros about their families and passions, but the single female pilot is given the one-line "Pilot X's girlfriend." It wasn't until they broke up, in season 2, that she got her own intro. Turns out she's been in Alaska four times longer than the other pilot, and hunts, fishes, and climbs ice walls, in addition to being an ace pilot.

But the narrative was "cannibalistic llama," and our eyes glazed over, and we stopped seeing her as anything else.

• • •

Language is a powerful thing, and it changes the way we view ourselves, and other people, in delightful and horrifying ways. Anyone with any knowledge of the military, or who pays attention to how the media talks about war, has likely caught on to this.

We don't kill "people." We kill "targets." (Or japs or gooks or ragheads). We don't kill "fifteen-year-old boys" but "enemy combatants" (yes, every boy fifteen and over killed in drone strikes now is automatically listed as an enemy combatant. Not a boy. Not a child.).

And when we talk about "people" we don't really mean "men and women." We mean "people and female people." We talk about "American Novelists" and "American Women Novelists" (theguardian.com/books/2013/apr/25/wikipedia-women-american-novelists). We talk about "Teenage Coders" and "Lady Teenage Coders" (tor.com/blogs/2013/05/lady-teenage-coder-fixes-your-twitter-so-no-one-can-spoil-game-of-thrones-for-you-again)

And when we talk about war, we talk about soldiers and female soldiers.

Because this is the way we talk, when we talk about history and use the word "soldiers" it immediately erases any women doing the fighting. Which is why it comes as no surprise that the folks excavating Viking graves didn't bother to check whether the graves they dug up were male or female. They were graves with swords in them. Swords are for soldiers. Soldiers are men.

It was years before they thought to even check the actual bones of the skeletons (content.usatoday.com/communities/sciencefair/post/2011/07/invasion-of-the-viking-women-unearthed), instead of just saying, "Sword means dude!" and realized their mistake.

Women fought, too.

In fact, women did all sorts of things we think they didn't do. In the middle ages, they were doctors and sheriffs (the-history-girls.blogspot.co.uk/2013/05/sword-and-scalpel-by-karen-maitland.html). In Greece they were...oh, sod it. Listen. Foz Meadows does a better job with all the linky-links, for those who desire "proof" (fozmeadows.wordpress.com/2012/12/08/psa-your-default-narrative-settings-are-not-apolitical). Let's just put it this way: If you think there's a thing—*anything*—women didn't do in the past, you're wrong. Women—now and then—even made a habit of peeing standing up. They wore dildos. So even things the funny-ha-ha folks immediately raise a hand to say "It's impossible; women didn't do X!" Well. They did it. Except maybe impregnate other women. But even then, there were, of course, intersex folks categorized as "women" who did just that.

But none of those things fit our narrative. What we want to talk about are women in one capacity: their capacity as wife, mother, sister, daughter to a man. I see this in fiction all the time. I see it in books and TV. I hear it in the way people talk.

All those cannibal llamas.

It makes it really hard for me to write about llamas who aren't cannibals.

• • •

James Tiptree, Jr. has a very interesting story called, "The Women Men Don't See." I read it when I was twenty, and I admit I had a difficult time understanding what the fuss was all about. This was the story? But...this wasn't the story! We're stuck for the full narrative inside the head of a man who does very little, who's traveling with a woman and her daughter. Like the man, of course, we as readers don't "see" them. We don't realize that they are, in fact, the heroes of the story until it's over.

This was the man's story, after all. That was his narrative. It's his story we were a part of. They were just passing objects, some NPCs in his limited landscape.

We didn't see them.

• • •

When I was sixteen, I wrote an essay about why women should remain barred from combat in the U.S. military. I found it recently while going through some old papers. My argument for why women shouldn't be in combat was because war was terrible, and families were important, and with all these men dying in war, why would we want women to die, too?

That was my entire argument.

"Women shouldn't go to war because, like men do now, they would die there."

I got an "A."

• • •

I often tell people that I'm the biggest self-aware misogynist I know.

I was writing a scene last night between a woman general and the man she helped put on the throne. I started writing in some romantic tension, and realized how lazy that was. There are other kinds of tension.

I made a passing reference to sexual slavery, which I had to cut. I nearly had him use a gendered slur against her. I growled at the screen. He wanted to help save her child…no. Her brother? Okay. She was going to betray him. Okay. He had some wives who died…ugh. No. Close advisors? Friends? Maybe somebody just…left him?

Even writing about societies where there is very little sexual violence, or no sexual violence against women, I find myself writing in the same tired tropes and motivations. "Well, this is a bad guy, and I need something traumatic to happen to this heroine, so I'll have him rape her." That was an actual thing I did in the first draft of my first book, which features a violent society where women outnumber men twenty-five to one. Because, of course, it's What You Do.

I actually watched a TV show recently that was supposedly about this traumatic experience a young girl went through, but was, in fact, simply tossed in so that the two male characters in the show could fight over it, and argue about which of them was at fault because of what happened to her. It was the most flagrant erasure of a female character and her experiences that I'd seen in some time. She's literally in the room with them while they fight about it, revealing all these character things about them while she sort of fades into the background.

We forget what the story's about. We erase women in our stories who, in our own lives, are powerful, forthright, intelligent, terrifying people. Women stab and maim and kill and lead and manage and own and run. We know that. We experience it every day. We *see* it.

But this is our narrative: two men fighting loudly in a room, and a woman snuffling in a corner.

• • •

What is "realism"? What is "truth"? People tell me that the truth is what they've experienced. But the trouble is, it's often hard to sort out what we actually experienced from what we're told we experienced, or what we should have experienced. We're social creatures, and fallible.

In disaster situations, the average person will ask for about four other opinions before forming their own (io9.com/the-frozen-calm-of-normalcy-bias-486764924), before taking action. You can train people to respond quickly in these types of situations through vigorous training (such as in the military), but for the most part, about seventy percent of human beings like to just go along with their everyday routine. We like our narrative. It takes overwhelming evidence and—more importantly—the words of many, many, many people around us, for us to take action.

You see this all the time in big cities. It's why people can get into fistfights and assault others on busy sidewalks. It's why people are killed in broad daylight, and homes are broken into even in areas with lots of foot traffic. Most people actually ignore things out of the ordinary. Or, worse, hope that someone else will take care of it.

I remember being on the train in Chicago in a car with about a dozen other people. On the other side of the car, a man suddenly fell off his seat. Just... toppled over into the aisle. He started convulsing. There were three people between me and him. But nobody said anything. Nobody did anything.

I stood up, "Sir?" I said, and started toward him.

And that's when everyone started to move. I called for someone at the back to push the operator alert button, to tell the train driver to call for an ambulance at the next stop. After I moved, there were suddenly three or four other people with me, coming to the man's aid.

But somebody had to move *first*.

I stood in a crowded, standing-room-only train on another day and watched a young woman standing near the door close her eyes and drop her papers and binder onto the floor. She was packed tight, surrounded by other people, and no one said anything.

Her body began to go limp. "Are you okay!?" I said loudly, leaning toward her, and then other people were looking, and she was sagging, and the buzz started, and somebody called up from the front of the car that he was a doctor, and someone gave up their seat, and people moved, moved, moved.

Somebody needs to be the person who says something is wrong. We can't pretend we don't see it. Because people have been murdered and assaulted on street corners where hundreds of people milled around, pretending everything was normal.

But pretending it was normal didn't make it so.

Somebody has to point it out. Somebody has to get folks to move.

Somebody has to *act*.

• • •

I shot my first gun at my boyfriend's house in high school: first a rifle, then a sawed-off shotgun. I have since gotten to be pretty decent with a Glock, still terrible with a rifle, and had the opportunity to shoot an AK-47, the gun of choice for revolutionary armies around the world, particularly in the '80s.

I knocked over my first 200 lb. punching bag with my fist when I was twenty-four.

The punch meant more. Anyone could shoot a gun. But now I knew how to hit things properly in the face. Hard.

Growing up, I learned that women fulfilled certain types of roles and did certain types of things. It wasn't that I didn't have great role models. The women in my family were hardworking matriarchs. But the stories I saw on TV and movies and even in many books said they were anomalies. They were furry, non-cannibalistic llamas. So rare.

But the stories were all wrong.

I spent two years in South Africa and another decade once I returned to the States finding out about all the women who fought. Women fought in every revolutionary army, I found, and those armies were often composed of fighting forces that were twenty to thirty percent women. But when we say "revolutionary army," what do we think of? What image does it conjure? Does the force in your mind include three women and seven men? Six women and fourteen men?

Women not only made bombs and guns in WWII—they picked up guns and drove tanks and flew airplanes. The Civil War, the Revolutionary War—point me to a war and I can point to an instance where women picked up a hat and a gun and went off to join it. And yes, Shaka Zulu employed female fighters as well. But when we say "Shaka Zulu's fighters," what image do we conjure in our minds? Do we think of these women? Or are they the ones we don't see? The ones who, if we included them in our stories, people would say weren't "realistic"?

Of course, we do talk about women who ran with Shaka Zulu. When I Google "women who fought for Shaka Zulu" I learn all about his "harem of 1200 women." And his mother, of course. And this line was very popular: "Women, cattle, and slaves." One breath.

It's easy to think women never fought, never led, when we are never seen.

• • •

What does it matter, if we tell the same old stories? If we share the same old lies? If women fight, and women lead, and women hold up half the sky, what do stories matter to the truth? We won't change the truth by writing people out of it.

Will we?

Stories tell us who we are. What we're capable of. When we go out looking for stories, we are, I think, in many ways going in search of ourselves, trying to find understanding of our lives, and the people around us. Stories and language tell us what's important.

If women are "bitches" and "cunts" and "whores" and the people we're killing are "gooks" and "japs" and "ragheads," then they aren't really people, are they? It makes them easier to erase. Easier to kill. To disregard. To un-see.

But the moment we re-imagine the world as a buzzing hive of individuals with a variety of genders and complicated sexes and unique, passionate narratives that have yet to be told—it makes them harder to ignore. They are no longer "women and cattle and slaves," but active players in their own stories.

And ours.

Because when we choose to write stories, it's not just an individual story we're telling. It's theirs. And yours. And ours. We all exist together. It all happens here. It's muddy and complex and often tragic and terrifying. But ignoring half of it, and pretending there's only one way a woman lives or has ever lived—in relation to the men that surround her—is not a single act of erasure, but a political erasure.

Populating a world with men, with male heroes, male people, and their "women, cattle, and slaves" is a political act. You are making a conscious choice to erase *half the world.*

As storytellers, there are more interesting choices we can make.

I can tell you all day that llamas have scales. I can draw you pictures. I can rewrite history. But I am a single storyteller, and my lies don't become narrative unless you agree with me. Unless you write just like me. Unless you, too, buy my lazy narrative and perpetuate it.

You must be complicit in this erasure for it to happen. You, me, all of us.

Don't let it happen.

Don't be lazy.

The llamas will thank you.

Real human people will, too.

~

Kameron Hurley is a Very Serious Writer who currently hacks out a living as a marketing and advertising scribe in Ohio. She spent much of her roaring twenties traveling, pretending to learn how to box, and trying not to die spectacularly. Along the way, she justified her nomadic lifestyle by picking up degrees in history from the University of Alaska and the University of Kwa-Zulu Natal. Today, she lives a comparatively boring life sustained by Coke Zero, Chipotle, low-carb cooking, and lots of words. She continues to work hard at not dying.

WRITING STORIES, WRINKLING TIME

KAT HOWARD

The very first work of science fiction I ever read was written by a woman, and featured a female lead. And the female characters in the book weren't limited to just the lead. There was an entire compelling and interesting cast of them. Not because this was some Amazonian dystopia where something happened to all the men but the one poor guy whose sad duty was to repopulate humanity, but just because! More than that, the book was given to me by a woman, by my mom's best friend. It was Madeleine L'Engle's *A Wrinkle in Time,* and it wasn't until I started writing in the field that I realized just how unusual this experience, so full of women, was when it came to SF.

I find myself in a field now that all too often seems convulsed by the idea that if women are doing it, it can't be SF. God knows, we shouldn't be writing it, because then we contaminate the lovely pristine science with feelings and relationships, and with women doing things they couldn't possibly be doing. That treats as exceptions the contributions of Mary Shelley and James Tiptree, Jr. and Joanna Russ and Connie Willis and Mary Doria Russell and Marie Curie and Rosalind Franklin and Ada Lovelace and Anita Borg and Grace Hopper to their respective fields.

I don't want to destroy science fiction, not really. I want to remind it that— at its best—it is the literature of extraordinary possibility. Of looking to the future, to the stars, to the place past the limits of current knowledge, and saying "there." There is what we can imagine. There is what we can be. There is what is possible. Of not just dreaming bigger, but dreaming better.

I want, quite desperately, to go back in time to the world of that seven-year-old girl who read *A Wrinkle in Time* and felt like she had found a book and a world she belonged in.

~

Kat Howard is the World Fantasy Award-nominated author of over twenty pieces of short fiction. Her work has been performed on NPR as part of "Selected Shorts," and has appeared in *Lightspeed*, *Subterranean*, and *Apex*, among other venues. Her novella, "The End of the Sentence," written with Maria Dahvana Headley, will be out in August from Subterranean Press. You can find her on twitter as @KatWithSword and she blogs at strangeink.blogspot.com.

WHERE ARE MY SF BOOKS?

DeAnna Knippling

A lot of the things I know now about women and SF, I didn't learn until my daughter was old enough to start reading chapter books. The two don't really seem to connect, do they? Chapter books (or early reader books) are for kids age six to eight-ish, and they're deadly dull. I'm sorry. I'm sure there are people out there who love *Magic Tree House* and that ilk with a passion, but we had trouble getting through them, reading them together. I turned to other books. What was I reading when I was that age? I couldn't remember, really, but I dipped back as far as I could into my memories, for things like *The Hobbit* and Narnia and Heinlein and Piers Anthony and whatnot.

My daughter wasn't interested in the things that I loved. Especially the SF.

She wanted adventure books (not that slow old Hobbit stuff), and she wanted books about girls. She did not see why she had to put up with boy main characters. Or boring stuff about girls, for that matter (Narnia? A snoozer). She had all kinds of other options than reading—so why waste her time on something that wasn't at least as good as *The Powerpuff Girls*?

That's when it started to snap into place.

SF was: a) All about Boys, b) Very Literary, or c) Not Otherwise Accessible to Kids. I'm not talking "not appropriate for kids," in the sense of being frightened of finding dirty words or sex. We ended up finding and liking Tamora Pierce, thank you very much, and have been vastly entertained by many inappropriate things since then. But on the SF side—not so much. *The Giver* went over well eventually, and so did *A Wrinkle in Time*. But I had a horrible time finding other things. I could have looked harder; I could have found other SF she might have liked. But in the end, we ended up with a great deal more fantasy than anything else. And liked it.

At the same time, I was realizing that I was reading far, far less SF. On the one hand, I wasn't reading it because I was digging into other genres, because I'm learning to write, and often when you're learning, it's easier to process hard lessons when you're not picking apart the things you love best. But on the other hand, I was finding the same problems that my daughter did: a) All about Boys, b) Very Literary, or c) Not Otherwise Accessible to ME.

I buy a lot of books every year, and I plow through scads more via the library. Where are my SF books?

I could dig down deep and find them (and I have in many cases). But what they should be doing is sitting right at the top of the lists—the award lists, the bestseller lists. Fantasy's figured this out. So has…pretty much every other genre. Except Westerns. And it's easy to see how well those sell.

You know what's selling like hotcakes right now for SF? Young adult SF… with some female protagonists, more action than literary, and all kinds of accessible, from realistic character flaws and a focus on science that's engaging rather than alienating and asking hard questions having to do with society instead of taking an easy way out. Admittedly, I think the YA stuff skews too far for female leads—look, we're trying to get *all* the readers to grow up loving the genre—but that's another topic, for another day. Right now, I just want to know where my books are…and why they aren't helping print SF in general hit the top of everyone's lists.

~

DeAnna Knippling, at the behest of her daughter, secretly writes pulp adventure fiction for kids (she tries to stick to about half boys and half girls) under the name De Kenyon (her daughter comes up with the best ideas). She also writes adult fiction under her own name as well as doing design and editing work. She has recently appeared in *Crossed Genres*, *Black Static*, *Big Pulp*, and more. She reads submissions for *Lightspeed* and dreams one day of editing a middle-grade pulp magazine with stories that would curl the hair on a Peterbald cat. You can find her at WonderlandPress.com.

READING THE LIBRARY ALPHABETICALLY

LIZ ARGALL

It started when I read the library alphabetically...

No, it started with *Superman III* and Richard Pryor's dream of what computers could be.

It started with *Doctor Who*: Tom Baker, the twinkle-eyed uncle with jelly babies; Peter Davison, the mean older brother; Sylvester McCoy, the whimsical daydreamer who cared too much. Sylvester McCoy, my doctor. Ace, my companion, who was nobody's victim, wore a bomber jacket with voluminous pockets and made her own explosives.

It started in school when I watched *Star Trek* and *Red Dwarf* so I could keep up and have something in common with the nerd girls (and even a few nerd boys) that I still love to this day.

But no, I didn't think of those shows as Science Fiction, not then. Not my Science Fiction with capital letters, the fiction that set me on a path and shaped me as the writer I would become. That came from reading the library alphabetically.

Reading the library alphabetically was a solitary pursuit, huddled away in the stacks on a mildewed couch with mice scuttling in my peripheral vision. It was a private thing, and a lonely thing. I read introductions to anthologies that gave me windows into faraway America, where people spoke with confidence about trends and best of's. They spoke with authority about battles in nomenclature that I only knew about as they argued to redefine the terms. The world those editors wrote about seemed almost as alien and impossible as Mars.

Asimov gave me a love of Mars. I read a lot of Asimov's robot series, way up there in the A's. He was so different to *Star Trek*, *D&D*, *TMNT*, *Doctor Who*

437

and cyberpunk. I loved his academic rigor. I loved his introductions where he spent so much time explaining how our understanding of the planets had changed since he wrote the story. I loved his robots. I loved their yearning, the way they stretched the limits of their programming or fell into traps, but always strove. Sincere, good-hearted striving and failing isn't something we see a lot of in non-"literary" fiction, but the robots were magnificent in their failures, often profound failures. The beauty and the tragedy of these characters created human-shaped entities in fiction I could relate to. Perhaps it says something that my comfort reading included Virginia Woolf, Jack London, Oscar Wilde, and short stories by Steinbeck.

And it may sound strange, given critiques he has received, but Asimov gave me my first memories of an adult female character I liked and admired! A strong woman who wasn't sexualized (at least to my twelve year-old eyes—I have not re-read), who seemed whole and complete and complicated. Susan Calvin, who was interested in her own story, achieving what she thought was important, was wonderfully competent and was in a position of power and authority. I loved that she didn't play nice and she was successful and that was a breath of fresh air. She wasn't pretty and I especially liked that. People have told me how nastily Asimov wrote Susan Calvin, but I think every time I came across a "negative" description of her I must have rejoiced. You can be older and not-pretty and have people think about your body in negative ways and be angry and capable and in authority and that is marvelous. How often do we get active female characters like that?

Working my way through Asimov, and Arthur C. Clarke (*Rama Revealed*, I didn't find *Rendezvous with Rama* for years), and many anthologies, it slowly dawned on me. I'd always known I wanted to be a writer, from the age of seven I'd known, but it crept up on me that I wanted to write Science Fiction. It terrified me. Even whispering the word in the depths of my own mind felt close to impossible. Gendered marketing and schoolyard politics had made it clear I was not welcome and trying to grapple with the vastness of the cosmos can be terrifying for any soul or gender. As my reading continued, I learned the acronyms SF, SFF, and the politics of the phrase "Speculative Fiction" over "Science Fiction." (After serious thought, I decided I would join team speculate.) "I want to write SF": I could whisper that in the quiet of my mind and not always slide off the edges.

I remember standing in the library, thinking about being a girl trying to write science fiction. (I wonder how different life would have been if Butler or Russ had graced our library shelves.) Thinking about being a girl trying to prove myself to a series of blank-faced male American faces (with maybe a few from the UK) made me feel very small. My dry, bookish world of science fiction seemed so different to the brightly colored fandom of my friends and I had been taught to be somewhat snobbish about pop culture—even as I smeared my nose against the glass looking in.

I remember standing in the middle of the library, suddenly caught short by a thought, tears welling in my eyes. Would I be forever lonely? Trying to break into boys' club after boys' club? I'd already learned that becoming good at handball just meant the boys stopped playing if I came near.

Then, working my way through the library, I got to Le Guin. I had loved *A Wizard of Earthsea*, LOVED it, but it never occurred to me that she would write beyond fantasy. Her science fiction blew my mind; her essays inspired me and gave me dreams to chase.

Part of me felt jealous. I wanted to be the first female Science Fiction Author (I'm sure I had read science fiction by women before that, but had categorized it differently, not hard enough, not marketed as such—the way dystopian futures written by women are still erased as kidsy or other ghettoizing notions that render women invisible in our field). A bigger part of me was relieved. Le Guin showed me that female writers could make it in the world. Just as *Aurealis* magazine appeared in my life and gave me stories in my geography and culture, stories where America wasn't always the center and the homes were more like my home.

For me, Le Guin had broken the path and written science fiction that resonated on so many levels. Her ansible, her exploration of space travel and diverse culture—one of her stories even made me feel angry and that radicalized my reading in a wonderful way.

Later I would properly tackle my own internalized misogyny, but for the time being me and Ursula Le Guin were the only female science fiction writers and we were going to change the world.

Mary Shelley, look at us now!

~

Liz Argall has been destroying science fiction in places like *Apex Magazine*, *Strange Horizons*, *Daily Science Fiction*, *Anywhere But Earth*, and *This Is How You Die: Stories of the Inscrutable, Infallible, Inescapable Machine of Death*. She creates the webcomic *Things Without Arms and Without Legs* and writes love songs to inanimate objects. She generally doesn't put her SFWA membership on her bio, she never mentioned her Australian Society of Authors membership back in the day, and once you start mentioning memberships and workshops (like Clarion or Launch Pad) the bio can get terribly long! SFWA membership just seemed relevant for this particular essay. Her previous incarnations include circus manager, refuge worker, artists' model, research officer for the Order of Australia Awards, and extensive work in the not-for-profit sector. Her roller derby name is Betsy Nails. She has a website lizargall.com.

STEPPING THROUGH
A PORTAL

BONNIE JO STUFFLEBEAM

I did not read much science fiction growing up. I liked what I did stumble upon: *Childhood's End; Alas, Babylon; A Scanner Darkly, Fahrenheit 451; Hitchhiker's Guide to the Galaxy.* But although these stories fascinated me, there was little in them to relate to for a bisexual teenage girl. What I read instead were YA books written for teens like me, all lacking in any element of the fantastical or science fictional: *Girl Walking Backwards; Dare, Truth, or Promise; Pages for You* (the reading of which was a steamy secret I kept from my parents). We were taught *Frankenstein* in school, of course, and in one particularly resonant AP English class we were required to read Margaret Atwood's *The Handmaid's Tale.* The boys in the class complained; it was too liberal, too feminist, not as classic as the other dystopian novels we were exploring—*Brave New World* and *1984.* "Why did we have to read *that*?" they asked.

It wasn't until college that I stumbled upon women writing science fiction, and it was like stepping through a portal to a whole new world. No one had ever told me about these books, about these writers—Ursula K. Le Guin, Octavia Butler, Alice Sheldon, Kelly Link—or, for that matter, about this niche of SFF, where lived the subtle, character-oriented stories I'd always longed to read—and write. I thought I had found a haven by and for women like me. Then I started to read the comments, the critiques, follow the controversies, and it became apparent that the utopia I thought I had discovered was not a utopia after all. Like in Le Guin's "The Ones Who Walk Away From Omelas," there was a darker side to paradise, a sinister presence lurking in comments sections, in bulletins and blogs, in reviews. It was just like in my high school English class, only the people who labeled these women-written stories as too feminist had bigger soapboxes from which to shout. It was a devastating blow for a young woman, one that dragged me down to a less rosy view of the science fiction world.

These days I try to see the bright side as much as possible, and there is certainly a light in the dark; more than one, in fact. Women continue to write genre-defying science fiction, which I continue to read, and magazines like *Tin House* (*Fantastic Women: 18 Tales of the Surreal and the Sublime*), the now-defunct *Electric Velocipede*, and, yes, *Lightspeed*, release issues devoted entirely to women and all their glorious destruction. I am proud to be part of this, to be one of the women working to tear down the gendered walls of SFF, so that in the future, teenage girls can easily find themselves in the science fiction that they read.

~

Bonnie Jo Stufflebeam lives in Texas with her husband and two literarily named cats: Gimli and Don Quixote. Her fiction and poetry has appeared in magazines such as *Clarkesworld*, *Strange Horizons*, *Goblin Fruit*, and *Daily Science Fiction*. She holds an MFA in Creative Writing from the University of Southern Maine's Stonecoast program and reviews short fiction at her blog, *Short Story Review*. You can visit her on Twitter @BonnieJoStuffle or through her website: bonniejostufflebeam.com.

THE WENDYBIRD

STINA LEICHT

When I was a little girl, my mother read *Peter Pan* aloud to me. As often happens, life got in the way. She stopped before she got to the end. Thus, for me the story ended when the Lost Boys shoot Wendy for hoping to set foot on Neverland. That was my first real experience of fantasy. Neverland was a place that killed girls. Still, I wanted to be a Knight of the Round Table. Dolls were okay, and so were tiaras, but I wanted to wear a pretty silk dress and slay my own dragons—better, I wanted to be good at it. And then I found SF through Madeline L'Engle. L'Engle said women could have adventures in SF. If females were only nominally present, at least no one would kill me for showing up. I thought SF was for smart, open-minded, forward-thinking people.

However, I soon discovered that SF wasn't all that different from Neverland.

The funny thing is that everyone assumes the most difficult part of being a woman in a white straight man's world is the struggle to be accepted. Sure, someone flipped over the "No Girls Allowed" sign on the clubhouse, but the sign still exists. The external world still informs you in one way or another that you don't count, and you never will. That's bad enough, but then there's the more powerful aspect—the internal voice.

Like it or not, people are partly a product of their environment. I was raised in a misogynistic culture. I have to double-think everything I write because if I'm not careful, I'll act in a way that runs against my own (and other women's) best interest. It sucks that I'm more comfortable writing in a male character's point of view than a female's. It sucks that I can't write for young kids or even write a sex scene without feeling like I'm selling out to a system that insists these are my only creative outlets. It sucks that when a man successfully writes from a female point of view, he's showered with praise, but if a woman successfully writes from a male point of view, it's shrugged off as just one of a million expected aspects of good writing. It sucks that every single time I tell someone I'm an author, I have to explain that no, I don't write children's books, nor do I write erotica. It sucks that I've never seen a male author asked those questions. It sucks that men's voices are given more importance than women's—so much so that whenever I see a piece mocking *Girls* on HBO, I'm left wondering if the show really is that banal or if it's just another moment where women's problems are belittled? I question everything. I have to. Being self-aware is survival, and when I hear men whine about being asked to do the same, I just want to say, "Welcome to my world."

~

Stina Leicht is a two-time Campbell Award nominee for Best New Writer (2012 and 2013.) Her debut novel *Of Blood and Honey*, a historical fantasy set in 1970s Northern Ireland, was short-listed for the Crawford Award. The sequel, *And Blue Skies from Pain*, is available now. Her shorter fiction is also featured in Ann and Jeff VanderMeer's surreal anthology *Last Drink Bird Head*, and in the anthology *Rayguns Over Texas*.

I Wanted to be the First Woman on the Moon

Sylvia Spruck Wrigley

When I was six years old, my teacher asked everyone to tell her what they wanted to be when they grew up. She went to each desk, one by one, and we were to whisper it in her ear, and then she would tell the class. When it was my turn, I whispered in her ear that I wanted to be the first woman on the moon.

"You what?"

The class tittered. I whispered it again. I wanted to be the first woman on the moon.

She smiled and nodded. But then she started giggling as she told the room. Everyone laughed. The class stared at me, uninterested in Becky, who wanted to be a mom and Tom, who wanted to be a fireman. I kept my head up and stared at the blackboard.

The principal walked past the classroom and our teacher beckoned him in. "Come here, you *have* to hear this. Sylvia, tell him what you told me."

So in front of the whole class, I said it again. I want to be the first woman on the moon.

He laughed and said, "But what if some other little girl, some little girl who is already sixteen, wants the same thing. What then?"

I chewed my lip, looked at my feet. He patted me on the head and left the room.

It was my first lesson that some things aren't worth trying for, because you aren't going to get them anyway.

No one said, hey, so you want to be an astronaut! No one noticed that I had already internalized that women were only in competition with one another. I didn't want to be the first person on Mars or the first person to explore to the edges of the solar system. The best that I hoped for was to be the first woman to do something that a man had already done. This was our world. This was how it had always been.

I gave up on that dream. When people asked what I wanted to be, I picked more realistic goals. A rock singer. A movie star. An author. And no one laughed anymore.

But I keep thinking about the past and the future and how that six-year-old could have been told being an astronaut was a worthy goal, whether or not she was the first. Luckily, my mother encouraged me to dream, so all those dreams about outer space made it onto paper…and still do. I write about recreating recipes on far-off colonies and the trials of living a million miles from Starbucks. I write about the daughters and the mothers and the great aunts. I write about the lack of Tampax. I write about those left behind. And in the end, I believe that, as a woman writing *real* science fiction, I bring more than I ever could have if I'd actually traveled to the moon. Although there's still time, maybe, if I act fast.

~

Sylvia Spruck Wrigley obsessively writes letters to her mother, her teenage offspring, her accountant, as well as to unknown beings in outer space. Only her mother admits to reading them. Born in Heidelberg, she spent her childhood in California and now splits her time between South Wales and Andalucía, two coastal regions with almost nothing in common. Her short fiction has most recently appeared in *Daily Science Fiction*, *Crossed Genres* and *Lightspeed*. You can find out more about her at intrigue.co.uk.

NEVER THINK OF YOURSELF AS LESS

HELENA BELL

Last spring I got a voicemail on my phone from an unknown number. After listening to it, I said, more to myself than to my parents, who happened to be in the room with me, "My story has been nominated for the Nebula Award."

"Oh," my father said. "Is that good?"

My mother immediately went to the shelf and started pulling down books: Kevin J. Anderson, Frank Herbert, Orson Scott Card.

"Here," she said. "Look." And she showed him back covers and inside flaps: writers my father had heard of mentioning here and there that yes, they too had once been nominated for or won a Nebula.

"Yes," she said. "It's good.

• • •

It was my mother who read the Timothy Zahn *Star Wars* novels to my brother and me as bedtime stories. She's the one who bought me a copy of *Jurassic Park* when I was ten, then *Congo*, *Sphere*, *The Andromeda Strain*.

She gave me other books too, of course: *Black Beauty*, *The Little Princess*, ALL the *Misty* books. But we always veered slowly back into science fiction.

Yet there was no Ursula K. Le Guin in her recommendations. No Russ, Tiptree, Asaro, or Bujold. By the time I finally started reading speculative short fiction, I could name a dozen favorite female poets, female literary writers, and essayists…But not a single female science fiction writer other than Ursula K. Le Guin, whom I only really knew thanks to *A Wizard of Earthsea*.

It's taken me years to slowly correct the course I was set upon, lovingly, by my mother. Last spring may have been the first time that she'd read any science fiction by women, as she quickly devoured all the stories nominated in my category. She liked Cat Rambo's story a lot. Less so Aliette's story "Immersion," because I told her it would win and, well, she's still my mom.

So no. She didn't hand me a battered copy of *The Left Hand of Darkness* or scour the SF section in the bookstore for female sounding names in order to broaden my (and her) reading tastes. She gave me the books she knew, that had been recommended to her by the few other people she knew who read SF—all of whom were men.

But she gave me *lots* of them. As many as I could read. SF, fantasy, horse books, princess books, Nancy Drew, and Judy Blume. And when my teachers wrote on my report card "Helena is very bright, but sometimes she reads during class when she should be paying attention," she just laughed and bought me more.

"Never let a teacher tell you to read less," she said. Or to write less. To dream less. To think of yourself as less.

So thanks, Mom. For everything.

~

Helena Bell is a writer living in Raleigh, NC, where she is an MFA Candidate in Fiction at North Carolina State University. She is a graduate of the Clarion West Workshop and her work has appeared in *Clarkesworld*, *The Indiana Review*, and *Electric Velocipede*. Her short story "Robot" was a nominee for the Nebula Award in 2012.

AN ABC OF KICKASS

OR A PARTIAL EXORCISM
OF MY TBR/TBRA* PILE

JUDE GRIFFIN

A is for Athena Andreadis's *To Seek Out New Life: The Biology of Star Trek*: an entertaining and erudite look at the strength of the science in the science fiction classic. (A is also for **A**nnoying my husband by bringing up her points like why the differing blood color of Vulcans and humans means no Spock.)

B is for Leigh **B**rackett, Queen of Space Opera, and her unbeatable story titles like "The Beast-Jewel of Mars," and "Purple Priestess of the Mad Moon."

C is for Margaret **C**avendish, Duchess of Newcastle, who wrote of submarines in the sixteen hundreds in *The Blazing-World*.

D is for Aliette **d**e Bodard's "The Heartless Light of Stars": "In space, distance is time."

E is for **E**katerina Sedia's "Herding Vegetable Sheep," where entertainment conglomerates run for and win presidencies.

F is forever for *Frankenstein*, written by the nineteen-year-old Mary Shelley, laying bare the hubris of science unhinged from ethics and one of the most important science fiction works ever written.

G is for Glotolog, documented in Joanna Russ's searing tale of the encompassing cultural oppression of the Whelk-finned Glotologs over the Crescent-finned, Spotty, and Mottled populations, *How to Suppress Women's Writing*.

H is for Nalo Hopkinson, whose science fiction is unconstrained by anyone's rules or expectations, who weaves together magic and science as suits the story, and who made a dress that hangs in my closet (shameless fangirling by me, sorry).

I is for "In Hiding," by Wilmar Shiras, a short story that became the first chapter of *Children of the Atom*—thought to be the inspiration for the *X-Men* comic books.

J is for Jezebels, sterilized, state-controlled prostitutes in Margaret Atwood's *The Handmaid's Tale*.

K is for Kameron Hurley, rescuing the history of soft, downy, non-cannibalistic llamas in "We Have Always Fought."

L is for Madeleine L'Engle: Her genre-busting science fiction and fantasy novel, *A Wrinkle In Time*, is one of the most marvelous introductions to SFF a child could have.

M is for Mistressworks: go.

N is for Nnedi Okorafor: vengeful swordfish, robotic spiders, rapacious multinationals, elgorts, clack beetles, aliens, apocalypses, and goddesses—what's not to love?

O is for Octavia Butler: the first science fiction writer ever to win the MacArthur Fellowship (aka, Genius Grant).

P is for Parrish Plessis, the star of Marianne de Pierres's rollicking SF action adventure series.

Q is for the Quetz, Joyce Chng's empathic, pterosaur-like creatures. With feathers!

R is for Rukbat 3, aka Pern, the setting for Anne McCaffrey's Dragonriders series.

S is for *Memoirs of a Spacewoman* by Naomi Mitchison, where space exploration is the skeleton for an exploration of empathy, binary thinking bias, sexuality, and whose own life is a fantastic tale of its own.

T is for Tiamat, home of the Winters and the Summers in Joan Vinge's *The Snow Queen*.

U is for Ursula Le Guin and her Hainish explorations of physics, gender, sexuality, politics, and religion. And who published her story "Nine Lives" in Playboy as "**U.K.** Le Guin" because, as an editor noted, "Many of our readers are frightened by stories by women."

V is for Eliza Victoria's *Project 17*: Orwell with robots! And world-building that feels all too real.

W is for Clare Winger Harris: the first woman to be published in SF publications and a visionary for her recognition that one gender need not embody all the courage, curiosity, intelligence, abilities, daring, and strength in a tale.

X is for all the names and stories and worlds and ideas lost to us through willful blindness, dismissal, fear, and antipathy.

Y is for Yod, the cyborg at the center of Marge Piercy's novel, *He, She, and It*, exploring love, gender, and identity in a corporate-controlled dystopia.

Z is for Zinzi December in *Zoo City*, Lauren Beukes's novel of an alternate South Africa, animalling, the music industry, and a criminal underworld. Bonus points for wearing a fake sloth while accepting the Arthur C. Clarke Award.

* TBRA=To Be Read Again

~

Jude Griffin is an envirogeek, writer, and photographer. She has trained llamas at the Bronx Zoo; was a volunteer EMT, firefighter, and HAZMAT responder; worked as a guide and translator for journalists covering combat in Central America; lived in a haunted village in Thailand; ran an international frog monitoring network; and loves happy endings. Bonus points for frolicking dogs and kisses backlit by a shimmering full moon. Jude is also an editorial assistant at *Lightspeed Magazine*.

STOCKING STUFFERS

ANAEA LAY

It's Christmas of 1998. I'm thirteen, in the eighth grade, and hate just about everything.

I'm supposed to get Confirmed in the spring, but have deep theological concerns that I want resolved first. You see, I'm very serious, very snobby, and commitments to omnipotent deities are not a thing I'm inclined to take lightly. Instead of getting answers, I'm warmly invited to stop coming to CCD.

That's upsetting, but there's more. I have to spend most of my time with other thirteen-year-olds, and they're busy doing the adolescent sexual awakening thing. None of it makes any sense to me since the amount of cheating via illicit hand-holding going on makes it pretty clear that exclusive relationships are a recipe for heart-break. I'm reeling with horror after a conversation with another girl wherein she confessed that she had a crush on two different boys and was sincerely worried that made her a slut. If being a slut is that easy, I'm convinced we're all doomed.

On top of that, all my peers think fart jokes are the funniest thing ever, and that finishing your classwork in ten minutes and spending the rest of the time reading is a social faux pas. Also, no matter how much I practice the flute, there is no overcoming the fact that I couldn't keep a beat if the fate of the universe depended on it. So, basically, being thirteen sucked for me just like it did for everybody before or since.

This Christmas is special, though. I go downstairs at my grandparent's house to pillage my stocking and in with the usual socks, lip gloss, and nail polish is a book. A weird book with cover art of carefully posed naked people swimming underwater. I give my Dad a *look*. A "Dad, are you nuts?" look. He disavows all knowledge of what the elves were up to. I put the book at the

451

bottom of my massive stack of Christmas-gift-books and figure I'll get to it if I run out of things to read before my birthday in June brings more.

Spring comes, and with it the eighth grade English class project on persecution. This is the unit where everybody reads one of four books: *The Diary of Anne Frank*, *1984*, *Animal Farm*, or *Fahrenheit 451*. I do not want to do one of those books. I also don't know how to pick out a book about persecution without having read it already. "Do you still have that book I gave you for Christmas?" my dad asks when I lament my conundrum at the dinner table. "Have I ever lost or given up a book?" I reply. "Read that book," he says.

I was not the first person to read *Stranger in a Strange Land* and have my mind a little bit blown. In fact, I was so far behind the curve there that only the cannibalism would cut it as a scandalous idea anymore. But it was the first time I ran into something that said, "Hey, you can be a good person without being Christian," and also said, "Monogamy is a bit messed up, don't you think?" These were things I really needed to hear, not because they were my introduction to those ideas, but because they were my introduction to the idea that I wasn't alone for having them. I wasn't even so weird that my dad couldn't notice what was going on and slip a message into my Christmas stocking.

Or maybe Dad just wanted us to have a literature canon in common and that was the Christmas I was finally old enough that the sexual content of later Heinlein wasn't too mature for me. It could have been an accident that he handed me the perfect book at the perfect moment. I've never asked and don't plan to; that'd risk ruining a really good story.

Story has been the lens I use to interact with the world for as long as I've been a conscious being. There was never a question about whether I'd be a writer, even as my dreams of becoming a rock star and concert flautist fell apart on me. From Christmas of 1998, there was never a question about whether I'd write science fiction. It was my first hint that I wasn't alone, that if I just gritted my teeth and waited, then I could go find the parts of the world that would make sense to me and then I could make them mine.

If that means I'm destroying SF, oh well. Someday I'm going to have nieces and nephews, and they're going to have to be thirteen, too. You'd better believe I'll do whatever it takes to make sure the perfect book for them winds up in their stocking.

~

Anaea Lay lives in Madison, Wisconsin where she sells real estate under a different name, writes, cooks, plays board games, spoils her cat, runs the *Strange Horizons* podcast, and plots to take over the world. Her work has appeared in a variety of venues, including *Strange Horizons*, *Lightspeed*, *Nightmare*, *Apex*, and *Daily Science Fiction*.

Breaching the Gap

Brooke Bolander

Unlike a lot of you, my fantastic voyage didn't start until some point in or around 1995. Science I've always loved; from five years old onwards, I wanted to be a paleontologist, and nothing in the intervening years caused my digging urges to dry up. The first thing I ever clearly remember reading, at the age of three or so, was a children's book on Roy Chapman Andrews and his trip to the Gobi Desert to excavate the fossilized nests of Protoceratops. Science fiction, however…well. Innocuous stuff like *Flight of the Navigator, Batteries Not Included*, and *Short Circuit* I could get away with watching, but my fundamentalist mother was convinced little gray aliens were actually little gray demons from the bowels of Dis, and so my exposure was severely limited.

At least until 1995 and *The X-Files*.

As you'll all no doubt be shocked to learn, I was something of a lonely, outcast nerd in junior high. As many a lonely, outcast nerd has done before and since, I retreated to the comforting cloisters of my bedroom on Friday nights. When ruining my eardrums with loud music and my eyeballs with JRPGs got too boring, I turned to my old babysitter, the television.

Scully was strong, stronger than any other woman I'd seen in science fiction. She was icy and arch and logical. She was a scientist, but sometimes she did impulsive, self-destructive shit, like everybody does once in a while. Her belly was soft in spots, but by no means was she ever portrayed as weak. Her relationship with Mulder was built on mutual love and respect, not some vapid *Moonlighting* "GOTTA GET ME A MAN AND GET LAID" headlong hormonal charge into non-autonomy. In short, she was shown as a fucking human being. Feminine without resorting to clichés, smart without implying that razor intelligence lessened her somehow as a woman.

I connected with that character in a way I'd never, ever connected with a fictional character before. I didn't even know you could identify with a made-up person that closely. I was a voracious reader as a child, but Scully just about broke my young heart.

Science fiction has always been to me, at its core, about relationships and the ways we interact with one another. The best of it—the stuff that sticks with you, the stuff you don't forget an hour after watching or reading—has god-damned heart. There's nothing more alien or unknowable than another person's thoughts. We travel through the world in insulated ships made of meat and bone. If you're lucky, you make contact with others. If you're extraordinarily lucky, you manage to find someone who understands you.

And if you are very, very lucky (we're talking lottery numbers and shipwreck survivors, here), you learn to put down words in such a way as to tell stories that everyone gets. Think about how phenomenal that is, to be able to connect with that many people. You're making contact with alien intelligences. You're breaching the gap.

Thanks for teaching me about that possibility, Scully. Thanks, Octavia Butler and Ursula Le Guin. If it weren't for amazing, trail-breaking, iconoclastic women, both fictional and gloriously real, I wouldn't be writing this today. I gratefully stand on the shoulders of Amazons.

~

Brooke Bolander attended the University of Leicester 2004-2007, studying History and Archaeology, and is an alum of the 2011 Clarion Writers' Workshop at UCSD. Her work has been featured in *Lightspeed*, *Strange Horizons*, *Nightmare*, *Reflection's Edge*, and the Prime Books anthology *Aliens: Recent Encounters*. She can be reached at @BBolander for the Twitter-inclined.

WOMEN WHO ARE MORE THAN STRONG

GEORGINA KAMSIKA

It might have taken a while for the world to cotton on to "geek stuff" being cool (despite *Star Wars* doing so well so long ago), but for as long as I can recall, science fiction has been my favourite genre for books and films.

I'm happy to say that I feel science fiction is really thriving. This is good, because it's not like we want to write for a small niche group alone. I love that it's okay for mums and grandmas and sons to read science fiction on the bus or the tube and no one stares. At the end of the day, it's all stories about people, even if some of them might be alien or undead.

The part that's missing, the part I really want to change, is for there to be more stories about people like me written by people like me. Women in the main role. Not a plucky sidekick, not a screaming damsel to be saved from the monster, but the leader. The protagonist (or antagonist) who drives the story forward, who has power and meaning and weight to her role. Women who are more than strong, who have personalities, friends, lovers, and enemies. Now that's science fiction I really want to read.

~

Georgina Kamsika is a speculative fiction writer born in Yorkshire, England, to Anglo-Indian immigrant parents and has spent most of her life explaining her English first name, Polish surname, and Asian features. She reads widely, everything from E.M. Forester to Chuck Palahniuk, and values her vast comics collection. She remembers being very proud when her story was chosen to be displayed on the wall (this was at infant school). Many years later, she began taking her writing seriously and has had numerous short stories published in magazines and the odd anthology. Her debut novel, *The Sulphur Diaries* (Legend Press), was released in November of 2011. Georgina is also a first reader for *Lightspeed Magazine*.

A
Science-Fictional
Woman

Cheryl Morgan

Last year, when we were going through one of the periodic "Worldcon is an evil conspiracy run by old, white men" phases in social media, I saw a young person say that what Worldcon needed to do to become relevant to the modern world was to start having some programming on LGBT issues. Ha!

The first Worldcon I attended, eighteen years earlier, had Samuel R. Delany as a Guest of Honor. I've done my share of LGBT panels at Worldcon since then. But truthfully, I felt at home in science fiction long before that.

As a kid growing up, changing gender was something that could only happen by magic. Later, when people like Christine Jorgensen and April Ashley entered my consciousness, I understood that life for me was possible. But that life was most definitely something that was a gift of *Science!* Being a transsexual was something that belonged to *The Future*. If you did it now, you were a freak, an outcast, someone who could only be at home in Professor Xavier's School for Gifted Youngsters. Or at a science fiction convention.

So what has gone wrong? How have we got to a place in which a simple request for more science fiction that doesn't assume a default gender binary can get treated as a greater threat to dude-kind than, say, banning football or beer? Why are works written fairly and squarely in a tradition established by Tiptree, Le Guin, and Russ suddenly viewed as something science fiction readers wouldn't buy?

Part of the problem is, I think, that The Future has happened. When Joe Haldeman postulated, in *The Forever War*, a future world in which homosexuality was the norm, everyone knew that he was just winding up the conservatives. Now those same conservatives are terrified that Haldeman might have actually been prescient. When I was a kid, being gay was a crime. These days in the UK, we have gay ministers in Parliament, and changing gender is a human right. Social changes are so less scary when viewed from the other end of a wormhole, or through the lens of relativistic time dilation.

The other issue is that we have won the culture war. Science fiction is no longer a haven for misfits and outcasts; it is part of mainstream society. People can no longer become science fiction fans because they don't feel welcome anywhere else. The ghetto doors are open. What happens here is reflective of what happens everywhere.

Women have, of course, always been destroying science fiction. Scholarly works such as Justine Larbalestier's *The Battle of the Sexes in Science Fiction* show this to be true. The dudebros of the day were just as terrified of catching cooties from Joanna Russ as their modern day equivalents are when faced down by Kameron Hurley. But these days the stakes are bigger. People like me are living proof that the gender binary isn't the immutable biological divide that we were taught it was in school. And if that wall crumbles, what future is there for patriarchy?

There will always be a need to destroy science fiction. Tearing down the old and bringing in the new is something that art does. But in one little corner of the genre, that corner concerned with gender, trans people have been busily taking science fiction and turning it into science fact. It is no wonder that the dudebros are scared. They can see that the tide has turned, and that their pretty little sandcastles of social privilege are about to be swept away. What sort of brave new world we end up in remains to be seen. Brit Mandelo's anthology, *Beyond Binary*, offers all sorts of possibilities. Some people may choose to abandon gender altogether. Others, like me, will be perfectly happy to live whatever gendered life suits them best.

Here's the rub, though. Iain Banks has said that when he came up with The Culture, he realized that if gender were mutable, and patriarchy still existed, then everyone would opt to be male. There's an argument to be made that the male-dominated science fiction of the so-called Golden Age is set in a world like that. Everyone lives as a man, and babies are made in tanks. It's science, right? A future in which women exist is a future that destroys that science fictional promise of no longer needing them. So there is still work to be done; still imagination needed; still a world to change.

Keep writing, ladies; we have a patriarchy to destroy.

～

Cheryl Morgan was, to her knowledge, the first openly trans person to win a Hugo Award. Science fiction was not destroyed as a result. She now runs a publishing company, Wizard's Tower Press (wizardstowerpress.com) and an ebook store, Wizard's Tower Books (wizardstowerbooks. com). This has not destroyed science fiction either. If at first you don't succeed ...

Your Future is Out of Date

Pat Murphy

I credit Robert Heinlein and the Holy Roman Catholic Church and San Francisco's Exploratorium with making me the writer I am today.

The Church gave me the time and tedium needed to practice skills I would later need. As a child, I accompanied my parents to mass each Sunday. I had no choice in the matter. I knelt, stood, and sat on cue while the priest droned on in Latin.

Since I wasn't allowed to read in church, I told myself stories. That is to say, I took stories that I had read and rewrote them in my imagination (while maintaining an appropriately pious look on my face). My rewrites almost always involved reworking a story's narrative to make a place for myself in the tale—an active role, where I could play the hero.

This was in the late '60s, and I was a fan of science fiction. The stories I read lacked heroic girls or women. In most science fiction of the time, technology had advanced, and yet somehow women were still mothers or helpers or secretaries or in need of rescue—if they were there at all.

It was a stretch to squeeze myself into these stories, but I managed it. I usually imagined a fictional me, dressed in boy's clothes and passing as a boy. In my version of *Tarzan*, a scrawny fourth-grade girl accompanied the lord of the jungle on his adventures. I credit all that exercise in daydreaming and plotting with forcing me to develop the skills I needed as a writer.

The church provided me the incentive to practice my plotting skills, but it was reading the work of Robert Heinlein that gave me the deep motivation to write. As a child, I discovered Heinlein's juveniles. Exciting stories—well told and compelling—like *Rocket Ship Galileo*, *Time for the Stars*, *Tunnel in the Sky*. Of course, creating active and interesting roles for myself in these stories required extensive reimagining, but I was used to that.

But then I read Heinlein's *Podkayne of Mars*, the story of a teenaged girl from Mars who was traveling to Venus. I was thrilled to find a girl in the novel's starring role. At last, I thought, I had found a story I would not have to rewrite. Podkayne's mother was a famous engineer; Podkayne wanted to be the captain of an explorer spaceship. It was perfect.

Unfortunately, as I read, I discovered that this was not a story for me after all. Podkayne talked about using her "feminine wiles" to learn astrogation from crewmembers. She wrote: "It is a mistake for a girl to beat a male at any test of physical strength," and "It does not do to let a male of any age know that one has brains."

Throughout the book, Podkayne proved incompetent at everything except taking care of babies and some social relations. In a time of crisis, she went to pieces and wanted to crawl back into her uncle's lap for comfort.

All this led her to alter her aspirations and accept a traditional woman's role. Her new opinion: "A baby is lots more fun than differential equations. Every starship has a crèche. So which is better? To study crèche engineering and pediatrics—and be a department head in a starship? Or buck for pilot training and make it…and wind up as a female pilot nobody wants to hire."

At age twelve, I found myself outraged. Heinlein was telling me about how the world worked—and I understood that was the way his world worked. But I didn't, I wouldn't, and couldn't believe in his teenage girl or his version of the world. I was jarred out of the story and out of Heinlein's future. It wasn't fair that Podkayne couldn't be a starship captain. It wasn't right that she had to act like she wasn't as smart as the men around her.

I was pissed. And that was when I realized something about the power of fiction writing.

Fiction writers have, in a limited sense, the power to control your mind. When you give yourself over to a good book, you come to believe in the author's world, the author's way of thinking about the way the world works. If a book is compelling, you believe in it on some very deep level. The world portrayed in the book seeps into your unconscious and becomes part of your experience of the world. The writer's truth—Heinlein's truth, my truth—becomes your truth.

As a child, I believed Heinlein's view of the world—until he wrote about something that I knew better than he did—the mind of a teenage girl. That's when he lost me. That was when his worldview bumped into something I believed in even more: my own ability to do whatever I wanted to do.

I realized that I wanted futures that were very different from the future that Heinlein described in *Podkayne of Mars*. To change the world, I had to write new futures, ones in which gender roles and social relationships were different from the ones deemed normal at the time.

My stories are viruses, carrying my version of the world. My goal is to control your mind for the duration of the story—and in the process to introduce you to different possibilities. If writing those new futures means the destruction of science fiction as we knew it, then so be it.

All that was long ago. I've been writing science fiction—and some might say destroying science fiction—for over thirty-five years. Along the way, Karen Fowler and I co-founded the Tiptree Award, which rewards those writers who are bold enough to contemplate shifts and changes in gender roles, a fundamental aspect of any society.

Recently, when I was visiting Japan, I found a copy of *Podkayne of Mars* in translation. I was surprised to see it—and even more surprised by the Japanese tagline on the cover. In loose translation, it read: "Shame on you, Mr. Heinlein. You have shattered the dreams of young girls."

I doubt that this tagline will sell the book, but I believe it nailed the essence of Heinlein's novel. It also described in a single line why I am committed to writing new futures. It warmed my heart.

∼

Pat Murphy has won numerous awards for her thoughtful, literary science fiction and fantasy writing, including two Nebula Awards, the Philip K. Dick Award, the World Fantasy Award, the Seiun Award, and the Theodore Sturgeon Memorial Award. She has published seven novels and many short stories for adults, including *Rachel in Love*, *The Falling Woman*, *The City Not Long After*, *Nadya*, and *Adventures in Time and Space with Max Merriwell*, a novel that *Publisher's Weekly* called the "cerebral equivalent of a roller-coaster ride." Her children's novel, *The Wild Girls*, won a Christopher Award in 2008. In 1991, with writer Karen Fowler, Pat co-founded the James Tiptree, Jr. Award, an annual literary prize for science fiction or fantasy that expands or explores our understanding of gender roles. This award is funded by grassroots efforts that include auctions and bake sales, harnessing the power of chocolate chip cookies in an ongoing effort to change the world. Pat enjoys looking for and making trouble. Her favorite color is ultraviolet. Her favorite book is whichever one she is working on right now.

STRAY OUTSIDE THE LINES

E. CATHERINE TOBLER

You speak your mind and they ask you what's wrong with you.

You question the words they've published and they say you want to censor their work.

You suggest a new path forward and they call you a fascist.

You see a problem and they wonder what the hell you're talking about.

They trip over themselves to tell you you're ugly, but to also not let the door hit your perky ass on the way out.

Every day, women are told and taught not to speak up. By the response our words garner, we are told our opinions are not wanted or valued. We are shown that our voices have no place alongside the words of male colleagues. Whether our words are fictional or not, we are told in subtle and blatant ways that we are still not entirely welcome to play with the boys.

You can speak, but know your place. Look to Barbie for a role model. Be quiet, be perfect, be pink, and if you stray outside the lines—

Stray outside the lines.

Be cheeky. Be bold.

They will say all manner of nasty things to you. About you. These aren't truths. Your friends will support you, and you will make new friends who share your sentiments. It's possible some will believe your criticism means their own years of hard work are worthless. This is another thing we are taught: that if X is true, so must Y be. This is not a truth. Your work is not without worth.

This is the future. This is the place we dreamed of. This is the place where everyone is supposed to be equal, no matter color, gender, age. This is the place our fictional words created—it is not by mistake, or random.

Science fiction tells us we can be equal, that we *are* equal—so don't you dare stay inside the lines. *Stray*, because sitting where you are told gets you nowhere. Science fiction taught you about the stars, science fiction told you there are better places. You aren't going to reach them without being cheeky.

~

E. Catherine Tobler lives and writes in Colorado—strange how that works out. Her Rings of Anubis series is available from Masque Books. Among others, her short fiction has appeared in *Daily Science Fiction, Fantasy Magazine, Realms of Fantasy, Clarkesworld,* and *Lady Churchill's Rosebud Wristlet.* She is a Sturgeon Award finalist and the senior editor at *Shimmer Magazine.*

MY LOVE CAN DESTROY

SEANAN MCGUIRE

I didn't choose the science fiction life. I want to make that very clear. By first grade I knew that there were "girl things" and "boy things," and that if you wanted to be the kind of girl who had friends and got invited to sleepovers and didn't sit alone in the weird kid corner of the classroom, you would like the things that were intended for you. I *yearned* for the world of the cool kids, the ones who floated in a cloud of crinoline and hair bows, who spoke authoritatively of Barbies and ponies and other acceptable hobbies. It wasn't that I didn't love those things—I did, and I still do, as my vast collection of creepy dolls and My Little Ponies will demonstrate—it was that I loved other things, too. Things that had a nasty tendency to come spilling out of my mouth every time I opened it.

Things like "I spent the weekend watching *Doctor Who* on channel 54," and "I want to go to Xavier's School for Gifted Youngsters next year," and "if unicorns are real, do you think they'd let us ride them?" The unicorn questions were less immediately isolating within my peer group, but as for the rest …

This isn't a long-winded way of saying "I wasn't like those other girls," because I was really just like those other girls. We all loved weird and wonderful things, and I know I wasn't the only female science fiction fan in my elementary school. I was just the only one with the runaway mouth, the one who couldn't learn that what I loved was aberrant and wrong.

One by one, I watched the other girls drop away and hide our shared interests, not because they didn't care about the voyages of the Starship Enterprise anymore, but because they couldn't stand the teasing. It came from the boys first, accusing us of being dumb, having cooties, and destroying the very things we purported to love. Then, it came from within, as the girls who had already learned to conceal their stripes whipped around and attacked the rest of us. *They* were good girls, who liked girl things, and the best way to show that was to shame the bad girls who liked boy things. *We* needed to be put in our place. So "we" dwindled, and dwindled, until it was just me, and I thought I would be alone forever.

Because see, that's the thing about being a woman in science fiction: We start getting told "you are destroying the thing you love" really, really early. It's in the marketing and the media. It's in the messages that are passed to our schoolmates, and hence the messages that are passed to us. It's in the social norms that everyone wants to enforce. Boys get giant robots, girls get fashion dolls. "Both" is never an option.

I didn't choose the science fiction life. The science fiction life chose me. If I had been able, as a child, to control what I loved, I would have chosen to love something that didn't come with the specter of "your love will be the end of everything." I would have chosen love without rejection, love without cooties, love that was viewed as gender normative, because I was living inside of a false binary. We create it, and then we enforce it, and we don't understand why everyone is unhappy all the time.

I'm down with the idea that my love is destroying science fiction. We can build it up again, and this time, it can have room for everybody.

Even me.

~

Seanan McGuire was born and raised in Northern California, resulting in a love of rattlesnakes and an absolute terror of weather. She shares a crumbling old farmhouse with a variety of cats, far too many books, and enough horror movies to be considered a problem. Seanan publishes about three books a year, and is widely rumored not to actually sleep. When bored, Seanan tends to wander into swamps and cornfields, which has not yet managed to get her killed (although not for lack of trying). She also writes as Mira Grant, filling the role of her own evil twin, and tends to talk about horrible diseases at the dinner table.

ACKNOWLEDGMENTS

We could not have put this issue together without the help and support of our wonderful Kickstarter backers—all 2801 of them!

One of the secondary Kickstarter rewards allowed backers to add their name to a list of donors that would appear in the published issue. About half of our backers chose this reward. We're excited to recognize them on the list below. (Note: Because some people did not include a last name, or included a business name, or Twitter handle, we have this sorted by first name.)

A. Kwong; A.C. Wise; A.E. Fisher; A.K. Harrison; A.T. Greenblatt; Aaron Canton; Aaron Zimmerman; Abigail Fine; Adam B. Levine; Adam Maloney; Adam Powell; Adela Torres; Adrien Robertson; Adrienne Martini; Ahmed Tedjini; Aidan Doyle; Aimee Picchi; A.J. Reardon; Aja Romano; Alan DeHaan; Alana Joli Abbott; Alasdair Semple; Alec Austin; Alex Bacon; Alex Barsk; Alex Brett; Alex Conall; Alex Fitzpatrick; Alex Hardison; Alex Melchor; Alex Schlow; Alex von der Linden; Alexander F. Burns; Alexandria Gray; Ali Hawke; Alice Bentley; Alice T.; Alison L. Doyle; Alison M. Brown; Alison Wilgus; Alistair McLean; Allen Nussbaumer; Alli Martin; Alliah; Allie Jones; Alma Vilić; Alumiere; Alyc Helms; Amanda Cales; Amanda Cobb; Amanda Dier; Amanda Helms; Amanda J. Moffett; Amanda Kelly; Amanda Miller; Amber Teasdale; Amy Browning; Amy C. Fredericks; Amy E. Goldman; Amy McLane; Amy McNally; An Owomoyela; Andi Ferguson; Andi Newton; Andre & Laura Kostur; André Nóbrega; Andrea Corbin; Andrea Cox; Andrea Fry; Andrea Gatley; Andreas Flögel; Andreas Skyman; Andres Rosado Sepulveda; Andrew Armstrong; Andrew Barton; Andrew Giffin; Andrew Liptak; Andrew Penn Romine; Andrija Popovic; Andy Barbieri; Andy Bartalone; Andy Dost; Andy Knox; Andy Konecny; Andy Mammel; Anelie Crighton; Ángel Lozano; Angela Auer; Angela Korra'ti; Angie Flunker; Aniko Hazi; Anke Wehner; Ann

Chatham; Ann Voelkel; Anna Andersen; Anna McDuff; Annabeth Leong; Anne Charnock; Anne M. Marble; Anne Petersen; Antha Ann Adkins; Anthony C. Lanni; Anthony R. Cardno; Anton Prosser; Apis Teicher; Aramada; Aria Stewart; Ariana Harradine; Ariel Marcy; Ariel Segall; Arkady Martine; Arlene Medder; Arun Srinivasan; Asa Maria Bradley; Ashley Chatneuff; Asia al-Massari; Astra Plumarum; Aubrey Kinlan; Aubrey Westbourne; Ayla Khan; B. Pearsall; B. Sonerud; B. Symons; Bailey S.R.; Barbara Barbex; Barbara E. Klein; Bárbara Morais; Barbara Shepard; Barbie Jones; Barney Walsh; Bartek Łopatka; Bear & Angela Philley; Beatrice McKeown; Becca Shea; Becky Bergmann; Bekki Callaway; Ben Babcock; Ben Cartwright; Benet Devereux; Benjamin Blattberg; Benjamin Dean; Benjamin Juang; Benjamin Luke Vreugdenburg; Bernard Chen; Beth Avila; Beth C.; Beth Johnson; Betsy Streeter; Beverly Bambury; Bill & Laura Pearson; Bill Carter; Bill Ruhsam; Bill Shirley; Bill Simoni; Bill Williams; Blair A. Nicholson; Bob Hanks; Bobby Harrell; Boman Hwang; Brandon High; Brandon Paul Salinas; Brenda Cooper; Brenda Noiseux; Brendan Hutt; Brendan N. Moody; Brian Carpenter; Brian Farrey-Latz; Brian K. Johnson; Brian York; Brian, Sarah, & Josh Williams; Brie Sheldon; Brigitte Winter; Britney Cain; Brittany Kearns; Brittany Warman; Bronwyn K. Allen; Brook & Julia West; Brooks Moses; Bruce Flinchum; C. Glen Williams; C. Parisi; C. Shuy; C.C. Finlay; C.C. Nelson; C.D. Covington; C.D. Thomas; C.D. Thomas; C.E. Hyun; C.J. Pierce; C.J. Vincent; C.M. Merritt; Caleb Huitt; Caley; Calle Dybedahl; Cameron Harris; Camille Griep; Cara Spindler; Carl Berger Sr.; Carl Engle-Laird; Carl Sjostrand; Carmen Maria Machado; Carol J. Guess; Caroline Herdman-Grant; Caroline Ratajski; Carolyn Livingston; Carolyn VanEseltine; Carrie & Gwen Seidman; Carrie Sessarego; Cass Morris; Cassandra Lease; Cat Langford; Cat Sparks; Cat Wilson; Catherine Asaro; Catherine Haines; Catherine Heloise; Catherine Lundoff; Cathriona Tobin; Cathy Douglas; Cathy Green; Cathy Lopez; Cathy Sweeney; Catie Coleman; Caylie Sadin; Cecilia Tan; Chad L. Peck; Charity Tahmaseb; Charles 'gaygeeksf' Boylan; Charles Fitt; Charles Nicolosi; Charlie Reeves; Charlotte Ashley; Charlotte Grubbs; Chelle Parker; Chelsea Biondolillo; Cheryl Chancellor; Cheryl Morgan; Chloe Long; Chris Darden; Chris Furst; Chris Limb; Chris McKeever; Chris Radley; Chris Salter; Chris Seebeck; Chris Tong; Christian Lindke; Christin LeXi Davies; Christina Castillo; Christina D.; Christina Lay; Christina Smart; Christine Bell; Christine Chen; Christoff Youngman; Christopher Barzak; Christopher Hunter; Christopher Lear (@sapha12); Christopher Mangum; Christy Shorey; Ciaran Conliffe; Cindy Womack; Claire Pullen; Claire Sims; Clare A. Bohn; Claus Nielsen; Cliff Winnig; CoachPaul; Colette Reap; Colin Eakins; Colin Simpson; Colleen Bunn; Colleen Reed; Connie Cockrell; Coral Moore; Count Darling IV; Craig E.; Craig L. Wittler; Cris de Borja; Crystal

Lynn Hilbert; Crystal M. Huff; Cydney Ferguson-Brey; Cynthia Bradburn; Cynthia Gonsalves; Cynthia Ward; D. Cardillo; D. Cordell; D. Joan Leib; D.A. Price; D.E.Wasser; D.H. Frisby; D.L. Thurston; D. Miller; D.N. Deng; d'Avid; Dagny Phillips-Stumberger; Dallas Taylor; Damien Angelica Walters; Dan Balgoyen; Dan Franklin; Dan Grace; Dan Raffensperger; Dan[i/iel] Franklin; Dani & Brian Daly; Daniel C.; Daniel Neve; Daniel P. Haeusser; Daniel Swensen; Danielle Bell; Danielle M. LeFevre; Danielle Pollock; Danielle Vazquez; Darcy Elliott; Darja Malcolm-Clarke; Dark Matter Zine; Dave Bower; Dave Chua; Dave Hutchinson; Dave Versace; David A. Poole; David Alexander; David Bonner; David Bower; David C.; David Fiander; David G. Lein; David Haan; David Soponski; David Stegora; Davis Beeman; Dawn Bonanno; Dea Haupt; Dean O'Donnell; Deanne Fountaine; Deb Anderson; Debbie Townsend; Déborah; Deborah A. Bailey; Deborah Install; Deborah J. Brannon; Debra Vega; Dee Mamora; Deirdre; Deirdre M. Murphy; Deirdre Saoirse Moen; Demi Benson; Denice J.D.; Denise Ganley; Denise Paolucci; Dennis Beebe; Dennis Skibsted Sorensen; Derek Groothuis; Derin K.; Devan S. Ruthra; Devin Singer; Diana Wadke; Diana Walter; Diane Hagen; Diane Severson (Mori); Diane Turnshek; Django Wexler; Don Pizarro; Don Stark; Donaithnen; Donald J. Bingle; Donald Stark; Donovan Corrick; Doug Bissell; Doug Riechel; Douglas E. Bischoff; Dr. Pete Meyers; Drew Beechum; Duncan Molloy; Dustin Faucheux; Dustin Fickle; Dylan Sara; E. Anderson; E. Bromley; E. Castillo; E. Catherine Tobler; E. DeShetler-McGann; E. Halvorson; E. McKinstry; E. Michael Kwan; E.A. Shkolnik; E.C. Myers; Eagle Archambeault; Eddie Cochrane; Effie Seiberg; Elaine Blank; Elana Houde; Eldritch; Elena Nunnenmann; Elias F. Combarro; Elise Anderson; Eliza Zhitnik; Elizabeth A. Denton; Elizabeth A. Janes; Elizabeth Alpert; Elizabeth Creegan; Elizabeth Davidson; Ellen Green; Elliott Kay; Elya Arrasmith; Emanuela Terravecchia; Emilie Collyer; Emily Albarillo; Emily De Rango; Emily Ferguson; Emily Gladstone Cole; Emily Goldman; Emily J. Porter; Emily Jiang; Emily Perper; Emily Rowan; Emily Taylor; Emily X.R. Pan; Emma Engel; Emma Mieko Candon; Emma Osborne; Emma Stickley; Emma Wearmouth; Empty Set Entertainment; Emy Peters; Enrico Barisione; Eoin Ryan; Epiphyllum; Eric Chase; Eric Floehr; Eric Rossing; Eric S. Bauman; Eric Tilton; Eric Toczek; Erica Feldscher; Erica McGillivray; Erica N. Whiting; Erik Johnson; Erika Vannerson; Erin Hawley; Erin Kowalski; Erin McClain Beck; Etai Klein; Ethan Fremen; Etienne Lebeuf-Daigneault; Eugene Johnson; Eugene LeRoy; Eugene Myers; Eva Forsom; Evan Dorn; Eve Rickert; Eve Stein (not Einstein); Ewa Patrycja Malc; Folly Blaine; Forth Sadler; Frances Rowat; Frances Silversmith; Francesca Rogers; Frank J. Skornia; Frank Mitchell; Fred C. Moulton; Fred Kiesche; Fred Paffhausen; Freddie Baer; Frederic Bernard Jones; Gabriel Rosas; Gabrielle Ley; Gabrielle Seaborn; Gail Z. Martin; Gale

Skipworth; Galen Dara; Galen Loram; Garner Halloran; Garret Reece; Garrick Pass; Garth Kidd; Gavin C. Pugh; GeekGirlsRule.net; GeekMom Kay Moore; Geoff "Euphonium" Brown; Georgina Kamsika; Geremy Carnes; Gerry Canavan; Gillian Daniels; Gin Grahame; Glen Mehn; Glenn Liddy; Glennis LeBlanc; Gopakumar Sethuraman; Grahm B. Eberhardt; Greg Weir; Gregory Norman Bossert; Greig Christie; Guillaume Laurent; Gwenhael Le Moine; H. Lynnea Johnson; H. Marable; H. O'Hearn; H.L. Nelson; Håkon Gaut; Haley Herfurth; Halo Garrity; Hans Ranke; Heather Clitheroe; Heather Goodlett; Heather Mayer; Heather McCulley; Heather Morris; Heather Roulo; Heather Wallace; Heathyre Redemann; Helen Barker; Helen Merrick; Helen Savore; Helene Wecker; Henry Szabranski; Holland Dougherty; Ian Llywelyn Brown; Ian Magee; Ian Seymour; Imogen Cassidy; Irfon-Kim Ahmad; Isabel Yap; J. Daniel Batt; J. Hepburn; J. Hussey; J. Spock; J. Straus; J.A. Campbell; J.A. Porter; J.B. Segal; J.C. Gloss; J.C. Hsyu; J.E. Nice; J.J. Irwin; J.J. Leggo; J.J. Litke; J.L. Couturier; J.R. Doddridge; J.R. Johnson; J.R. Murdock; J.S. Sawyer; J.V. Ackermann; J.W. Alden; J.W. Cooper; J.Y. Yang; Jack Myers; Jacquelyne Drainville; Jae Young Kim; Jaenen; Jaime Kimbrel; Jake L. Woodworth; James "@realjimbob" Spinks; James "Stew" Stewart; James Bryant; James Bywater; James Chen; James D. Tackett III; James Frederick Leach; James H. Murphy Jr.; James J. Channell; James Q. Pearce; James Wilson Smith; Jami Nord; Jamie Grey; Jamie Lynne Powell-Herbold; Jamie Scotto; Jana W.; Jane Hammons; Jane Showalter; Janet Holden; Janice Kewley Anitsakis; Janico Greifenberg; Janine K. Spendlove; Janne Tørklep; Jarrod Farquhar-Nicol; Jasmine Stairs; Jason & Kai Wodicka; Jason A. Zwiker; Javier Gijón; Jay Lofstead; Jay Oliver; Jay Summet; Jay Wolf; Jean Harrison; Jean-Philippe Turcotte; Jeanne Kramer-Smyth; Jedediah Berry; Jeff Rutherford; Jeff Seymour; Jeff Soesbe (yeff); Jeff Xilon; Jeffery Lawler; Jeffrey Scott Petersen; Jeffrey Weston; Jefri Knazan; Jen D. Cencak; Jen Lammey; Jen R. Albert; Jen Warren; Jen Woods; Jen1701D; Jenn FavorsFire Mercer; Jenna Shively; Jenni Copeland; Jennifer B. Powell; Jennifer Brown; Jennifer Brozek; Jennifer Foehner Wells; Jennifer Fransen Gould; Jennifer Kahng; Jennifer Lyn Parsons; Jennifer Simonovich; Jennifer Steinhurst; Jennifer Tifft; Jennifer Wheelock; Jennifer Willis & Mike Volk; Jeremiah Britt; Jeremy Andrew DeFatta; Jeremy Bargen; Jeremy G. Kahn; Jeremy Penner; Jeremy Rowland; Jess Hyslop; Jess Lethbridge; Jess Sharbaugh; Jesse C.; Jesse Toldness; Jessica Abel; Jessica Alden; Jessica Fritsche; Jessica K. Meade; Jessica Marie Zibung; Jessica Stokes; Jessica Winn; Jessie Harker; Jessie Kwak; Jill Heather Flegg; Jill Seidenstein; Jill W.; Jim & Rachel Trigg; Jim DeVona; Jim Peterson; Jim Steel; Jim Sweeney; Jimmosk; Jimmy Sandinista; Joan & Isaac Wolkerstorfer; Joanna Freeman; Joanne B; Jocelyn Paige Kelly; Jodi McIsaac; Joe Loveland; Joe McTee; Joe Monti; Joel Purton; John 'johnkzin' Rudd; John Cowell; John Daily Jr.;

John Devenny; John E.O. Stevens; John Eddy; John Green; John Klima; John R. Platt; John S. Costello; John Tobin; Joie Young; Jolie Gendel; Jon Schjelderup; Jonah Sutton-Morse; Jonathan "Dr Archeville" Howell; Jono Hayward; Joseph Oliveira; Josh Larios; Josh Medin; Josh Putman; Josh Small; Josh Thomson; Joshua Bowers; Joshua Daniel; Joshua Hair; Joshua Hockenberry; Joshua J. Ziegler; Joshua R. English; Joy Ralph; Judy Webster; Julia Patt; Julia Svaganovic; Julie C. Day; Julie Lindsey; Julie Winningham; Juliette Wade; Justin Evans; Justus Hepburn; K. Rowe, Sturgeon Creek Publishing; K.J. Russell; K.L. Neidecker; K.L. Rieck; K.L. Wagoner; Kai Charles; Kara Hartz; Kara Prior; Kara Sowles; Kara Stephens; Karen G. Anderson; Karen Mahoney; Karen McKenna; Karen S.; Kari Love; Karianne Kleve; Karlo Yeager-Rodríguez; Kassia; Kat Reisdorf; Kat Smith; Kate Dollarhyde; Kate Elliott; Kate Gardner; Kate Heartfield; Kate MacLeod; Katherine Boag; Katherine Malloy; Katherine Prevost; Katherine S.; Katherine Weinstein; Kathrin Köhler; Kathryn Tungate; Kathy Faircloth; Kathy Whitlock; Katie Dunn; Katie Puckett; Katja Bell; Katrina Lehto; Kay Evans; Keith Bissett; Kelley J.; Kelly Beebe; Kelly Brandt Haskins; Kelly Keck; Kelly Myers; Kelly Robson & Alyx Dellamonica; Kelly Smith; Kelly Stiles; Kelly Thompson; Ken Holt; Ken McConnell; Kent Wayson; Keri Bas; Keri Orstad; Keri Stevens; Kevin F. Wilson; Kevin Henderson; Kevin Hogan; Kevin J. Maroney; Kevin Makice; Kevin Staggers; Kevin Wadlow; Kier Duros; Kilian Metcalf; Kim Hanfelt; Kim Nohr; Kim Unertl; Kimberly Bea; Kimi Nakaki; Kirk Hedden; Kirsten D.M. Kowalewski; Kris Ann Regeth; Kris Ligman; Kristen Fredericksen; Kristin H.; Kristin L. Lundgren; Kristin Luna; Kristin Lundgren; Kristina Lawton; Kristyn Willson; Kyle Barger; Kyle Bunker; Kyle R. Schlichter; Kyle Regan; Kylie White; Kymberlie R. McGuire; Kyra Freestar; L.J. Vaughn; L.M. Kane; L.S.K.; Lala Hulse; Lane Russo; Lara Eakins; Laura & Bill Pearson; Laura Almasy; Laura Aponte-Blizzard; Laura Cárdenas; Laura Clements; Laura E. Hall; Laura Host; Laura Laycock; Laura Quilter; Laura Schmidli; Laura Wilkinson; Laura Woods; Laurel Amberdine; Lauren C. Teffeau; Lauren Kramer; Lauren M. Roy; Lauren Scanlan; Lauren Wallace; Laurie Whiteley; Lee Guille; Lee Hallison; Lee Kathryn Rawles; Leife Shallcross; Leigh Saunders; Lene Taylor; Leo Zumpetta; Leonard Richardson; Leonardo Gedraite; Leonce Bowie III; Lesley Mitchell; Leslie Lee Sanders; Leticia Saoki; Lia Kawaguchi; Liam Dwyer; Libero Della Piana; Lila Sadkin; Lilian Og; Lilly Ibelo; Lisa Martincik; Lisa Mece; Lisa Paul; Lisa Rabey; Lisa Rodgers; Liz Ahl; Liz Argall; Liz Bada; Liz Gorinsky; Liz Harkness; Liz Pulido; Lizzie Newell; Lizzy Boden; Locallunatic; Logan Means; Loki Carbis; Lorena Dinger; Lorena O'English; Lori Propheter; Louis Sylvester; Louise Angrilli; Louise Löwenspets; Luce Correa; Lucius Annaeus Seneca; Lucy H. Lin; Luke Hannafin; Luke Rokich; Lura McCartney; Lyda Morehouse; Lynda Kennard; Lynn E. O'Connacht;

Lynne McCullough; M. Montella; M. Whittam; M. Adrian Sellers; M. Huw Evans; M. LaPlante; M. Medzihradszky; M. Oxamendi; M. Parker; M.C. Matz; M.E. Garber; M.R. Innes; Madeleine Ayling; Madeleine Holly-Rosing; Madison Dusome; Maggie Allen; Malcolm SW Wilson; Malia Kawaguchi; Malnpudl; Mandy Tonks; Mara Wood; Marc Wilson; Marcheto Algernon; Marcia Franklin; Margaret Colville; Margaret M. St. John; Margaret Treanor Frey; Marian D. Moore; Marian Weaver; Mariarosa Milazzo; Marion Deeds; Mark Gerrits; Mark Helwig Ostler; Mark Lindan; Mark Pantoja; Mark Williams; Marla Bracken; Marta Randall; Martin Cahill; Martin McGrath; Mary Alice Wuerz; Mary Anne Walker; Mary Gaughan; Mary Katherine Southern; Mary Kay Kare; Mary Mark Ockerbloom; Mathew Allan Garcia; Matt "Vinco" Taylor; Matt & Nykki Boersma; Matt Drown; Matt Hébert; Matt Leitzen; Matt Sell; Matthew 'Fish' Dockrey; Matthew Cranor; Matthew Sheahan; Matthew W. Quinn; Maty Claire Cropley; Maureen Kincaid Speller; Maurice Strubel; Max Vähling; Max Veit; Max Woerner Chase; Meagan Proctor Kavouras; Meagen K. Voss; Meason Kolkhorst; Megan D. Jones; Megan Hungerford; Megan Kurashige; Megan Lee Beals; Megan Peterson; Meghan McKinney; Mekenzie Larsen; Melanie Johnston; Melisande Von Funk; Melissa Burkart; Melissa Glasser; Melissa Harkness; Melissa House; Melissa Huston Taylor; Melissa J. Lytton; Melissa Shumake; Melissa Tabon; Melissa Trepanier; Melissa Turner; Melodie A. Selby, PE; Memory Scarlett; Meredith Jeanne Gillies; Merkku Sovijärvi; Michael "The CodingMerc" Henke; Michael "The Mad Hatter" Pye; Michael & Kassie Jennings; Michael A. Burstein; Michael Abbott; Michael Andersson; Michael Bernardi; Michael Brewer; Michael D. Woods; Michael Donoghue; Michael Fedrowitz; Michael Hanscom; Michael Kohne; Michael Lee; Michael Murphy; Michael Penrow; Michael Ray; Michael Reilly; Michael Sigmond; Michael Worrall; Michael Wyatt; Michele McCarthy; Michele Picard; Michele Savery; Michelle Cramer; Michelle Katz; Michelle L. Dupler; Michelle L. Palmer; Michelle Muenzler; Michelle Pardy; Mik Ishmael; Mike E.G./FreemadeSF; Mike Patterson; Mike Pignatella; Mike Rende; Miki Habryn; Miki Rodríguez Ramos; Mikko Parviainen; Minna Heimola; Miranda Nero; Miriam Krause; Miriam Rocke; Miriam Weinberg; Miss Banana; Mitchell Pittman; Morgan J. McCoy Albertson; Morgan S. Brilliant; Mortoc; Morva Bowman & Alan Pollard; Moyaccercchi; Muhamad Haiz Shamsudin; Muriel Jackson; N. Gerschwitz; Nadya Duke; Nai Eklund; Nancy Feldman; Naomi Mercer; Nat Lanza; Natalia Chwialkowski; Natalia Theodoridou; Natalie; Natalie Bueno Vasquez; Natalie Luhrs; Nathan Burgoine; Nathan Graves; Nathan Rosen; Natisha L-D; Neile Graham; Nell Scovell; Nelly Geraldine García-Rosas; Nicholas Devenish; Nicholas Hansen; Nick Bate; Nick Suffolk; Nick Tyler; Nicola Collie; Nicole Carlson; Nicole DeGennaro; Nicole Denae Stolpa; Nicole Walters;

Nicole Williams; Niels Erik Knudsen; Nigel Johnson; Nik Whitehead; Nina Niskanen; Nivair H. Gabriel; Noah Iliinsky; Noel Rappin; Nora Grosvenor; Noreen Duffy; Nyx A. Iron; Olivia Gillham; Olna Jenn Smith; Owen Zahorcak; P.M. Wolohan; Pamela Dubyak; Pat Hayes; Pat Murphy; Patricia (TrishEM) Matson; Patrick Ley; Patrick Tran; Paul & Rebecca Verlinden; Paul Cardullo; Paul Durrant; Paul J. Mendoza; Paul Rehac; Paul Sabourin-Hertzog; Paul Was; Paul Weimer; Paula Morehouse; Paula S. Jordan; Peggy Kolm; Penelope Millar; Penwing; Peter Brannen; Peter C. Roberts; Peter Chiykowski; Peter Gregg; Peter Hansen; Peter Jones; Peter Kempson; Peter Niblett; Petri Wessman; Phil Bowman; Phil Reiman; Philip Weiss; Phoebe Chase; Phronk; Pienaru Adrian; Pirx Danford; Priscila Santa Rosa; Priscila Simoes Tchorbadjian; Pseudopod. org Staff; Quinn Parrott; R. Brail; R. Eyres; R. Gates; R. James Whitley; R.C. Lewis; R.C. Nowack; R.D. Sullivan; R.E. Stearns; R.J. Young; R.S. Hunter; Rachael Acks; Rachael K. Jones; Rachel Ayers; Rachel Giesbers; Rachel Grinti; Rachel Sasseen; Rachel Sclare; Rachelle Chang; Rachelle Grein; Rafia Mirza; Randall Andrews; Raven Kavanagh; Raymond W.M. Chan; Rebecca Brewer; Rebecca Dominguez; Rebecca Gade; Rebecca Newman; Rebecca Null; Rebecca Stefoff; Reg Levy; Regis M. Donovan; Ren Tomovcik; Rene Tang; Renee Reese; Revek; Reyhan Sadaka; Rhiannon Floyd; Rhiannon Z. Llewellyn; Rhonda Parrish; Rich Griffith; Richard Eaton; Richard Guion; Richard Kadrey; Richard Leaver; Rick Cook Jr.; Rik Spruitenburg; Rita K. Hertel; Rob McMonigal; Rob Weber; Robert "Rev. Bob" Hood; Robert Burke; Robert E. Stutts; Robert Head; Robert Schweizer; Robin Postlethwaite; Roger Goun; Ron & Tara Oakes; Ron Mansolino; Ron Wodaski; Ronald Wanders; Ronny Aviram; Rose Beetem; Rose Eveleth; Rose Fox; Rowan Fae; Roy Sachleben; Roy Steves; Rrain Prior; Rudi Dornemann; Ruslan Dzhankhotov; Ryan Lelache; Ryan Olson; S. Kay Nash; S. Montalvo; S.A. Bryan; S.B. Divya; S.L. Durnford; S.R. Anderson; S.R. Pirie-Shepherd; Sal Manzo; Sally Qwill Janin; Sam Carpenter; Sam J. Miller; Samantha Brock; Samantha Dunaway Bryant; Samantha J. Sargent; Samantha M. Derr; Sandor Silverman; Sandy Macmillan; Sara Cleto; Sara Glassman; Sara H. Brosnan; Sara Harville; Sara Lovescarl; Sara M. Samuel; Sara Mitchell; Sara Pyle; Sara Stredulinsky; Sara Weiss; Sarah Baum; Sarah Bolland; Sarah Brand; Sarah Chislett; Sarah Cosgrove; Sarah Edie; Sarah Goslee; Sarah Grey; Sarah Hans; Sarah Liberman; Sarah M. Stewart; Sarah Mack; Sarah Milne; Sarah Nelson; Sarah Overall; Sarah Read; Sarah Stewart; Sarah Townson; Sarah Watson; Sarah Weiner; Sarah Wilson; Sarena Ulibarri; Sass Young; Sativa Quinn; Saundra Mitchell; Schondy; Scorcha; Scott Blomquist (sblom); Scott Fitzgerald Gray; Scott Madin; Scott Sweeny; Sean G.; Sean Wallace; Selene O'Rourke; Serge Broom; Seth Elgart; Shane Alonso; Shane O'Riordan; Shannon Rush; Shara Saunsaucie White; Sharon R. Turner; Sharon Wood; Shaun Kronenfeld;

Shauna Kosoris; Shauna Roberts; Shawn Andrew Mitchell; Shawn Camo; Shawn Hollyfield; Shay Darrach; Shean, Semeicha, & Sapphira Mohammed; Shel Graves; Sheraz Khan Niazi; Shervyn; Sheryl R. Hayes; Shiloh Williams; Sidsel Nørgaard Pedersen; Simon McNeil; Simone Macrae; Siobhan MacLean; Sky McKinnon; Smashingsuns; Snezana Nedeski; Snow Dragonwyck; Sofie Bird; Sofie Håkansson; Solvi Ericson; Sonya Galima; Sonya Lawson; SorchaRei; Stacey Becker; Stacey Hale Hankins; Stant Litore; Stef Maruch; Stefan Linden; Stefan Raets; Stephanie L. Weippert; Stephanie Logwood; Stephanie M. Grossman; Stephanie Swanson; Stephen Goudge; Stephen MacNeil; Stephen Spencer; Stephenie Sheung; Steve Gooch; Steve Hiner; Steve Irwin; Steve Lowe; Steve McHugh; Steve Stormoen; Steven A. Berger; Steven Gould, President SFWA; Steven Salter; Steven Saus; Steven Shaviro; Stina Leicht; Streator; Su J. Sokol; Sujin Headrick; Sunil Patel; Susan Connolly; Susan Harrington; Susan Schomburg; Susan Weiner; Svend Andersen; Sylvia Richardson; Sylvia Spruck Wrigley; T. Andersen; T. Bohm; T. Claar; T. Rob; T. Van Eeuwen; T.D. Walker; T.E. Stacy; T.K. Appleton; Tad Ottman; Taissa Reis; Tamara L. DeGray; Tami Veldura; Tania Clucas; Tania Lotia; Tanith K. Korravai; Tanja W.; Tansy Rayner Roberts; Tanya N. Kutasz; Tanya Spackman; Tara & Ron Oakes; Tara Ridgeway; Tarja Rainio; Tasha Turner; Taylor Davis; Tehani Wessely; Tera Fulbright; Terrance Averett; Terry Madden; Terry Weyna; Tess Grantham; Thalita Carvalho; The Hennis Family; Thea Orozco; TheBookMunkie.tumblr.com; Theresa DeLucci; Therese Godfree; Thersa Matsuura; ThinkBannedThoughts; Thom Slattery; Thomas Pither; Thomas Werner; Thor Muller; Tibs; Tiffany E. Wilson; Tim Moore; Tim Morgan; Tim Pratt; Tim Wormus; Timo Weimer; Tina Bounds; Tobias Asplund; Tobias S. Buckell; Tod McCoy; Todd Wheeler; Tom "Awesome Cakes" Carlson; Tom Barclay; Tom Hunter; Tom Savola; Tom Underberg; Tomas Burgos-Caez; Tone Berg; Toni P. Adams; Tony Downs; Tony Fiorentino; Tony Pisculli; Tor André Wigmostad; Tory Hoke; Tournevis; Tracey J. Pennington; Tracy Benton; Tracy Pinkelton; Travis Y.; Tricia Barr; Trina L. Short; Trina Marie Phillips; Trisha Commo; Trista & Daniel Robichaud; Trudy Haley; Tucker McKinnon; Tychoxi; Uhura B. Jones; V. Hanson; Valérie Lavigne; Valoise Armstrong; Valya Dudycz Lupescu; Valya Lupescu; Vanessa Torline; Verity Allan; Veronica Schwarz; Vian Lawson; Vicki Woodbury; Victor Merling; Victoria Boulton; Vincent Docherty; Virginia Pruitt; W. Donohue; W.S. Too; Wade Woodson; Wayne A. Arthurton; Wayne Carey; Wendy A.B. Whipple; Wendy Barron; Wendy Zdrodowski; Wes Hilton; Whitney L. Robinson; William Leisner; William Preston; William T. Vandemark; Wm Henry Morris; Wolf von Wolkenfels; Xap Esler; Yohan Odivart; Yong Jia Yaik; Zachery Bir; Zainah Alrujaib; Zakelro!; Zoey K. Jones; Zoraida Cordova; @atleb; @boxscorehaiku; @cheffojeffo; @hello_americans; @kindofstrange.

Coming Attractions

Coming up in July, in *Lightspeed* . . .

We'll have original science fiction by Adam-Troy Castro ("The New Provisions") and Carrie Vaughn ("Harry and Marlowe Versus the Haunted Locomotive of the Rockies"), along with SF reprints by Jo Walton ("The Panda Coin") and Howard Waldrop ("All About Strange Monsters of the Recent Past").

Plus, we'll have original fantasy by Theodora Goss ("Cimmeria: From the Journal of Imaginary Anthropology") and Matthew Hughes ("A Hole in the World"), and fantasy reprints by Aliette de Bodard ("Prayers of Forges and Furnaces") and Emma Bull ("De La Tierra").

For our ebook readers, our ebook-exclusive novella will be "Forlesen" by Gene Wolfe, and of course we'll have our usual assortment of author and artist spotlights, along with feature interviews with award-winning author Karl Schroeder and legendary video game designer Richard Garriott.

It's another great issue, so be sure to check it out. And while you're at it, please tell a friend about *Lightspeed*.

• • •

Looking ahead beyond next month, we've also got MORE DESTRUCTION TO COME. In October, our sister-magazines, *Fantasy* and *Nightmare*, will destroy fantasy and horror, respectively, with their Women Destroy Fantasy! and Women Destroy Horror! special issues. Women Destroy Fantasy! Is guest-edited by long-time Fantasy Magazine editor Cat Rambo, and Women Destroy Horror! Is guest-edited by legendary editor Ellen Datlow.

Then, in 2015, stay tuned for…QUEERS DESTROY SCIENCE FICTION! guest-edited by bestselling, award-winning author Seanan McGuire.

Thanks for reading!

SUBSCRIPTIONS & EBOOKS

Subscriptions: If you enjoyed this issue reading *Lightspeed,* please consider subscribing. It's a great way to support the magazine, and you'll get your issues in the convenient ebook format of your choice. All purchases from the *Lightspeed* store are provided in epub, mobi, and pdf format. A 12-month subscription to *Lightspeed* includes 96 stories (about 480,000 words of fiction, plus assorted nonfiction). The cost is just $35.88 ($12 off the cover price)—what a bargain! For more information, visit lightspeedmagazine.com/subscribe. Note: *Lightspeed* subscriptions (and regular issues) are currently only available in digital formats.

Ebooks & Bundles: We also have individual ebook issues available at a variety of ebook vendors ($3.99 each), and we now have Ebook Bundles available in the *Lightspeed* ebookstore, where you can buy in bulk and save! We currently have a number of ebook bundles available: Year One (issues 1-12), Year Two (issues 13-24), Year Three (issues 25-36), the Mega Bundle (issues 1-36), and the Supermassive Bundle (issues 1-48). Buying a bundle gets you a copy of every issue published during the named period. So if you need to catch up on *Lightspeed,* that's a great way to do so. Visit lightspeedmagazine.com/store for more information.

• • •

All caught up on *Lightspeed*? Good news! We also have lots of ebooks available from our sister-publications:

***Nightmare* Ebooks, Bundles, & Subscriptions:** Like *Lightspeed,* our sister-magazine *Nightmare* (nightmare-magazine.com) also has ebooks, bundles, and subscriptions available as well. For instance, you can get the complete first year (12 issues) of *Nightmare* for just $24.99; that's savings of $11 off buying the issues individually. Or, if you'd like to subscribe, a 12-month subscription to *Nightmare* includes 48 stories (about 240,000 words of fiction, plus assorted nonfiction), will cost you just $25 (about $11 off the cover price).

Fantasy Magazine Ebooks & Bundles: We also have ebook back issues—and ebook back issue bundles—of *Lightspeed*'s (now dormant) sister-magazine, *Fantasy*. To check those out, just visit fantasy-magazine.com/store. You can buy each *Fantasy* bundle for $24.99, or you can buy the complete run of *Fantasy Magazine*—all 57 issues—for just $114.99 (that's $10 off buying all the bundles individually, and more than $55 off the cover price!).

ABOUT THE WOMEN DESTROY SCIENCE FICTION! STAFF

CHRISTIE YANT,
GUEST EDITOR

Christie Yant is a science fiction and fantasy writer, and Assistant Editor for *Lightspeed Magazine*. Her fiction has appeared in anthologies and magazines including *Year's Best Science Fiction & Fantasy 2011* (Horton), *Armored, Analog Science Fiction & Fact, Beneath Ceaseless Skies, io9, Wired.com*, and *China's Science Fiction World*. Her work has received honorable mentions in *Year's Best Science Fiction* (Dozois) and *Best Horror of the Year* (Datlow), and has been long-listed for StorySouth's Million Writers Award. She lives on the central coast of California with two writers, an editor, and assorted four-legged nuisances. Follow her on Twitter @christieyant.

RACHEL SWIRSKY,
REPRINT EDITOR

Rachel Swirsky holds a master's degree in fiction from the Iowa Writers Workshop, and graduated from Clarion West in 2005. She's published over 50 short stories in venues including the *New Haven Review, Clarkesworld Magazine*, and Tor.com. Her short fiction has been nominated for the Hugo Award, the Locus Award, and the Sturgeon Award, and in 2010, her novella "The Lady Who Plucked Red Flowers Beneath the Queen's Window" won the Nebula. If it were an option, she might choose to replace her hair with feathers, preferably bright macaw feathers.

ROBYN LUPO,
FLASH FICTION EDITOR

Robyn Lupo has been known to frequent southwestern Ontario with her graduate student husband and elderly dog. She writes, reads, and plays video games. She is personal assistant to three cats, and an Assistant Editor for *Lightspeed Magazine*.

WENDY N. WAGNER,
NONFICTION & MANAGING EDITOR

Wendy N. Wagner's short fiction has appeared in magazines and anthologies including *Beneath Ceaseless Skies*, *The Lovecraft eZine*, *Armored*, *The Way of the Wizard*, and *Heiresses of Russ 2013: The Year's Best Lesbian Speculative Fiction*. Her first novel, *Skinwalkers*, is a Pathfinder Tales adventure. She served as the Assistant Editor of *Fantasy Magazine* and is currently the Managing/Associate Editor of *Lightspeed* and *Nightmare*. An avid gamer and gardener, she lives in Portland, Oregon, with her very understanding family. Follow her on Twitter @wnwagner.

GABRIELLE DE CUIR,
PODCAST PRODUCER

Gabrielle de Cuir has narrated over one hundred titles specializing in fantasy, humor, and titles requiring extensive foreign language and accent skills. Her "velvet touch" as an actors' director has earned her a special place in the audiobook world as the foremost choice for best-selling authors and celebrities. She is the writer and director of the Award winning short film *The Delivery*, which deals with an Alice-in-Wonderland version of audiobooks. Her own film credits include *Ghostbusters*, *American President*, and *Fright Night*. She spent her childhood in Rome growing up with her wildly artistic and cinematic father, John de Cuir, four-time Academy Award winning Production Designer, an upbringing that led her to be fluent in Romance languages and to have an unusual appetite for visual delights.

GALEN DARA,
ART DIRECTOR & COVER ARTIST

Galen Dara sits in a dark corner listening to the voices in her head. She has a love affair with the absurd and twisted, and an affinity for monsters, mystics, and dead things. She has illustrated for 47 North, Edge Publishing, *Lightspeed*, *Fireside Magazine*, Apex Publications, *Lackington Magazine* and *Goblin Fruit*. Recent book covers include *War Stories*, *Glitter & Mayhem*, and *Oz Reimagined*. She won the 2013 Hugo for Best Fan Artist and is nominated for the 2014

Hugo for Best Professional Artist. Her website is galendara.com, and you can follow her on Twitter @galendara. Her illustrations for *Lightspeed* are collected at: lightspeedmagazine.com/tag/illustrated-by-galen-dara.

JUDE GRIFFIN,
ASSISTANT & AUTHOR SPOTLIGHTS EDITOR

Jude Griffin is an envirogeek, writer, and photographer. She has trained llamas at the Bronx Zoo; was a volunteer EMT, firefighter, and HAZMAT responder; worked as a guide and translator for journalists covering combat in Central America; lived in a haunted village in Thailand; ran an international frog monitoring network; and loves happy endings. Bonus points for frolicking dogs and kisses backlit by a shimmering full moon.

SANDRA ODELL,
AUTHOR SPOTLIGHT INTERVIEWER

Sandra Odell is an avid reader, compulsive writer, and rabid chocoholic. She attended Clarion West in 2010. Her first collection of short stories was released from Hydra House Books in 2012. She is currently hard at work avoiding her first novel.

LEE HALLISON,
AUTHOR SPOTLIGHT INTERVIEWER

Lee Hallison writes fiction in an old Seattle house where she lives with her patient spouse, an impatient teen, two lovable dogs, and the memories of several wonderful cats. She's held many jobs—among them a bartender, a pastry chef, a tropical plant-waterer, a CPA, and a university lecturer. An East Coast transplant, she simply cannot fathom cherry blossoms in March.

LAUREL AMBERDINE, AUTHOR SPOTLIGHT
INTERVIEWER & ASSISTANT COPY EDITOR

Laurel Amberdine was raised by cats in the suburbs of Chicago. She's good at naps, begging for food, and turning ordinary objects into toys. She recently moved to San Francisco with her husband, and is enjoying its vastly superior weather. Between naps she's working on polishing up a few science fiction and fantasy novels, and hopes to send them out into the world soon.

Additional Staff

Publisher:
John Joseph Adams

Podcast Host:
Mur Lafferty

Copy Editor:
Dana Watson

Crowdfunding Logo Design:
Jenn Reese

Cover Design:
Karen Jones

Illustrators:
Li Grabenstetter
Elizabeth Leggett
Christine Mitzuk
Hillary Pearlman
Galen Dara (cover art)

Book Cover Design:
Jason Gurley

Book Production & Layout:
Michael Lee

Proofreaders:
Debra Jess
Rachael Jones
Amanda Mitchell
Sarah Slatton

First Readers:
Laurel Amberdine
Lisa Andrews
Amber Barkley
Kristi Charish
Kate Galey
Britt Gettys
Jude Griffin
Alyc Helms
Sylvia Hiven
Andrea Johnson
Georgina Kamsika
Louise Kane
Sarah Kirkpatrick
DeAnna Knippling
Stephanie Lorée
Gail Marsella
Laura Newsholme
Lianna Palkovick
Stephanie Sursi
Samantha Thomas
Nicole Walters
LaShawn Wanak
Gwen Whiting
Sandra Wickham

They Tell Me There Will Be No Pain

Rachael Acks

O, me alone! Make you a sword of me?
—*Coriolanus* 1.6

Colonel Rathbone attends my final debriefing. I'm wearing a paper hospital gown that doesn't cover my ass; I've got a breeze where no breeze has any right to be, from the back of my neck right down where the good Lord split me. But despite that I'm sweating, the backs of my thighs sticking to the paper covering the hospital table. The metal contacts set all around my head feel cold, sending little shocks that make my teeth itch.

"Sure you don't want to re-up?" the Colonel asks. He's got a deep voice. Jolly. Like a murderous Santa Claus, shaved into military trim. "You've got a solid record, all kills, no collateral, no fails. We sure could use you."

One of those things is a lie and we both know it. I smile at him with my rattling teeth. "Got to go home and take care of things, sir." Got to get out of here, sir.

"Hate to lose you, son." Rathbone calls everyone son, whether you got a cock or tits. He digs his datapad out of his pocket, calls up the SMOP and starts to read like a robot. No, worse than a robot; robots sound almost human these days.

Don't you, Phoebe?

". . .as agreed upon in your contract as signed, upon termination of your service you will return all government property issued to you upon entry, including all surgical and neural enhancements. Do you understand and still agree to these terms?"

I find I've pressed one finger against the visual link terminal on my right temple, like it's the starter on a car. The scent of lemons floods over my tongue. "I understand and agree, sir."

He shuts off the datapad and tucks it back away, claps me on the shoulder. "Then that's that. Good luck on the outside, son." Then he turns to go, broad back in olive drab, his crew cut salt and pepper above the stiff collar.

"Sir?"

"What?" His eyebrows ask me if I'm changing my mind.

"They said it won't hurt."

He gives me a kind, lying goddamn smile. "You did three tours, son. You're tough."

The door shuts behind him and I fiddle, peeling slowly at my hangnails. I used to do manicures with my big sister. Nail polish isn't regulation, not that I could keep from picking it off like I peel away my own skin.

There will be no pain, Phoebe whispers past my ear and into my spine.

"Shut the fuck up."

· · ·

So this is how it goes, son.

Ten years ago, you're a snot-nosed chicken shit fast food drone in the making. Bronze medal in high school track and field, chorus line parts only in high school drama, grades that aren't quite bad enough to justify the way mommy and daddy keep cutting back your allowance. Your older sister is the star quarterback of the family team. Full ride to Titan Tech, ships out on the first terraforming mission to Juno, calls home twice a week like a dutiful daughter and runs the hydroponics lab while she watches her kid sister paint her fingernails on the video feed. You still use her soap on days when you miss her; it smells like flowers and baby powder.

You're special, she tells you. Don't listen to anyone else. Join up in the corps, come out to Juno, we'll be partners.

You know what happens next. As far as Earth's concerned, there's only one thing that happened ten years ago. Only one thing that's happened in the last ten years because every goddamn one of us ripped our shirts off and wrote it across our hearts in blood.

The Drop. Julynine. Starfall. Lots of names, one result. A shattered habitat, a woman with wild eyes and a gold cross tattooed on her forehead screaming that her army, they got their authority straight from Jesus Christ hisself for our racial impurity and *hubris,* and your big sister, blown out into space, just one of ten thousand meat snowflakes floating in the black. Only you imagine her lying like a broken doll on the floor of the hydroponics lab, tight black curls sprinkled with dust and ice crystals and her fingernails Bahama Coral

Pink, tapping faintly in a pool of blood. The same shade she wore the day she took out a pair of tweezers and came at your eyebrows, saying, "Don't be a wuss, this doesn't *hurt*."

And just like everyone else on the goddamn planet, you cheer until your head just *thumps* with it when we make our war of vengeance.

Contract signing, swearing in, intake, ceremonies, first uniform, boot camp, none of that shit matters. It's all standard. The point is to make you into a unit, one little cog in the big machine of the Allied (ha!) Earth Special Forces.

This is the point where it matters. Where it starts to matter. Where it stops mattering.

Head wrapped in bandages, skull aching from newly drilled holes, random flavors running across your tongue (cantaloupe, cayenne, crawdad bake, we're in the Cs now) as the nano wires finish bonding to your neurons, you've got to focus, soldier, *focus,* this is important.

You look at the blank standard issue datapad screen, shoulders twitching every time a new ghost runs across your vision. A line of green text scrolls up, like you've jumped back to the goddamn twentieth century, but instead of *Want to play a game* or some shit like that, it reads:

Hello, I am your Tactical Analysis and Oversight Guidance (TAOG) system. My name is_____.

Fill in the blank. Your right shoulder twists as a metallic screech runs up the scale in your ear.

Well, what other name could you pick? You can only think of one right now, with the wires in your head all scrambled and crossed and reminding you about that one time you called the teacher "Mom" in third grade.

P-h-o-e-b-e.

Hello Charlie, I am your Tactical Analysis and Oversight Guidance (TAOG) system. My name is Phoebe. She whispers that as a formless voice now given form by your choice, past your ear, deep into your meat. *I'm looking forward to working with you.*

• • •

That's how it goes, only you're not you, you're me.

And you had a big sister named Phoebe.

• • •

Life outside AESF is one big vacation, only the vacation doesn't end and I don't get to go home because technically, I am home, permanently downside.

But I'm enjoying it. Really, I am. I take the train down to the beach every day, because that's what you do on vacation. Brightly colored plastic umbrellas, all shapes and colors and patterns, bob outside, shielding the civilians from the unending assault of the sun.

Take one of those umbrellas, line it with foil, it can be used to hide an explosive or a person from casual drone scans, only it makes a neat circle cut-out in transmissions that screams for attention after you've run your electronic eyes over it a good hundred times.

It's the middle of the day. Seven people on the train as it hums along over its superconductors: three teenaged boys (could be a threat, one of them's got a backpack who knows what's in that), one young mother with two sub-five-year-olds (probably okay), one old lady with a parasol (sunlight glancing off the gold cross she wears on her neck, is she one of them, one of the sectarians ohshitohshitohshit call it in—)

No response, Phoebe says. They told me my TAOG would go silent after surgery. They also told me removing the neural links wouldn't hurt. *Disconnected, Charlie. Recalibration necessary.*

Breathe. Breathe. That's right. My hands haven't fallen off. I just don't have drones any more. I'm just me. The old lady is just an old lady. She's out for the sunlight on her old bones. But I let her get off the train first, and keep my ass in the seat until I'm two stops down.

Then I go out onto the beach. The sand feels so strange under my shoes, squashing and shushing and kicking up in little clouds. I don't think I've run on anything but concrete or tarmac or metal decking for almost a decade. It feels different, so I smile about that, and my teeth itch in the cool breeze.

• • •

This is what it's like, the first time you hook into your cloud. Your consciousness shatters into a hundred pieces, one for each module.

There's the eyes and ears (SASbots), jammers (ESIMbots), guns and missiles (TWINs) and you're all of them at once, trying to hold them in formation and run them through patterns. You scream. It's cool. Everyone screams the first time, not because it *hurts*, but because it's so overwhelming your body pulls a random choice out of: (a) scream, (b) cry, or (c) laugh hysterically. Crying and screaming is better, it doesn't freak your observers out nearly as much.

But then goddamn it's the biggest rush in the world. You are a god with a thousand fingers that you can spike down into the ground like lightning. You fly, atmosphere or space it doesn't matter. Because when you're hooked into your cloud, you're out there with the drones, and your meat is left behind in the closet.

Calibration complete. Phoebe whispers these magical words to rhyme with "I love you."

A taste like blood floods your mouth. It's nauseating. Don't worry. You get used to it.

• • •

Life outside the drone cloud is blindness. I can't *see* anything. What kind of bullshit is the visual spectrum after you've gotten used to having infrared, ultraviolet, radio, all piped into your head from over a hundred different eyes? I used to be a fucking titan, heavy armor mach 6 in a thousand different directions, and now I'm small, naked. Just meat.

No jobs yet, but I don't need the money. My severance hasn't run out, I just need something to do. Being a drone pilot isn't much of a marketable skill in the real world. Doesn't help you smile at assholes and sell them cars, or new computers, or vacation packages to resorts where the only people who look like you scrub the toilets. Doesn't help with flipping burgers, either. I've developed this really worrying twitch in my left hand, I think it's from one of the nanowires fizzing in my brain. Makes it hard for me to sleep, I'll be drifting off and then suddenly my hand jerks under the covers and I'm wide awake.

It's bad enough I go to the nearest VA hospital, which takes a thirty minute train ride—

(two workmen, one of them has a hammer and veins bulging out from his bare forearms; typical nuclear family with a kid in a stroller who knows what's hidden in there; students, more students, more students in navy blue uniform jackets and at least someone's laughing around here but fuck why won't they hold still for five minutes; *No threat, no threat, no threat,* Phoebe assures me in a murmur that runs along my jawbone and makes me yawn)

—and then a two hour wait in a room that smells faintly of sweat and metal. The data signal there is jacked and all the paper magazines are at least three years old, so I just listen to two other vets make stilted conversation about their dogs.

"That's impossible," the doc at the VA tells me once it's my turn in the carefully refrigerated exam room. "They removed all your links before discharge. I've got the signed order from Colonel Rathbone."

"But what if the nanowires are still there?" I can fucking *feel* them, burrowing into my neurons.

The look he gives me is a lot like the manager of the last place I applied at, some joint that makes pizza. *You've got to be kidding, right?*

But they told me a lot of things, in the service. This will be a cakewalk. You'll go home a hero. We'll pull all the wires out of your brain and it won't hurt one bit, you're tough. "What about the TAOG, did they remove that too?"

His eyes widen slightly. "Are you hearing voices?"

I hold up my hands. The left twitches—See, I'm not just making this up. "No. Shit no. I'm not crazy." I know what happens to people who say shit like that. They go away and never come back. "Look, I just want to know my brain isn't turning into black pudding behind my eyes, okay? I busted my ass for you guys downside for nine years. Cut me a break."

The doctor sighs. "I'll put you in the queue for some testing. It'll take a few weeks, we're pretty overloaded. Though if you can travel—"

Being on the train for hours and hours, people constantly walking in and out and back and forth behind me and beside me and no thanks man, sounds like hell, I can't keep track of them all, too many threats. *Acquiring targets*—I shake my head. "Got no scratch. Got a form I can fill out for that?"

"Afraid not. All right. I'll send the appointment confirmation to your calendar."

As I slouch on out of the hospital, they run a guy past on a palette. He's got a cardio pack on his chest, a vent over the lower half of his face, red soaked bandages at his wrists. His face is the color of unbaked clay. He's also got a circle of white dimples around his head like a crown.

Corporal Dan Weston, Second Battalion, Third Squadron, retired, Phoebe murmurs up through my meat and into my left ear. *No threat, target deceased, permission not needed.*

I press my finger where the visual link used to be on my temple, and find nothing but a smooth, slick dimple of scar tissue.

My teeth itch.

• • •

So then you score a berth on a Predator-Class carrier, space-based command and dispatch center. Calories carefully counted, AG coming off perfectly calibrated spin so you can still do full PT every morning. Your body's all tight with wiry muscle for when you put it on the shelf and abandon it ten hours a day.

They assign you the easy missions first, out into the moons. Ones where you just drop dome busters, and the closest you get is doing an infrared check to make sure all the bodies are cooling off in their individual puddles of effluvia. Or you do spy runs, where you run the SASbots around and it's like a video game, and you'll get the high score and the achievement at the end if you find the princess. And by princess I mean the scumbag you paint down with a targeting laser so one of your big brothers can sweep in like justice in an atomized cloud and light that shit up better than Christmas.

But then you get your first real mission. No fanfare, no warning, you just walk in one day, hook into the cloud and launch off. Then Phoebe says, *Target acquired, authorization go.*

And that's it. You take the TWINs out to play, and the bad guys die. *Clean kill, stand down,* Phoebe tells you.

Years. You do it for *years.* Then:

Target acquired, authorization go.

"Getting a lot of noise. Confirm." The SASbots show a place crawling with heat signatures, like they're having a convention in that dumpy little building. Stats and dimensions scroll through your brain.

A green flash shivers over the view. Targeting laser, some new pilot double checking your shit.

Authorization go, Phoebe repeats. *Insurgents confirmed. Action is justified.*

You are so fucking justified. You send in the TWINs, and you flatten that little hovel. You turn it into a smear of gravel and ash. Then there's a spike of automatic weapons fire a click and a half west. Two SASbots go dead, a little blind spot in your brain.

Secondary threat, authorization go, Phoebe says. *Assistance incoming.*

A second wave of TWINs joins in the bombardment. You make the night go *white.* In the dim recesses of the drone bay, you hear one of the other jocks whoop. Well, look at those accuracy numbers. You sure can't blame him. You feel pretty fucking badass yourself.

You sweep in with SASbots again, check and confirm the kills, catalog what you just took out. You'd rather just send in recordings than fill out the paperwork. Secondary site is closer, so that gets done first. Shredded remains of fifteen adults, explosive residue that doesn't belong to us. First site—

she's lying in a puddle of blood, eyes wide and white all around, curly black hair stuck to the floor, legs a mist of bone and flesh

—there's kids, there's a goddamn kid, another one with his head half gone, and another, and a woman in an apron like you blew up a fucking daycare, and, and—

Charlie, your heartrate is spiking, Phoebe says. *What's wrong?*

"Kids," you say. "You said this was an authorized target." She told you to do it, told you, said it was okay. But terrorists don't play with plastic horses, don't have pigtails and purple barrettes. "Look at her! She's trying to scream!"

Death is instant, Phoebe calmly whispers into the skin of your neck. *Residual electrical spikes. There is no pain.*

But the girl looks at your hovering thimble-sized SASbot with eyes to drown in and tremblestremblestrembles her fingernails (glittering with nail polish is that Bahama Coral Pink oh fuck me fuck me fuck me) tapping the ground as she gurgles out breath after breath into the poisonous atmosphere.

• • •

This is how it goes, only you're not you, you're me.

And you (I mean me) realize this terrible truth: Phoebe's just there to tell you it's okay to pull the trigger. She's a wad of ones and zeroes that stands in for your conscience so you don't hesitate.

Phoebe isn't real.

Phoebe is a liar.

Phoebe is a sin eater.

• • •

I can't sleep any more. My hand won't stop jumping. Everything I eat tastes like electricity and motor oil. The VA test results say the nanowires in my head don't exist, but I can feel them rotting out and turning my brain into something black and gooey, blood on tarmac while Phoebe whispers battle plans onto the backs of my knees. All I have is vids, I can't focus enough to read any more, not that I was into books before.

And the vids? It's just bullshit bullshit bullshit, plastic people with perfect teeth in clothes worth more than my entire severance having cat fights about their boyfriends, cooking shows, action movies where a single guy with a gun fires more bullets than a clip can hold, softcore porn. It's like there's not even a fucking war on, and I just have to *move* before the tar in my head overflows.

I take the train down to the beach, late at night. The car is full of drunks, big guys, little guys, and they stand too goddamn close and breathe like furnaces. I finger my pocket, the stunted shape of a ceramic pistol. I don't have a drone cloud to protect me anymore. It's just me, just my pathetic meat and Phoebe, and we're never safe.

"Hey there," one of the guys says. "Where you going?" He smells like money and beer.

"Not anywhere you are." I stare straight ahead. My hand twitches at my side. I could snap his neck. He's crowding me.

"Don't be nasty." Leans even closer. "What are those marks on your head? You some kind of holy roller?"

I get asked that all the time. Like no one knows what soldiers look like if we're not dressed up like a GI Joe. Maybe no one bothers watching the news. Maybe they think the clouds of heavily-armed robots just fly themselves now, but shouldn't that scare everyone shitless?

He breathes on the side of my head, too close, too close. My teeth itch.

Threat detected. Phoebe breathes on the other side of my head.

I pull the pistol from my pocket, smooth like butter, slam my other fist into the guy's sternum to get him to back off and give me room. My pistol is the only steady thing in the world as I focus down the barrel at his head framed by gum advertisements and the blank windows looking out into black night. "Back off! Back the fuck off!"

"Whoa! Whoa lady! Chill! Chill!" Suddenly all the drunk guys are shouting.

"All of you! Shut the fuck up! Back off!"

Hands raise around the train car. A dark stain spreads over the front of my target's pants. "Don't do it. I didn't mean nothin'. I didn't mean nothin'!" The train halts, a cool rush of night air as the doors behind me open, I know exactly where they are, always know where your exits are.

Threat detected. Authorization go.

My trigger finger squeezes even as my hand jerks to the side. The bullet only makes a soft pop—I don't like loud noises, I wouldn't buy a loud gun are you kidding me—and the window behind the man shatters.

Everyone starts yelling all at once. Hands grab at my arm. I scream and break one of my knuckles on someone's nose. Then I run.

It's cold. There are clouds over the moon, so it's just a glowing, indistinct circle, like a puckered scar in the sky. I only notice when I get to the beach because the ground beneath my sneakers starts shushing me. I keep running until I'm not afraid any more.

Who the fuck am I kidding? I'm always afraid.

I walk out by the waves, where I can watch them crest into white foam, and sit on the damp sand. I take my datapad out of my other pocket, and the screen comes back on to the news vid I saw when I decided I had to get the fuck out of my house: *At Last, War Without Death.* I watch the bland-faced narrator silently mouth the words, "AESF reports zero casualties in the last two years of the conflict." Well no shit. We're all just clouds of robots now.

Targets don't count. That's authorized.

Retired don't count either.

My hand twitches. My teeth itch.

Disconnected, Charlie. Reactualizing neural connections, Phoebe says calmly, laying the words up my spine.

I pull the pistol from my pocket. My head throbs, hot and sharp under the scars. The barrel feels so cool and soothing, pressed against what used to be the visual link terminal on my right temple. The taste of blood floods my mouth.

There will be no pain, Phoebe whispers into my ear.

I close my eyes. "Liar."

I smell flowers and baby powder. *Authorization go.*

—For Mr. T. H.

~

Rachael Acks is a writer, geologist, and sharp-dressed sir. In addition to her steampunk novella series from Musa Publishing, she's had short stories in *Strange Horizons, Crossed Genres, Waylines, Daily Science Fiction, Penumbra,* and more. Rachael lives in Houston (where she bicycles, drinks tea, and twirls her ever so dapper mustache) with her two furry little bastards. For more information, see her website (rachaelacks.com) or watch her tweet (@katsudonburi) way too often.

THE APOCALYPSE TRIPTYCH

EDITED BY JOHN JOSEPH ADAMS AND HUGH HOWEY

BEFORE THE APOCALYPSE	DURING THE APOCALYPSE	AFTER THE APOCALYPSE
MARCH 2014	SEPTEMBER 2014	MARCH 2015
Trade Paperback ($17.95)	Trade Paperback ($17.95)	Trade Paperback ($17.95)
Ebook ($6.99)	Ebook ($6.99)	Ebook ($6.99)
Audiobook ($24.95)	Audiobook ($24.95)	Audiobook ($24.95)
ISBN: 978-1495471179	ISBN: 978-1497484375	ISBN: 978-1497484405

FEATURING ALL-NEW, NEVER-BEFORE-PUBLISHED STORIES BY

Charlie Jane Anders	Tananarive Due	Ken Liu	Scott Sigler
Megan Arkenberg	Jamie Ford	Jonathan Mayberry	Robin Wasserman
Paolo Bacigalupi	Hugh Howey	Matthew Mather	David Wellington
Annie Bellet	Jake Kerr	Jack McDevitt	Ben H. Winters
Desirina Boskovich	Nancy Kress	Seanan McGuire	...and more!
Tobias S. Buckell	Sarah Langan	Will McIntosh	